PENULTIMATE QUEST

STORY AND ART BY LARS BROWN
COLORS BY BEX GLENDINING

ALMA'S QUEST DRAWN BY JOHN KANTZ

IRON CIRCUS COMICS

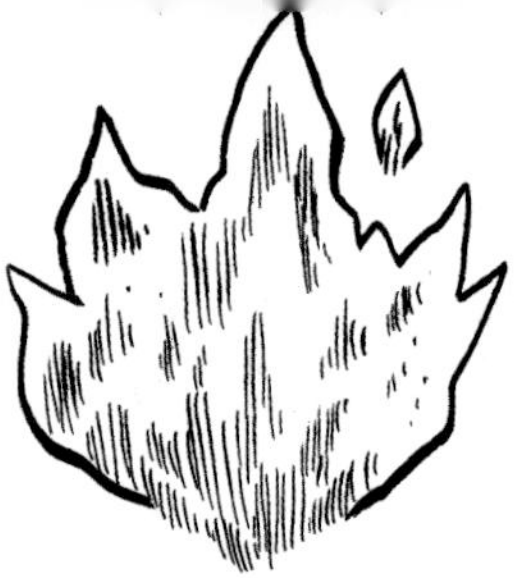

Story & Art: Lars Brown
Colors: Bex Glendining
"Alma's Quest" Drawn By: John Kantz

Publisher: C. Spike Trotman
Editor: Andrea Purcell
Art Director & Cover Design: Matt Sheridan
Proofreader: Abby Lehrke
Print Technician & Book Design: Beth Scorzato

Published By
Iron Circus Comics
329 West 18th Street
Suite 604
Chicago, IL 60616
ironcircus.com

First Edition: August 2020

ISBN: 978-1-945820-50-2

10 9 8 7 6 5 4 3 2 1

Printed in China

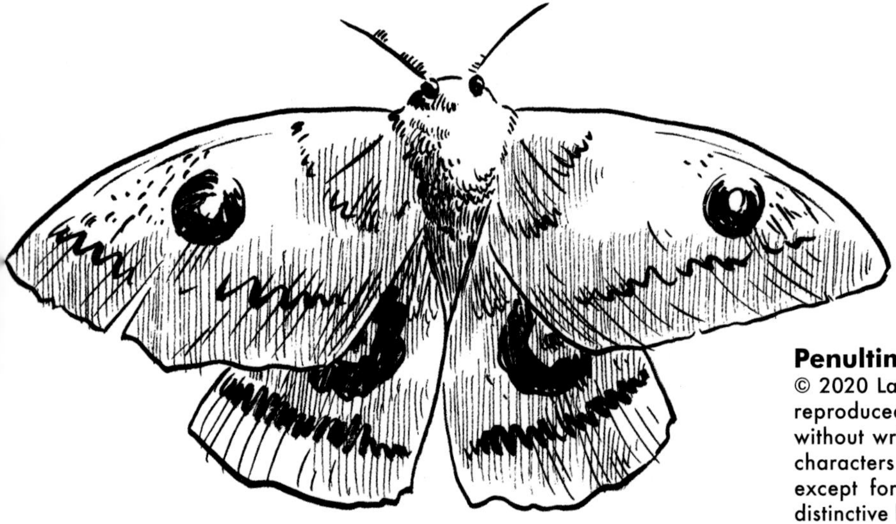

Penultimate Quest

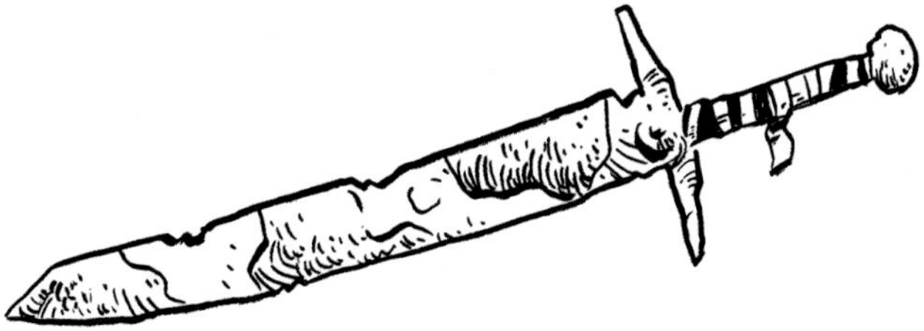

Publisher's Cataloging-In-Publication Data
(Prepared by The Donohue Group, Inc.)

Names: Brown, Lars, 1983- author, illustrator. | Glendining, Bex, colorist. | Kantz, John, illustrator.
Title: Penultimate quest / story and art by Lars Brown ; colors by Bex Glendining ; Alma's quest drawn by John Kantz.
Description: First edition. | Chicago, IL : Iron Circus Comics, 2020. | Interest age level: 013-018. | Summary: "In a philosophical fantasy adventure, warriors living through a role playing game must learn the difference between diversion and escape as they try to break the cycle of a never ending quest"-- Provided by publisher.
Identifiers: ISBN 9781945820502 (paperback)
Subjects: LCSH: Soldiers--Comic books, strips, etc. | Fantasy games--Comic books, strips, etc. Quests (Expeditions)--Comic books, strips, etc. | CYAC: Soldiers--Fiction. | Fantasy games--Fiction. | Quests (Expeditions)--Fiction. | LCGFT: Graphic novels. | Fantasy fiction.
Classification: LCC PZ7.7.B784 Pe 2020 | DDC 741.5973 [Fic]--dc23

ACROSS A DARK SEA LIES A MYSTERIOUS ISLAND...

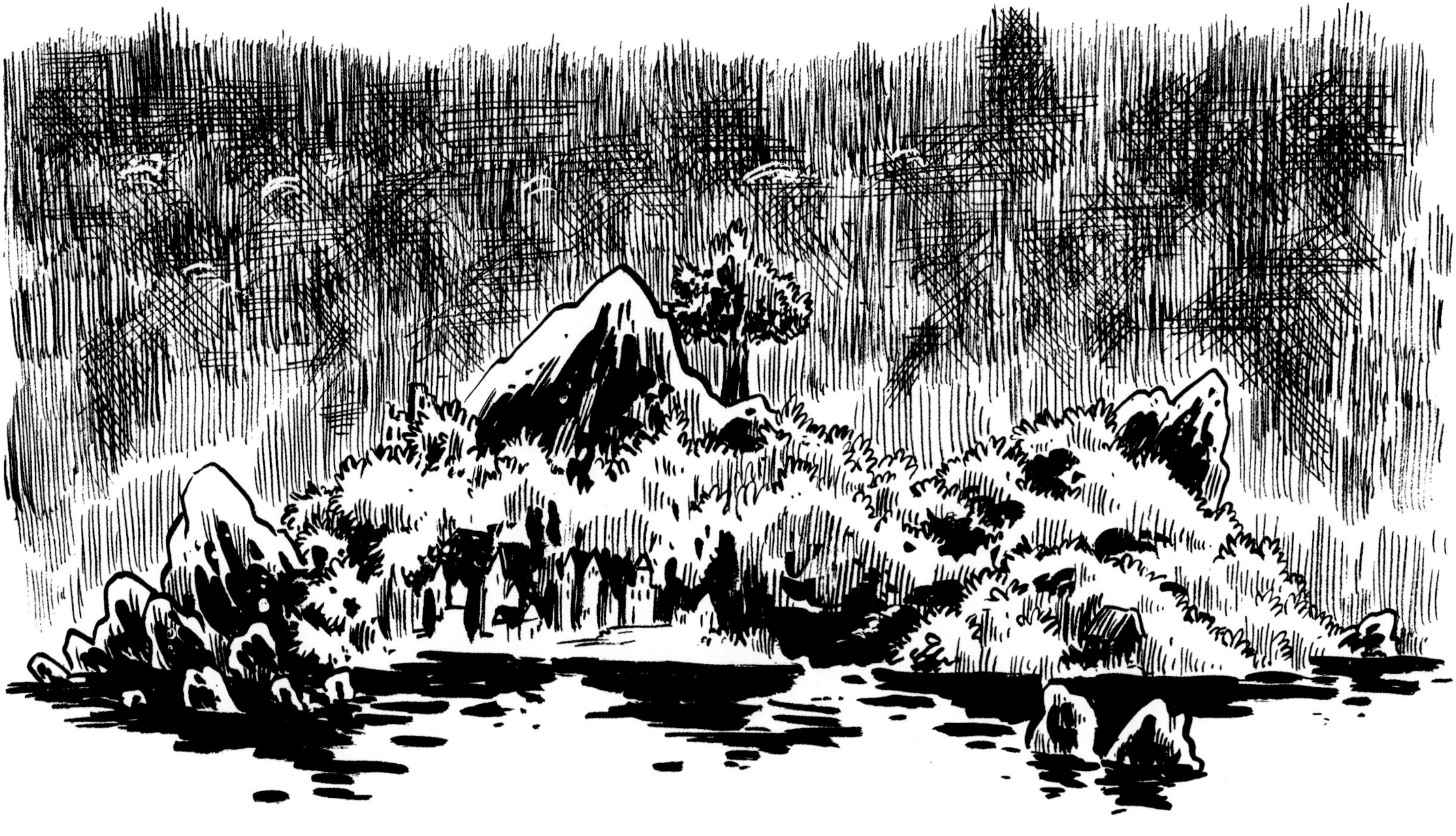

Thank you to Ames, always. Thank you to Bex, your colors have brought this book to life! And thank you to Spike, Andrea and Matthew at Iron Circus!

-Lars

Thank you to Olivia Stephens, for recommending me. Thank you to Lars, for letting me be a part of the captivating Penultimate Quest world. And thank you to Spike and Andrea at Iron Circus!

-Bex

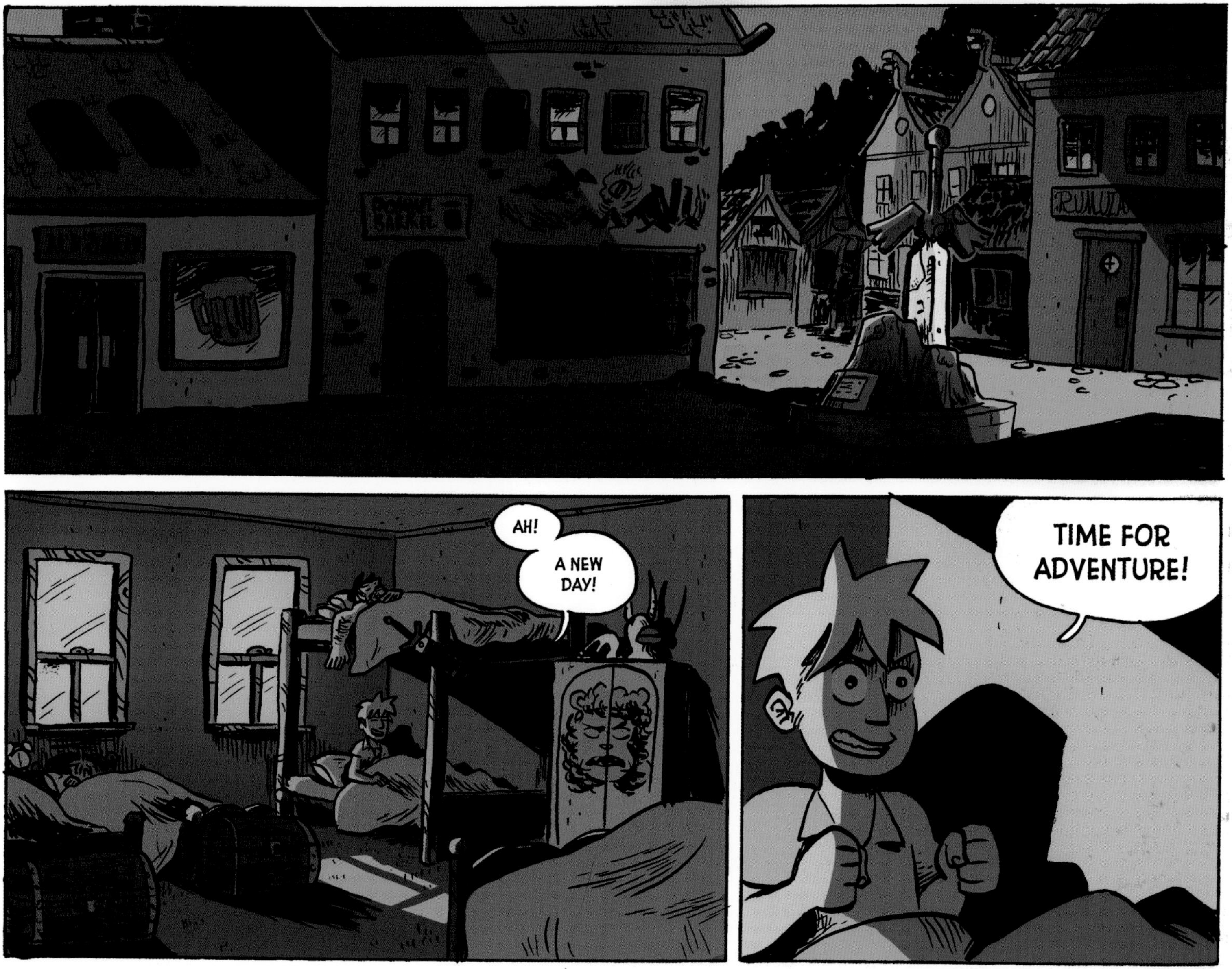
AH!
A NEW DAY!
TIME FOR ADVENTURE!

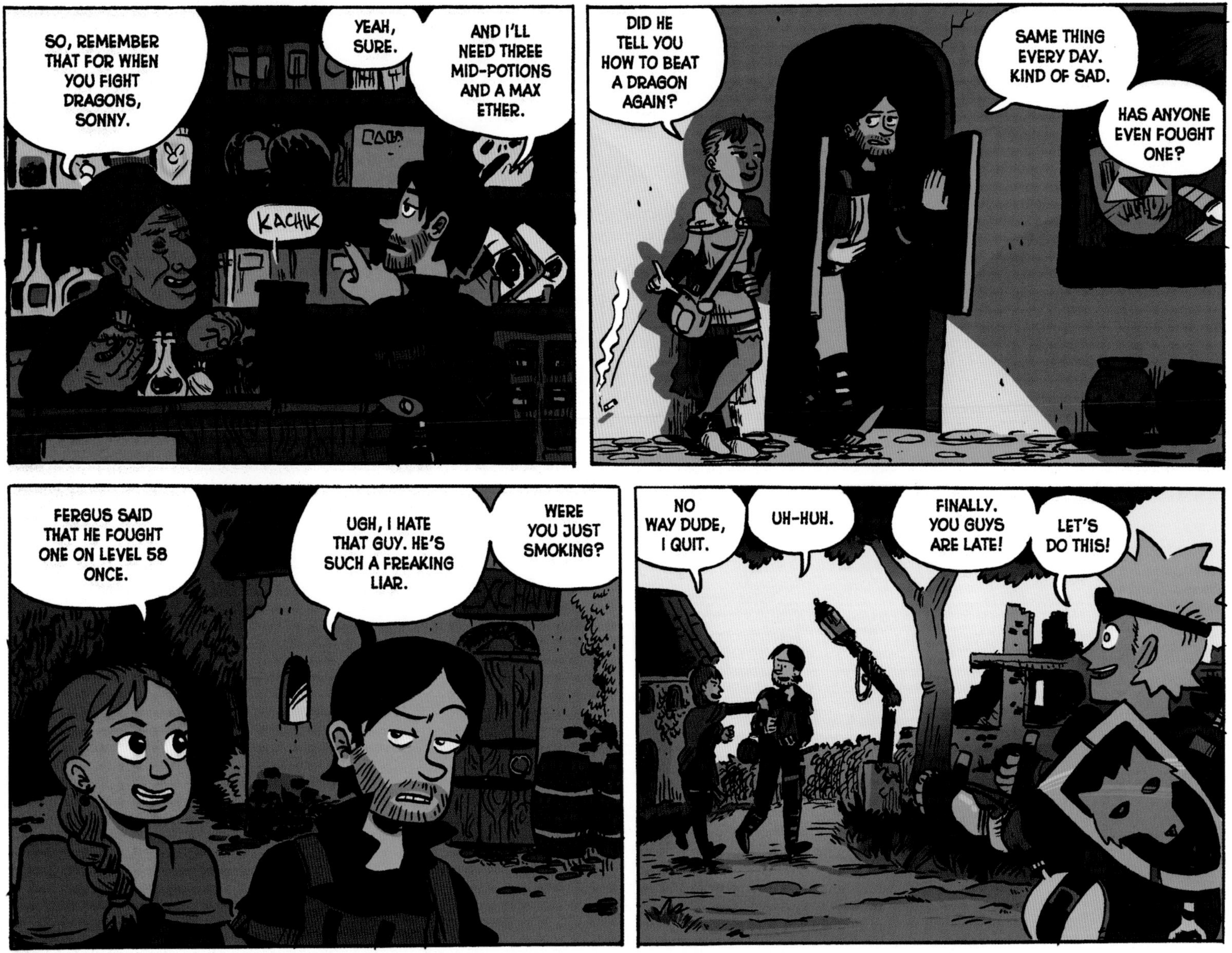
SO, REMEMBER THAT FOR WHEN YOU FIGHT DRAGONS, SONNY.
YEAH, SURE.
AND I'LL NEED THREE MID-POTIONS AND A MAX ETHER.
KACHIK
DID HE TELL YOU HOW TO BEAT A DRAGON AGAIN?
SAME THING EVERY DAY. KIND OF SAD.
HAS ANYONE EVEN FOUGHT ONE?
FERGUS SAID THAT HE FOUGHT ONE ON LEVEL 58 ONCE.
UGH, I HATE THAT GUY. HE'S SUCH A FREAKING LIAR.
WERE YOU JUST SMOKING?
NO WAY DUDE, I QUIT.
UH-HUH.
FINALLY. YOU GUYS ARE LATE!
LET'S DO THIS!

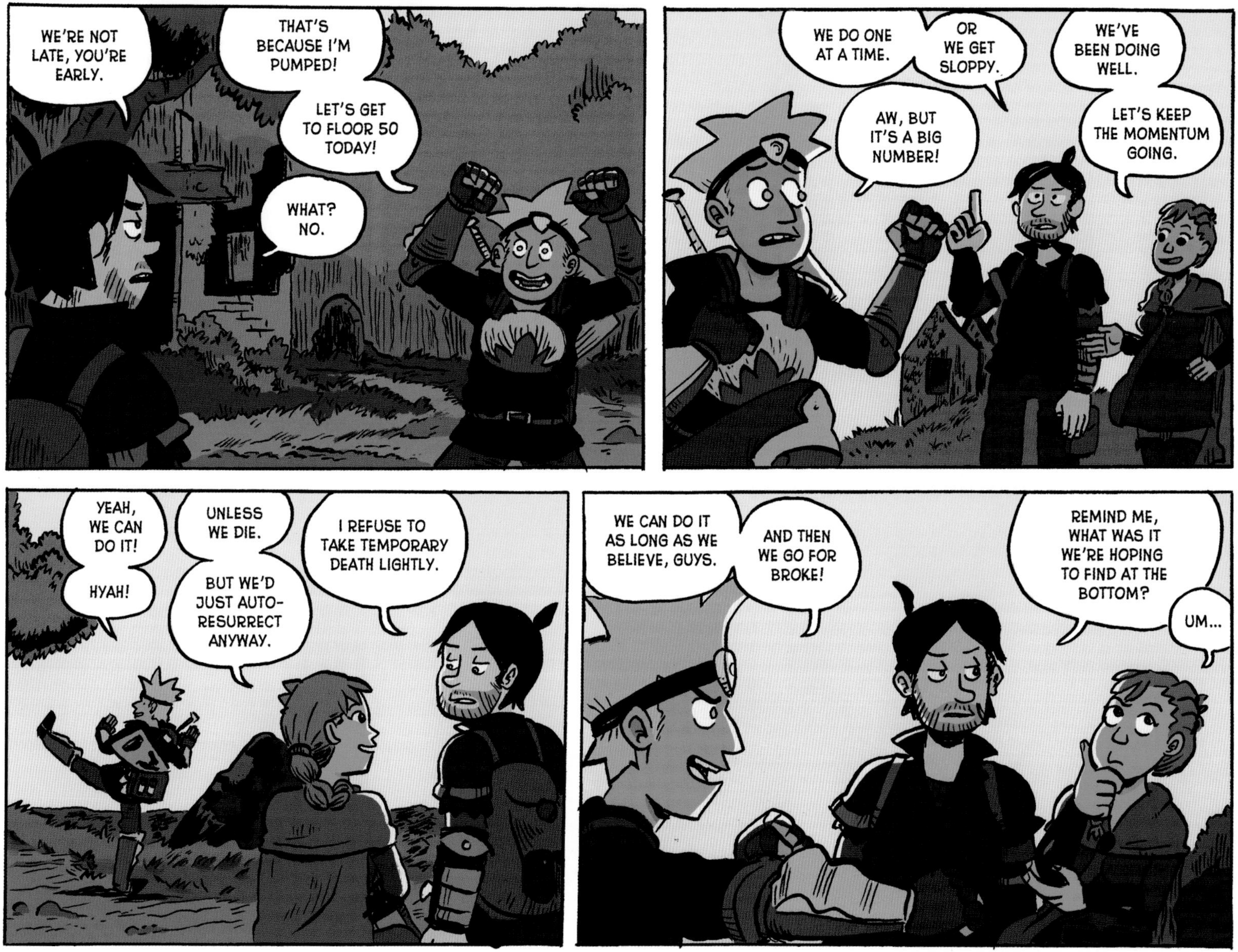
WE'RE NOT LATE, YOU'RE EARLY.
THAT'S BECAUSE I'M PUMPED!
LET'S GET TO FLOOR 50 TODAY!
WHAT? NO.
WE DO ONE AT A TIME.
OR WE GET SLOPPY.
AW, BUT IT'S A BIG NUMBER!
WE'VE BEEN DOING WELL.
LET'S KEEP THE MOMENTUM GOING.
YEAH, WE CAN DO IT!
HYAH!
UNLESS WE DIE.
BUT WE'D JUST AUTO-RESURRECT ANYWAY.
I REFUSE TO TAKE TEMPORARY DEATH LIGHTLY.
WE CAN DO IT AS LONG AS WE BELIEVE, GUYS.
AND THEN WE GO FOR BROKE!
REMIND ME, WHAT WAS IT WE'RE HOPING TO FIND AT THE BOTTOM?
UM...

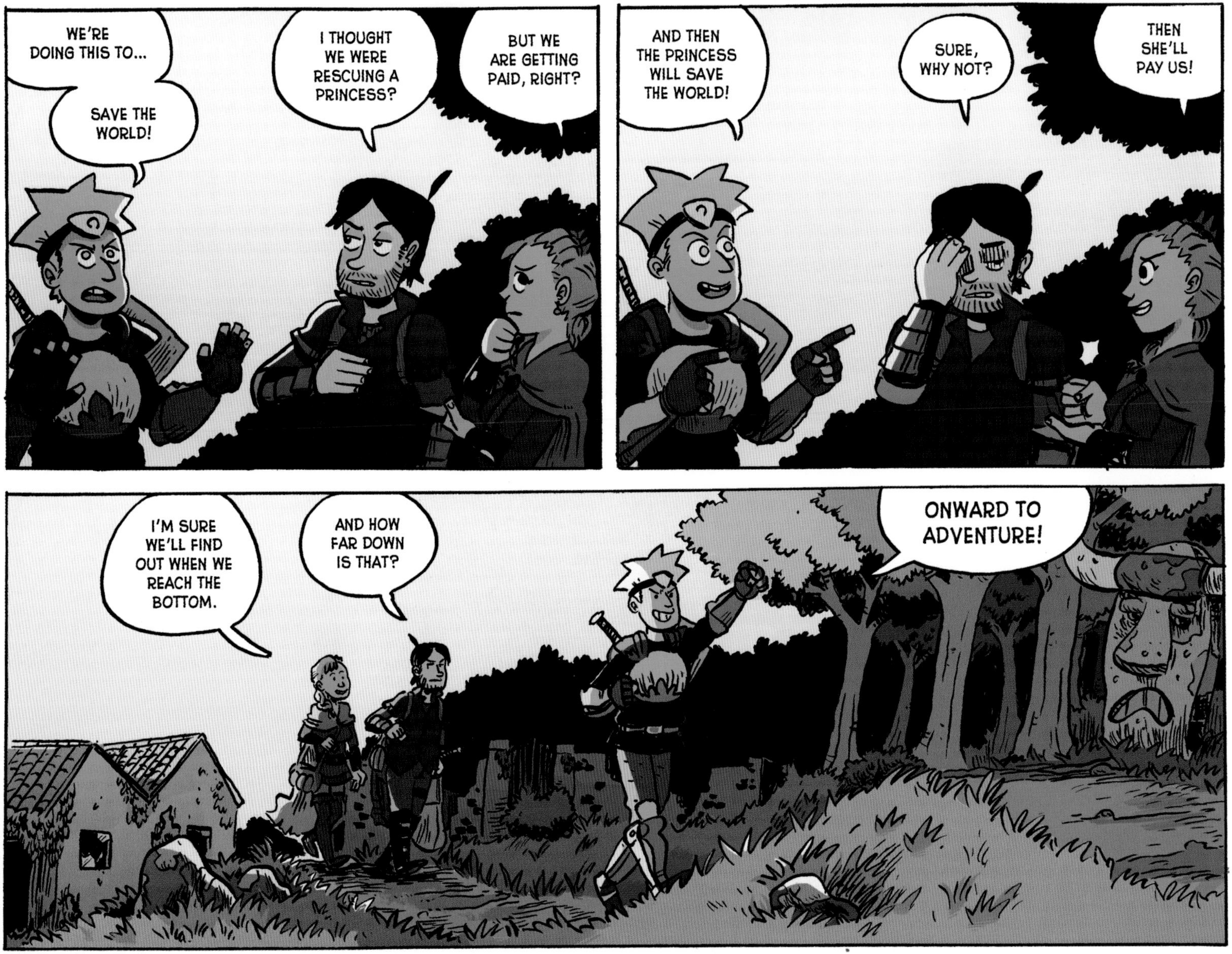
WE'RE DOING THIS TO...
SAVE THE WORLD!
I THOUGHT WE WERE RESCUING A PRINCESS?
BUT WE ARE GETTING PAID, RIGHT?
AND THEN THE PRINCESS WILL SAVE THE WORLD!
SURE, WHY NOT?
THEN SHE'LL PAY US!
I'M SURE WE'LL FIND OUT WHEN WE REACH THE BOTTOM.
AND HOW FAR DOWN IS THAT?
ONWARD TO ADVENTURE!

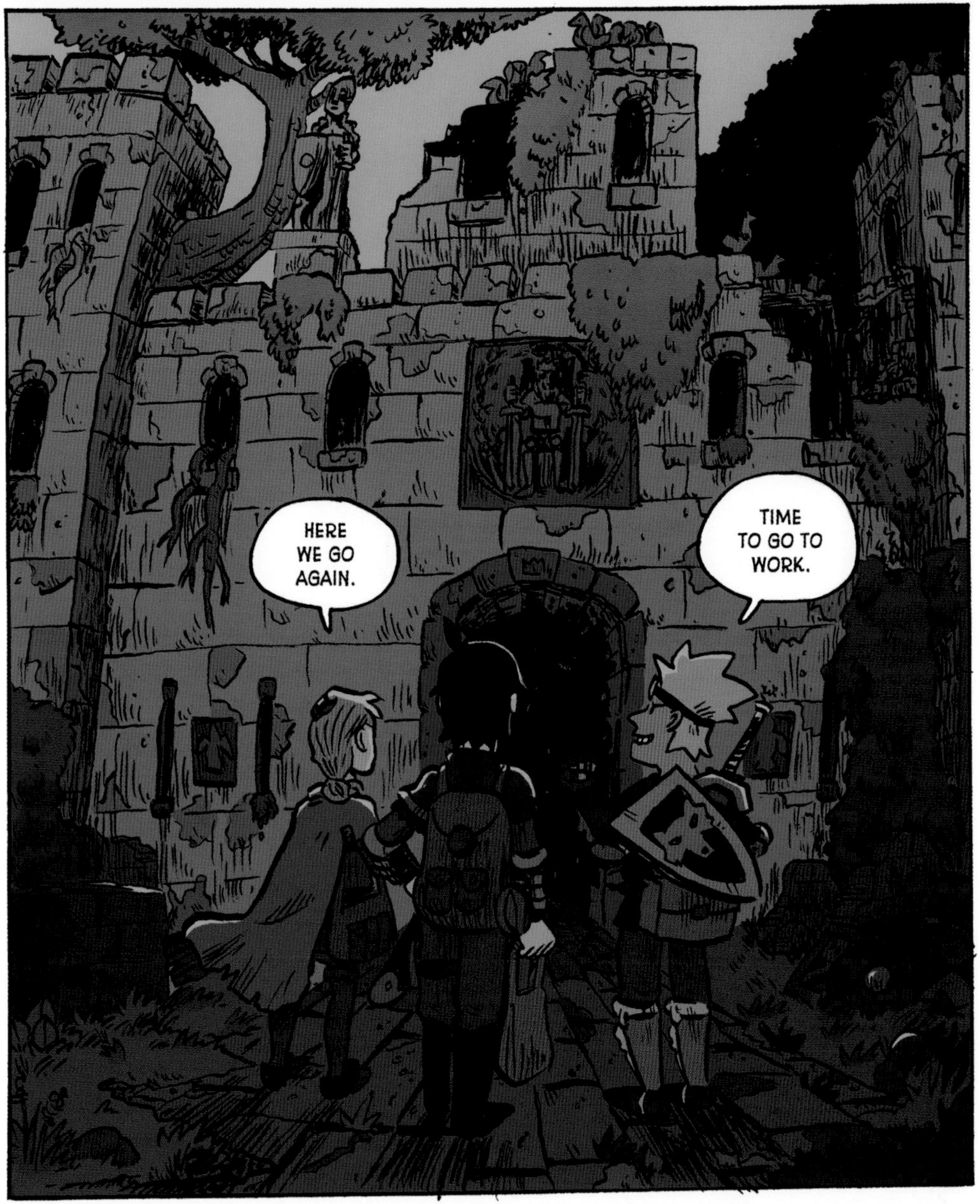
HERE WE GO AGAIN.
TIME TO GO TO WORK.

HEALING SALVE–

FOR BURNS AND MINOR CUTS. SOOTHING ALOE.

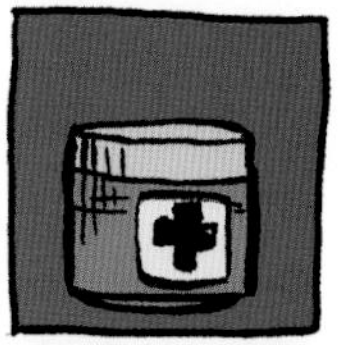

MID–POTION–

HEALS DAMAGE AND RELIEVES WEARINESS... SOMEHOW.

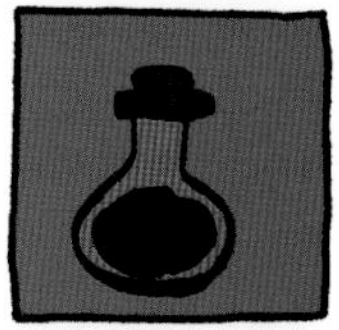

GREEN POWDER–

RESTORES THE ABILITY TO CAST SPELLS FOR WIZARDS.

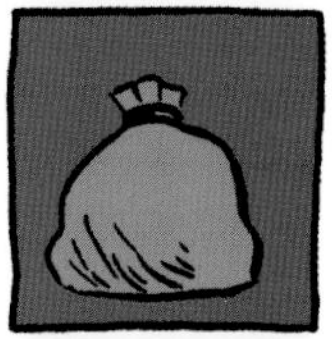

MINI BOMB–

USEFUL FOR REVEALING HIDDEN PASSAGEWAYS, AND BLOWING THINGS UP.

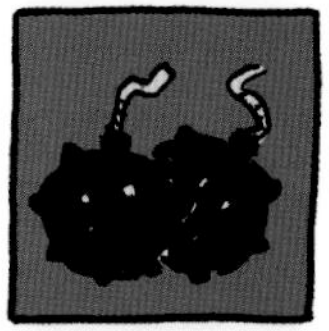

FIRE KIT –

MATCHES AND OIL FOR LIGHTING MAKESHIFT TORCHES.

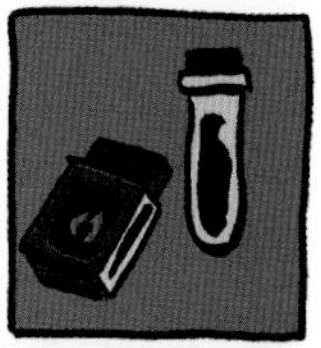

RETURN GEM–

SUMMONS THE ENTIRE PARTY OUT OF THE DUNGEON. EVERYONE ON THE ISLAND HAS ONE.

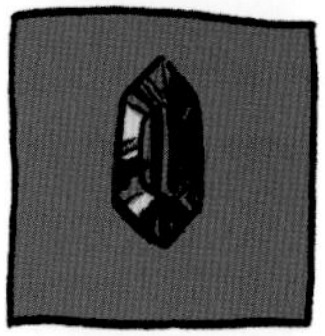

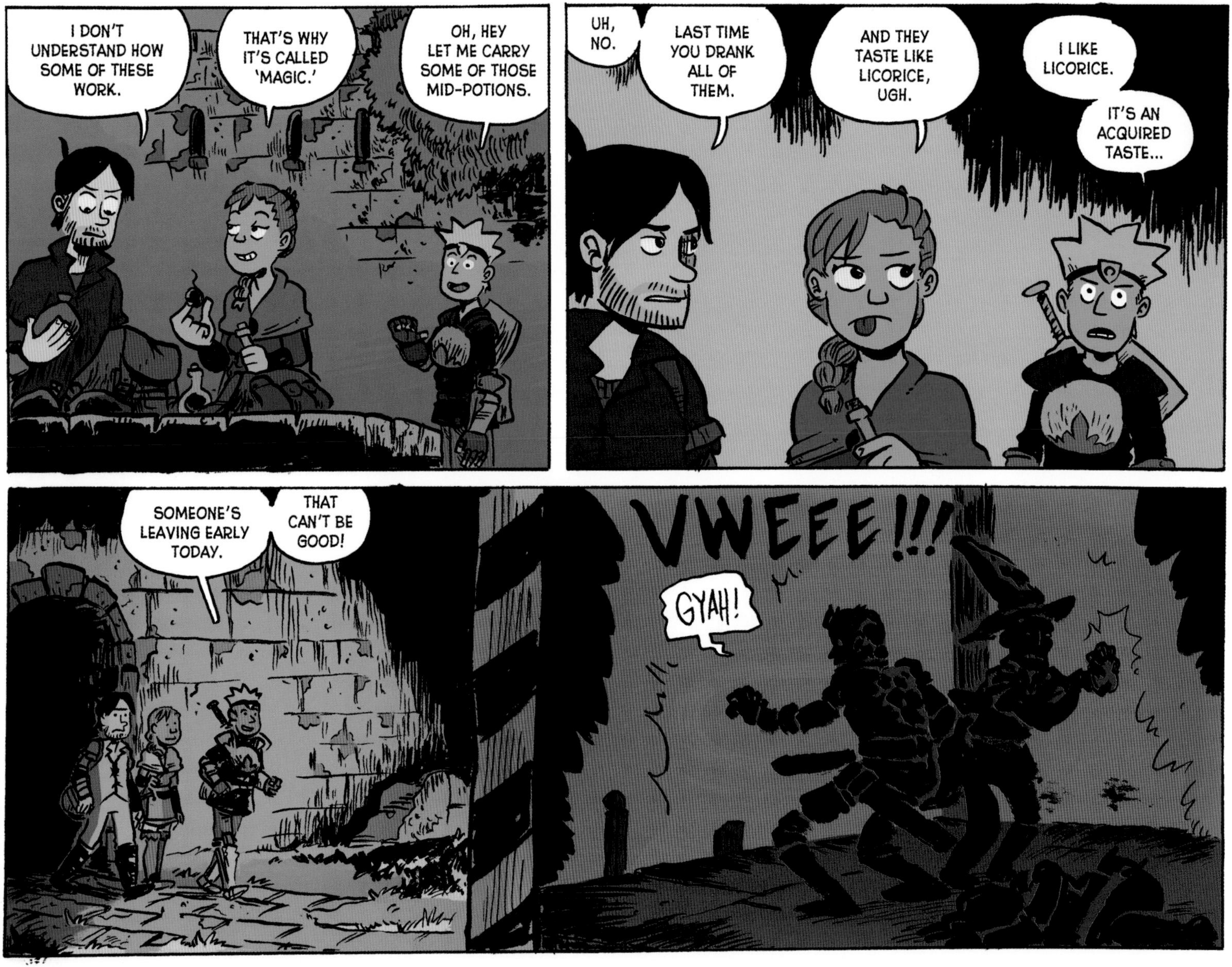
I DON'T UNDERSTAND HOW SOME OF THESE WORK.
THAT'S WHY IT'S CALLED 'MAGIC.'
OH, HEY LET ME CARRY SOME OF THOSE MID-POTIONS.
UH, NO.
LAST TIME YOU DRANK ALL OF THEM.
AND THEY TASTE LIKE LICORICE, UGH.
I LIKE LICORICE.
IT'S AN ACQUIRED TASTE...
SOMEONE'S LEAVING EARLY TODAY.
THAT CAN'T BE GOOD!
VWEEE!!!
GYAH!

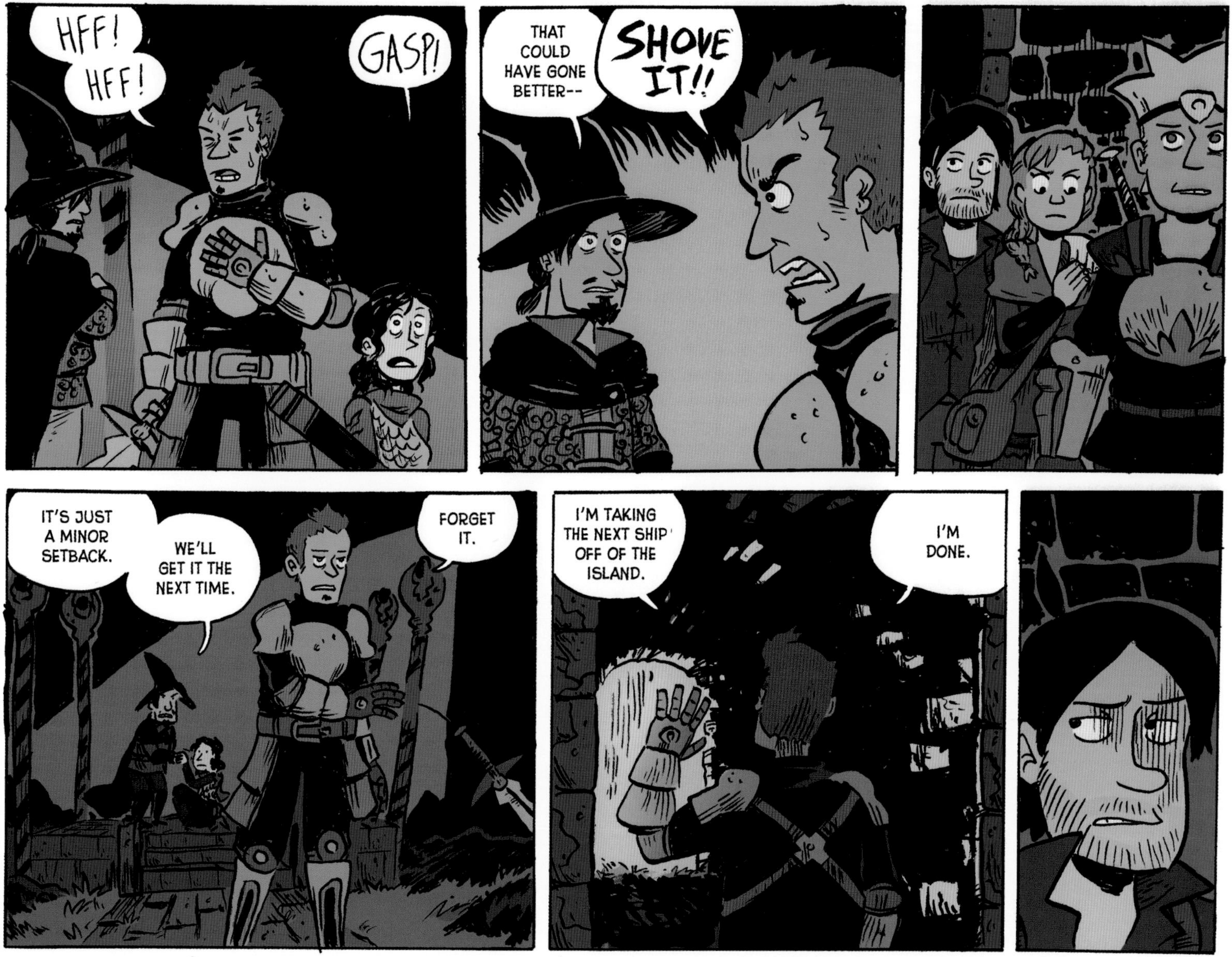
HFF! HFF!
GASP!
THAT COULD HAVE GONE BETTER--
SHOVE IT!!
IT'S JUST A MINOR SETBACK.
WE'LL GET IT THE NEXT TIME.
FORGET IT.
I'M TAKING THE NEXT SHIP OFF OF THE ISLAND.
I'M DONE.

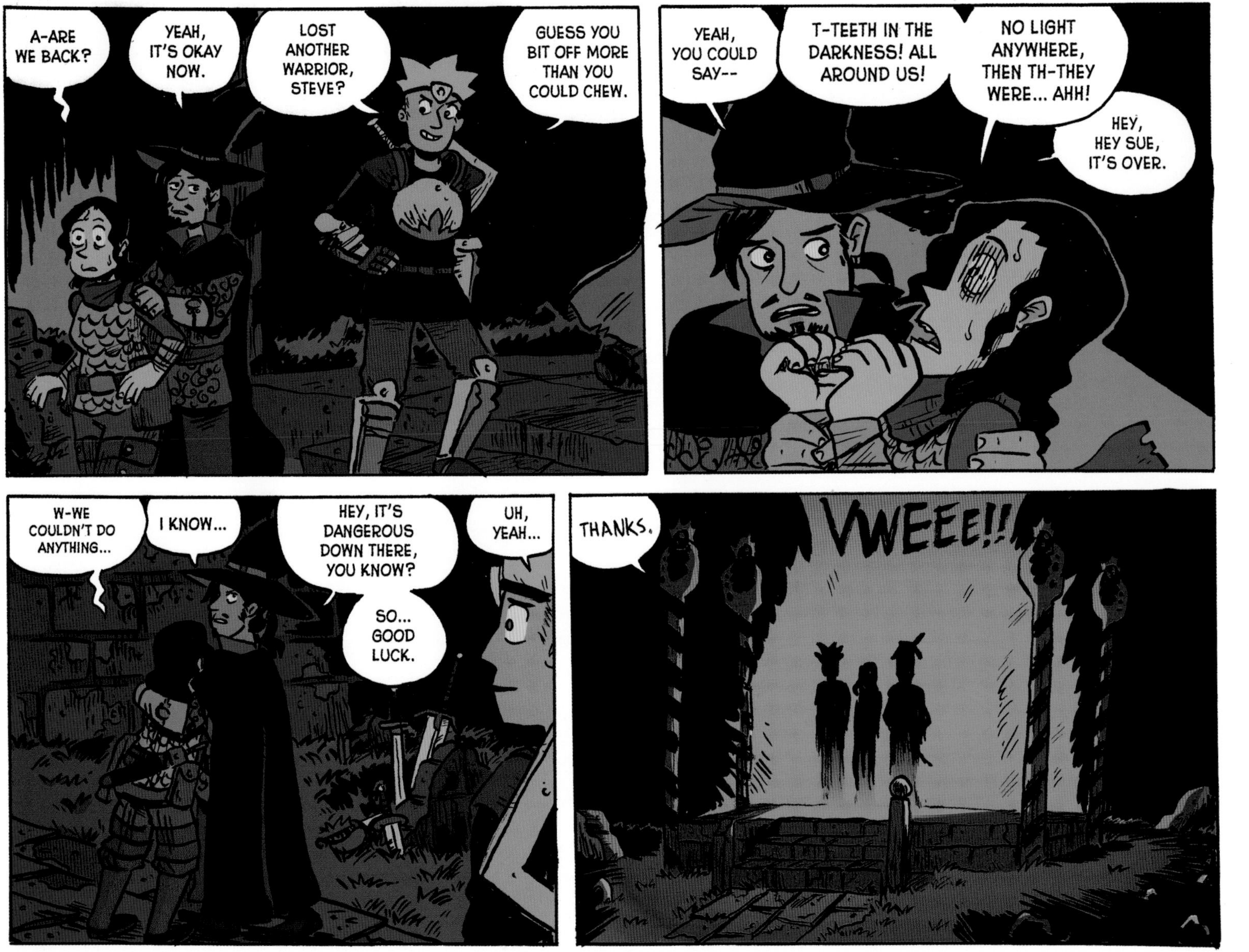
A-ARE WE BACK?
YEAH, IT'S OKAY NOW.
LOST ANOTHER WARRIOR, STEVE?
GUESS YOU BIT OFF MORE THAN YOU COULD CHEW.
YEAH, YOU COULD SAY--
T-TEETH IN THE DARKNESS! ALL AROUND US!
NO LIGHT ANYWHERE, THEN TH-THEY WERE... AHH!
HEY, HEY SUE, IT'S OVER.
W-WE COULDN'T DO ANYTHING...
I KNOW...
HEY, IT'S DANGEROUS DOWN THERE, YOU KNOW?
SO... GOOD LUCK.
UH, YEAH...
THANKS.
VWEEE!!

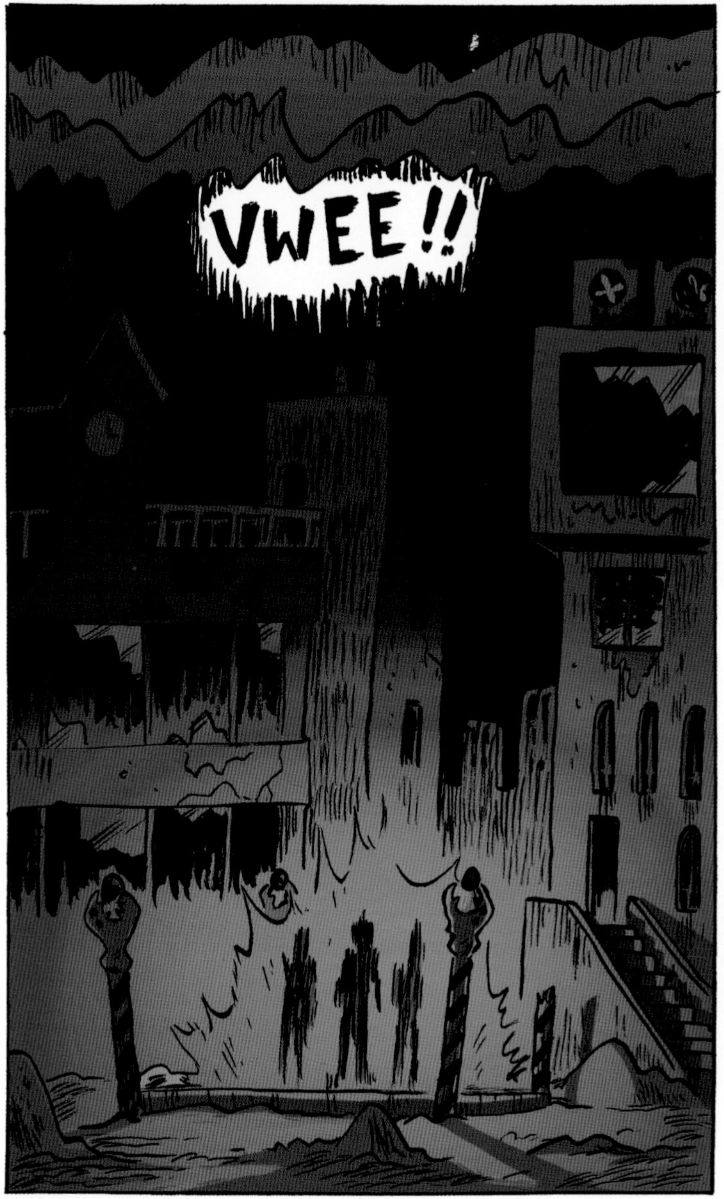
VWEE!!

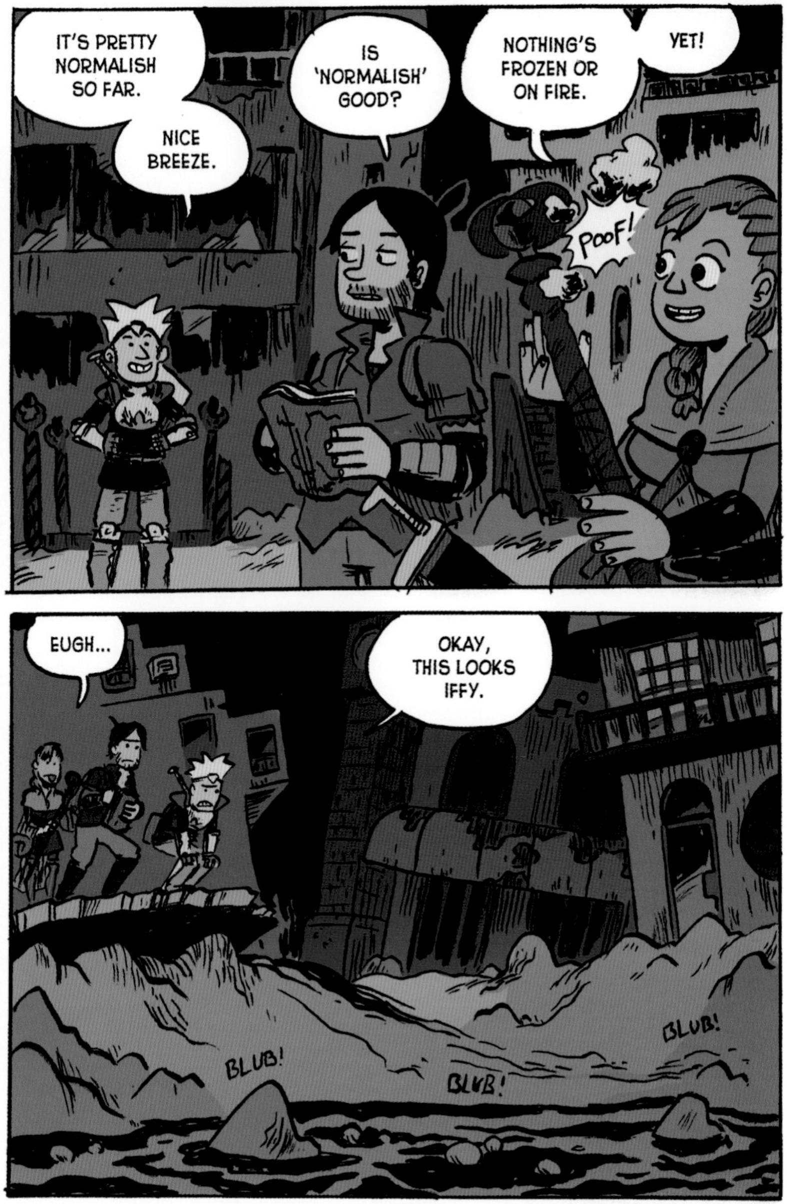
IT'S PRETTY NORMALISH SO FAR.
NICE BREEZE.
IS 'NORMALISH' GOOD?
NOTHING'S FROZEN OR ON FIRE.
YET!
POOF!
EUGH...
OKAY, THIS LOOKS IFFY.
BLUB!
BLUB!
BLUB!

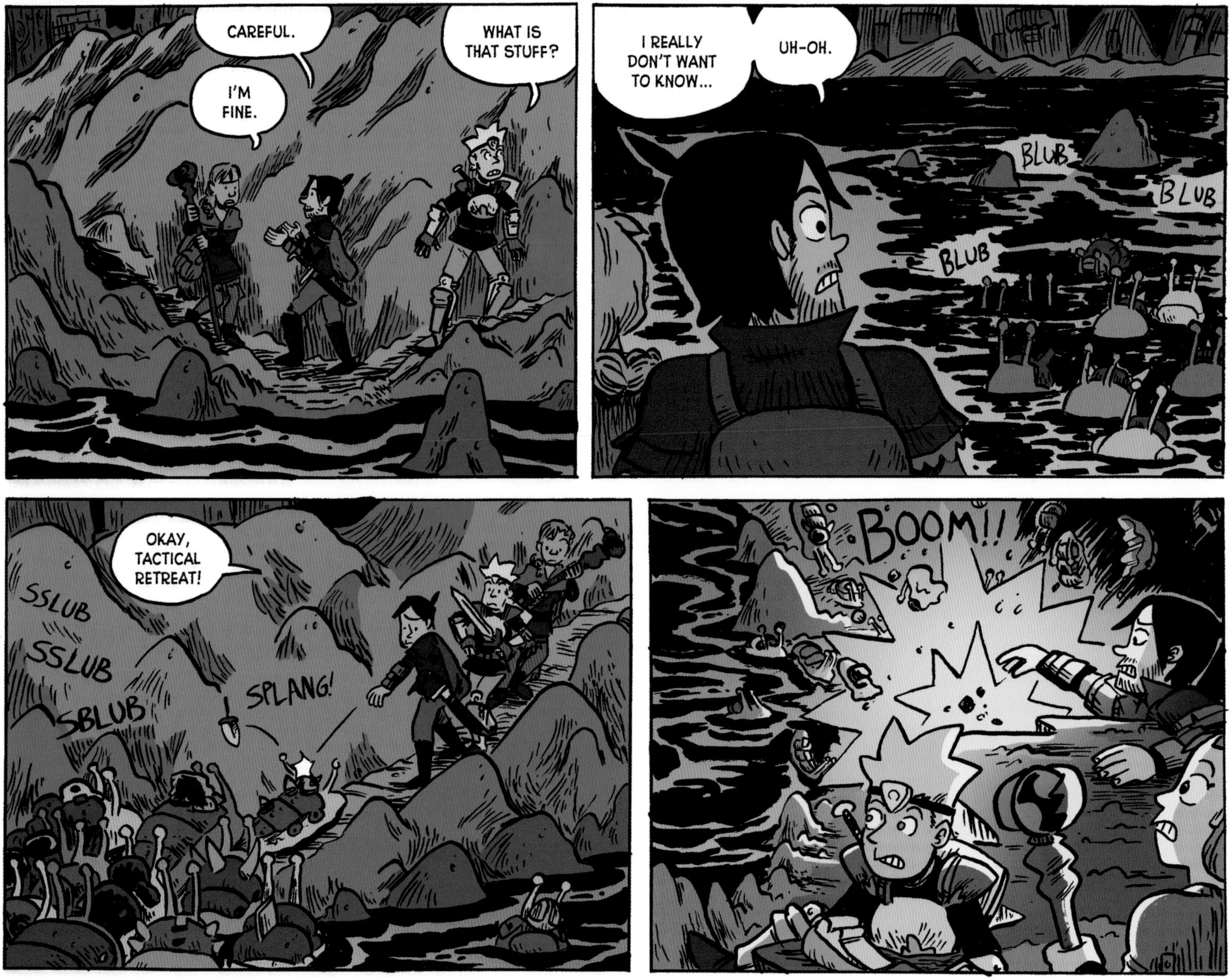
CAREFUL.
I'M FINE.
WHAT IS THAT STUFF?
I REALLY DON'T WANT TO KNOW...
UH-OH.
BLUB
BLUB
BLUB
OKAY, TACTICAL RETREAT!
SSLUB
SSLUB
SBLUB
SPLANG!
BOOM!!

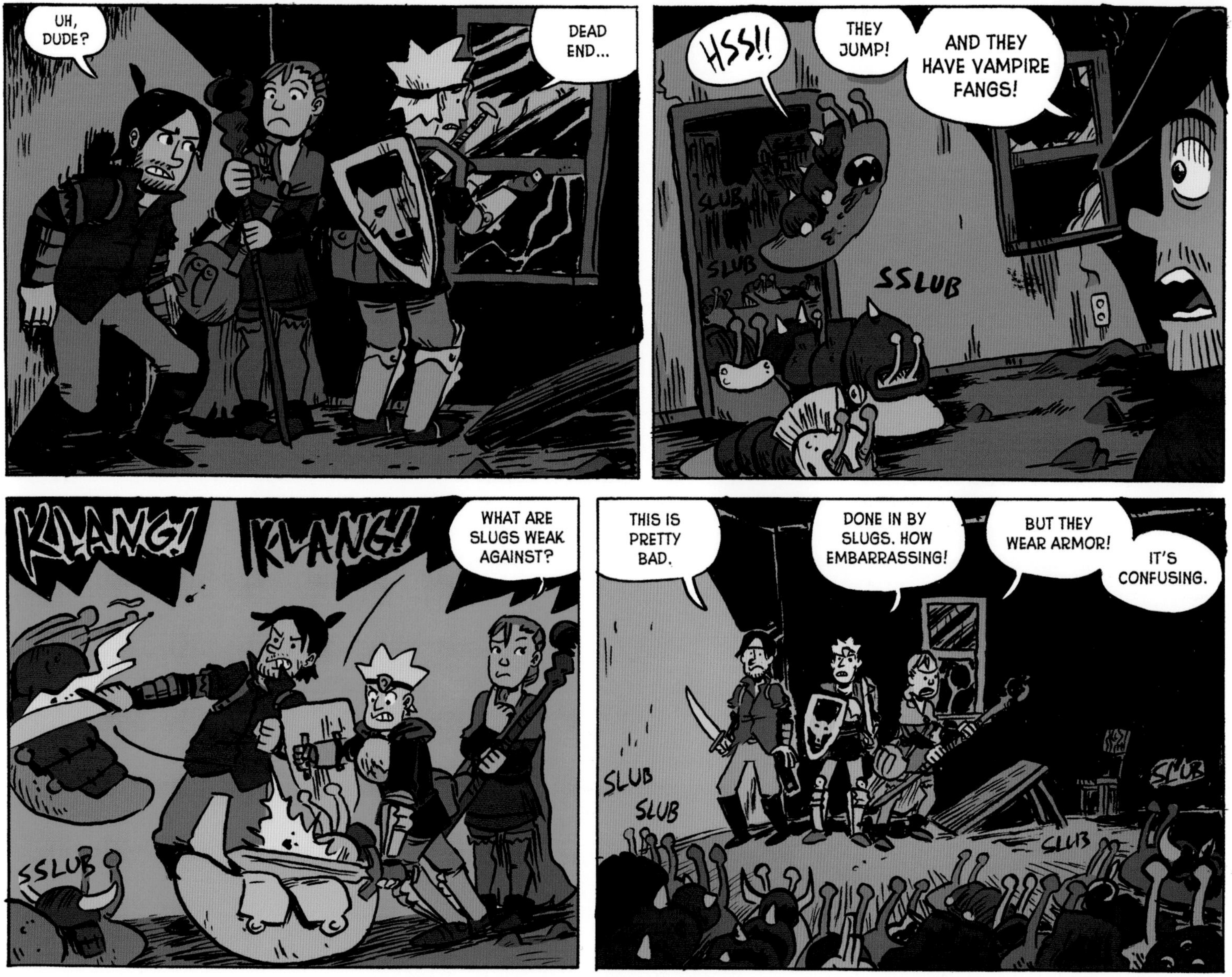
UH, DUDE?
DEAD END...
HSS!!
THEY JUMP!
AND THEY HAVE VAMPIRE FANGS!
SLUB
SLUB
SSLUB
KLANG!
KLANG!
WHAT ARE SLUGS WEAK AGAINST?
SSLUB
THIS IS PRETTY BAD.
DONE IN BY SLUGS. HOW EMBARRASSING!
BUT THEY WEAR ARMOR!
IT'S CONFUSING.
SLUB
SLUB
SLUB
SLUB

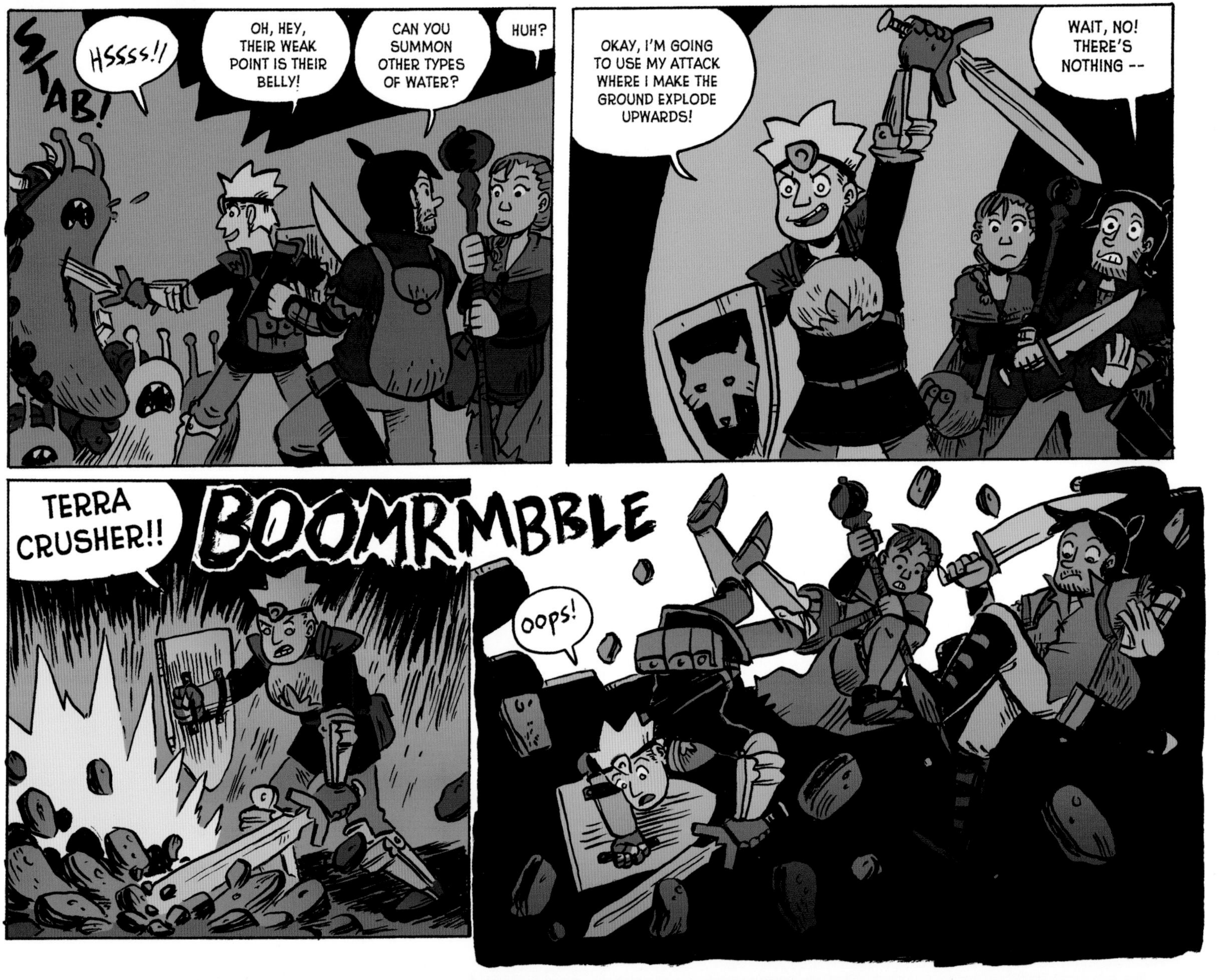
STAB!
HSSSS!!
OH, HEY, THEIR WEAK POINT IS THEIR BELLY!
CAN YOU SUMMON OTHER TYPES OF WATER?
HUH?
OKAY, I'M GOING TO USE MY ATTACK WHERE I MAKE THE GROUND EXPLODE UPWARDS!
WAIT, NO! THERE'S NOTHING --
TERRA CRUSHER!!
BOOMRMBBLE
OOPS!

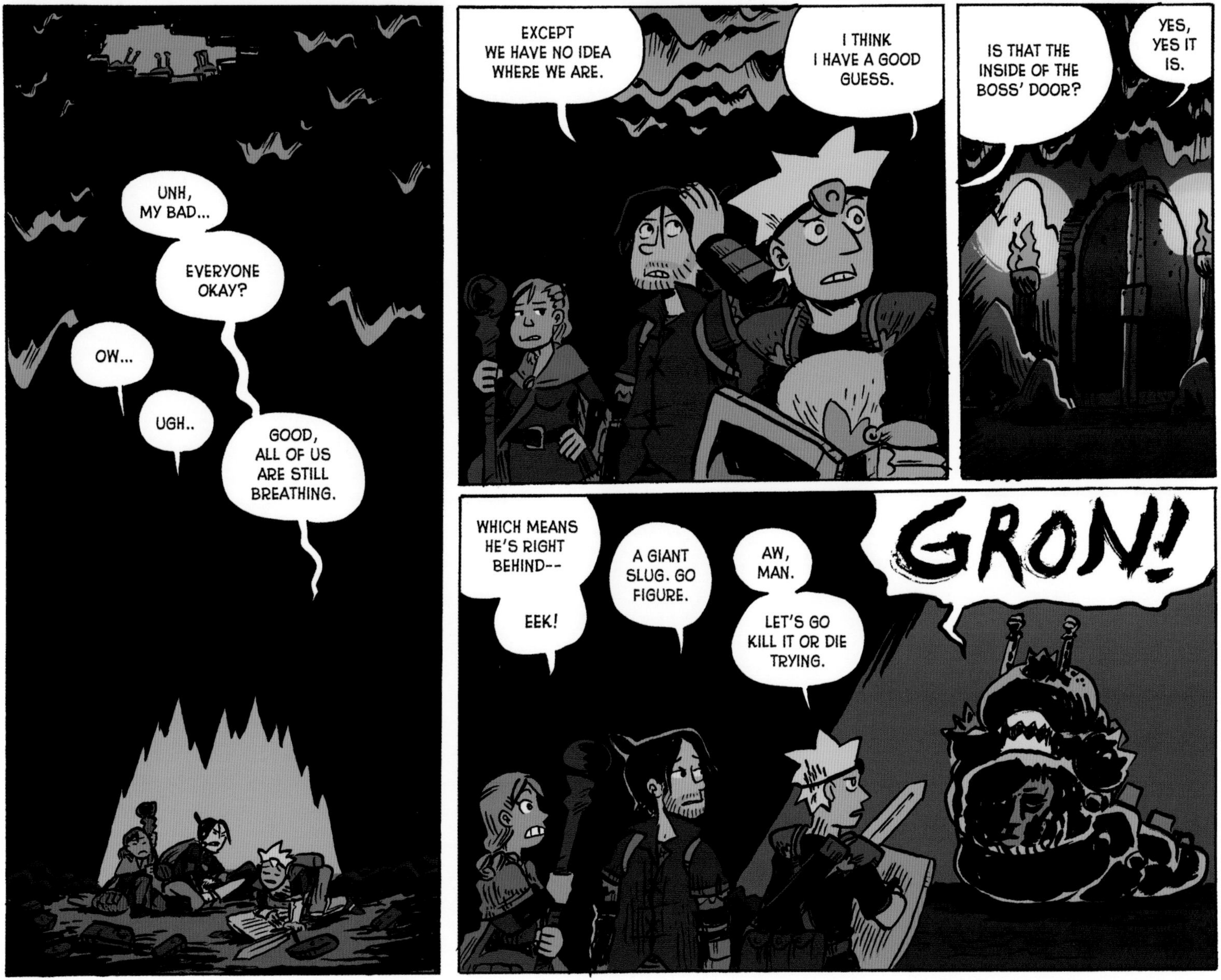
UNH, MY BAD...
EVERYONE OKAY?
OW...
UGH..
GOOD, ALL OF US ARE STILL BREATHING.
EXCEPT WE HAVE NO IDEA WHERE WE ARE.
I THINK I HAVE A GOOD GUESS.
IS THAT THE INSIDE OF THE BOSS' DOOR?
YES, YES IT IS.
WHICH MEANS HE'S RIGHT BEHIND--
GRON!
EEK!
A GIANT SLUG. GO FIGURE.
AW, MAN.
LET'S GO KILL IT OR DIE TRYING.

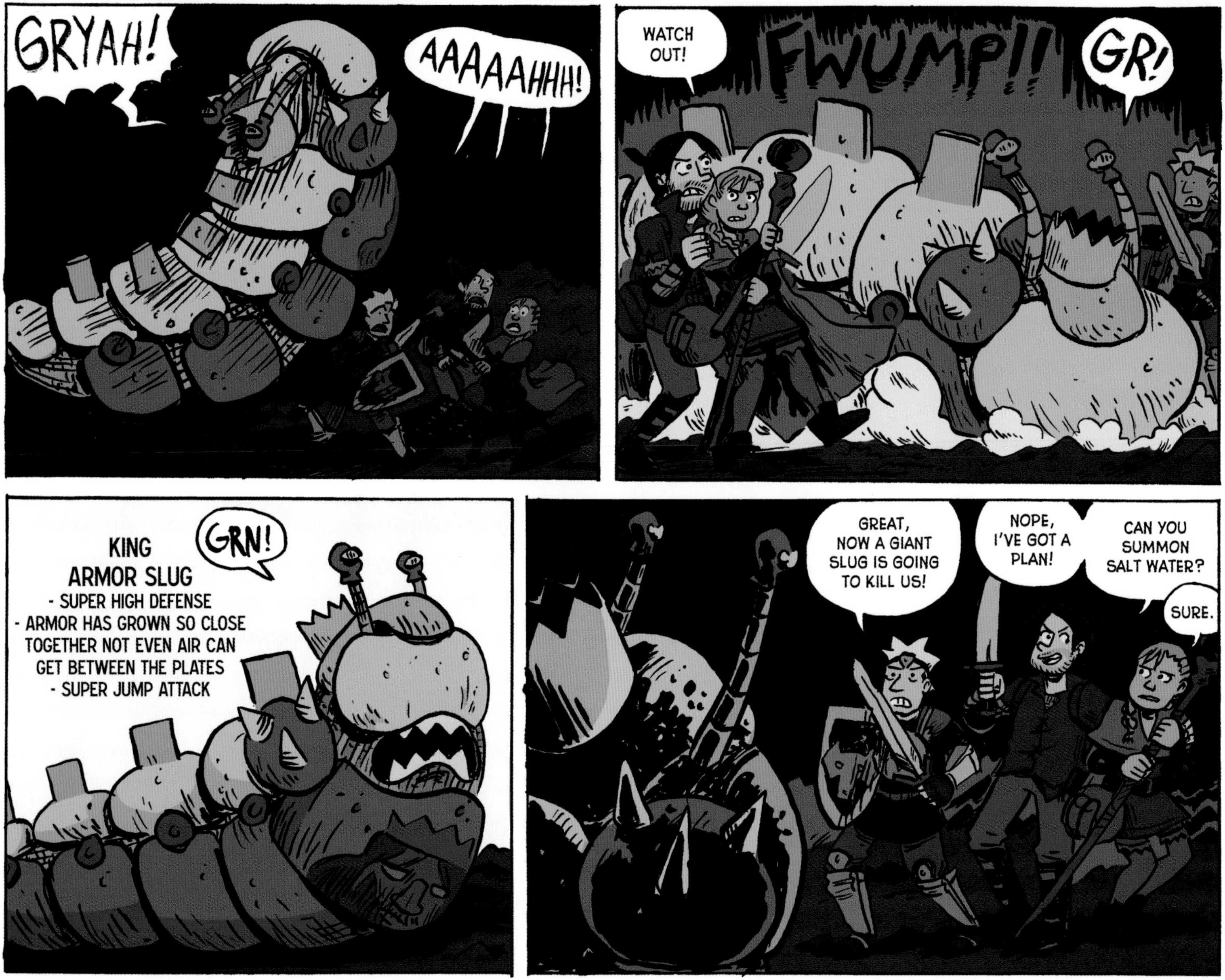
GRYAH!
AAAAAHHH!
WATCH OUT!
FWUMP!!
GR!
KING ARMOR SLUG
- SUPER HIGH DEFENSE
- ARMOR HAS GROWN SO CLOSE TOGETHER NOT EVEN AIR CAN GET BETWEEN THE PLATES
- SUPER JUMP ATTACK
GRN!
GREAT, NOW A GIANT SLUG IS GOING TO KILL US!
NOPE, I'VE GOT A PLAN!
CAN YOU SUMMON SALT WATER?
SURE.

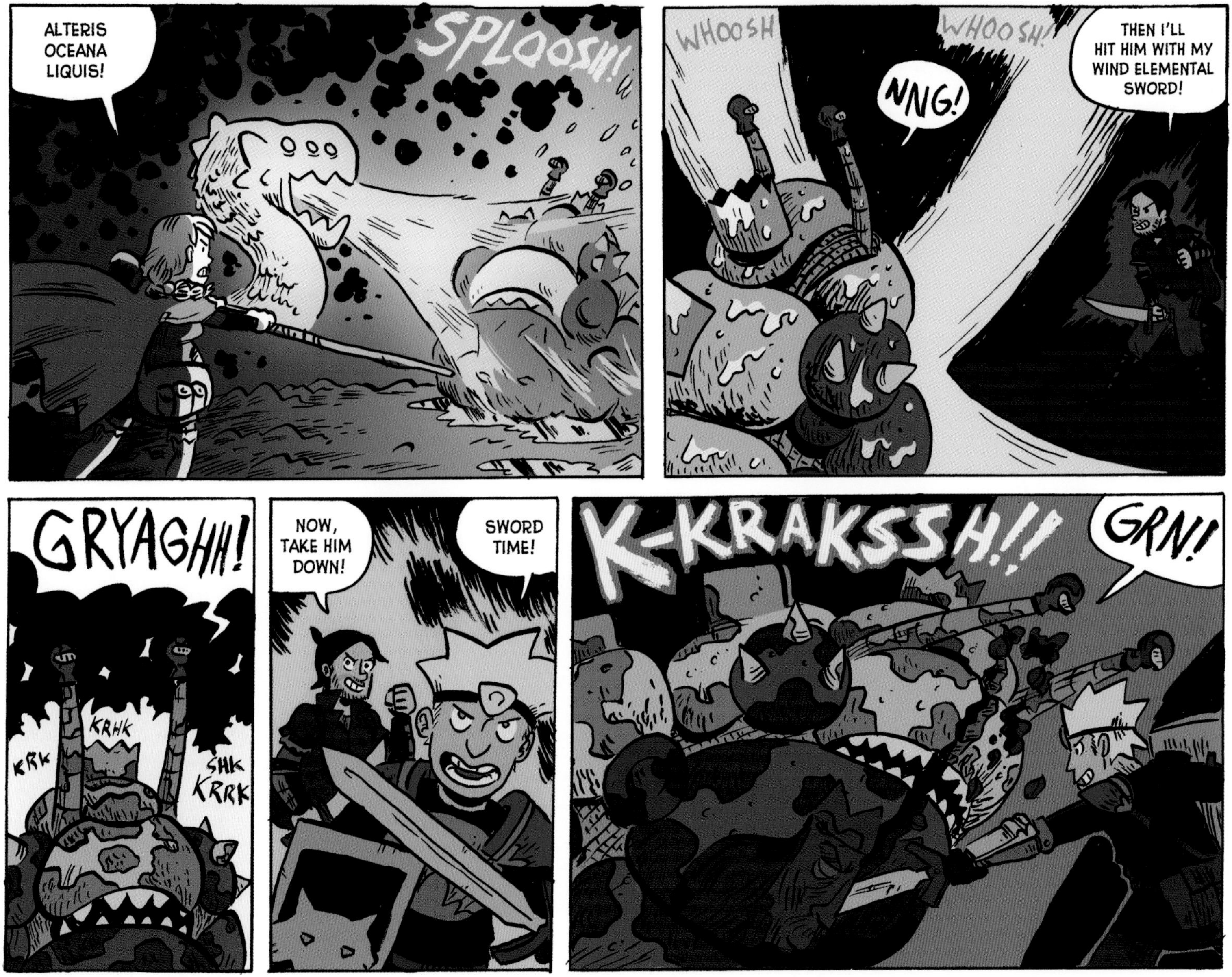
ALTERIS OCEANA LIQUIS!
SPLOOSH!
WHOOSH
WHOOSH!
NNG!
THEN I'LL HIT HIM WITH MY WIND ELEMENTAL SWORD!
GRYAGHH!
KRHK
KRK
SHK KRRK
NOW, TAKE HIM DOWN!
SWORD TIME!
K-KRAKSSH!!
GRN!

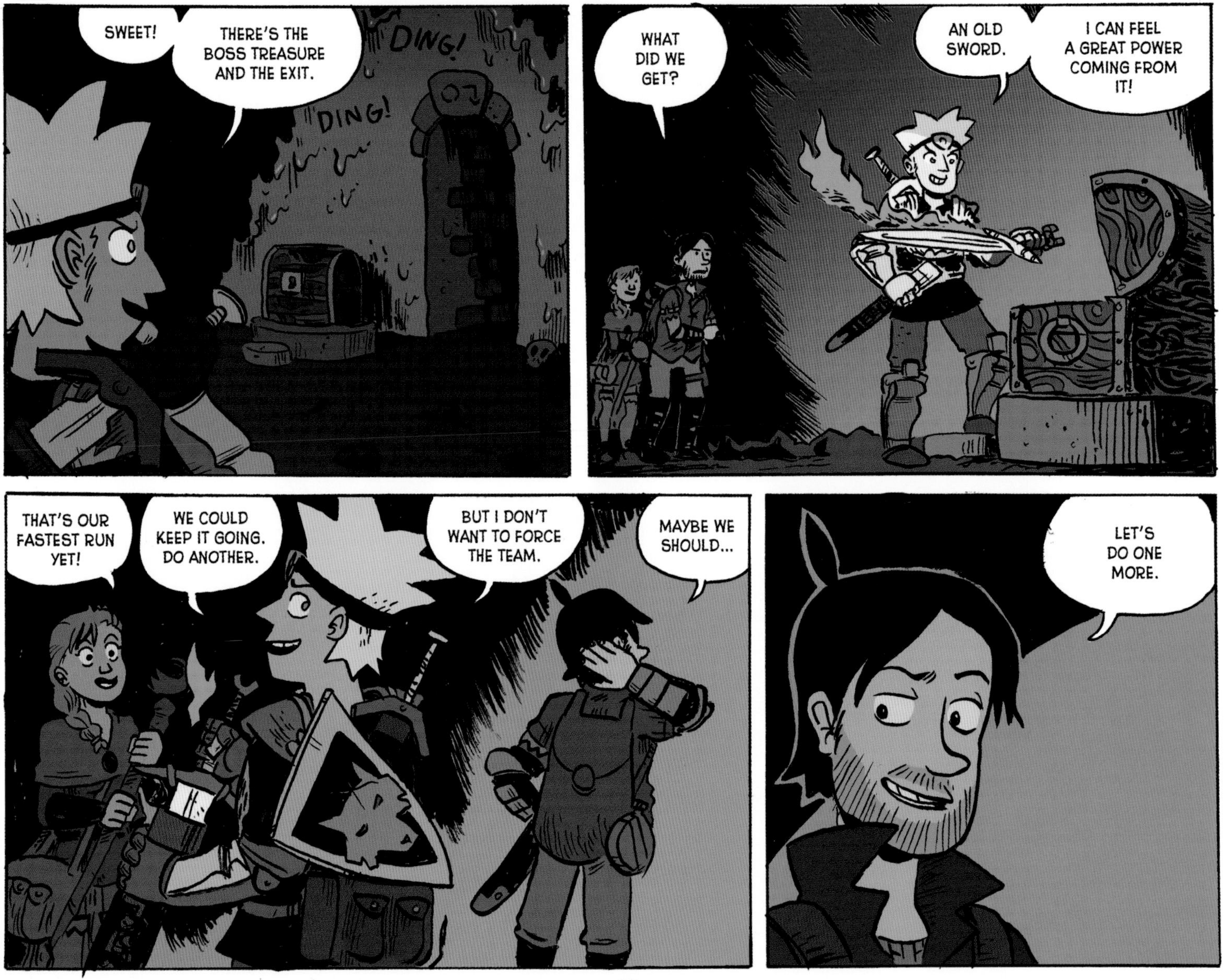
SWEET!
THERE'S THE BOSS TREASURE AND THE EXIT.
DING!
DING!
WHAT DID WE GET?
AN OLD SWORD.
I CAN FEEL A GREAT POWER COMING FROM IT!
THAT'S OUR FASTEST RUN YET!
WE COULD KEEP IT GOING. DO ANOTHER.
BUT I DON'T WANT TO FORCE THE TEAM.
MAYBE WE SHOULD...
LET'S DO ONE MORE.

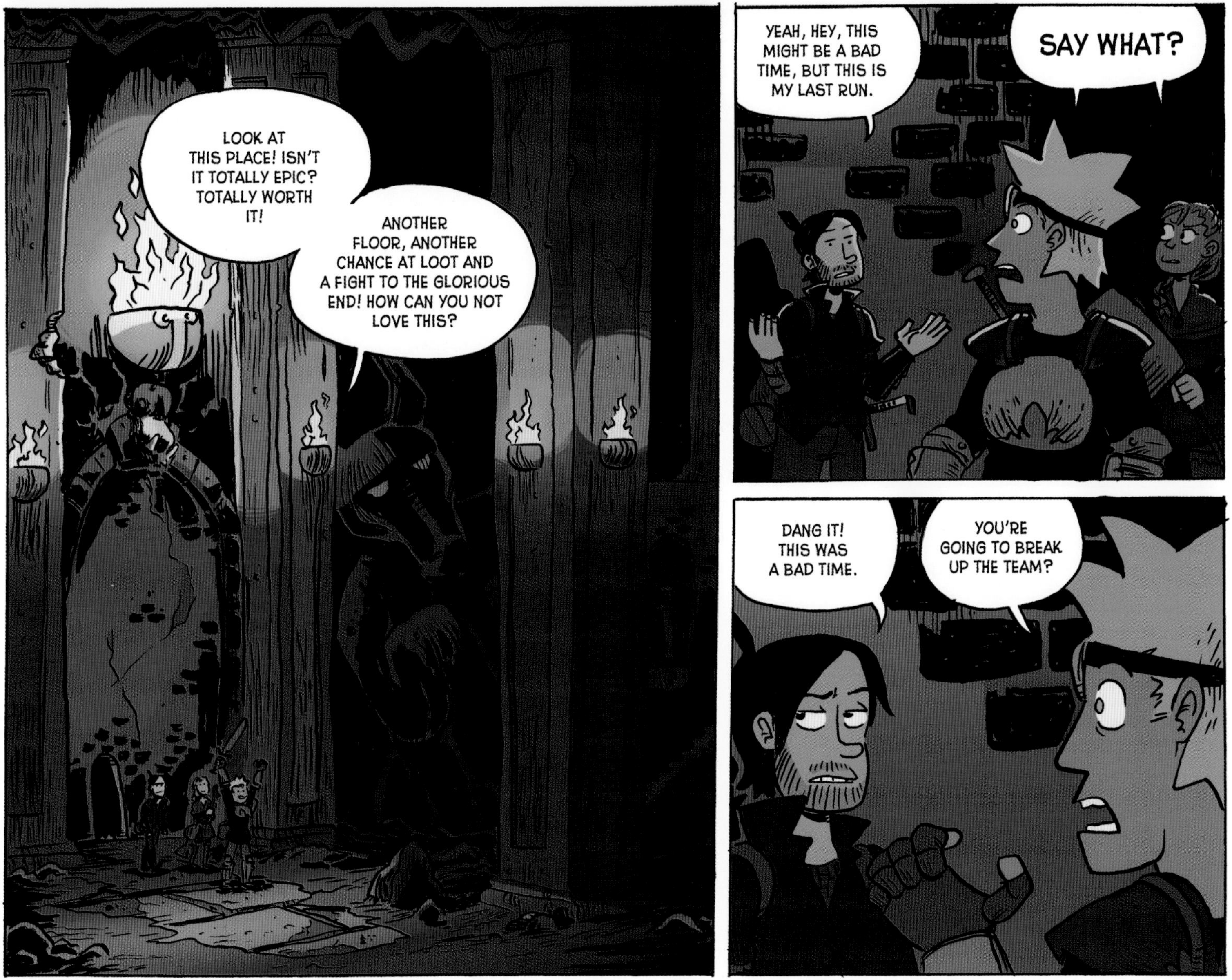
LOOK AT THIS PLACE! ISN'T IT TOTALLY EPIC? TOTALLY WORTH IT!
ANOTHER FLOOR, ANOTHER CHANCE AT LOOT AND A FIGHT TO THE GLORIOUS END! HOW CAN YOU NOT LOVE THIS?
YEAH, HEY, THIS MIGHT BE A BAD TIME, BUT THIS IS MY LAST RUN.
SAY WHAT?
DANG IT! THIS WAS A BAD TIME.
YOU'RE GOING TO BREAK UP THE TEAM?

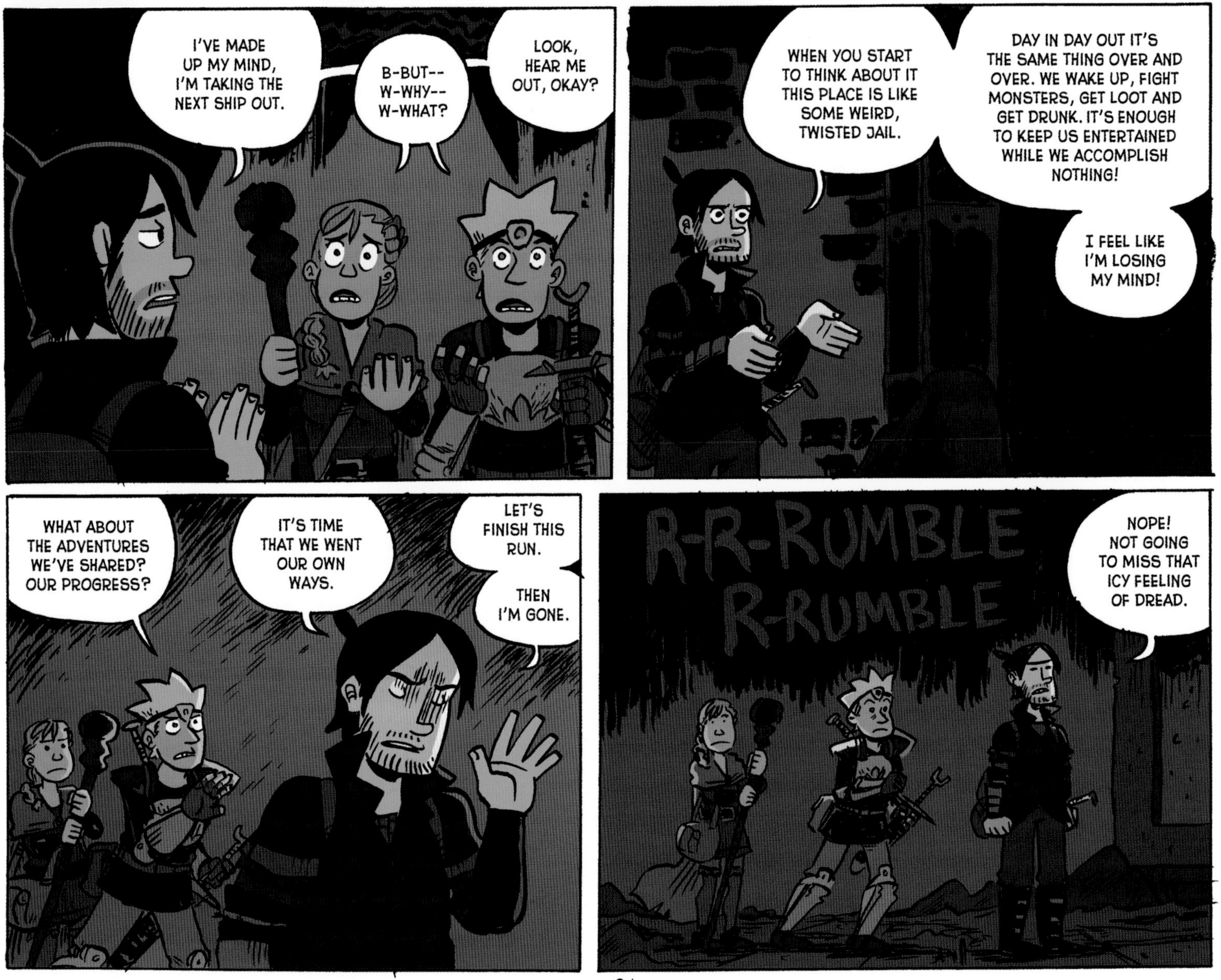
I'VE MADE UP MY MIND, I'M TAKING THE NEXT SHIP OUT.
B-BUT-- W-WHY-- W-WHAT?
LOOK, HEAR ME OUT, OKAY?
WHEN YOU START TO THINK ABOUT IT THIS PLACE IS LIKE SOME WEIRD, TWISTED JAIL.
DAY IN DAY OUT IT'S THE SAME THING OVER AND OVER. WE WAKE UP, FIGHT MONSTERS, GET LOOT AND GET DRUNK. IT'S ENOUGH TO KEEP US ENTERTAINED WHILE WE ACCOMPLISH NOTHING!
I FEEL LIKE I'M LOSING MY MIND!
WHAT ABOUT THE ADVENTURES WE'VE SHARED? OUR PROGRESS?
IT'S TIME THAT WE WENT OUR OWN WAYS.
LET'S FINISH THIS RUN.
THEN I'M GONE.
R-R-RUMBLE
R-RUMBLE
NOPE! NOT GOING TO MISS THAT ICY FEELING OF DREAD.

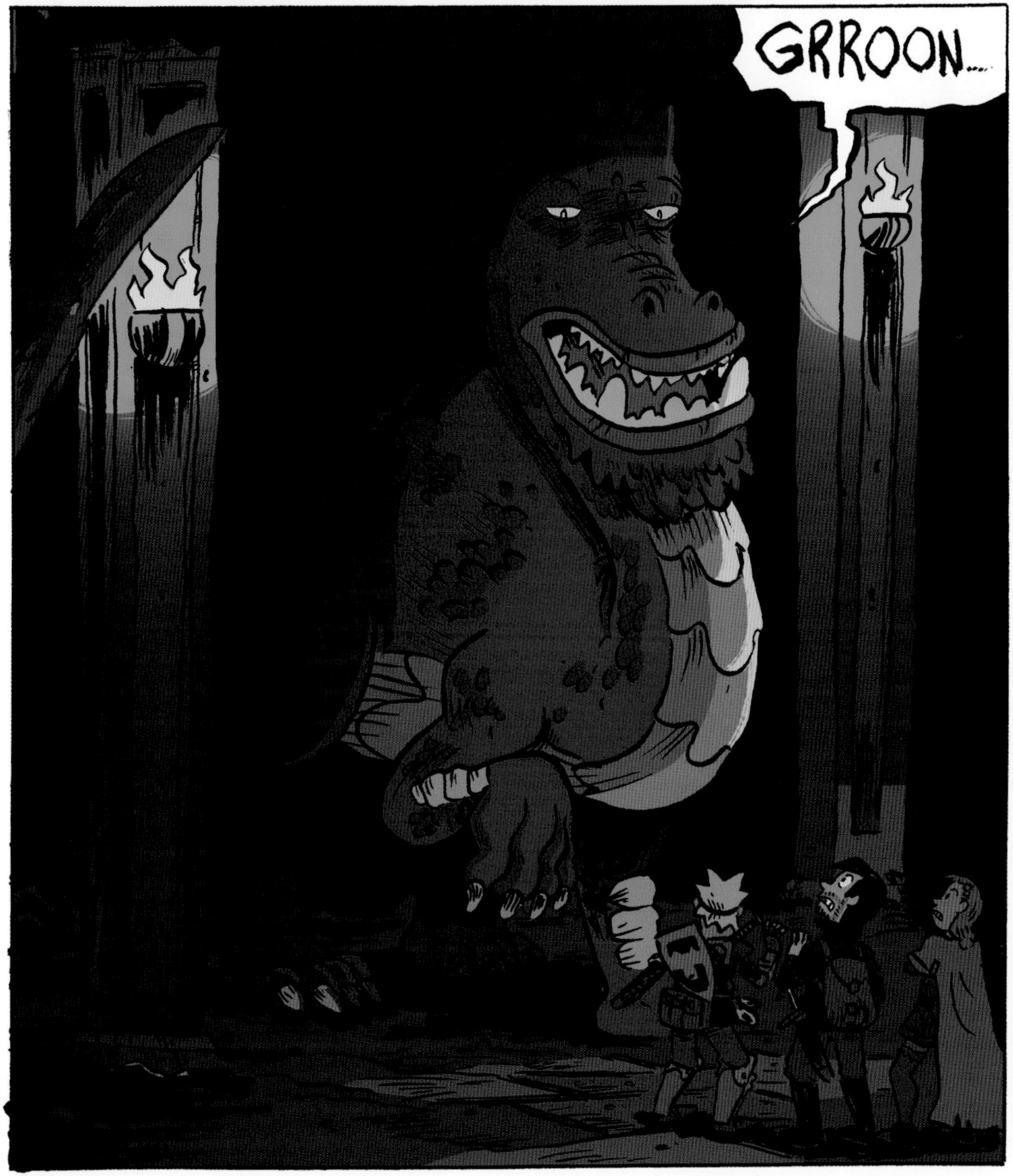
GRROON...

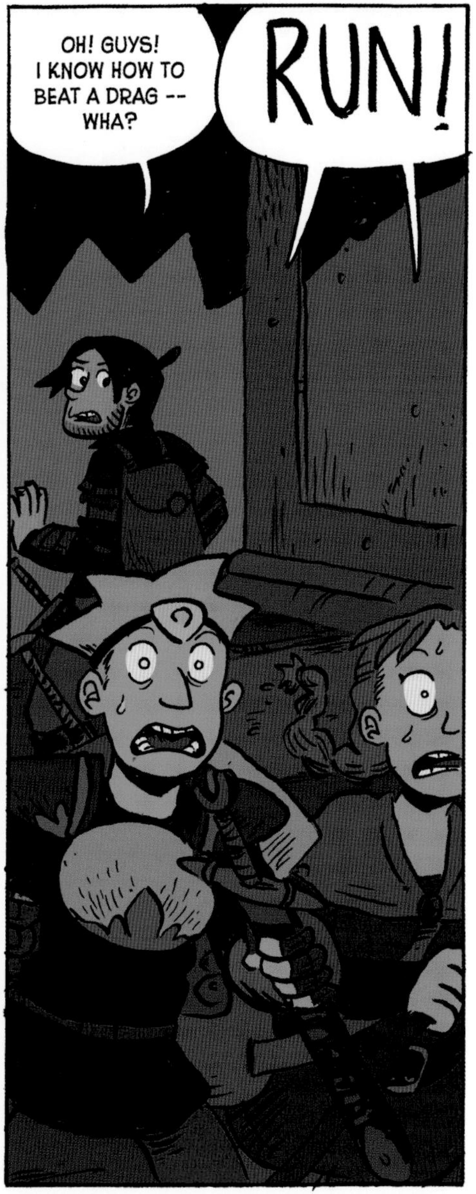
OH! GUYS! I KNOW HOW TO BEAT A DRAG -- WHA?
RUN!

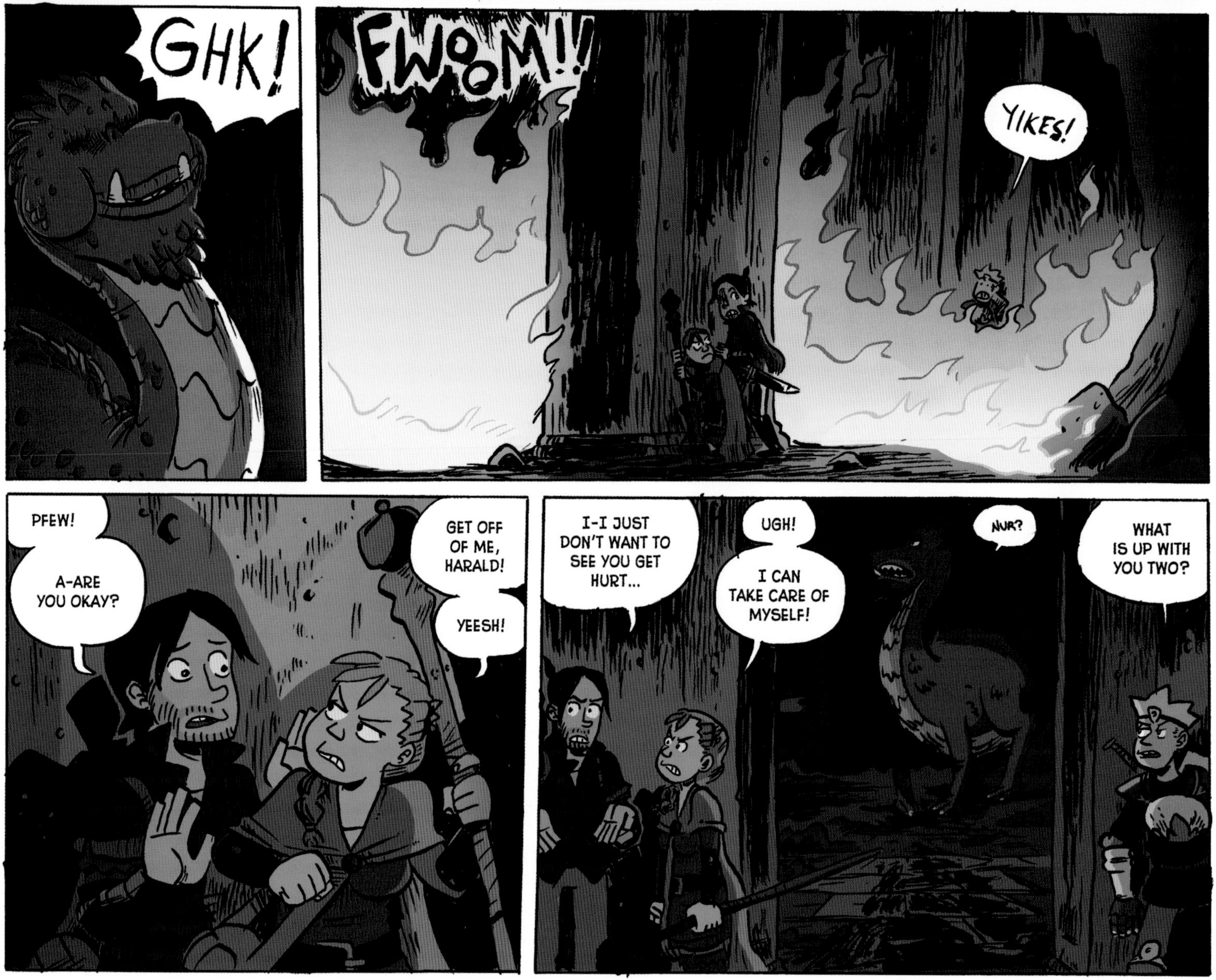
GHK!
FWOOM!!
YIKES!
PFEW!
A-ARE YOU OKAY?
GET OFF OF ME, HARALD!
YEESH!
I-I JUST DON'T WANT TO SEE YOU GET HURT...
UGH!
I CAN TAKE CARE OF MYSELF!
NUR?
WHAT IS UP WITH YOU TWO?

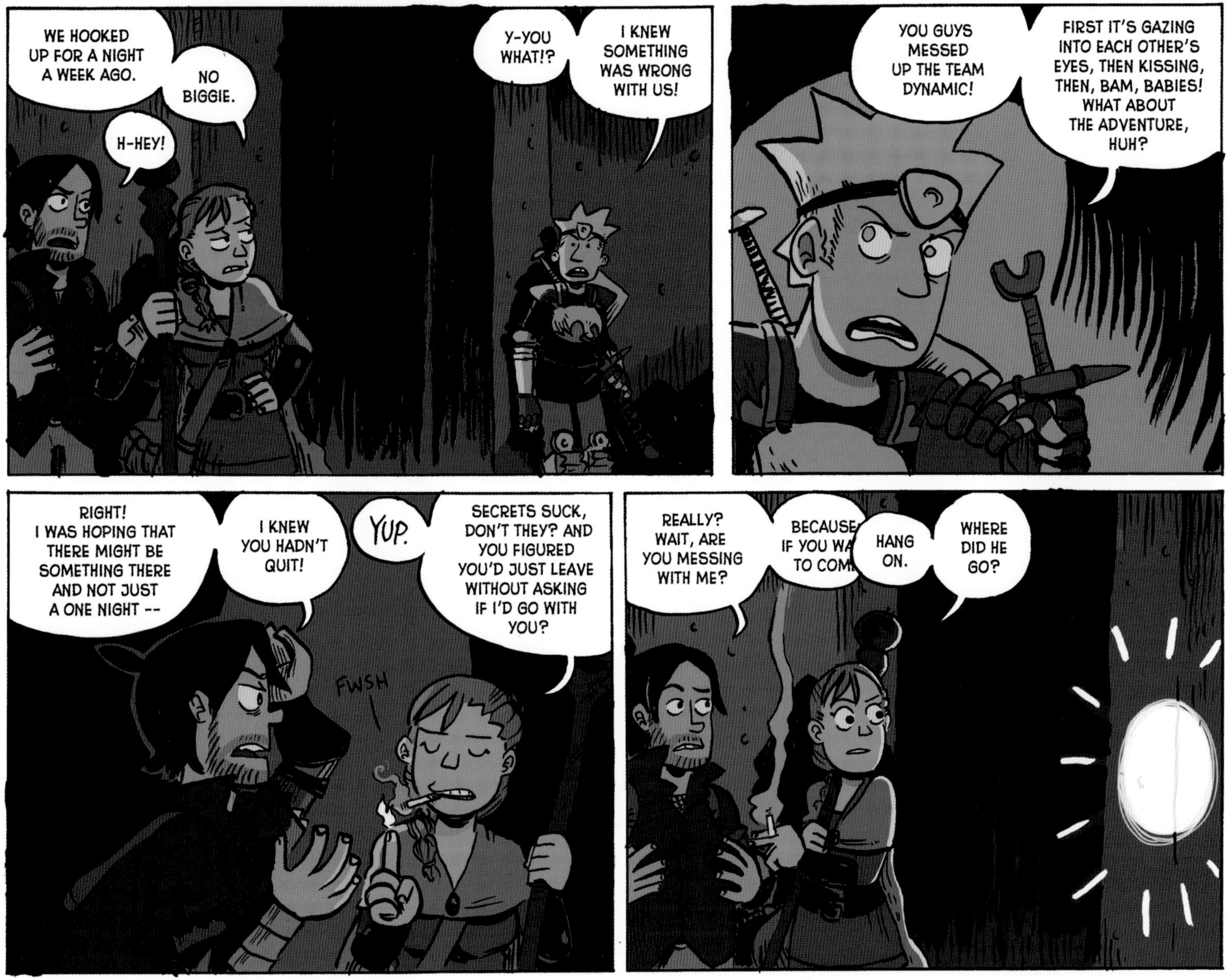
WE HOOKED UP FOR A NIGHT A WEEK AGO.
H-HEY!
NO BIGGIE.
Y-YOU WHAT!?
I KNEW SOMETHING WAS WRONG WITH US!
YOU GUYS MESSED UP THE TEAM DYNAMIC!
FIRST IT'S GAZING INTO EACH OTHER'S EYES, THEN KISSING, THEN, BAM, BABIES! WHAT ABOUT THE ADVENTURE, HUH?
RIGHT! I WAS HOPING THAT THERE MIGHT BE SOMETHING THERE AND NOT JUST A ONE NIGHT --
I KNEW YOU HADN'T QUIT!
YUP.
SECRETS SUCK, DON'T THEY? AND YOU FIGURED YOU'D JUST LEAVE WITHOUT ASKING IF I'D GO WITH YOU?
FWSH
REALLY? WAIT, ARE YOU MESSING WITH ME?
HANG ON.
WHERE DID HE GO?

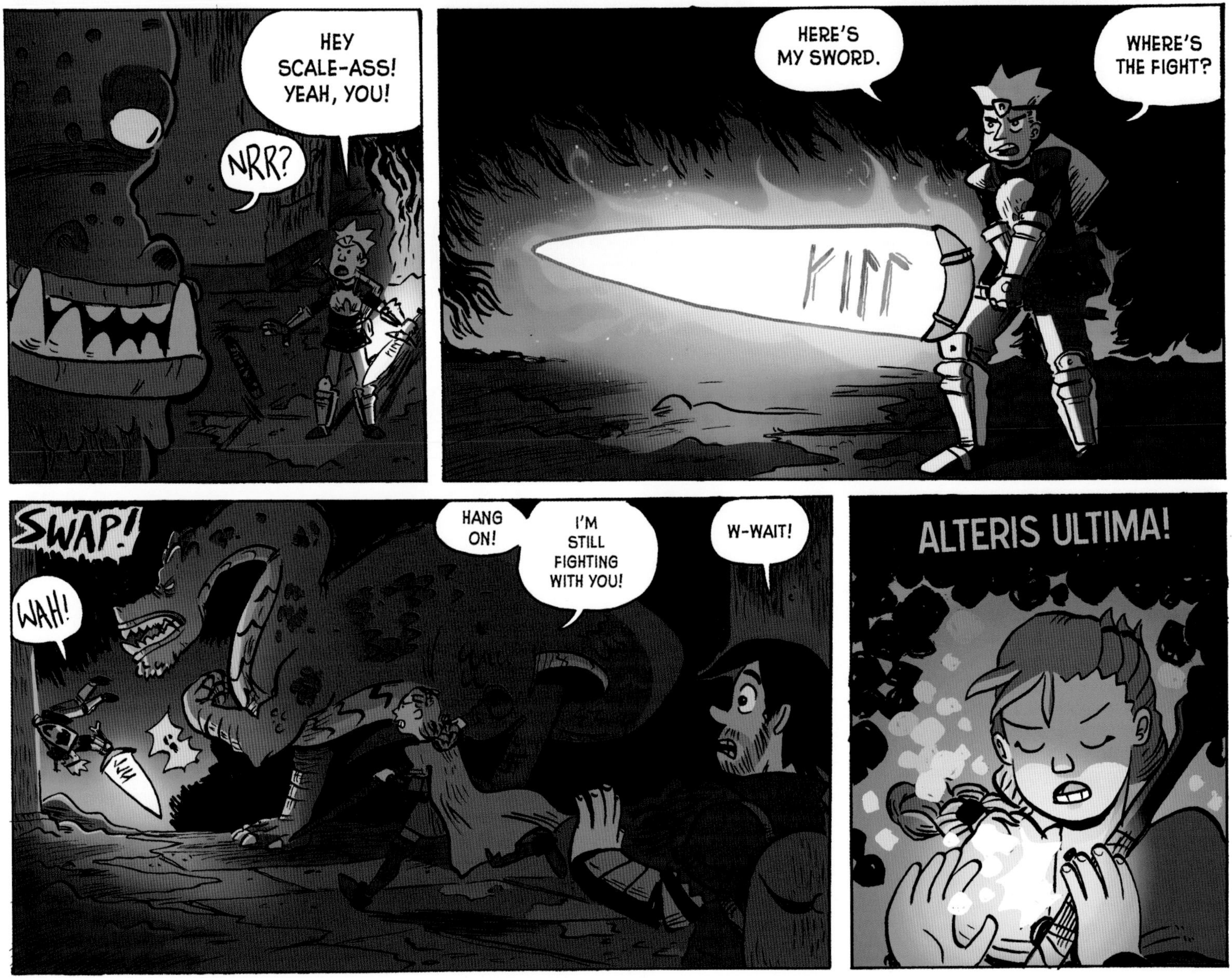
HEY SCALE-ASS! YEAH, YOU!
NRR?
HERE'S MY SWORD.
WHERE'S THE FIGHT?
SWAP!
WAH!
HANG ON!
I'M STILL FIGHTING WITH YOU!
W-WAIT!
ALTERIS ULTIMA!

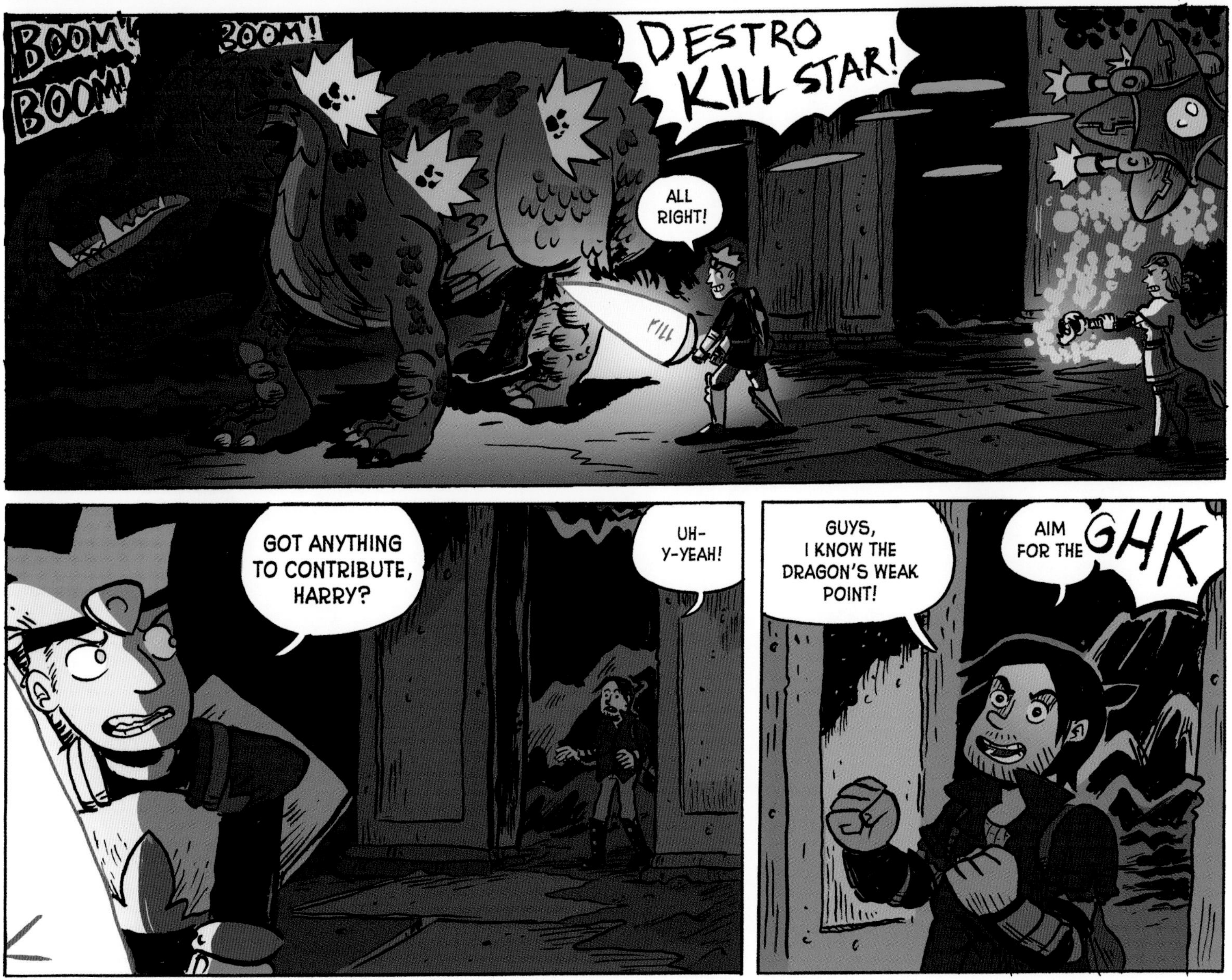
BOOM!
BOOM!
BOOM!
DESTRO KILL STAR!
ALL RIGHT!
GOT ANYTHING TO CONTRIBUTE, HARRY?
UH- Y-YEAH!
GUYS, I KNOW THE DRAGON'S WEAK POINT!
AIM FOR THE
GHK

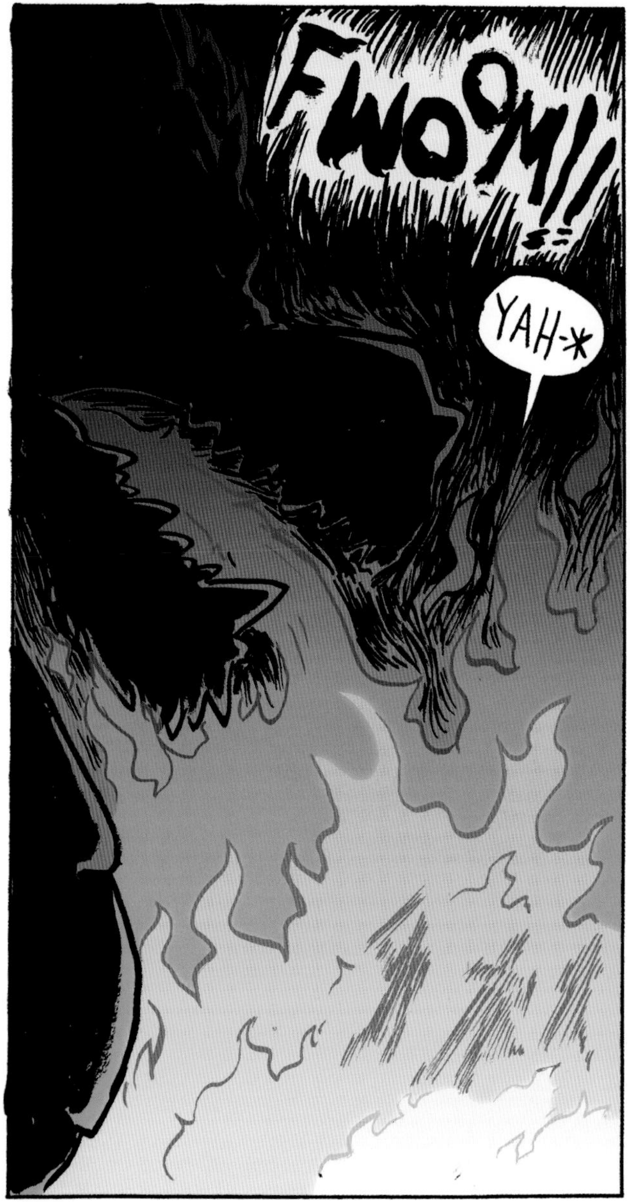
FWOOM!!
YAH-*
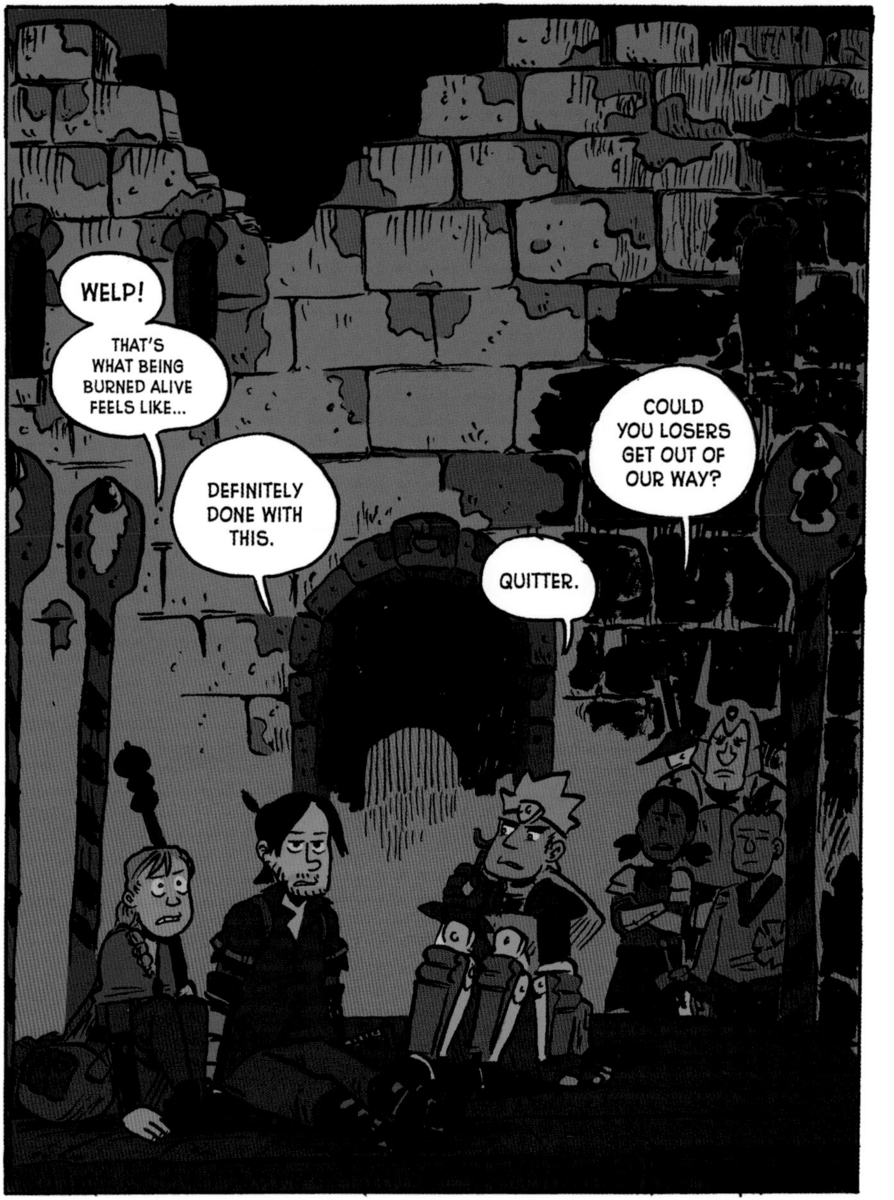
WELP!
THAT'S WHAT BEING BURNED ALIVE FEELS LIKE...
DEFINITELY DONE WITH THIS.
QUITTER.
COULD YOU LOSERS GET OUT OF OUR WAY?

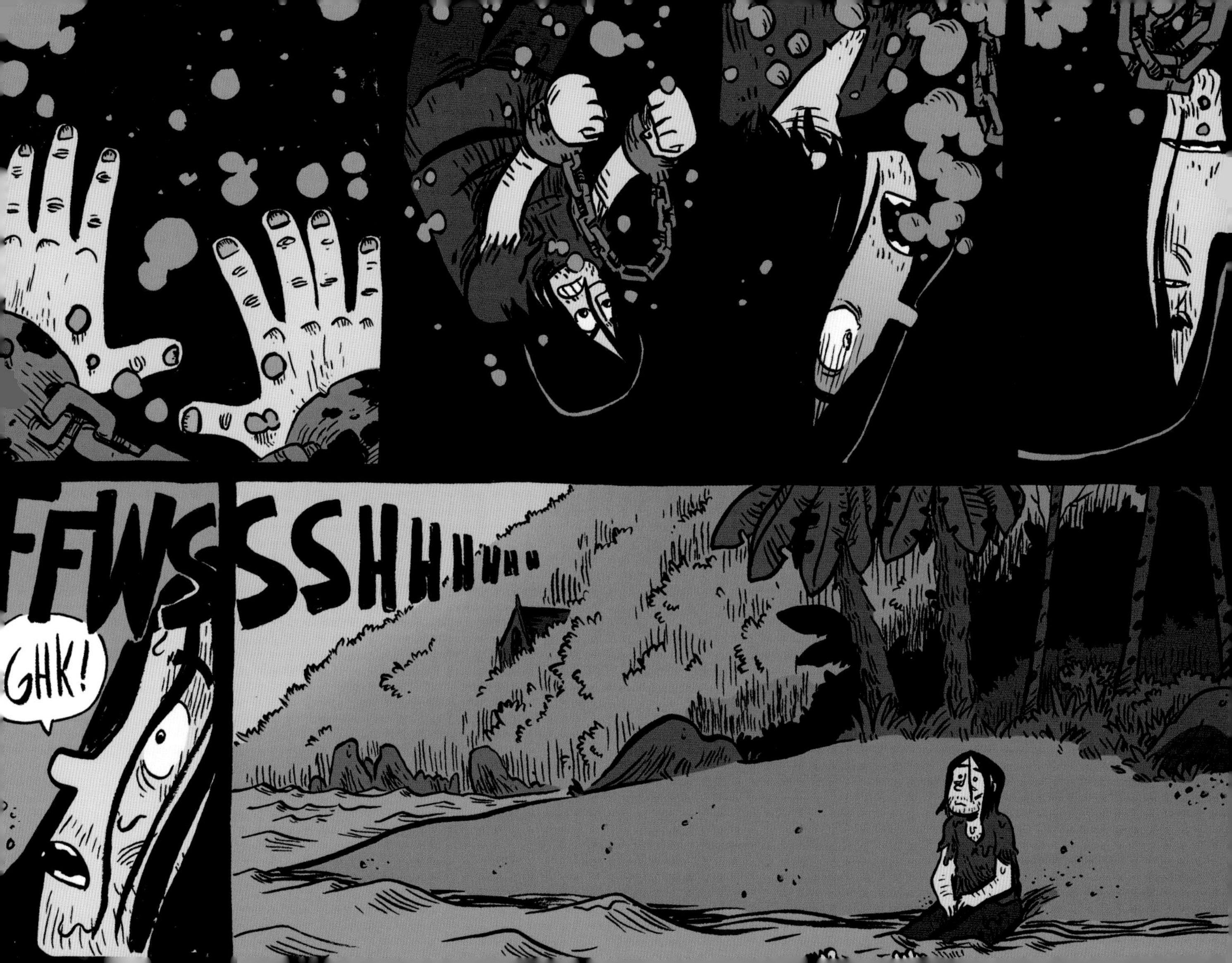
FFWSSSHHHHHH
GHK!

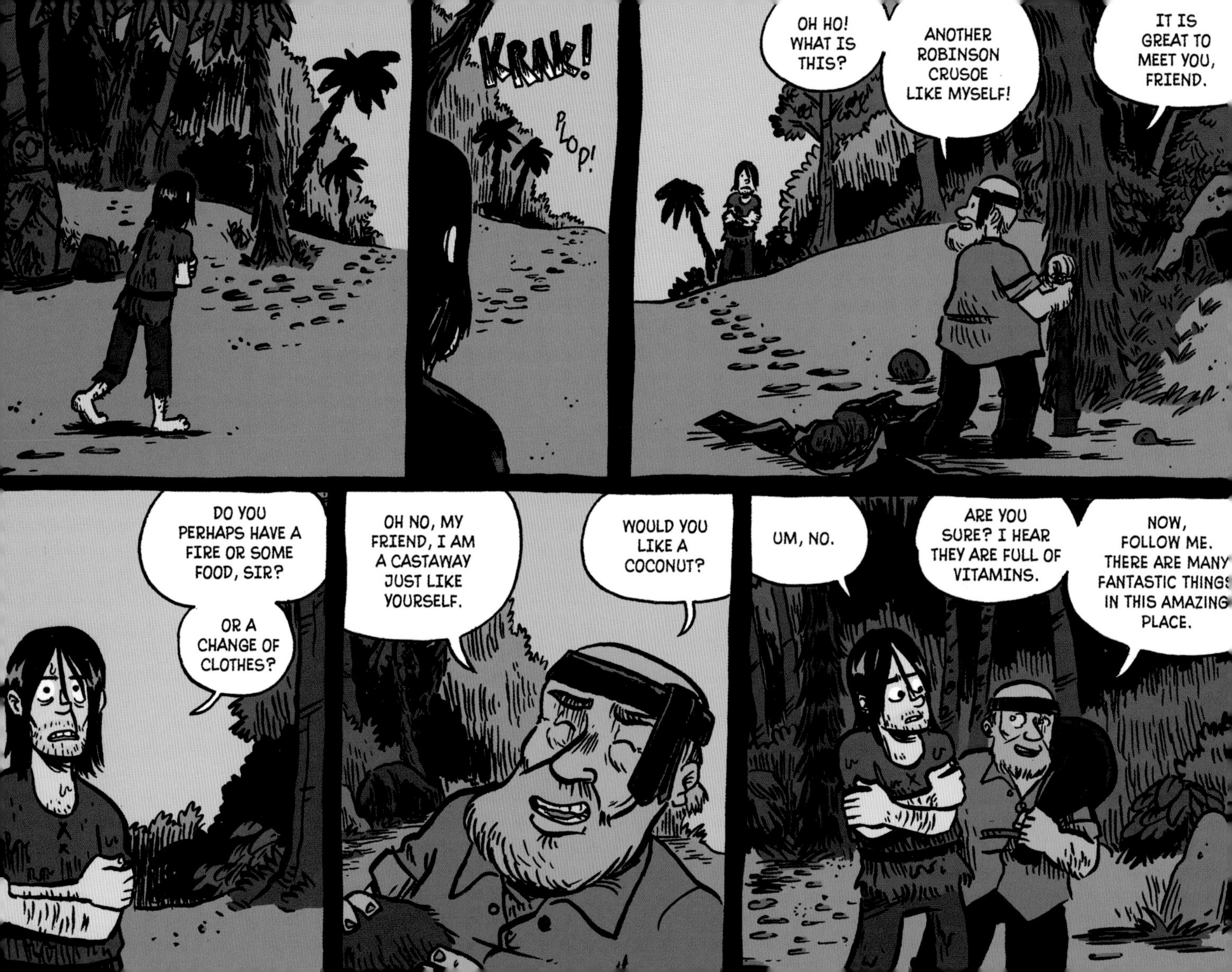
KRAK!
PLOP!
OH HO! WHAT IS THIS?
ANOTHER ROBINSON CRUSOE LIKE MYSELF!
IT IS GREAT TO MEET YOU, FRIEND.
DO YOU PERHAPS HAVE A FIRE OR SOME FOOD, SIR?
OR A CHANGE OF CLOTHES?
OH NO, MY FRIEND, I AM A CASTAWAY JUST LIKE YOURSELF.
WOULD YOU LIKE A COCONUT?
UM, NO.
ARE YOU SURE? I HEAR THEY ARE FULL OF VITAMINS.
NOW, FOLLOW ME. THERE ARE MANY FANTASTIC THINGS IN THIS AMAZING PLACE.

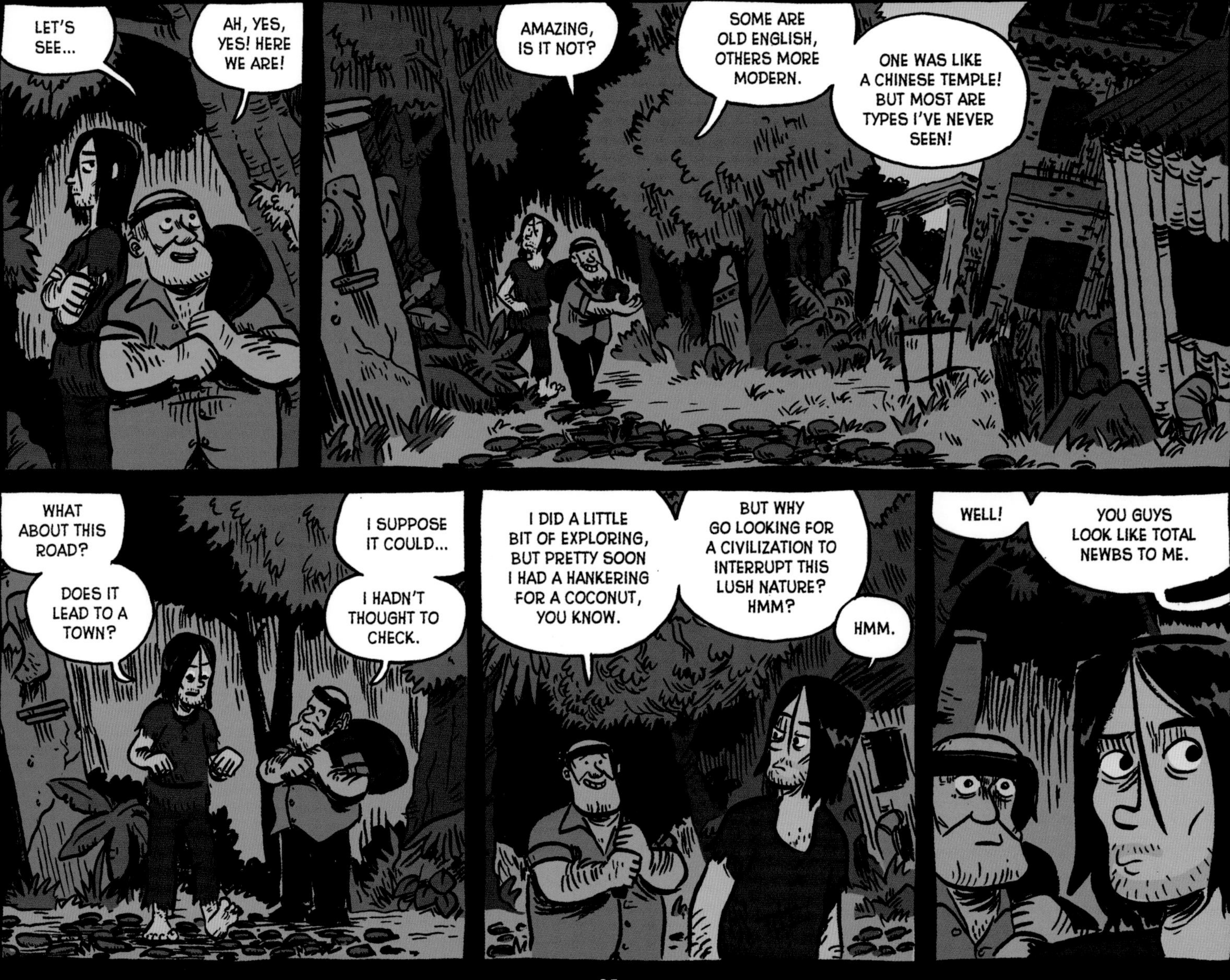
LET'S SEE...
AH, YES, YES! HERE WE ARE!
AMAZING, IS IT NOT?
SOME ARE OLD ENGLISH, OTHERS MORE MODERN.
ONE WAS LIKE A CHINESE TEMPLE! BUT MOST ARE TYPES I'VE NEVER SEEN!
WHAT ABOUT THIS ROAD?
DOES IT LEAD TO A TOWN?
I SUPPOSE IT COULD...
I HADN'T THOUGHT TO CHECK.
I DID A LITTLE BIT OF EXPLORING, BUT PRETTY SOON I HAD A HANKERING FOR A COCONUT, YOU KNOW.
BUT WHY GO LOOKING FOR A CIVILIZATION TO INTERRUPT THIS LUSH NATURE? HMM?
HMM.
WELL!
YOU GUYS LOOK LIKE TOTAL NEWBS TO ME.

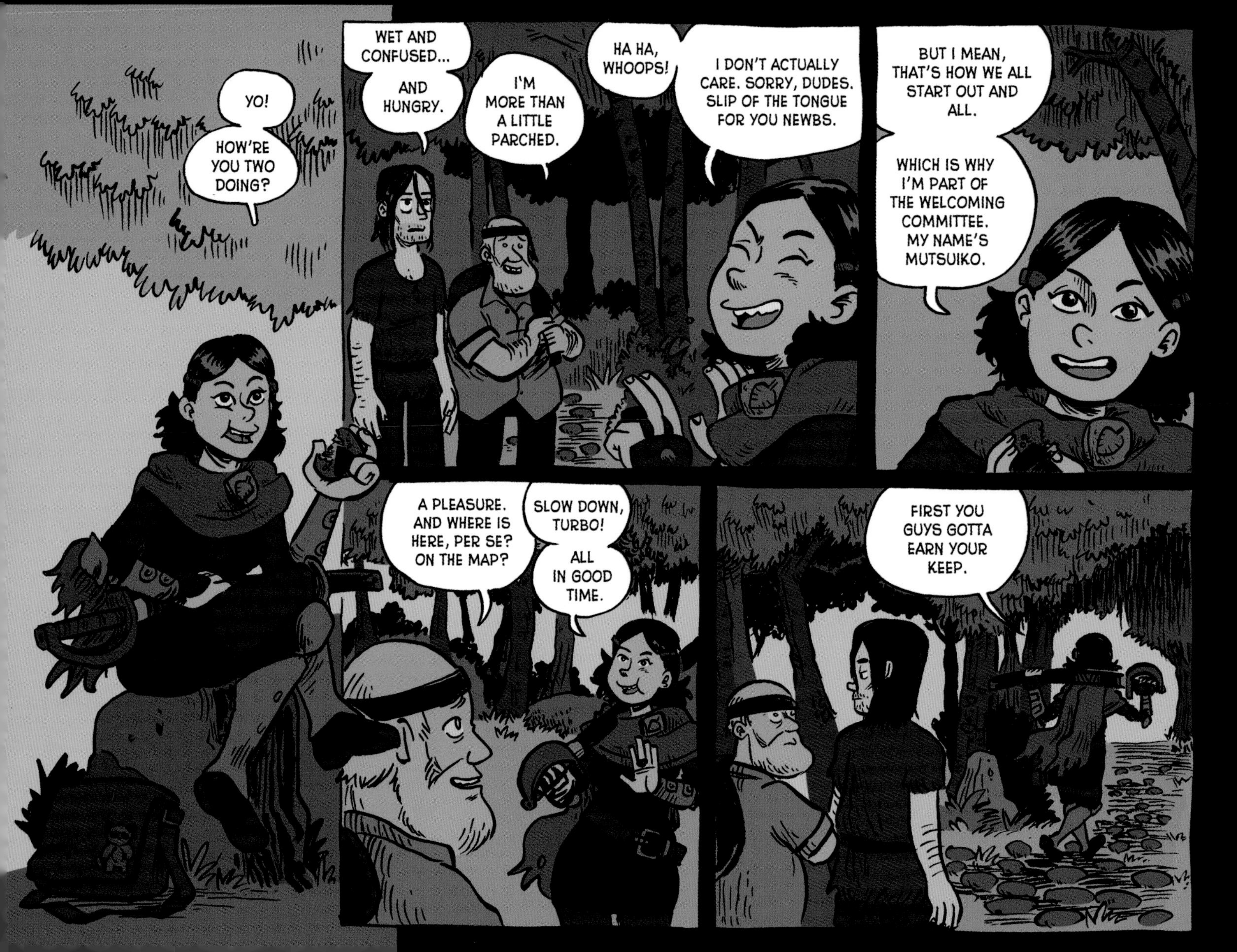
YO!
HOW'RE YOU TWO DOING?
WET AND CONFUSED...
AND HUNGRY.
I'M MORE THAN A LITTLE PARCHED.
HA HA, WHOOPS!
I DON'T ACTUALLY CARE. SORRY, DUDES. SLIP OF THE TONGUE FOR YOU NEWBS.
BUT I MEAN, THAT'S HOW WE ALL START OUT AND ALL.
WHICH IS WHY I'M PART OF THE WELCOMING COMMITTEE. MY NAME'S MUTSUIKO.
A PLEASURE. AND WHERE IS HERE, PER SE? ON THE MAP?
SLOW DOWN, TURBO!
ALL IN GOOD TIME.
FIRST YOU GUYS GOTTA EARN YOUR KEEP.

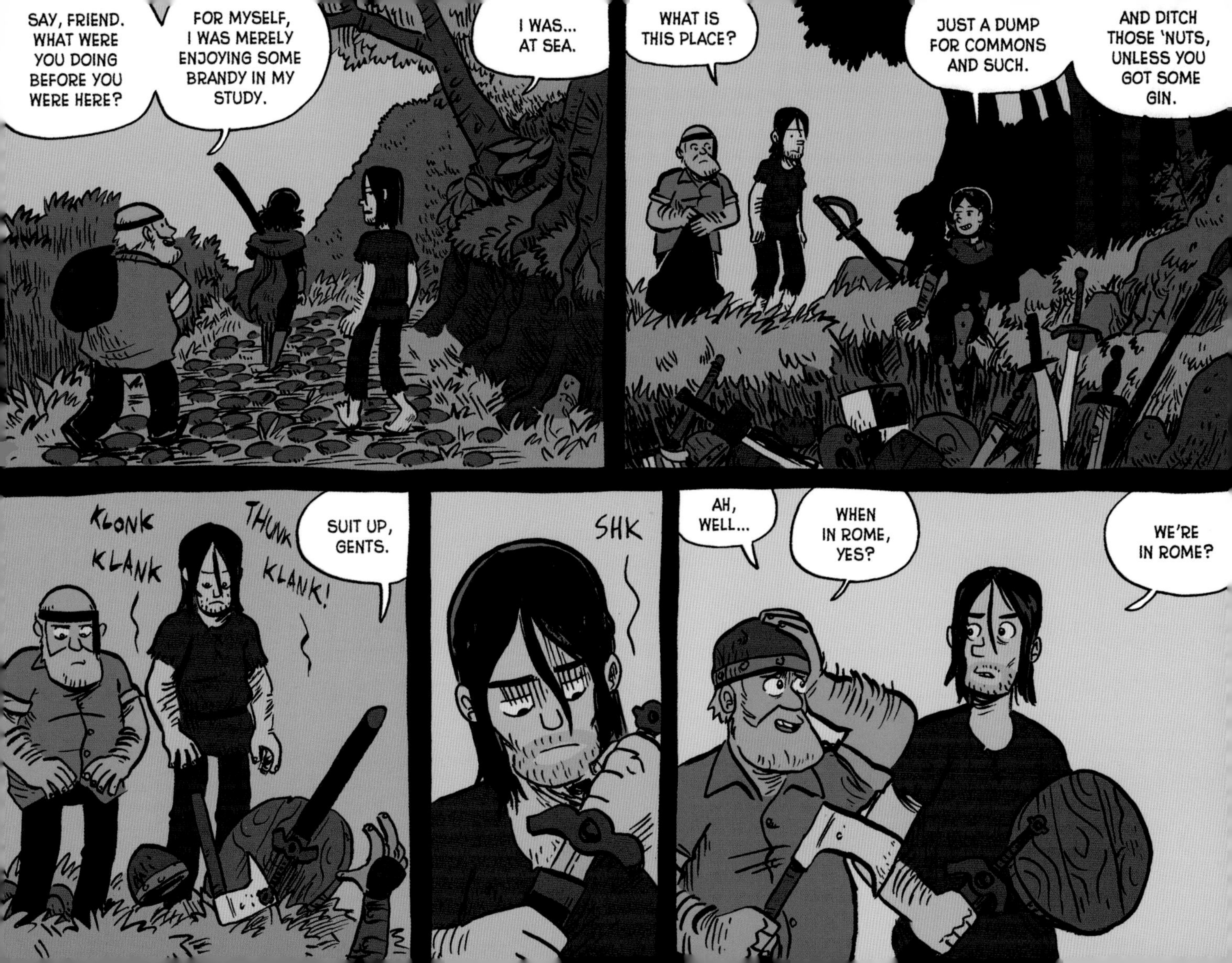
SAY, FRIEND. WHAT WERE YOU DOING BEFORE YOU WERE HERE?
FOR MYSELF, I WAS MERELY ENJOYING SOME BRANDY IN MY STUDY.
I WAS... AT SEA.
WHAT IS THIS PLACE?
JUST A DUMP FOR COMMONS AND SUCH.
AND DITCH THOSE 'NUTS, UNLESS YOU GOT SOME GIN.
KLONK
KLANK
THUNK
KLANK!
SUIT UP, GENTS.
SHK
AH, WELL...
WHEN IN ROME, YES?
WE'RE IN ROME?

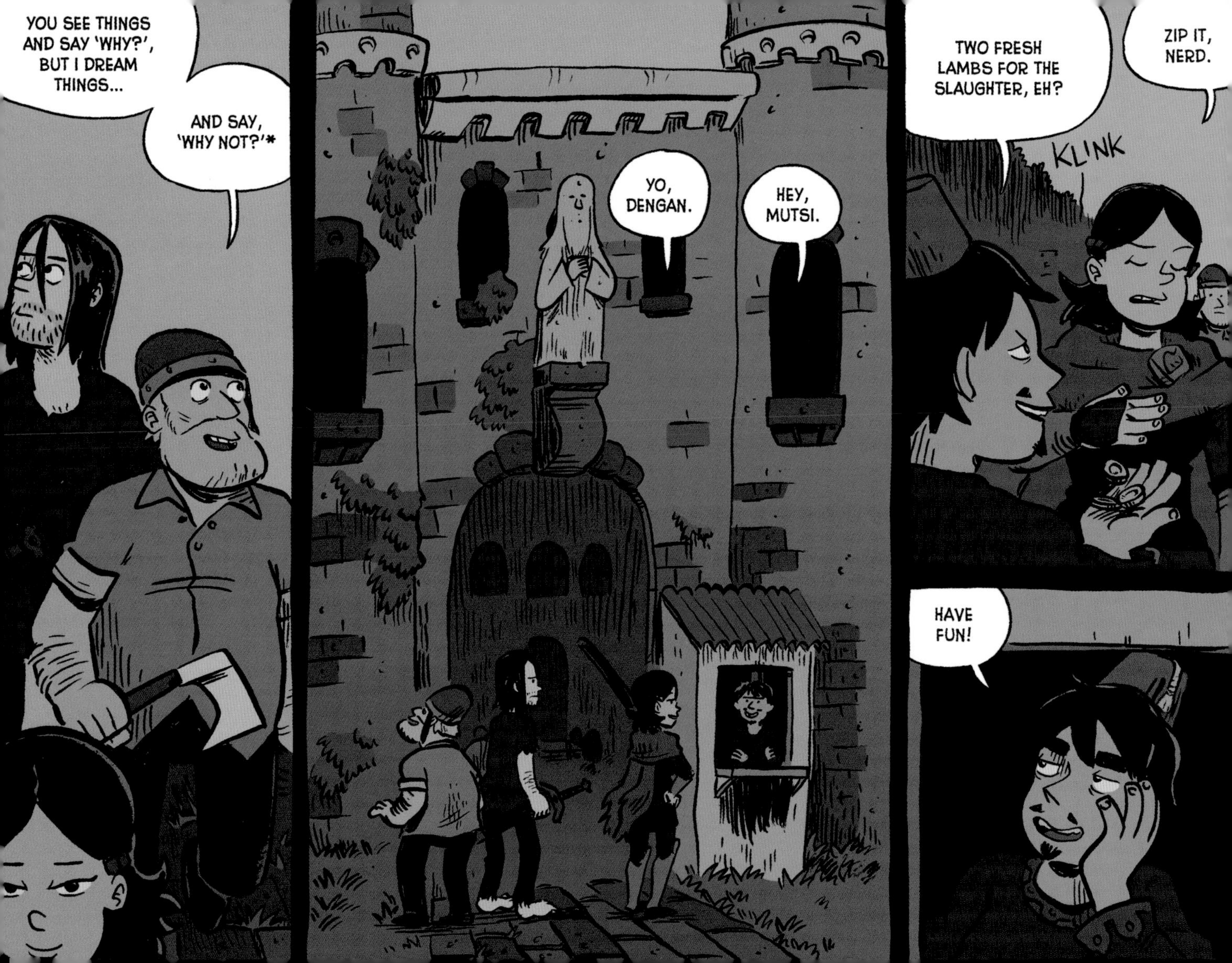
YOU SEE THINGS AND SAY 'WHY?', BUT I DREAM THINGS...
AND SAY, 'WHY NOT?'*
YO, DENGAN.
HEY, MUTSI.
TWO FRESH LAMBS FOR THE SLAUGHTER, EH?
ZIP IT, NERD.
KLINK
HAVE FUN!

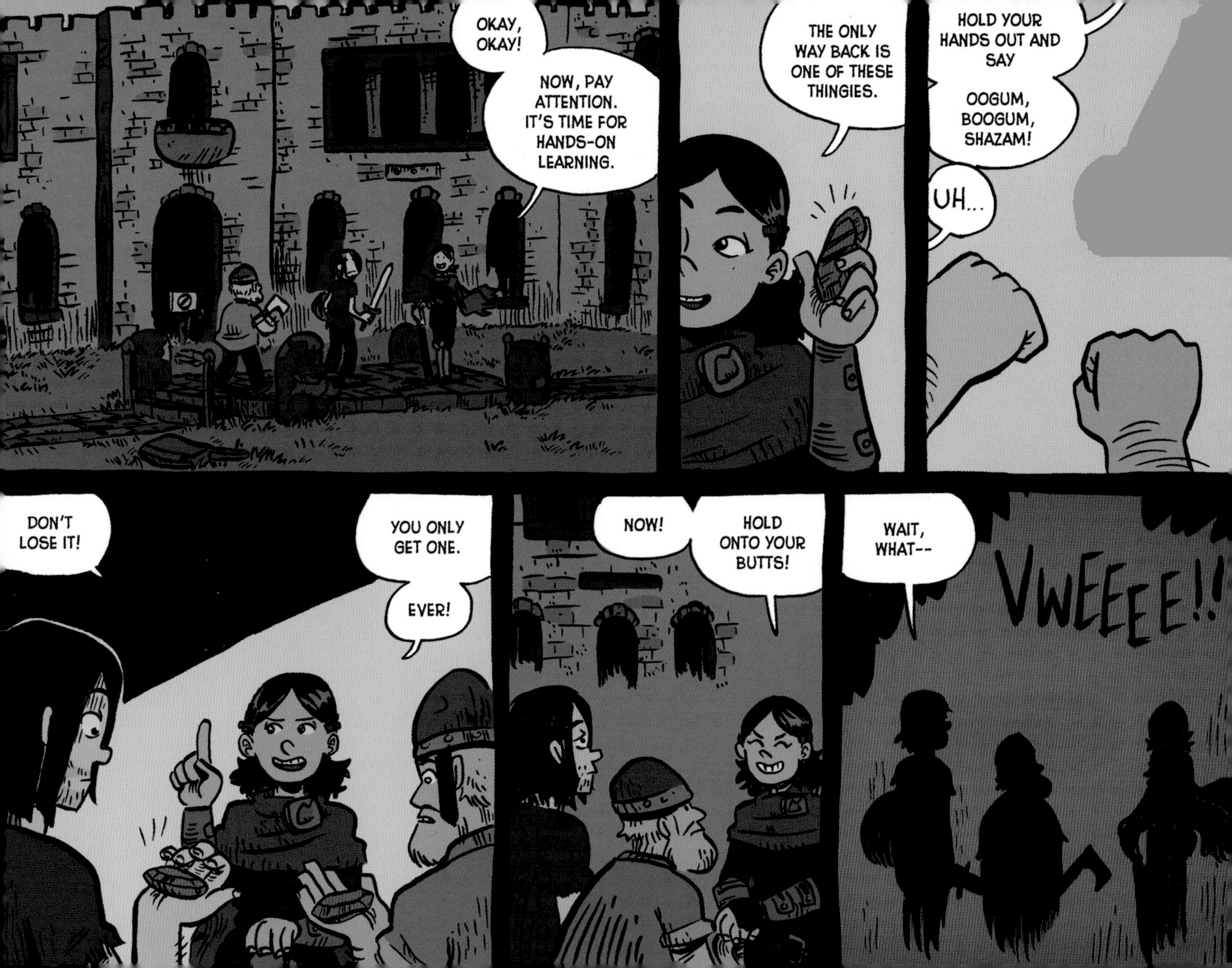
OKAY, OKAY!
NOW, PAY ATTENTION. IT'S TIME FOR HANDS-ON LEARNING.
THE ONLY WAY BACK IS ONE OF THESE THINGIES.
HOLD YOUR HANDS OUT AND SAY
OOGUM, BOOGUM, SHAZAM!
UH...
DON'T LOSE IT!
YOU ONLY GET ONE.
EVER!
NOW!
HOLD ONTO YOUR BUTTS!
WAIT, WHAT--
VWEEEEE!!

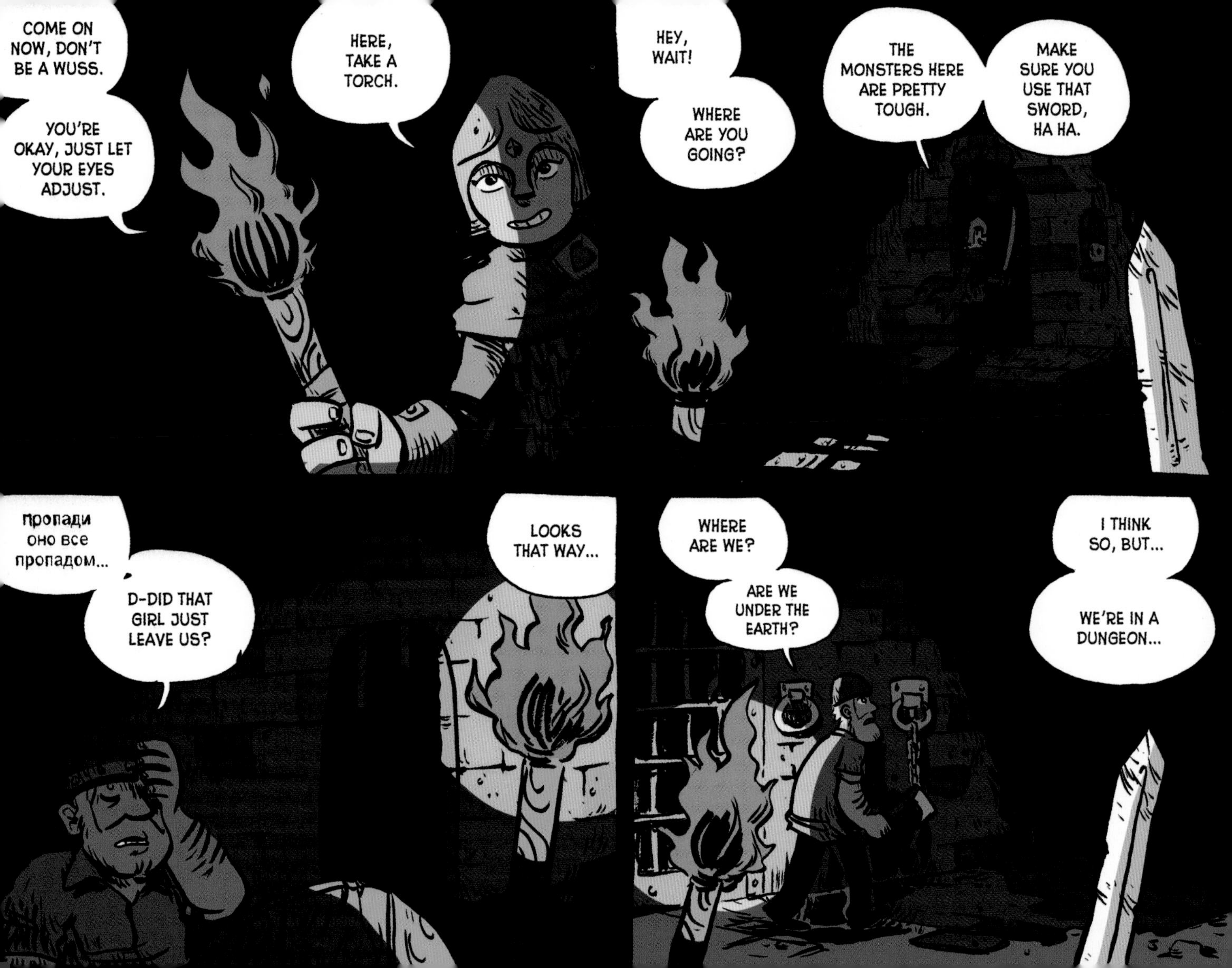
COME ON NOW, DON'T BE A WUSS.
YOU'RE OKAY, JUST LET YOUR EYES ADJUST.
HERE, TAKE A TORCH.
HEY, WAIT!
WHERE ARE YOU GOING?
THE MONSTERS HERE ARE PRETTY TOUGH.
MAKE SURE YOU USE THAT SWORD, HA HA.
пропади оно все пропадом...
D-DID THAT GIRL JUST LEAVE US?
LOOKS THAT WAY...
WHERE ARE WE?
ARE WE UNDER THE EARTH?
I THINK SO, BUT...
WE'RE IN A DUNGEON...

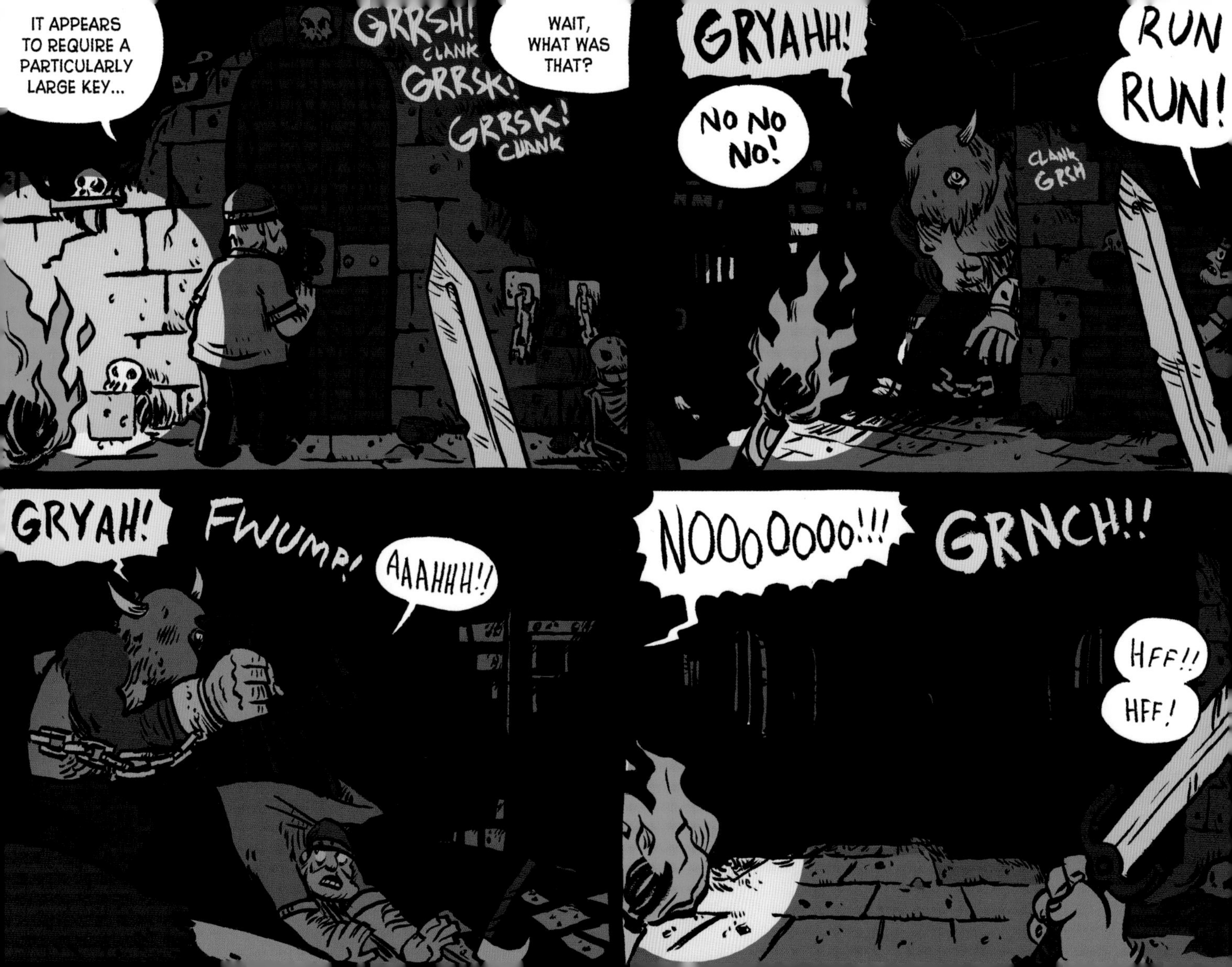
IT APPEARS TO REQUIRE A PARTICULARLY LARGE KEY...
GRRSH!
CLANK
GRRSK!
GRRSK!
CLANK
WAIT, WHAT WAS THAT?
GRYAHH!
NO NO NO!
CLANK
GRSH
RUN RUN!
GRYAH!
FWUMP!
AAAHHH!!
NOOOOOOO!!!
GRNCH!!
HFF!!
HFF!

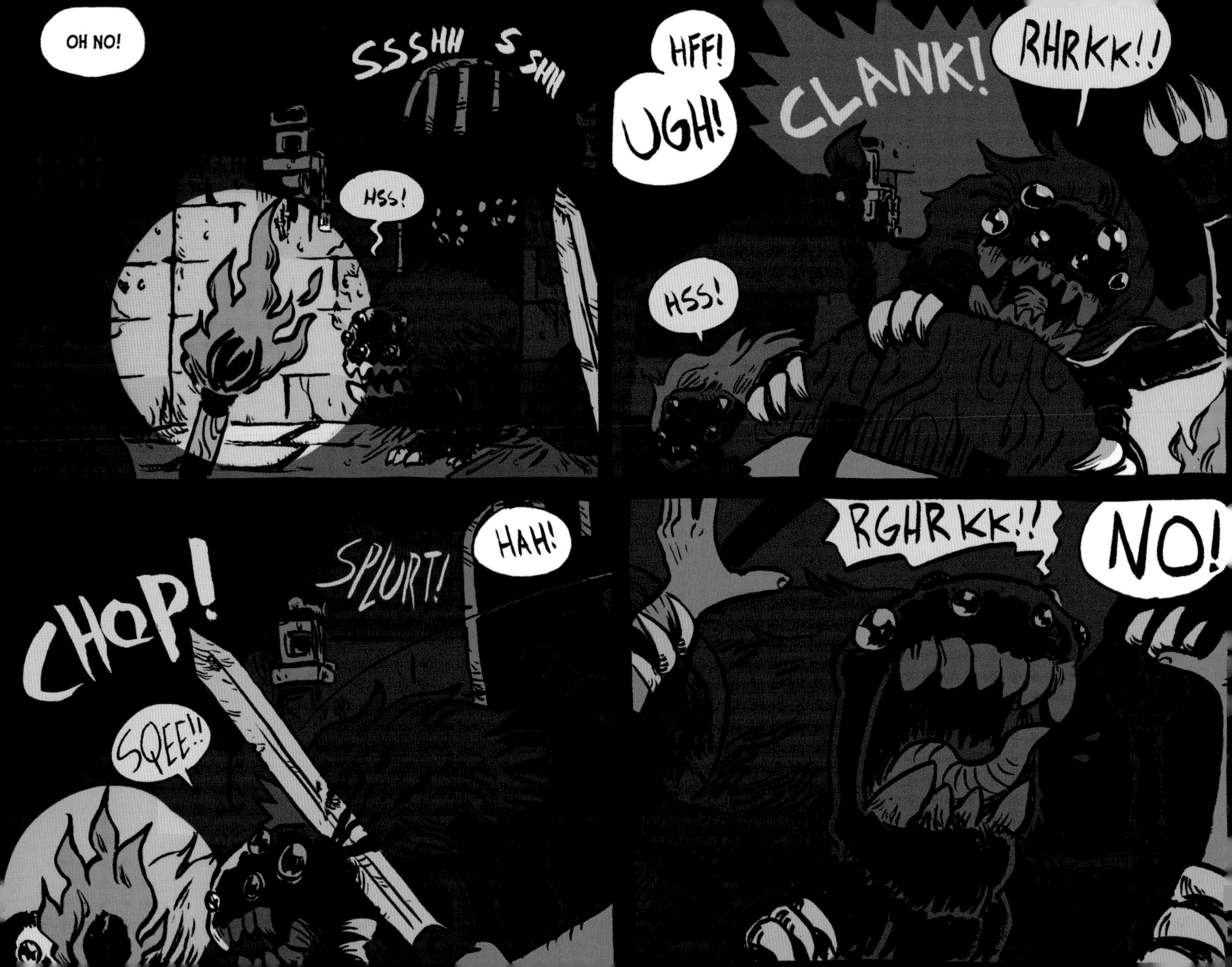
OH NO!
SSSHH S SHH
HSS!
HFF!
UGH!
CLANK!
RHRKK!!
HSS!
CHOP!
SPLURT!
HAH!
SQEE!!
RGHRKK!!
NO!

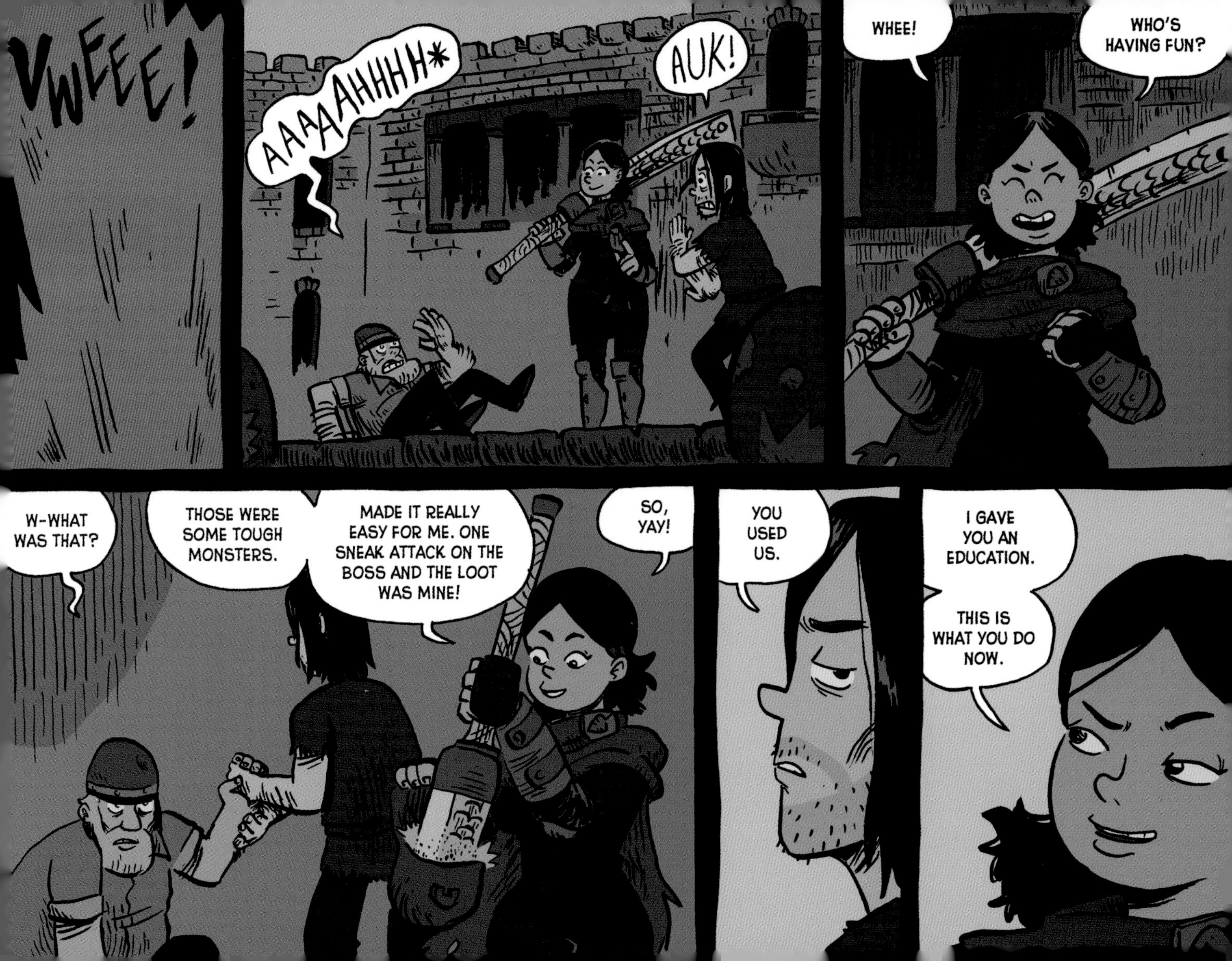
VWEEE!
AAAAAHHHH*
AUK!
WHEE!
WHO'S HAVING FUN?
W-WHAT WAS THAT?
THOSE WERE SOME TOUGH MONSTERS.
MADE IT REALLY EASY FOR ME. ONE SNEAK ATTACK ON THE BOSS AND THE LOOT WAS MINE!
SO, YAY!
YOU USED US.
I GAVE YOU AN EDUCATION.
THIS IS WHAT YOU DO NOW.

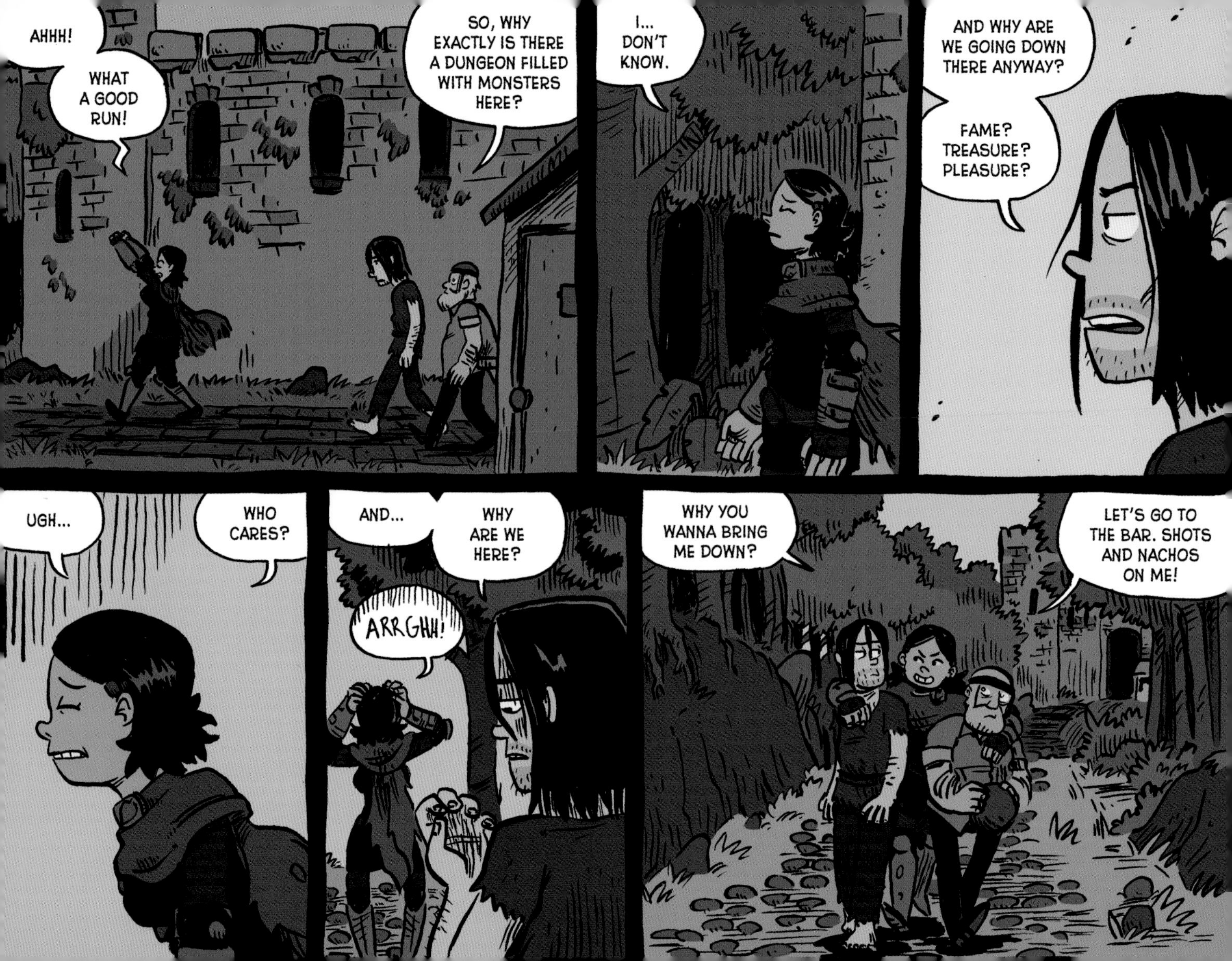
AHHH!
WHAT A GOOD RUN!
SO, WHY EXACTLY IS THERE A DUNGEON FILLED WITH MONSTERS HERE?
I... DON'T KNOW.
AND WHY ARE WE GOING DOWN THERE ANYWAY?
FAME? TREASURE? PLEASURE?
UGH...
WHO CARES?
AND...
WHY ARE WE HERE?
ARRGHH!
WHY YOU WANNA BRING ME DOWN?
LET'S GO TO THE BAR. SHOTS AND NACHOS ON ME!

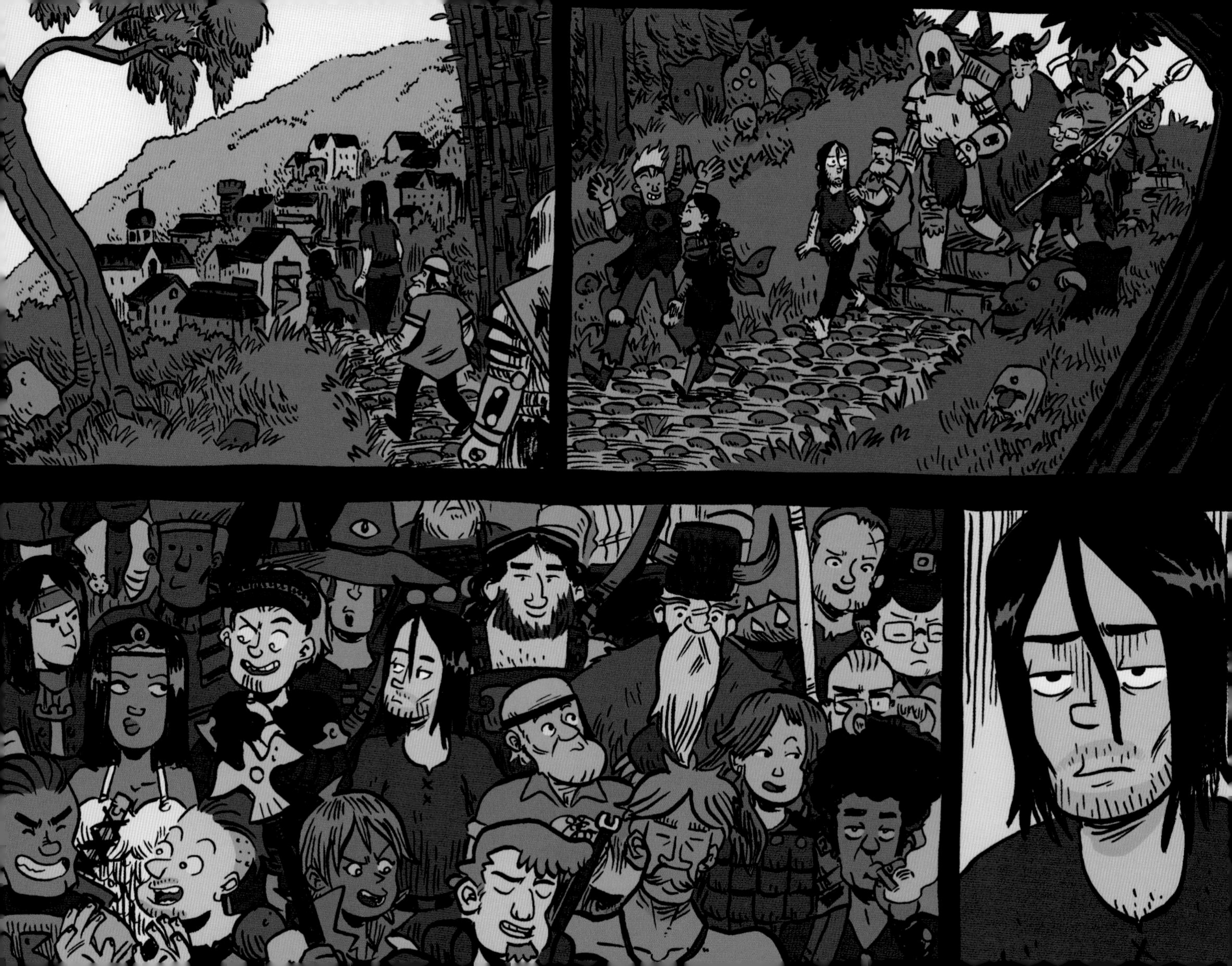

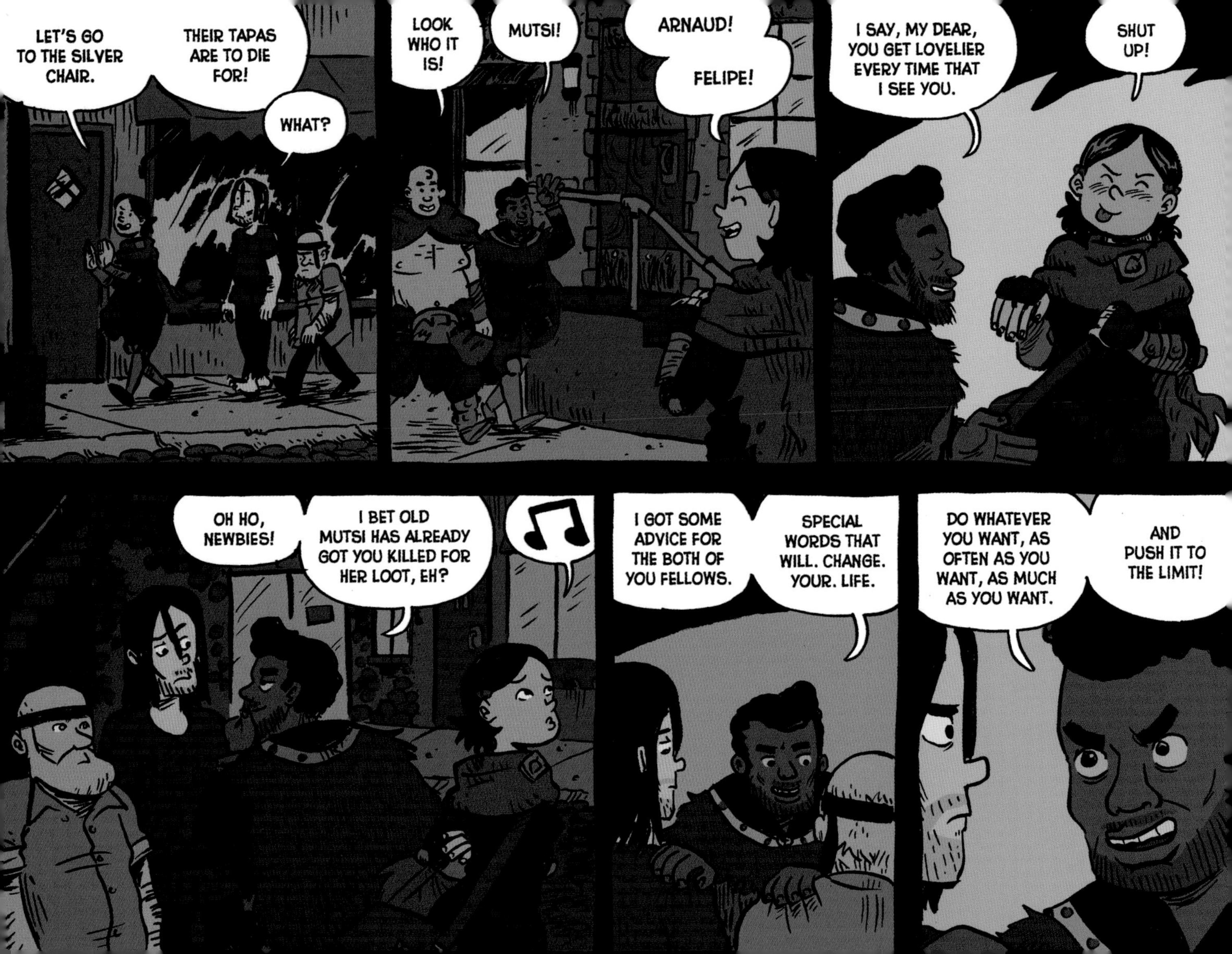
LET'S GO TO THE SILVER CHAIR.
THEIR TAPAS ARE TO DIE FOR!
WHAT?
LOOK WHO IT IS!
MUTSI!
ARNAUD!
FELIPE!
I SAY, MY DEAR, YOU GET LOVELIER EVERY TIME THAT I SEE YOU.
SHUT UP!
OH HO, NEWBIES!
I BET OLD MUTSI HAS ALREADY GOT YOU KILLED FOR HER LOOT, EH?
I GOT SOME ADVICE FOR THE BOTH OF YOU FELLOWS.
SPECIAL WORDS THAT WILL. CHANGE. YOUR. LIFE.
DO WHATEVER YOU WANT, AS OFTEN AS YOU WANT, AS MUCH AS YOU WANT.
AND PUSH IT TO THE LIMIT!

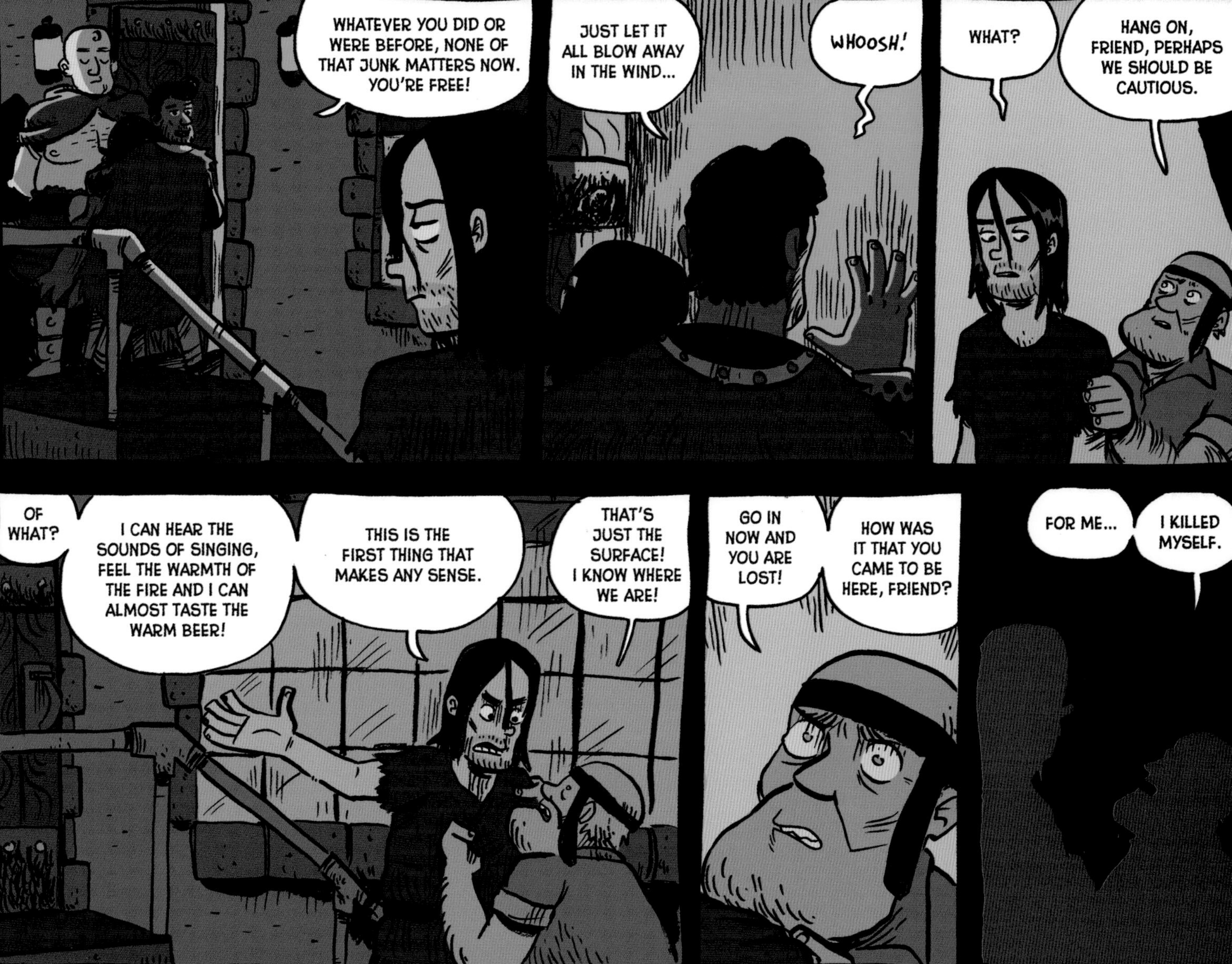
WHATEVER YOU DID OR WERE BEFORE, NONE OF THAT JUNK MATTERS NOW. YOU'RE FREE!
JUST LET IT ALL BLOW AWAY IN THE WIND...
WHOOSH!
WHAT?
HANG ON, FRIEND, PERHAPS WE SHOULD BE CAUTIOUS.
OF WHAT?
I CAN HEAR THE SOUNDS OF SINGING, FEEL THE WARMTH OF THE FIRE AND I CAN ALMOST TASTE THE WARM BEER!
THIS IS THE FIRST THING THAT MAKES ANY SENSE.
THAT'S JUST THE SURFACE! I KNOW WHERE WE ARE!
GO IN NOW AND YOU ARE LOST!
HOW WAS IT THAT YOU CAME TO BE HERE, FRIEND?
FOR ME...
I KILLED MYSELF.

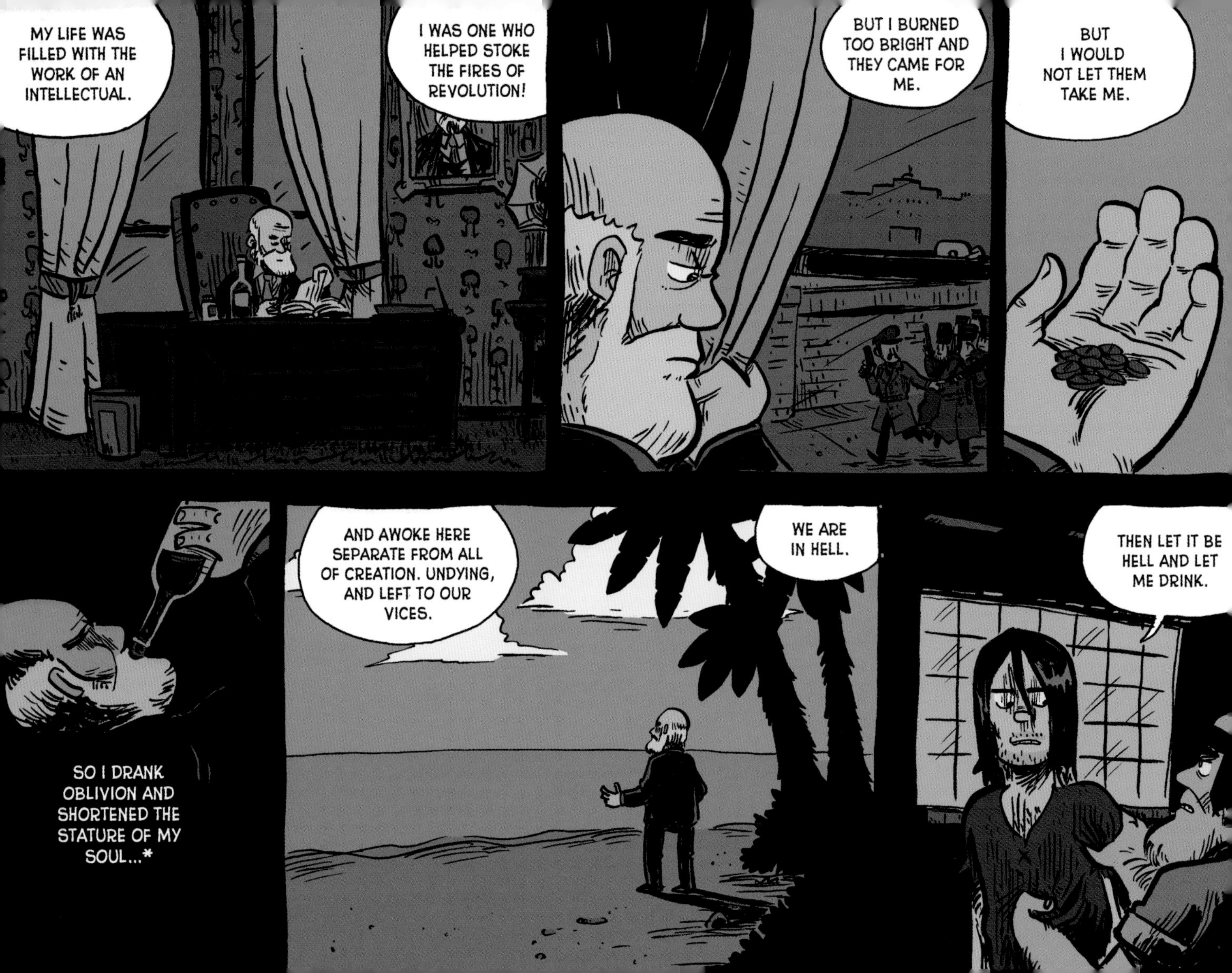
MY LIFE WAS FILLED WITH THE WORK OF AN INTELLECTUAL.
I WAS ONE WHO HELPED STOKE THE FIRES OF REVOLUTION!
BUT I BURNED TOO BRIGHT AND THEY CAME FOR ME.
BUT I WOULD NOT LET THEM TAKE ME.
SO I DRANK OBLIVION AND SHORTENED THE STATURE OF MY SOUL...*
AND AWOKE HERE SEPARATE FROM ALL OF CREATION. UNDYING, AND LEFT TO OUR VICES.
WE ARE IN HELL.
THEN LET IT BE HELL AND LET ME DRINK.

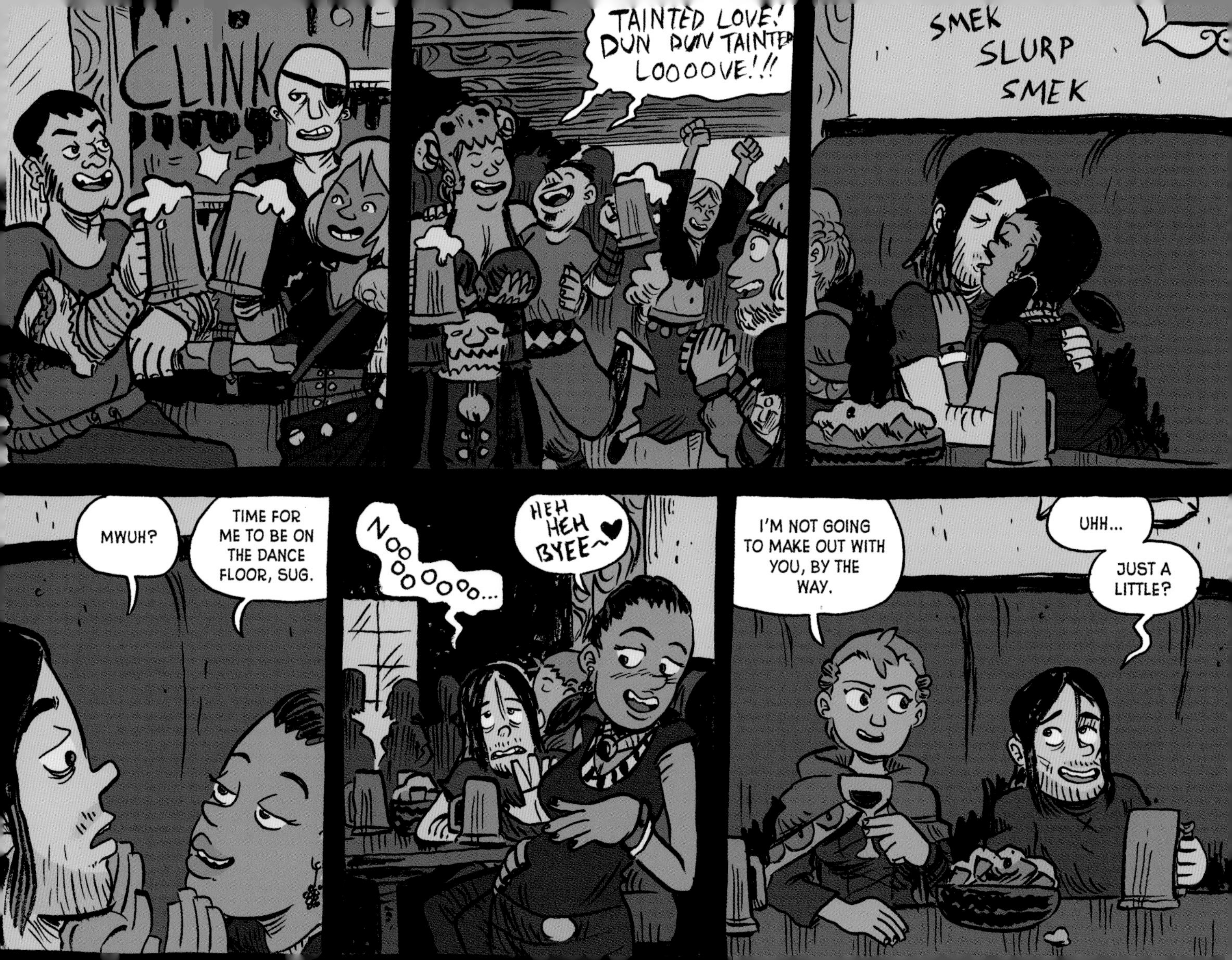
CLINK
TAINTED LOVE! DUN DUN TAINTED LOOOOVE!!!
SMEK SLURP SMEK
MWUH?
TIME FOR ME TO BE ON THE DANCE FLOOR, SUG.
NOOOOOoo...
HEH HEH BYEE~♥
I'M NOT GOING TO MAKE OUT WITH YOU, BY THE WAY.
UHH...
JUST A LITTLE?

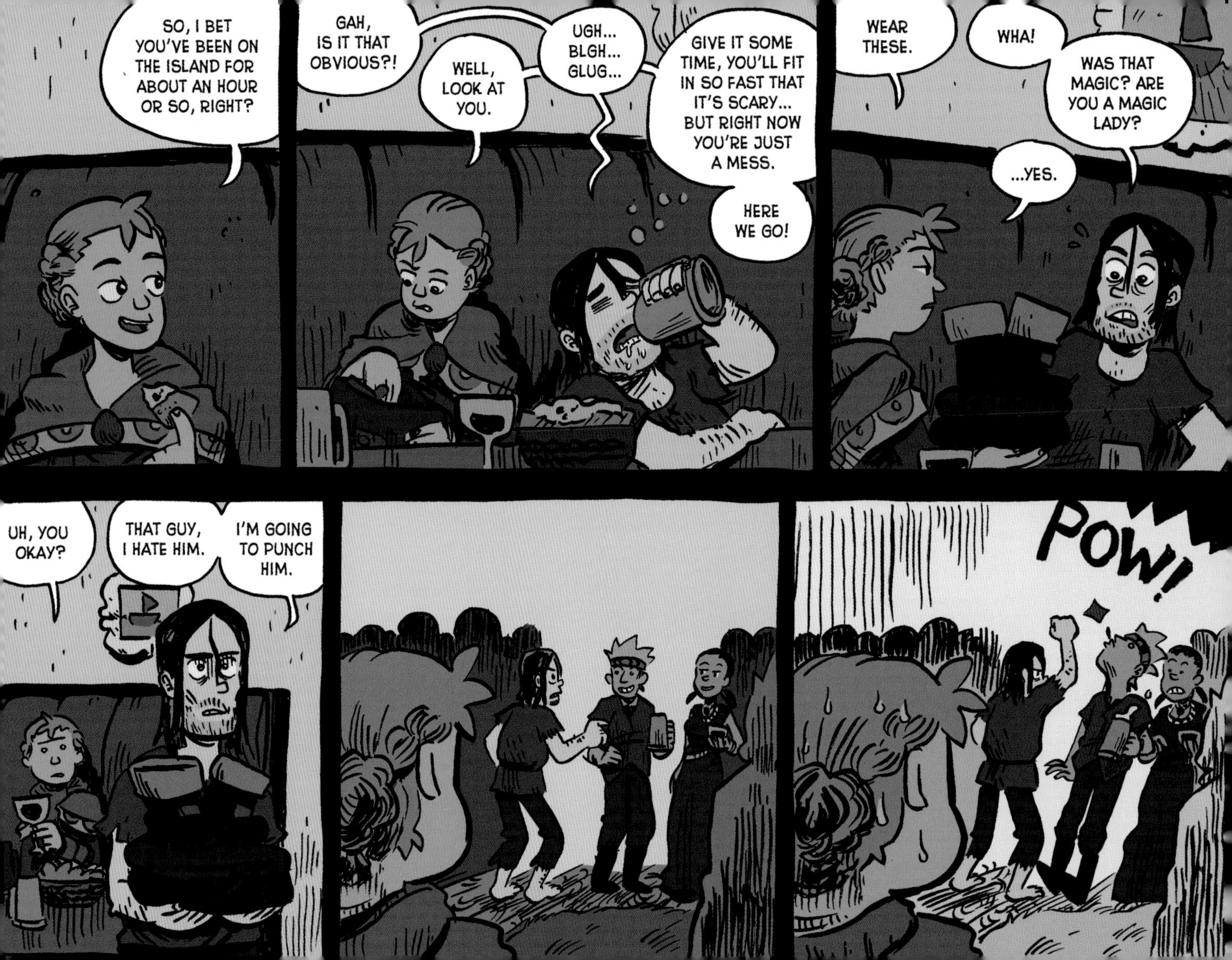
SO, I BET YOU'VE BEEN ON THE ISLAND FOR ABOUT AN HOUR OR SO, RIGHT?
GAH, IS IT THAT OBVIOUS?!
WELL, LOOK AT YOU.
UGH... BLGH... GLUG...
GIVE IT SOME TIME, YOU'LL FIT IN SO FAST THAT IT'S SCARY... BUT RIGHT NOW YOU'RE JUST A MESS.
HERE WE GO!
WEAR THESE.
WHA!
WAS THAT MAGIC? ARE YOU A MAGIC LADY?
...YES.
UH, YOU OKAY?
THAT GUY, I HATE HIM.
I'M GOING TO PUNCH HIM.
POW!

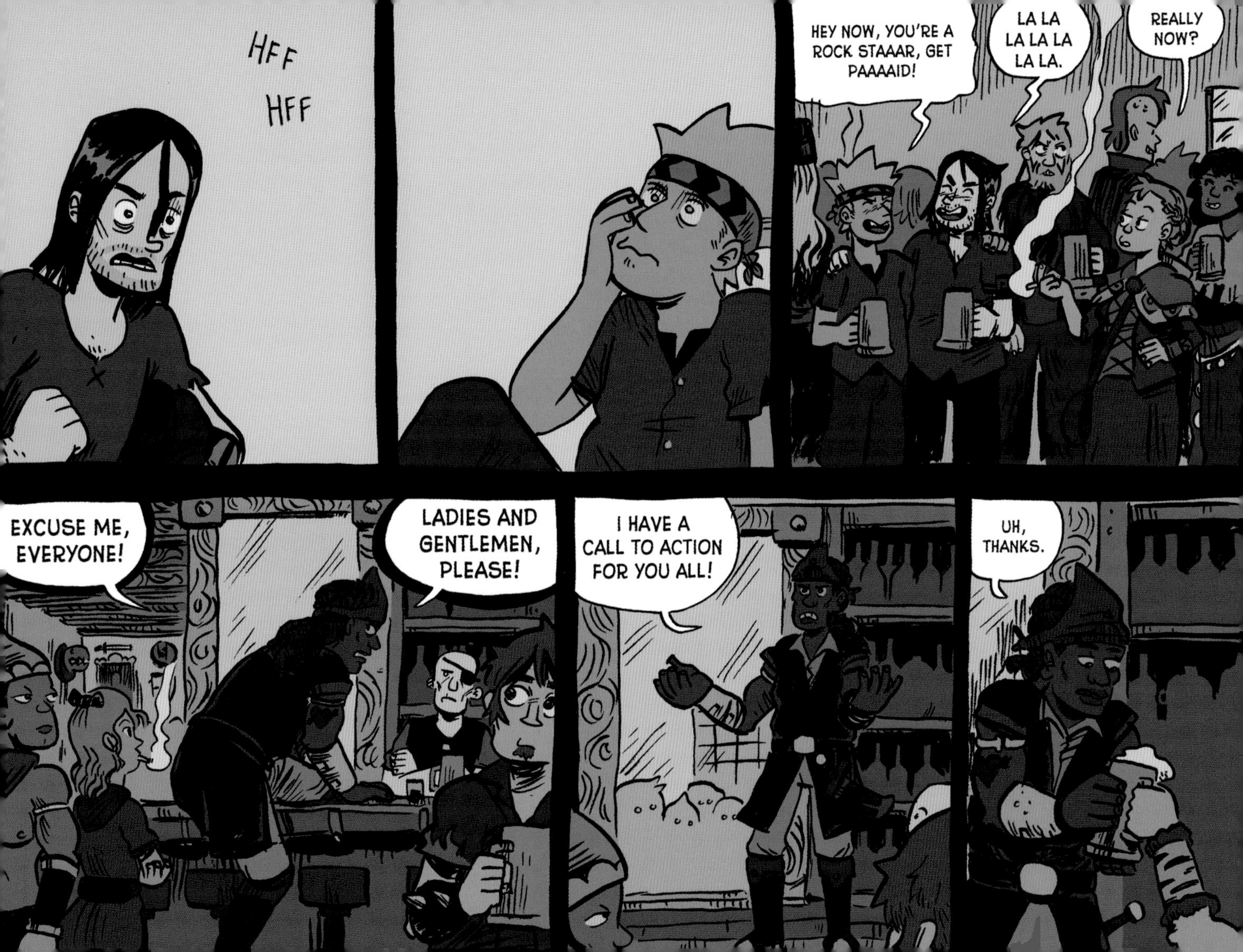
HFF
HFF
HEY NOW, YOU'RE A ROCK STAAAR, GET PAAAAID!
LA LA LA LA LA LA LA.
REALLY NOW?
EXCUSE ME, EVERYONE!
LADIES AND GENTLEMEN, PLEASE!
I HAVE A CALL TO ACTION FOR YOU ALL!
UH, THANKS.

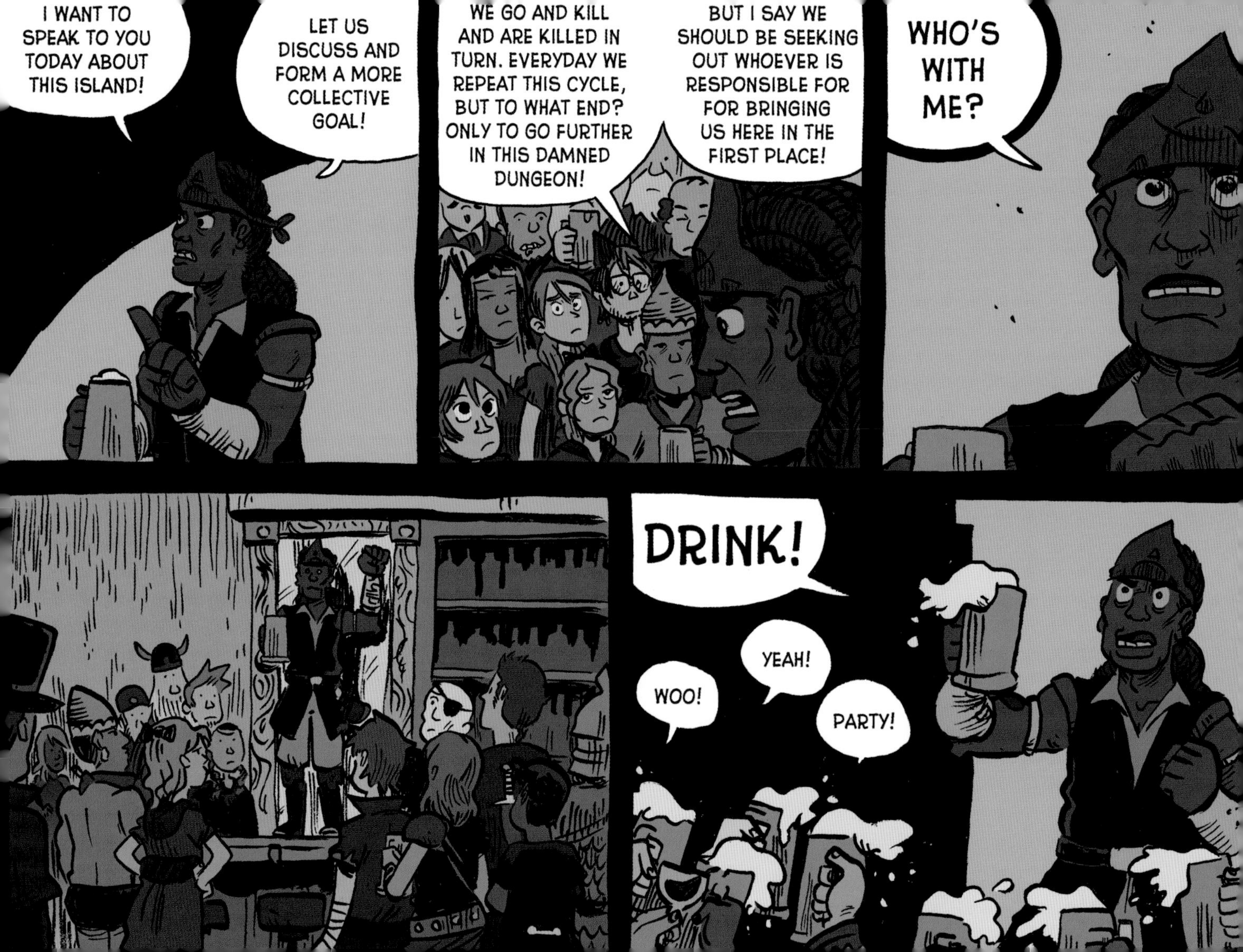
I WANT TO SPEAK TO YOU TODAY ABOUT THIS ISLAND!
LET US DISCUSS AND FORM A MORE COLLECTIVE GOAL!
WE GO AND KILL AND ARE KILLED IN TURN. EVERYDAY WE REPEAT THIS CYCLE, BUT TO WHAT END? ONLY TO GO FURTHER IN THIS DAMNED DUNGEON!
BUT I SAY WE SHOULD BE SEEKING OUT WHOEVER IS RESPONSIBLE FOR FOR BRINGING US HERE IN THE FIRST PLACE!
WHO'S WITH ME?
DRINK!
WOO!
YEAH!
PARTY!

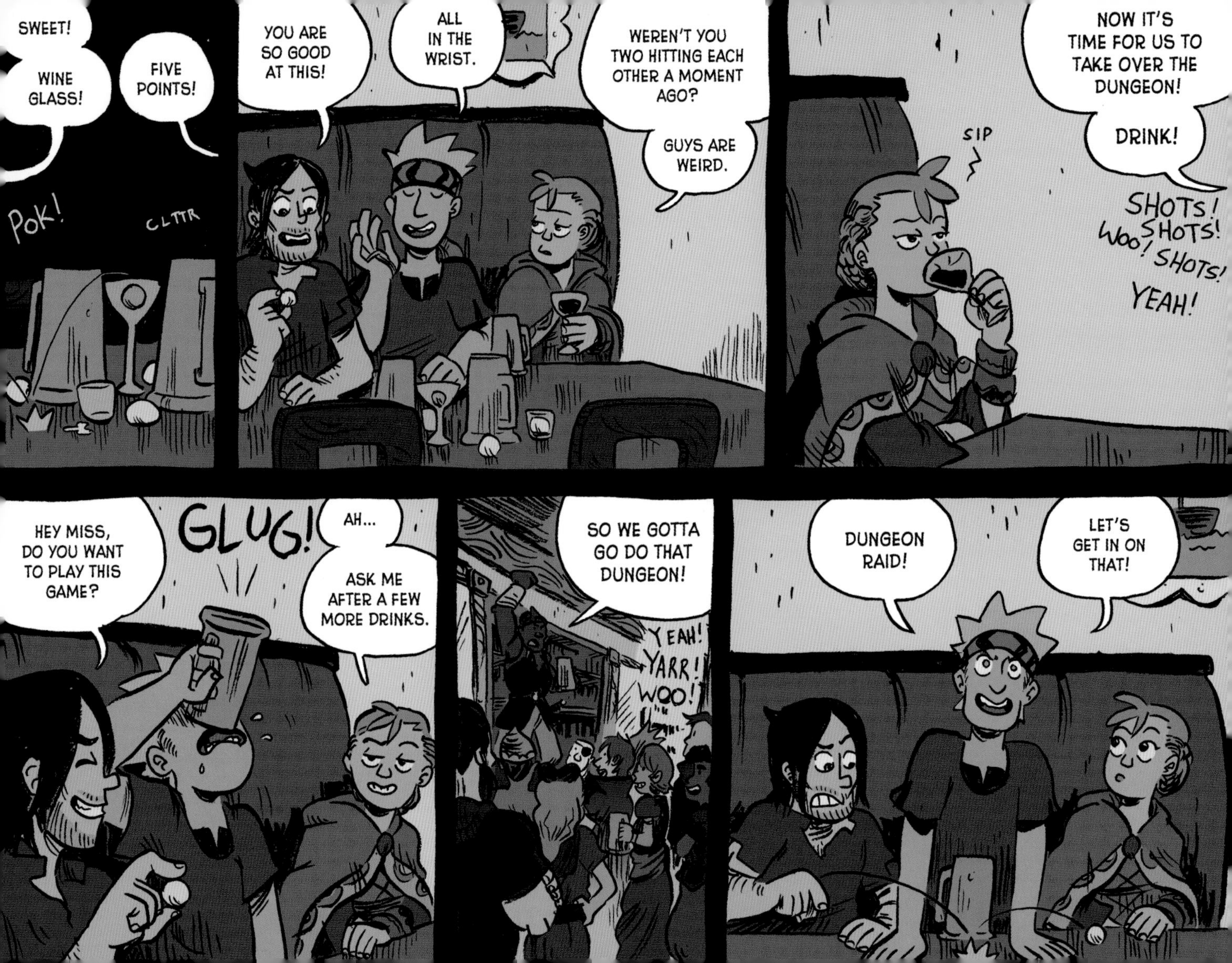
SWEET!
WINE GLASS!
FIVE POINTS!
POK!
CLTTR
YOU ARE SO GOOD AT THIS!
ALL IN THE WRIST.
WEREN'T YOU TWO HITTING EACH OTHER A MOMENT AGO?
GUYS ARE WEIRD.
SIP
NOW IT'S TIME FOR US TO TAKE OVER THE DUNGEON!
DRINK!
SHOTS! SHOTS! WOO! SHOTS! YEAH!
HEY MISS, DO YOU WANT TO PLAY THIS GAME?
GLUG!
AH...
ASK ME AFTER A FEW MORE DRINKS.
SO WE GOTTA GO DO THAT DUNGEON!
YEAH! YARR! WOO!
DUNGEON RAID!
LET'S GET IN ON THAT!

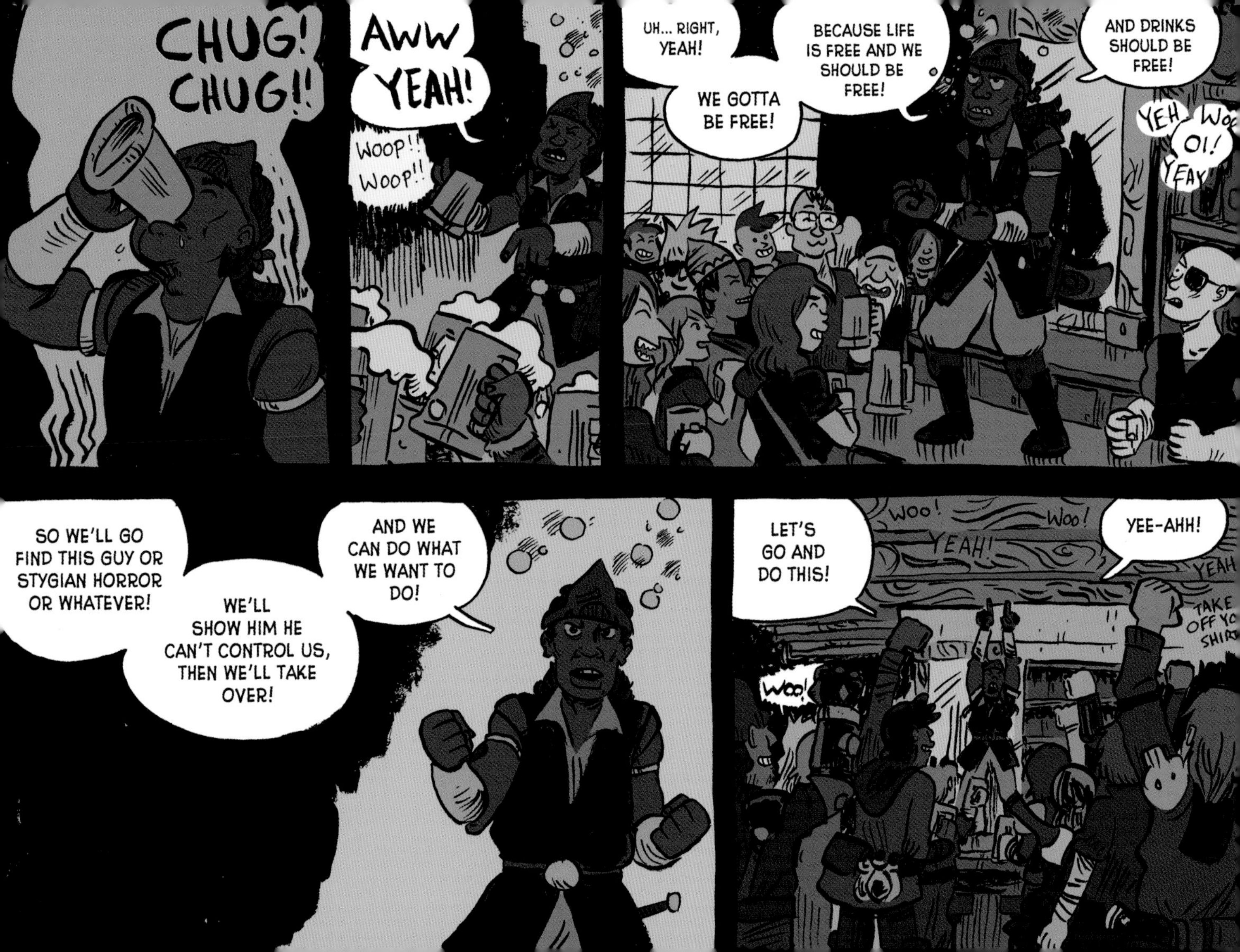
CHUG! CHUG!!
AWW YEAH!
WOOP!! WOOP!!
UH... RIGHT, YEAH!
WE GOTTA BE FREE!
BECAUSE LIFE IS FREE AND WE SHOULD BE FREE!
AND DRINKS SHOULD BE FREE!
YEH
OI!
YEAY
SO WE'LL GO FIND THIS GUY OR STYGIAN HORROR OR WHATEVER!
WE'LL SHOW HIM HE CAN'T CONTROL US, THEN WE'LL TAKE OVER!
AND WE CAN DO WHAT WE WANT TO DO!
LET'S GO AND DO THIS!
WOO!
WOO!
YEAH!
YEE-AHH!
YEAH
TAKE OFF
WOO!

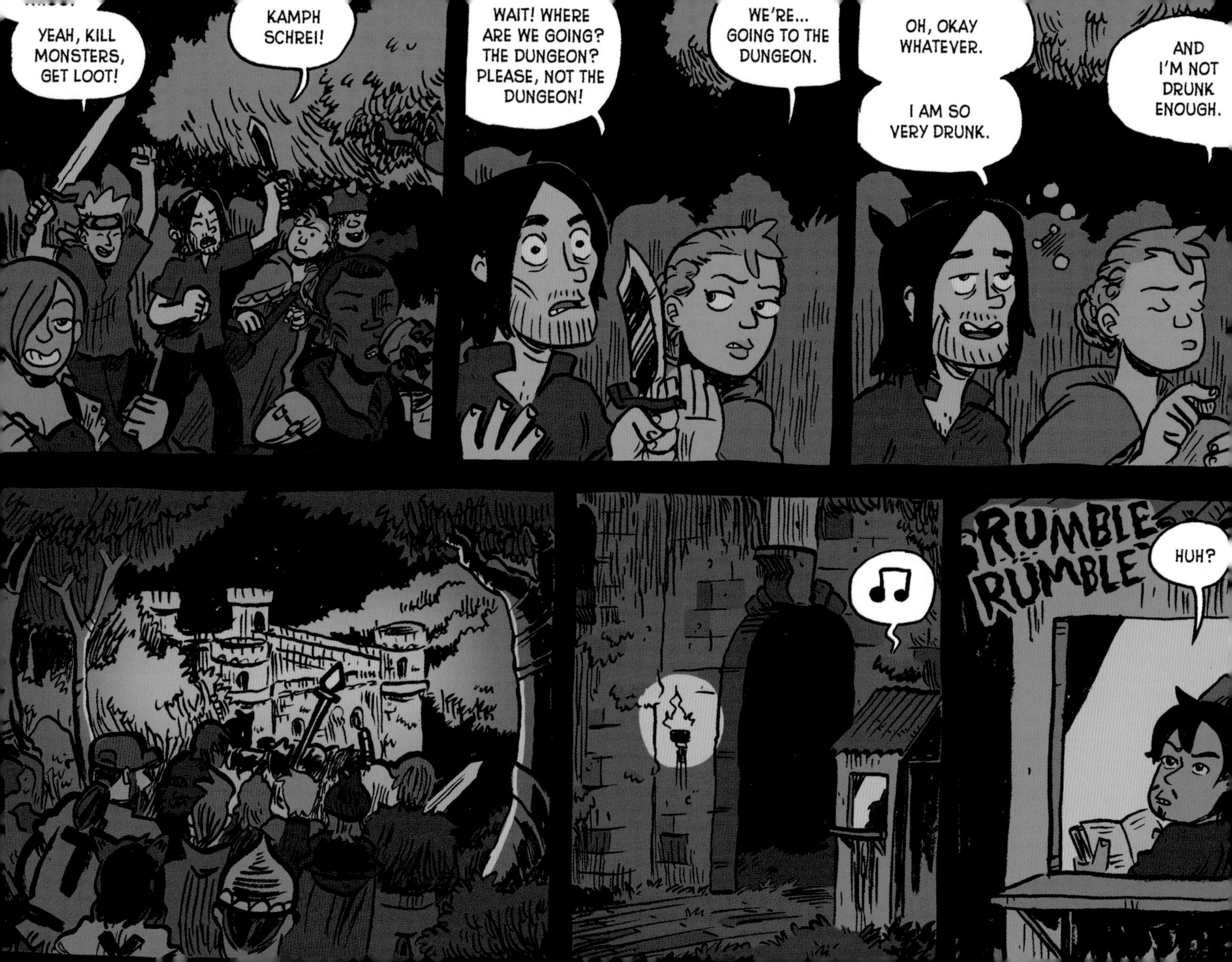
YEAH, KILL MONSTERS, GET LOOT!
KAMPH SCHREI!
WAIT! WHERE ARE WE GOING? THE DUNGEON? PLEASE, NOT THE DUNGEON!
WE'RE... GOING TO THE DUNGEON.
OH, OKAY WHATEVER.
I AM SO VERY DRUNK.
AND I'M NOT DRUNK ENOUGH.
♫
RUMBLE RUMBLE
HUH?

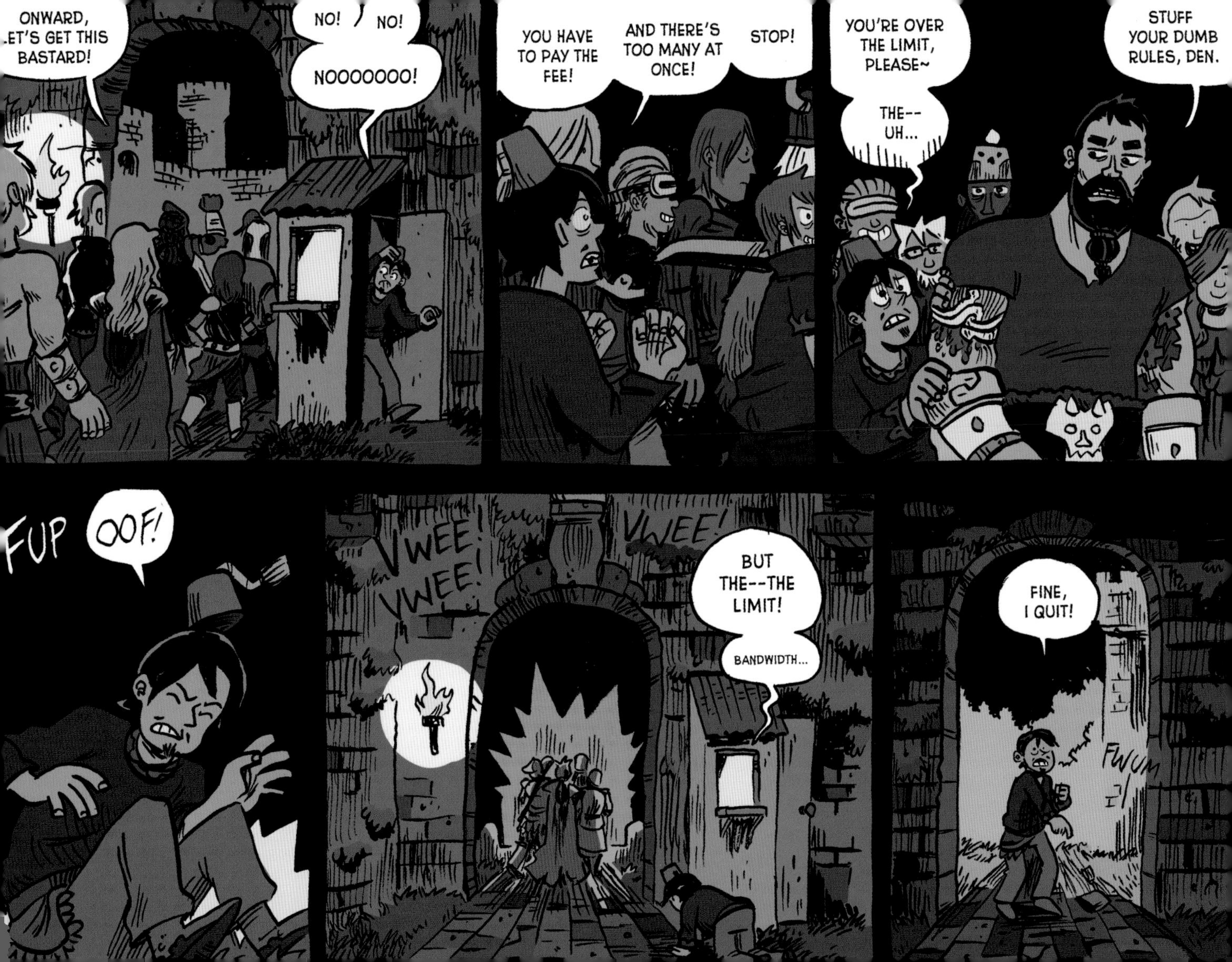
ONWARD, LET'S GET THIS BASTARD!
NO! NO!
NOOOOOOO!
YOU HAVE TO PAY THE FEE!
AND THERE'S TOO MANY AT ONCE!
STOP!
YOU'RE OVER THE LIMIT, PLEASE~
THE-- UH...
STUFF YOUR DUMB RULES, DEN.
FUP
OOF!
VWEE! VWEE!
VWEE!
BUT THE--THE LIMIT!
BANDWIDTH...
FINE, I QUIT!
FWUM

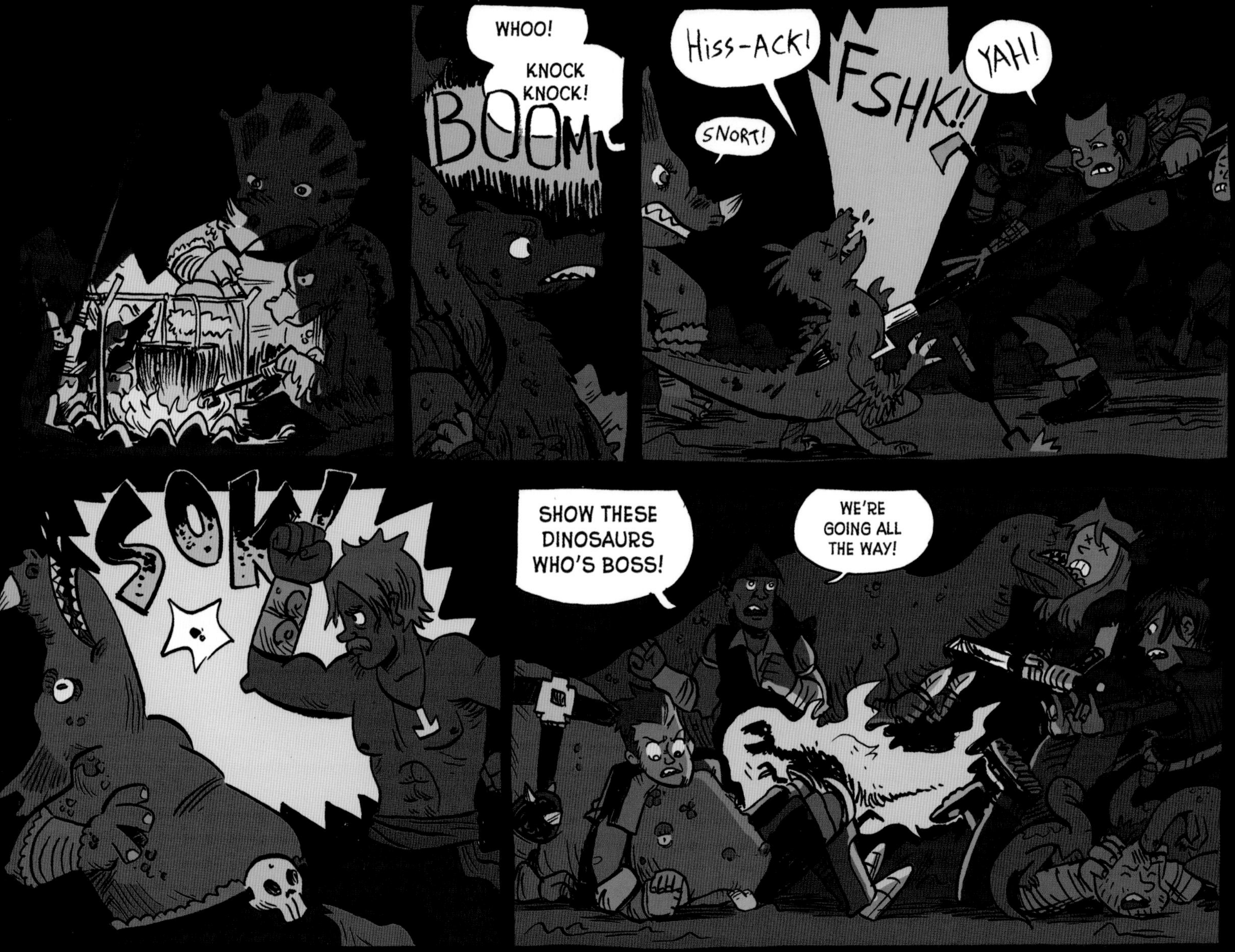
WHOO!
KNOCK KNOCK!
BOOM
Hiss-ACK!
SNORT!
FSHK!!
YAH!
SHOW THESE DINOSAURS WHO'S BOSS!
WE'RE GOING ALL THE WAY!

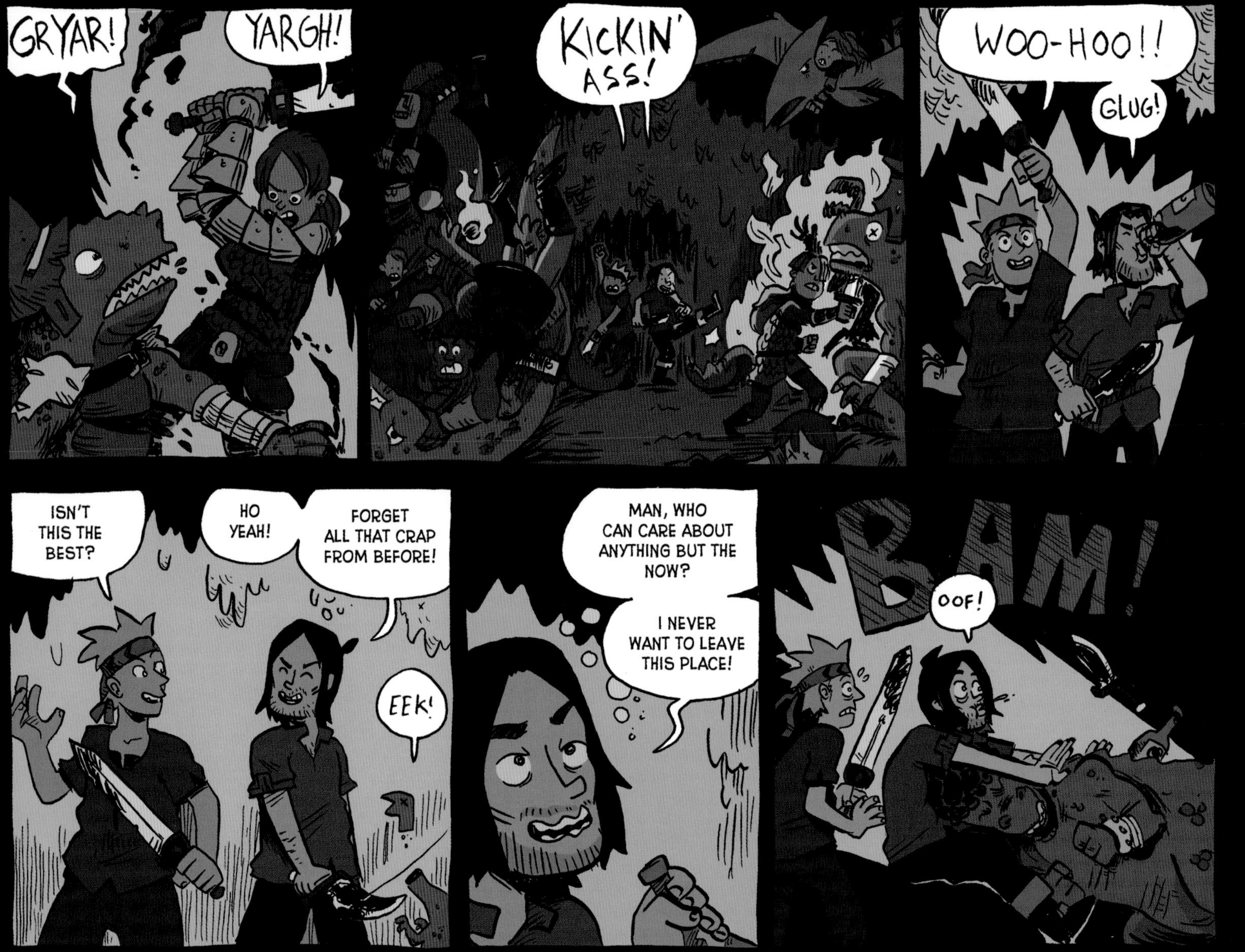
GRYAR!
YARGH!
KICKIN' ASS!
WOO-HOO!!
GLUG!
ISN'T THIS THE BEST?
HO YEAH!
FORGET ALL THAT CRAP FROM BEFORE!
EEK!
MAN, WHO CAN CARE ABOUT ANYTHING BUT THE NOW?
I NEVER WANT TO LEAVE THIS PLACE!
BAM!
OOF!

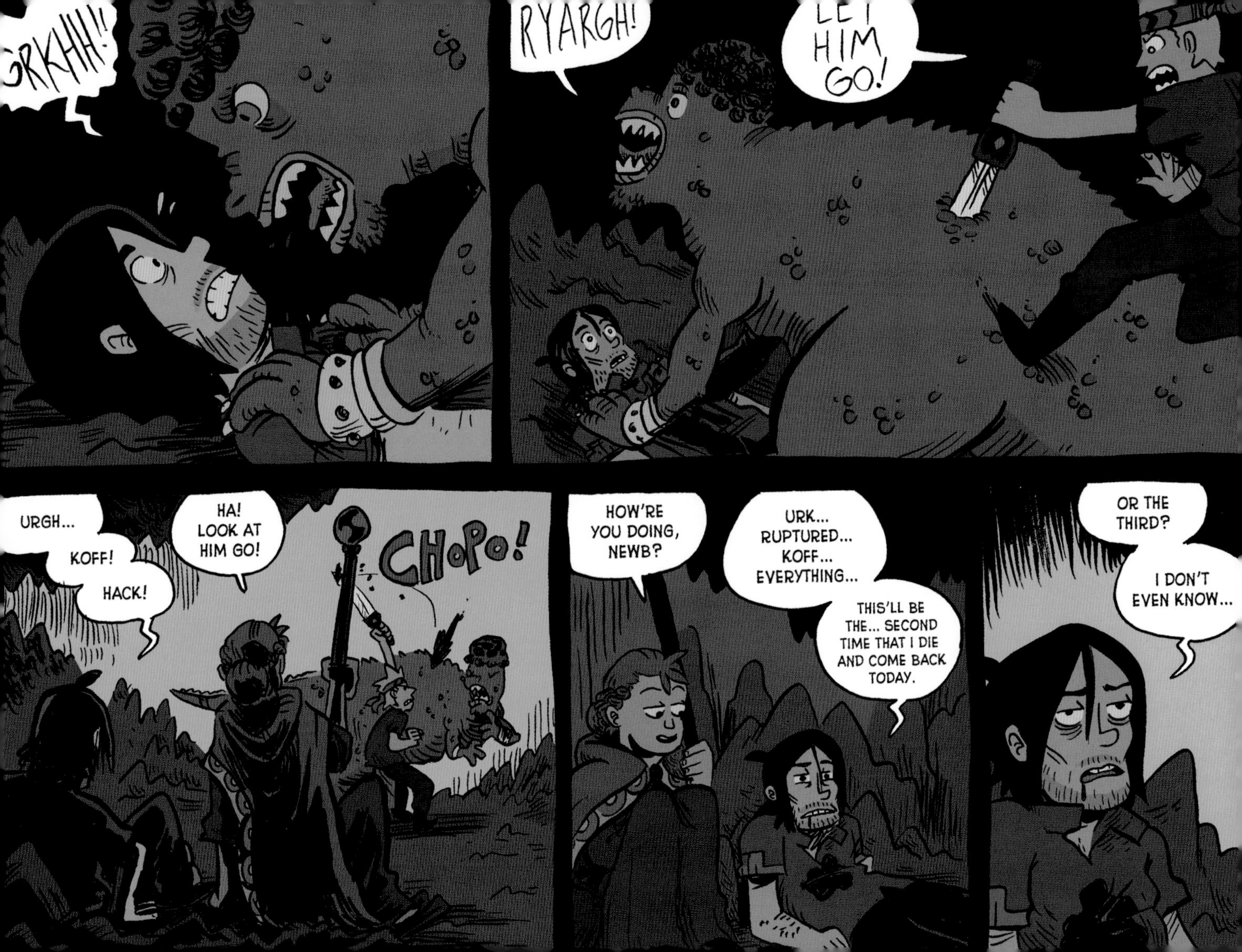
GRKHH!!
RYARGH!
LET HIM GO!
URGH...
KOFF!
HACK!
HA! LOOK AT HIM GO!
CHOPO!
HOW'RE YOU DOING, NEWB?
URK... RUPTURED... KOFF... EVERYTHING...
THIS'LL BE THE... SECOND TIME THAT I DIE AND COME BACK TODAY.
OR THE THIRD?
I DON'T EVEN KNOW...

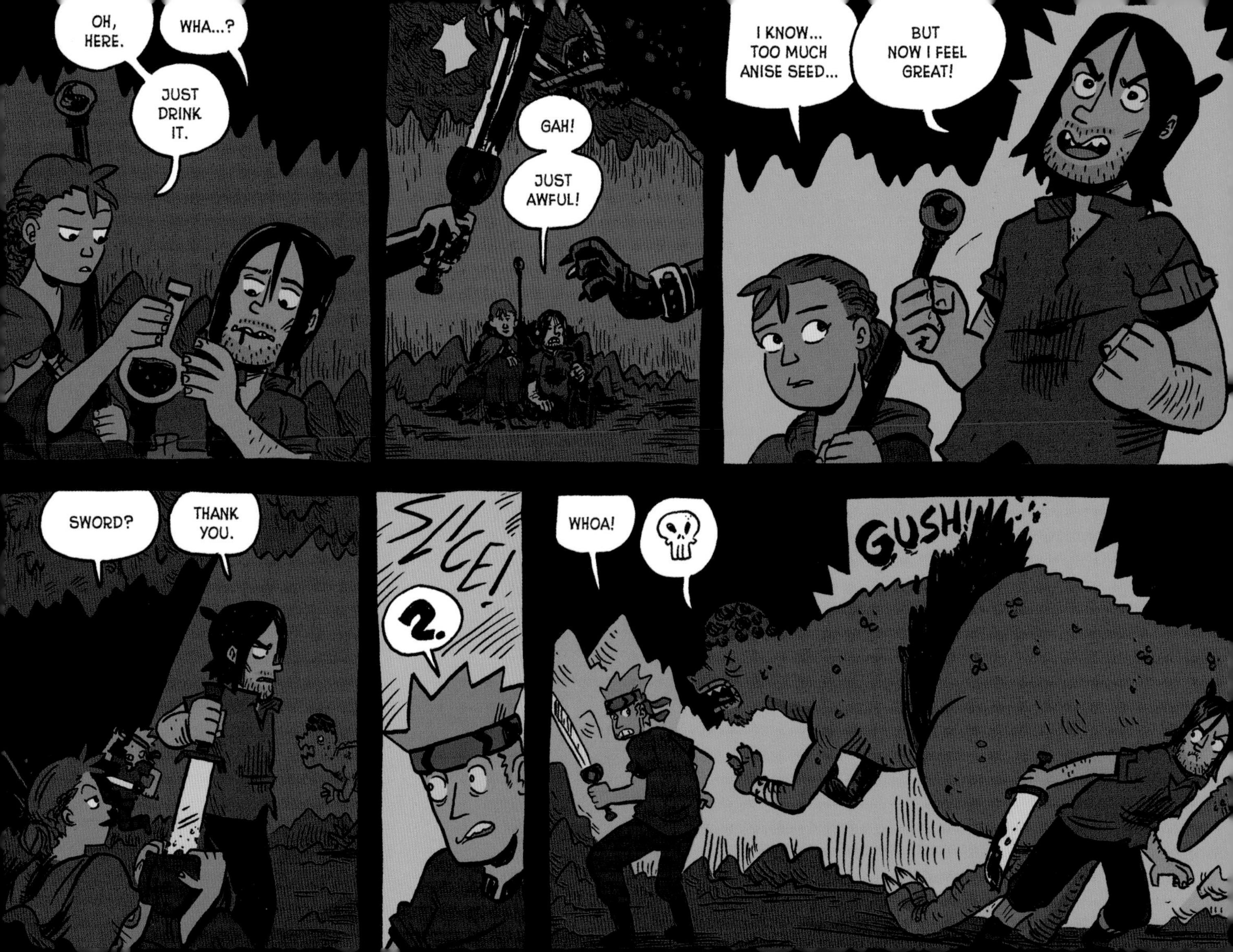
OH, HERE.
WHA...?
JUST DRINK IT.
GAH!
JUST AWFUL!
I KNOW... TOO MUCH ANISE SEED...
BUT NOW I FEEL GREAT!
SWORD?
THANK YOU.
SLICE!
?
WHOA!
GUSH!

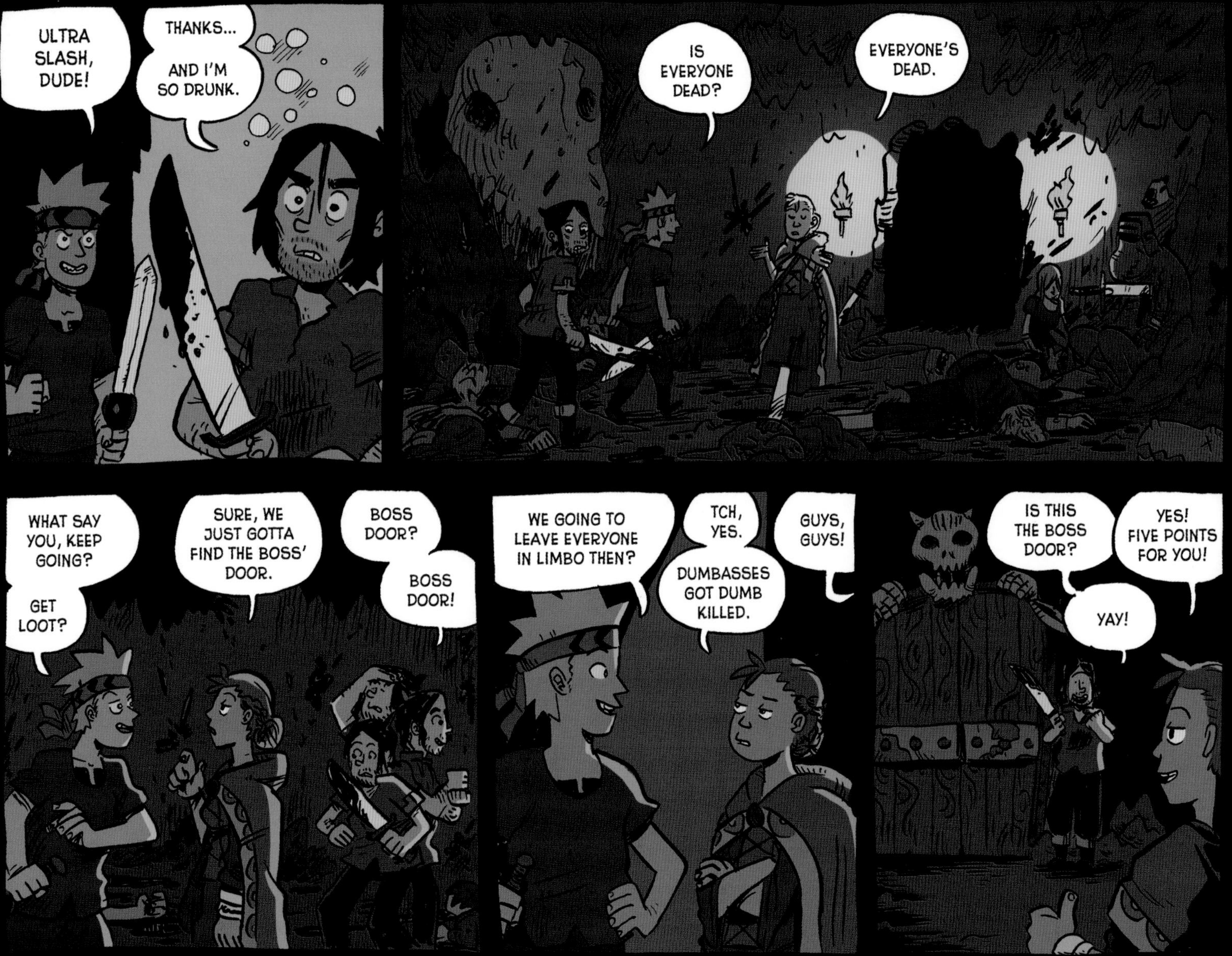

ULTRA SLASH, DUDE!
THANKS... AND I'M SO DRUNK.
IS EVERYONE DEAD?
EVERYONE'S DEAD.
WHAT SAY YOU, KEEP GOING?
GET LOOT?
SURE, WE JUST GOTTA FIND THE BOSS' DOOR.
BOSS DOOR?
BOSS DOOR!
WE GOING TO LEAVE EVERYONE IN LIMBO THEN?
TCH, YES.
DUMBASSES GOT DUMB KILLED.
GUYS, GUYS!
IS THIS THE BOSS DOOR?
YES! FIVE POINTS FOR YOU!
YAY!

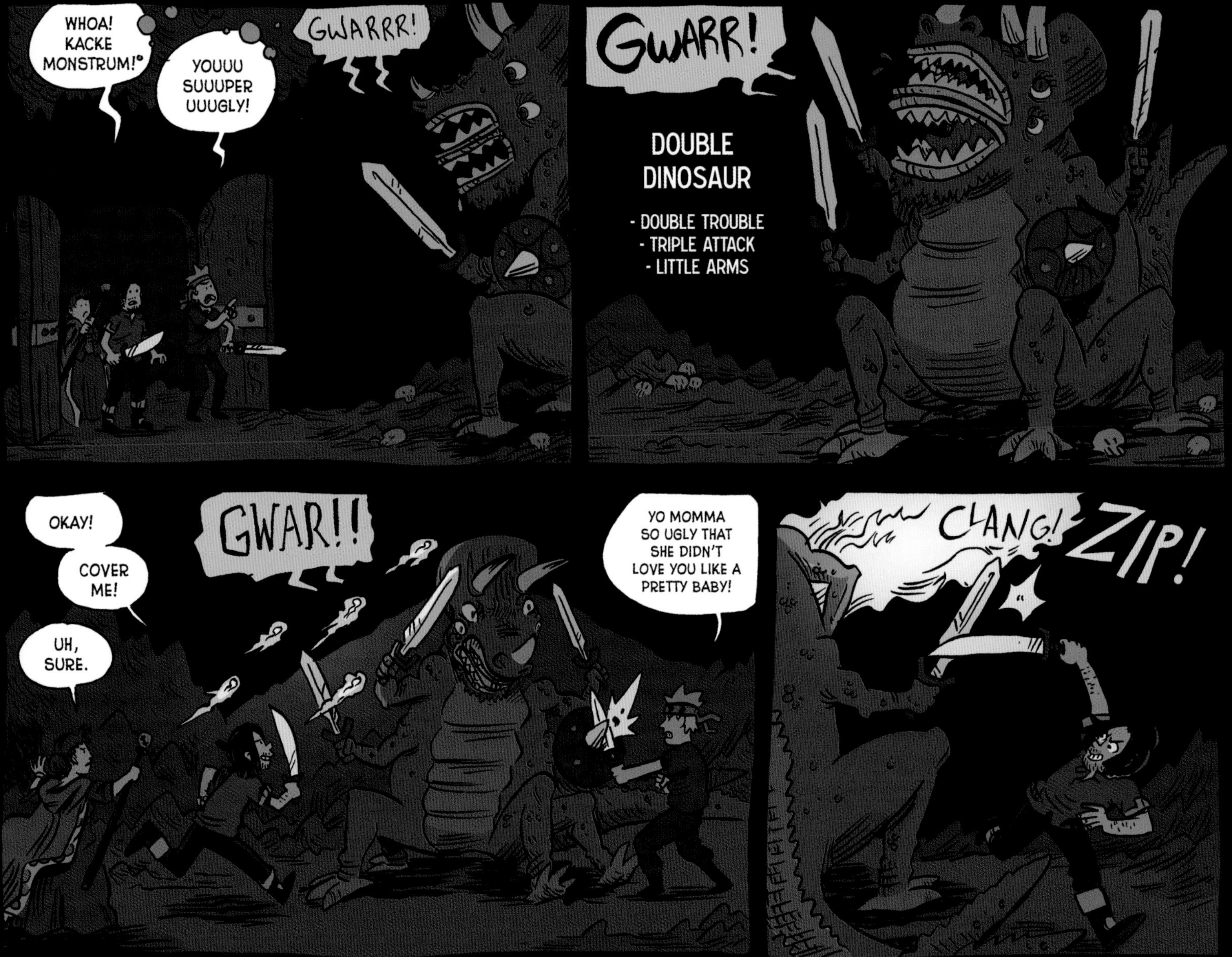
WHOA! KACKE MONSTRUM!*
YOUUU SUUUPER UUUGLY!
GWARRR!
GWARR!
DOUBLE DINOSAUR
- DOUBLE TROUBLE
- TRIPLE ATTACK
- LITTLE ARMS
OKAY!
COVER ME!
UH, SURE.
GWAR!!
YO MOMMA SO UGLY THAT SHE DIDN'T LOVE YOU LIKE A PRETTY BABY!
CLANG!
ZIP!

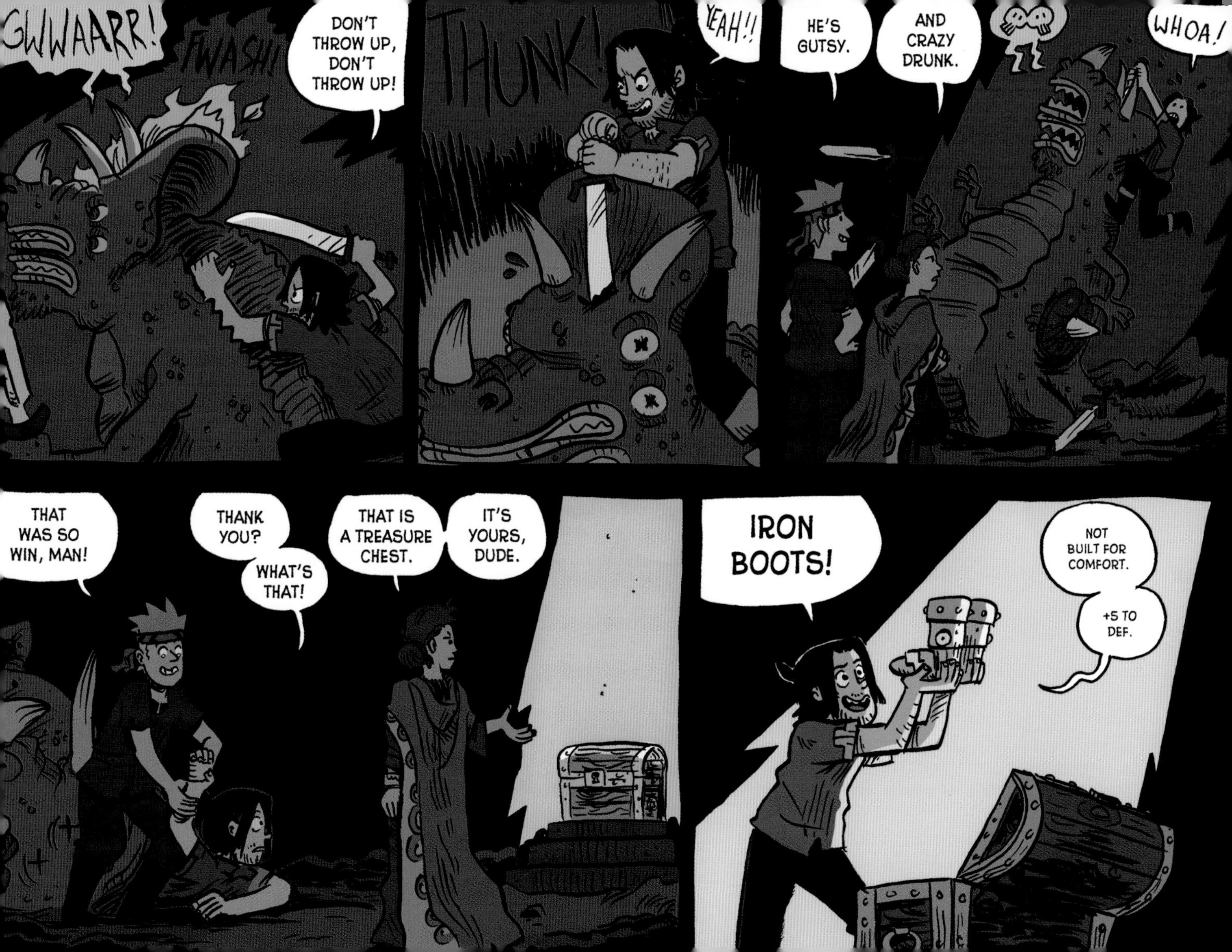
GWWAARR!
FWASH!
DON'T THROW UP, DON'T THROW UP!
THUNK!
YEAH!!
HE'S GUTSY.
AND CRAZY DRUNK.
WHOA!
THAT WAS SO WIN, MAN!
THANK YOU?
WHAT'S THAT!
THAT IS A TREASURE CHEST.
IT'S YOURS, DUDE.
IRON BOOTS!
NOT BUILT FOR COMFORT.
+5 TO DEF.

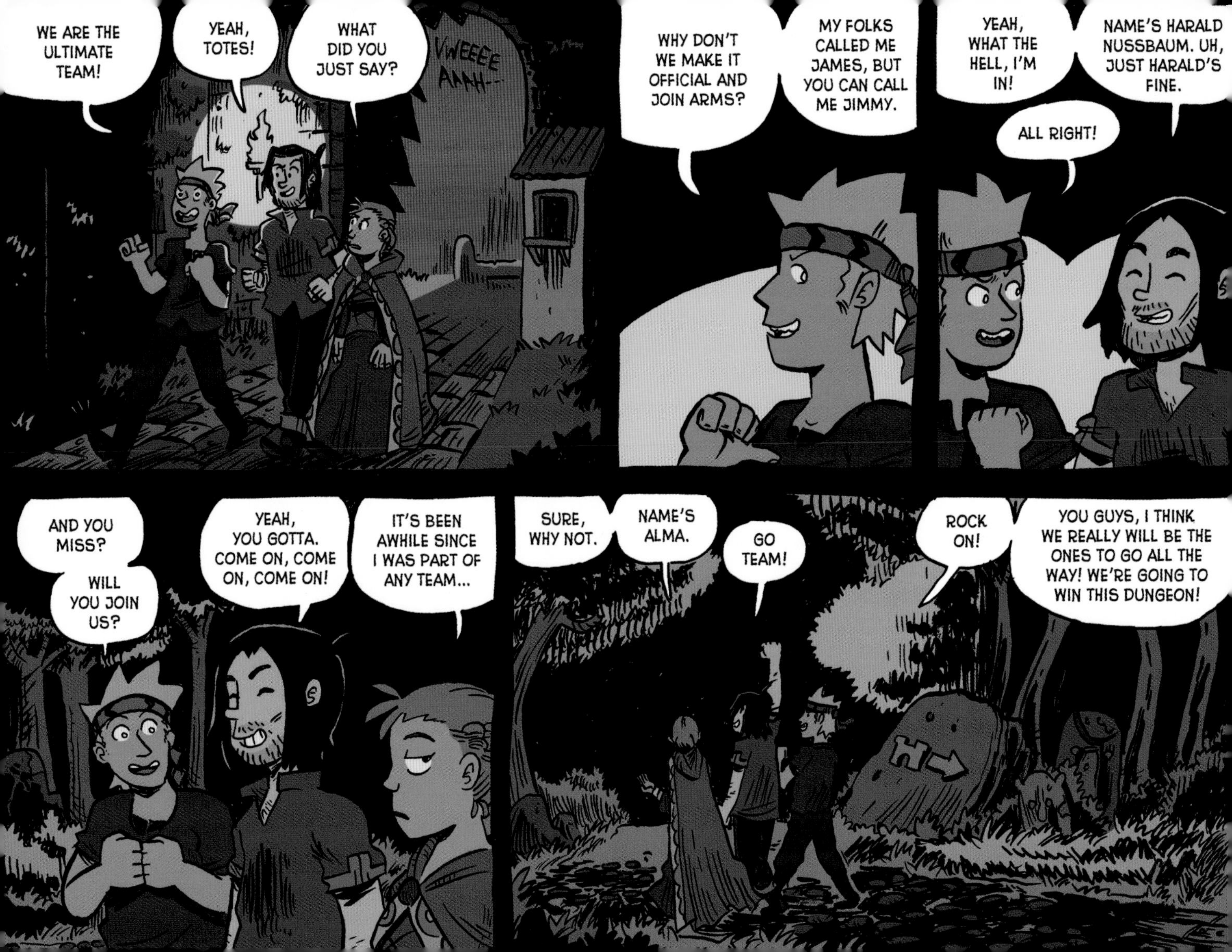
WE ARE THE ULTIMATE TEAM!
YEAH, TOTES!
WHAT DID YOU JUST SAY?
VWEEEE AAAH--
WHY DON'T WE MAKE IT OFFICIAL AND JOIN ARMS?
MY FOLKS CALLED ME JAMES, BUT YOU CAN CALL ME JIMMY.
YEAH, WHAT THE HELL, I'M IN!
NAME'S HARALD NUSSBAUM. UH, JUST HARALD'S FINE.
ALL RIGHT!
AND YOU MISS?
WILL YOU JOIN US?
YEAH, YOU GOTTA. COME ON, COME ON, COME ON!
IT'S BEEN AWHILE SINCE I WAS PART OF ANY TEAM...
SURE, WHY NOT.
NAME'S ALMA.
GO TEAM!
ROCK ON!
YOU GUYS, I THINK WE REALLY WILL BE THE ONES TO GO ALL THE WAY! WE'RE GOING TO WIN THIS DUNGEON!

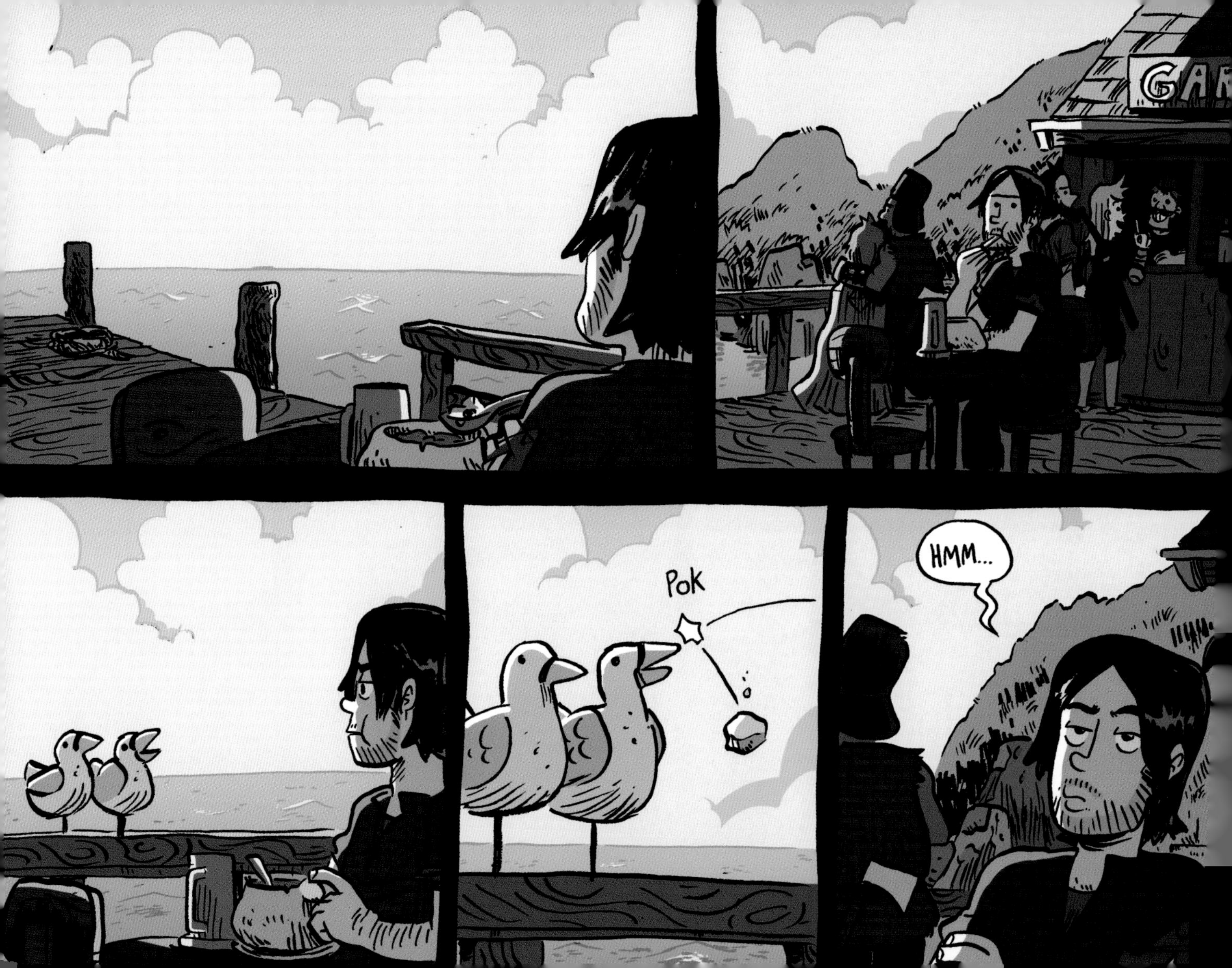
GAR
POK
HMM...

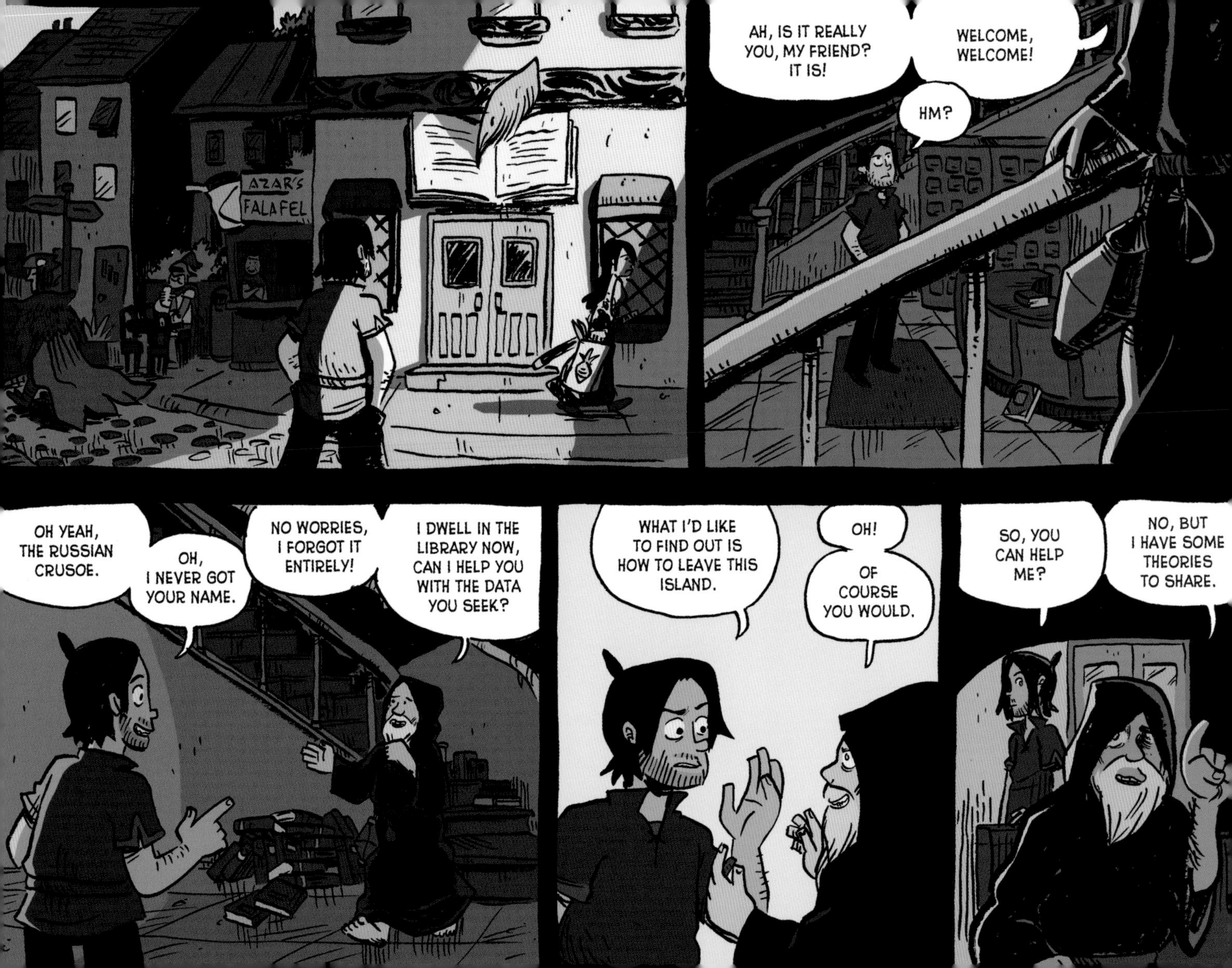
AZAR'S FALAFEL
AH, IS IT REALLY YOU, MY FRIEND? IT IS!
WELCOME, WELCOME!
HM?
OH YEAH, THE RUSSIAN CRUSOE.
OH, I NEVER GOT YOUR NAME.
NO WORRIES, I FORGOT IT ENTIRELY!
I DWELL IN THE LIBRARY NOW, CAN I HELP YOU WITH THE DATA YOU SEEK?
WHAT I'D LIKE TO FIND OUT IS HOW TO LEAVE THIS ISLAND.
OH!
OF COURSE YOU WOULD.
SO, YOU CAN HELP ME?
NO, BUT I HAVE SOME THEORIES TO SHARE.

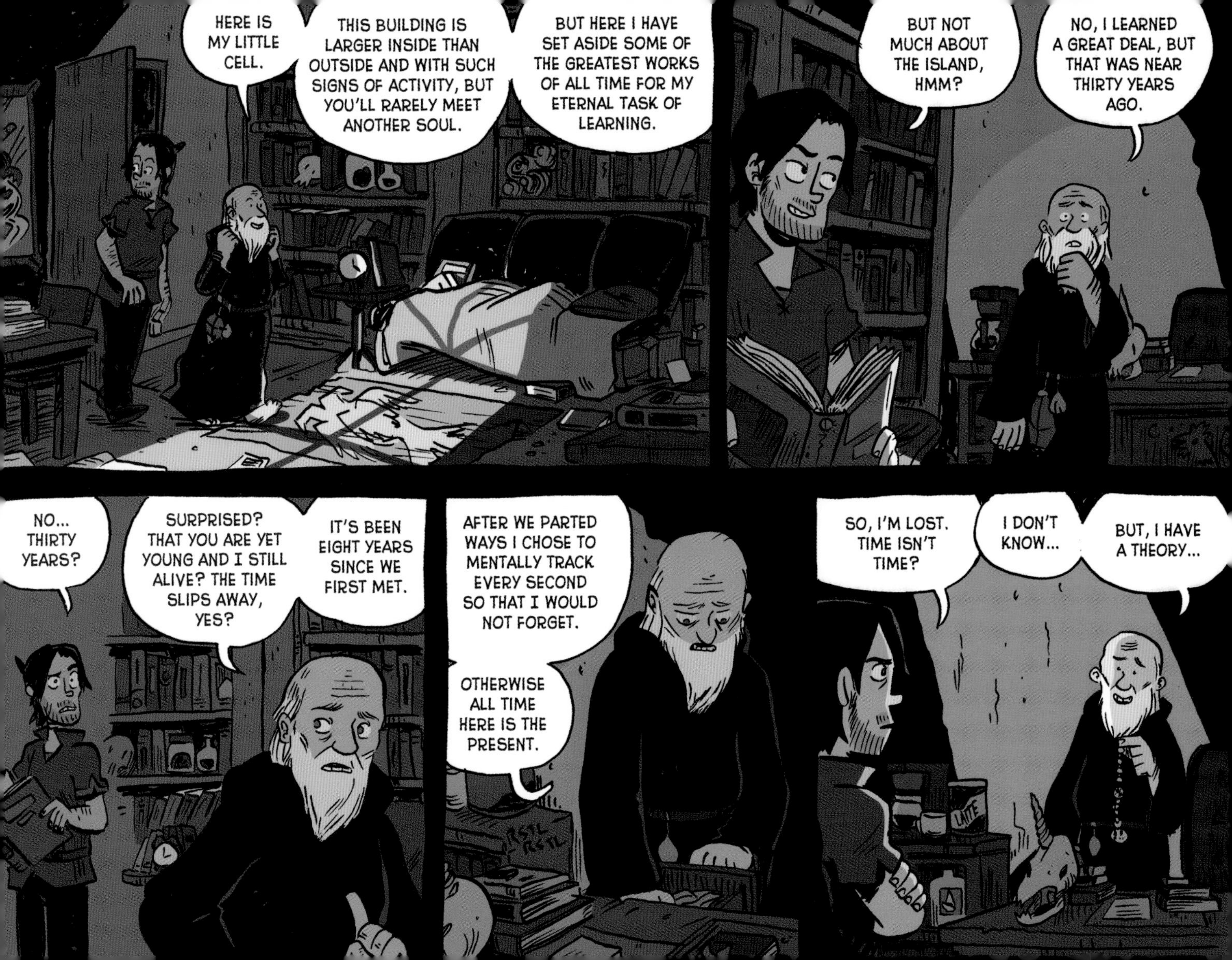
HERE IS MY LITTLE CELL.
THIS BUILDING IS LARGER INSIDE THAN OUTSIDE AND WITH SUCH SIGNS OF ACTIVITY, BUT YOU'LL RARELY MEET ANOTHER SOUL.
BUT HERE I HAVE SET ASIDE SOME OF THE GREATEST WORKS OF ALL TIME FOR MY ETERNAL TASK OF LEARNING.
BUT NOT MUCH ABOUT THE ISLAND, HMM?
NO, I LEARNED A GREAT DEAL, BUT THAT WAS NEAR THIRTY YEARS AGO.
NO... THIRTY YEARS?
SURPRISED? THAT YOU ARE YET YOUNG AND I STILL ALIVE? THE TIME SLIPS AWAY, YES?
IT'S BEEN EIGHT YEARS SINCE WE FIRST MET.
AFTER WE PARTED WAYS I CHOSE TO MENTALLY TRACK EVERY SECOND SO THAT I WOULD NOT FORGET.
OTHERWISE ALL TIME HERE IS THE PRESENT.
RSTL RSTL
SO, I'M LOST. TIME ISN'T TIME?
I DON'T KNOW...
BUT, I HAVE A THEORY...
LATTE

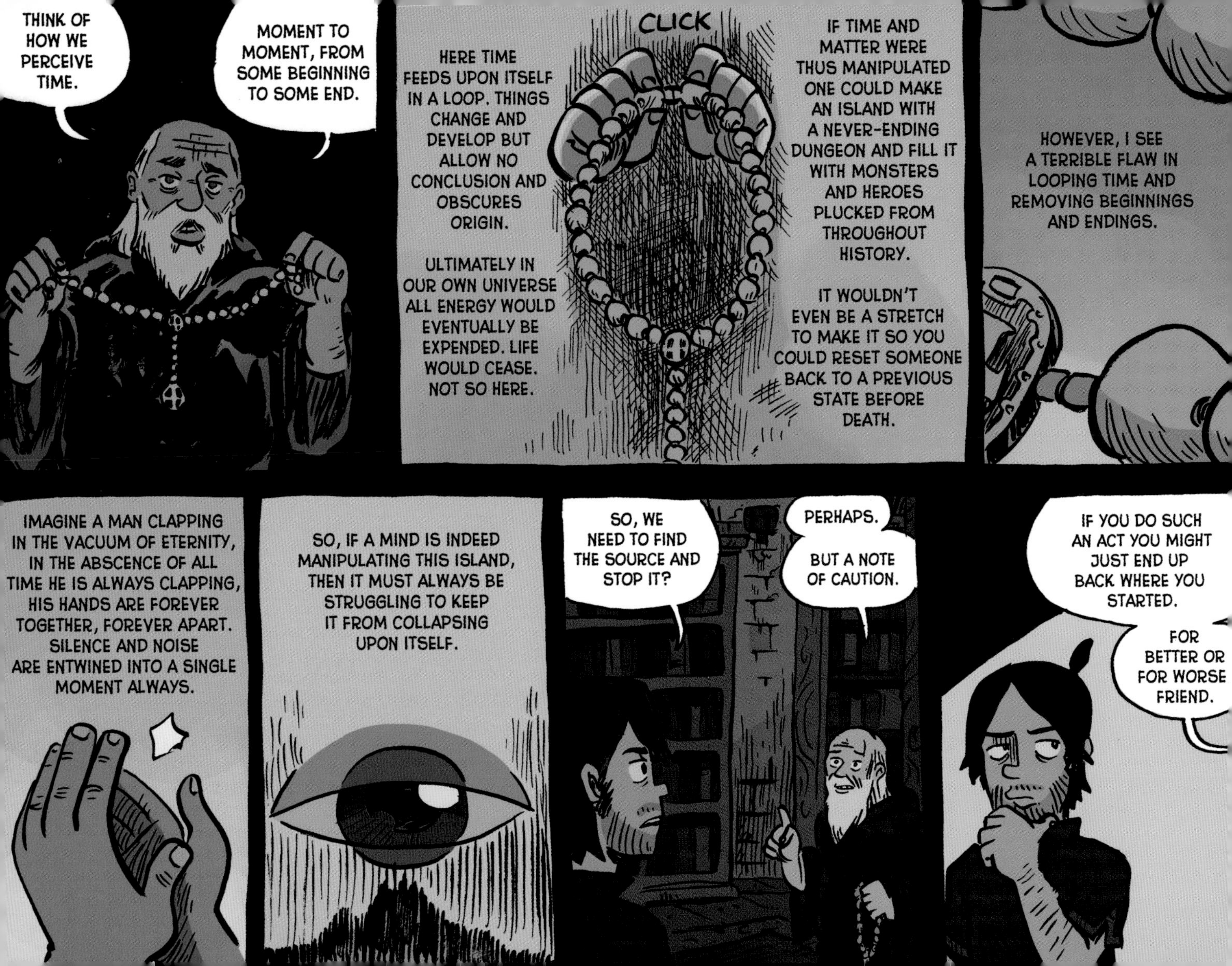
THINK OF HOW WE PERCEIVE TIME.
MOMENT TO MOMENT, FROM SOME BEGINNING TO SOME END.
HERE TIME FEEDS UPON ITSELF IN A LOOP. THINGS CHANGE AND DEVELOP BUT ALLOW NO CONCLUSION AND OBSCURES ORIGIN.
ULTIMATELY IN OUR OWN UNIVERSE ALL ENERGY WOULD EVENTUALLY BE EXPENDED. LIFE WOULD CEASE. NOT SO HERE.
CLICK
IF TIME AND MATTER WERE THUS MANIPULATED ONE COULD MAKE AN ISLAND WITH A NEVER-ENDING DUNGEON AND FILL IT WITH MONSTERS AND HEROES PLUCKED FROM THROUGHOUT HISTORY.
IT WOULDN'T EVEN BE A STRETCH TO MAKE IT SO YOU COULD RESET SOMEONE BACK TO A PREVIOUS STATE BEFORE DEATH.
HOWEVER, I SEE A TERRIBLE FLAW IN LOOPING TIME AND REMOVING BEGINNINGS AND ENDINGS.
IMAGINE A MAN CLAPPING IN THE VACUUM OF ETERNITY, IN THE ABSCENCE OF ALL TIME HE IS ALWAYS CLAPPING, HIS HANDS ARE FOREVER TOGETHER, FOREVER APART. SILENCE AND NOISE ARE ENTWINED INTO A SINGLE MOMENT ALWAYS.
SO, IF A MIND IS INDEED MANIPULATING THIS ISLAND, THEN IT MUST ALWAYS BE STRUGGLING TO KEEP IT FROM COLLAPSING UPON ITSELF.
SO, WE NEED TO FIND THE SOURCE AND STOP IT?
PERHAPS.
BUT A NOTE OF CAUTION.
IF YOU DO SUCH AN ACT YOU MIGHT JUST END UP BACK WHERE YOU STARTED.
FOR BETTER OR FOR WORSE FRIEND.

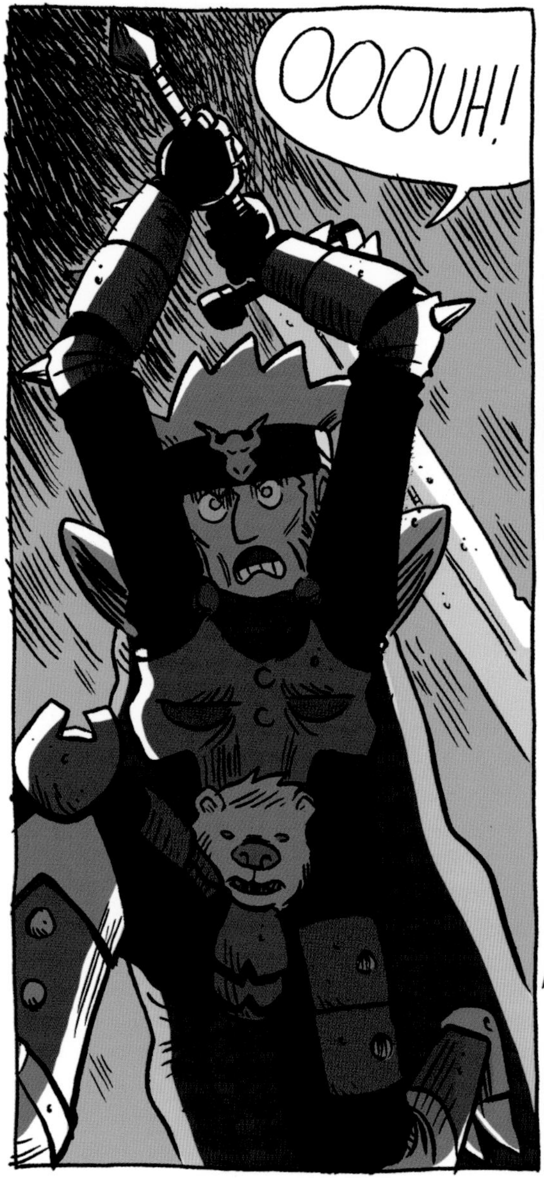
OOOUH!

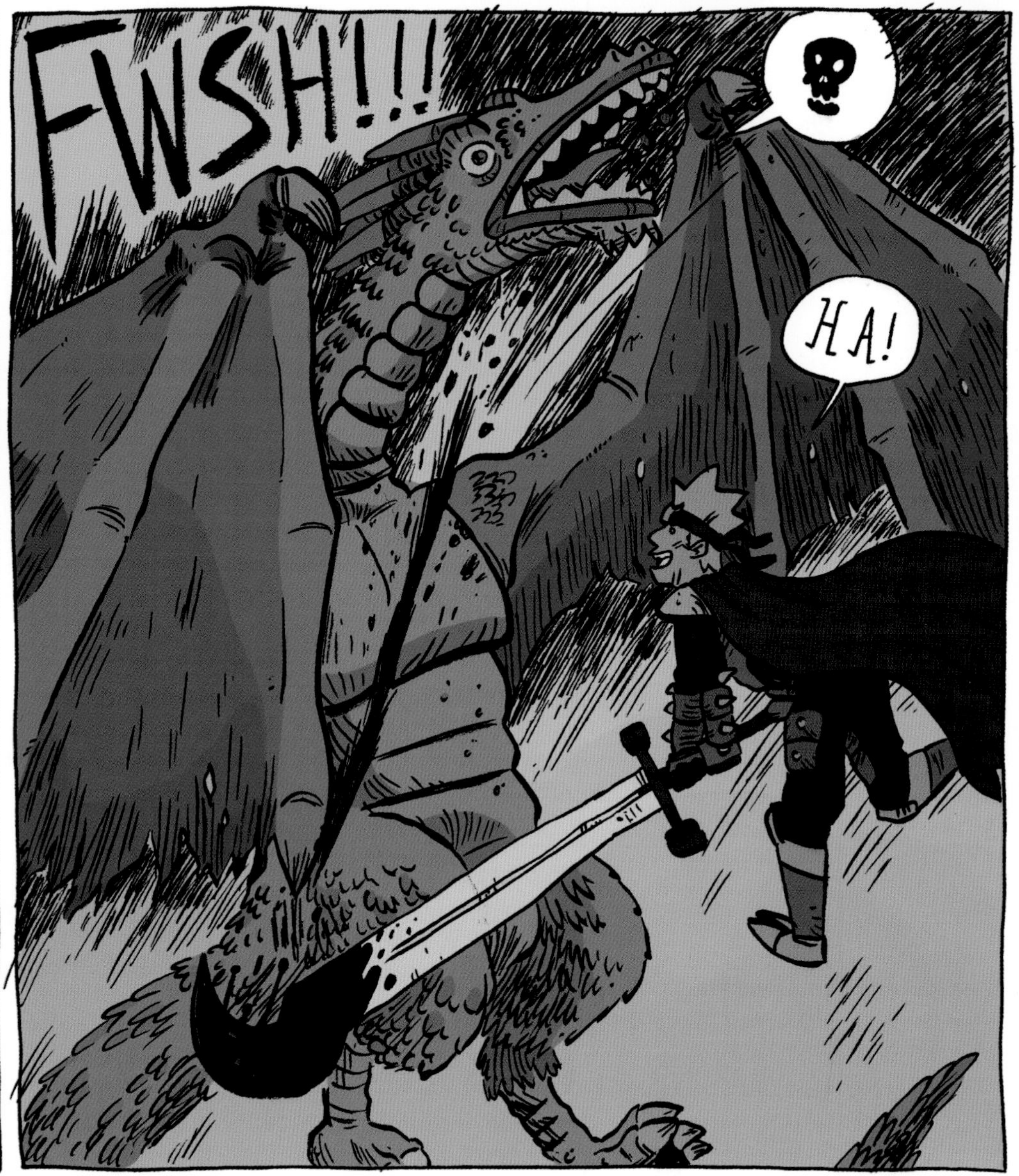
FWSH!!!
HA!

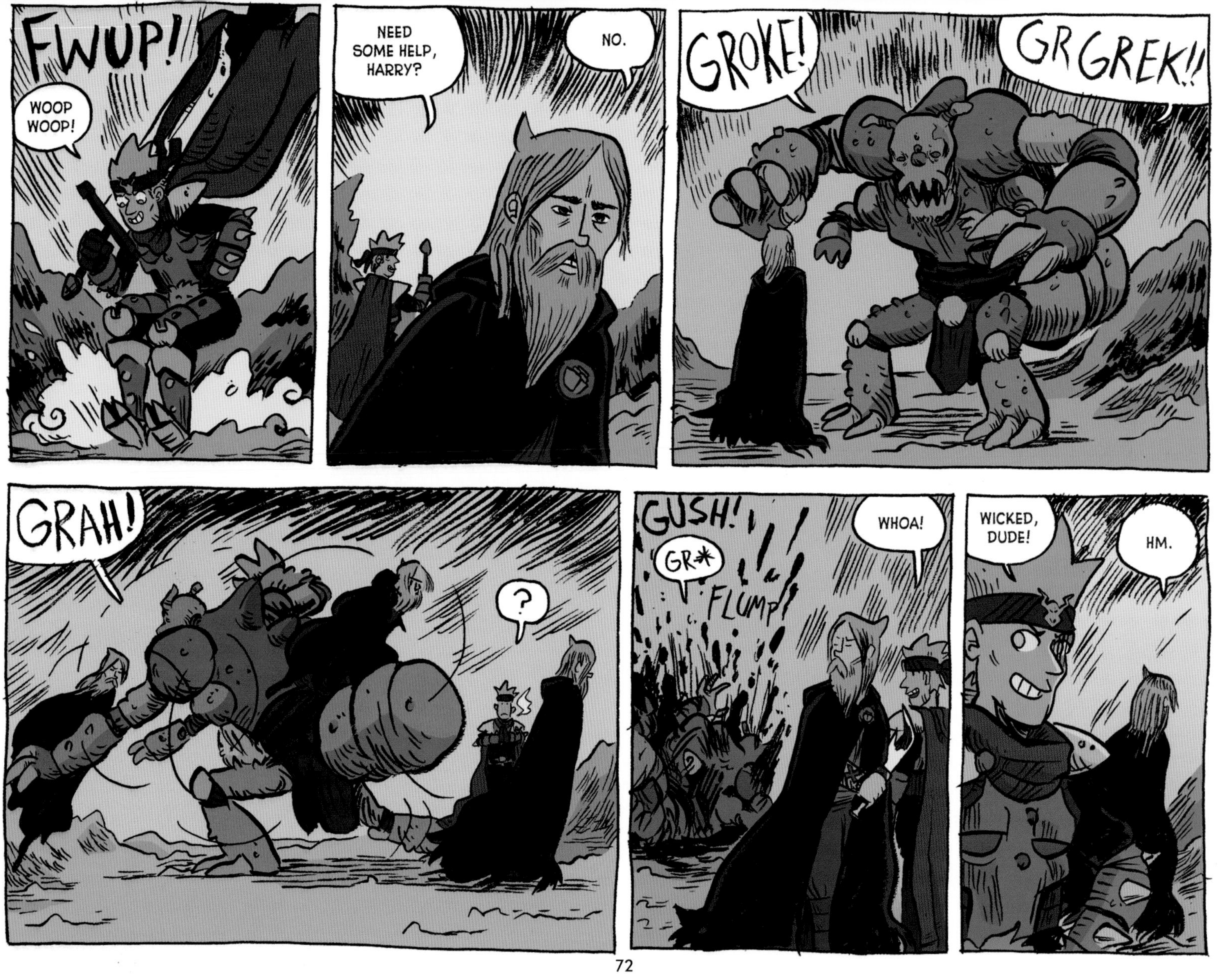
FWUP!
WOOP WOOP!
NEED SOME HELP, HARRY?
NO.
GROKE!
GRGREK!!
GRAH!
?
GUSH!
GR*
FLUMP
WHOA!
WICKED, DUDE!
HM.

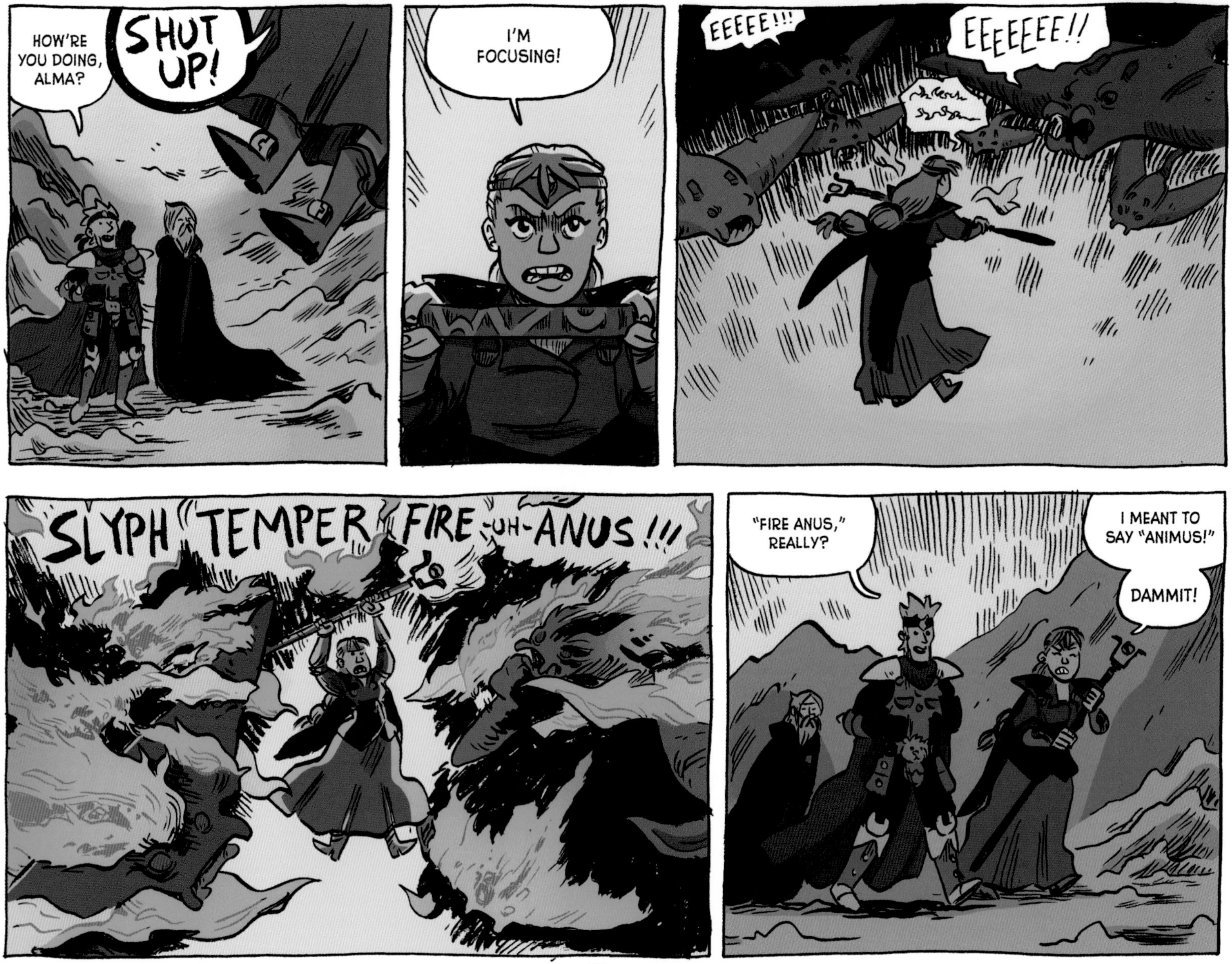
HOW'RE YOU DOING, ALMA?
SHUT UP!
I'M FOCUSING!
EEEEE!!!
EEEEEEE!!
SLYPH TEMPER FIRE-UH-ANUS!!!
"FIRE ANUS," REALLY?
I MEANT TO SAY "ANIMUS!"
DAMMIT!

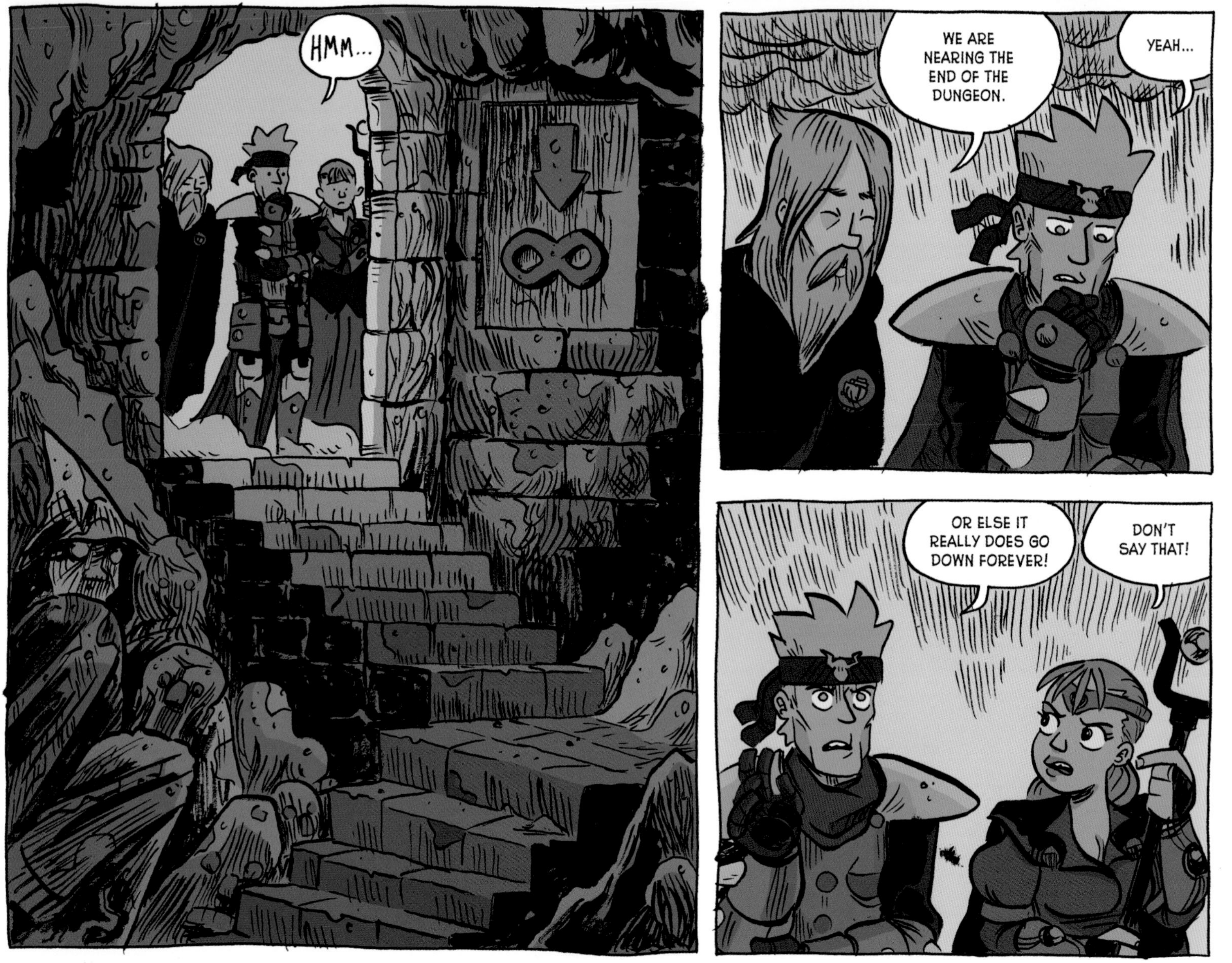
HMM...
WE ARE NEARING THE END OF THE DUNGEON.
YEAH...
OR ELSE IT REALLY DOES GO DOWN FOREVER!
DON'T SAY THAT!

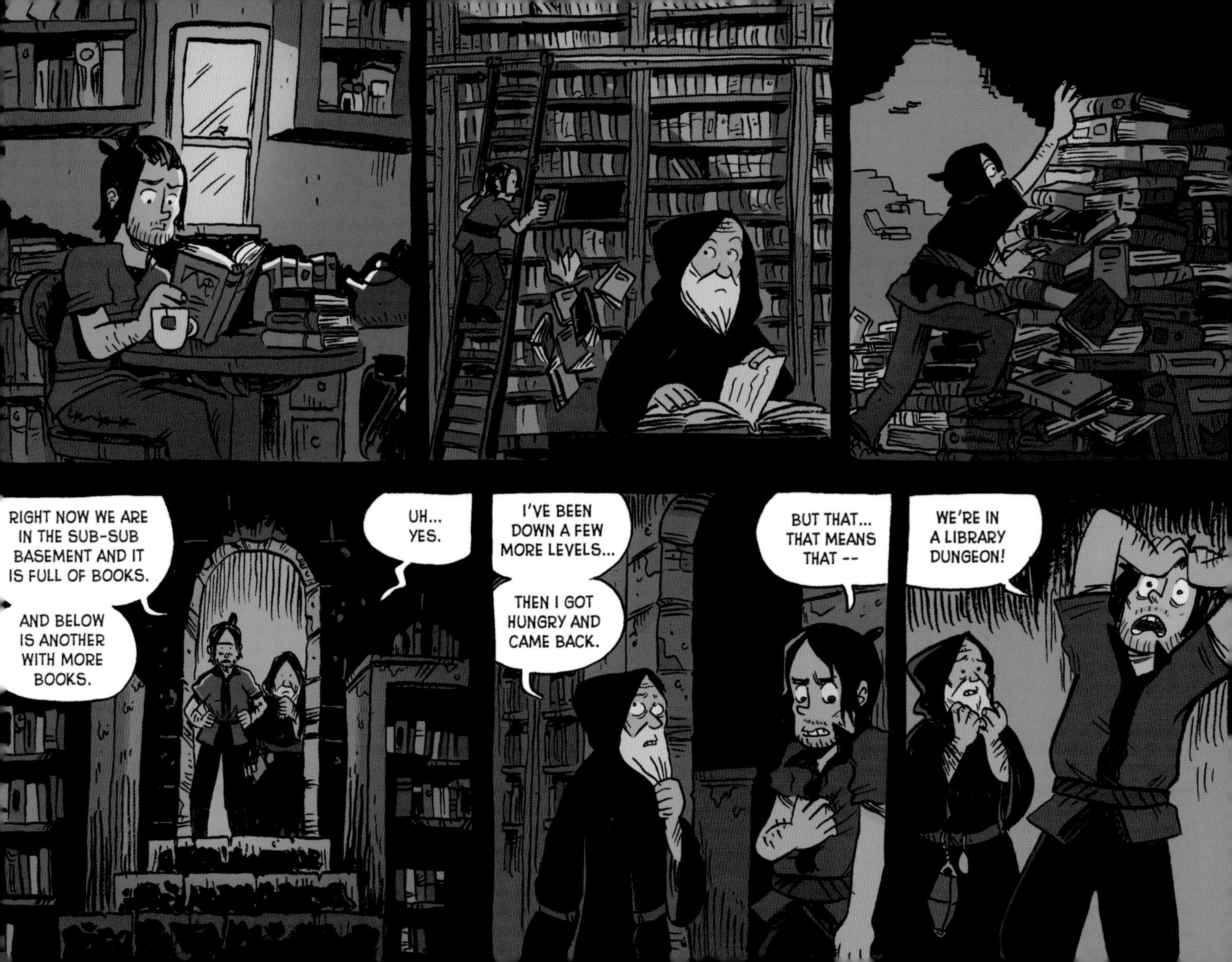
RIGHT NOW WE ARE IN THE SUB-SUB BASEMENT AND IT IS FULL OF BOOKS.
AND BELOW IS ANOTHER WITH MORE BOOKS.
UH... YES.
I'VE BEEN DOWN A FEW MORE LEVELS...
THEN I GOT HUNGRY AND CAME BACK.
BUT THAT... THAT MEANS THAT --
WE'RE IN A LIBRARY DUNGEON!

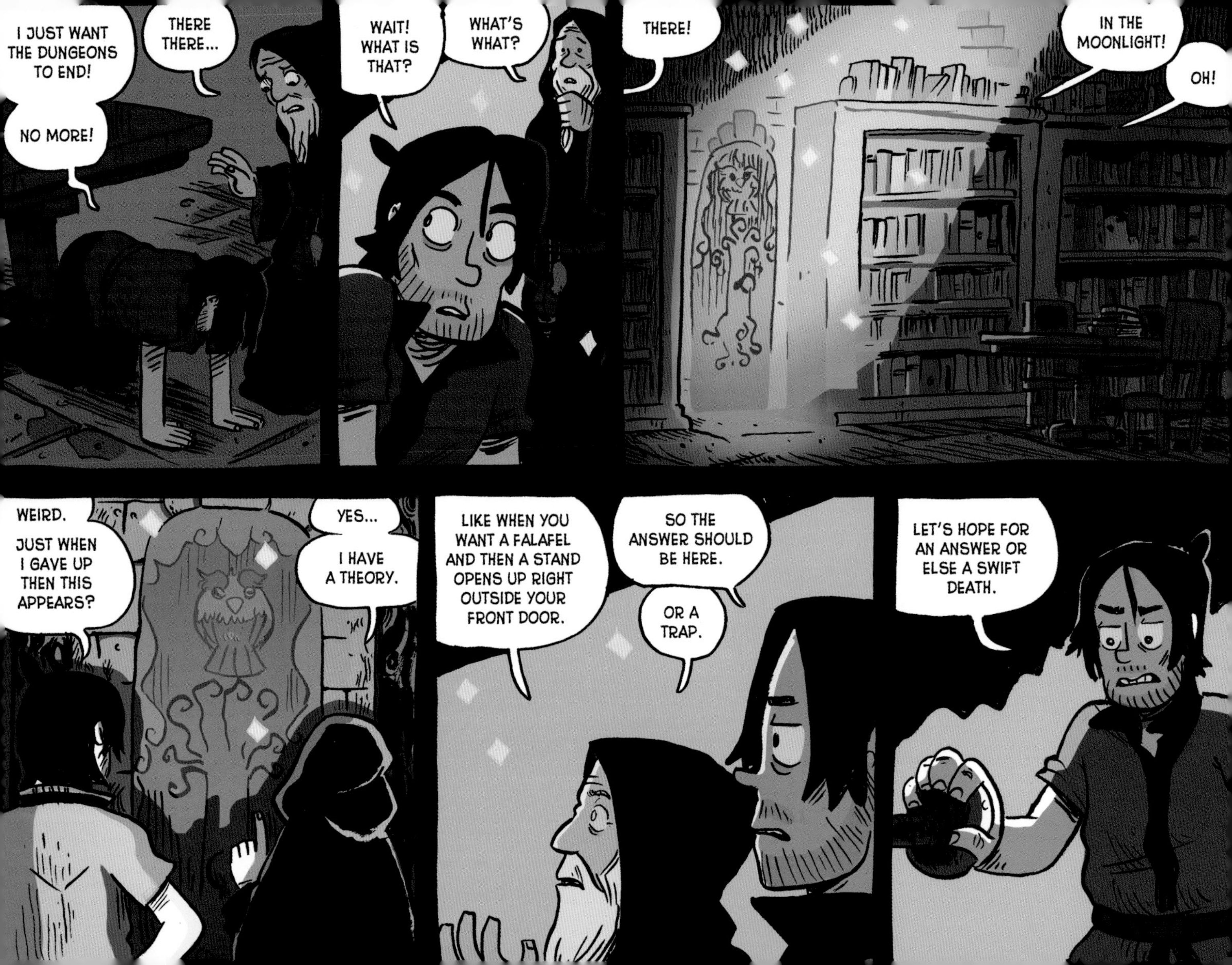
I JUST WANT THE DUNGEONS TO END!
THERE THERE...
NO MORE!
WAIT! WHAT IS THAT?
WHAT'S WHAT?
THERE!
IN THE MOONLIGHT!
OH!
WEIRD.
JUST WHEN I GAVE UP THEN THIS APPEARS?
YES...
I HAVE A THEORY.
LIKE WHEN YOU WANT A FALAFEL AND THEN A STAND OPENS UP RIGHT OUTSIDE YOUR FRONT DOOR.
SO THE ANSWER SHOULD BE HERE.
OR A TRAP.
LET'S HOPE FOR AN ANSWER OR ELSE A SWIFT DEATH.

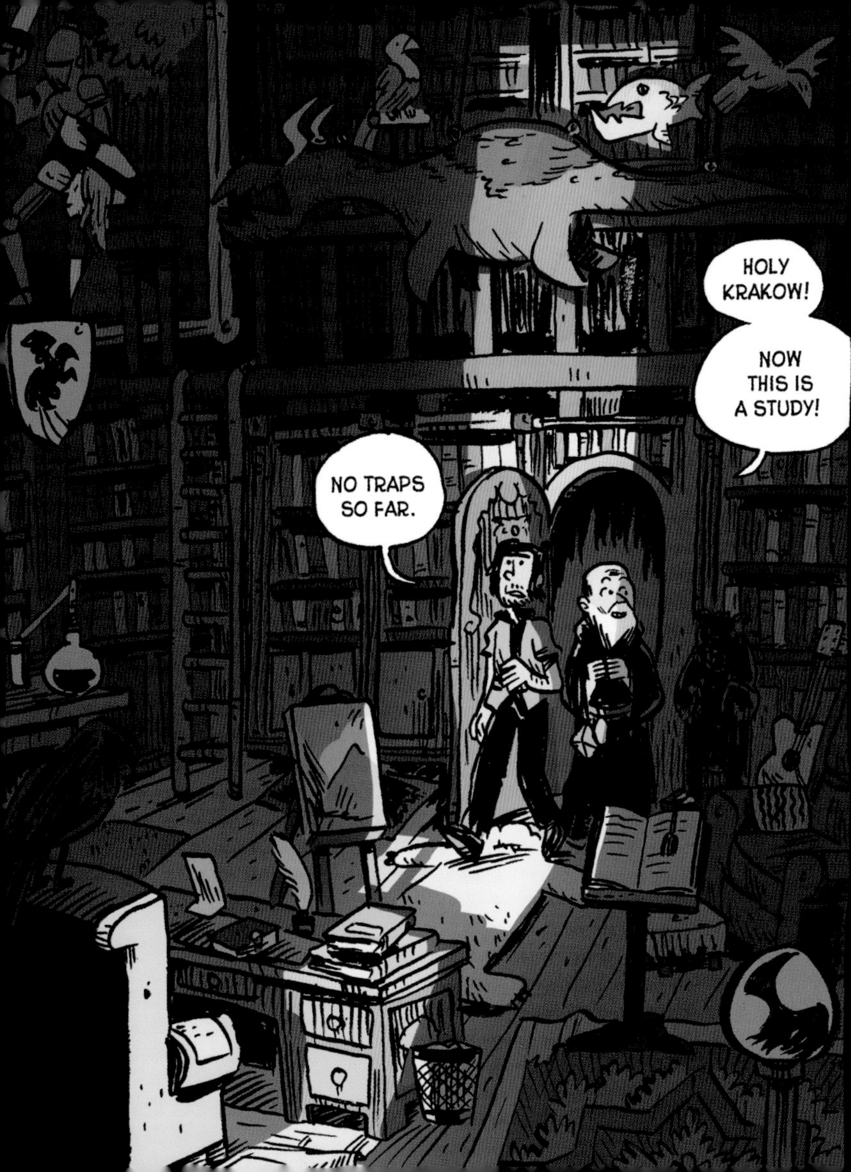
HOLY KRAKOW!
NOW THIS IS A STUDY!
NO TRAPS SO FAR.

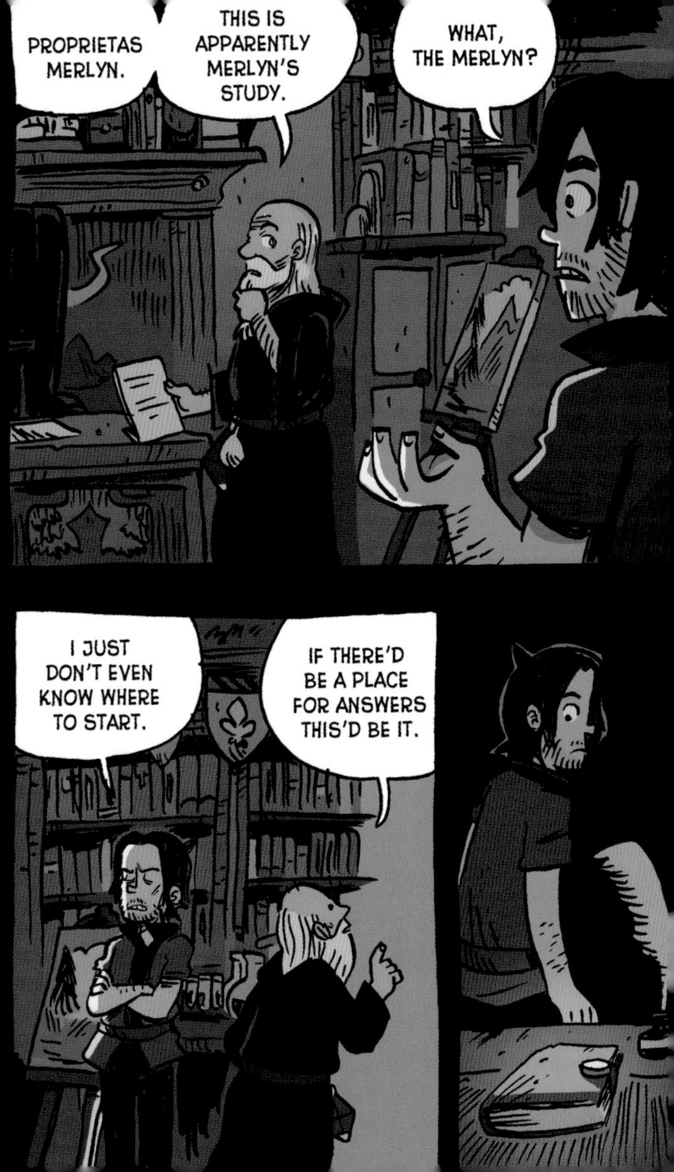
PROPRIETAS MERLYN.
THIS IS APPARENTLY MERLYN'S STUDY.
WHAT, THE MERLYN?
I JUST DON'T EVEN KNOW WHERE TO START.
IF THERE'D BE A PLACE FOR ANSWERS THIS'D BE IT.

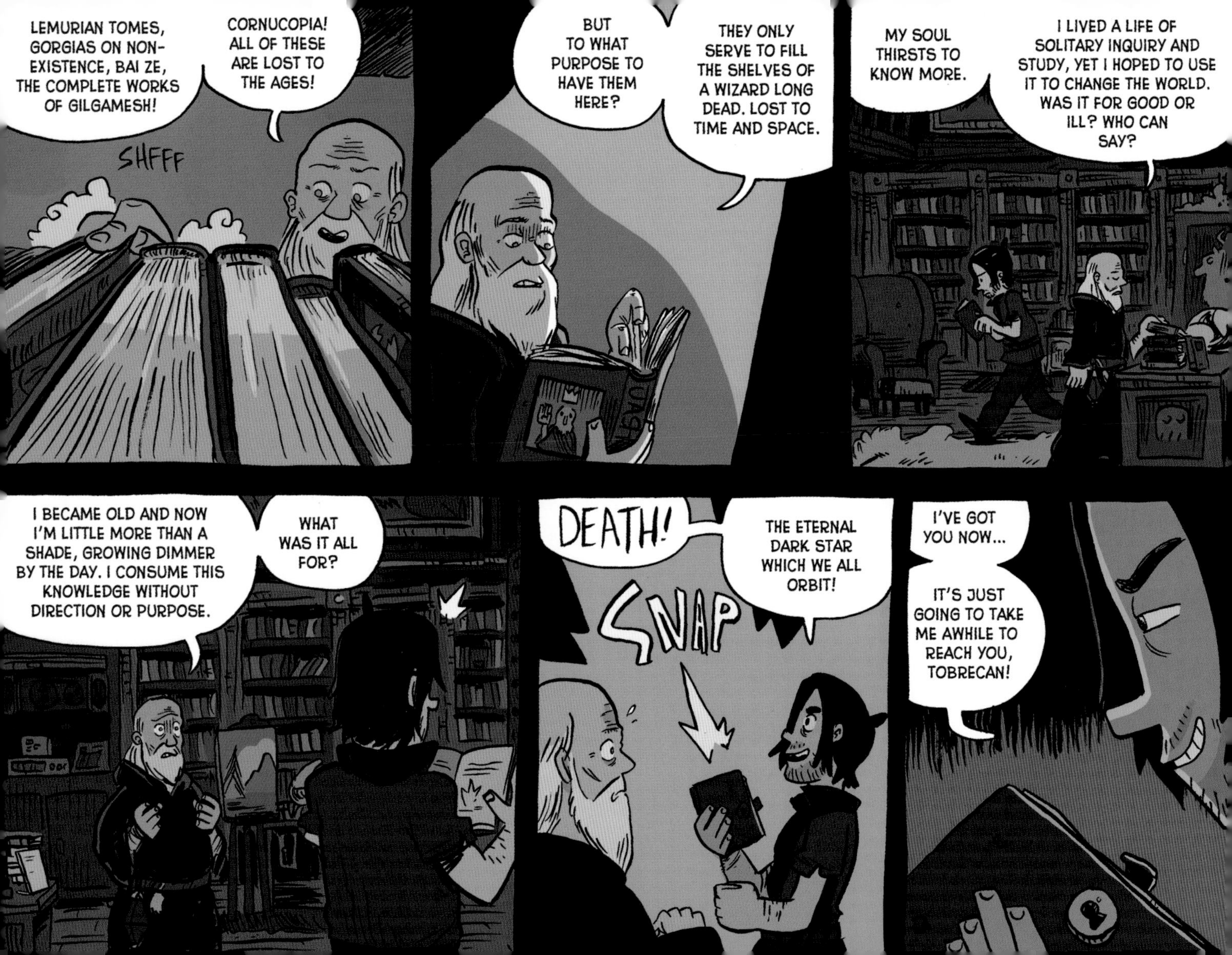
LEMURIAN TOMES, GORGIAS ON NON-EXISTENCE, BAI ZE, THE COMPLETE WORKS OF GILGAMESH!
CORNUCOPIA! ALL OF THESE ARE LOST TO THE AGES!
SHFFF
BUT TO WHAT PURPOSE TO HAVE THEM HERE?
THEY ONLY SERVE TO FILL THE SHELVES OF A WIZARD LONG DEAD. LOST TO TIME AND SPACE.
MY SOUL THIRSTS TO KNOW MORE.
I LIVED A LIFE OF SOLITARY INQUIRY AND STUDY, YET I HOPED TO USE IT TO CHANGE THE WORLD. WAS IT FOR GOOD OR ILL? WHO CAN SAY?
I BECAME OLD AND NOW I'M LITTLE MORE THAN A SHADE, GROWING DIMMER BY THE DAY. I CONSUME THIS KNOWLEDGE WITHOUT DIRECTION OR PURPOSE.
WHAT WAS IT ALL FOR?
DEATH!
THE ETERNAL DARK STAR WHICH WE ALL ORBIT!
SNAP
I'VE GOT YOU NOW...
IT'S JUST GOING TO TAKE ME AWHILE TO REACH YOU, TOBRECAN!

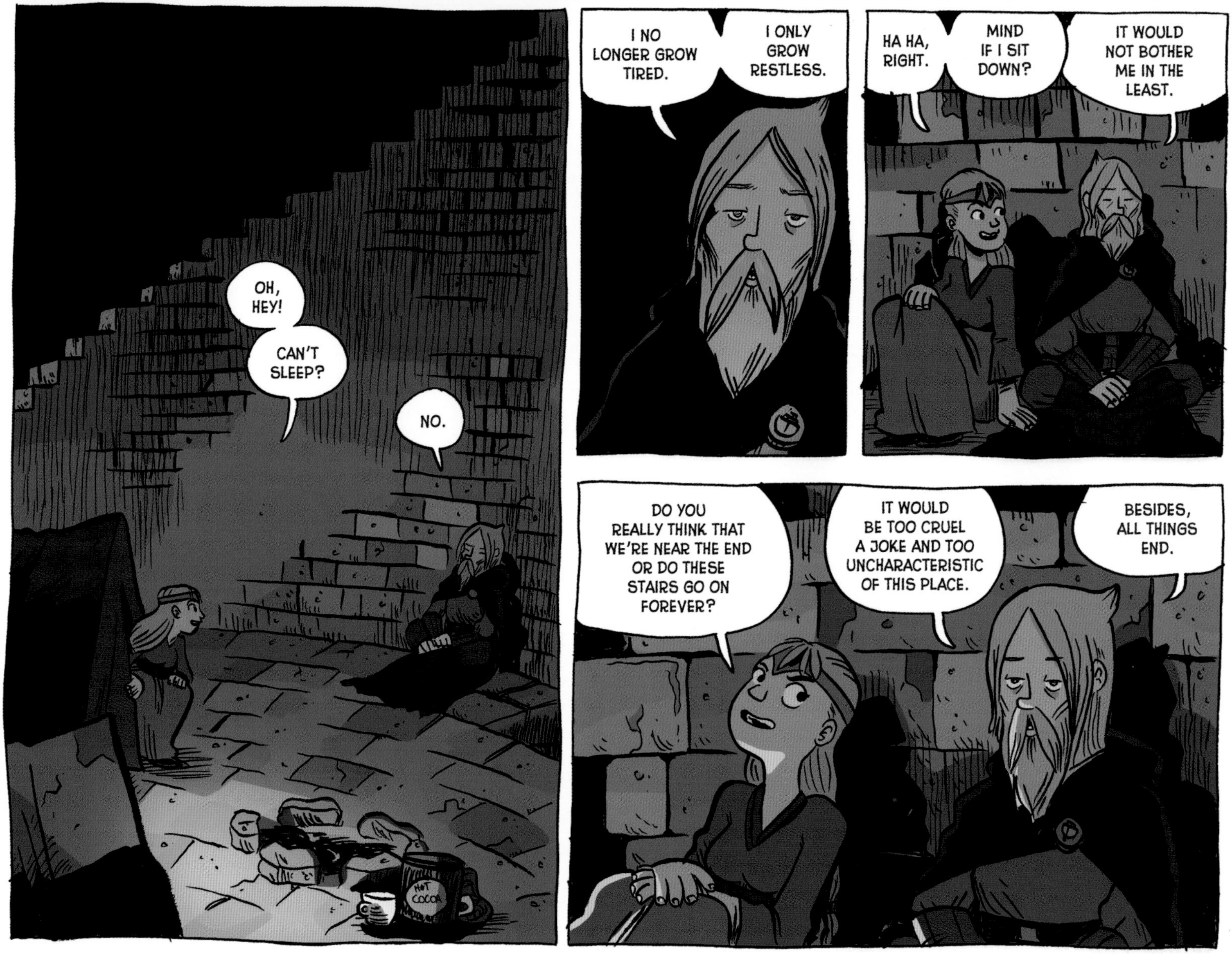
OH, HEY!
CAN'T SLEEP?
NO.
HOT COCOA
I NO LONGER GROW TIRED.
I ONLY GROW RESTLESS.
HA HA, RIGHT.
MIND IF I SIT DOWN?
IT WOULD NOT BOTHER ME IN THE LEAST.
DO YOU REALLY THINK THAT WE'RE NEAR THE END OR DO THESE STAIRS GO ON FOREVER?
IT WOULD BE TOO CRUEL A JOKE AND TOO UNCHARACTERISTIC OF THIS PLACE.
BESIDES, ALL THINGS END.

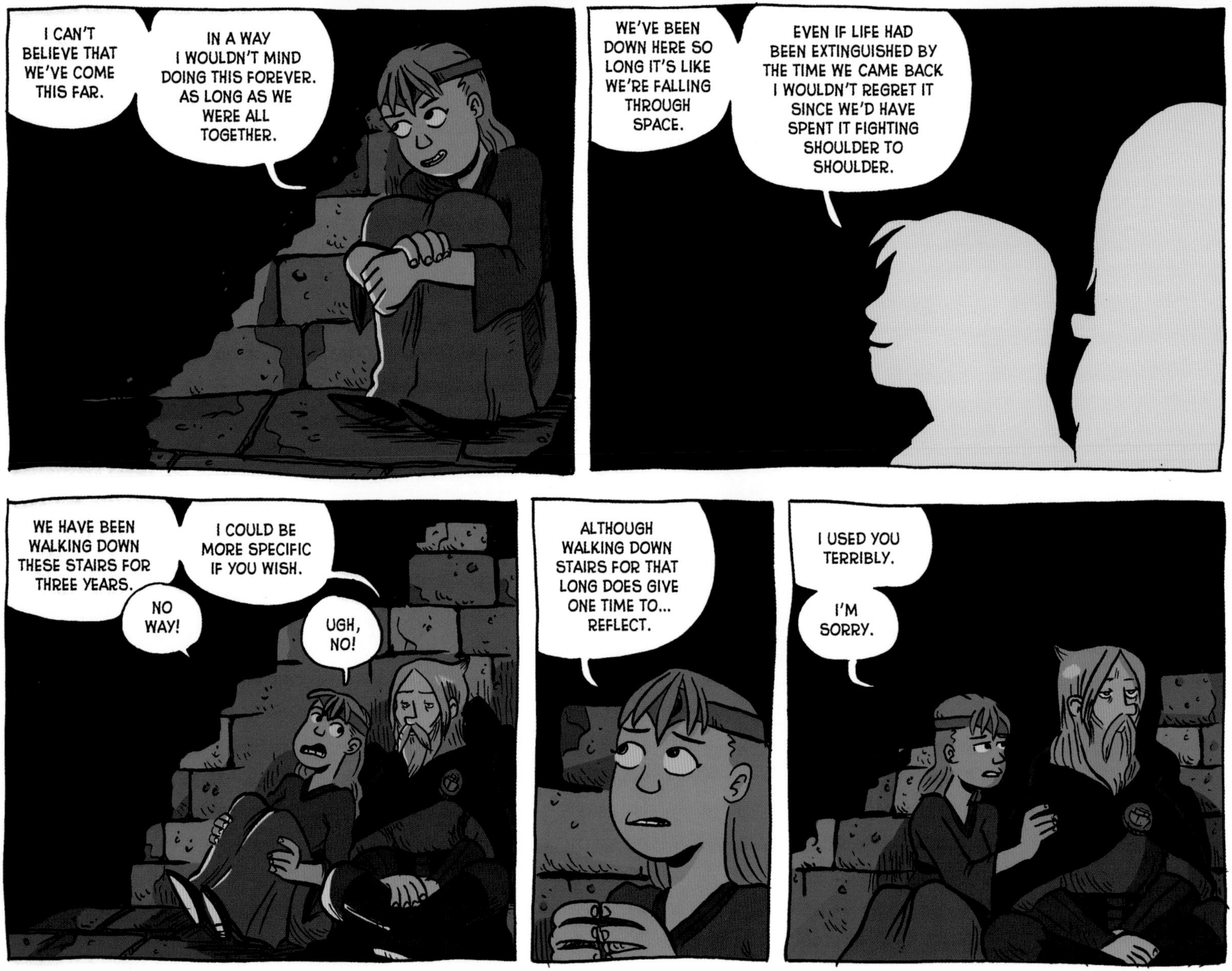
I CAN'T BELIEVE THAT WE'VE COME THIS FAR.
IN A WAY I WOULDN'T MIND DOING THIS FOREVER. AS LONG AS WE WERE ALL TOGETHER.
WE'VE BEEN DOWN HERE SO LONG IT'S LIKE WE'RE FALLING THROUGH SPACE.
EVEN IF LIFE HAD BEEN EXTINGUISHED BY THE TIME WE CAME BACK I WOULDN'T REGRET IT SINCE WE'D HAVE SPENT IT FIGHTING SHOULDER TO SHOULDER.
WE HAVE BEEN WALKING DOWN THESE STAIRS FOR THREE YEARS.
I COULD BE MORE SPECIFIC IF YOU WISH.
NO WAY!
UGH, NO!
ALTHOUGH WALKING DOWN STAIRS FOR THAT LONG DOES GIVE ONE TIME TO... REFLECT.
I USED YOU TERRIBLY.
I'M SORRY.

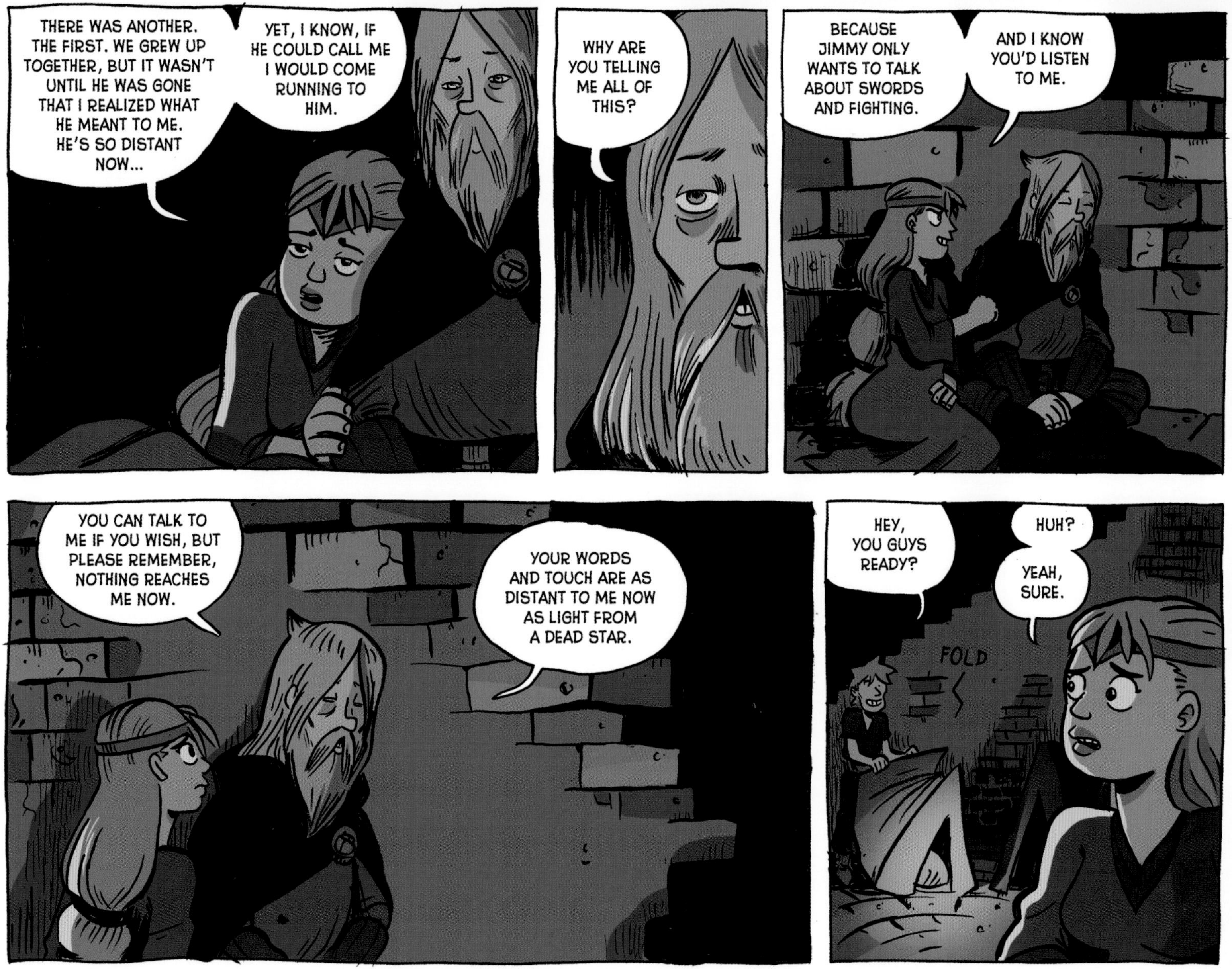
THERE WAS ANOTHER. THE FIRST. WE GREW UP TOGETHER, BUT IT WASN'T UNTIL HE WAS GONE THAT I REALIZED WHAT HE MEANT TO ME. HE'S SO DISTANT NOW...
YET, I KNOW, IF HE COULD CALL ME I WOULD COME RUNNING TO HIM.
WHY ARE YOU TELLING ME ALL OF THIS?
BECAUSE JIMMY ONLY WANTS TO TALK ABOUT SWORDS AND FIGHTING.
AND I KNOW YOU'D LISTEN TO ME.
YOU CAN TALK TO ME IF YOU WISH, BUT PLEASE REMEMBER, NOTHING REACHES ME NOW.
YOUR WORDS AND TOUCH ARE AS DISTANT TO ME NOW AS LIGHT FROM A DEAD STAR.
HEY, YOU GUYS READY?
HUH?
YEAH, SURE.
FOLD

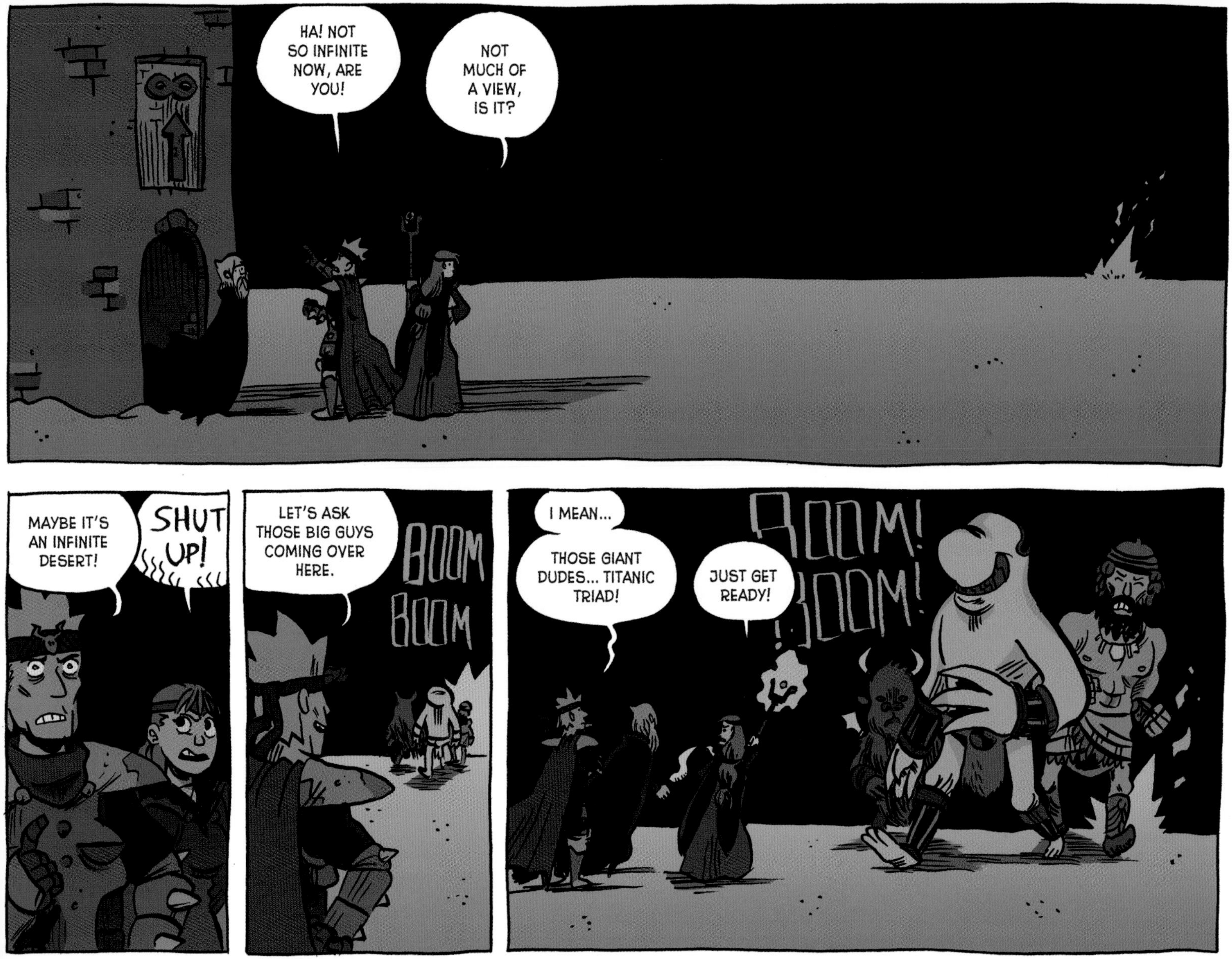
HA! NOT SO INFINITE NOW, ARE YOU!
NOT MUCH OF A VIEW, IS IT?
MAYBE IT'S AN INFINITE DESERT!
SHUT UP!
LET'S ASK THOSE BIG GUYS COMING OVER HERE.
BOOM BOOM
I MEAN...
THOSE GIANT DUDES... TITANIC TRIAD!
JUST GET READY!
BOOM! BOOM!

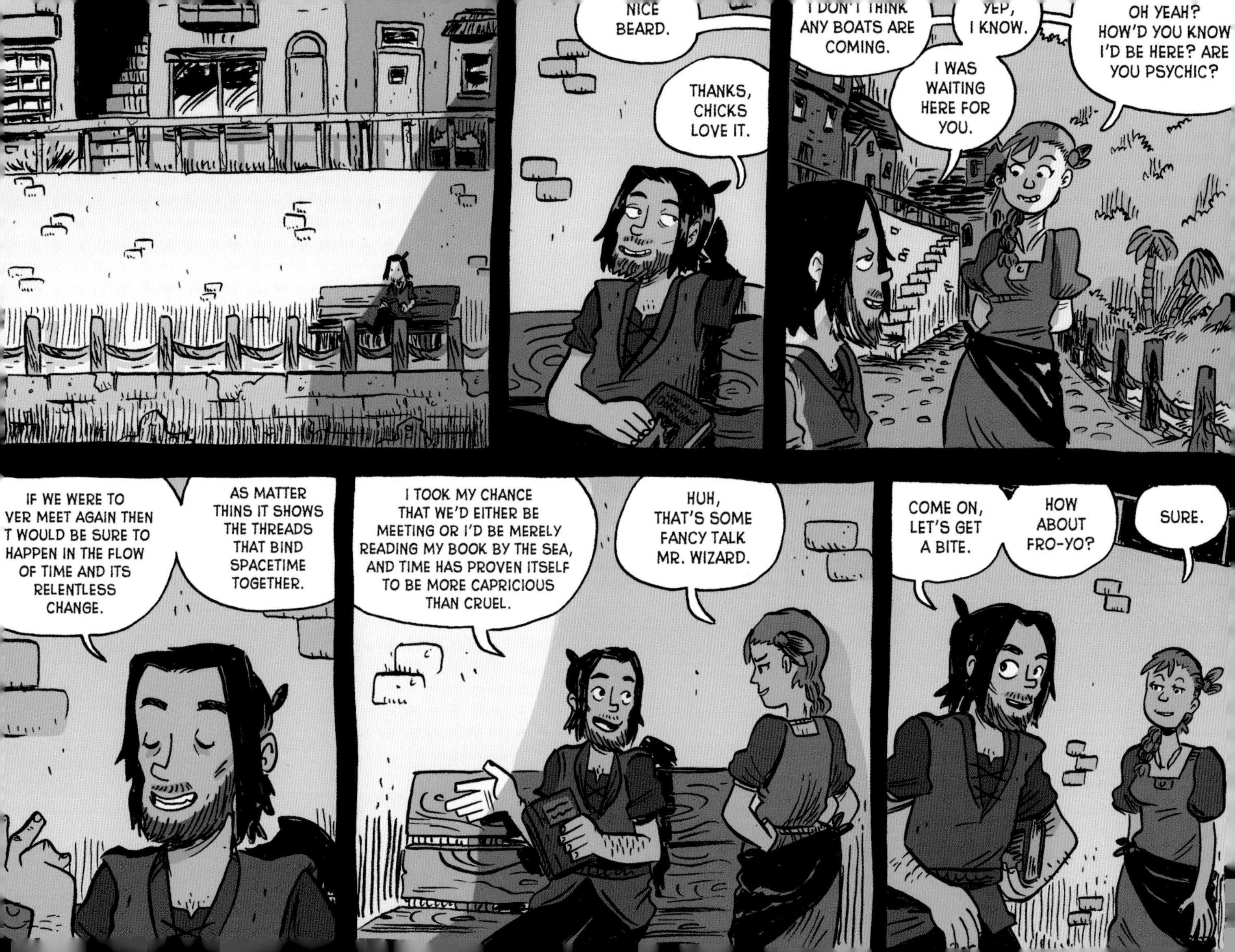
NICE BEARD.
THANKS, CHICKS LOVE IT.
I DON'T THINK ANY BOATS ARE COMING.
YEP, I KNOW.
I WAS WAITING HERE FOR YOU.
OH YEAH? HOW'D YOU KNOW I'D BE HERE? ARE YOU PSYCHIC?
IF WE WERE TO VER MEET AGAIN THEN T WOULD BE SURE TO HAPPEN IN THE FLOW OF TIME AND ITS RELENTLESS CHANGE.
AS MATTER THINS IT SHOWS THE THREADS THAT BIND SPACETIME TOGETHER.
I TOOK MY CHANCE THAT WE'D EITHER BE MEETING OR I'D BE MERELY READING MY BOOK BY THE SEA, AND TIME HAS PROVEN ITSELF TO BE MORE CAPRICIOUS THAN CRUEL.
HUH, THAT'S SOME FANCY TALK MR. WIZARD.
COME ON, LET'S GET A BITE.
HOW ABOUT FRO-YO?
SURE.

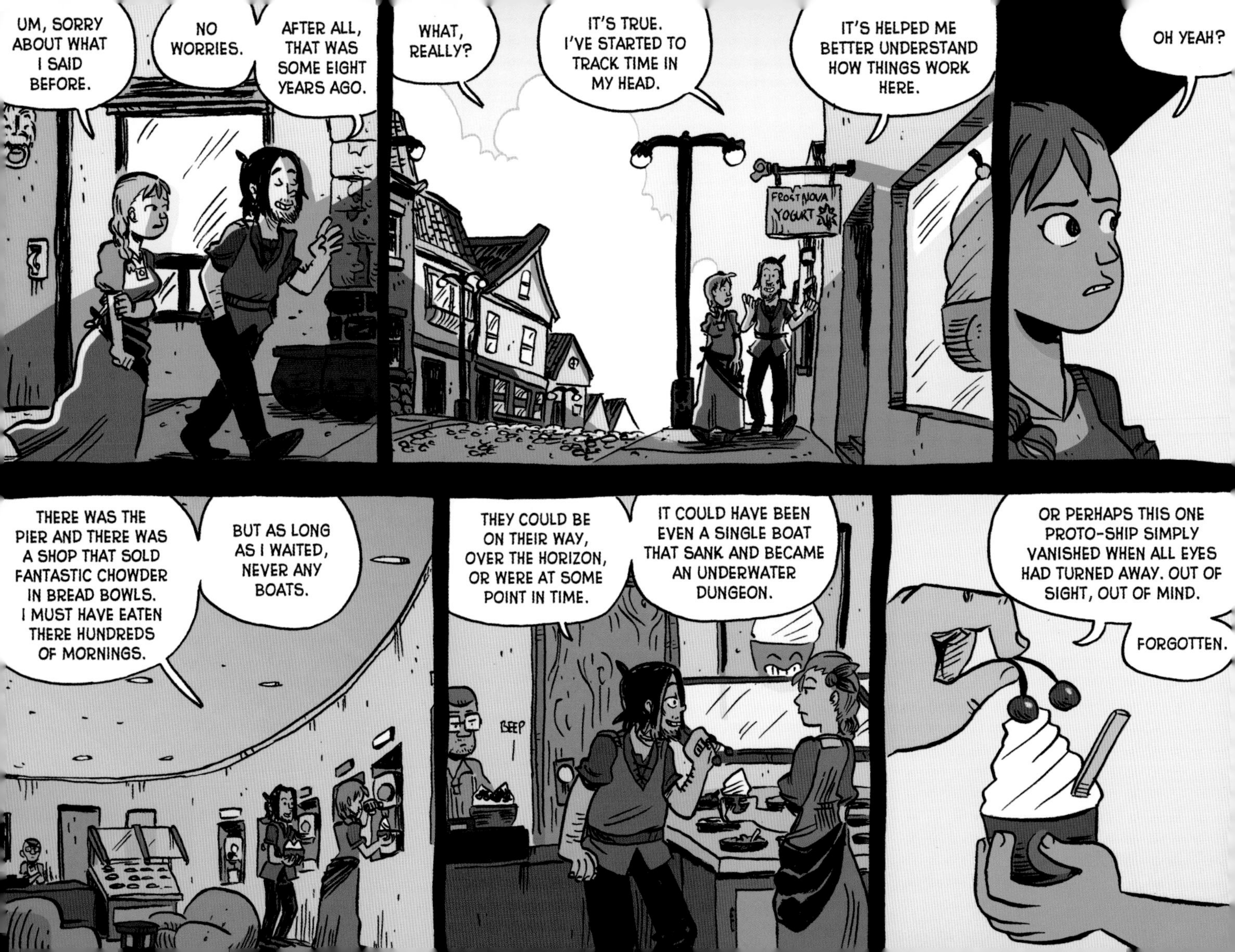

UM, SORRY ABOUT WHAT I SAID BEFORE.
NO WORRIES.
AFTER ALL, THAT WAS SOME EIGHT YEARS AGO.
WHAT, REALLY?
IT'S TRUE. I'VE STARTED TO TRACK TIME IN MY HEAD.
IT'S HELPED ME BETTER UNDERSTAND HOW THINGS WORK HERE.
FROST NOVA YOGURT
OH YEAH?
THERE WAS THE PIER AND THERE WAS A SHOP THAT SOLD FANTASTIC CHOWDER IN BREAD BOWLS. I MUST HAVE EATEN THERE HUNDREDS OF MORNINGS.
BUT AS LONG AS I WAITED, NEVER ANY BOATS.
THEY COULD BE ON THEIR WAY, OVER THE HORIZON, OR WERE AT SOME POINT IN TIME.
IT COULD HAVE BEEN EVEN A SINGLE BOAT THAT SANK AND BECAME AN UNDERWATER DUNGEON.
BEEP
OR PERHAPS THIS ONE PROTO-SHIP SIMPLY VANISHED WHEN ALL EYES HAD TURNED AWAY. OUT OF SIGHT, OUT OF MIND.
FORGOTTEN.

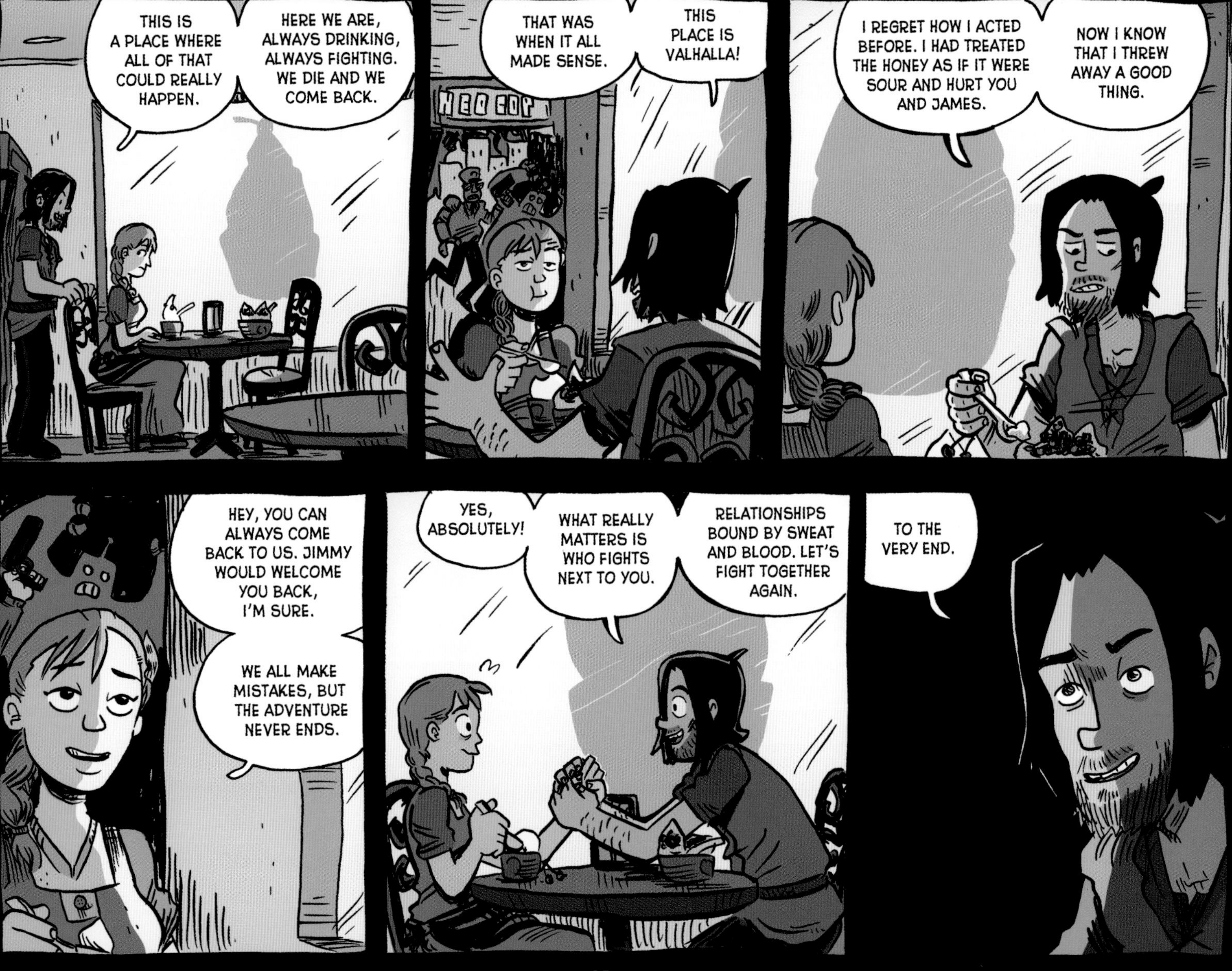
THIS IS A PLACE WHERE ALL OF THAT COULD REALLY HAPPEN.
HERE WE ARE, ALWAYS DRINKING, ALWAYS FIGHTING. WE DIE AND WE COME BACK.
THAT WAS WHEN IT ALL MADE SENSE.
THIS PLACE IS VALHALLA!
I REGRET HOW I ACTED BEFORE. I HAD TREATED THE HONEY AS IF IT WERE SOUR AND HURT YOU AND JAMES.
NOW I KNOW THAT I THREW AWAY A GOOD THING.
HEY, YOU CAN ALWAYS COME BACK TO US. JIMMY WOULD WELCOME YOU BACK, I'M SURE.
WE ALL MAKE MISTAKES, BUT THE ADVENTURE NEVER ENDS.
YES, ABSOLUTELY!
WHAT REALLY MATTERS IS WHO FIGHTS NEXT TO YOU.
RELATIONSHIPS BOUND BY SWEAT AND BLOOD. LET'S FIGHT TOGETHER AGAIN.
TO THE VERY END.

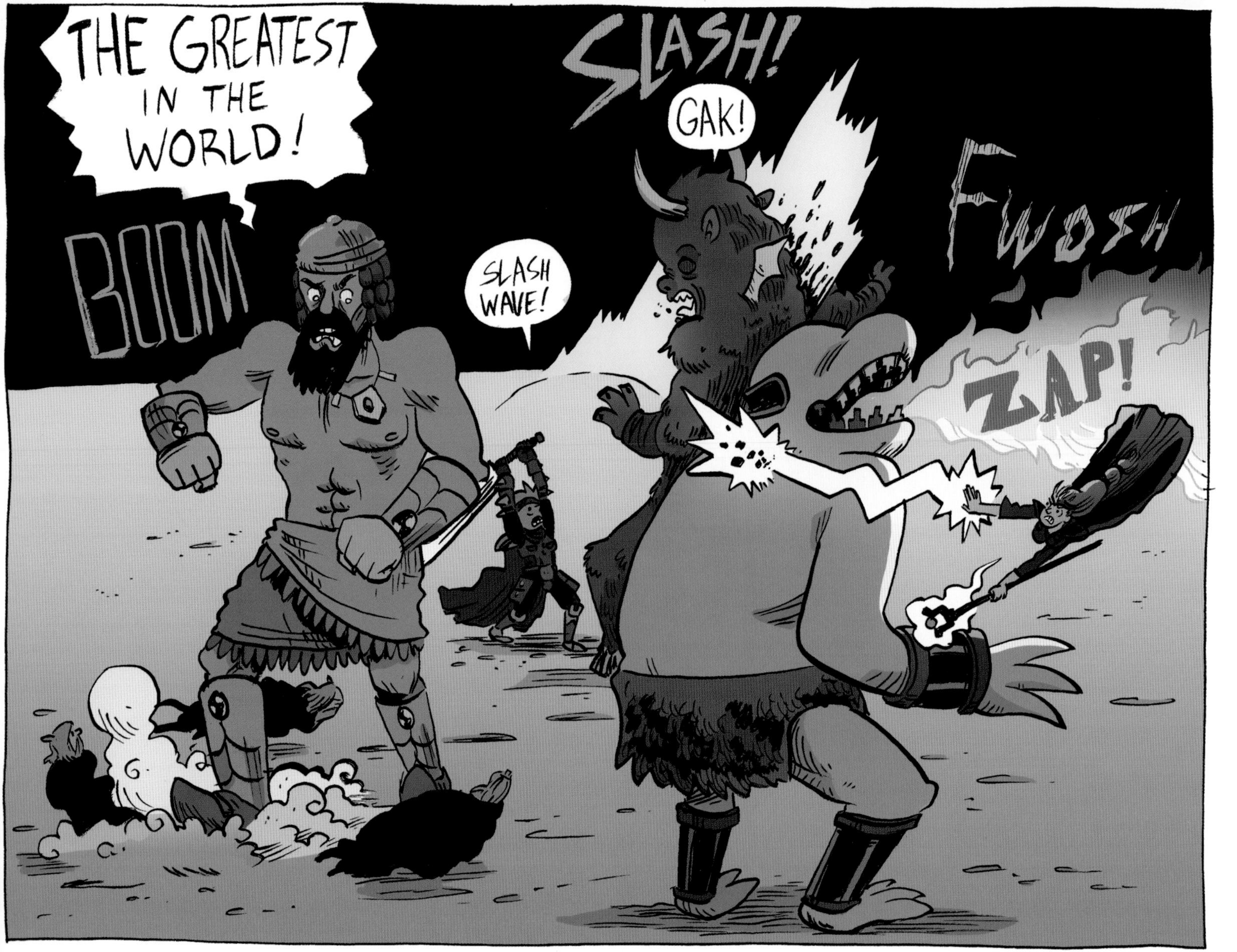
THE GREATEST IN THE WORLD!
BOOM
SLASH WAVE!
SLASH!
GAK!
FWOSH
ZAP!

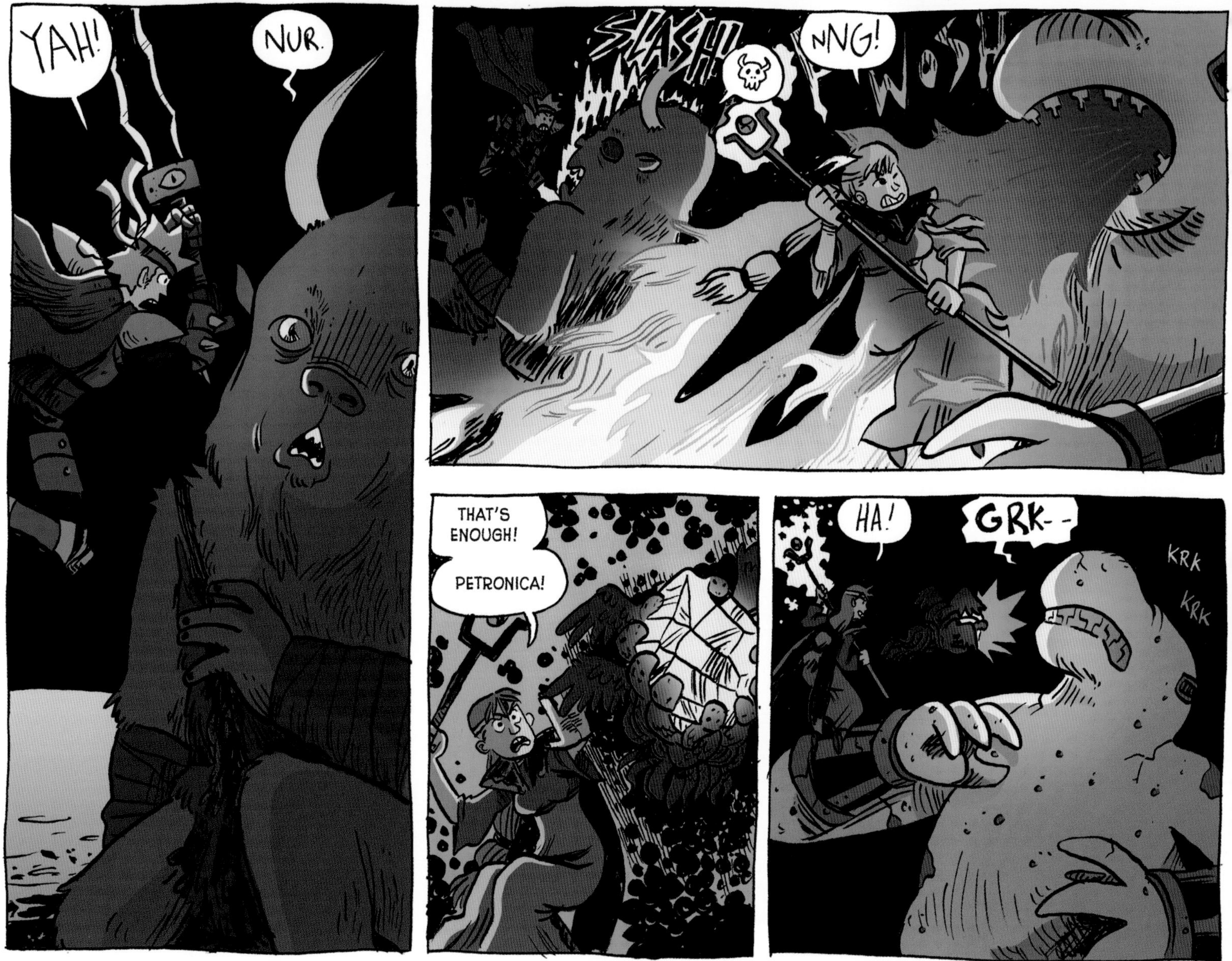
YAH!
NUR.
SLASH!
NNG!
PWOSH!
THAT'S ENOUGH!
PETRONICA!
HA!
GRK--
KRK
KRK

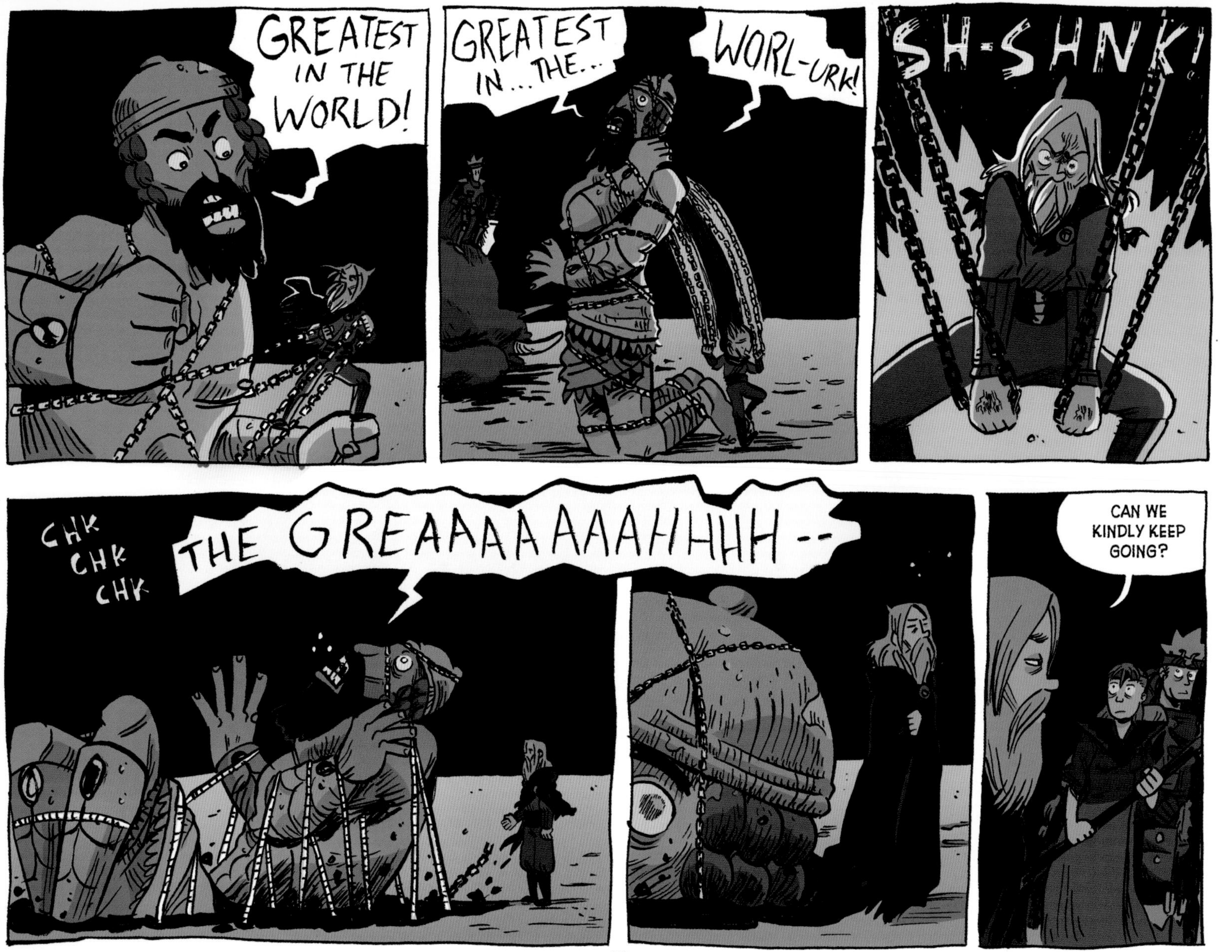
GREATEST IN THE WORLD!
GREATEST IN... THE...
WORL-URK!
SH-SHNK!
CHK CHK CHK
THE GREAAAAAAAHHHH--
CAN WE KINDLY KEEP GOING?

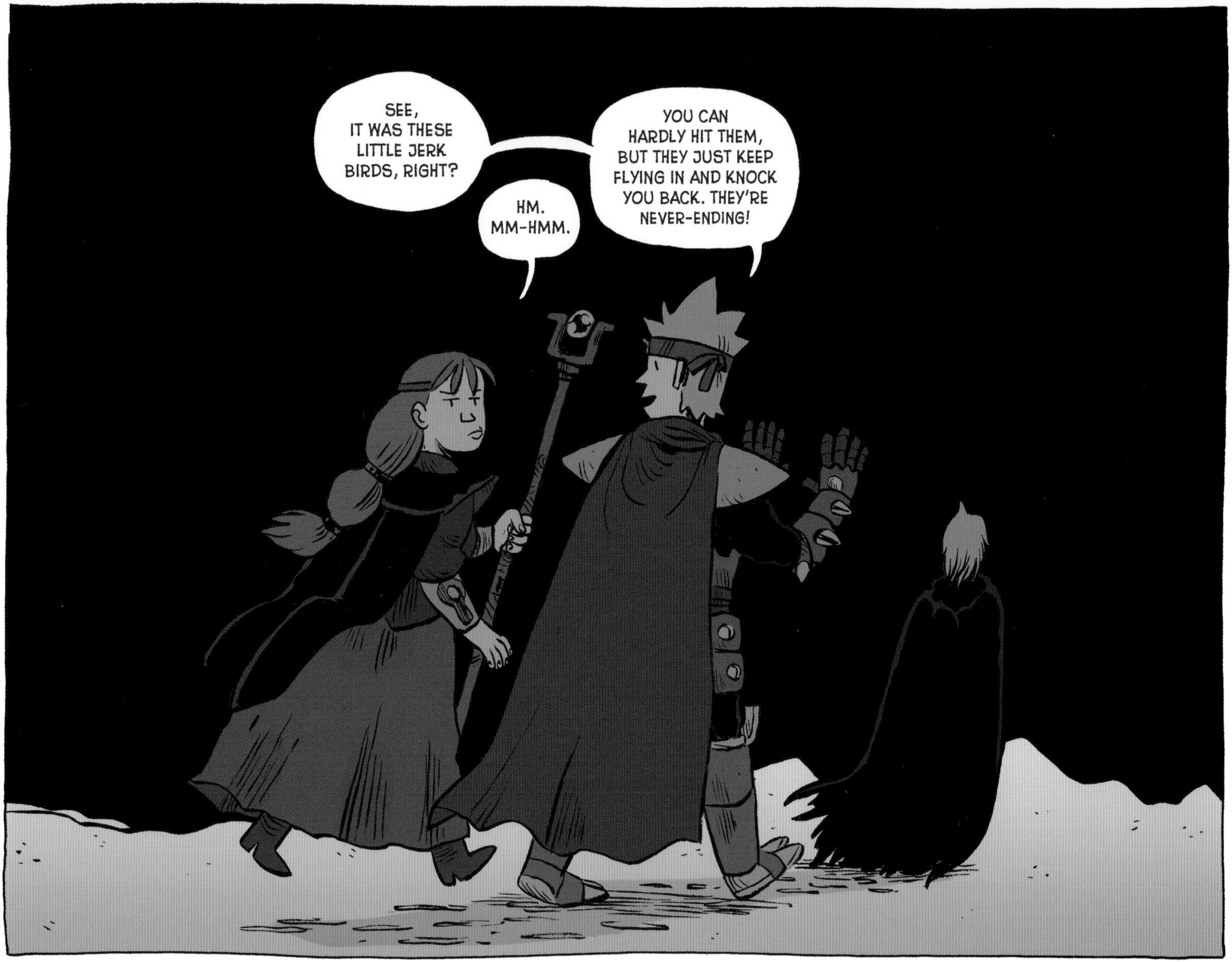
SEE, IT WAS THESE LITTLE JERK BIRDS, RIGHT?
HM. MM-HMM.
YOU CAN HARDLY HIT THEM, BUT THEY JUST KEEP FLYING IN AND KNOCK YOU BACK. THEY'RE NEVER-ENDING!

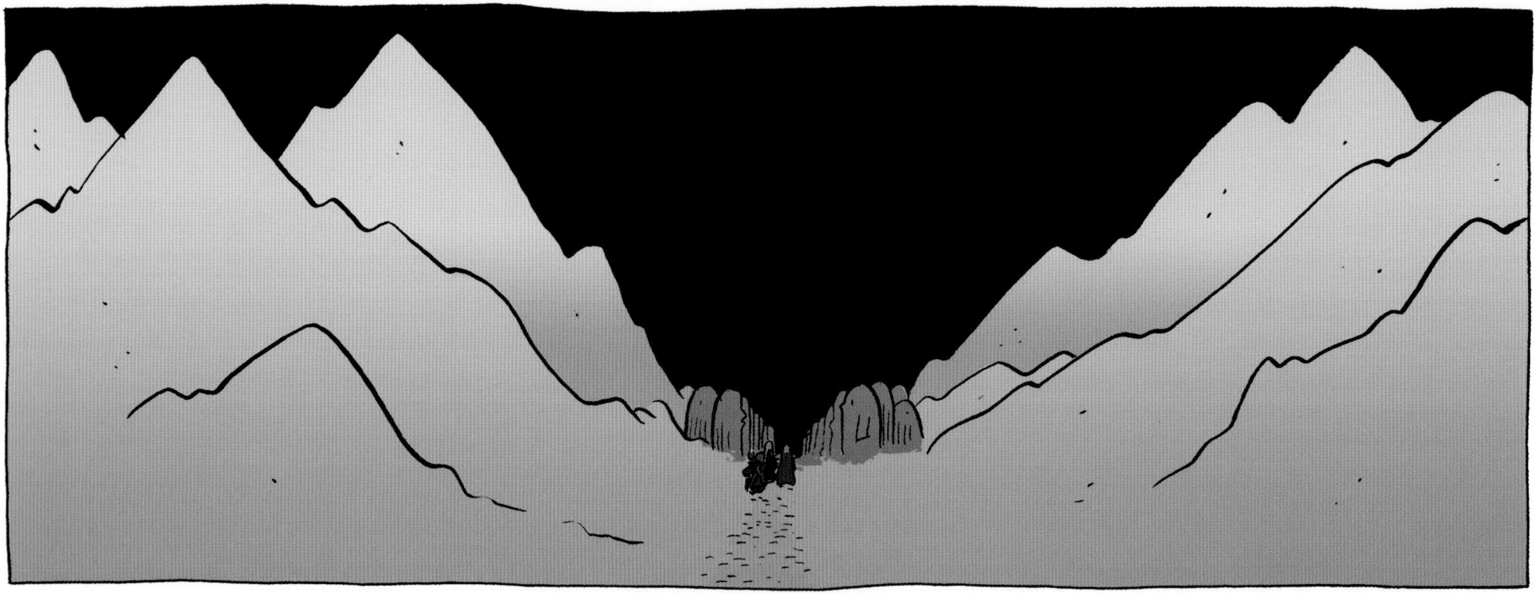

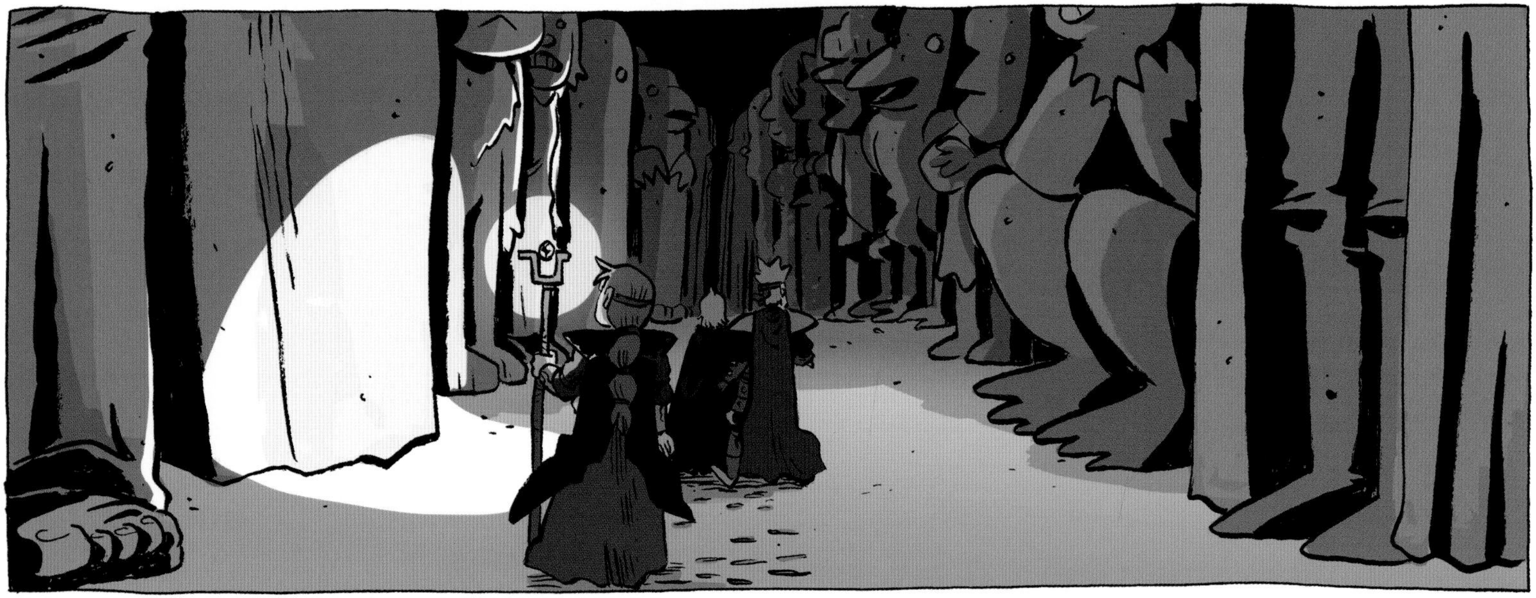

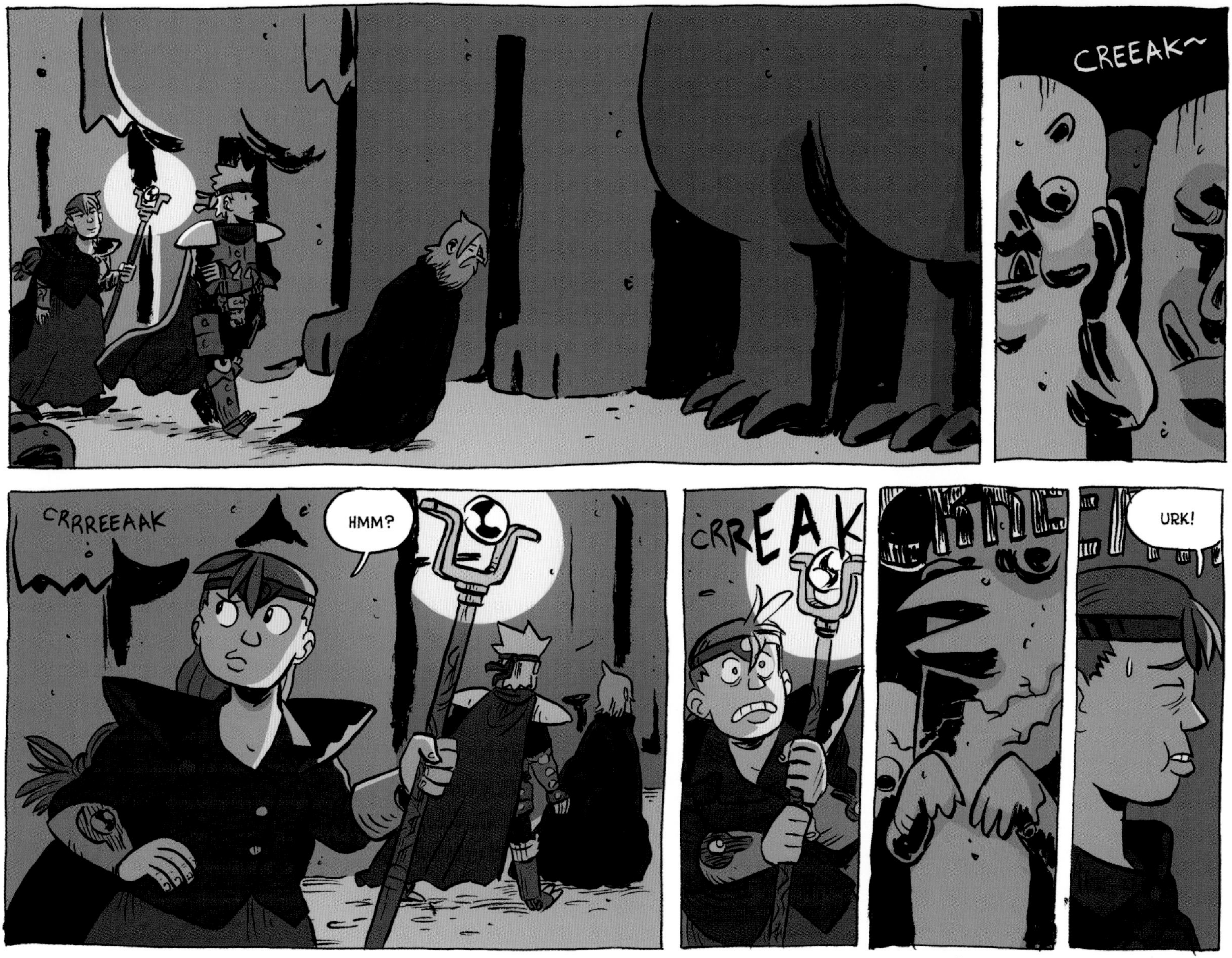
CREEAK~
CRRREEAAK
HMM?
CRREAK
URK!

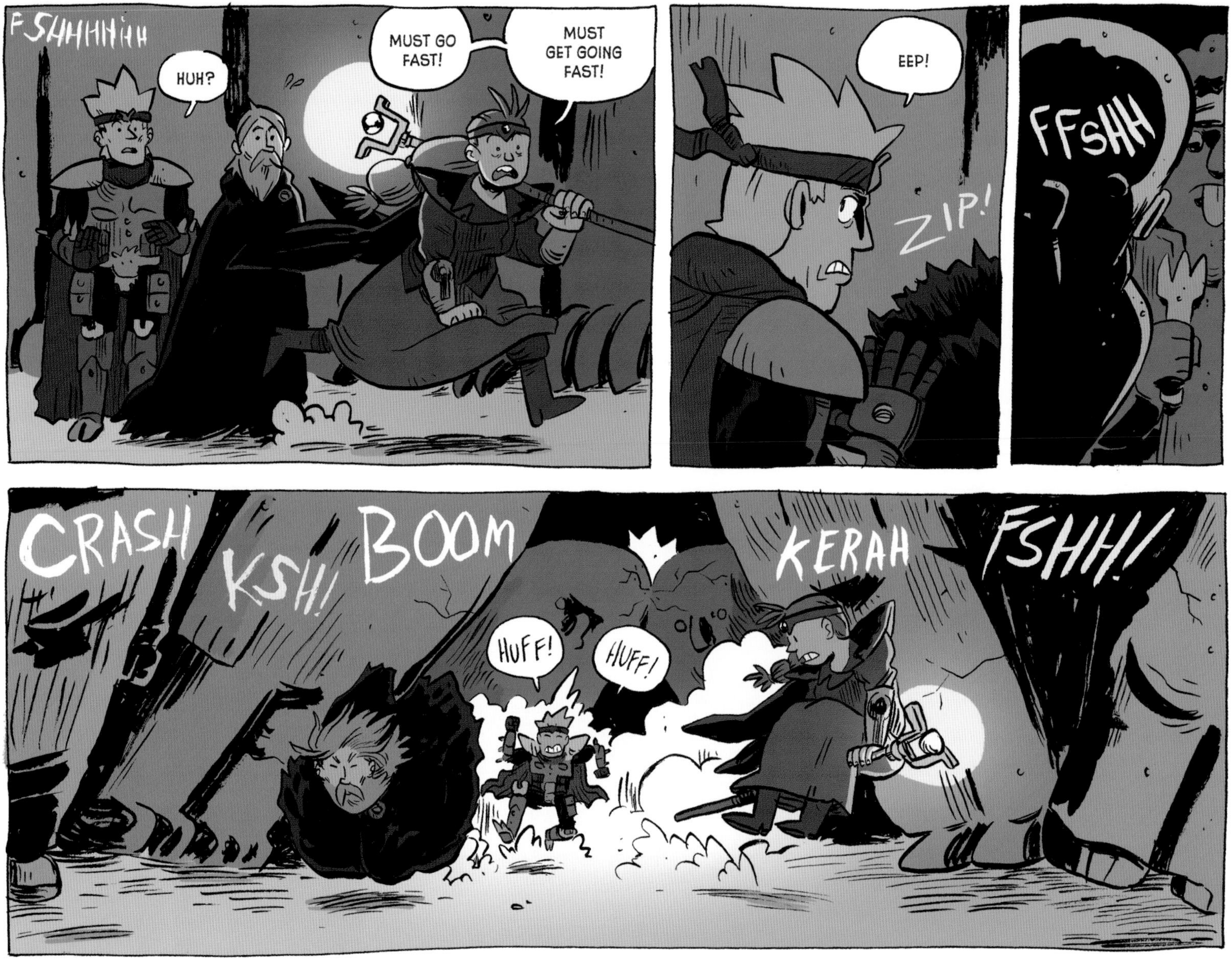
FSHHHHHH
HUH?
MUST GO FAST!
MUST GET GOING FAST!
EEP!
ZIP!
FFSHH
CRASH
KSH!
BOOM
HUFF!
HUFF!
KERAH
FSHH!

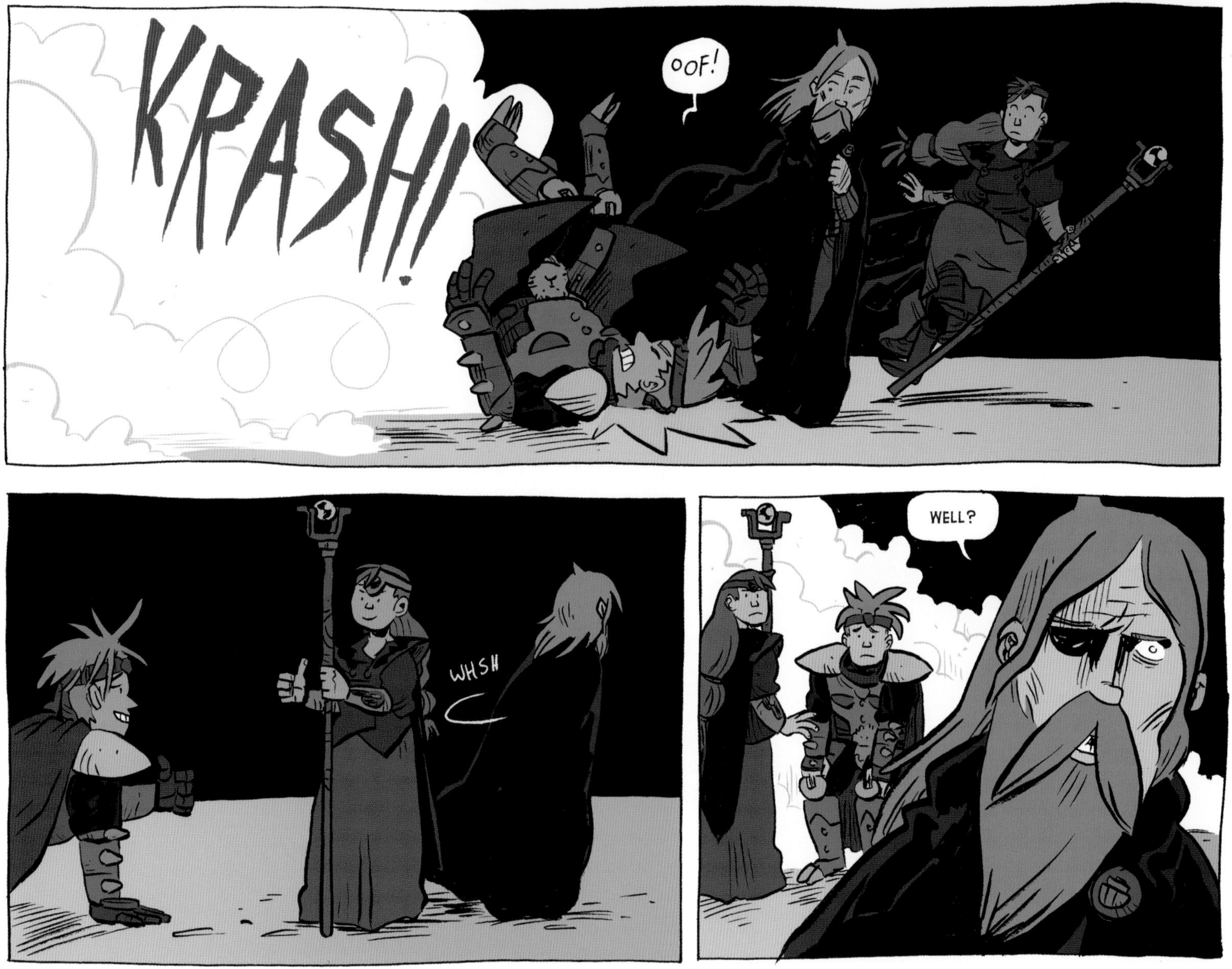
KRASH!
OOF!
WHSH
WELL?

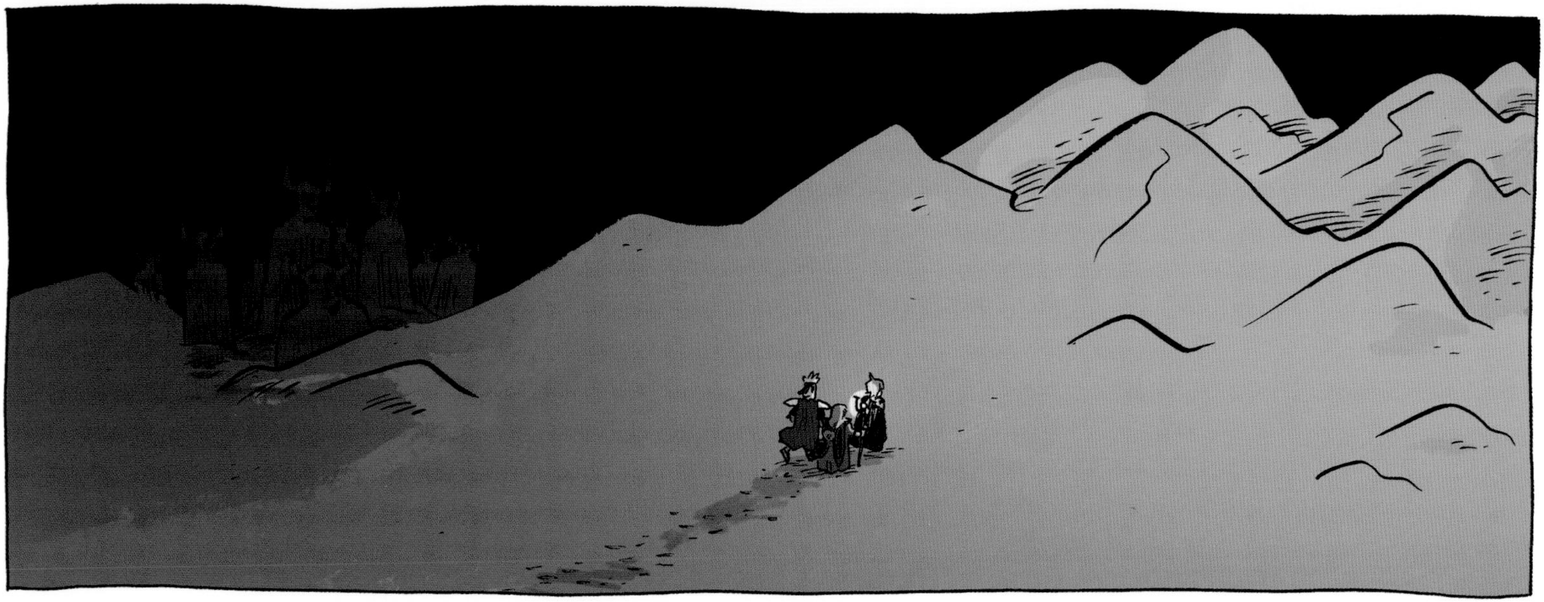

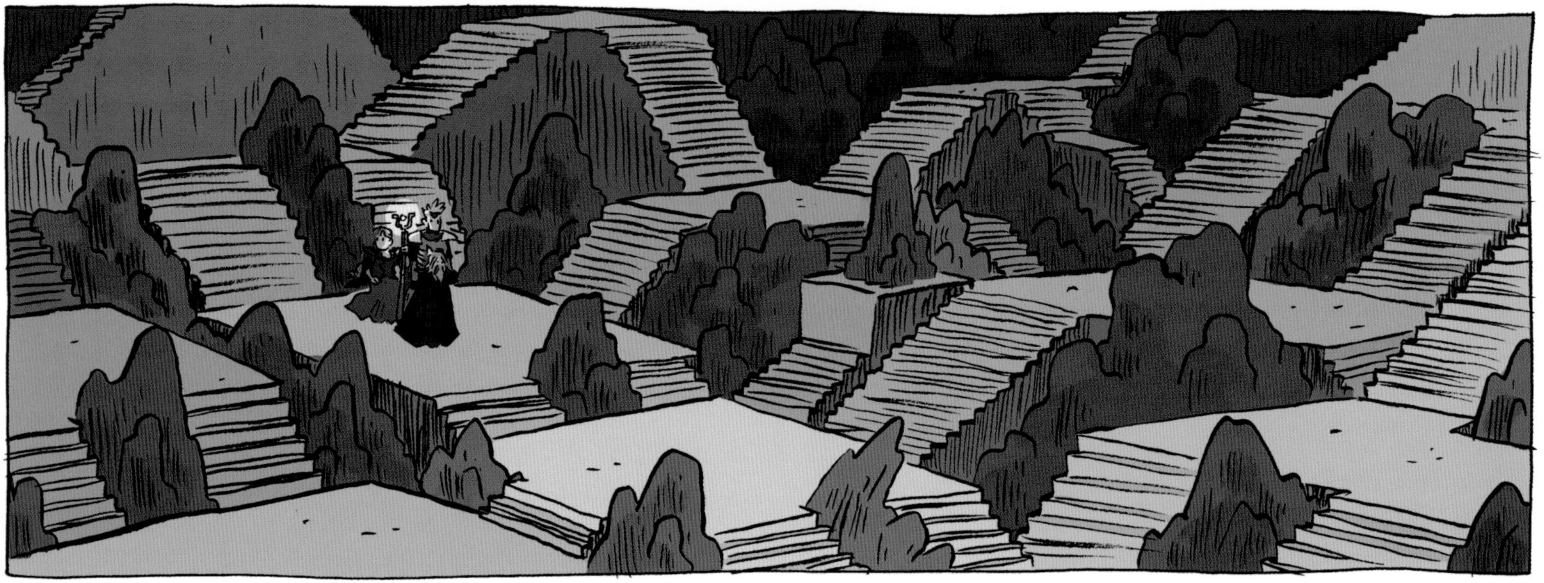

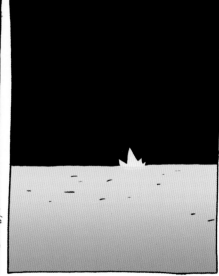

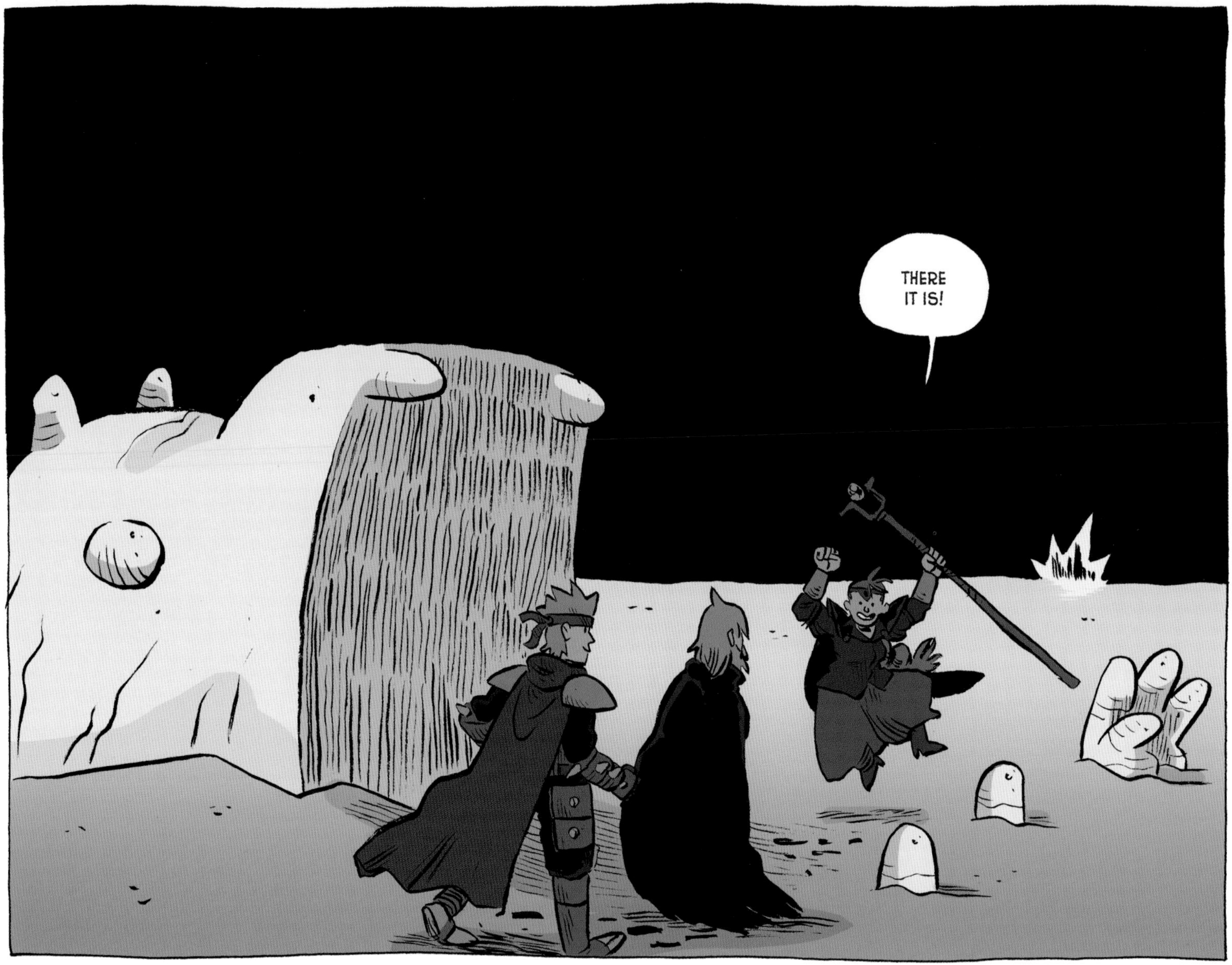
THERE IT IS!

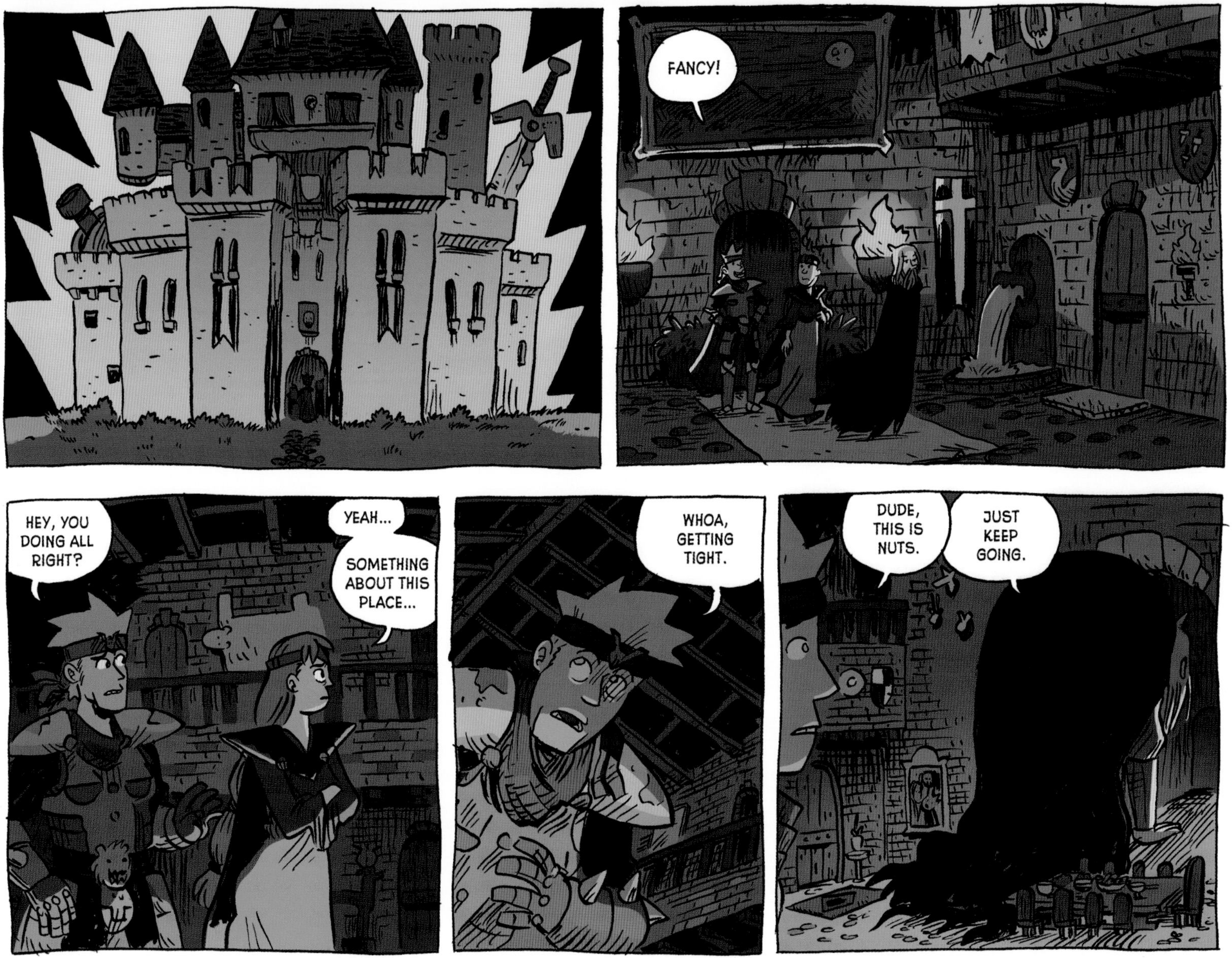
FANCY!
HEY, YOU DOING ALL RIGHT?
YEAH...
SOMETHING ABOUT THIS PLACE...
WHOA, GETTING TIGHT.
DUDE, THIS IS NUTS.
JUST KEEP GOING.

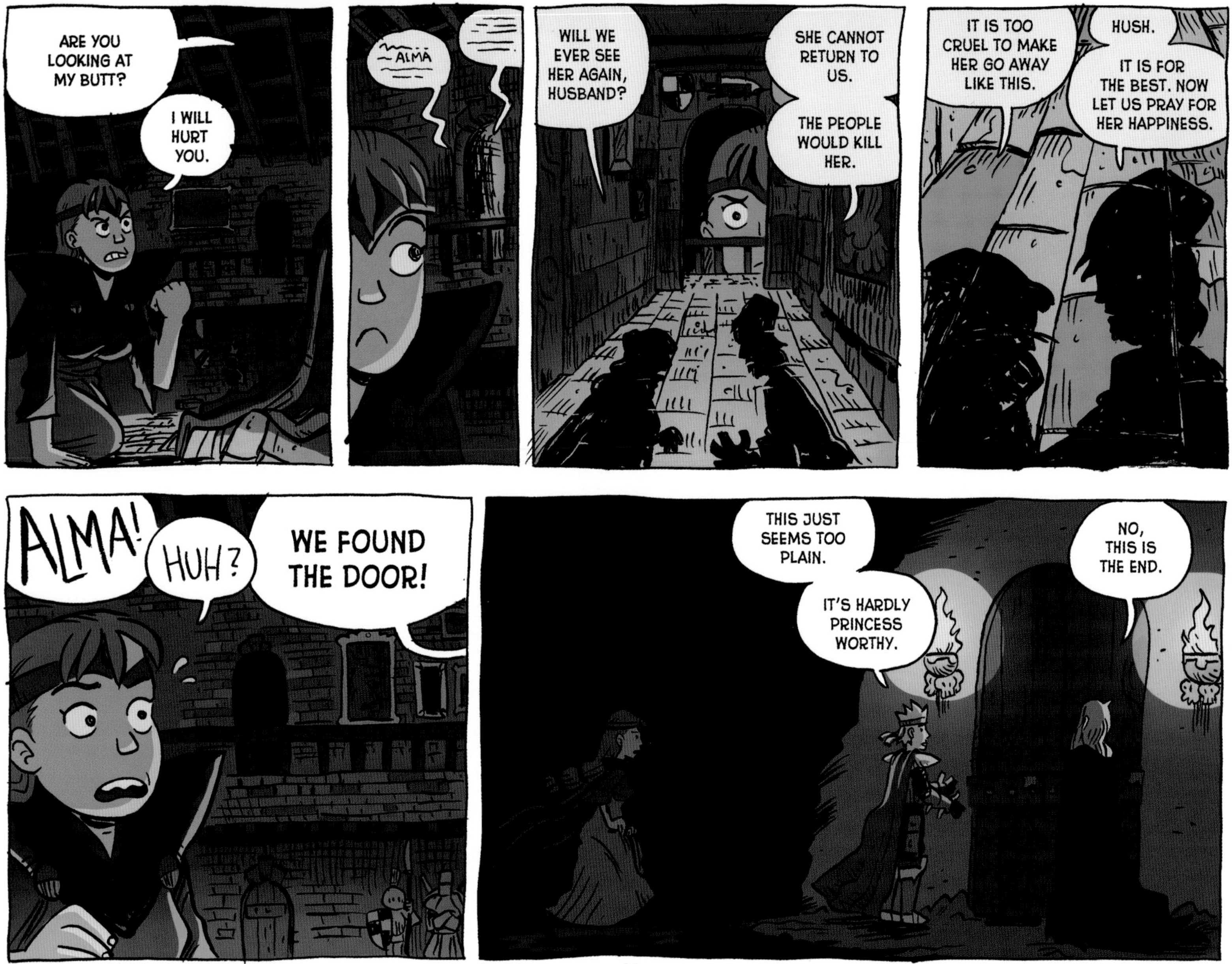

ARE YOU LOOKING AT MY BUTT?
I WILL HURT YOU.
ALMA
WILL WE EVER SEE HER AGAIN, HUSBAND?
SHE CANNOT RETURN TO US.
THE PEOPLE WOULD KILL HER.
IT IS TOO CRUEL TO MAKE HER GO AWAY LIKE THIS.
HUSH.
IT IS FOR THE BEST. NOW LET US PRAY FOR HER HAPPINESS.
ALMA!
HUH?
WE FOUND THE DOOR!
THIS JUST SEEMS TOO PLAIN.
IT'S HARDLY PRINCESS WORTHY.
NO, THIS IS THE END.

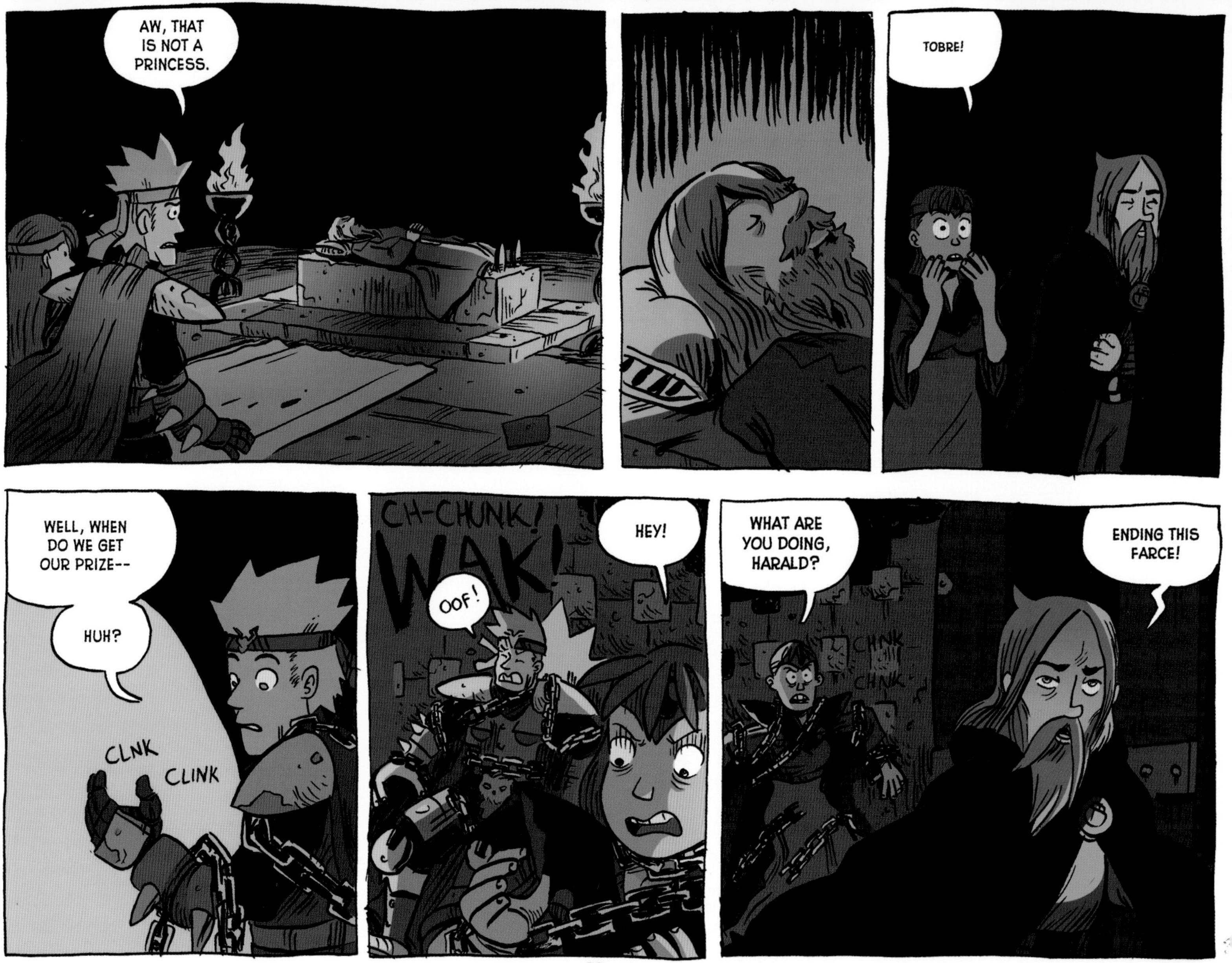
AW, THAT IS NOT A PRINCESS.
TOBRE!
WELL, WHEN DO WE GET OUR PRIZE--
HUH?
CLNK
CLINK
CH-CHUNK!
WAK!
OOF!
HEY!
WHAT ARE YOU DOING, HARALD?
CHNK
CHNK
ENDING THIS FARCE!

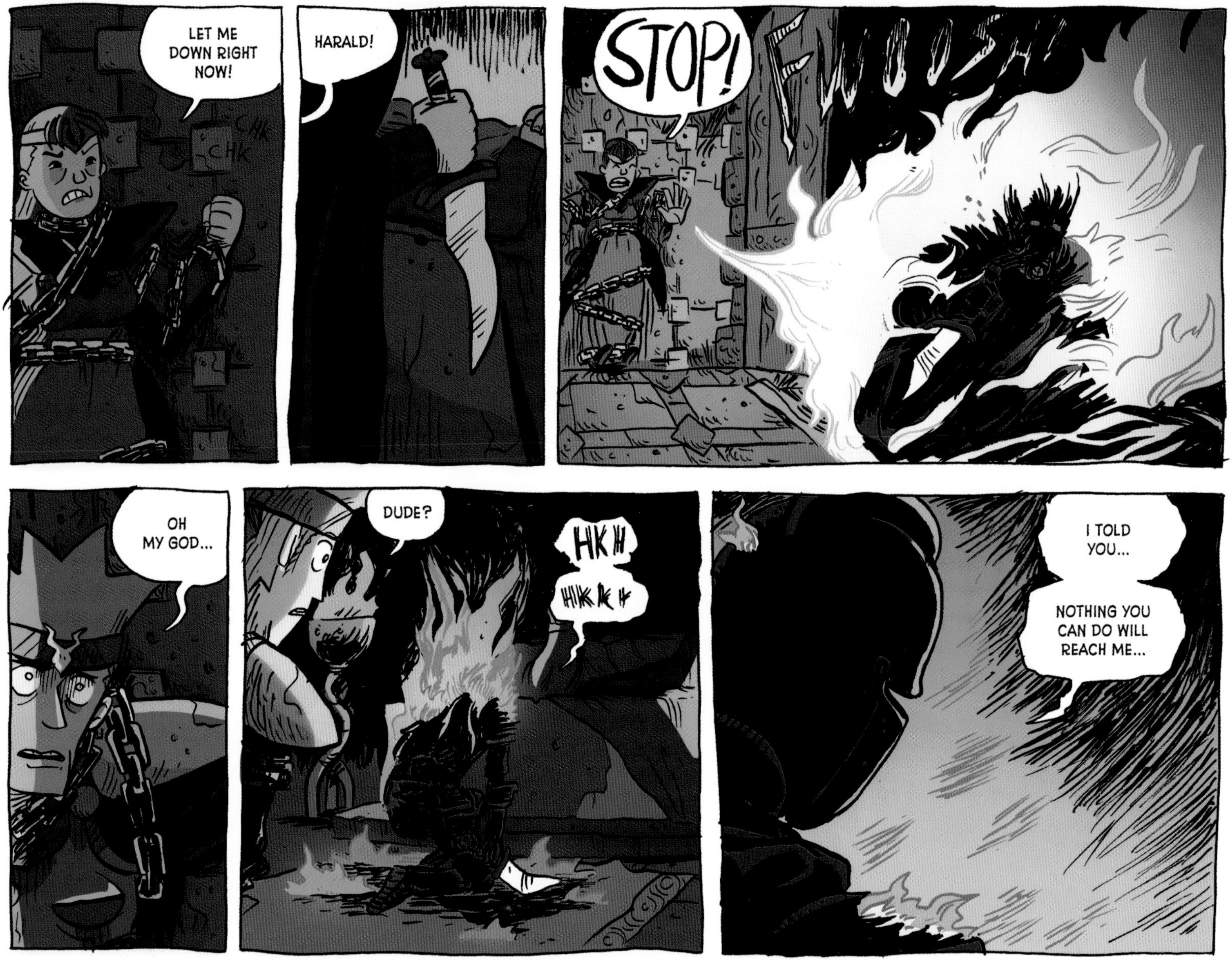
LET ME DOWN RIGHT NOW!
CHK CHK
HARALD!
STOP!
FWOOOSH
OH MY GOD...
DUDE?
HKH
HKKH
I TOLD YOU...
NOTHING YOU CAN DO WILL REACH ME...

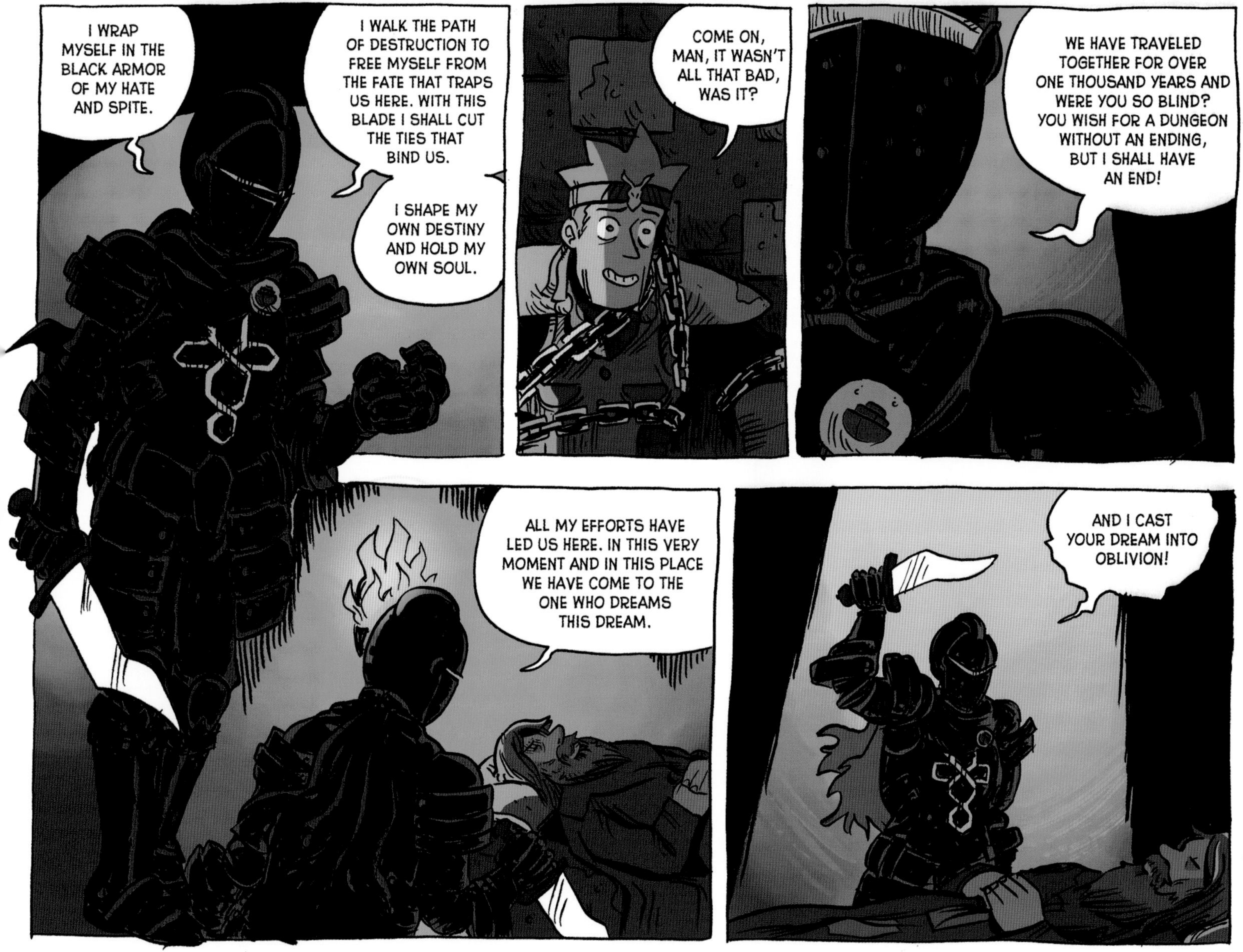
I WRAP MYSELF IN THE BLACK ARMOR OF MY HATE AND SPITE.
I WALK THE PATH OF DESTRUCTION TO FREE MYSELF FROM THE FATE THAT TRAPS US HERE. WITH THIS BLADE I SHALL CUT THE TIES THAT BIND US.
I SHAPE MY OWN DESTINY AND HOLD MY OWN SOUL.
COME ON, MAN, IT WASN'T ALL THAT BAD, WAS IT?
WE HAVE TRAVELED TOGETHER FOR OVER ONE THOUSAND YEARS AND WERE YOU SO BLIND? YOU WISH FOR A DUNGEON WITHOUT AN ENDING, BUT I SHALL HAVE AN END!
ALL MY EFFORTS HAVE LED US HERE. IN THIS VERY MOMENT AND IN THIS PLACE WE HAVE COME TO THE ONE WHO DREAMS THIS DREAM.
AND I CAST YOUR DREAM INTO OBLIVION!

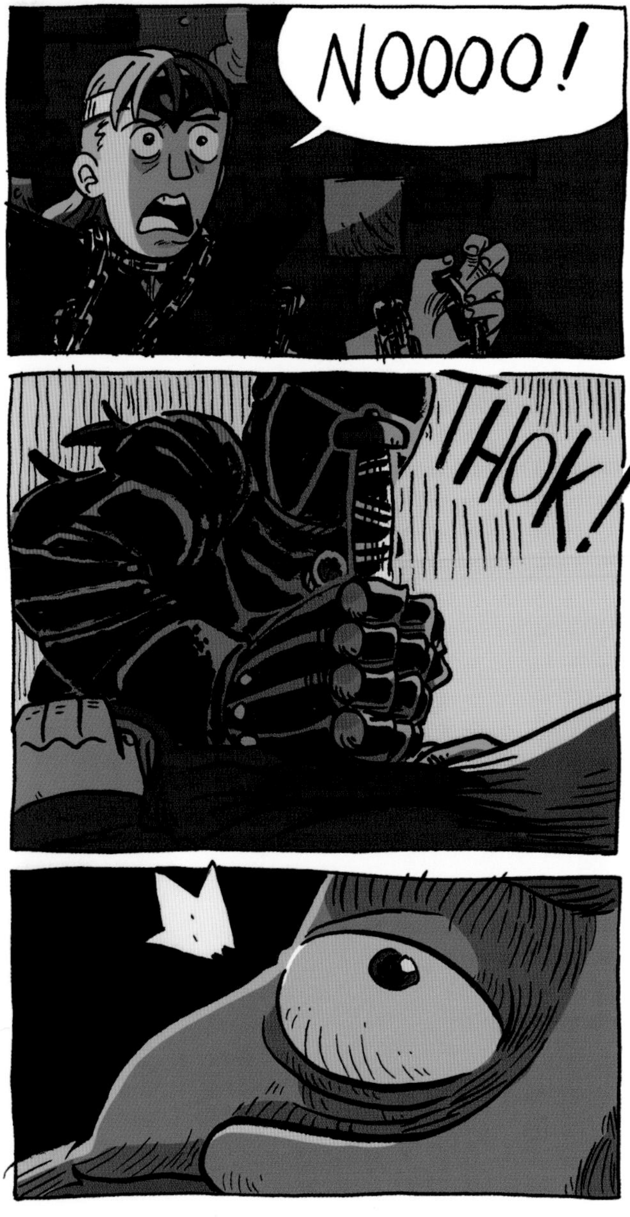
NOOOO!
THOK!
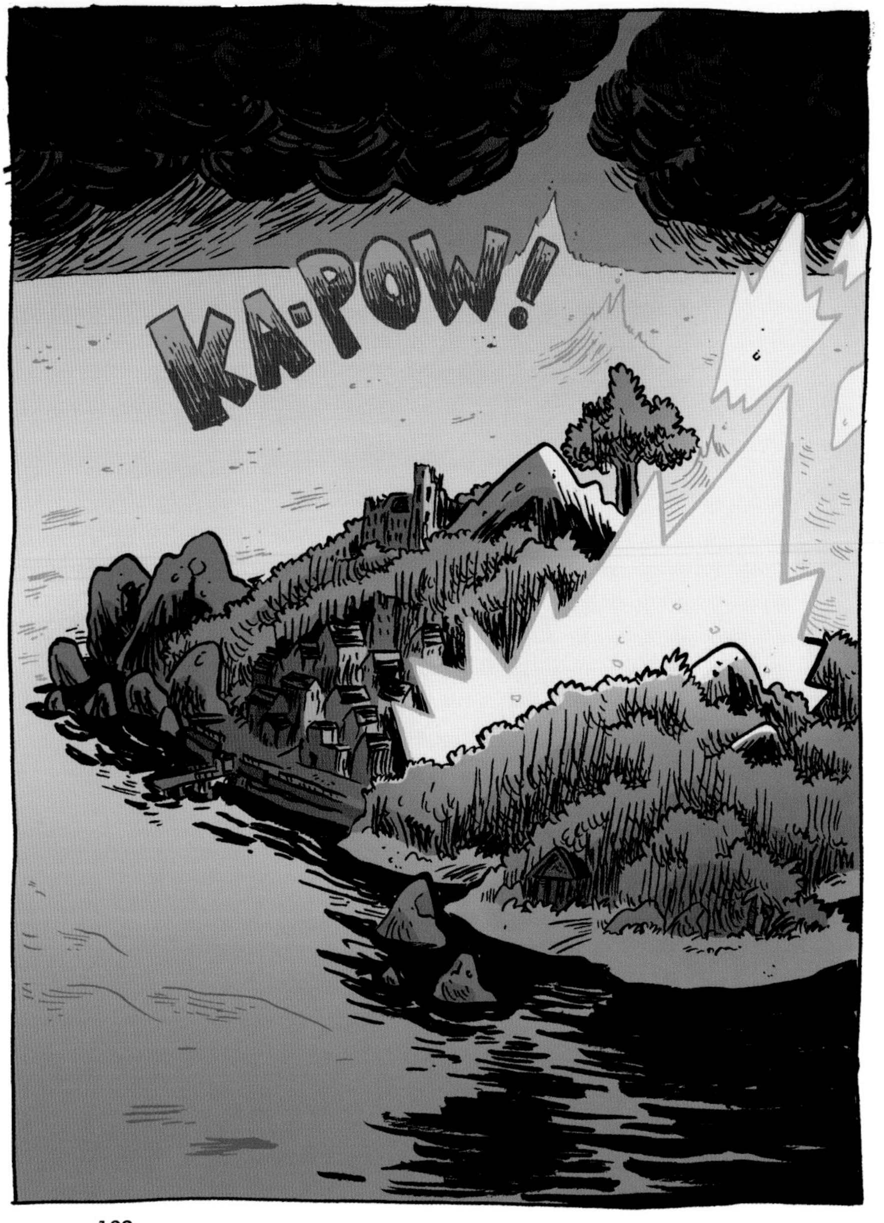
KA-POW!

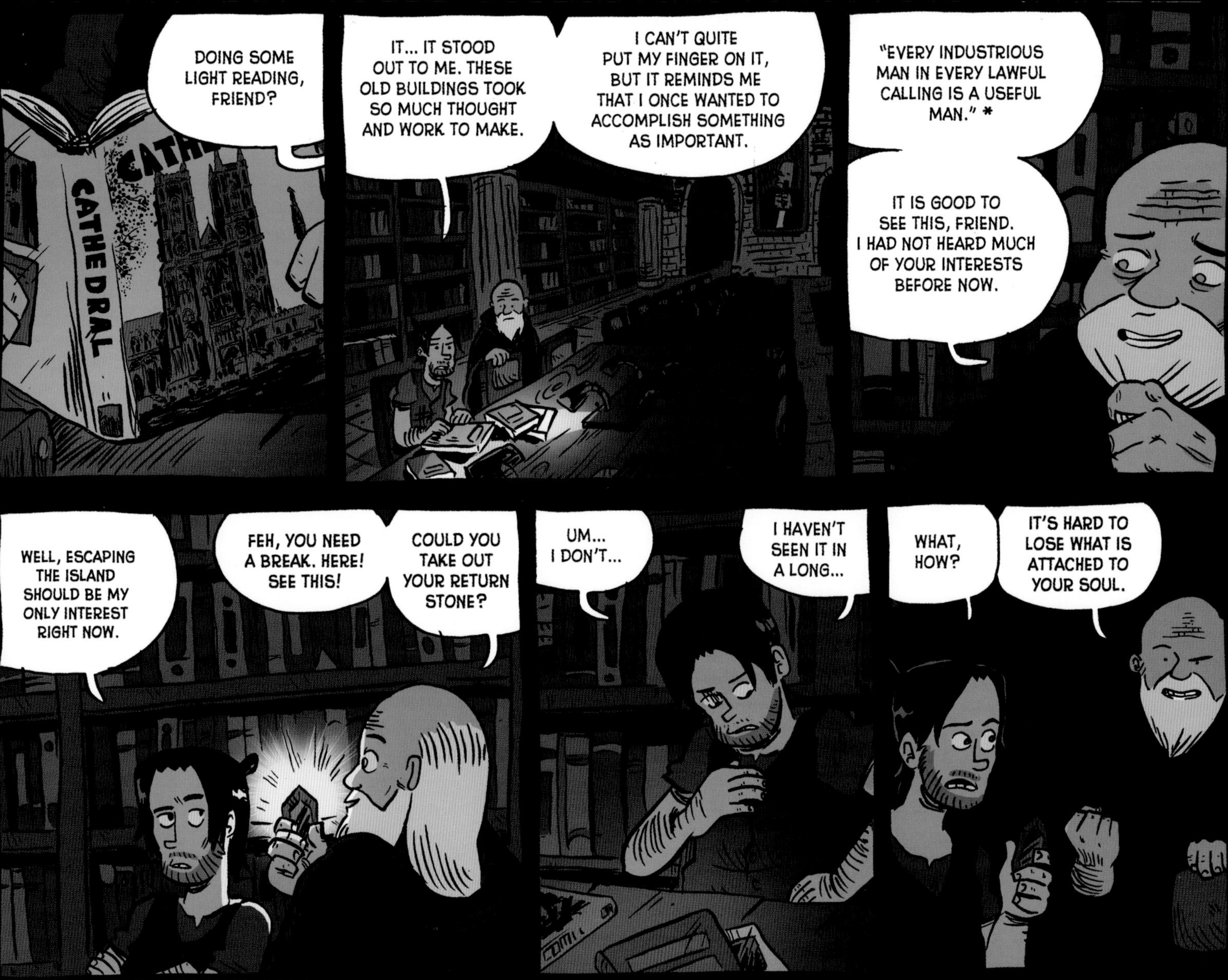
DOING SOME LIGHT READING, FRIEND?
CATHEDRAL
IT... IT STOOD OUT TO ME. THESE OLD BUILDINGS TOOK SO MUCH THOUGHT AND WORK TO MAKE.
I CAN'T QUITE PUT MY FINGER ON IT, BUT IT REMINDS ME THAT I ONCE WANTED TO ACCOMPLISH SOMETHING AS IMPORTANT.
"EVERY INDUSTRIOUS MAN IN EVERY LAWFUL CALLING IS A USEFUL MAN." *
IT IS GOOD TO SEE THIS, FRIEND. I HAD NOT HEARD MUCH OF YOUR INTERESTS BEFORE NOW.
WELL, ESCAPING THE ISLAND SHOULD BE MY ONLY INTEREST RIGHT NOW.
FEH, YOU NEED A BREAK. HERE! SEE THIS!
COULD YOU TAKE OUT YOUR RETURN STONE?
UM... I DON'T...
I HAVEN'T SEEN IT IN A LONG...
WHAT, HOW?
IT'S HARD TO LOSE WHAT IS ATTACHED TO YOUR SOUL.

* RALPH WALDO EMERSON 1803-1882

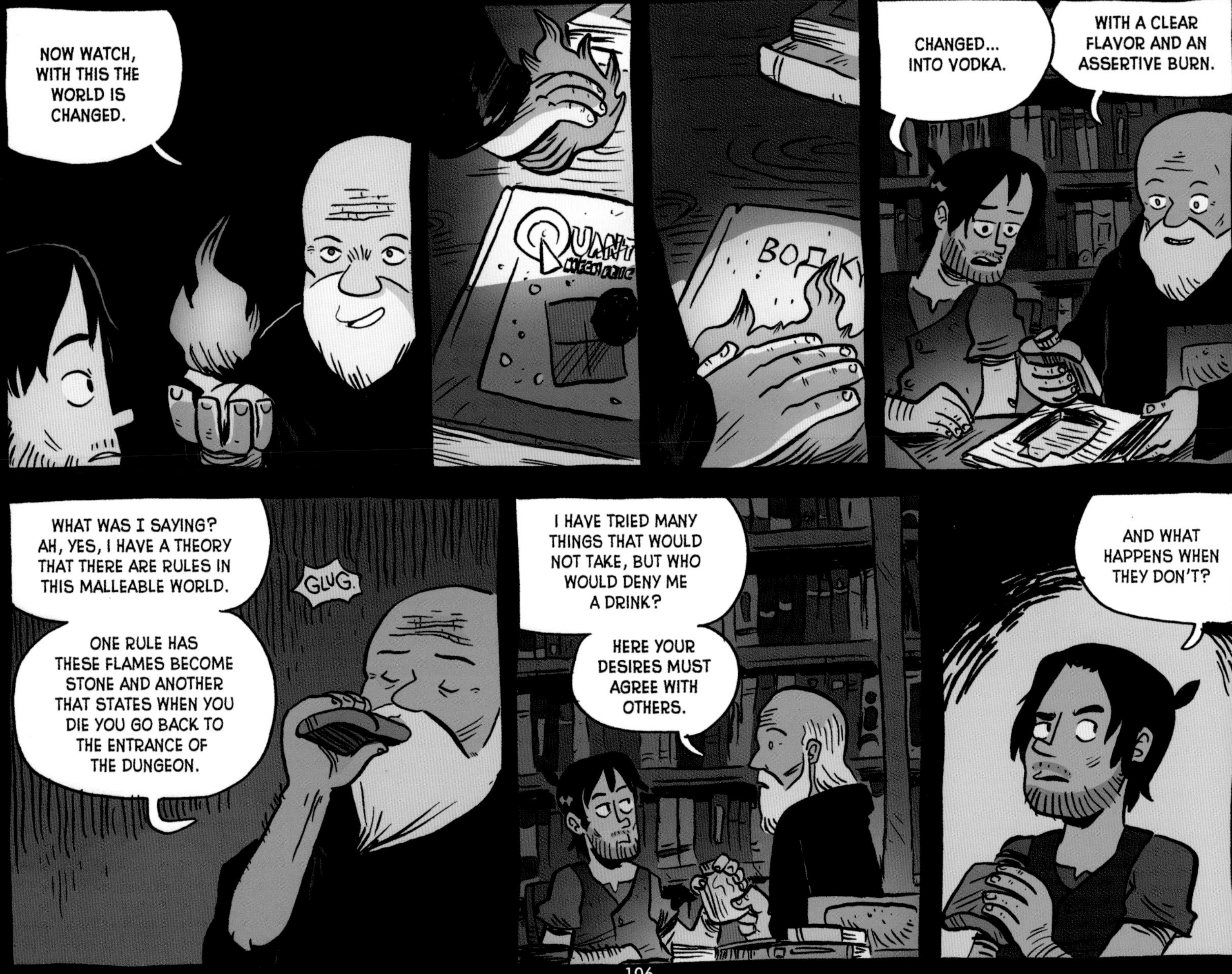
NOW WATCH, WITH THIS THE WORLD IS CHANGED.
CHANGED... INTO VODKA.
WITH A CLEAR FLAVOR AND AN ASSERTIVE BURN.
WHAT WAS I SAYING? AH, YES, I HAVE A THEORY THAT THERE ARE RULES IN THIS MALLEABLE WORLD.
GLUG.
ONE RULE HAS THESE FLAMES BECOME STONE AND ANOTHER THAT STATES WHEN YOU DIE YOU GO BACK TO THE ENTRANCE OF THE DUNGEON.
I HAVE TRIED MANY THINGS THAT WOULD NOT TAKE, BUT WHO WOULD DENY ME A DRINK?
HERE YOUR DESIRES MUST AGREE WITH OTHERS.
AND WHAT HAPPENS WHEN THEY DON'T?

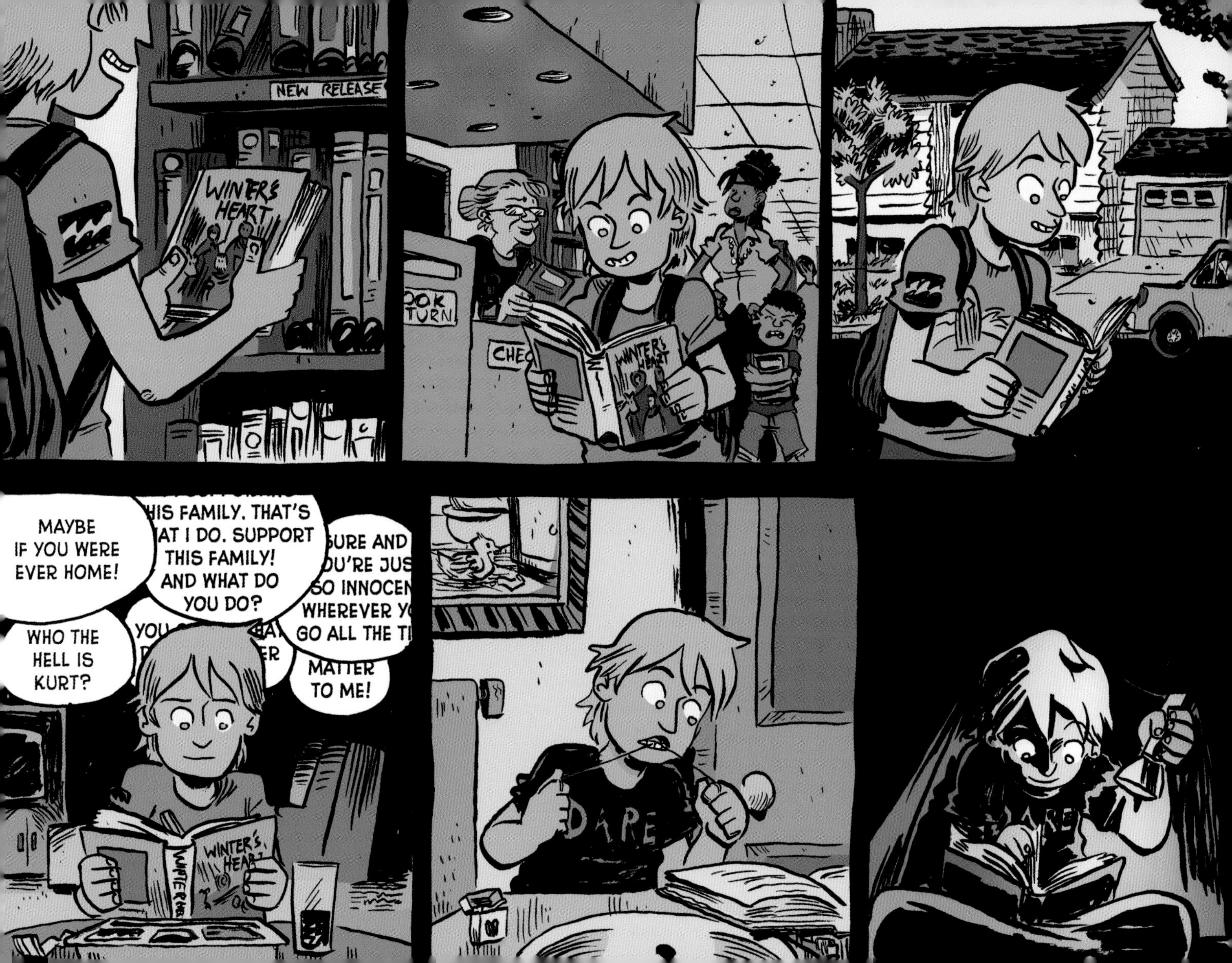
NEW RELEASE
WINTER'S HEART
OOK
TURN
CHEC
WINTER'S HEART
MAYBE IF YOU WERE EVER HOME!
HIS FAMILY. THAT'S
AT I DO. SUPPORT THIS FAMILY! AND WHAT DO YOU DO?
SURE AND
OU'RE JUS
SO INNOCEN
WHEREVER Y
GO ALL THE TI
WHO THE HELL IS KURT?
MATTER TO ME!
WINTER'S HEART
DARE

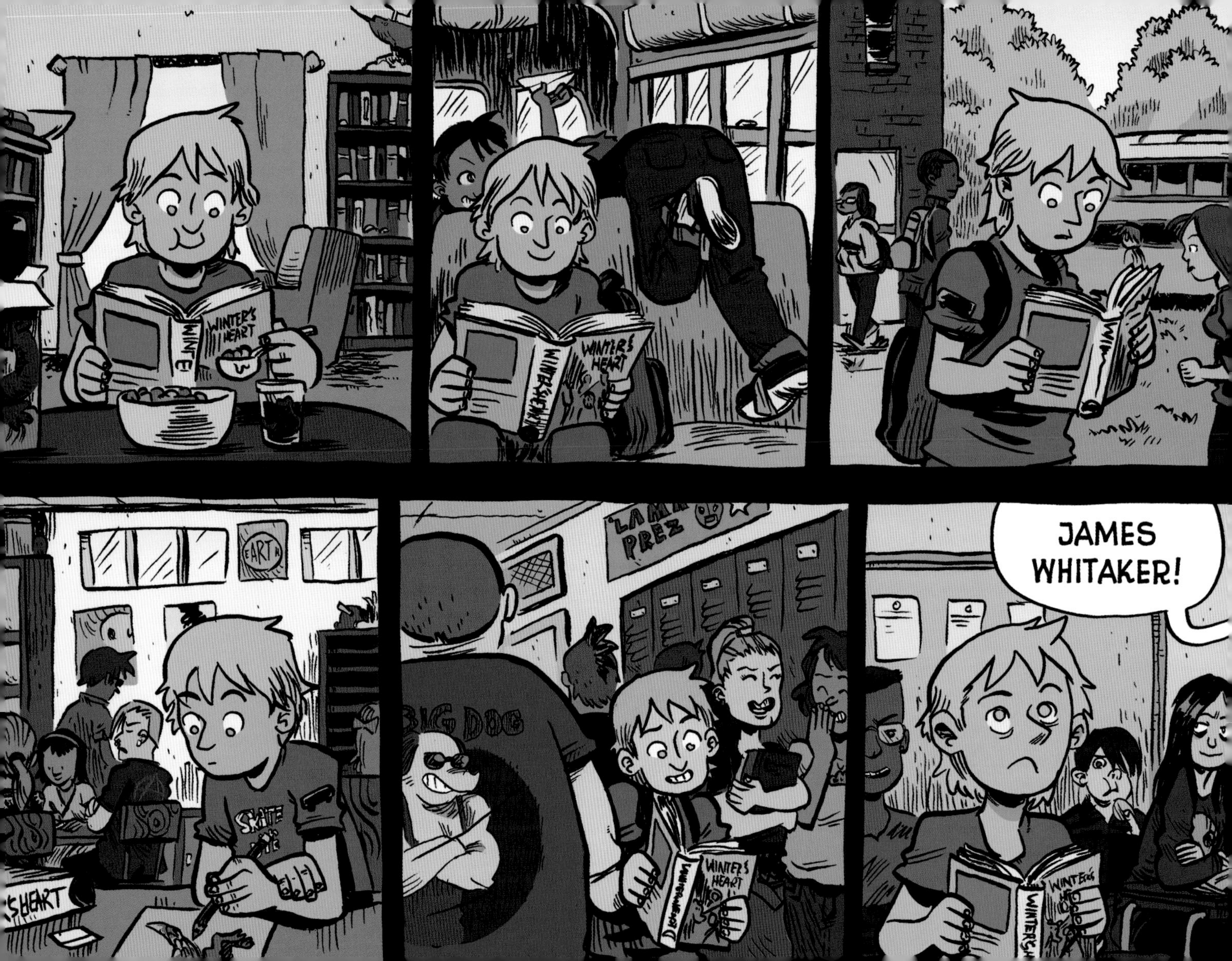
WINTER'S HEART
WINTER'S HEART
ART
'S HEART
BIG DOG
WINTER'S HEART
JAMES WHITAKER!

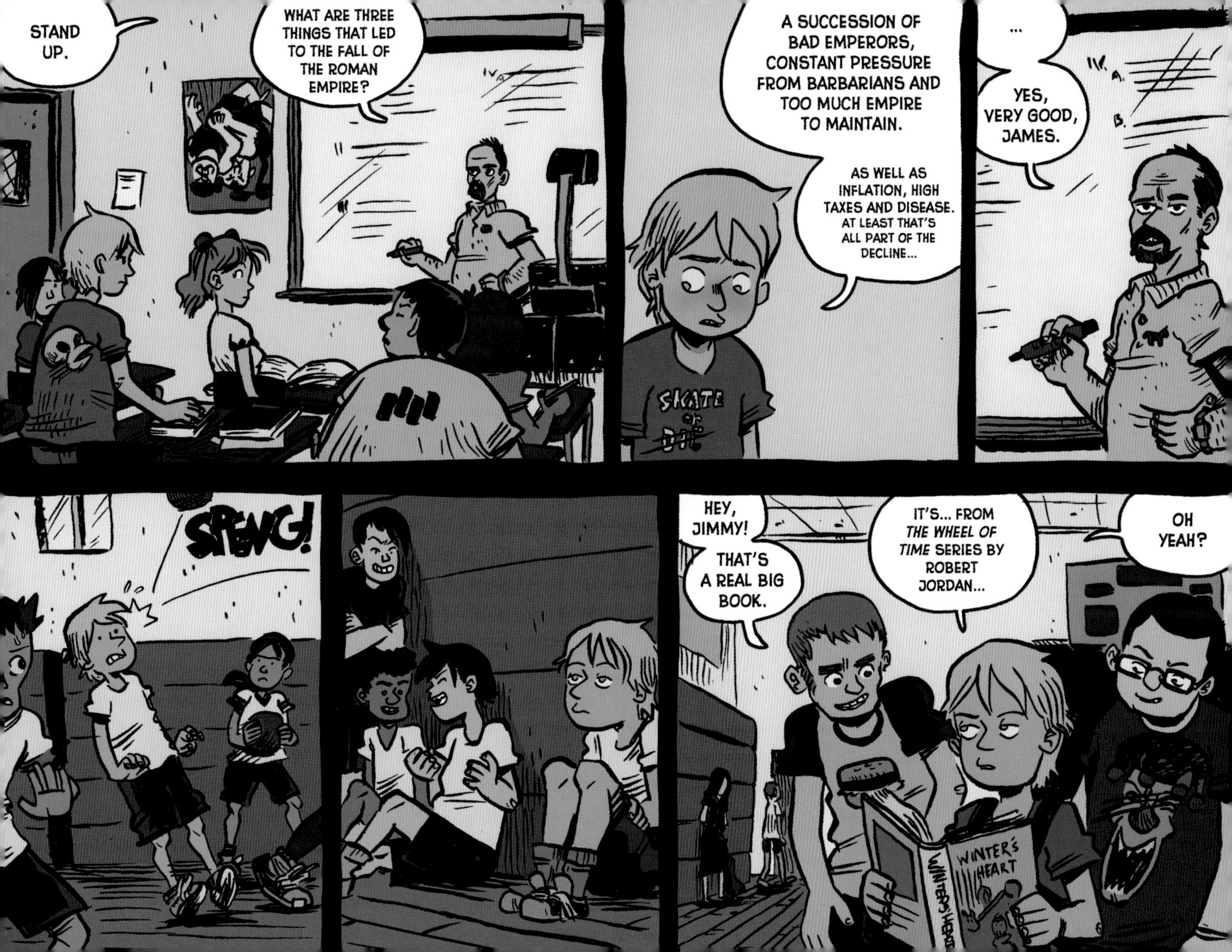
STAND UP.
WHAT ARE THREE THINGS THAT LED TO THE FALL OF THE ROMAN EMPIRE?
A SUCCESSION OF BAD EMPERORS, CONSTANT PRESSURE FROM BARBARIANS AND TOO MUCH EMPIRE TO MAINTAIN.
AS WELL AS INFLATION, HIGH TAXES AND DISEASE. AT LEAST THAT'S ALL PART OF THE DECLINE...
SKATE or DIE
...
YES, VERY GOOD, JAMES.
SPENG!
HEY, JIMMY!
THAT'S A REAL BIG BOOK.
IT'S... FROM *THE WHEEL OF TIME* SERIES BY ROBERT JORDAN...
OH YEAH?
WINTER'S HEART

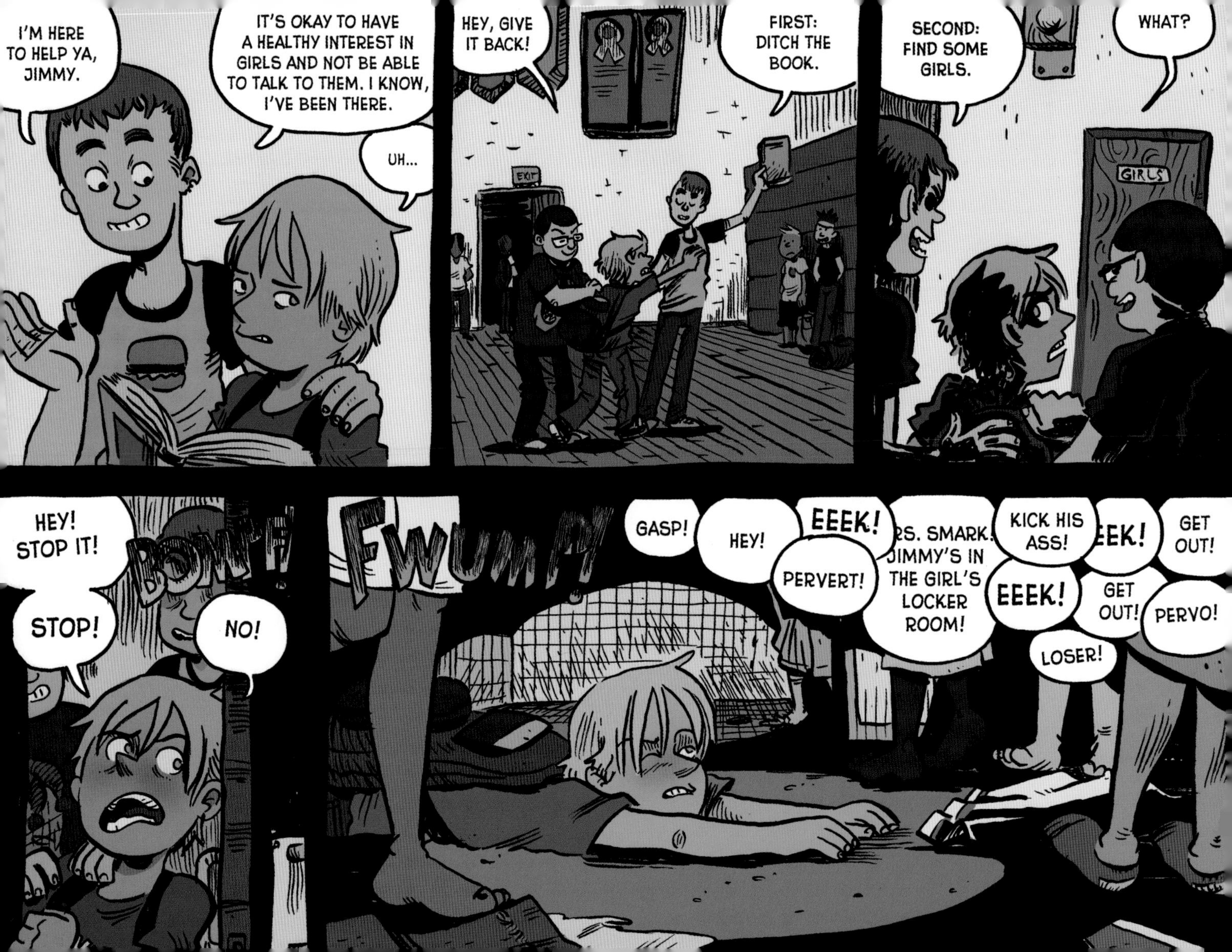

I'M HERE TO HELP YA, JIMMY.
IT'S OKAY TO HAVE A HEALTHY INTEREST IN GIRLS AND NOT BE ABLE TO TALK TO THEM. I KNOW, I'VE BEEN THERE.
UH...
HEY, GIVE IT BACK!
EXIT
FIRST: DITCH THE BOOK.
SECOND: FIND SOME GIRLS.
WHAT?
GIRLS
HEY! STOP IT!
BOMF!
STOP!
NO!
FWUMP!
GASP!
HEY!
EEEK!
PERVERT!
RS. SMARK. JIMMY'S IN THE GIRL'S LOCKER ROOM!
KICK HIS ASS!
EEK!
EEEK!
GET OUT!
GET OUT!
PERVO!
LOSER!

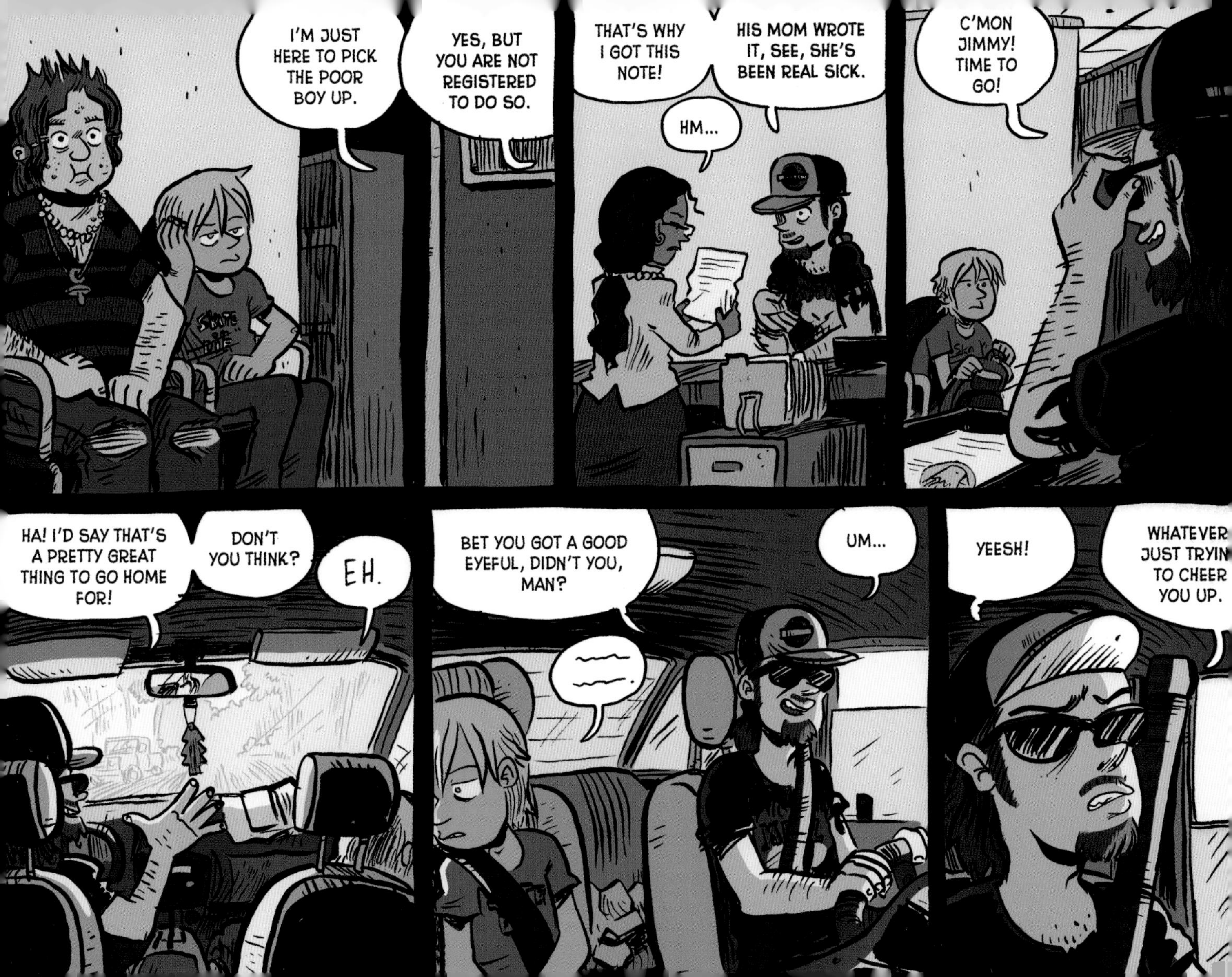
I'M JUST HERE TO PICK THE POOR BOY UP.
YES, BUT YOU ARE NOT REGISTERED TO DO SO.
THAT'S WHY I GOT THIS NOTE!
HIS MOM WROTE IT, SEE, SHE'S BEEN REAL SICK.
HM...
C'MON JIMMY! TIME TO GO!
HA! I'D SAY THAT'S A PRETTY GREAT THING TO GO HOME FOR!
DON'T YOU THINK?
EH.
BET YOU GOT A GOOD EYEFUL, DIDN'T YOU, MAN?
UM...
YEESH!
WHATEVER JUST TRYIN TO CHEER YOU UP.

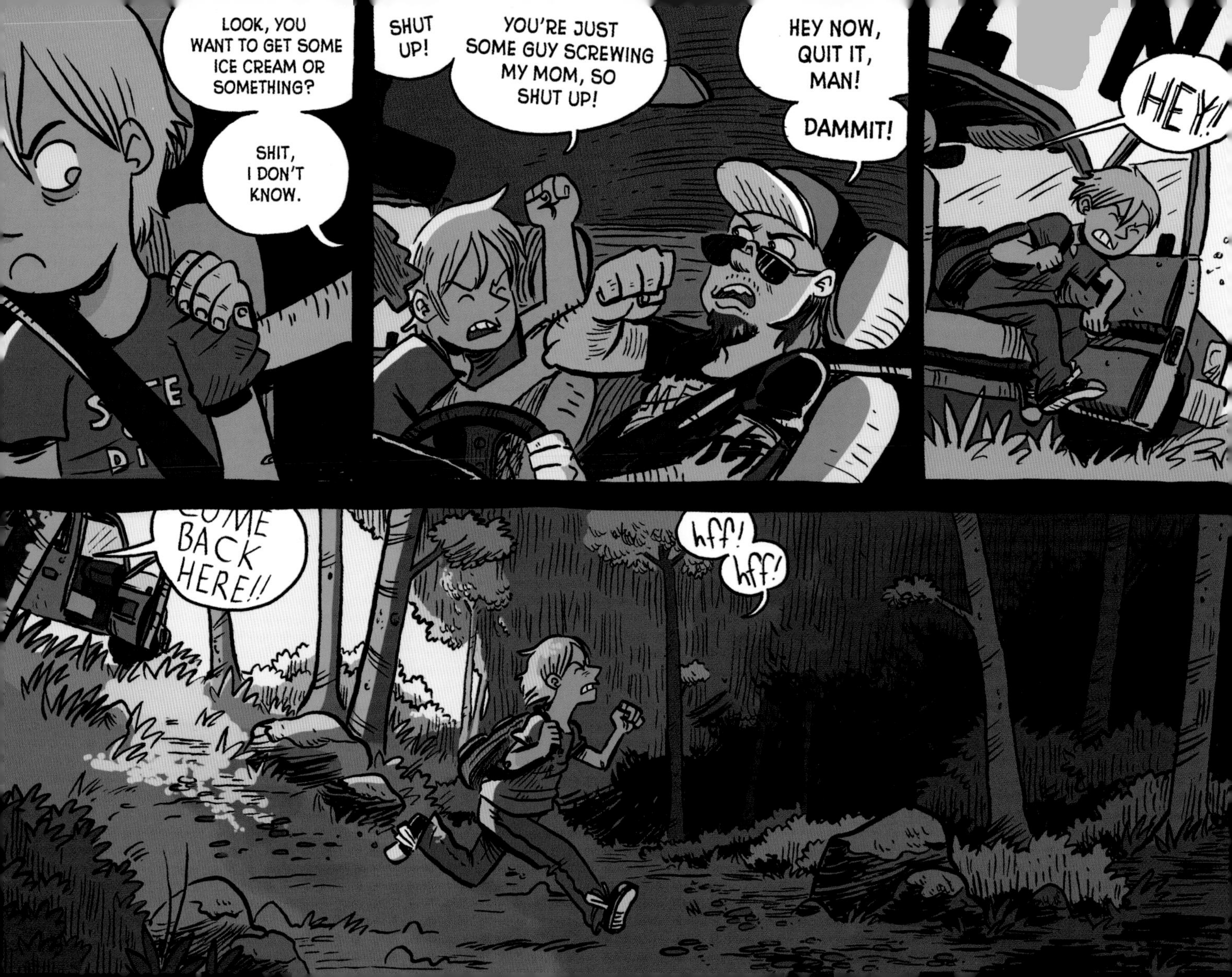
LOOK, YOU WANT TO GET SOME ICE CREAM OR SOMETHING?
SHIT, I DON'T KNOW.
SHUT UP!
YOU'RE JUST SOME GUY SCREWING MY MOM, SO SHUT UP!
HEY NOW, QUIT IT, MAN!
DAMMIT!
HEY!!
BACK HERE!!
hff! hff!

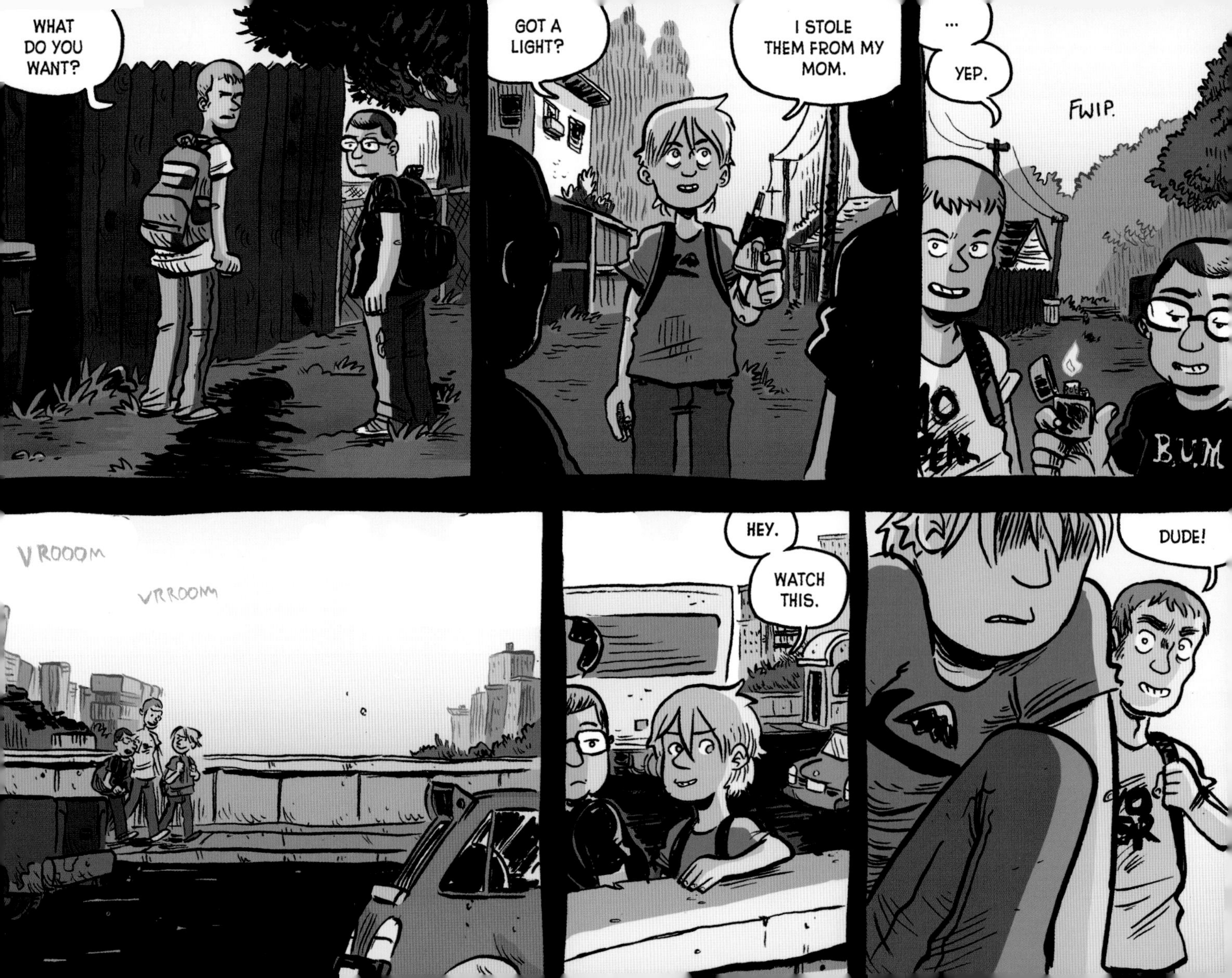
WHAT DO YOU WANT?
GOT A LIGHT?
I STOLE THEM FROM MY MOM.
...
YEP.
FWIP.
B.U.M
VROOOM
VRROOM
HEY.
WATCH THIS.
DUDE!

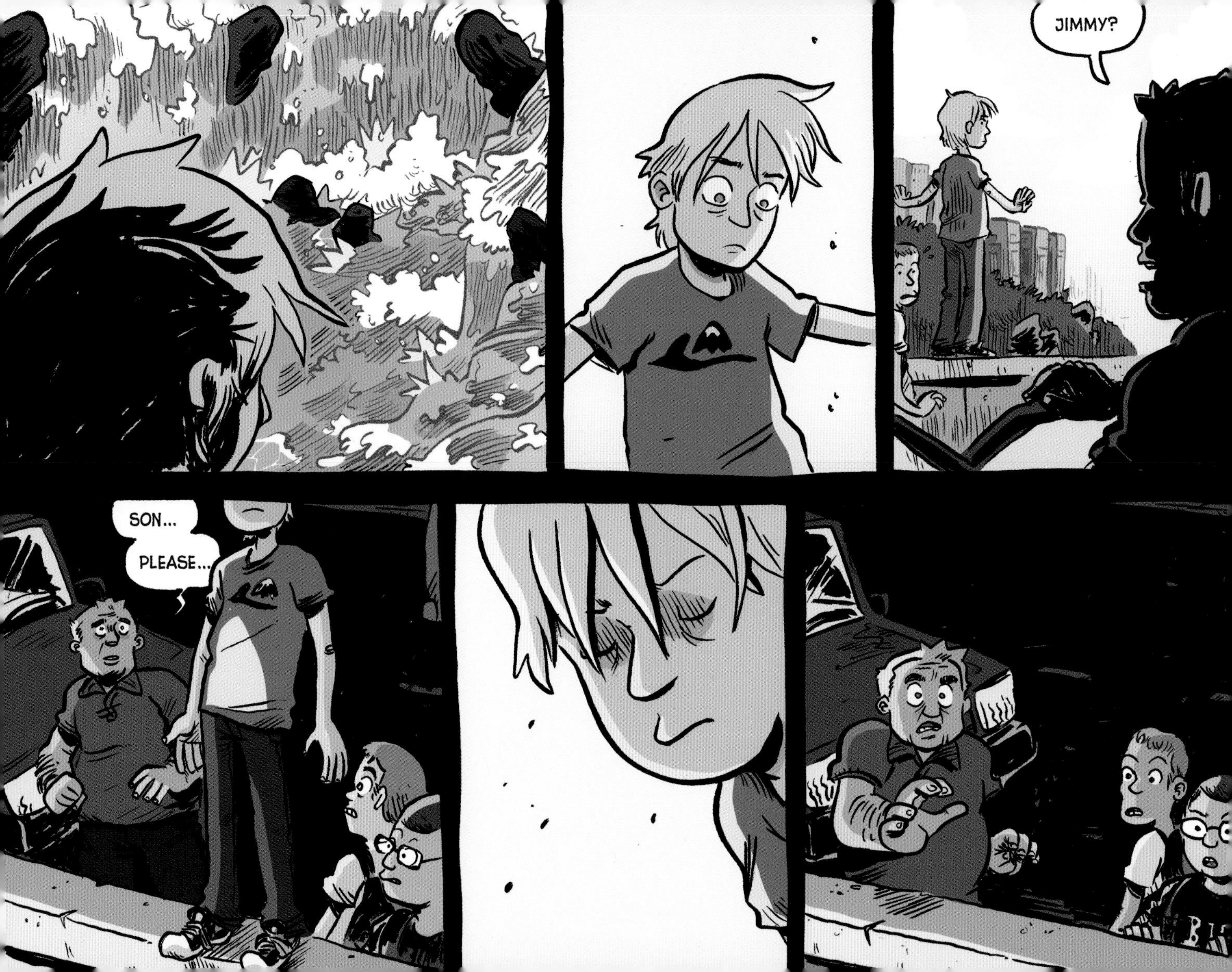
JIMMY?
SON...
PLEASE...

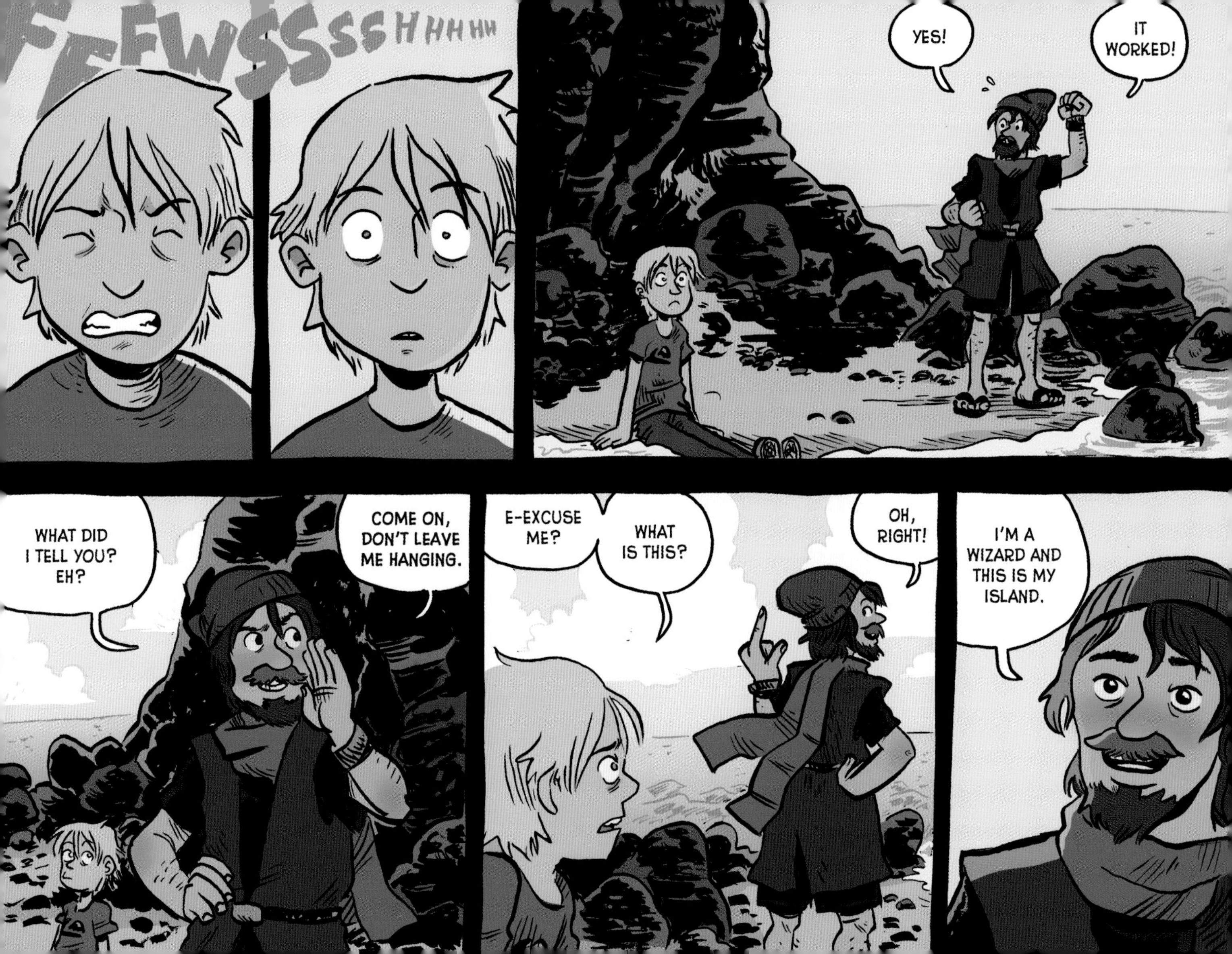
FFFWSSSSSHHHHH
YES!
IT WORKED!
WHAT DID I TELL YOU? EH?
COME ON, DON'T LEAVE ME HANGING.
E-EXCUSE ME?
WHAT IS THIS?
OH, RIGHT!
I'M A WIZARD AND THIS IS MY ISLAND.

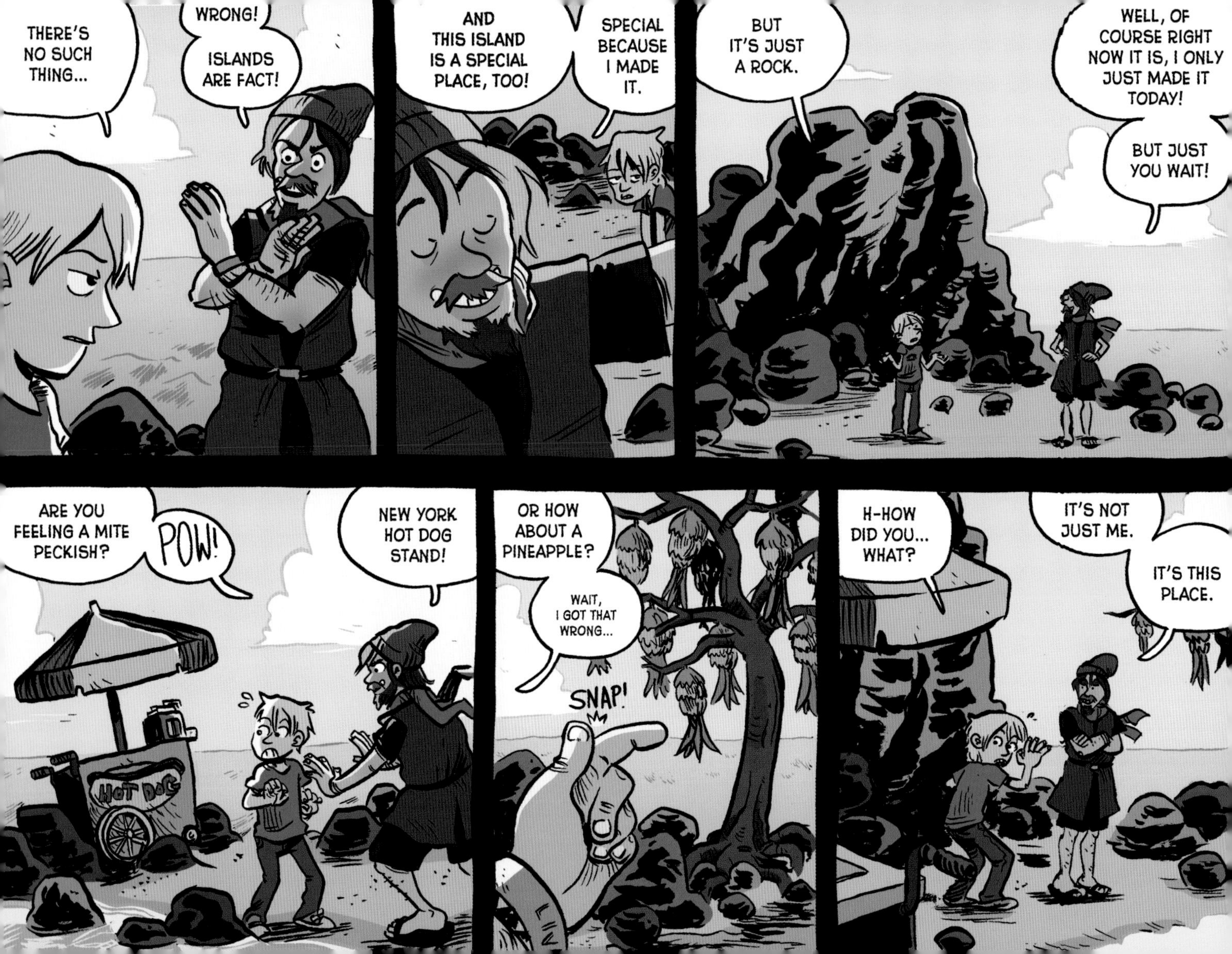
THERE'S NO SUCH THING...
WRONG!
ISLANDS ARE FACT!
AND THIS ISLAND IS A SPECIAL PLACE, TOO!
SPECIAL BECAUSE I MADE IT.
BUT IT'S JUST A ROCK.
WELL, OF COURSE RIGHT NOW IT IS, I ONLY JUST MADE IT TODAY!
BUT JUST YOU WAIT!
ARE YOU FEELING A MITE PECKISH?
POW!
NEW YORK HOT DOG STAND!
HOT DOG
OR HOW ABOUT A PINEAPPLE?
WAIT, I GOT THAT WRONG...
SNAP!
H-HOW DID YOU... WHAT?
IT'S NOT JUST ME.
IT'S THIS PLACE.

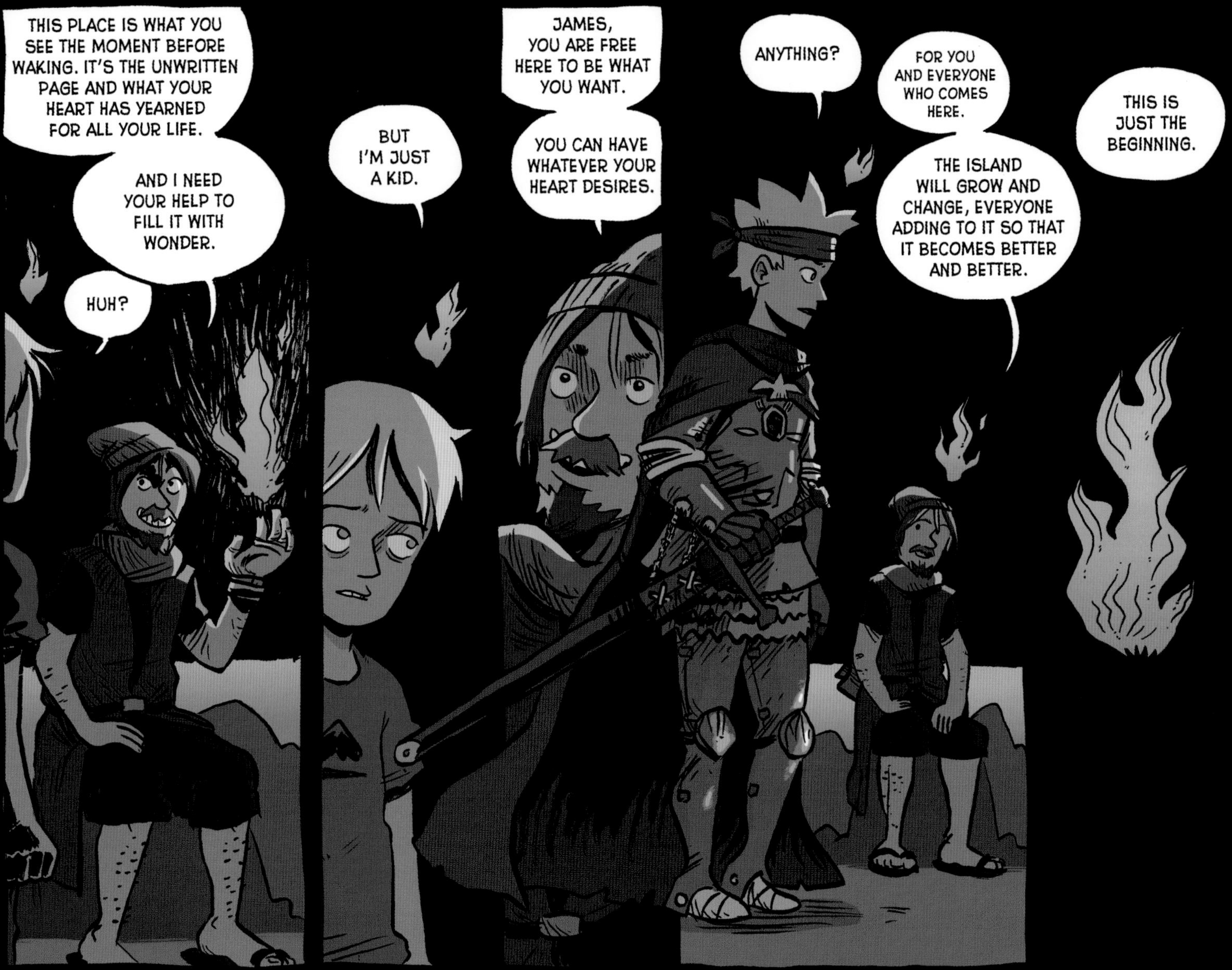
THIS PLACE IS WHAT YOU SEE THE MOMENT BEFORE WAKING. IT'S THE UNWRITTEN PAGE AND WHAT YOUR HEART HAS YEARNED FOR ALL YOUR LIFE.
AND I NEED YOUR HELP TO FILL IT WITH WONDER.
HUH?
BUT I'M JUST A KID.
JAMES, YOU ARE FREE HERE TO BE WHAT YOU WANT.
YOU CAN HAVE WHATEVER YOUR HEART DESIRES.
ANYTHING?
FOR YOU AND EVERYONE WHO COMES HERE.
THE ISLAND WILL GROW AND CHANGE, EVERYONE ADDING TO IT SO THAT IT BECOMES BETTER AND BETTER.
THIS IS JUST THE BEGINNING.

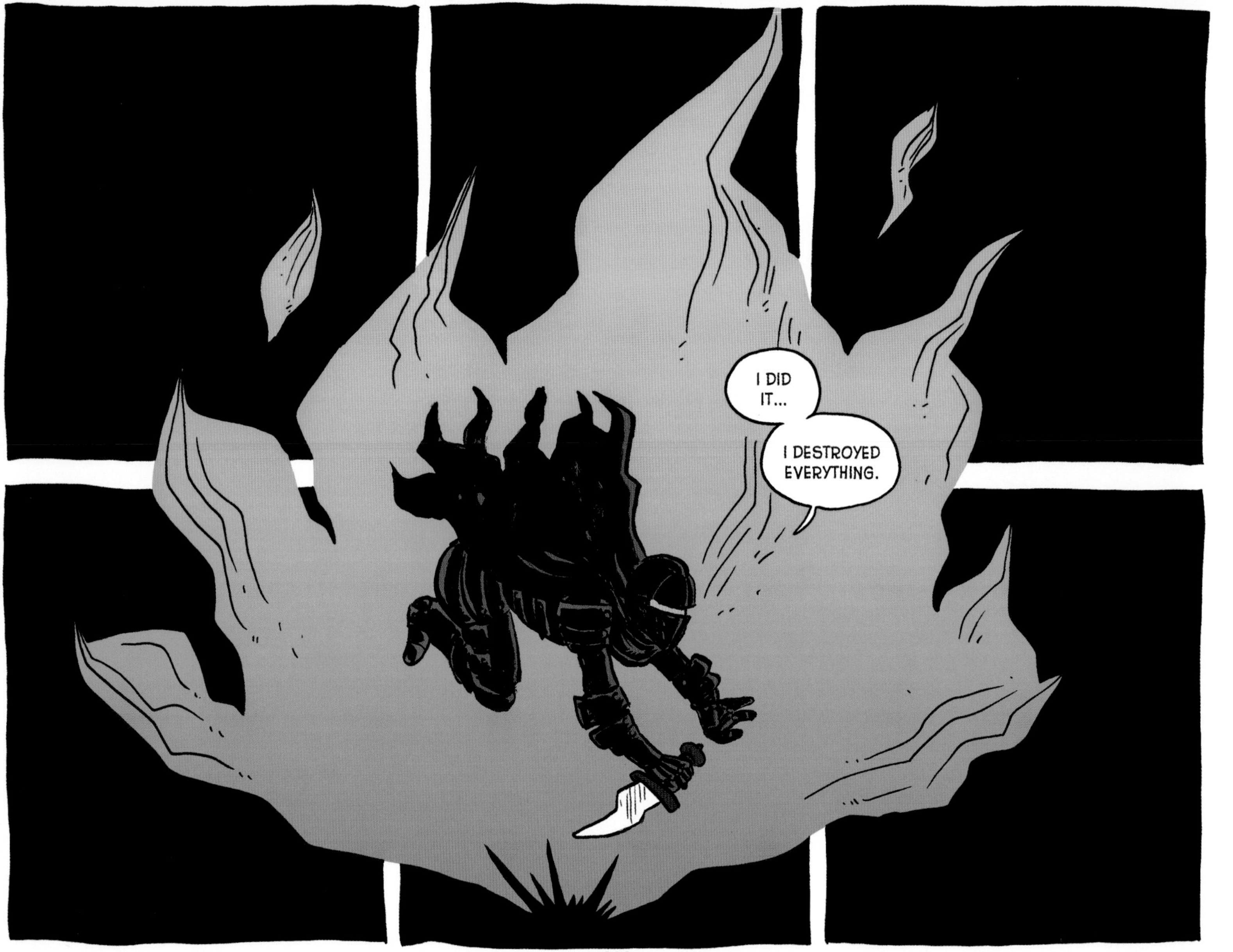
I DID IT...
I DESTROYED EVERYTHING.

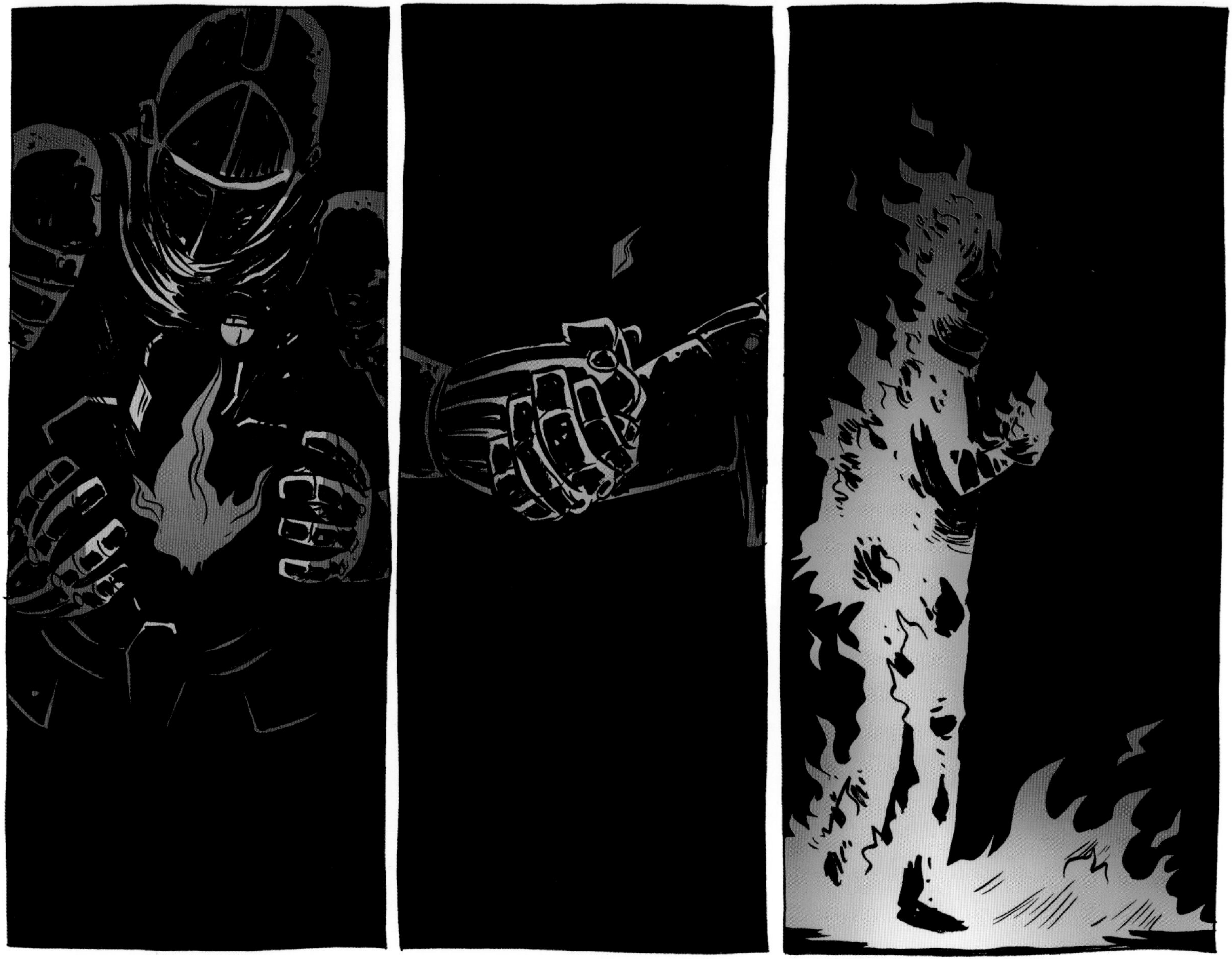

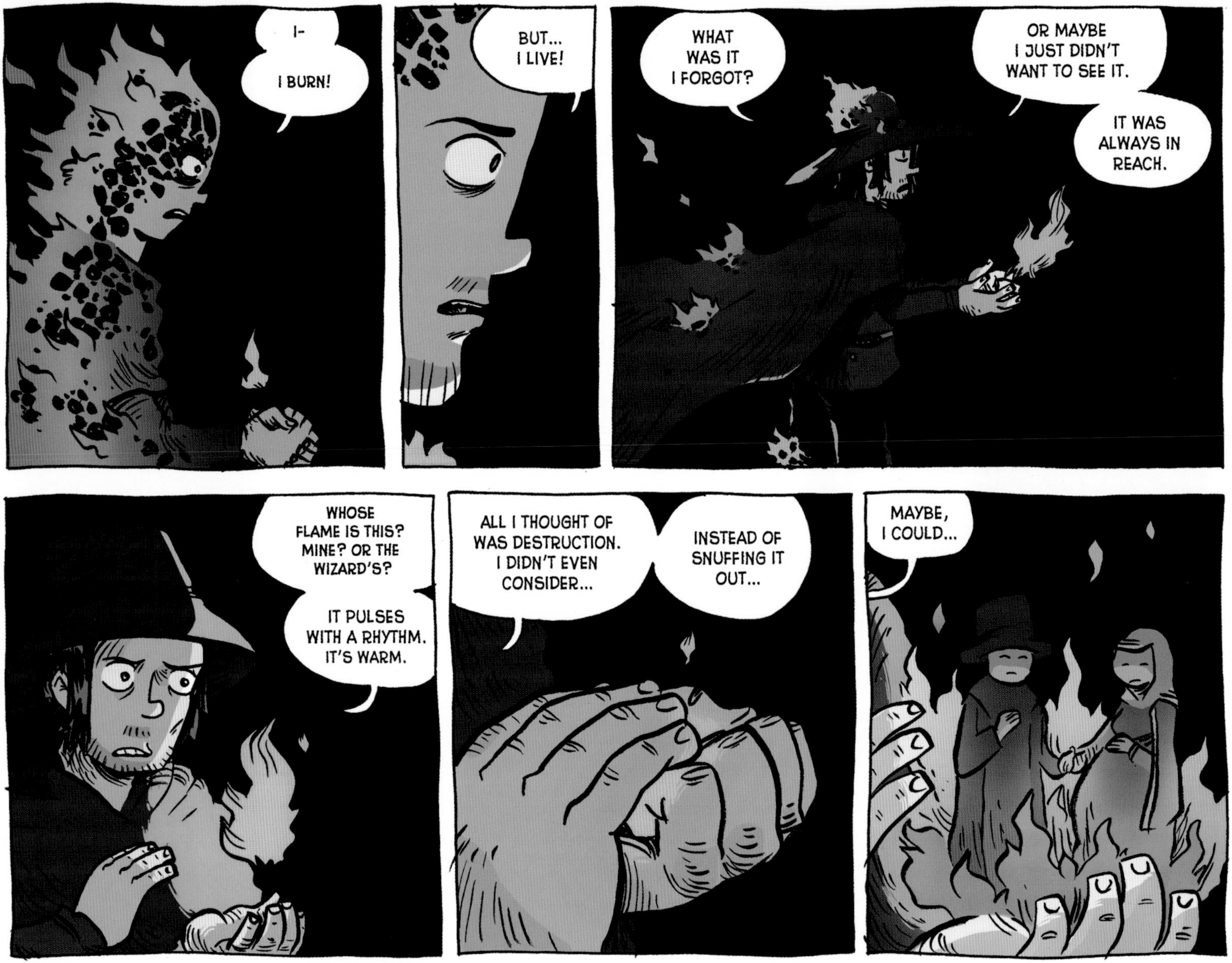

I-
I BURN!
BUT... I LIVE!
WHAT WAS IT I FORGOT?
OR MAYBE I JUST DIDN'T WANT TO SEE IT.
IT WAS ALWAYS IN REACH.
WHOSE FLAME IS THIS? MINE? OR THE WIZARD'S?
IT PULSES WITH A RHYTHM. IT'S WARM.
ALL I THOUGHT OF WAS DESTRUCTION. I DIDN'T EVEN CONSIDER...
INSTEAD OF SNUFFING IT OUT...
MAYBE, I COULD...

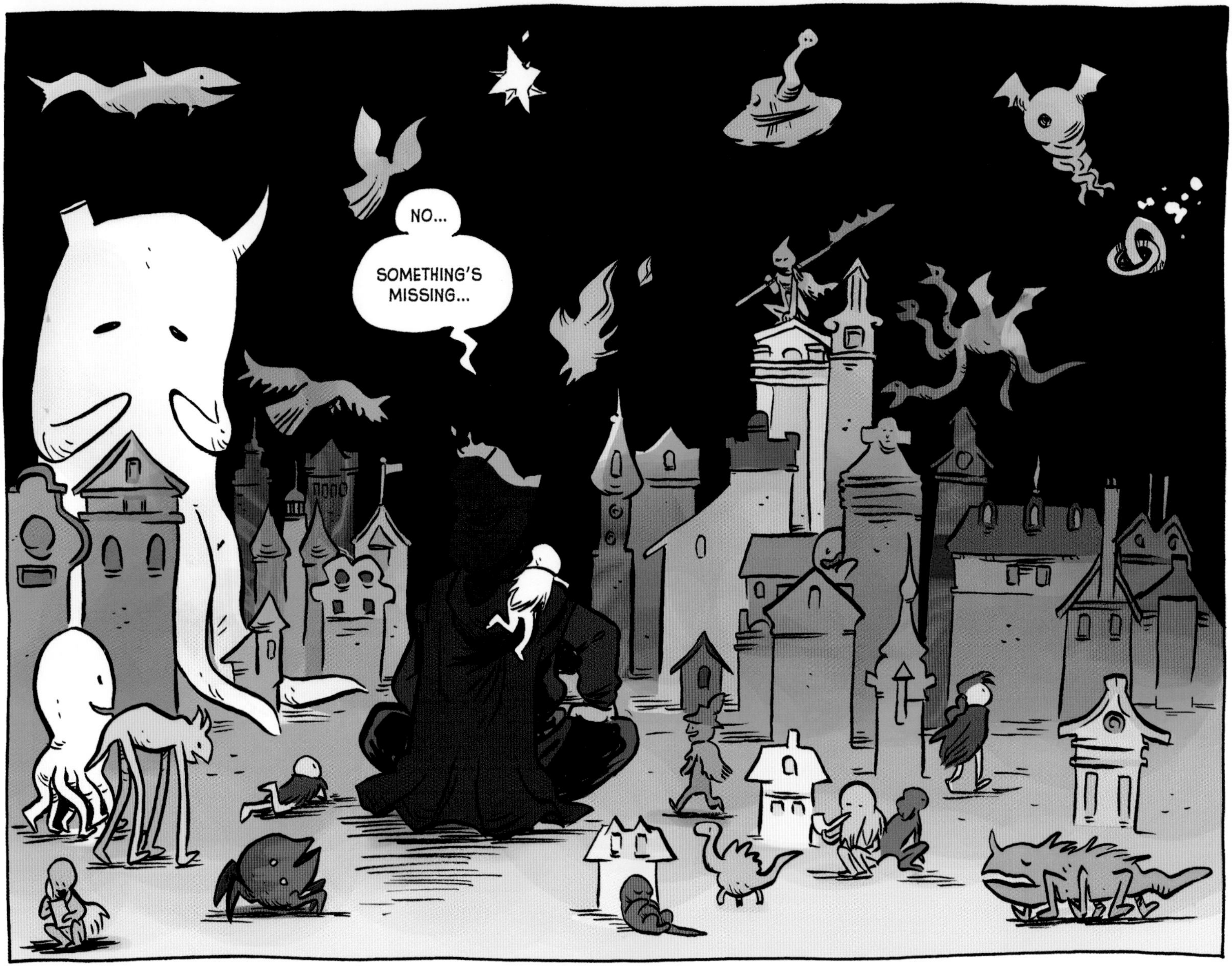
NO...
SOMETHING'S MISSING...

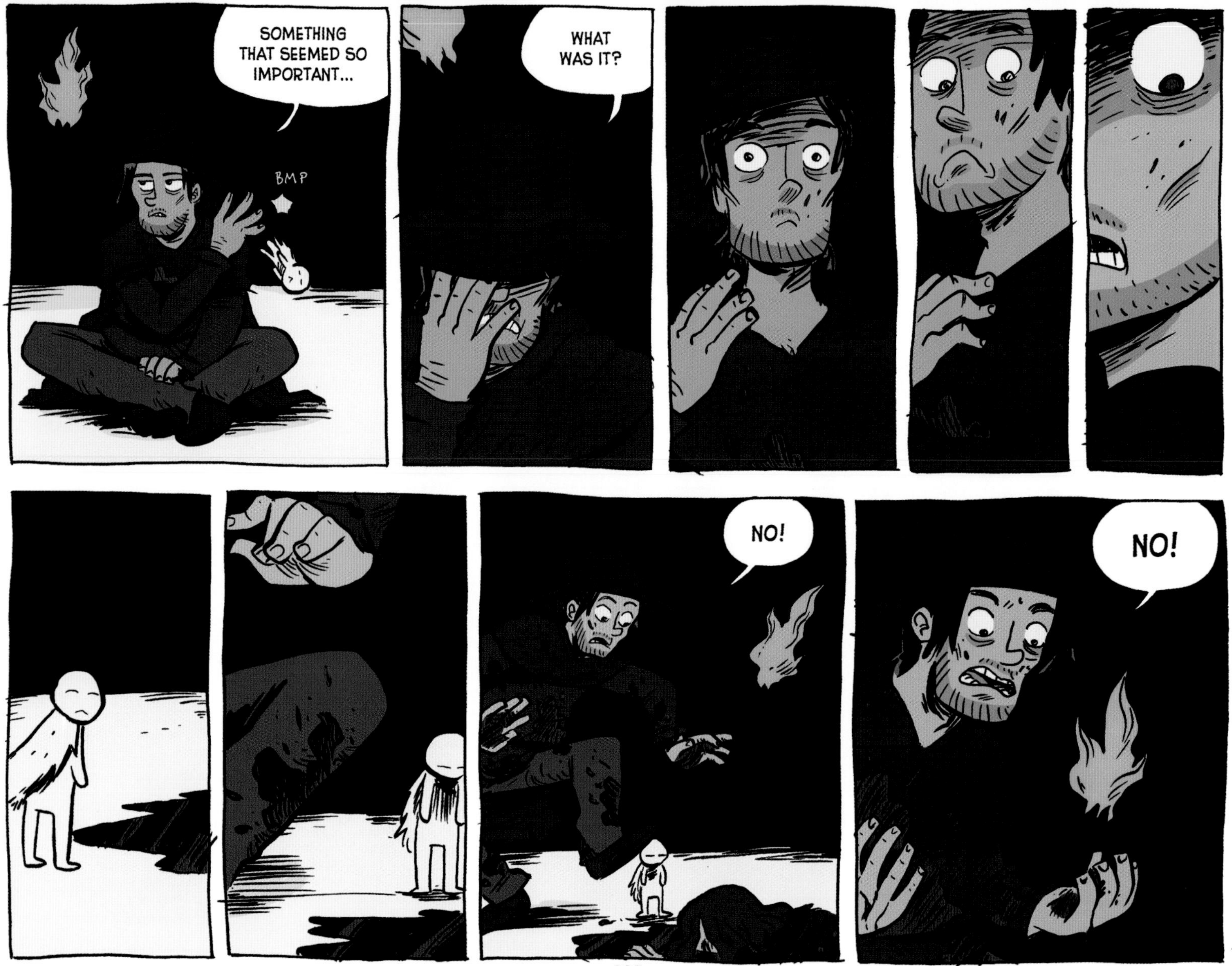
SOMETHING THAT SEEMED SO IMPORTANT...
BMP
WHAT WAS IT?
NO!
NO!

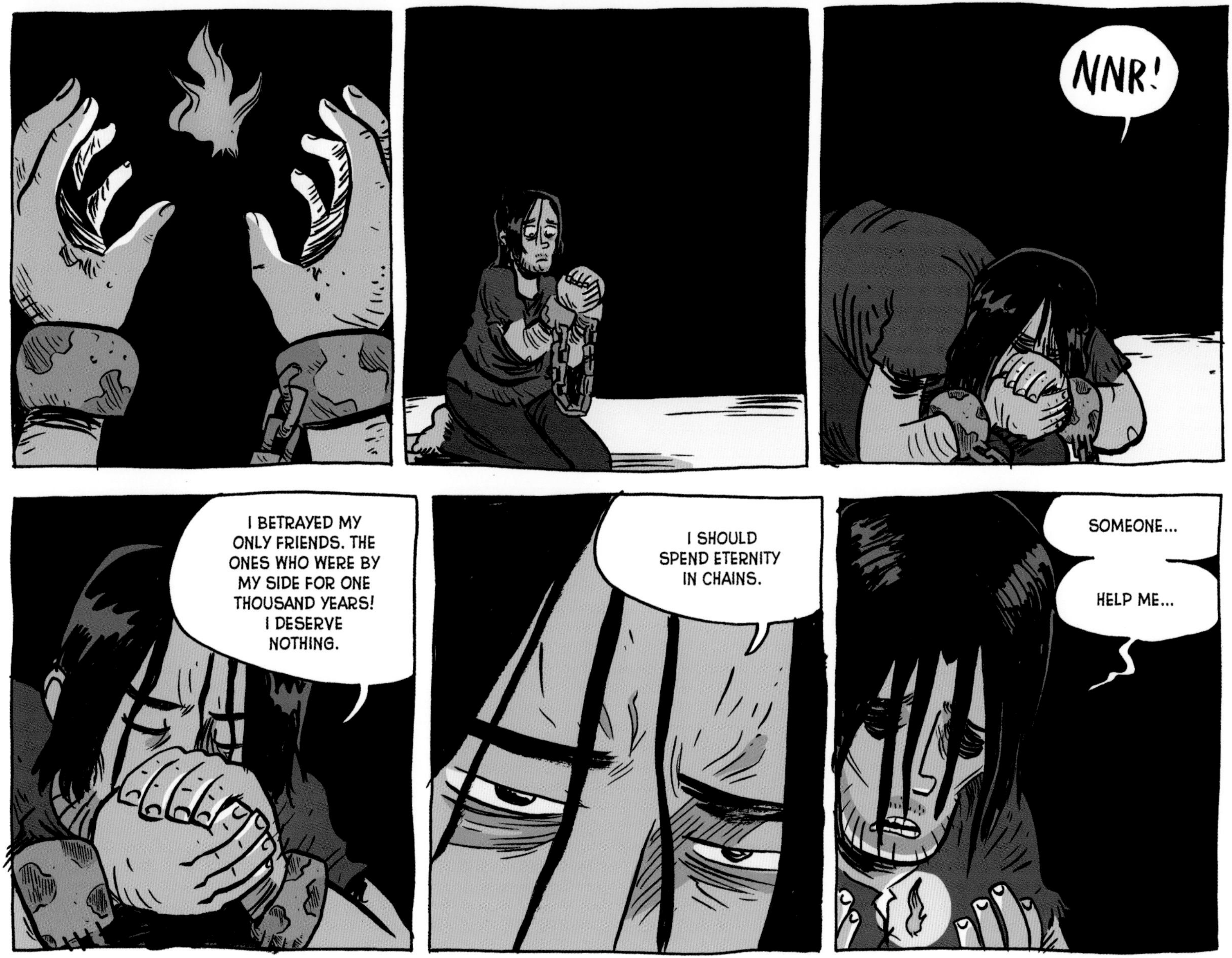
NNR!
I BETRAYED MY ONLY FRIENDS. THE ONES WHO WERE BY MY SIDE FOR ONE THOUSAND YEARS! I DESERVE NOTHING.
I SHOULD SPEND ETERNITY IN CHAINS.
SOMEONE...
HELP ME...

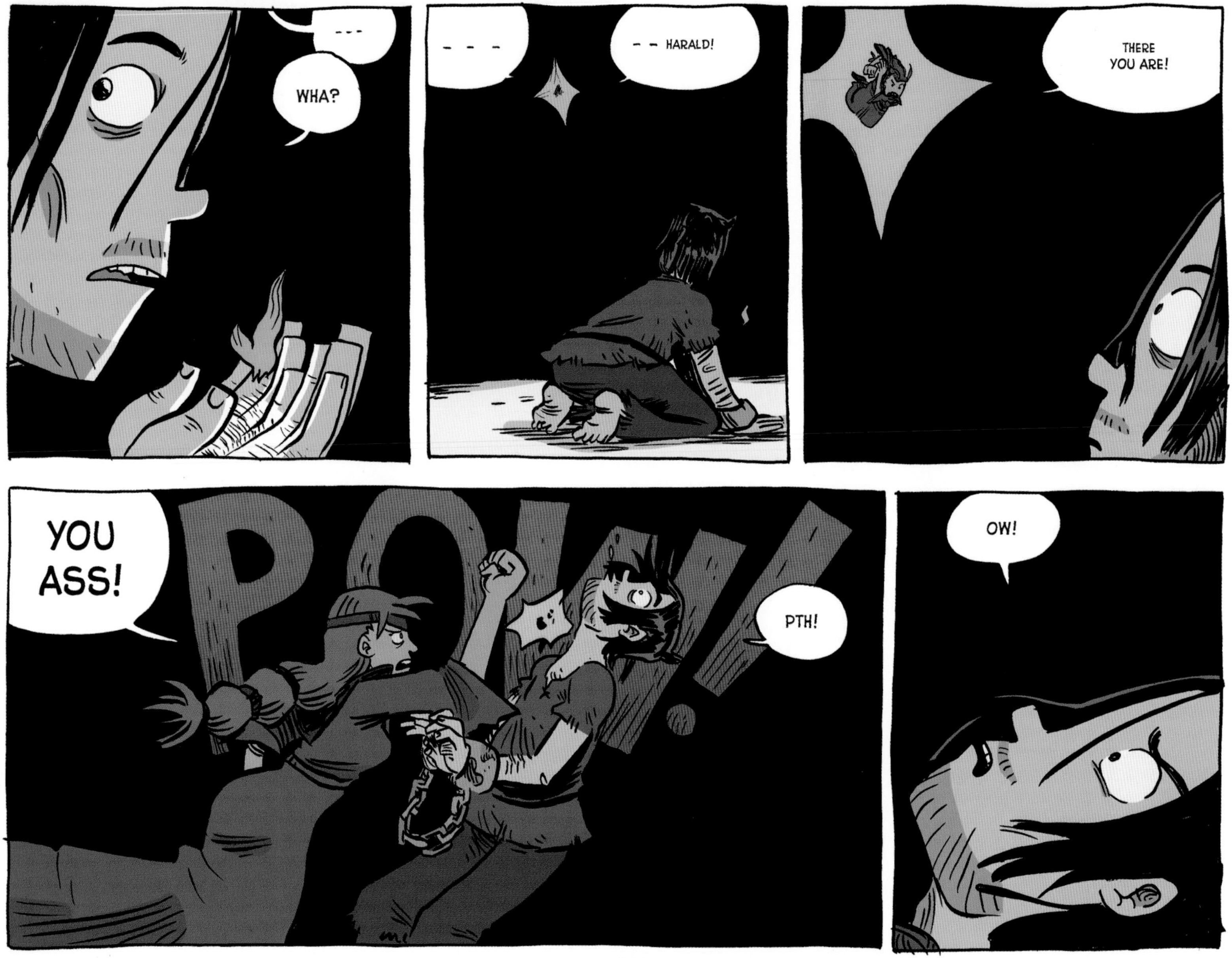

WHA?
- - -
- - HARALD!
THERE YOU ARE!
YOU ASS!
POW!!
PTH!
OW!

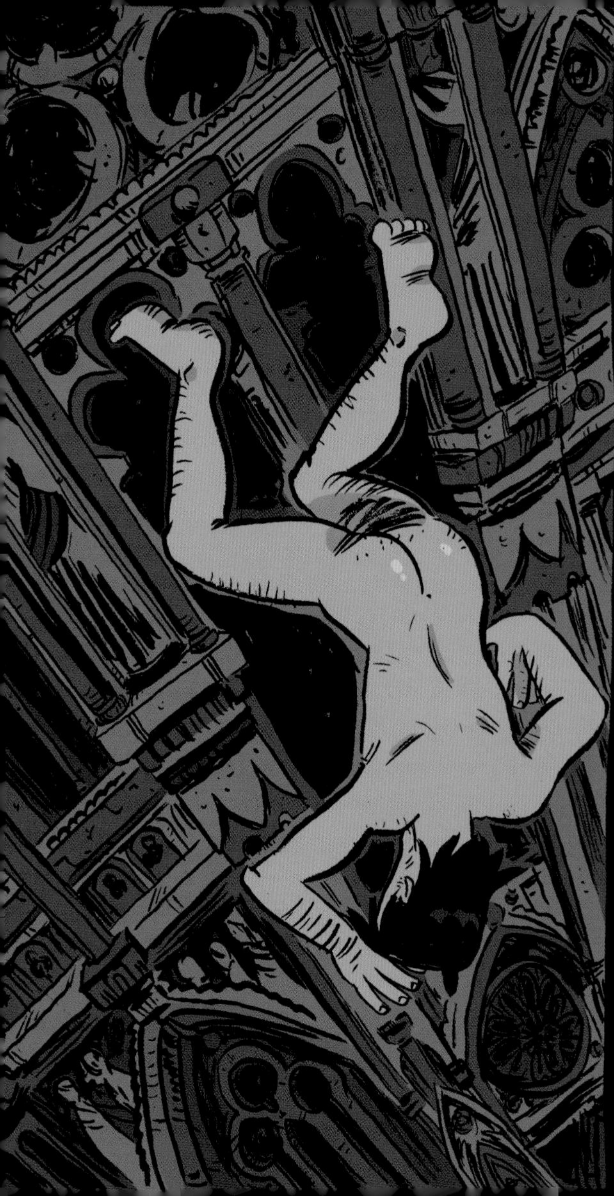

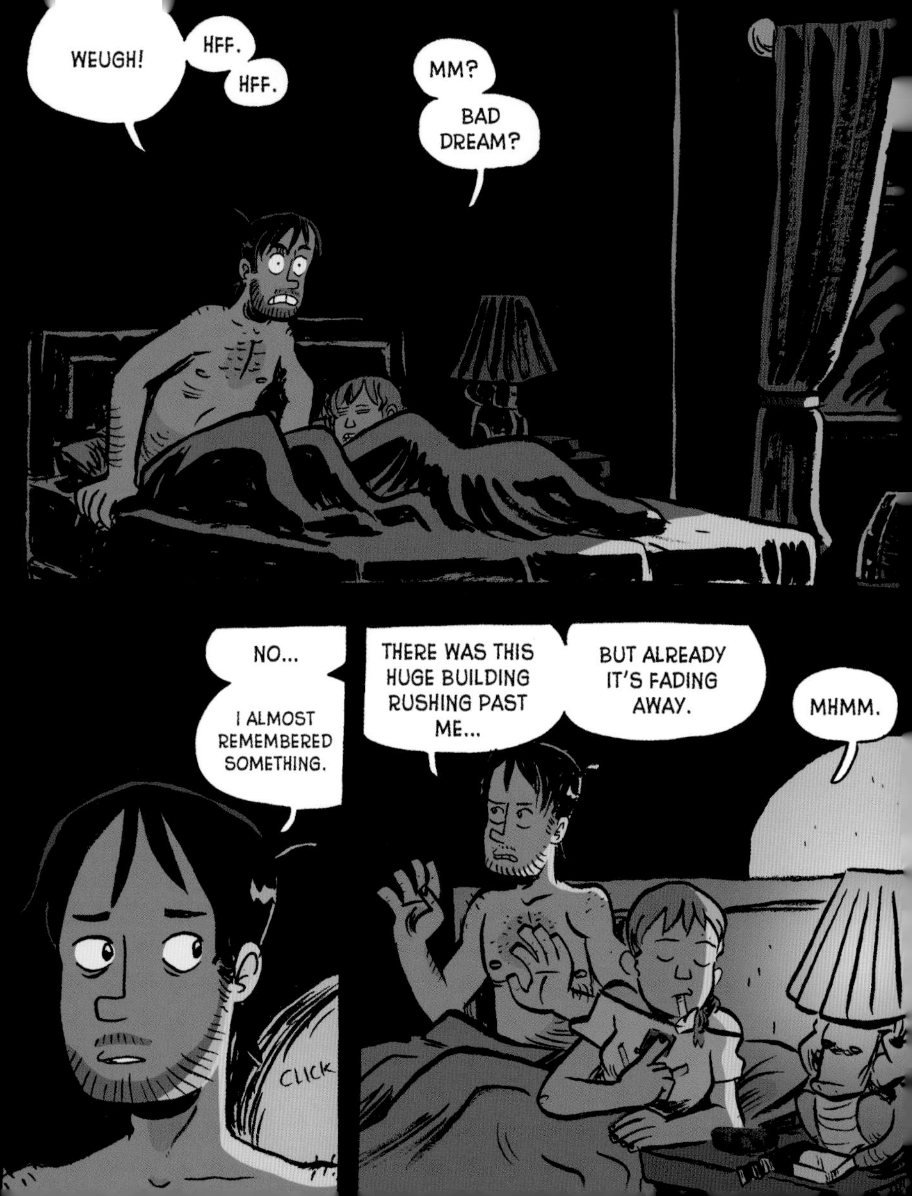
WEUGH!
HFF.
HFF.
MM?
BAD DREAM?
NO...
I ALMOST REMEMBERED SOMETHING.
CLICK
THERE WAS THIS HUGE BUILDING RUSHING PAST ME...
BUT ALREADY IT'S FADING AWAY.
MHMM.

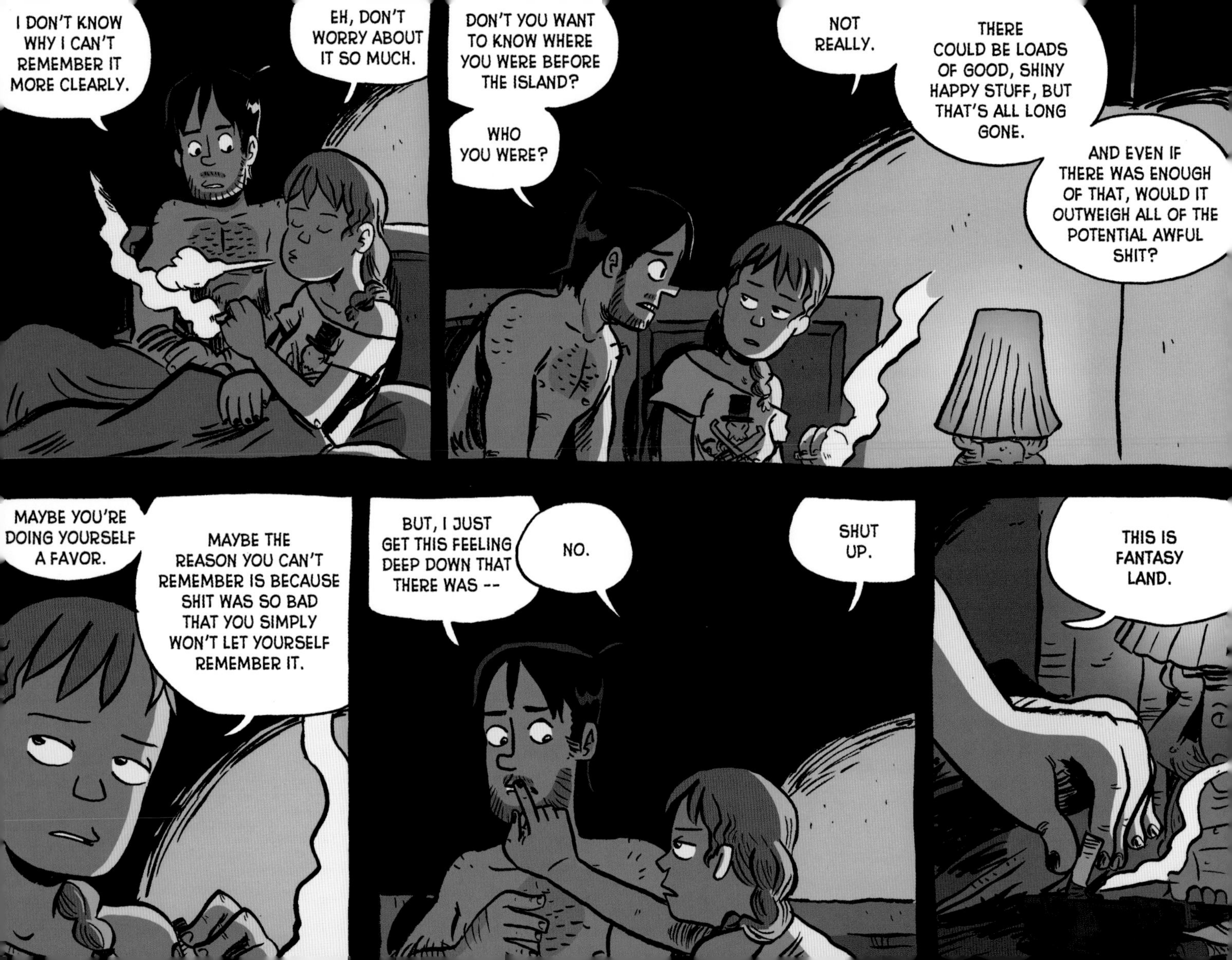
I DON'T KNOW WHY I CAN'T REMEMBER IT MORE CLEARLY.
EH, DON'T WORRY ABOUT IT SO MUCH.
DON'T YOU WANT TO KNOW WHERE YOU WERE BEFORE THE ISLAND?
WHO YOU WERE?
NOT REALLY.
THERE COULD BE LOADS OF GOOD, SHINY HAPPY STUFF, BUT THAT'S ALL LONG GONE.
AND EVEN IF THERE WAS ENOUGH OF THAT, WOULD IT OUTWEIGH ALL OF THE POTENTIAL AWFUL SHIT?
MAYBE YOU'RE DOING YOURSELF A FAVOR.
MAYBE THE REASON YOU CAN'T REMEMBER IS BECAUSE SHIT WAS SO BAD THAT YOU SIMPLY WON'T LET YOURSELF REMEMBER IT.
BUT, I JUST GET THIS FEELING DEEP DOWN THAT THERE WAS --
NO.
SHUT UP.
THIS IS FANTASY LAND.

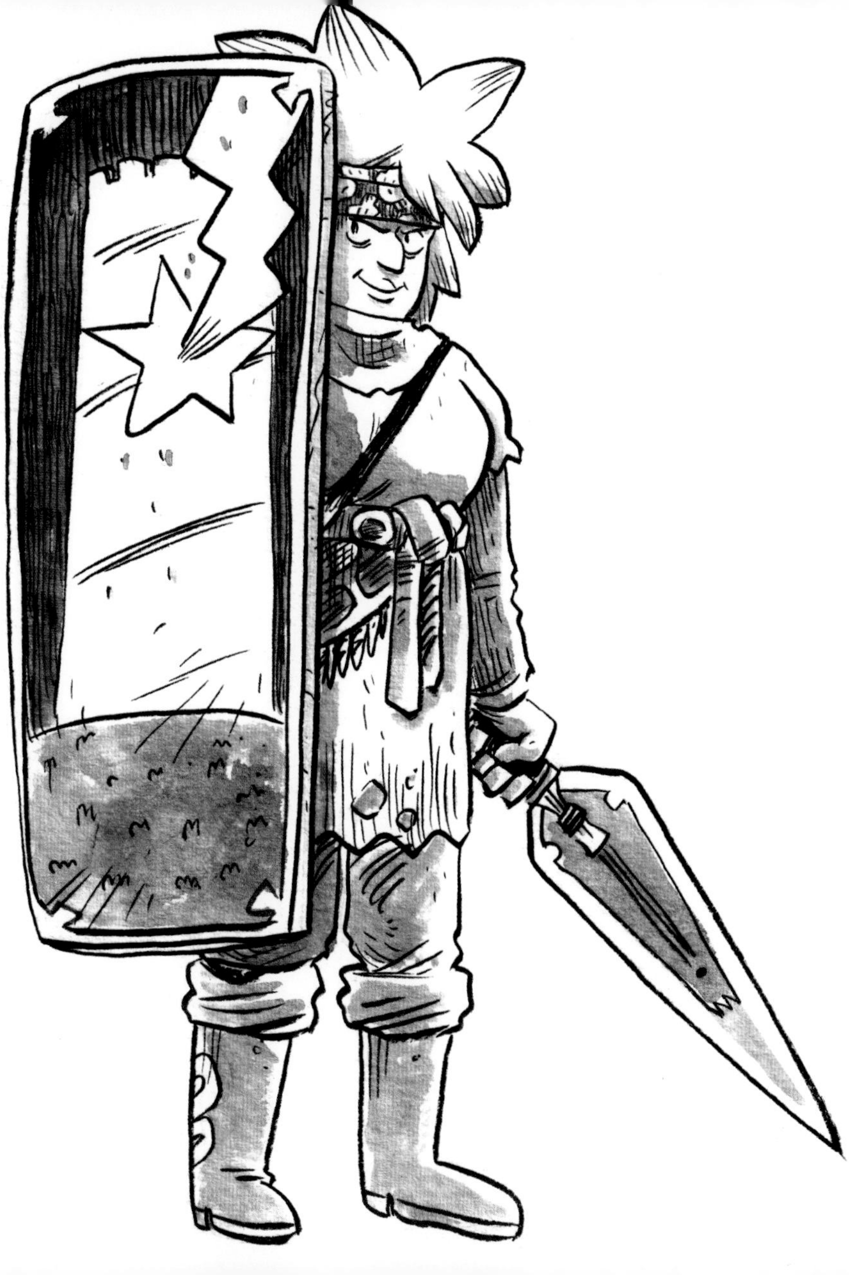

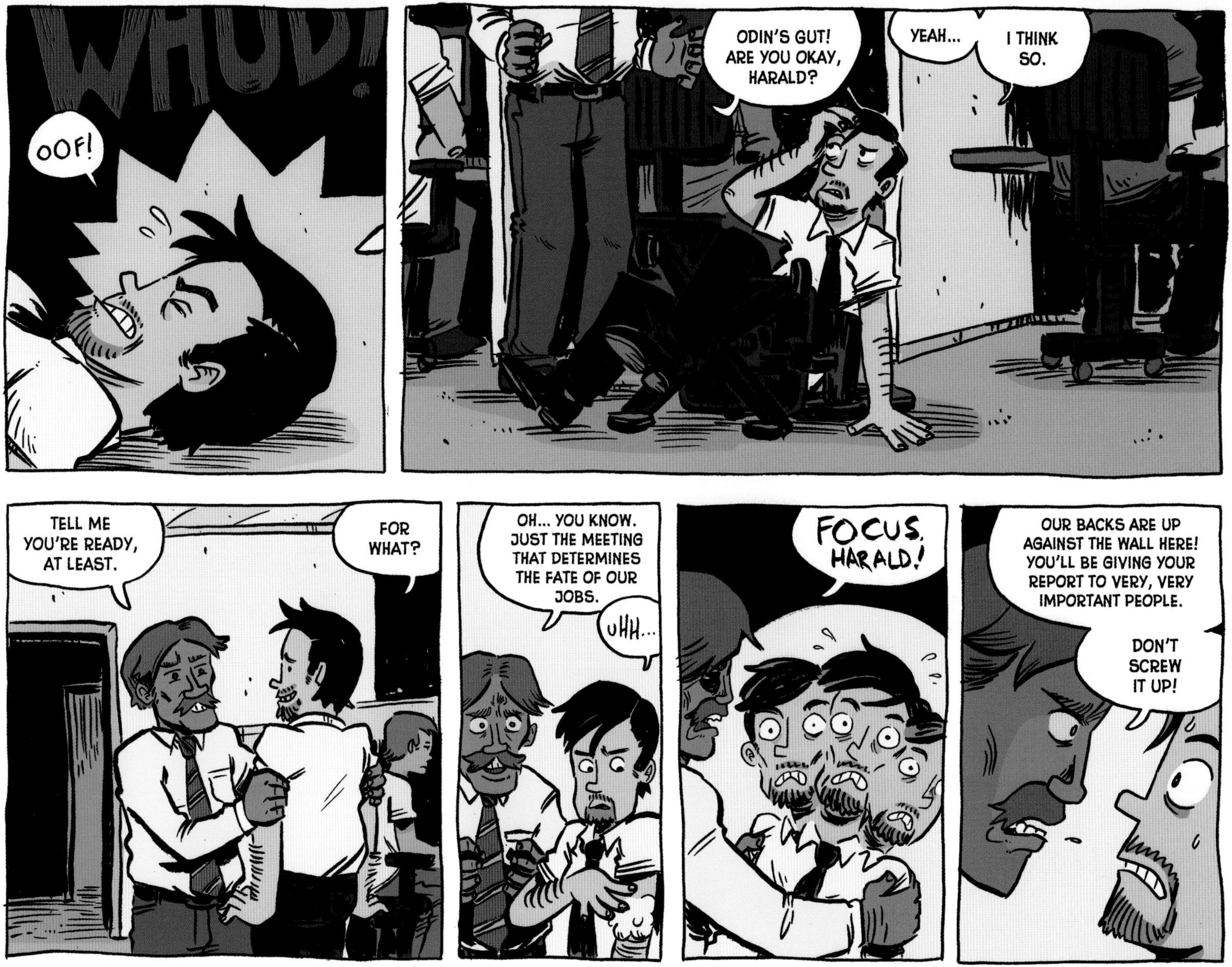
WHUD!
OOF!
ODIN'S GUT! ARE YOU OKAY, HARALD?
YEAH...
I THINK SO.
TELL ME YOU'RE READY, AT LEAST.
FOR WHAT?
OH... YOU KNOW. JUST THE MEETING THAT DETERMINES THE FATE OF OUR JOBS.
UHH...
FOCUS, HARALD!
OUR BACKS ARE UP AGAINST THE WALL HERE! YOU'LL BE GIVING YOUR REPORT TO VERY, VERY IMPORTANT PEOPLE.
DON'T SCREW IT UP!

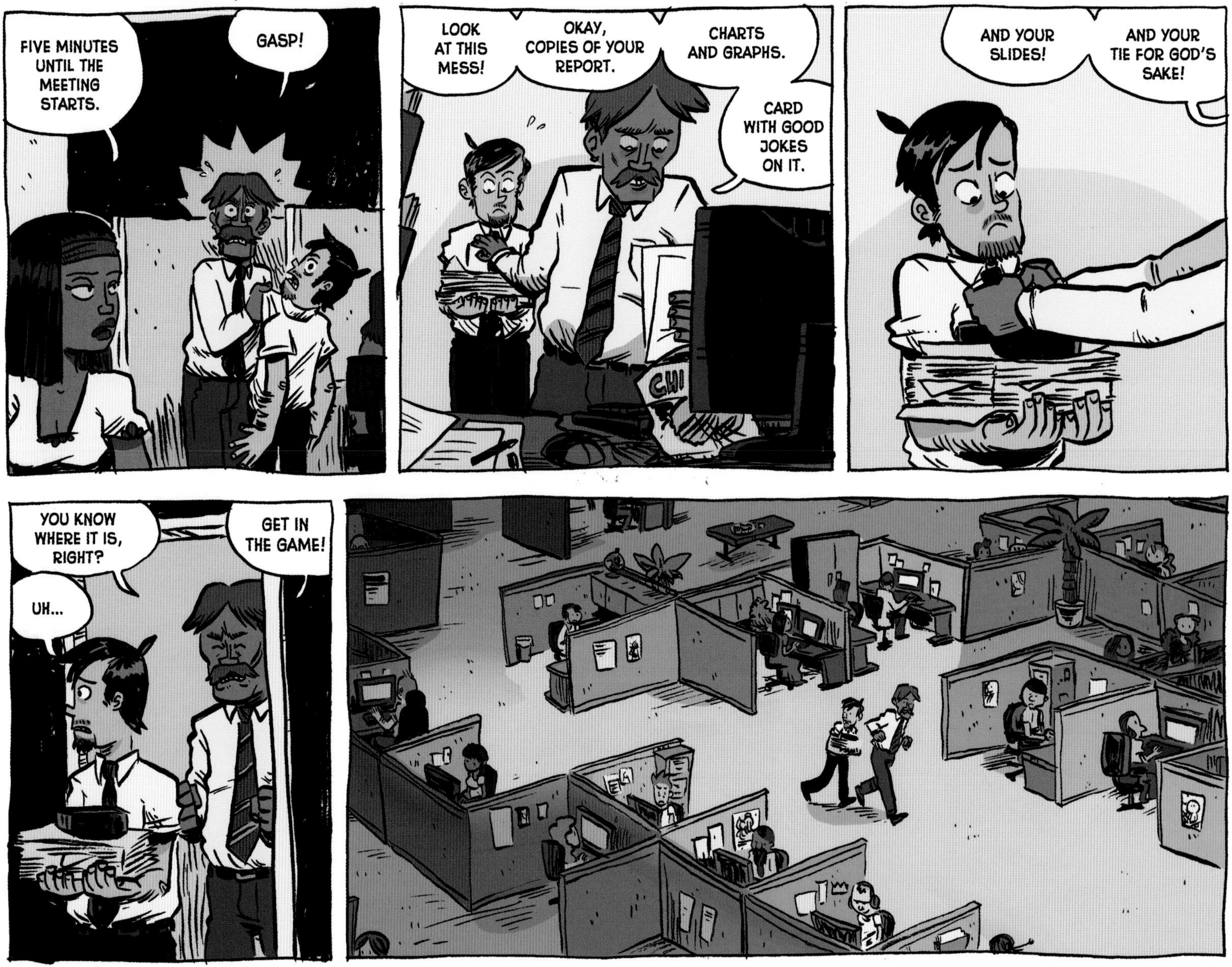
FIVE MINUTES UNTIL THE MEETING STARTS.
GASP!
LOOK AT THIS MESS!
OKAY, COPIES OF YOUR REPORT.
CHARTS AND GRAPHS.
CARD WITH GOOD JOKES ON IT.
AND YOUR SLIDES!
AND YOUR TIE FOR GOD'S SAKE!
YOU KNOW WHERE IT IS, RIGHT?
GET IN THE GAME!
UH...

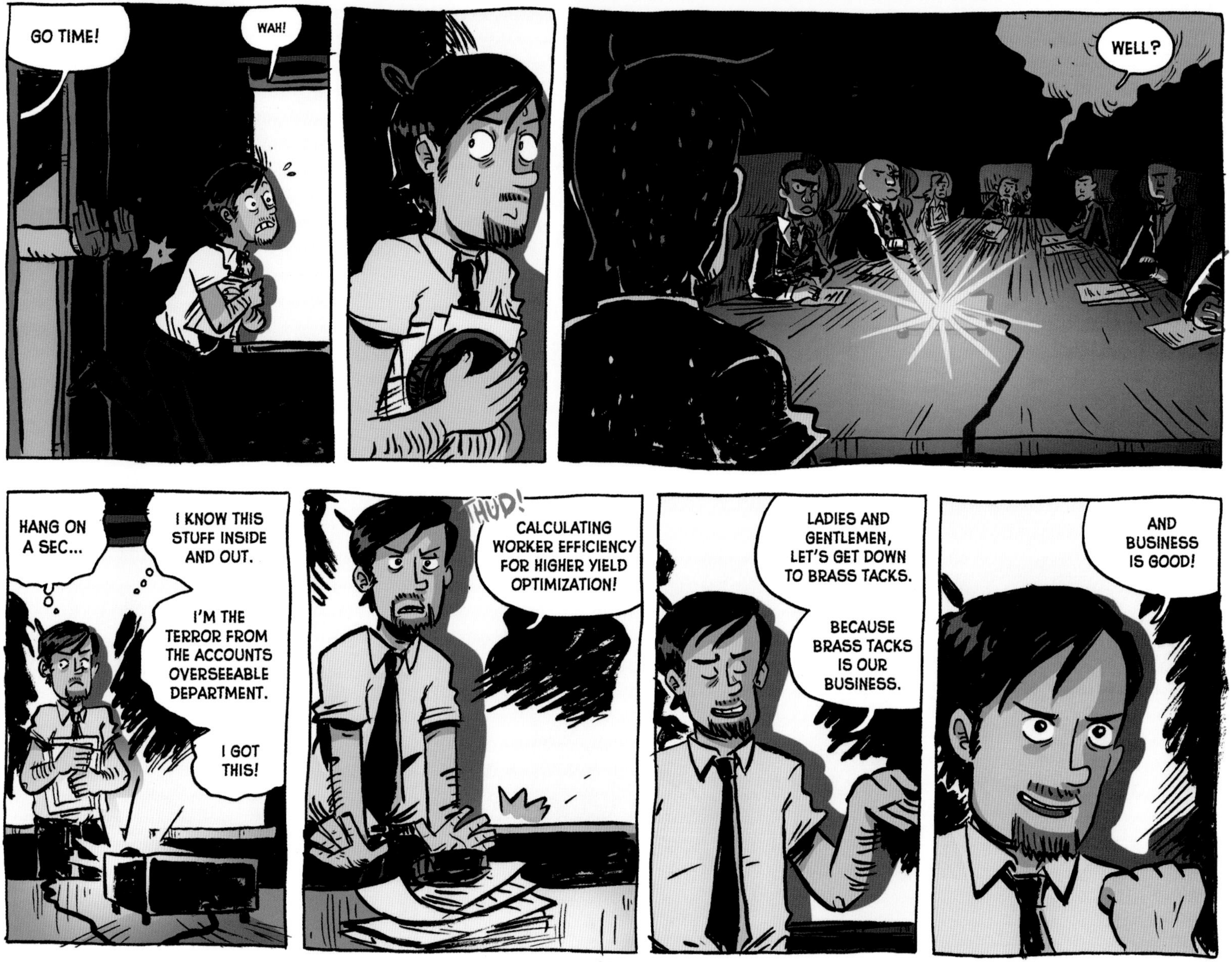
GO TIME!
WAH!
WELL?
HANG ON A SEC...
I KNOW THIS STUFF INSIDE AND OUT.
I'M THE TERROR FROM THE ACCOUNTS OVERSEEABLE DEPARTMENT.
I GOT THIS!
THUD!
CALCULATING WORKER EFFICIENCY FOR HIGHER YIELD OPTIMIZATION!
LADIES AND GENTLEMEN, LET'S GET DOWN TO BRASS TACKS.
BECAUSE BRASS TACKS IS OUR BUSINESS.
AND BUSINESS IS GOOD!

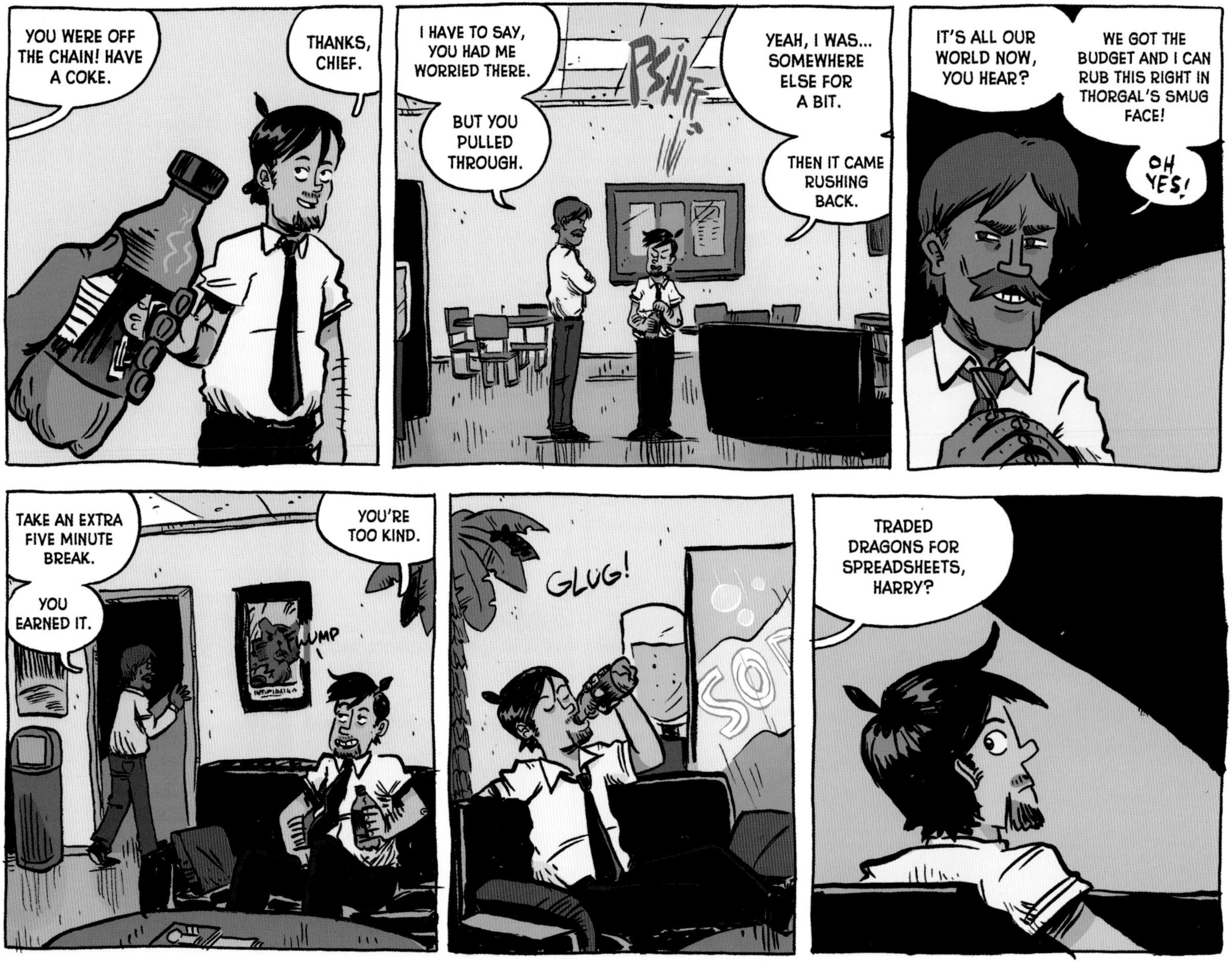
YOU WERE OFF THE CHAIN! HAVE A COKE.
THANKS, CHIEF.
I HAVE TO SAY, YOU HAD ME WORRIED THERE.
BUT YOU PULLED THROUGH.
PSHFF
YEAH, I WAS... SOMEWHERE ELSE FOR A BIT.
THEN IT CAME RUSHING BACK.
IT'S ALL OUR WORLD NOW, YOU HEAR?
WE GOT THE BUDGET AND I CAN RUB THIS RIGHT IN THORGAL'S SMUG FACE!
OH YES!
TAKE AN EXTRA FIVE MINUTE BREAK.
YOU EARNED IT.
YOU'RE TOO KIND.
FWUMP
GLUG!
TRADED DRAGONS FOR SPREADSHEETS, HARRY?

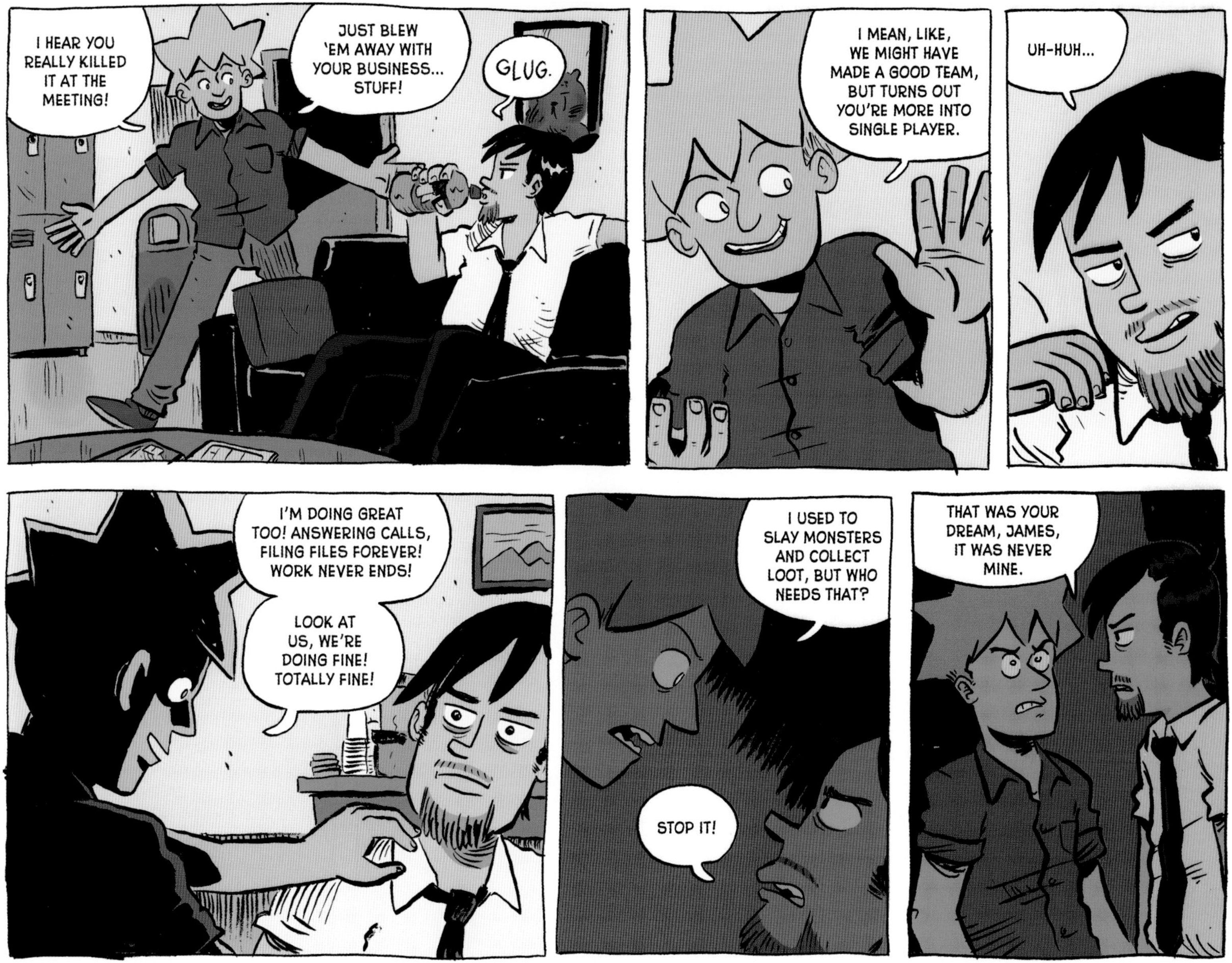
I HEAR YOU REALLY KILLED IT AT THE MEETING!
JUST BLEW 'EM AWAY WITH YOUR BUSINESS... STUFF!
GLUG.
I MEAN, LIKE, WE MIGHT HAVE MADE A GOOD TEAM, BUT TURNS OUT YOU'RE MORE INTO SINGLE PLAYER.
UH-HUH...
I'M DOING GREAT TOO! ANSWERING CALLS, FILING FILES FOREVER! WORK NEVER ENDS!
LOOK AT US, WE'RE DOING FINE! TOTALLY FINE!
I USED TO SLAY MONSTERS AND COLLECT LOOT, BUT WHO NEEDS THAT?
STOP IT!
THAT WAS YOUR DREAM, JAMES, IT WAS NEVER MINE.

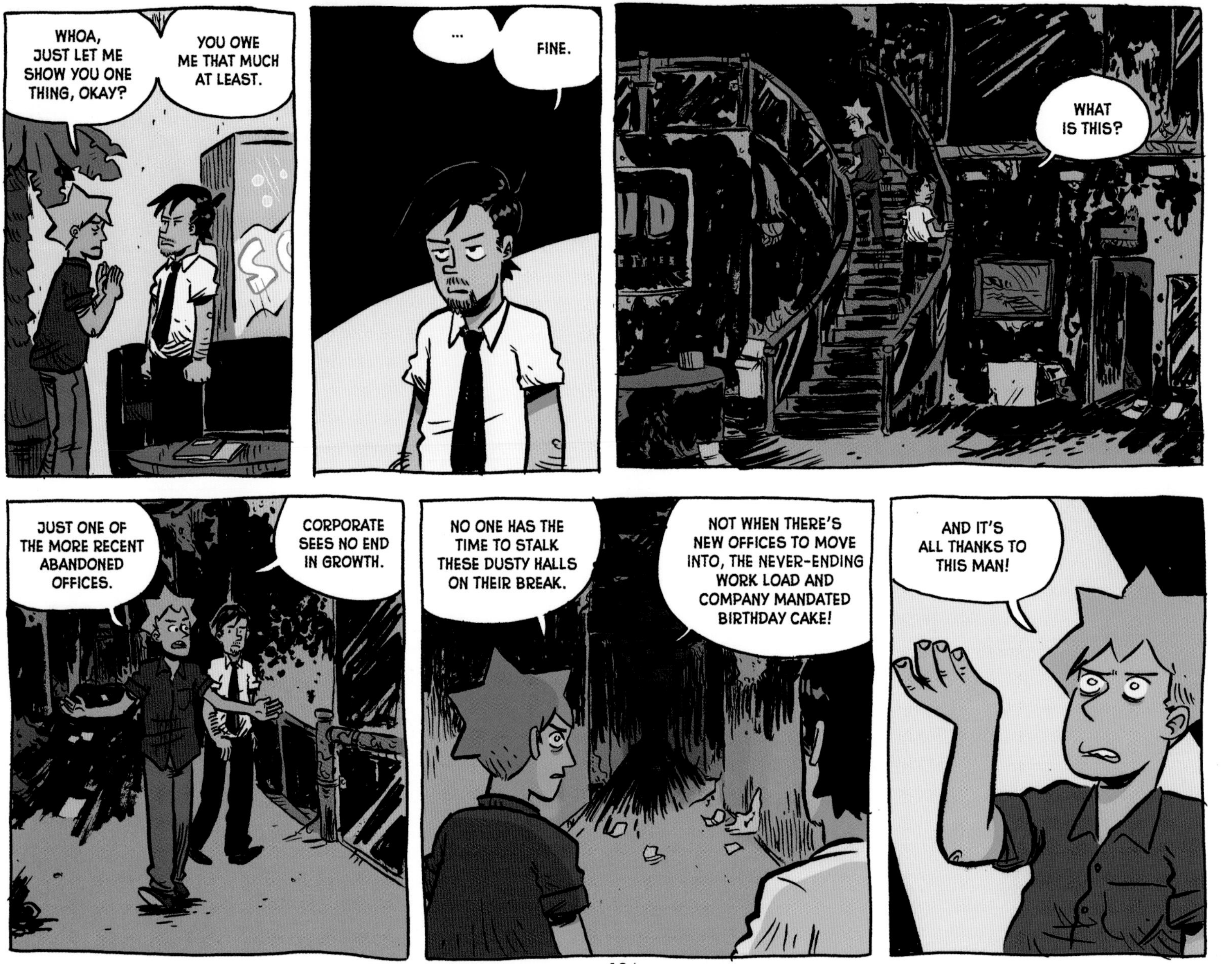
WHOA, JUST LET ME SHOW YOU ONE THING, OKAY?
YOU OWE ME THAT MUCH AT LEAST.
...
FINE.
WHAT IS THIS?
JUST ONE OF THE MORE RECENT ABANDONED OFFICES.
CORPORATE SEES NO END IN GROWTH.
NO ONE HAS THE TIME TO STALK THESE DUSTY HALLS ON THEIR BREAK.
NOT WHEN THERE'S NEW OFFICES TO MOVE INTO, THE NEVER-ENDING WORK LOAD AND COMPANY MANDATED BIRTHDAY CAKE!
AND IT'S ALL THANKS TO THIS MAN!

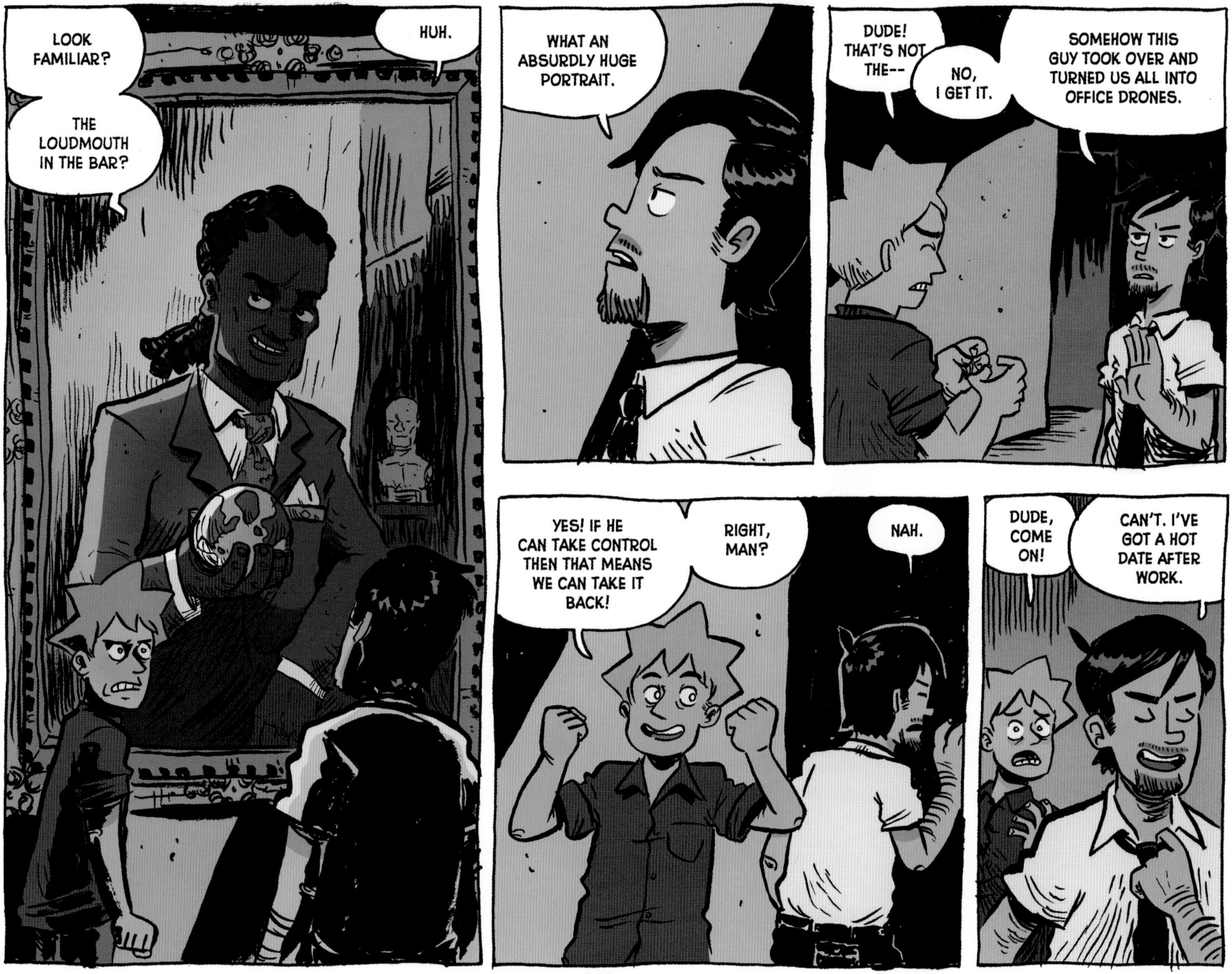
LOOK FAMILIAR?
THE LOUDMOUTH IN THE BAR?
HUH.
WHAT AN ABSURDLY HUGE PORTRAIT.
DUDE! THAT'S NOT THE--
NO, I GET IT.
SOMEHOW THIS GUY TOOK OVER AND TURNED US ALL INTO OFFICE DRONES.
YES! IF HE CAN TAKE CONTROL THEN THAT MEANS WE CAN TAKE IT BACK!
RIGHT, MAN?
NAH.
DUDE, COME ON!
CAN'T. I'VE GOT A HOT DATE AFTER WORK.

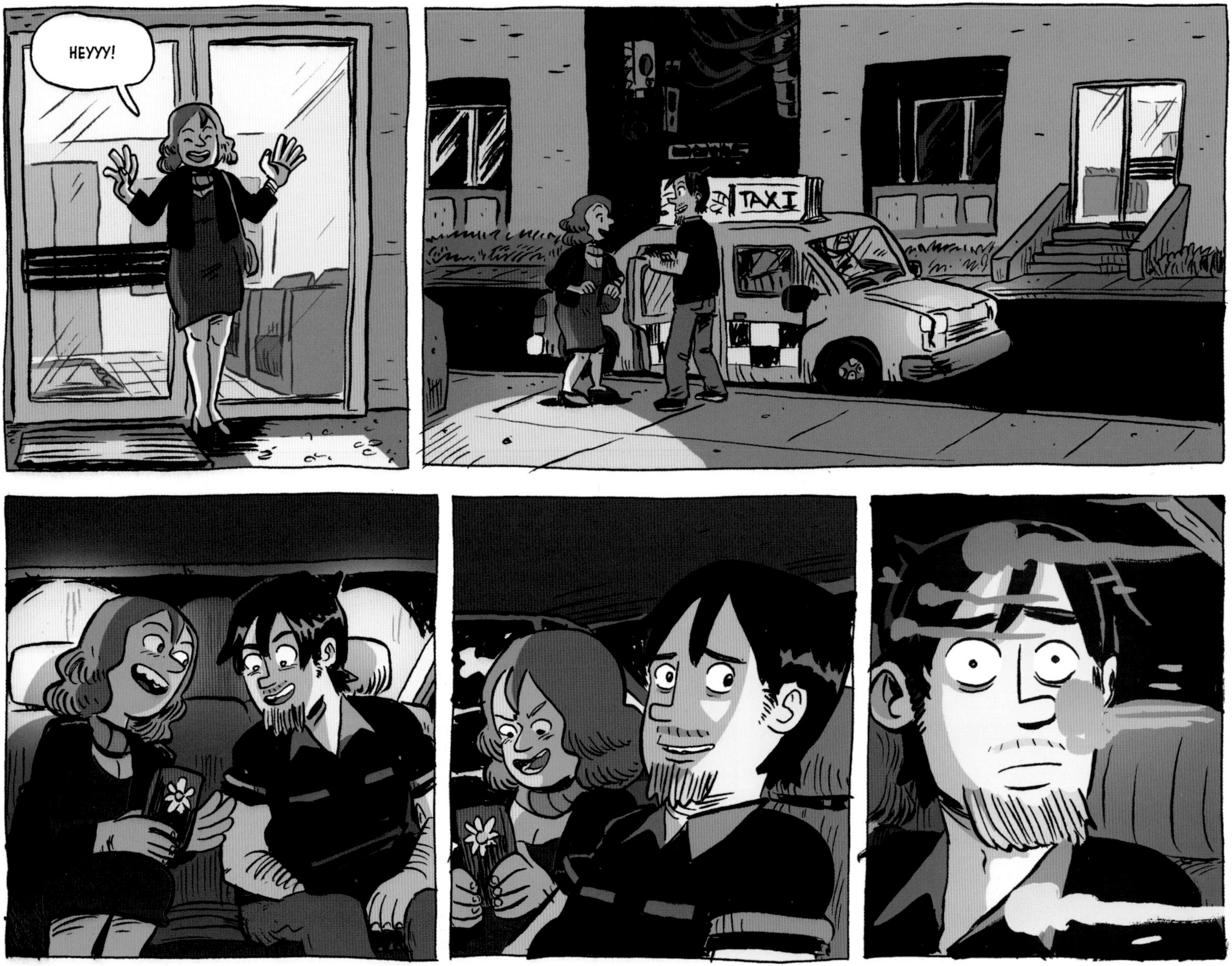
HEYYY!
TAXI

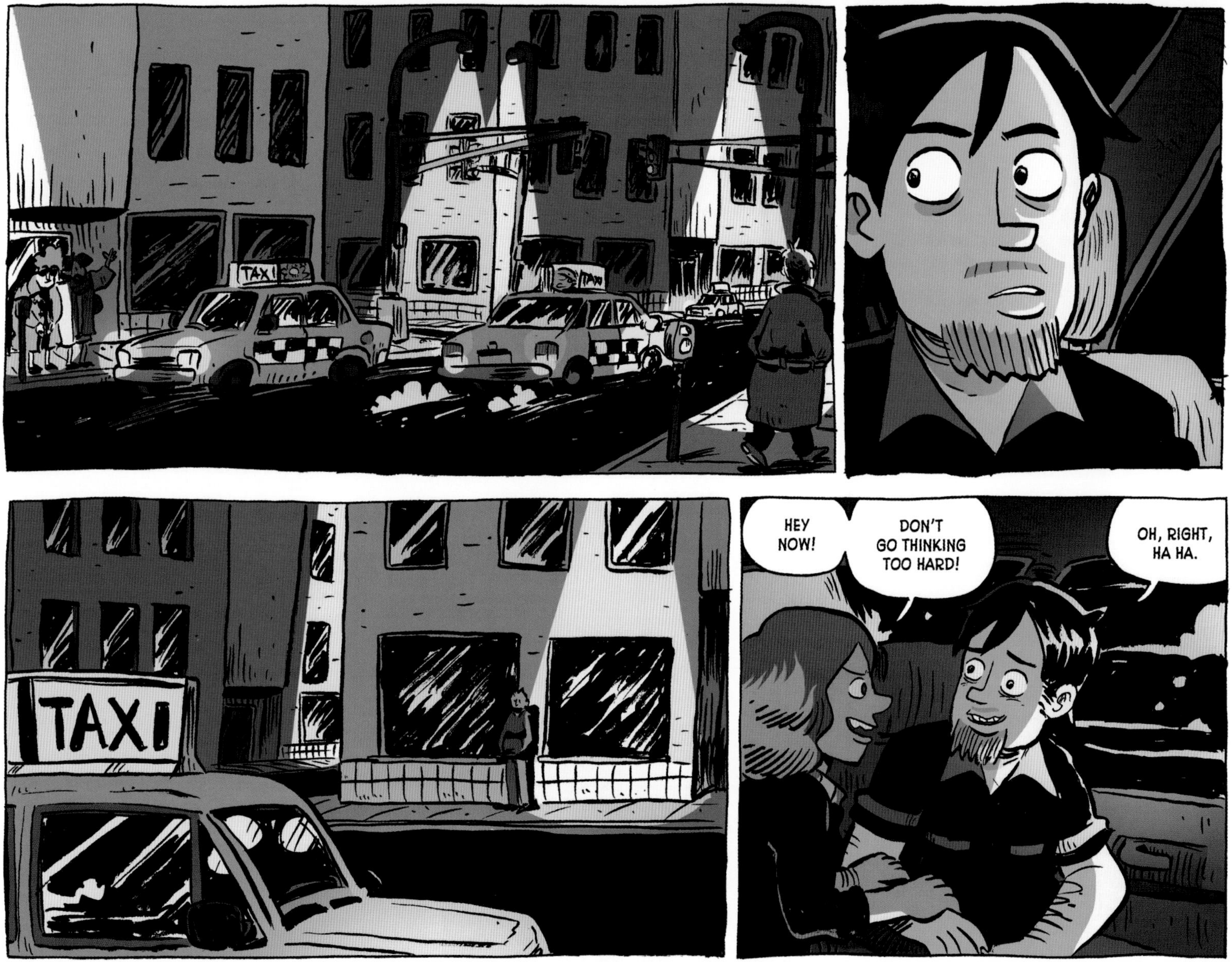
TAXI
TAXI
HEY NOW!
DON'T GO THINKING TOO HARD!
OH, RIGHT, HA HA.

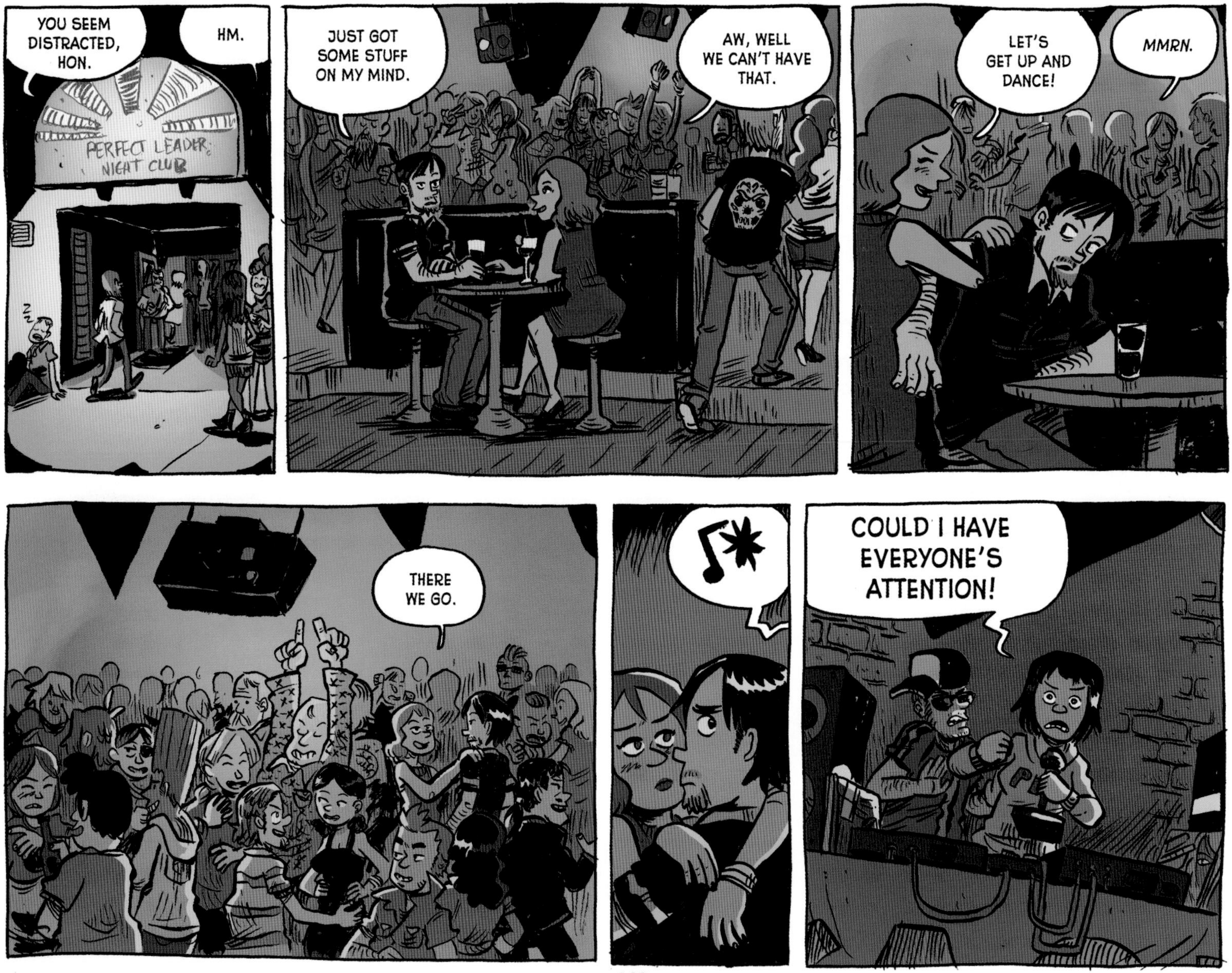
YOU SEEM DISTRACTED, HON.
HM.
PERFECT LEADER NIGHT CLUB
JUST GOT SOME STUFF ON MY MIND.
AW, WELL WE CAN'T HAVE THAT.
LET'S GET UP AND DANCE!
MMRN.
THERE WE GO.
COULD I HAVE EVERYONE'S ATTENTION!

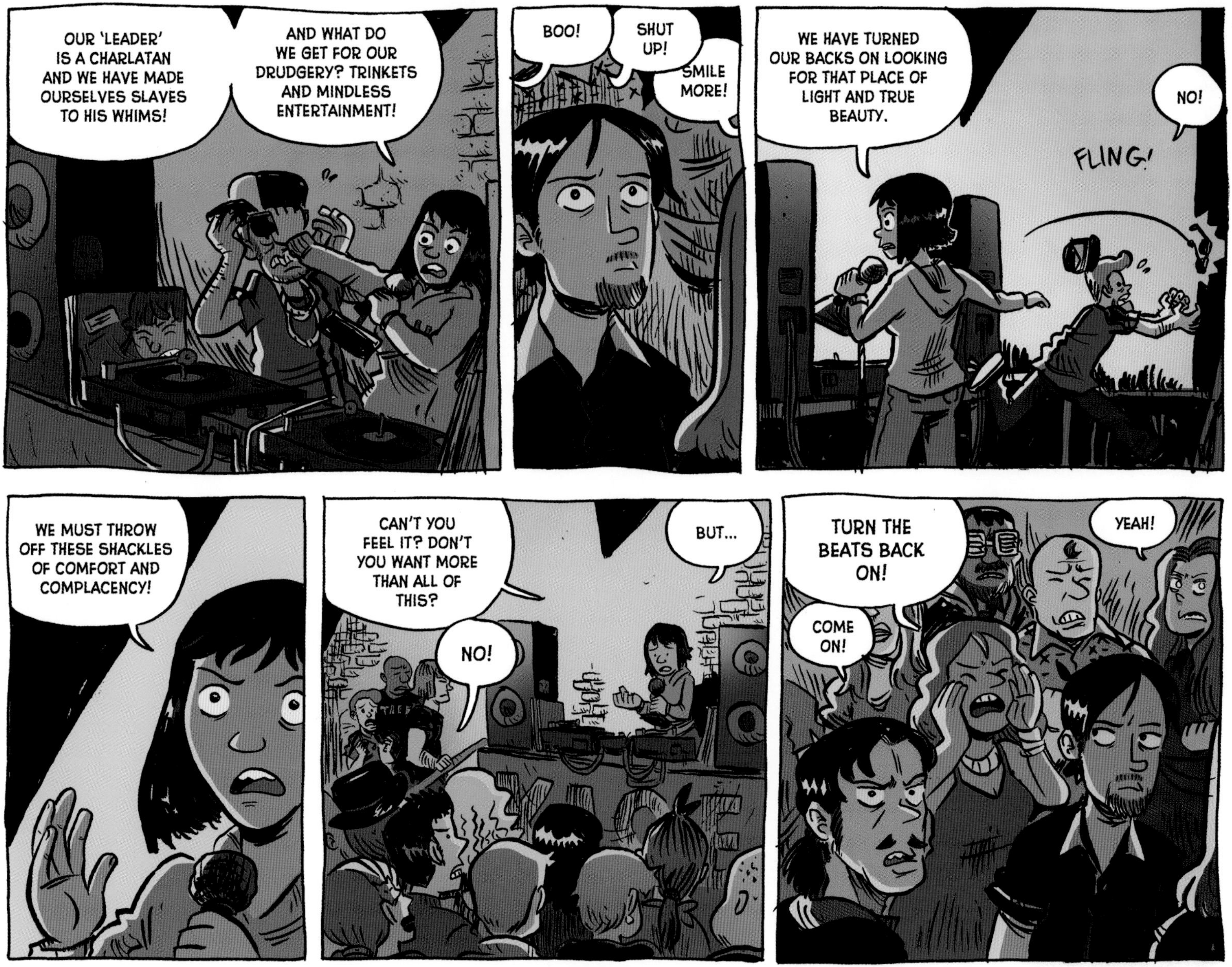
OUR 'LEADER' IS A CHARLATAN AND WE HAVE MADE OURSELVES SLAVES TO HIS WHIMS!
AND WHAT DO WE GET FOR OUR DRUDGERY? TRINKETS AND MINDLESS ENTERTAINMENT!
BOO!
SHUT UP!
SMILE MORE!
WE HAVE TURNED OUR BACKS ON LOOKING FOR THAT PLACE OF LIGHT AND TRUE BEAUTY.
NO!
FLING!
WE MUST THROW OFF THESE SHACKLES OF COMFORT AND COMPLACENCY!
CAN'T YOU FEEL IT? DON'T YOU WANT MORE THAN ALL OF THIS?
BUT...
NO!
TURN THE BEATS BACK ON!
YEAH!
COME ON!

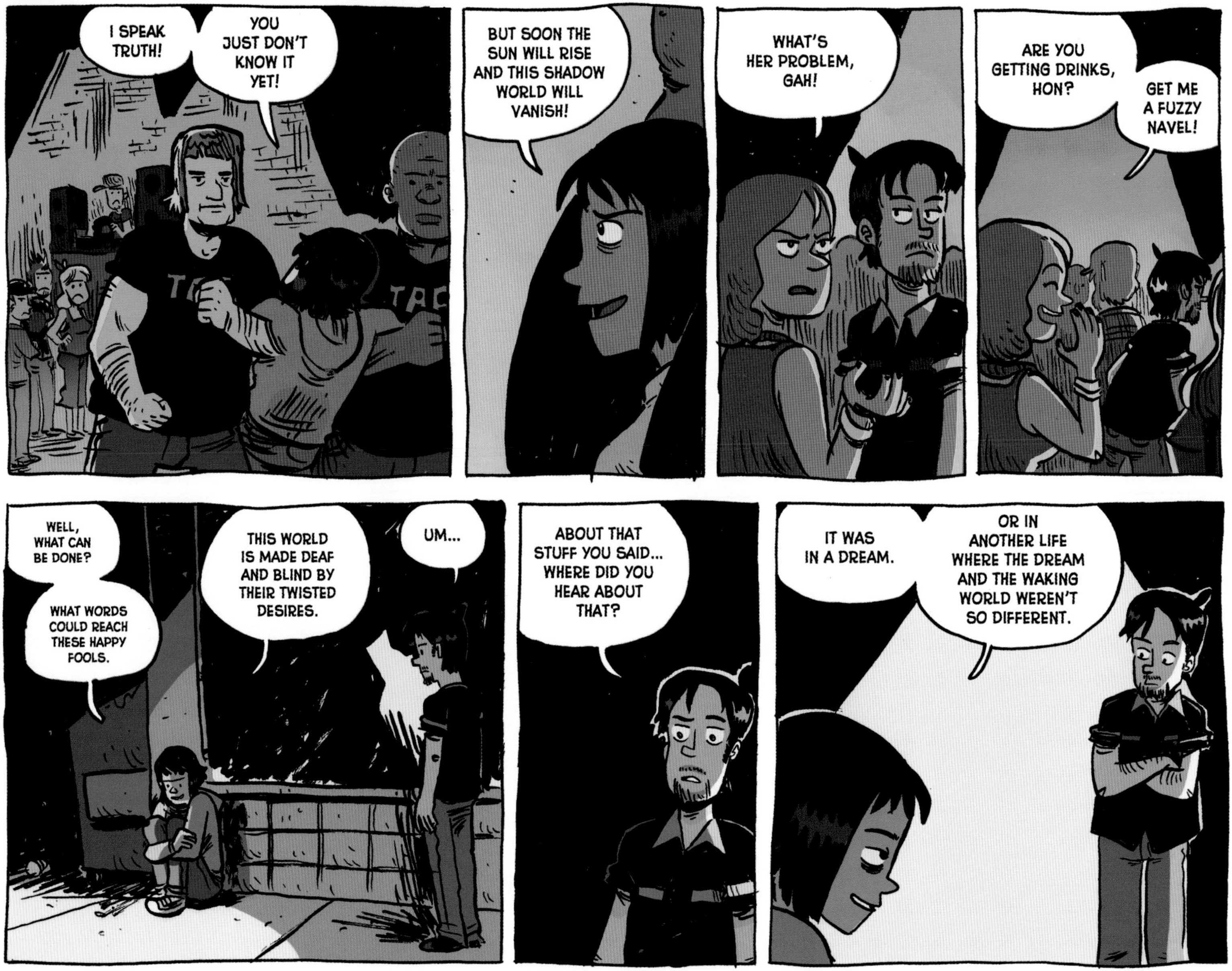
I SPEAK TRUTH!
YOU JUST DON'T KNOW IT YET!
BUT SOON THE SUN WILL RISE AND THIS SHADOW WORLD WILL VANISH!
WHAT'S HER PROBLEM, GAH!
ARE YOU GETTING DRINKS, HON?
GET ME A FUZZY NAVEL!
WELL, WHAT CAN BE DONE?
WHAT WORDS COULD REACH THESE HAPPY FOOLS.
THIS WORLD IS MADE DEAF AND BLIND BY THEIR TWISTED DESIRES.
UM...
ABOUT THAT STUFF YOU SAID... WHERE DID YOU HEAR ABOUT THAT?
IT WAS IN A DREAM.
OR IN ANOTHER LIFE WHERE THE DREAM AND THE WAKING WORLD WEREN'T SO DIFFERENT.

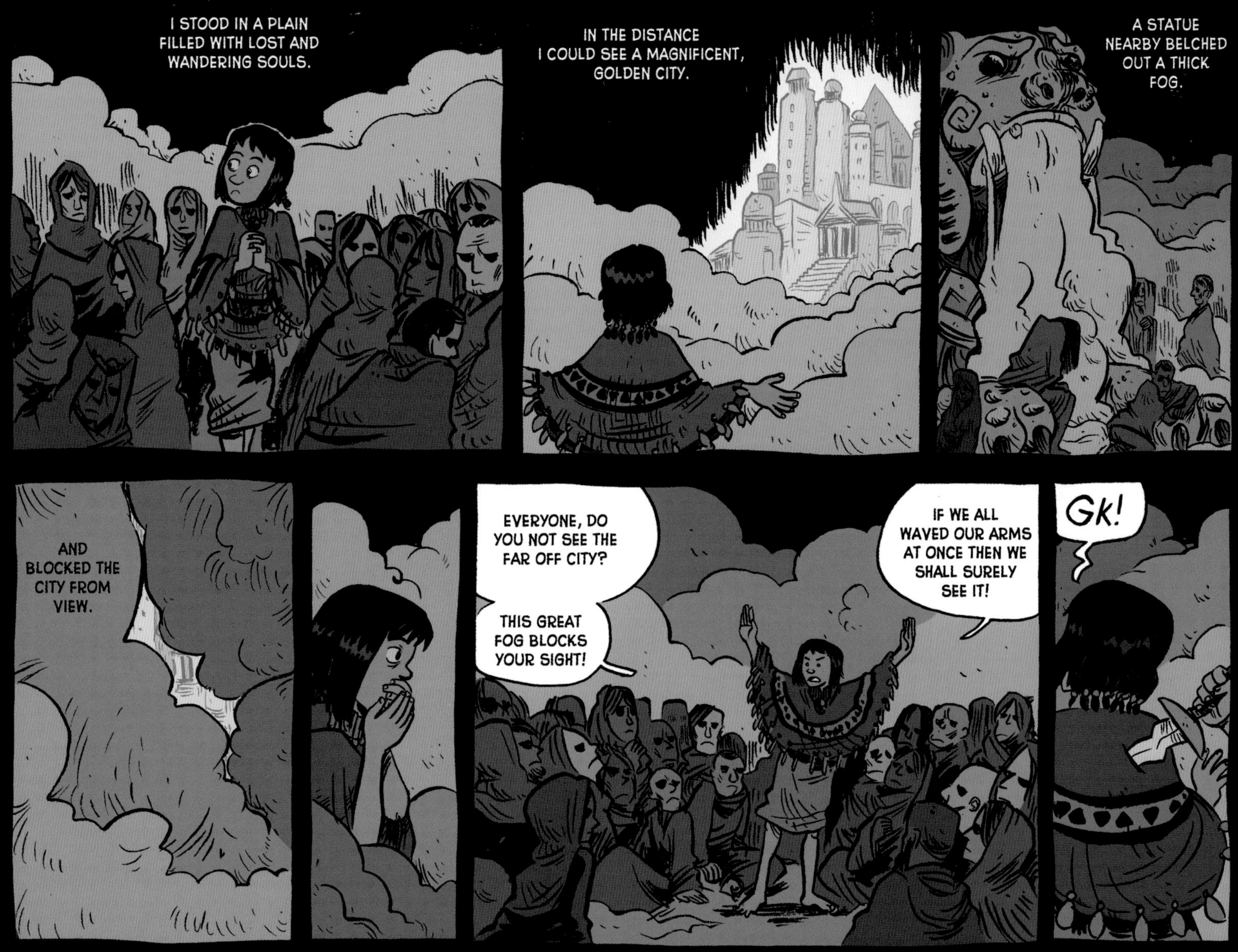
I STOOD IN A PLAIN FILLED WITH LOST AND WANDERING SOULS.
IN THE DISTANCE I COULD SEE A MAGNIFICENT, GOLDEN CITY.
A STATUE NEARBY BELCHED OUT A THICK FOG.
AND BLOCKED THE CITY FROM VIEW.
EVERYONE, DO YOU NOT SEE THE FAR OFF CITY?
THIS GREAT FOG BLOCKS YOUR SIGHT!
IF WE ALL WAVED OUR ARMS AT ONCE THEN WE SHALL SURELY SEE IT!
Gk!

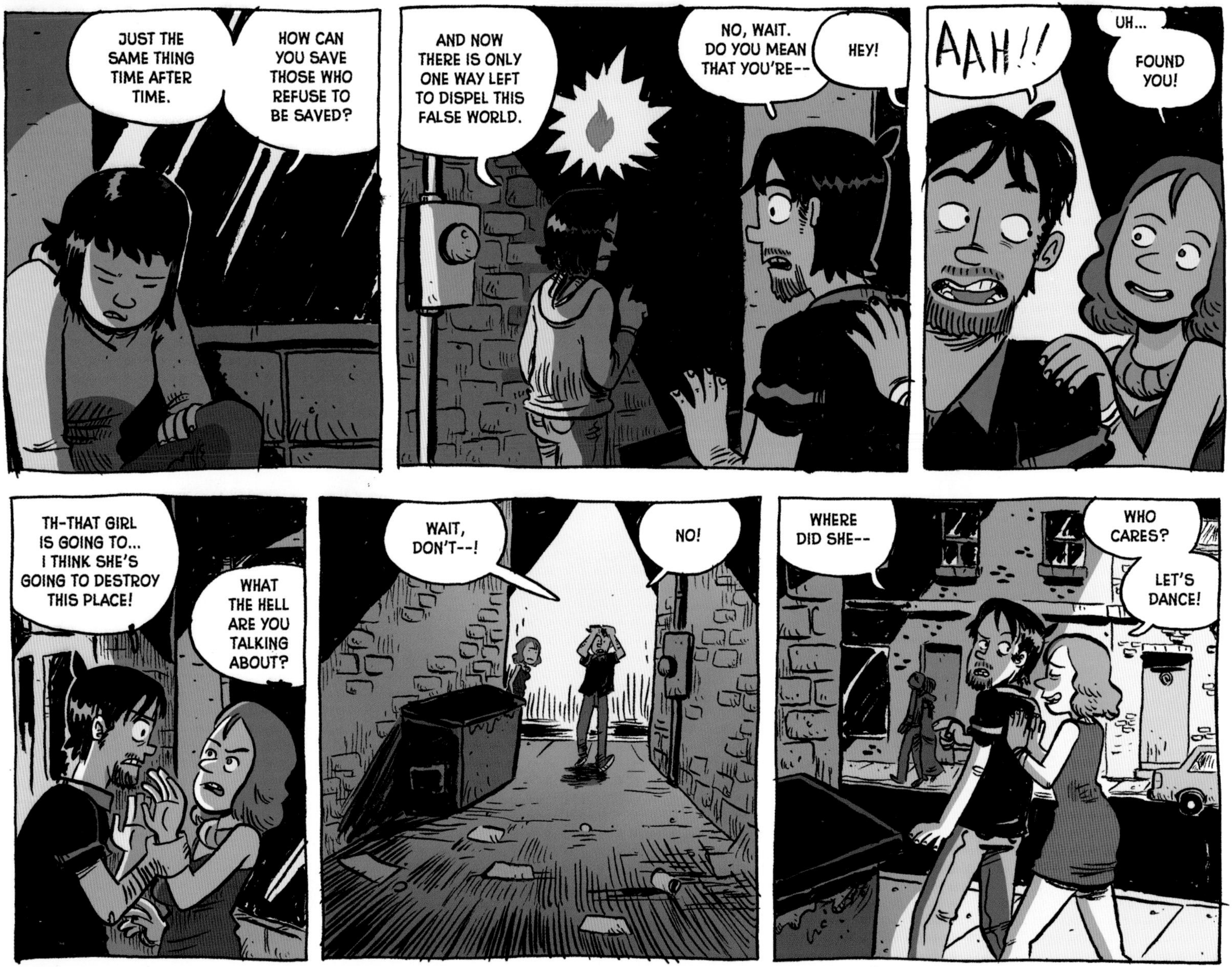
JUST THE SAME THING TIME AFTER TIME.
HOW CAN YOU SAVE THOSE WHO REFUSE TO BE SAVED?
AND NOW THERE IS ONLY ONE WAY LEFT TO DISPEL THIS FALSE WORLD.
NO, WAIT. DO YOU MEAN THAT YOU'RE--
HEY!
AAH!!
UH...
FOUND YOU!
TH-THAT GIRL IS GOING TO... I THINK SHE'S GOING TO DESTROY THIS PLACE!
WHAT THE HELL ARE YOU TALKING ABOUT?
WAIT, DON'T--!
NO!
WHERE DID SHE--
WHO CARES?
LET'S DANCE!

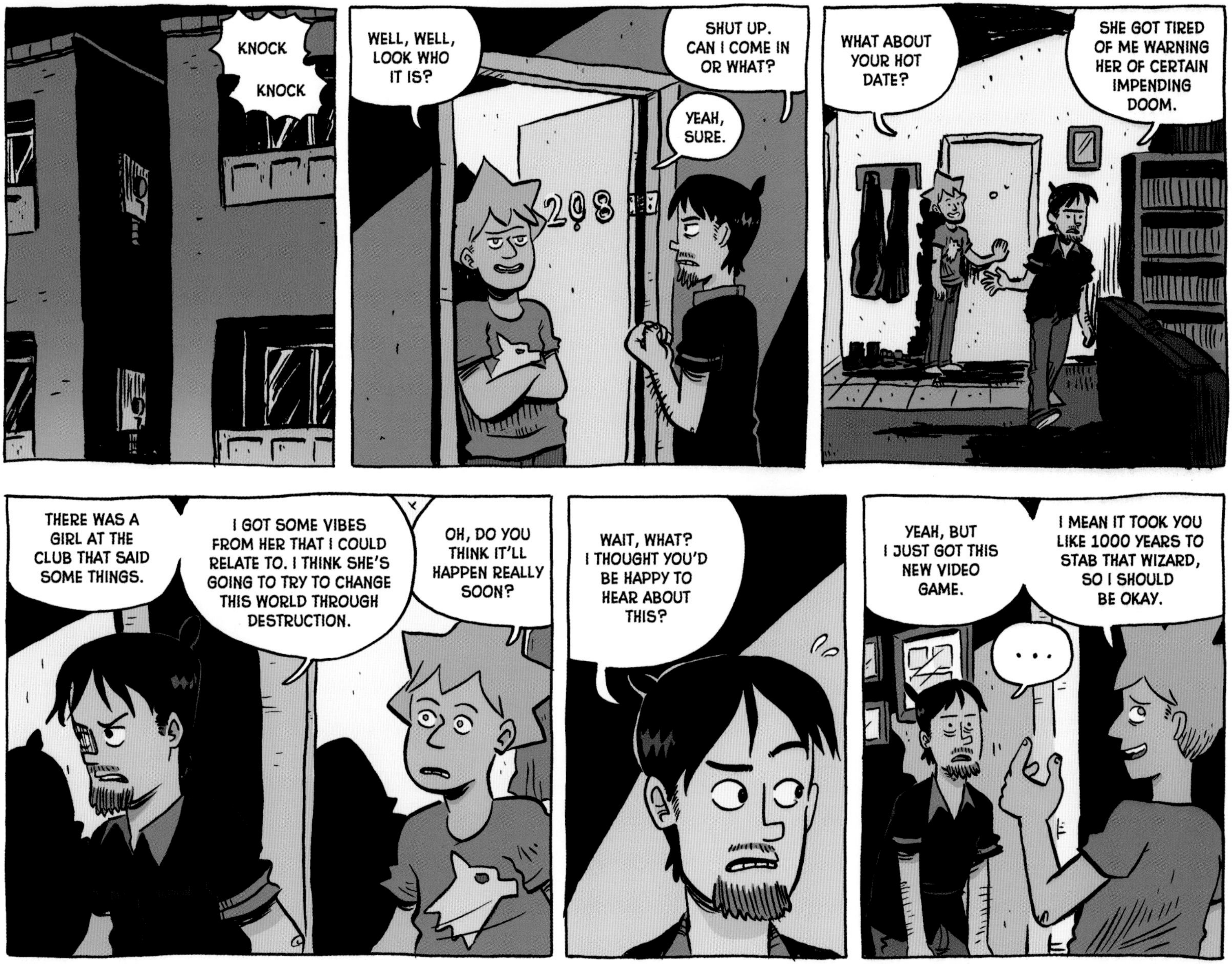
KNOCK
KNOCK
WELL, WELL, LOOK WHO IT IS?
SHUT UP. CAN I COME IN OR WHAT?
YEAH, SURE.
208
WHAT ABOUT YOUR HOT DATE?
SHE GOT TIRED OF ME WARNING HER OF CERTAIN IMPENDING DOOM.
THERE WAS A GIRL AT THE CLUB THAT SAID SOME THINGS.
I GOT SOME VIBES FROM HER THAT I COULD RELATE TO. I THINK SHE'S GOING TO TRY TO CHANGE THIS WORLD THROUGH DESTRUCTION.
OH, DO YOU THINK IT'LL HAPPEN REALLY SOON?
WAIT, WHAT? I THOUGHT YOU'D BE HAPPY TO HEAR ABOUT THIS?
YEAH, BUT I JUST GOT THIS NEW VIDEO GAME.
I MEAN IT TOOK YOU LIKE 1000 YEARS TO STAB THAT WIZARD, SO I SHOULD BE OKAY.
...

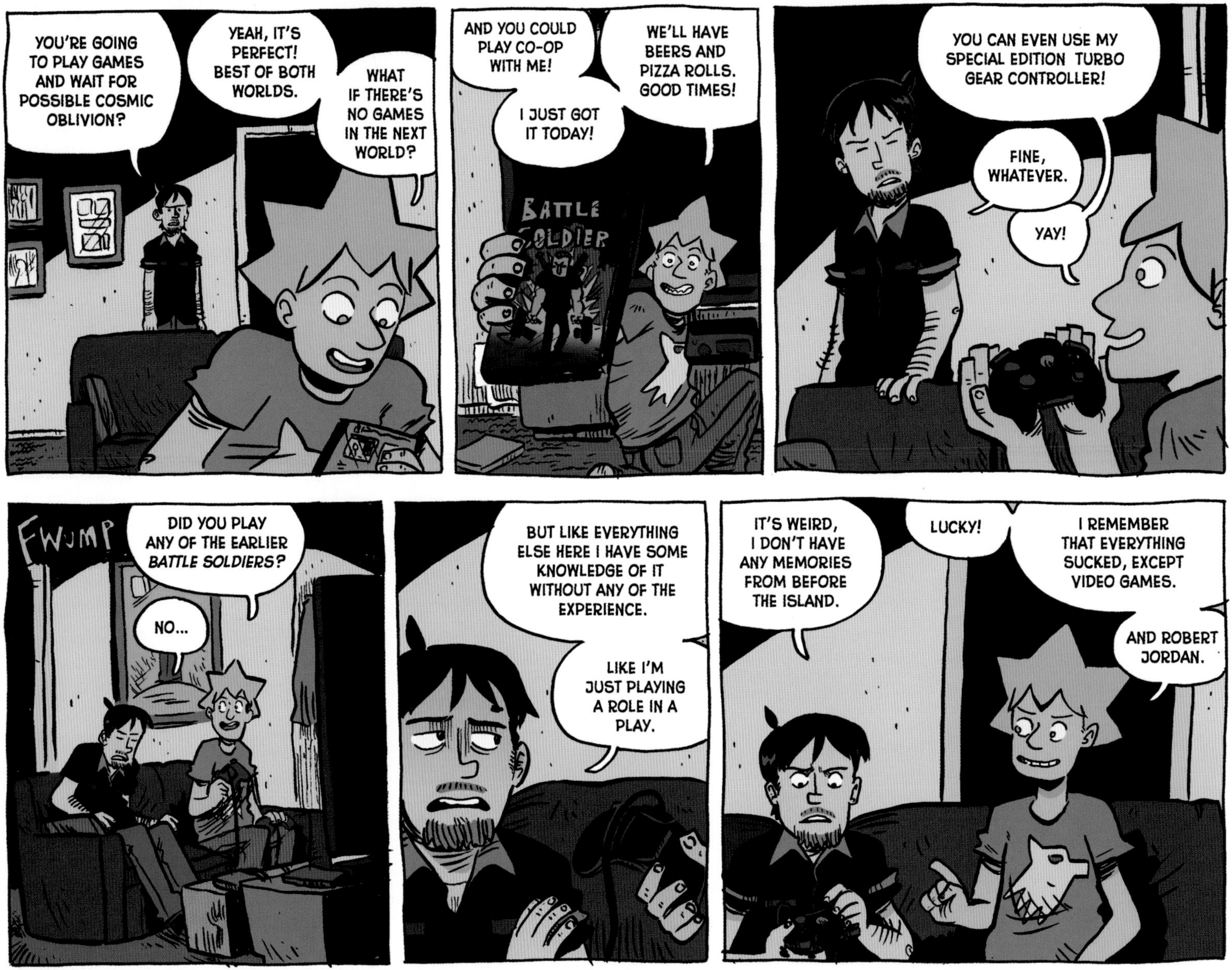
YOU'RE GOING TO PLAY GAMES AND WAIT FOR POSSIBLE COSMIC OBLIVION?
YEAH, IT'S PERFECT! BEST OF BOTH WORLDS.
WHAT IF THERE'S NO GAMES IN THE NEXT WORLD?
AND YOU COULD PLAY CO-OP WITH ME!
I JUST GOT IT TODAY!
WE'LL HAVE BEERS AND PIZZA ROLLS. GOOD TIMES!
BATTLE SOLDIER
YOU CAN EVEN USE MY SPECIAL EDITION TURBO GEAR CONTROLLER!
FINE, WHATEVER.
YAY!
FWUMP
DID YOU PLAY ANY OF THE EARLIER *BATTLE SOLDIERS?*
NO...
BUT LIKE EVERYTHING ELSE HERE I HAVE SOME KNOWLEDGE OF IT WITHOUT ANY OF THE EXPERIENCE.
LIKE I'M JUST PLAYING A ROLE IN A PLAY.
IT'S WEIRD, I DON'T HAVE ANY MEMORIES FROM BEFORE THE ISLAND.
LUCKY!
I REMEMBER THAT EVERYTHING SUCKED, EXCEPT VIDEO GAMES.
AND ROBERT JORDAN.

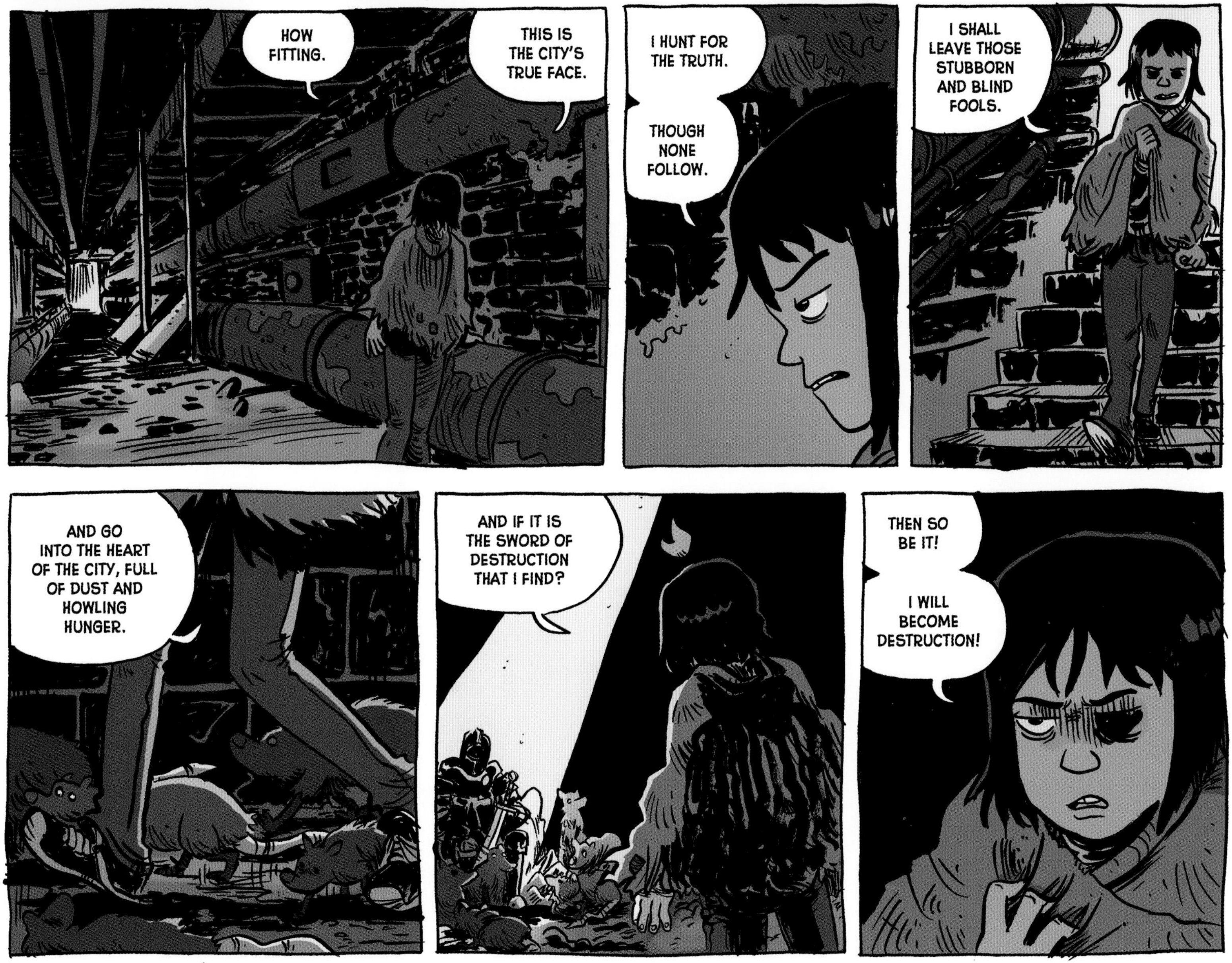
HOW FITTING.
THIS IS THE CITY'S TRUE FACE.
I HUNT FOR THE TRUTH.
THOUGH NONE FOLLOW.
I SHALL LEAVE THOSE STUBBORN AND BLIND FOOLS.
AND GO INTO THE HEART OF THE CITY, FULL OF DUST AND HOWLING HUNGER.
AND IF IT IS THE SWORD OF DESTRUCTION THAT I FIND?
THEN SO BE IT!
I WILL BECOME DESTRUCTION!

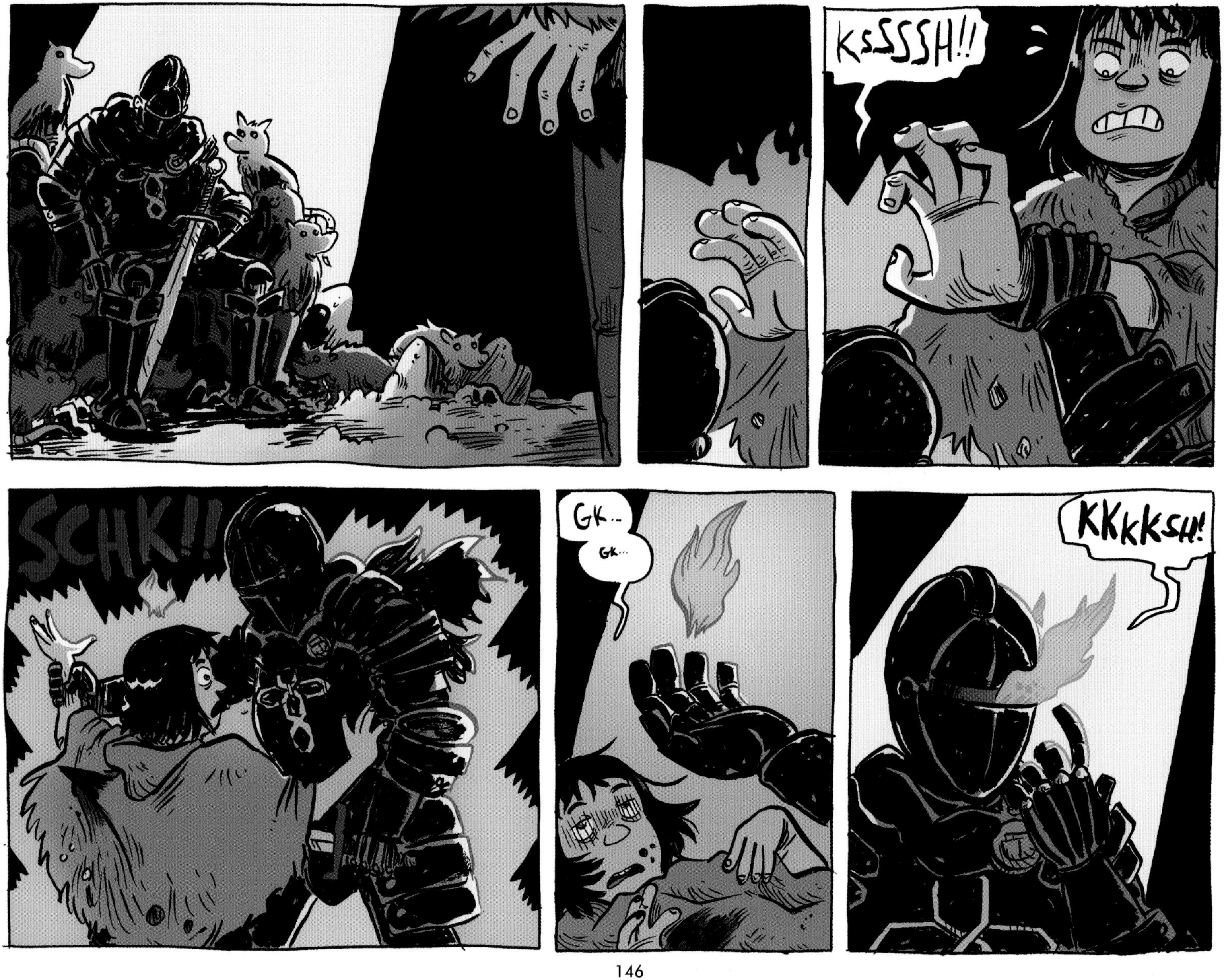
KsSSSSH!!
SCHK!!
GK...
GK...
KKKKSH!

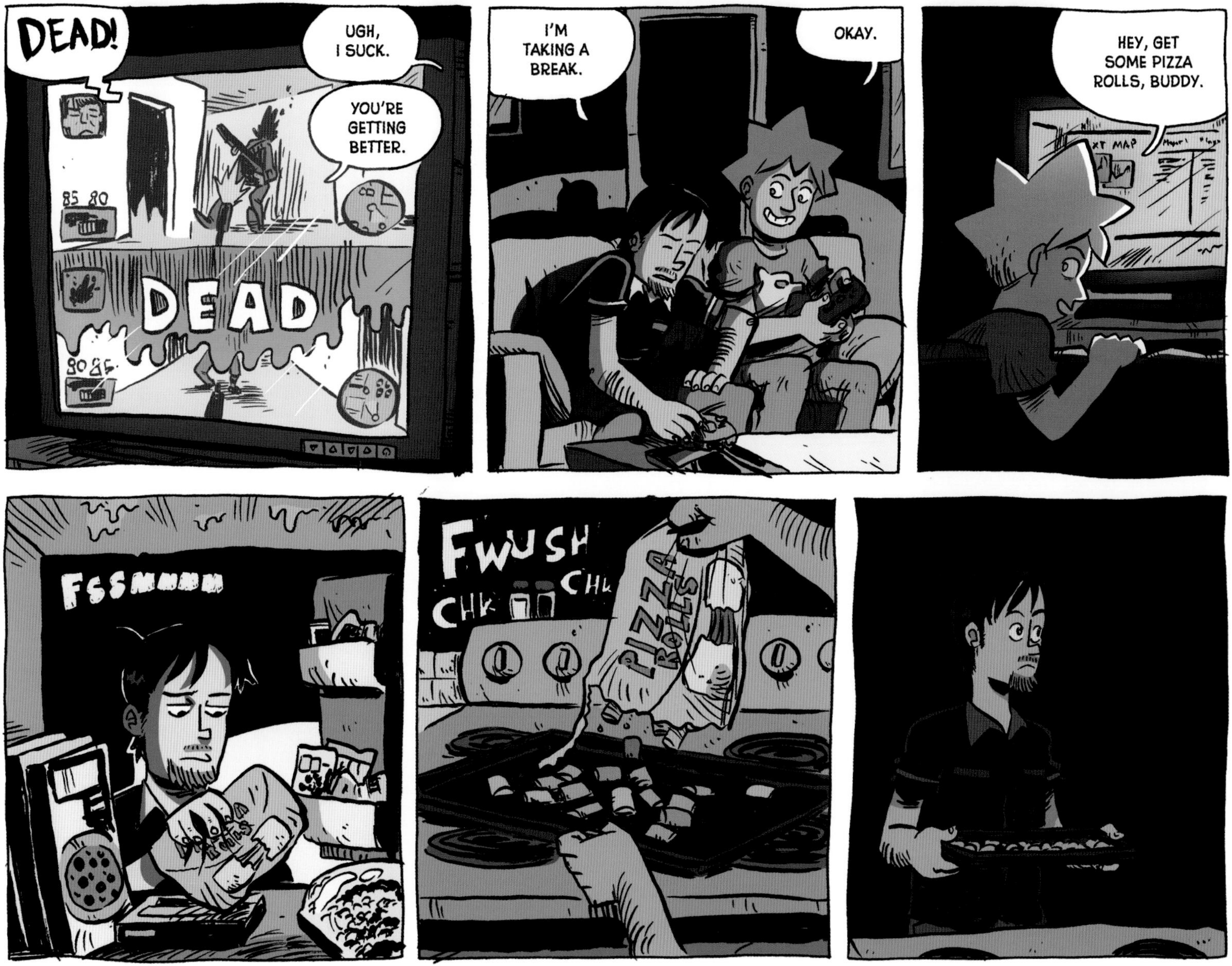
DEAD!
UGH, I SUCK.
YOU'RE GETTING BETTER.
DEAD
I'M TAKING A BREAK.
OKAY.
HEY, GET SOME PIZZA ROLLS, BUDDY.
FWUSH
CHK
PIZZA ROLLS

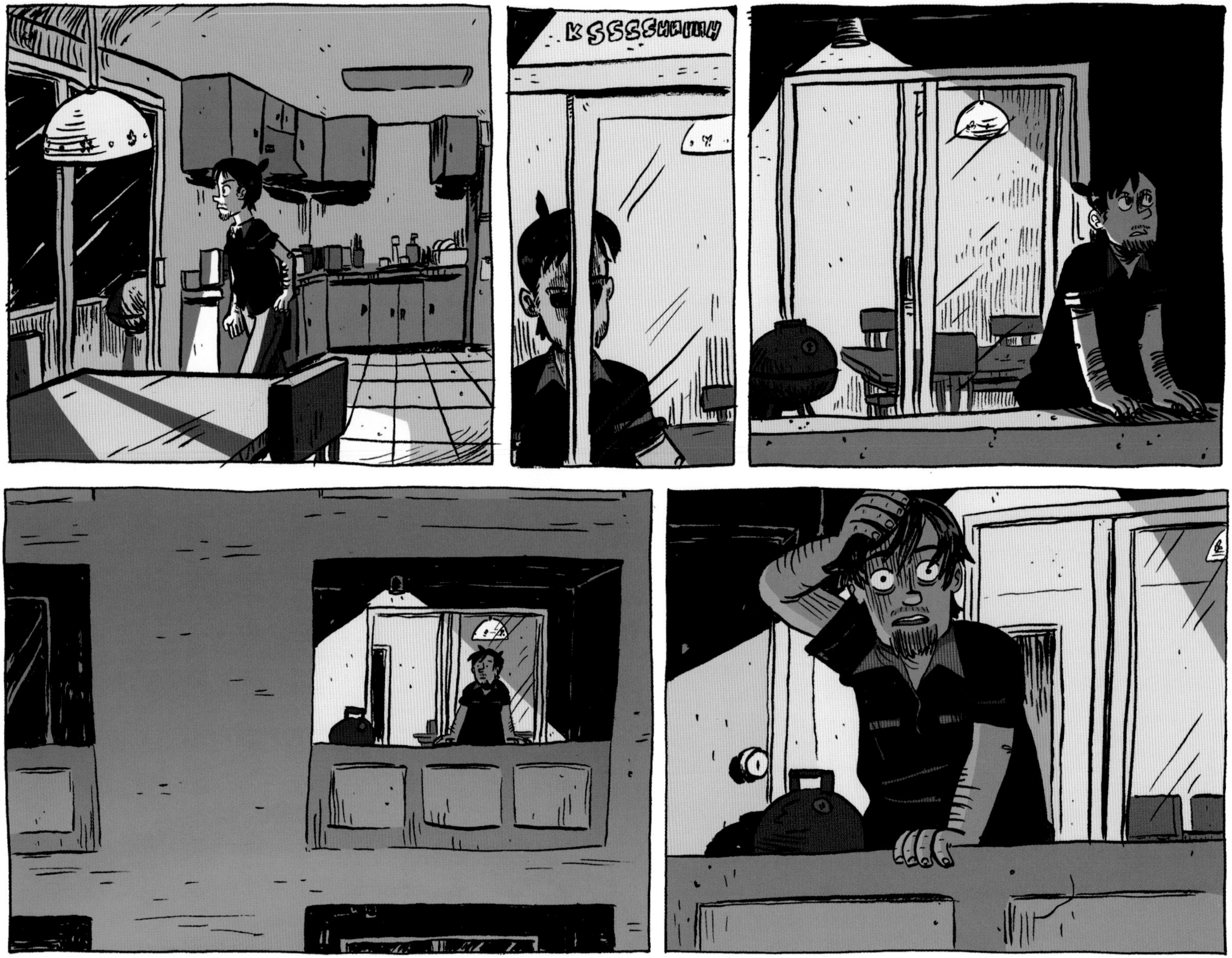
KSSSSHHHHH

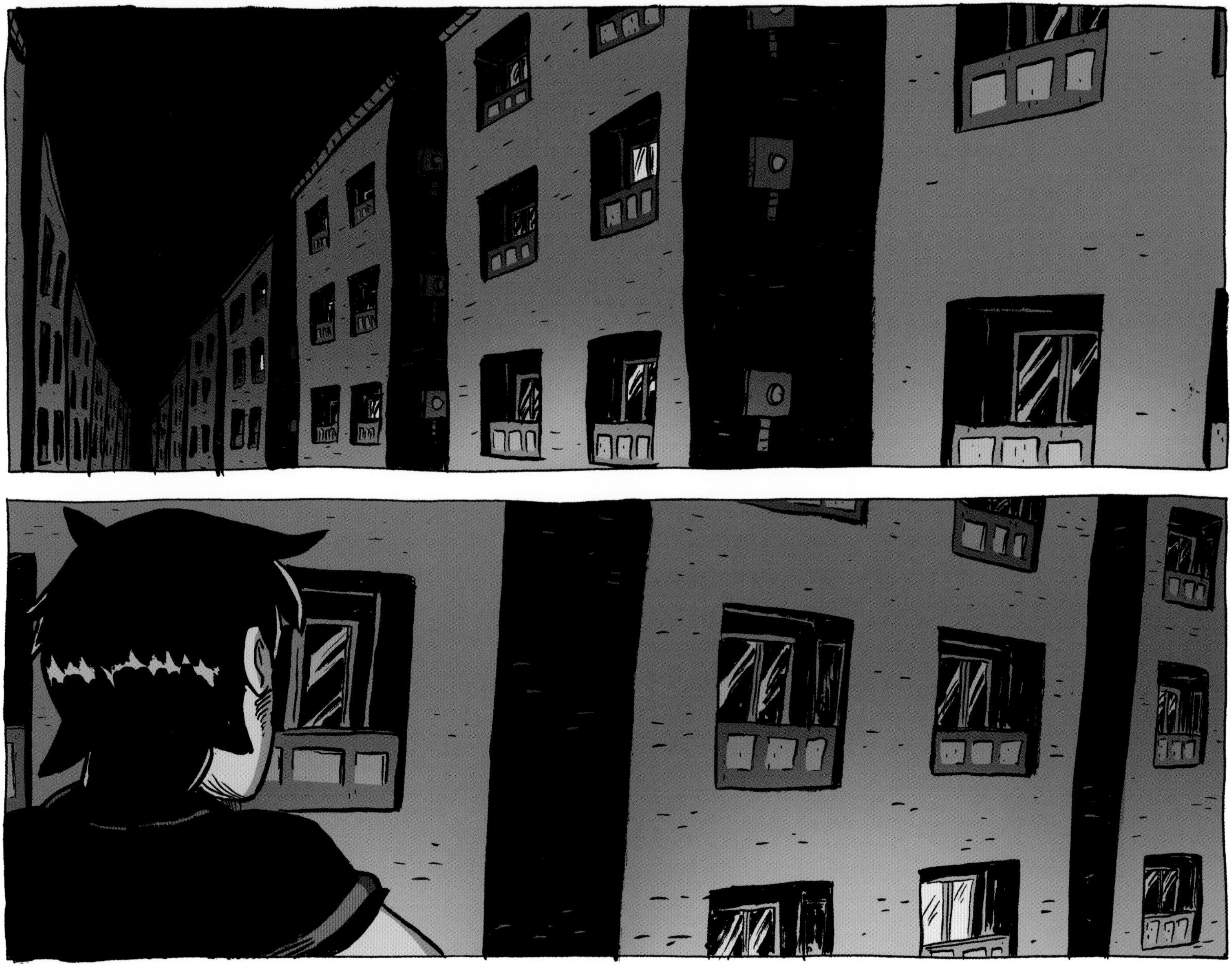

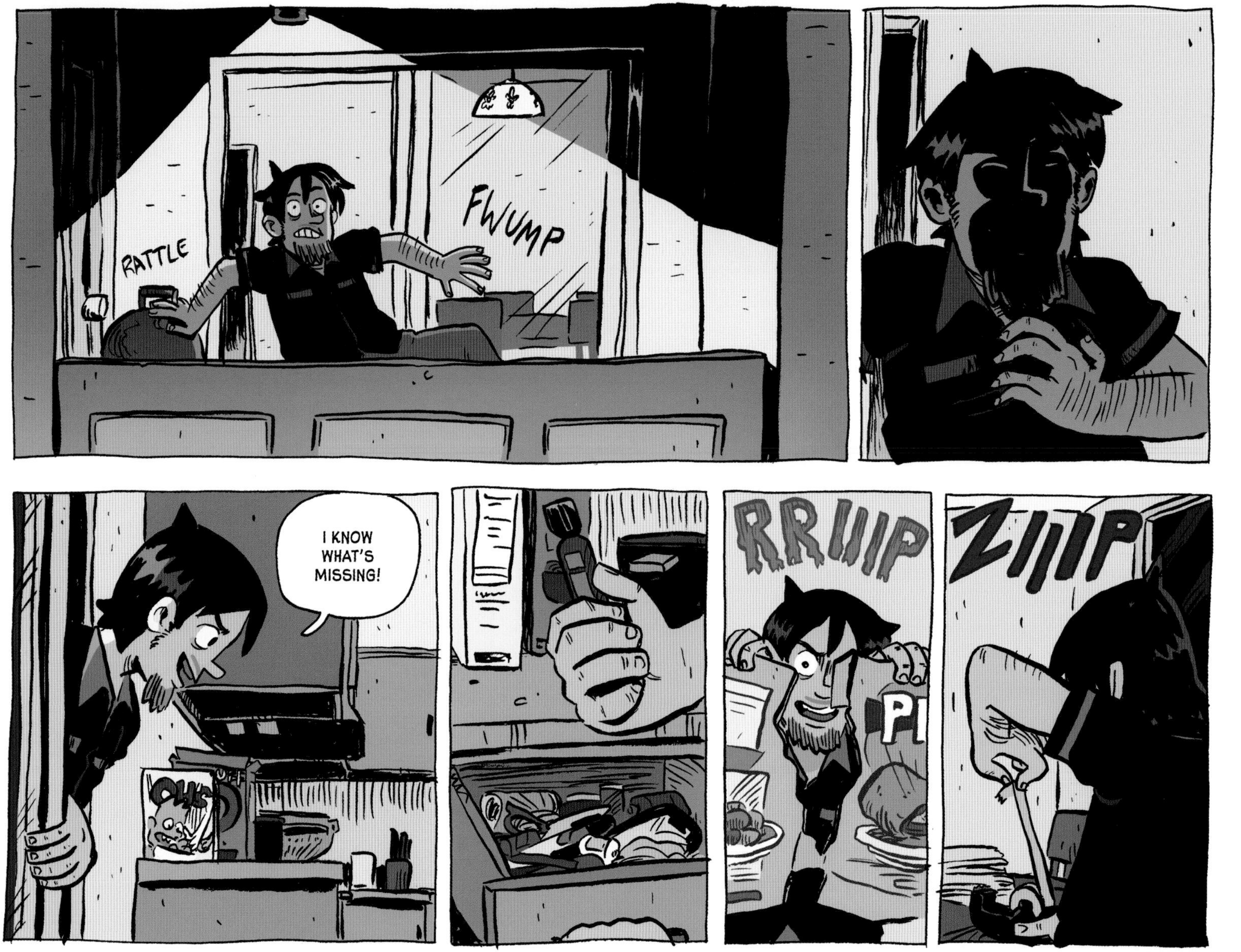
RATTLE
FWUMP
I KNOW WHAT'S MISSING!
RRIIIP
ZIIIP

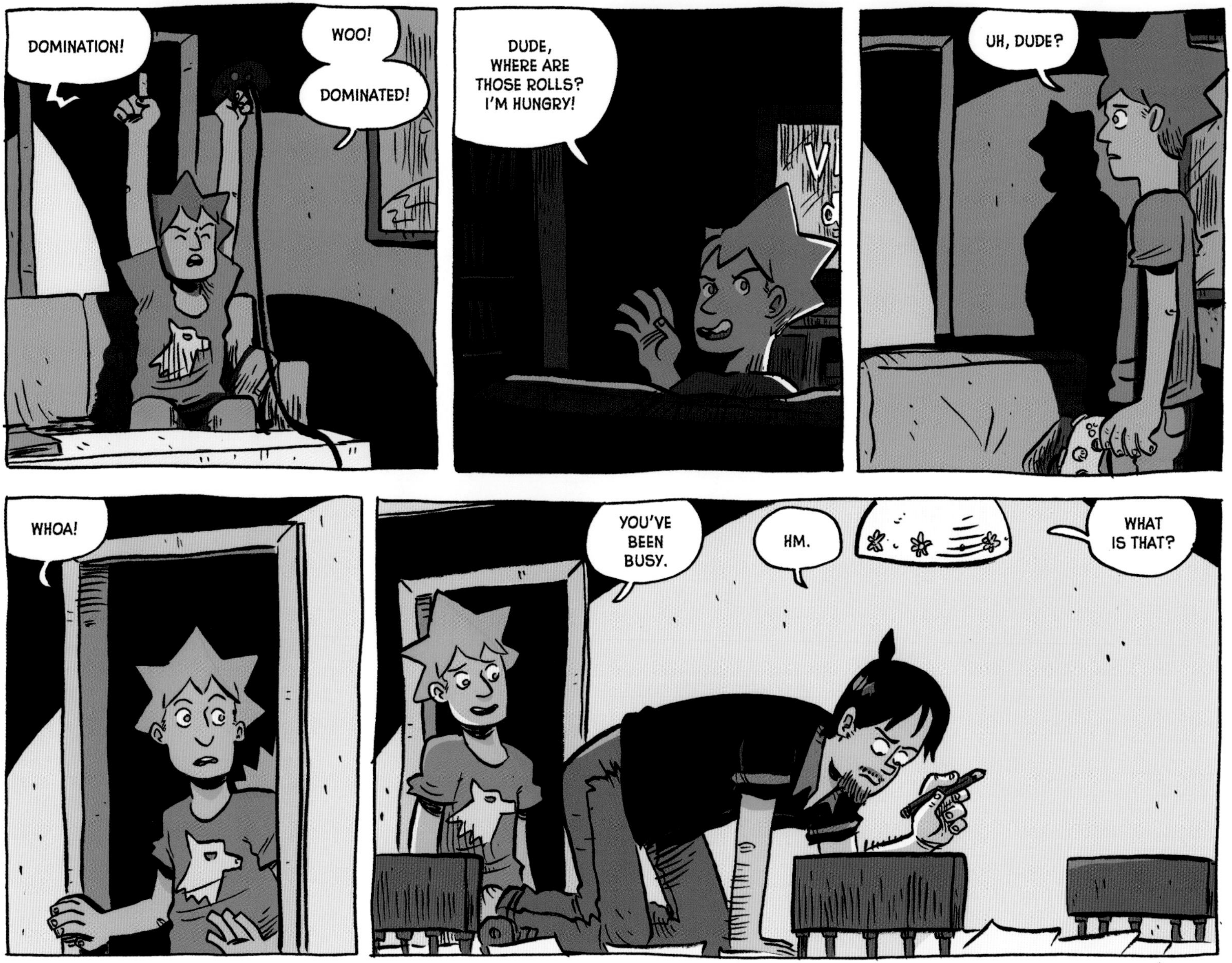
DOMINATION!
WOO!
DOMINATED!
DUDE, WHERE ARE THOSE ROLLS? I'M HUNGRY!
UH, DUDE?
WHOA!
YOU'VE BEEN BUSY.
HM.
WHAT IS THAT?

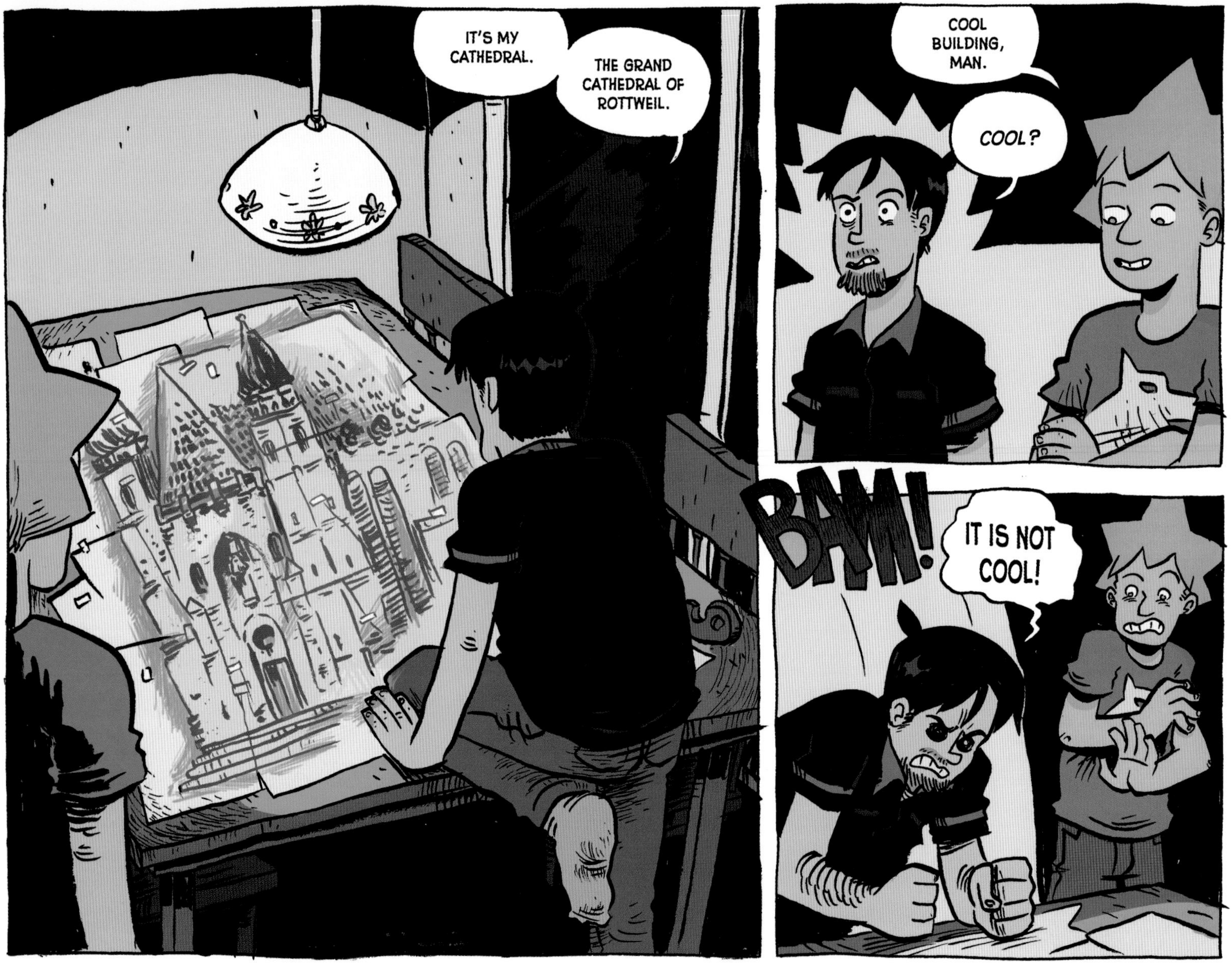
IT'S MY CATHEDRAL.
THE GRAND CATHEDRAL OF ROTTWEIL.
COOL BUILDING, MAN.
COOL?
BAM!
IT IS NOT COOL!

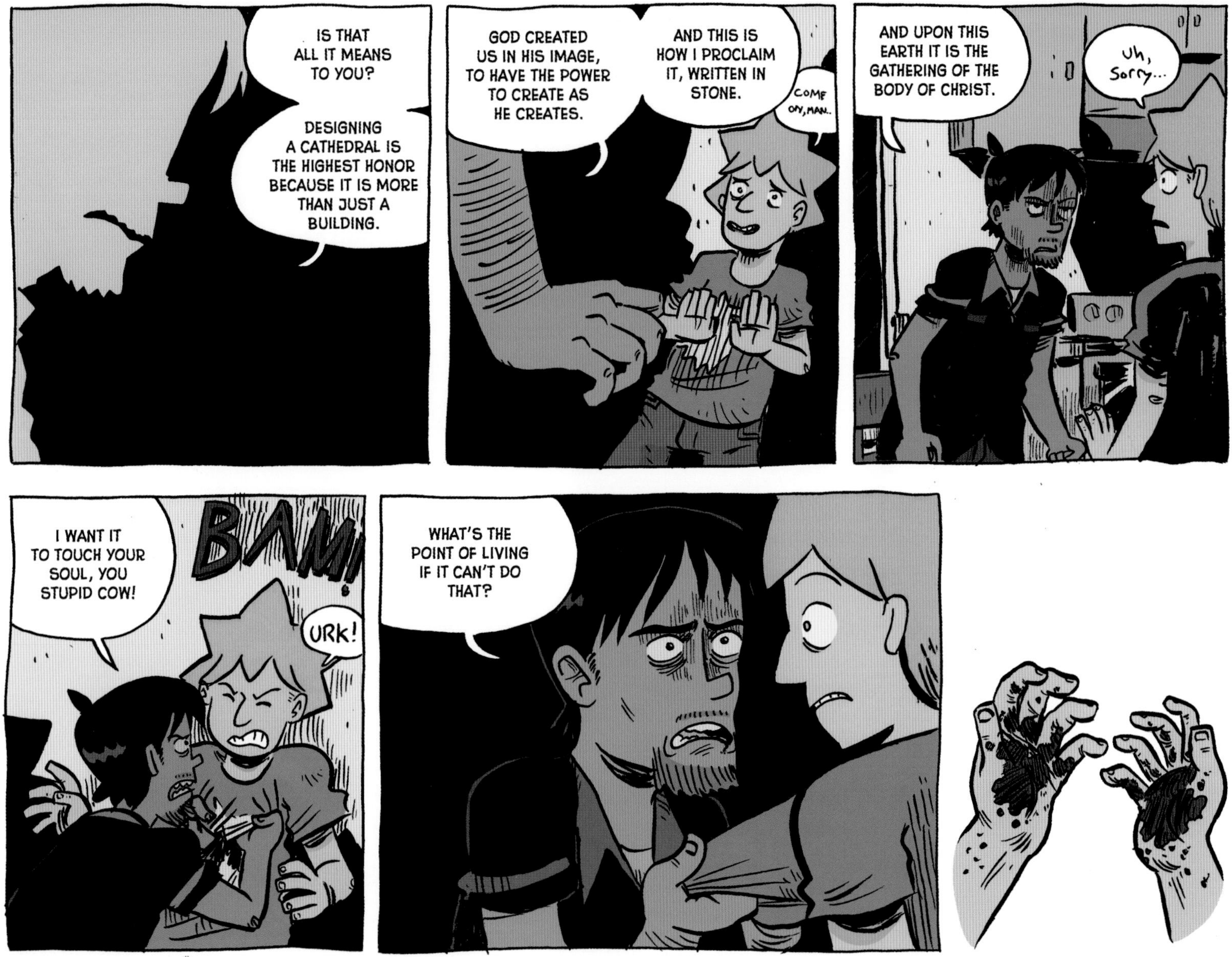
IS THAT ALL IT MEANS TO YOU?
DESIGNING A CATHEDRAL IS THE HIGHEST HONOR BECAUSE IT IS MORE THAN JUST A BUILDING.
GOD CREATED US IN HIS IMAGE, TO HAVE THE POWER TO CREATE AS HE CREATES.
AND THIS IS HOW I PROCLAIM IT, WRITTEN IN STONE.
COME ON, MAN..
AND UPON THIS EARTH IT IS THE GATHERING OF THE BODY OF CHRIST.
Uh, Sorry...
I WANT IT TO TOUCH YOUR SOUL, YOU STUPID COW!
BAM!
URK!
WHAT'S THE POINT OF LIVING IF IT CAN'T DO THAT?

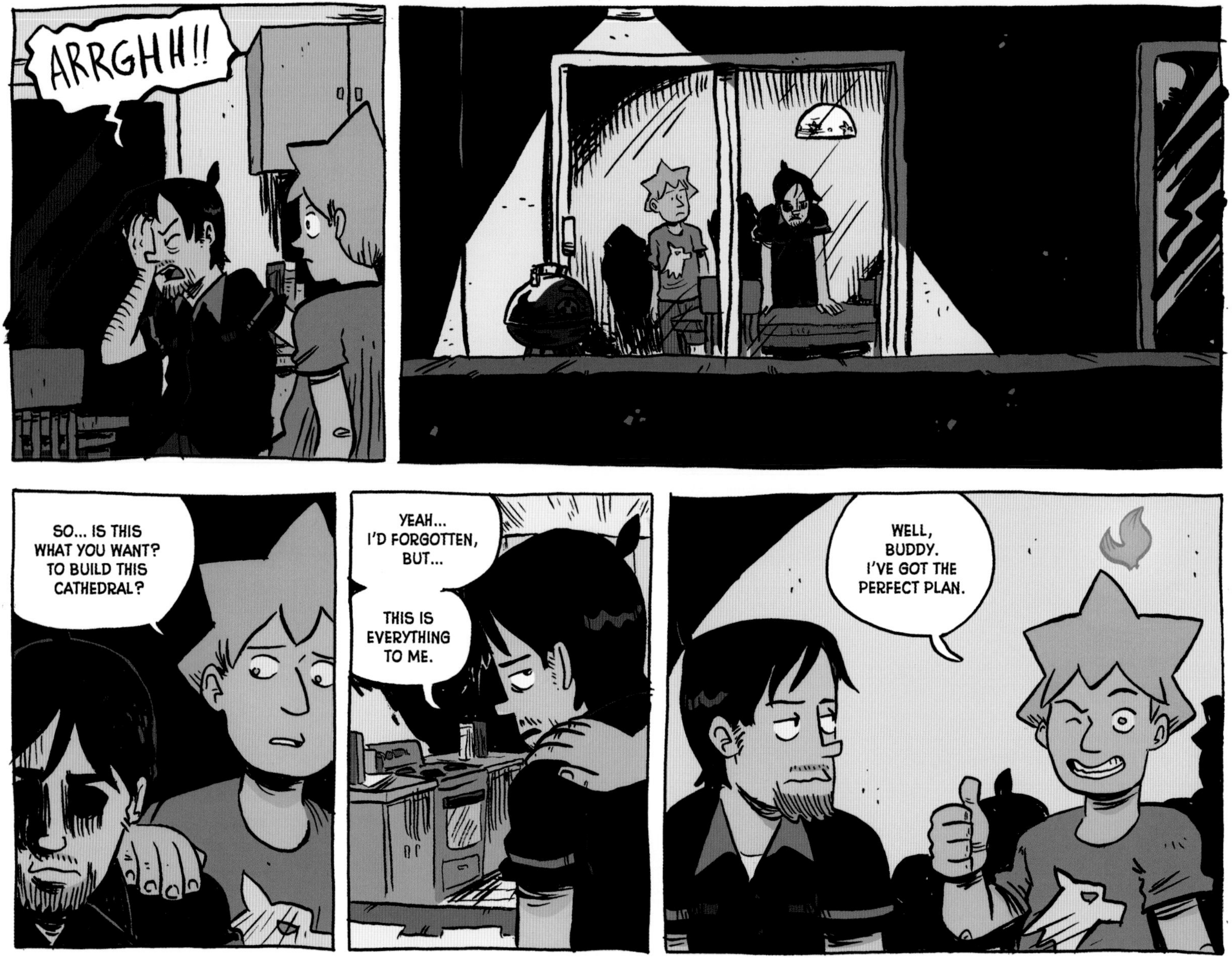
ARRGHH!!
SO... IS THIS WHAT YOU WANT? TO BUILD THIS CATHEDRAL?
YEAH... I'D FORGOTTEN, BUT...
THIS IS EVERYTHING TO ME.
WELL, BUDDY. I'VE GOT THE PERFECT PLAN.

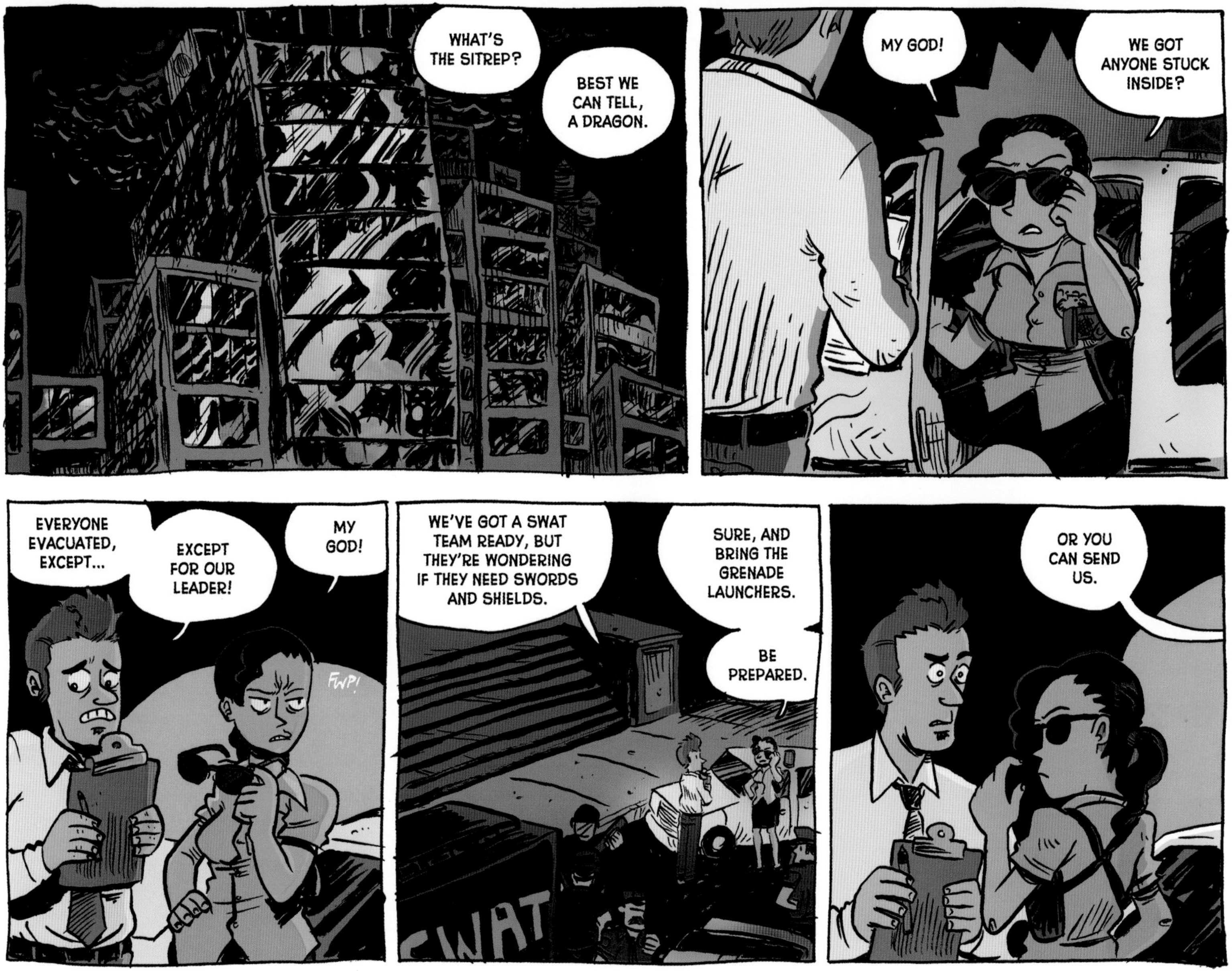
WHAT'S THE SITREP?
BEST WE CAN TELL, A DRAGON.
MY GOD!
WE GOT ANYONE STUCK INSIDE?
EVERYONE EVACUATED, EXCEPT...
EXCEPT FOR OUR LEADER!
MY GOD!
FWP!
WE'VE GOT A SWAT TEAM READY, BUT THEY'RE WONDERING IF THEY NEED SWORDS AND SHIELDS.
SURE, AND BRING THE GRENADE LAUNCHERS.
BE PREPARED.
SWAT
OR YOU CAN SEND US.

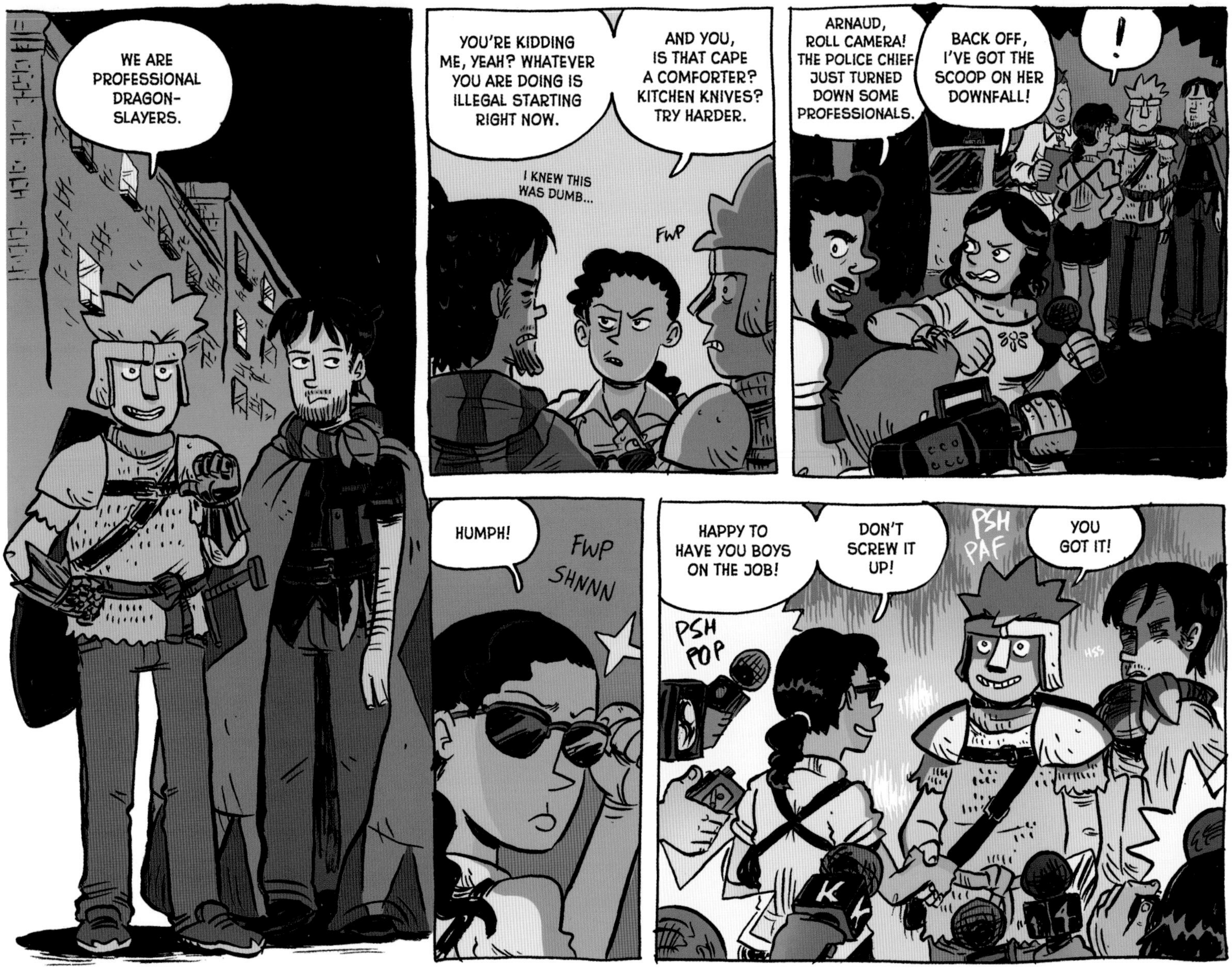
WE ARE PROFESSIONAL DRAGON-SLAYERS.
YOU'RE KIDDING ME, YEAH? WHATEVER YOU ARE DOING IS ILLEGAL STARTING RIGHT NOW.
AND YOU, IS THAT CAPE A COMFORTER? KITCHEN KNIVES? TRY HARDER.
I KNEW THIS WAS DUMB...
FWP
ARNAUD, ROLL CAMERA! THE POLICE CHIEF JUST TURNED DOWN SOME PROFESSIONALS.
BACK OFF, I'VE GOT THE SCOOP ON HER DOWNFALL!
!
HUMPH!
FWP
SHNNN
HAPPY TO HAVE YOU BOYS ON THE JOB!
DON'T SCREW IT UP!
PSH
PAF
YOU GOT IT!
PSH
POP

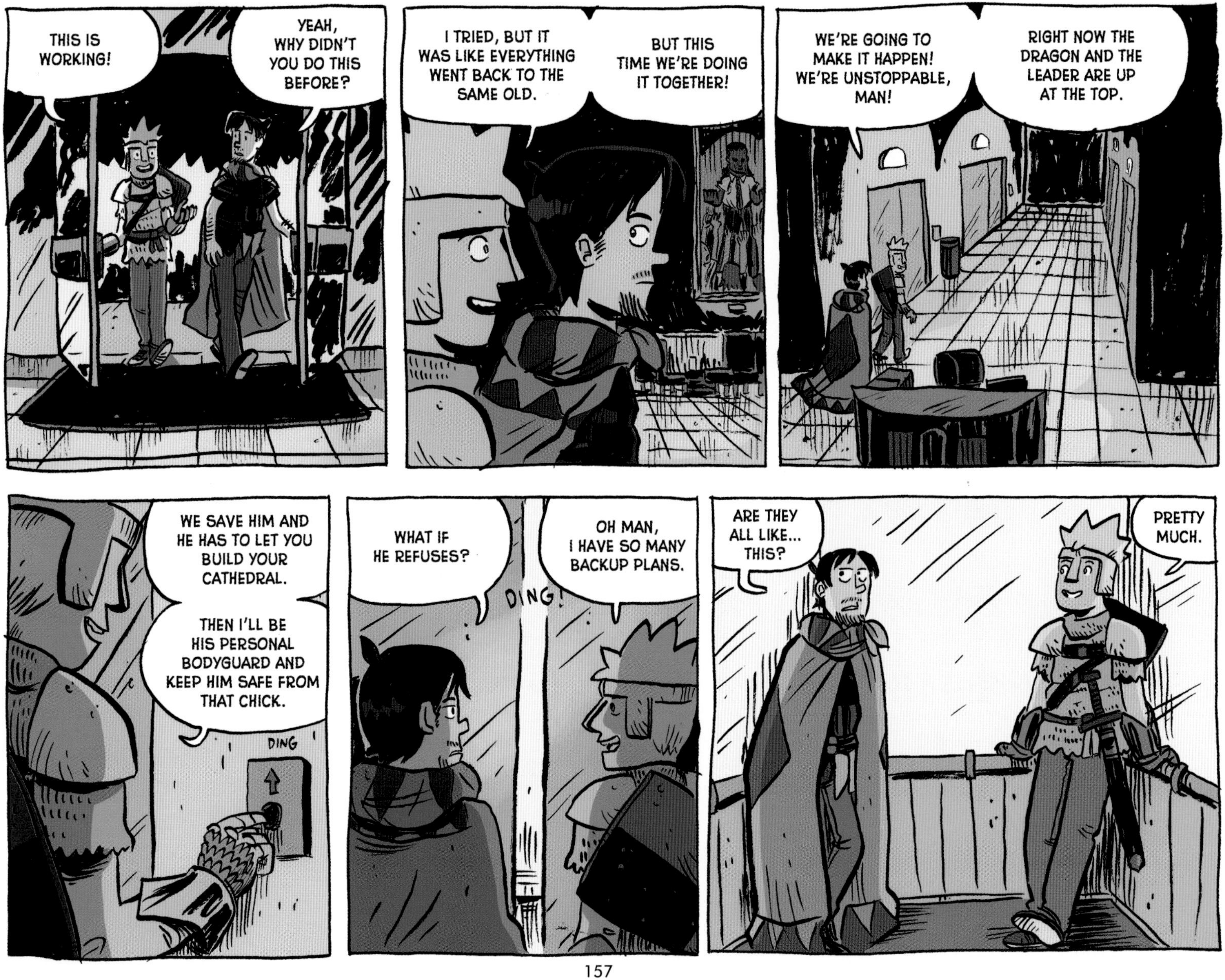
THIS IS WORKING!
YEAH, WHY DIDN'T YOU DO THIS BEFORE?
I TRIED, BUT IT WAS LIKE EVERYTHING WENT BACK TO THE SAME OLD.
BUT THIS TIME WE'RE DOING IT TOGETHER!
WE'RE GOING TO MAKE IT HAPPEN! WE'RE UNSTOPPABLE, MAN!
RIGHT NOW THE DRAGON AND THE LEADER ARE UP AT THE TOP.
WE SAVE HIM AND HE HAS TO LET YOU BUILD YOUR CATHEDRAL.
THEN I'LL BE HIS PERSONAL BODYGUARD AND KEEP HIM SAFE FROM THAT CHICK.
DING
WHAT IF HE REFUSES?
DING!
OH MAN, I HAVE SO MANY BACKUP PLANS.
ARE THEY ALL LIKE... THIS?
PRETTY MUCH.

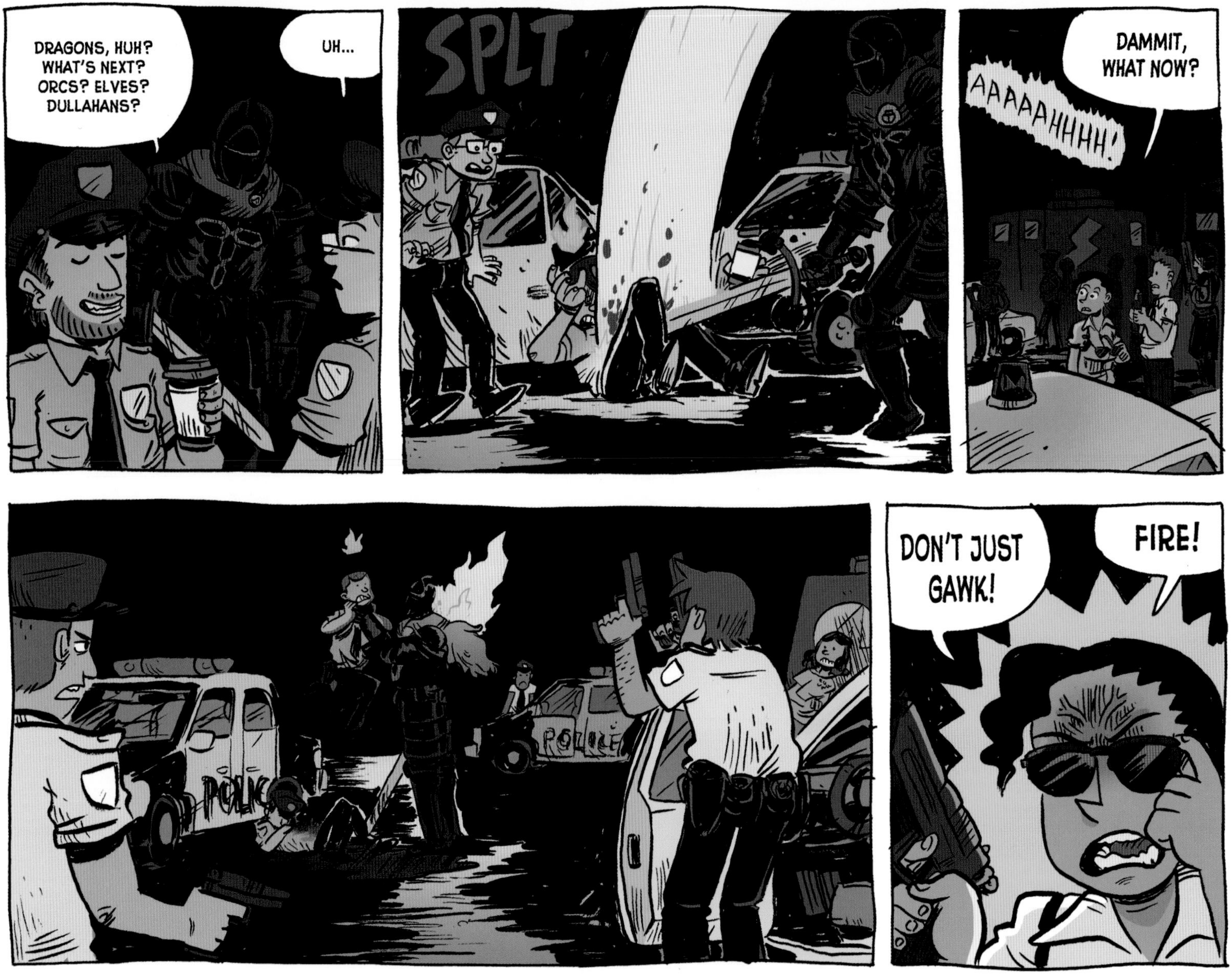
DRAGONS, HUH? WHAT'S NEXT? ORCS? ELVES? DULLAHANS?
UH...
SPLT
AAAAAHHHHH!
DAMMIT, WHAT NOW?
POLICE
POLIC
DON'T JUST GAWK!
FIRE!

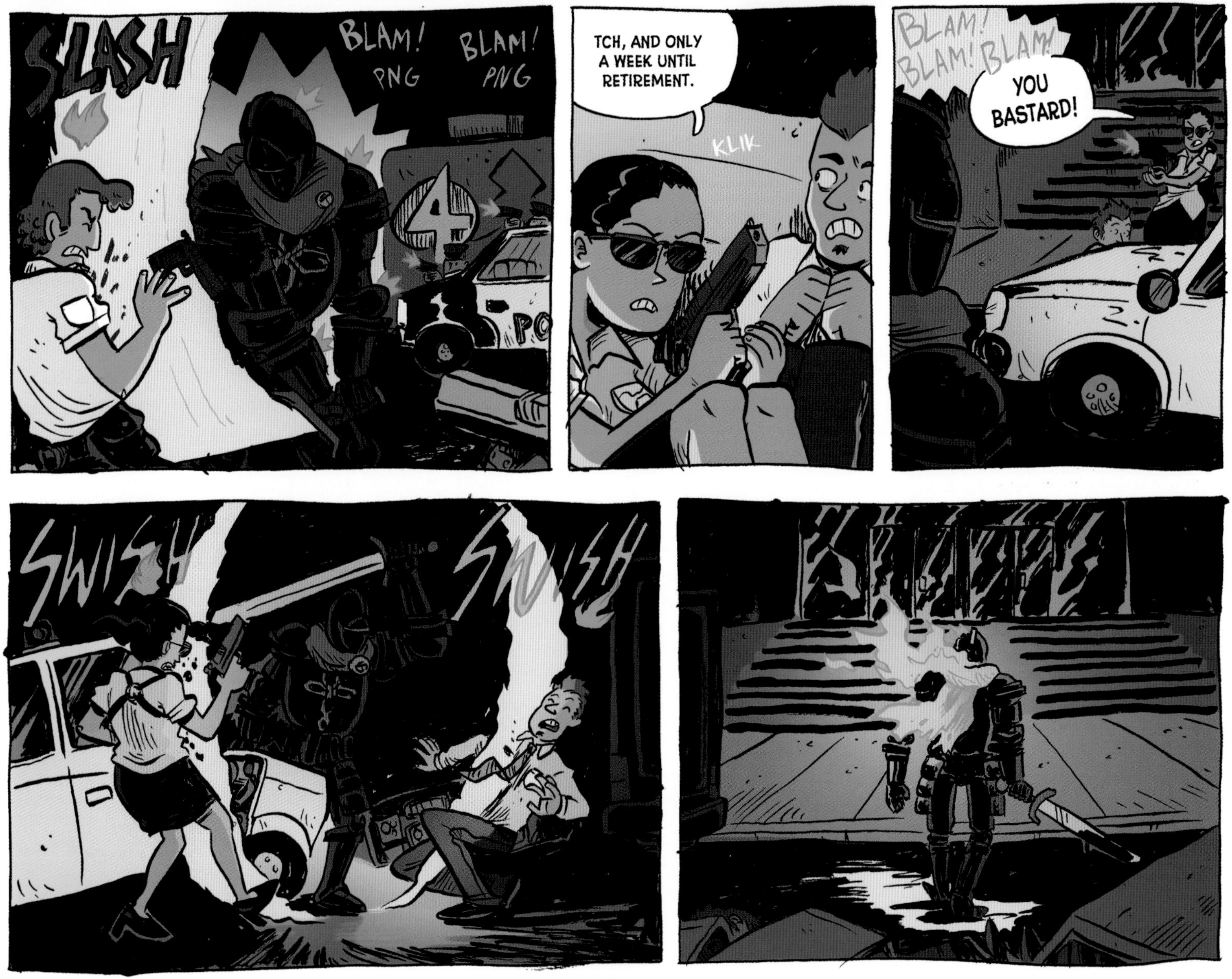
SLASH
BLAM! PNG
BLAM! PNG
TCH, AND ONLY A WEEK UNTIL RETIREMENT.
KLIK
BLAM! BLAM! BLAM!
YOU BASTARD!
SWISH
SWISH

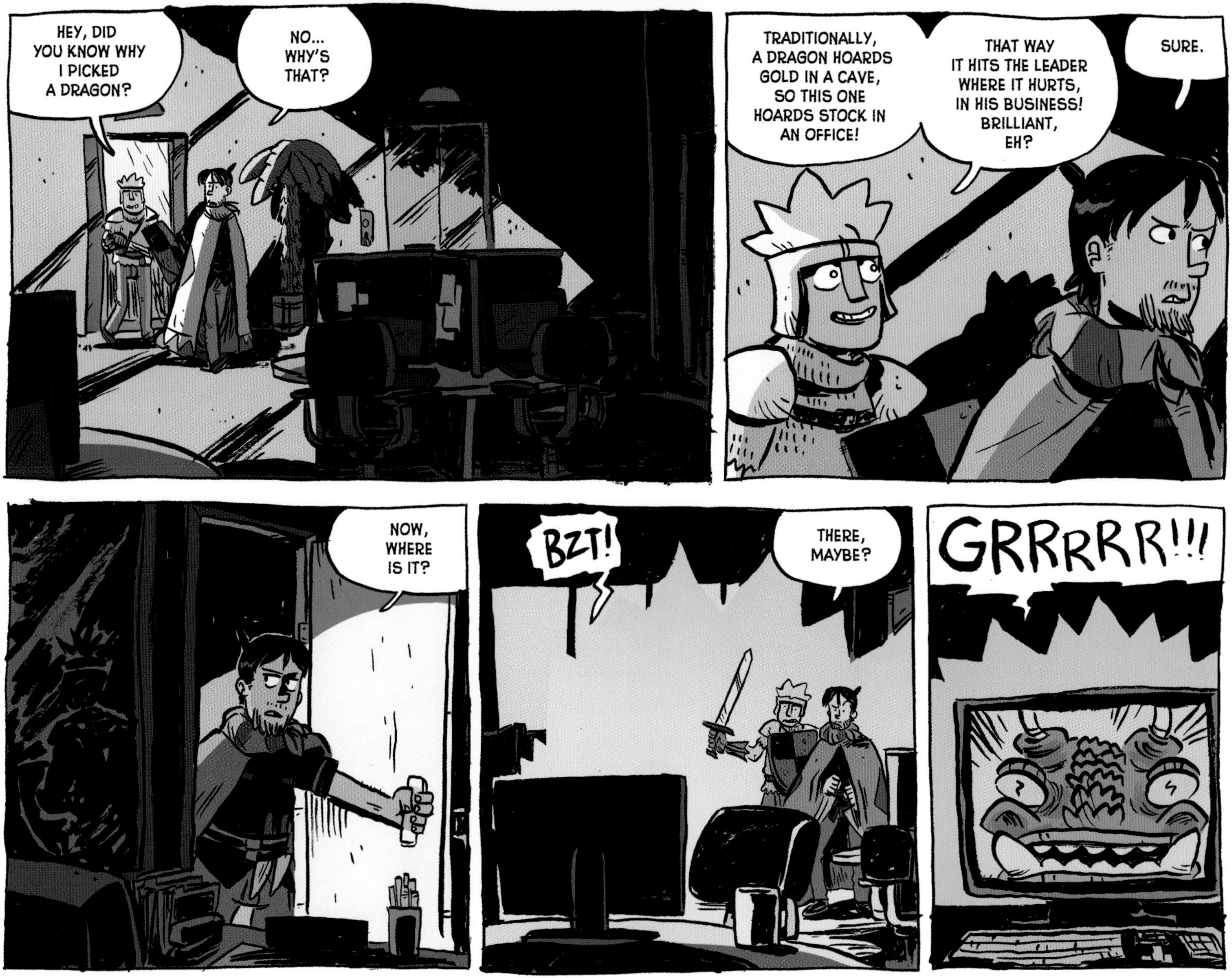
HEY, DID YOU KNOW WHY I PICKED A DRAGON?
NO... WHY'S THAT?
TRADITIONALLY, A DRAGON HOARDS GOLD IN A CAVE, SO THIS ONE HOARDS STOCK IN AN OFFICE!
THAT WAY IT HITS THE LEADER WHERE IT HURTS, IN HIS BUSINESS! BRILLIANT, EH?
SURE.
NOW, WHERE IS IT?
BZT!
THERE, MAYBE?
GRRRRRR!!!

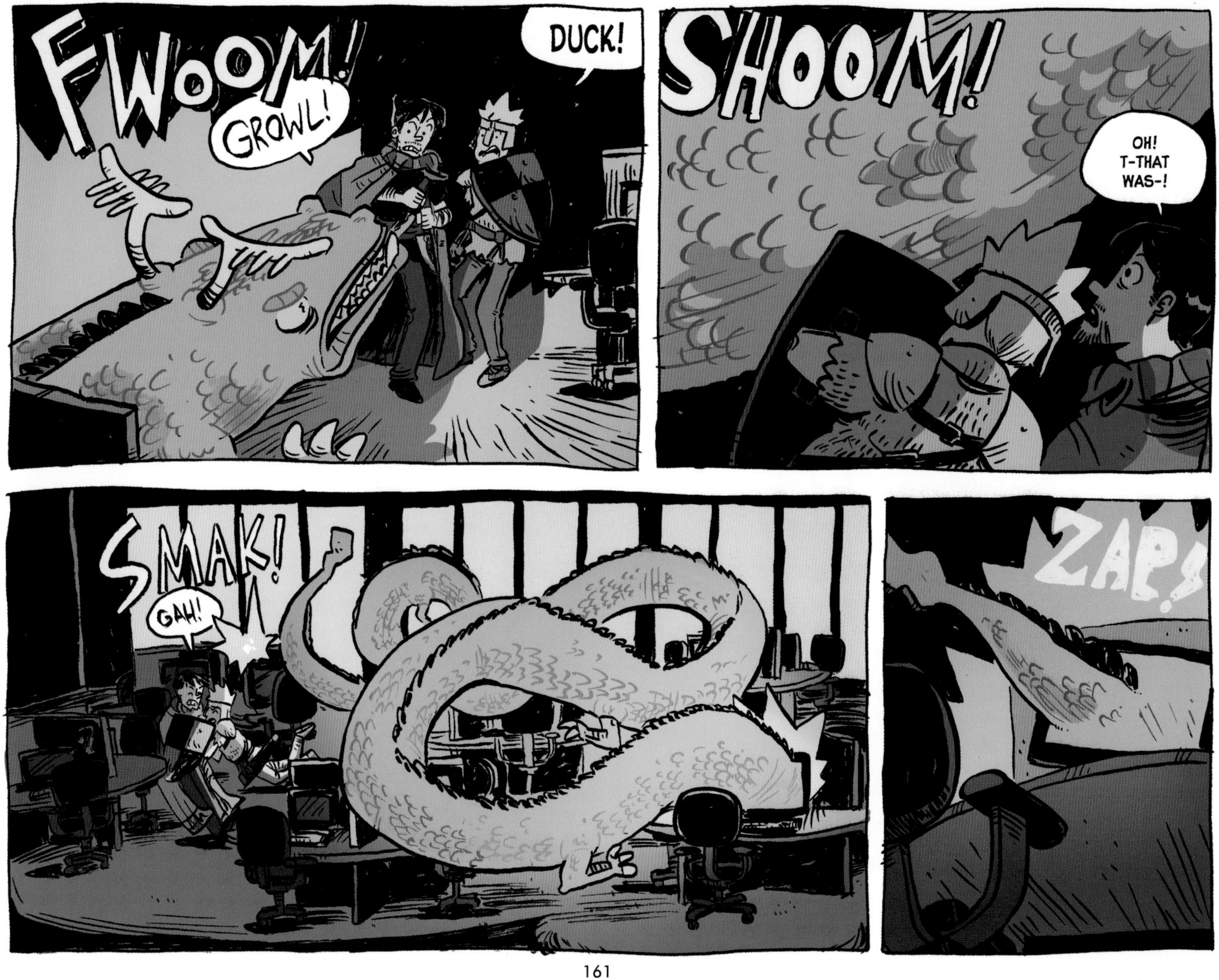
FWOOM!
GROWL!
DUCK!
SHOOM!
OH! T-THAT WAS-!
SMAK!
GAH!
ZAP!

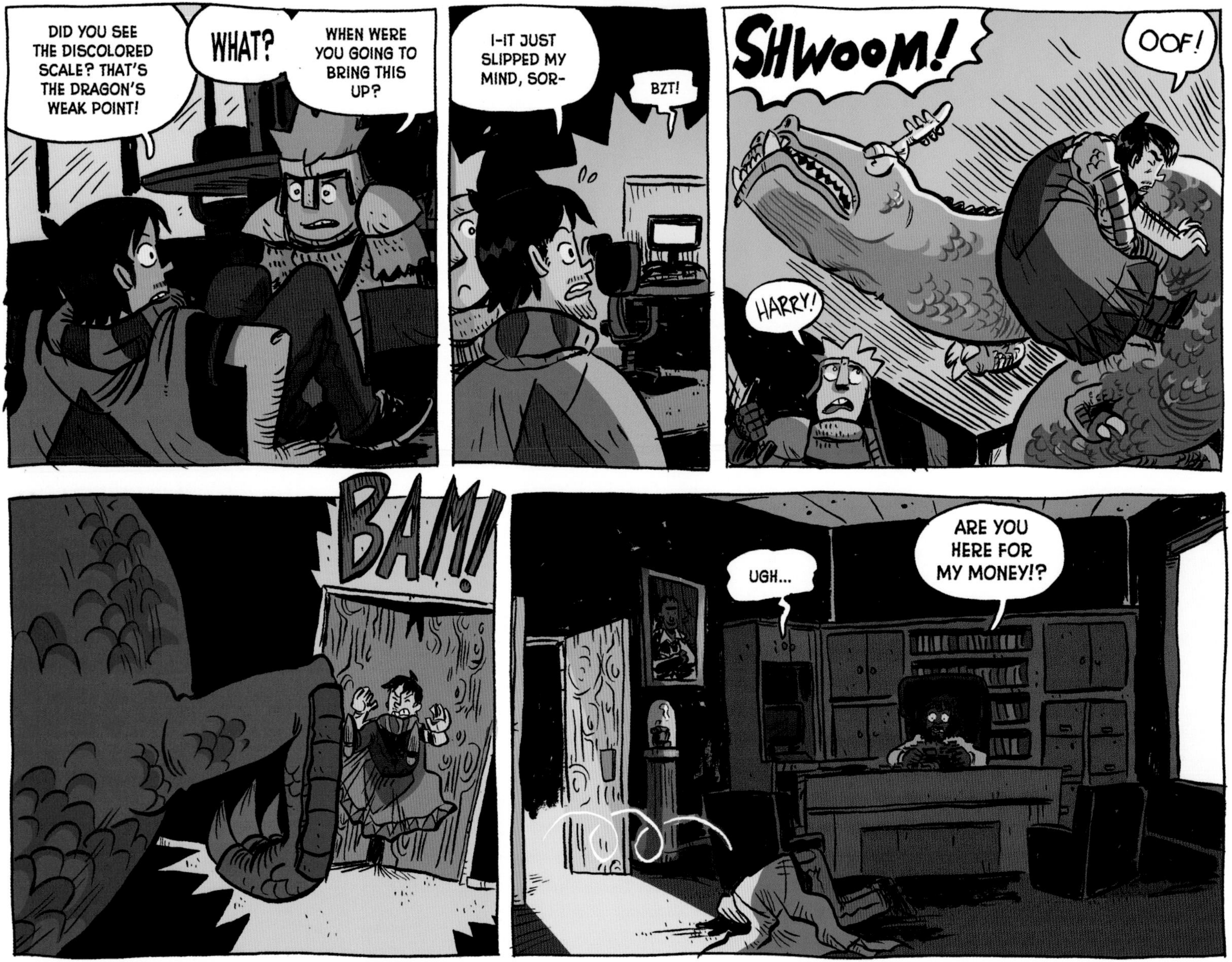
DID YOU SEE THE DISCOLORED SCALE? THAT'S THE DRAGON'S WEAK POINT!
WHAT?
WHEN WERE YOU GOING TO BRING THIS UP?
I-IT JUST SLIPPED MY MIND, SOR-
BZT!
SHWOOM!
OOF!
HARRY!
BAM!
UGH...
ARE YOU HERE FOR MY MONEY!?

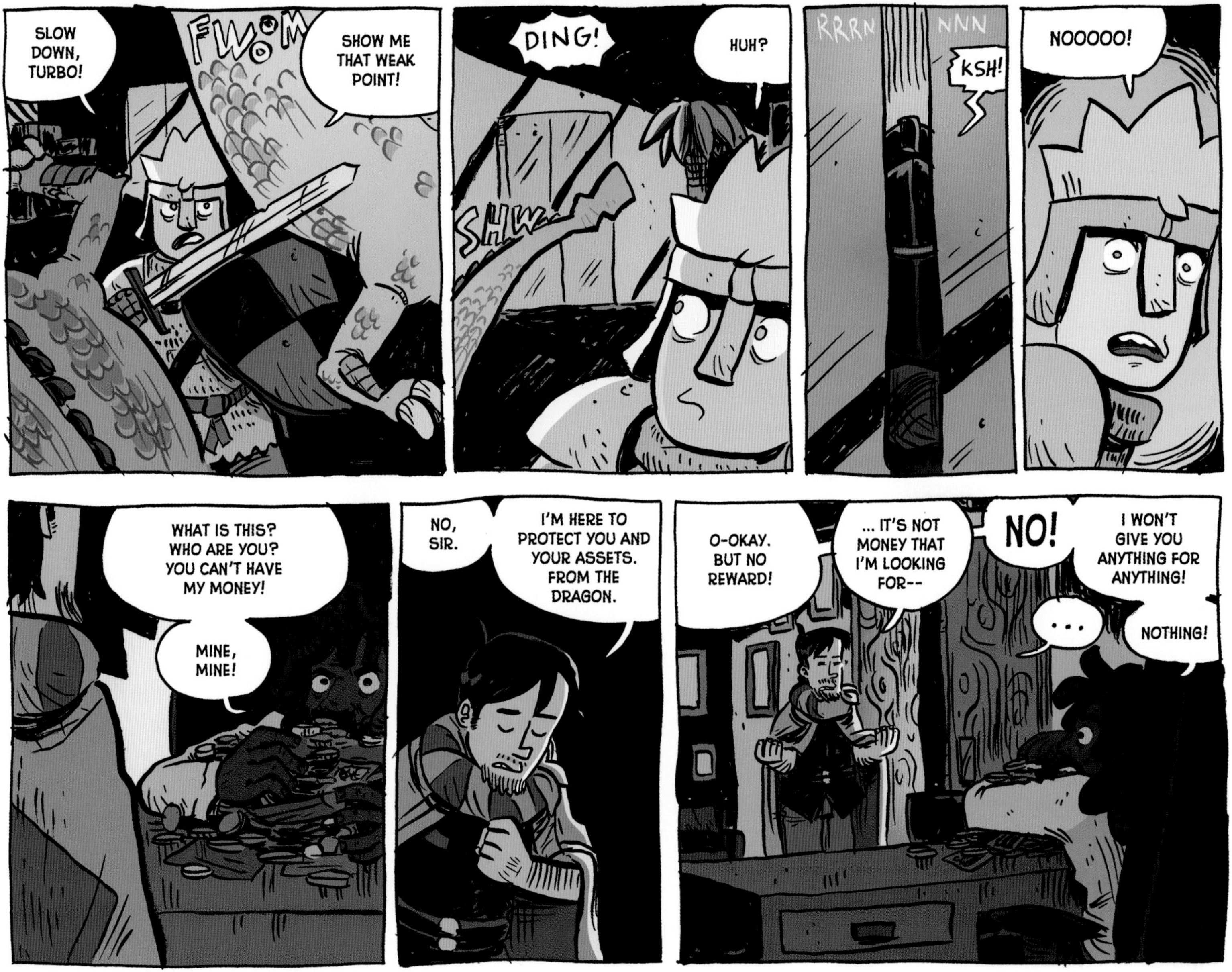
SLOW DOWN, TURBO!
FWOOM
SHOW ME THAT WEAK POINT!
DING!
HUH?
SHW
RRRN NNN
KSH!
NOOOOO!
WHAT IS THIS? WHO ARE YOU? YOU CAN'T HAVE MY MONEY!
MINE, MINE!
NO, SIR.
I'M HERE TO PROTECT YOU AND YOUR ASSETS. FROM THE DRAGON.
O-OKAY. BUT NO REWARD!
... IT'S NOT MONEY THAT I'M LOOKING FOR--
NO!
I WON'T GIVE YOU ANYTHING FOR ANYTHING!
...
NOTHING!

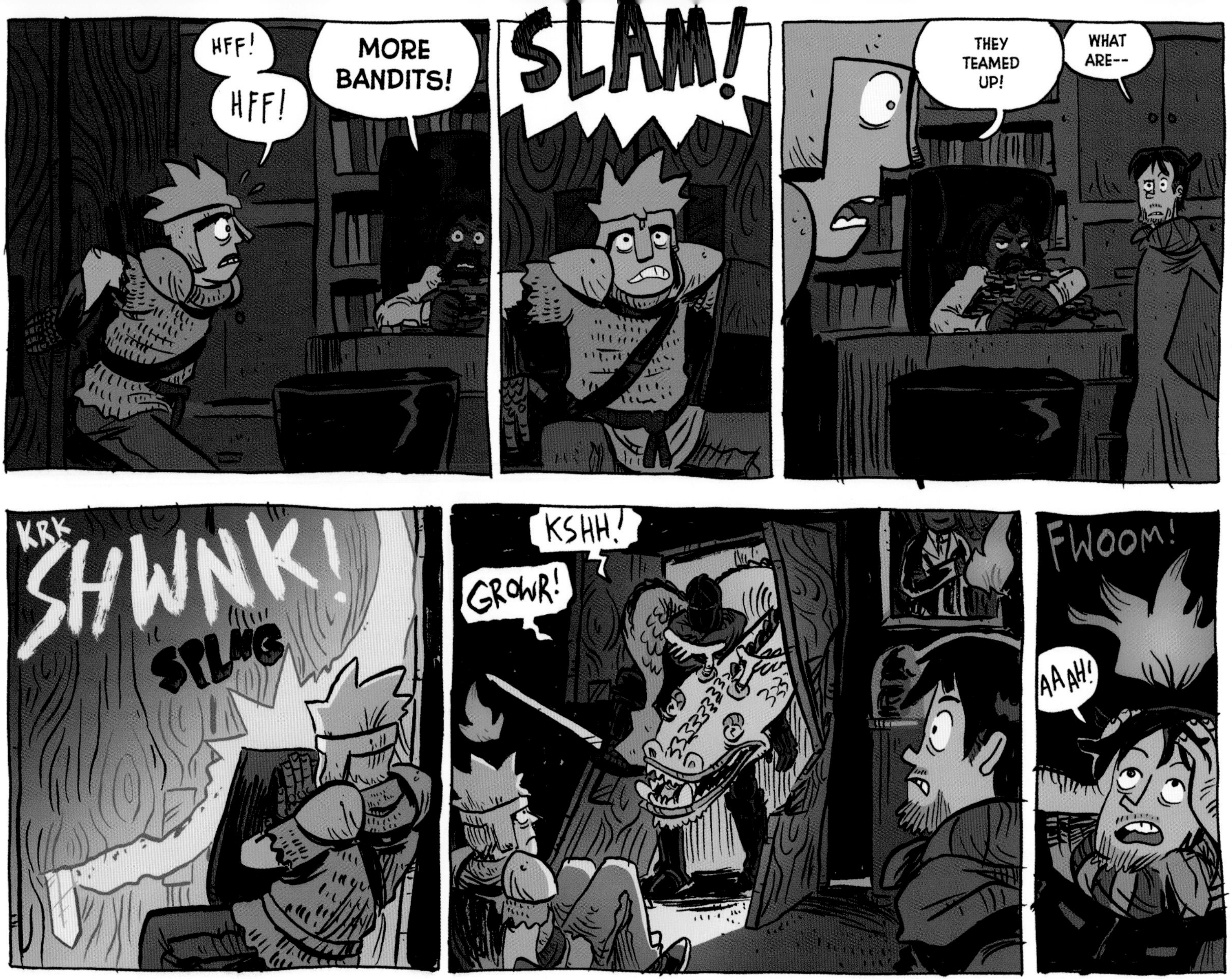
HFF!
HFF!
MORE BANDITS!
SLAM!
THEY TEAMED UP!
WHAT ARE--
KRK
SHWNK!
SPLNG
KSHH!
GROWR!
FWOOM!
AAAH!

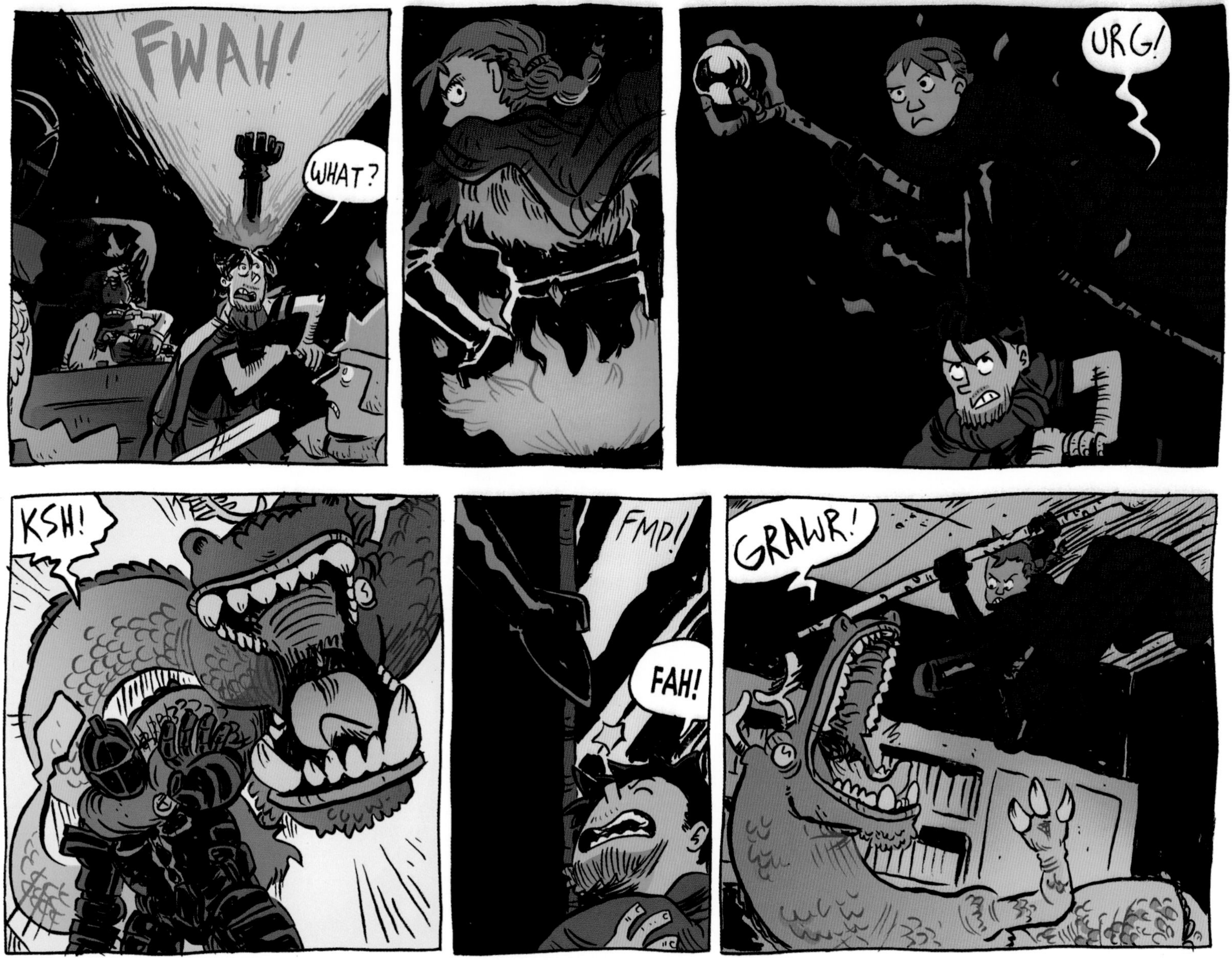
FWAH!
WHAT?
URG!
KSH!
FMP!
FAH!
GRAWR!

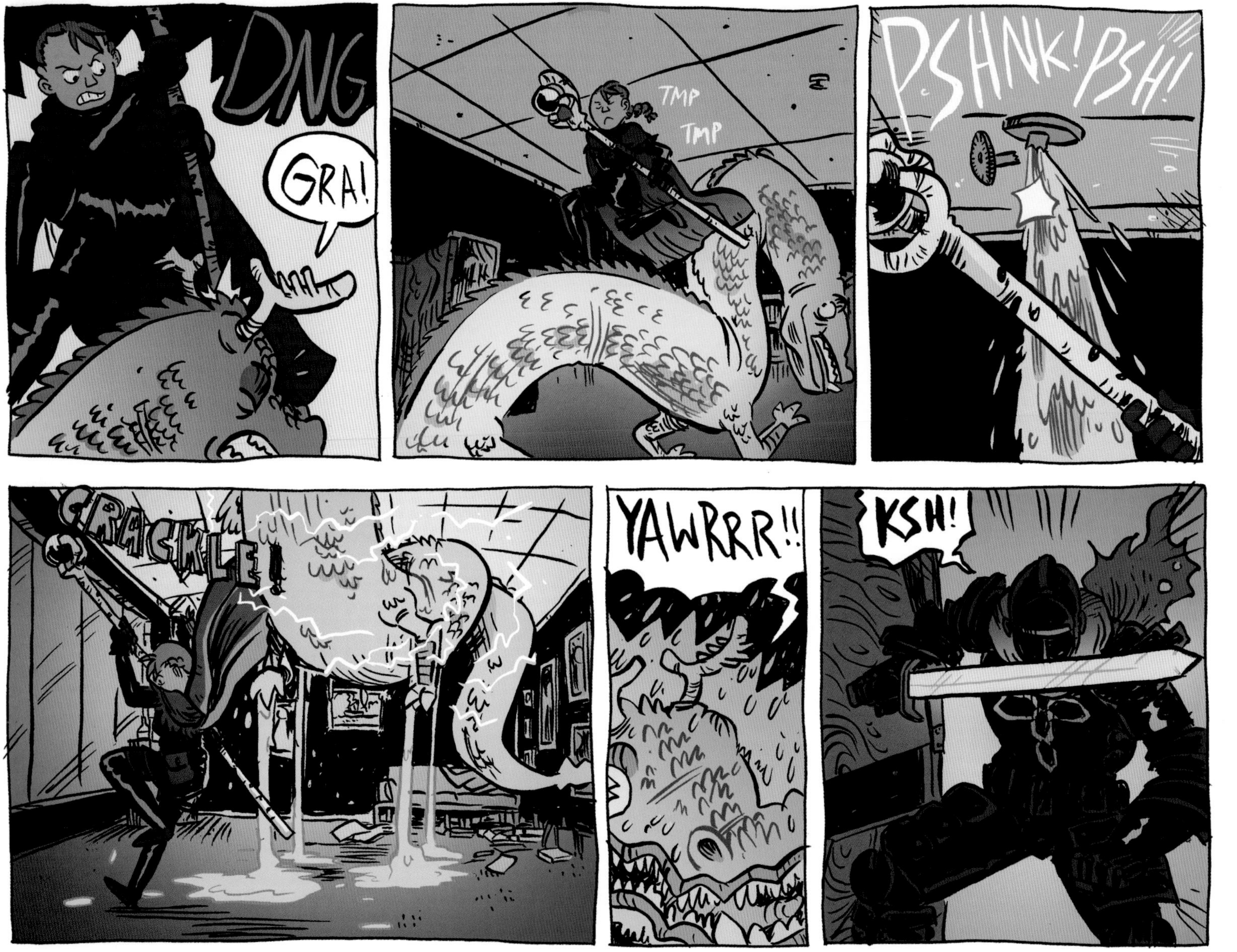
DNG
GRA!
TMP
TMP
PSHNK! PSH!
CRACKLE!
YAWRRR!!
KSH!

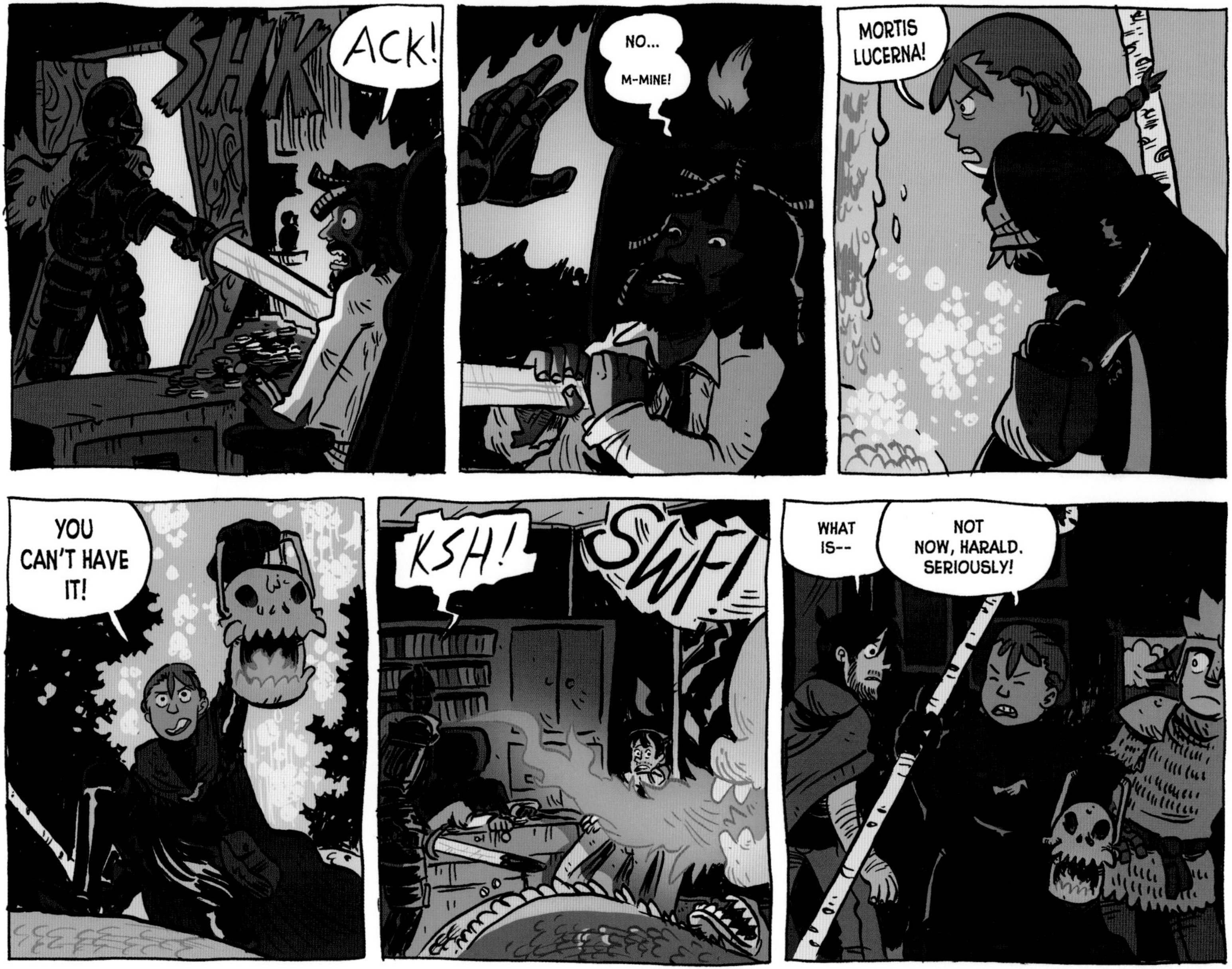
SHK
ACK!
NO...
M-MINE!
MORTIS LUCERNA!
YOU CAN'T HAVE IT!
KSH!
SWF!
WHAT IS--
NOT NOW, HARALD. SERIOUSLY!

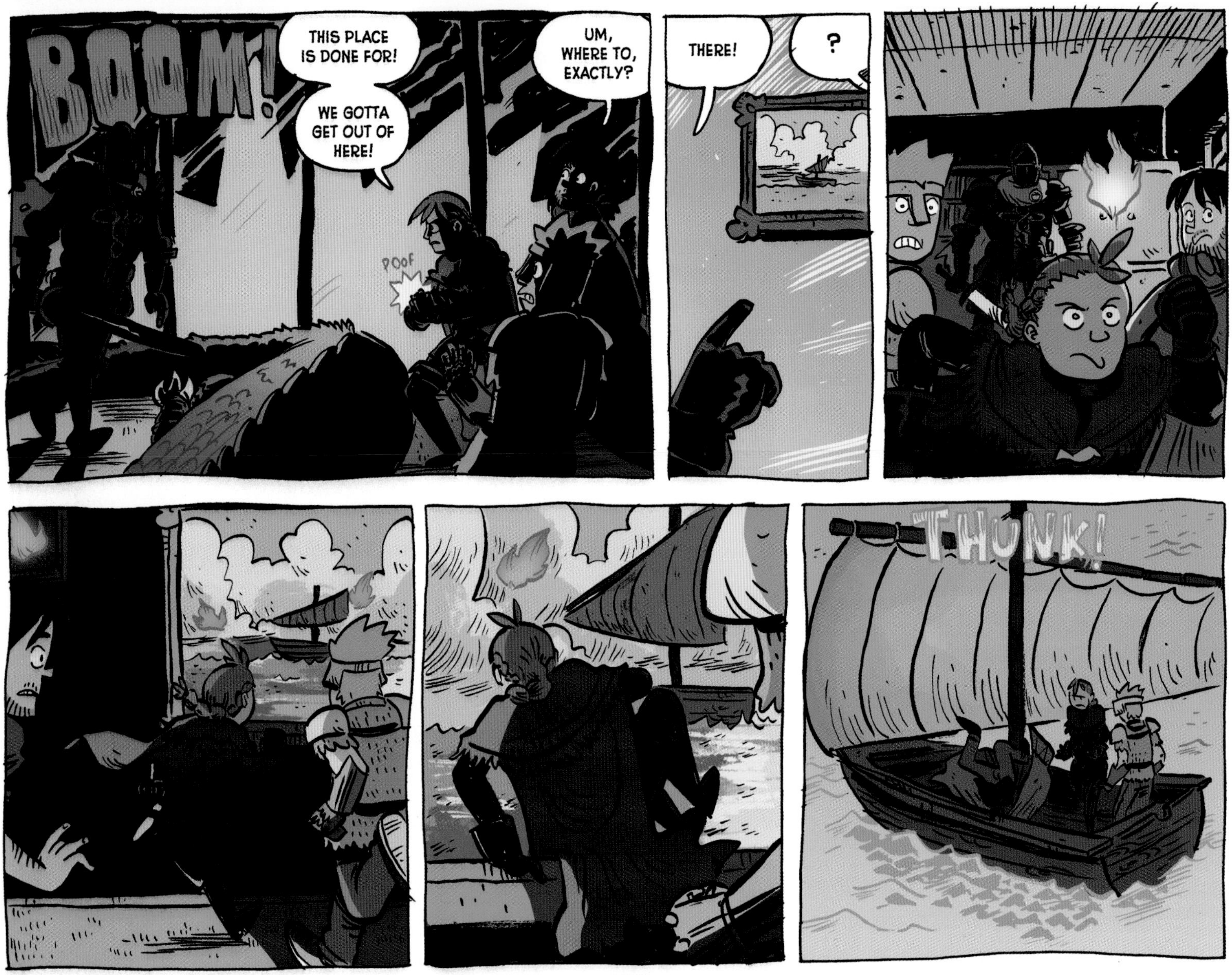
BOOM!
THIS PLACE IS DONE FOR!
WE GOTTA GET OUT OF HERE!
POOF
UM, WHERE TO, EXACTLY?
THERE!
?
THUNK!

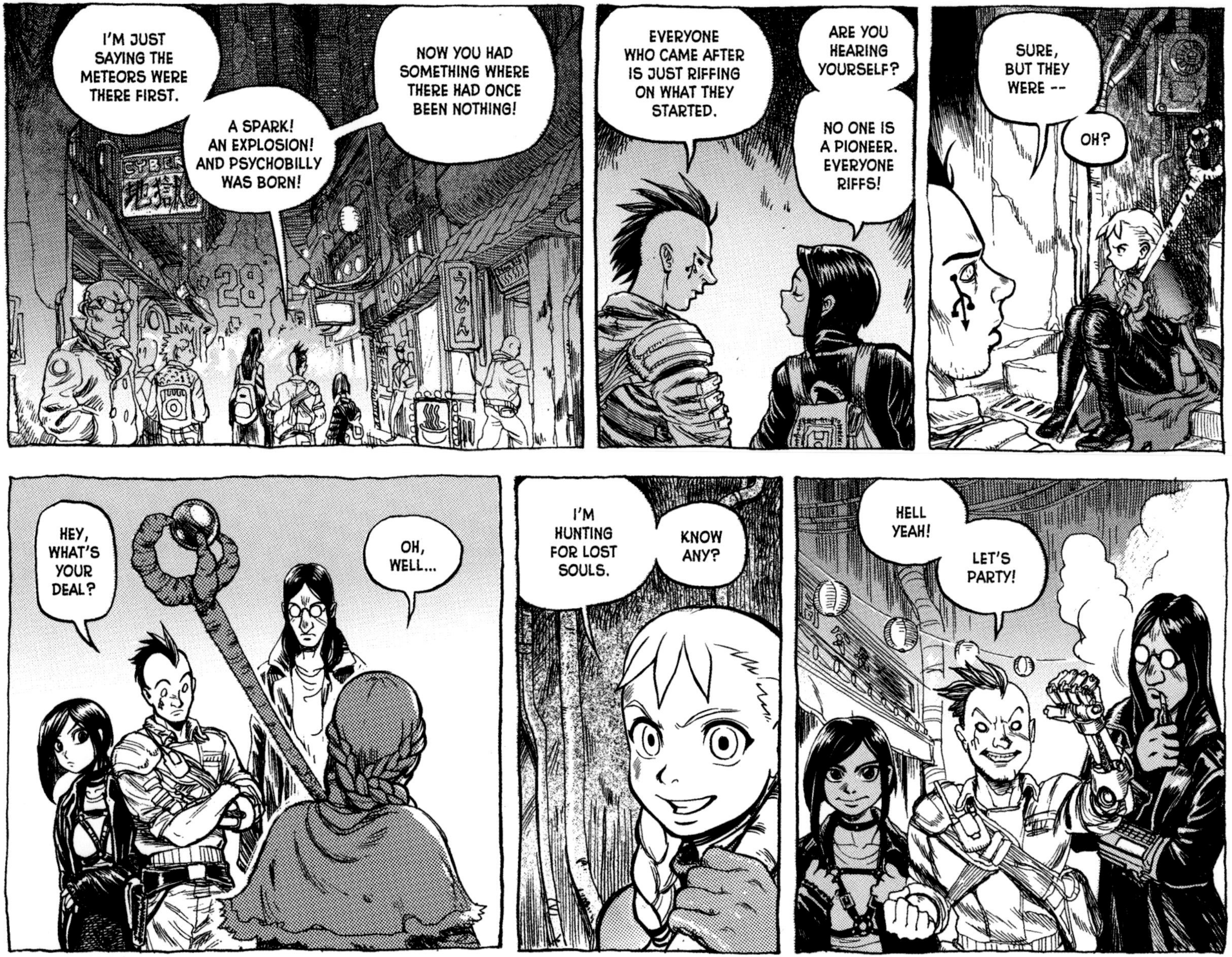
I'M JUST SAYING THE METEORS WERE THERE FIRST.
NOW YOU HAD SOMETHING WHERE THERE HAD ONCE BEEN NOTHING!
A SPARK! AN EXPLOSION! AND PSYCHOBILLY WAS BORN!
EVERYONE WHO CAME AFTER IS JUST RIFFING ON WHAT THEY STARTED.
ARE YOU HEARING YOURSELF?
NO ONE IS A PIONEER. EVERYONE RIFFS!
SURE, BUT THEY WERE --
OH?
HEY, WHAT'S YOUR DEAL?
OH, WELL...
I'M HUNTING FOR LOST SOULS.
KNOW ANY?
HELL YEAH!
LET'S PARTY!

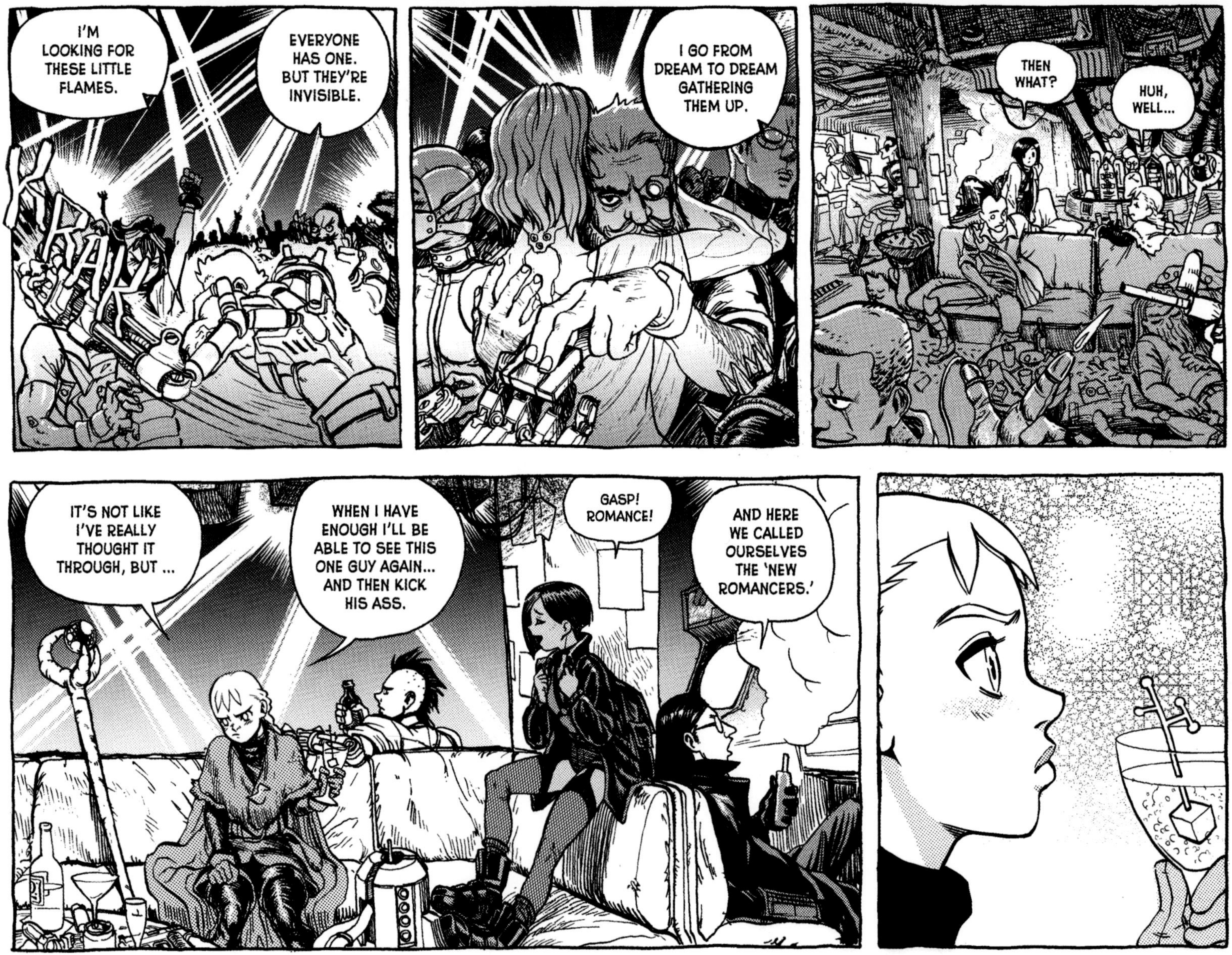
I'M LOOKING FOR THESE LITTLE FLAMES.
EVERYONE HAS ONE. BUT THEY'RE INVISIBLE.
KRAK
I GO FROM DREAM TO DREAM GATHERING THEM UP.
THEN WHAT?
HUH, WELL...
IT'S NOT LIKE I'VE REALLY THOUGHT IT THROUGH, BUT ...
WHEN I HAVE ENOUGH I'LL BE ABLE TO SEE THIS ONE GUY AGAIN... AND THEN KICK HIS ASS.
GASP! ROMANCE!
AND HERE WE CALLED OURSELVES THE 'NEW ROMANCERS.'

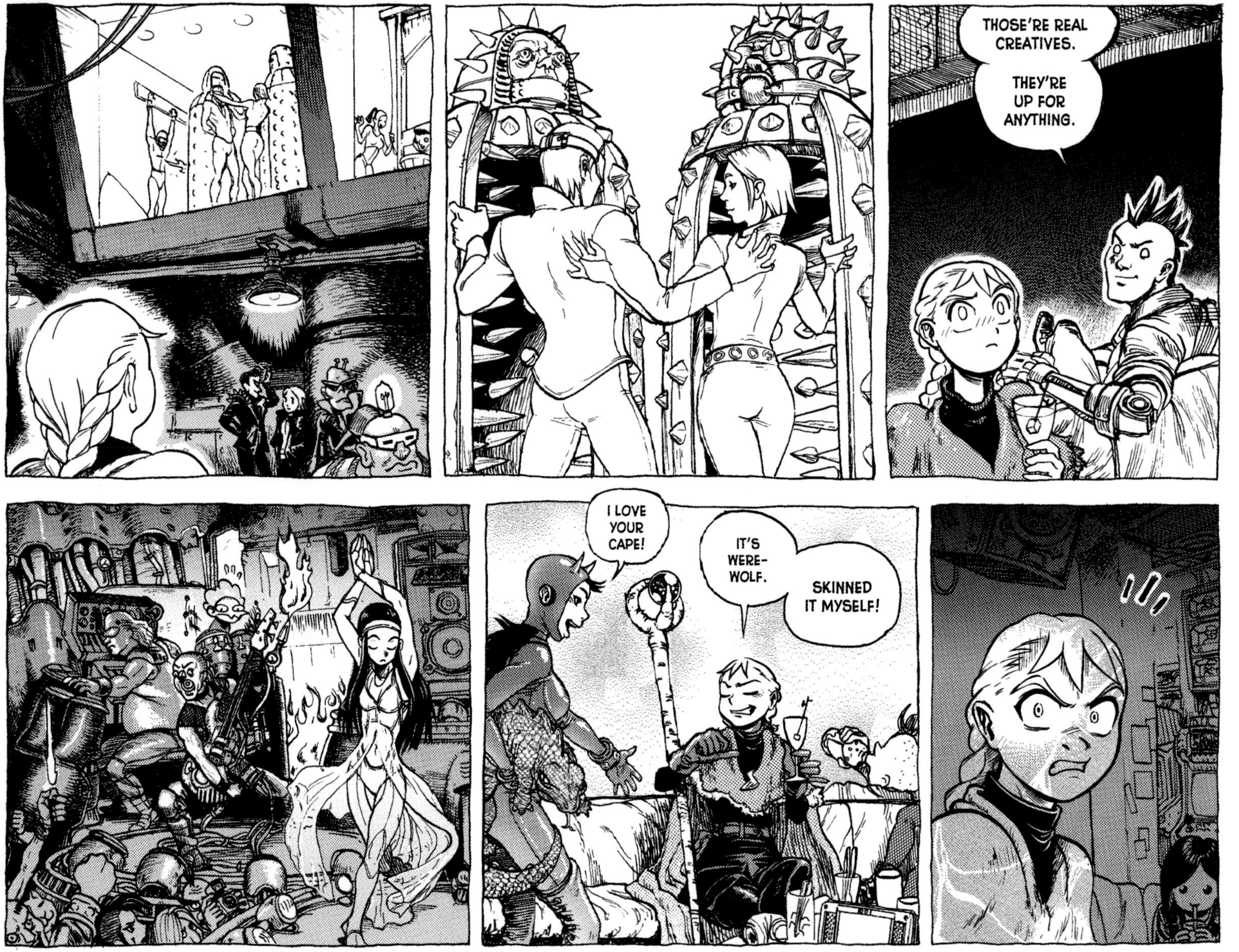
THOSE'RE REAL CREATIVES.
THEY'RE UP FOR ANYTHING.
I LOVE YOUR CAPE!
IT'S WERE-WOLF.
SKINNED IT MYSELF!

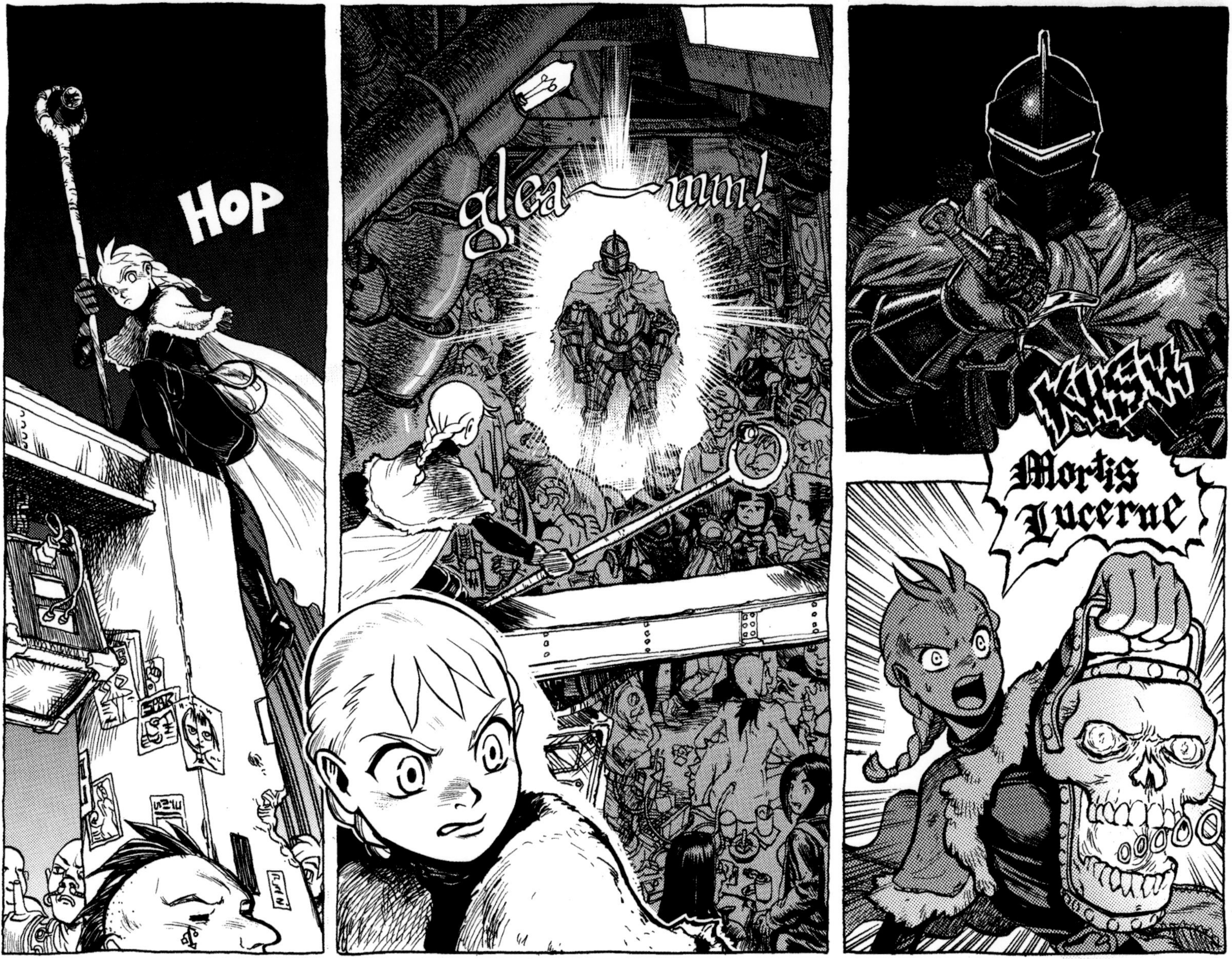
HOP
glea——mm!
KHSK
Mortis Lucerne

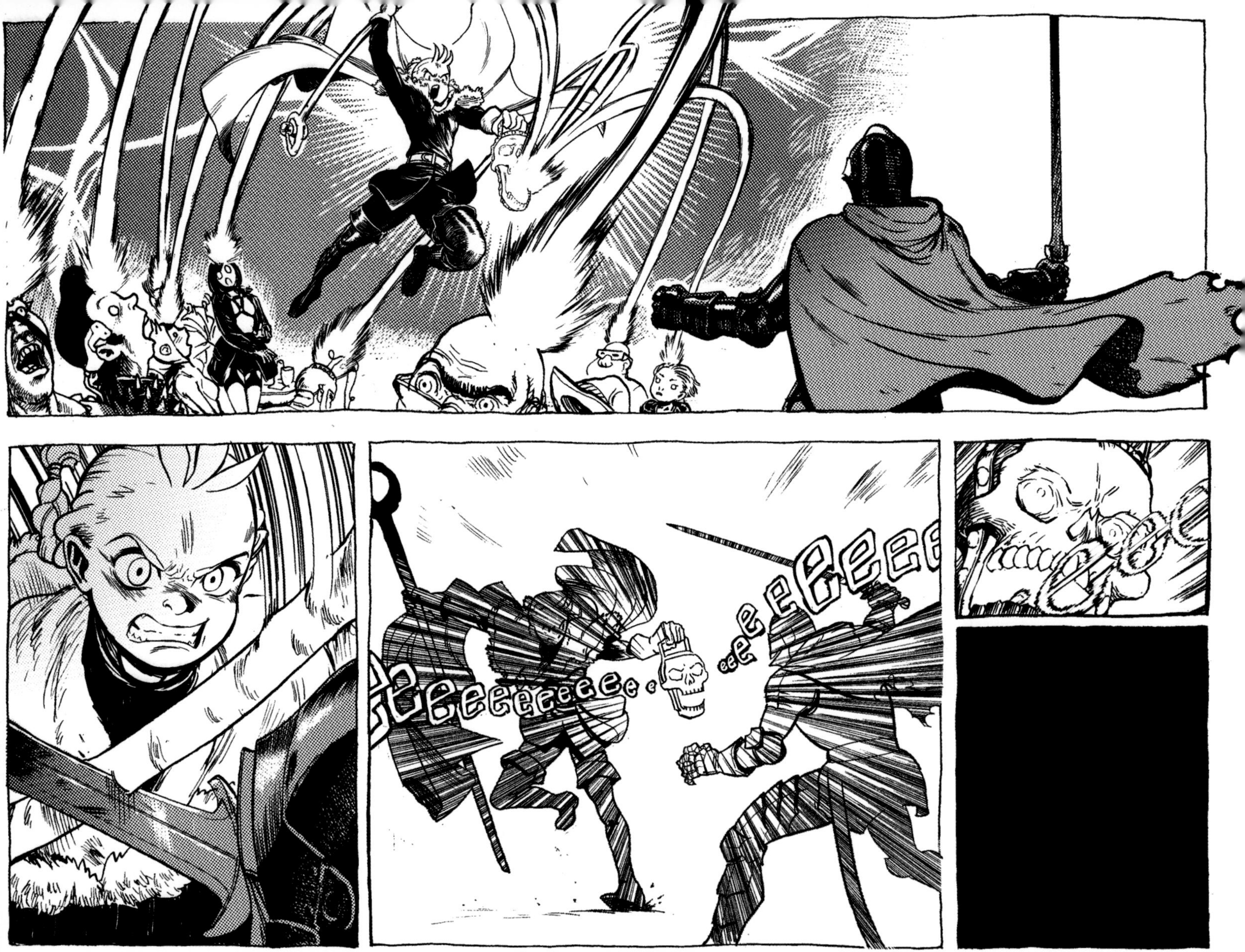
eeeeeeeeeeee e e eee eeeeeeeee

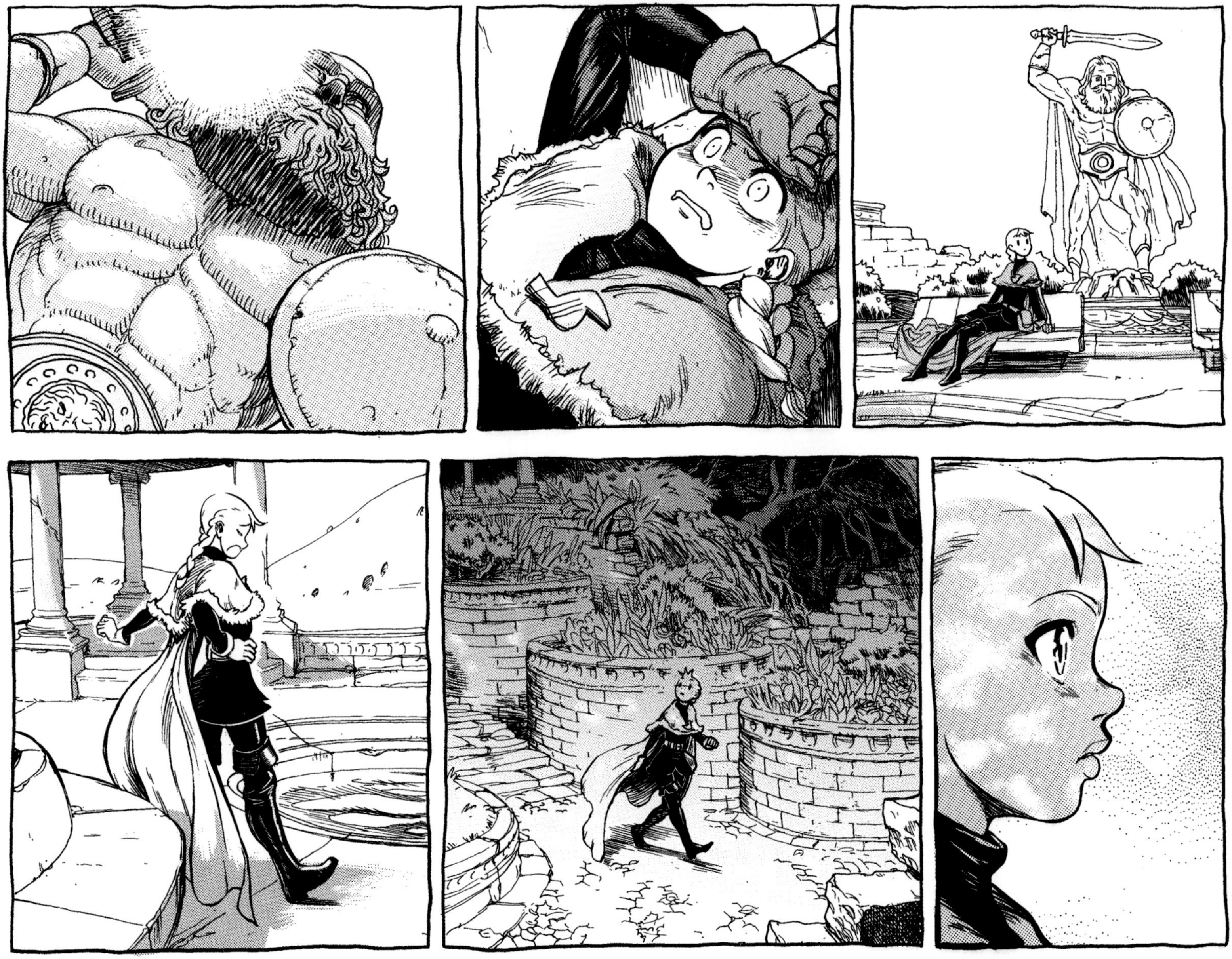

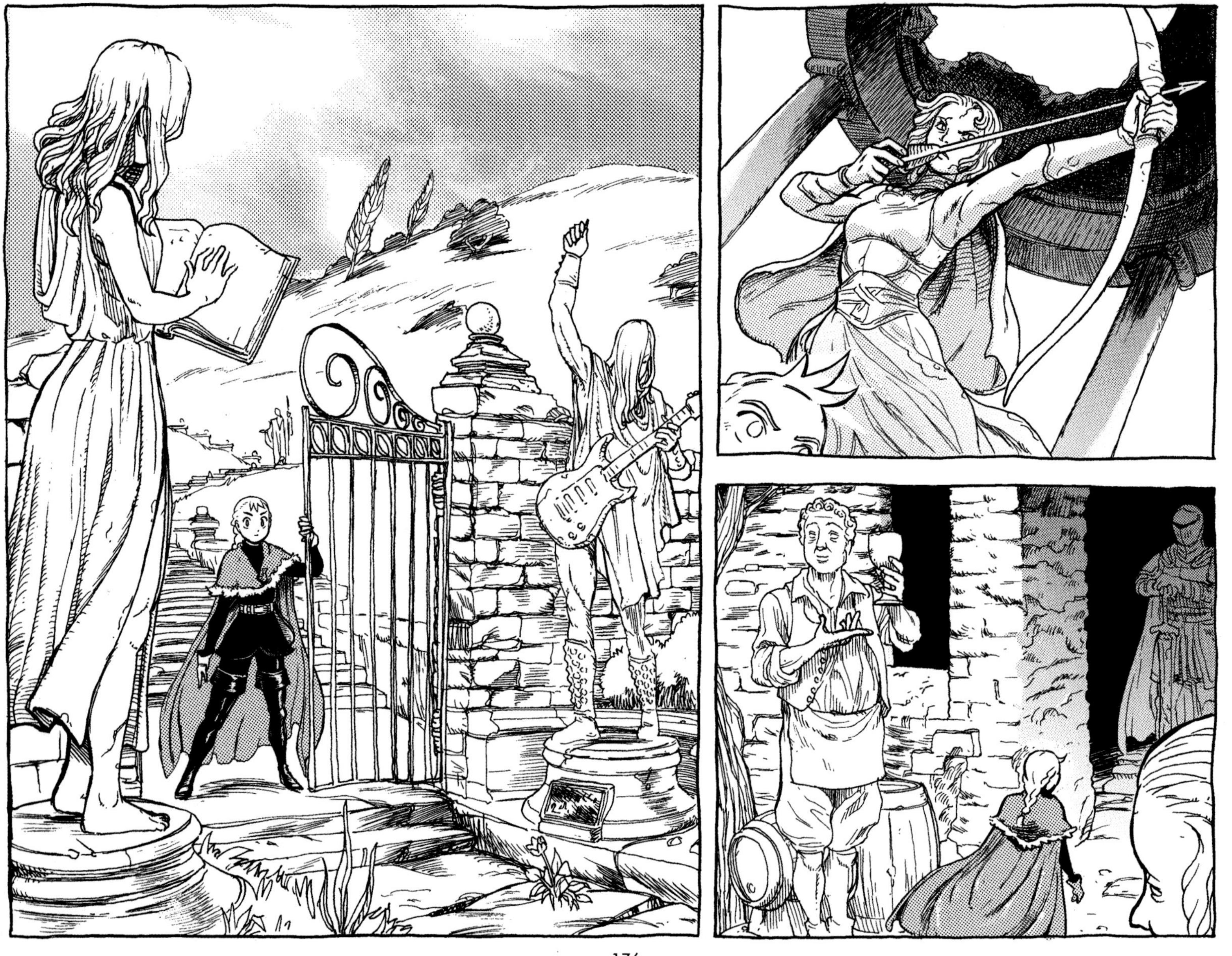

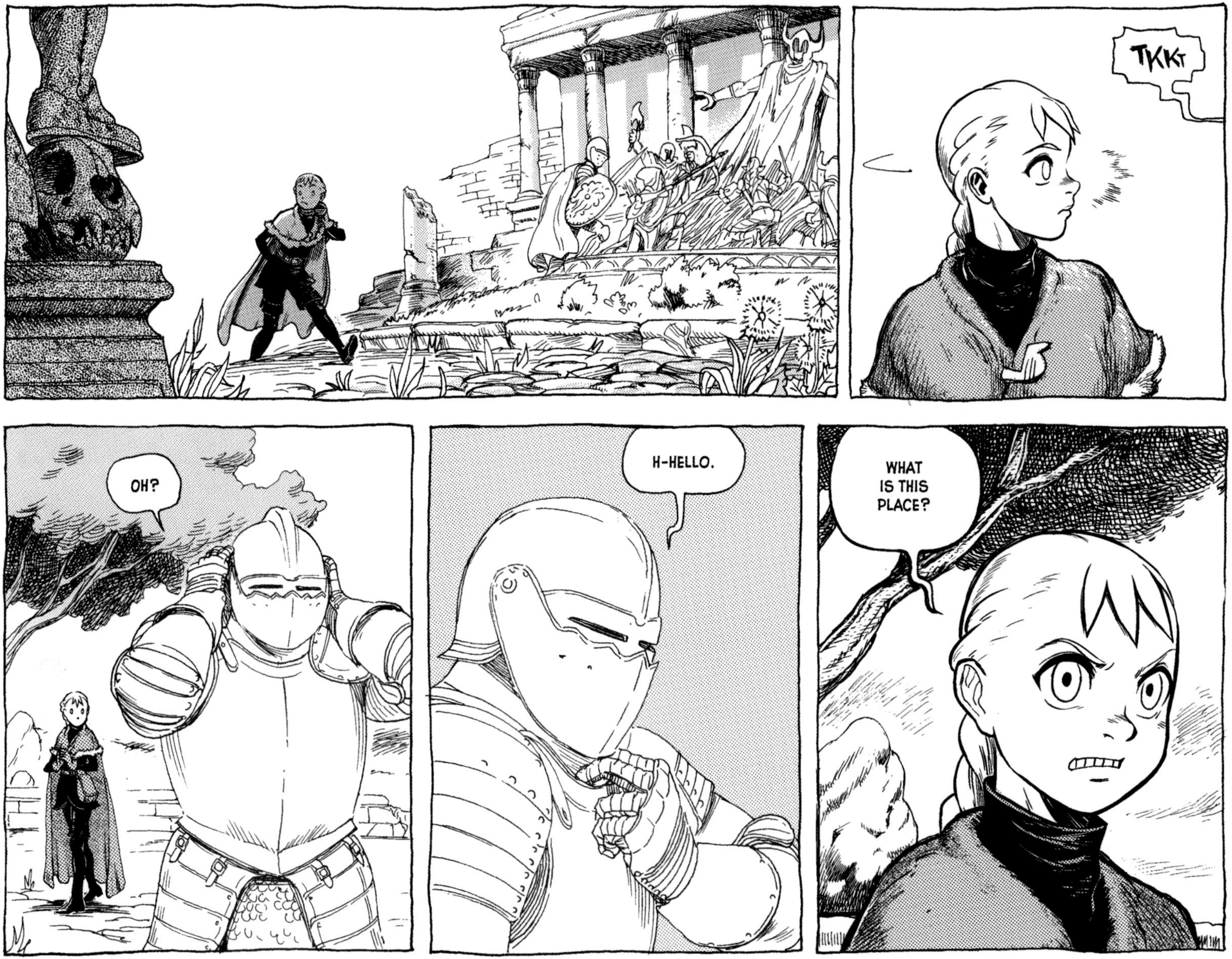
TKKT
OH?
H-HELLO.
WHAT IS THIS PLACE?

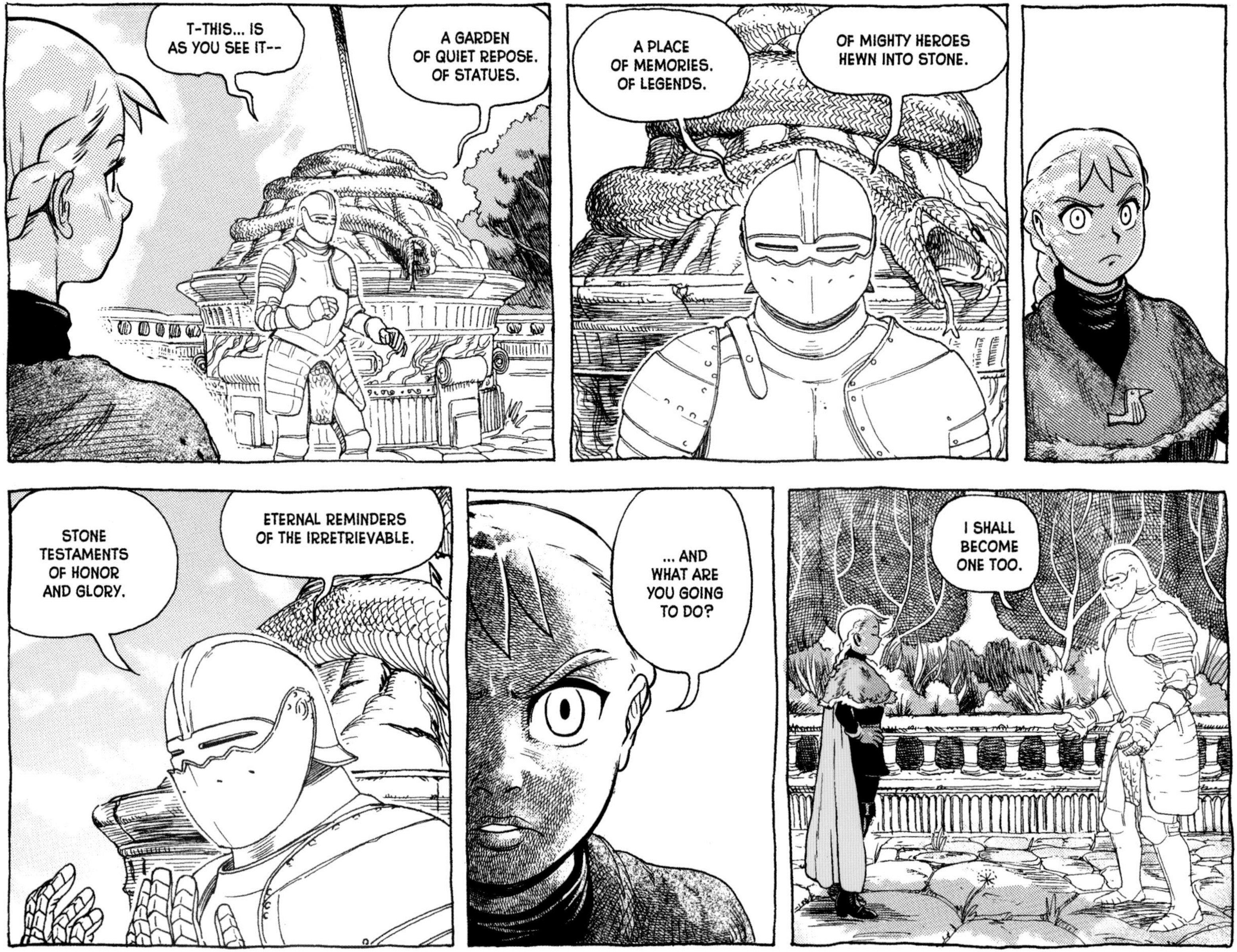
T-THIS... IS AS YOU SEE IT--
A GARDEN OF QUIET REPOSE. OF STATUES.
A PLACE OF MEMORIES. OF LEGENDS.
OF MIGHTY HEROES HEWN INTO STONE.
STONE TESTAMENTS OF HONOR AND GLORY.
ETERNAL REMINDERS OF THE IRRETRIEVABLE.
... AND WHAT ARE YOU GOING TO DO?
I SHALL BECOME ONE TOO.

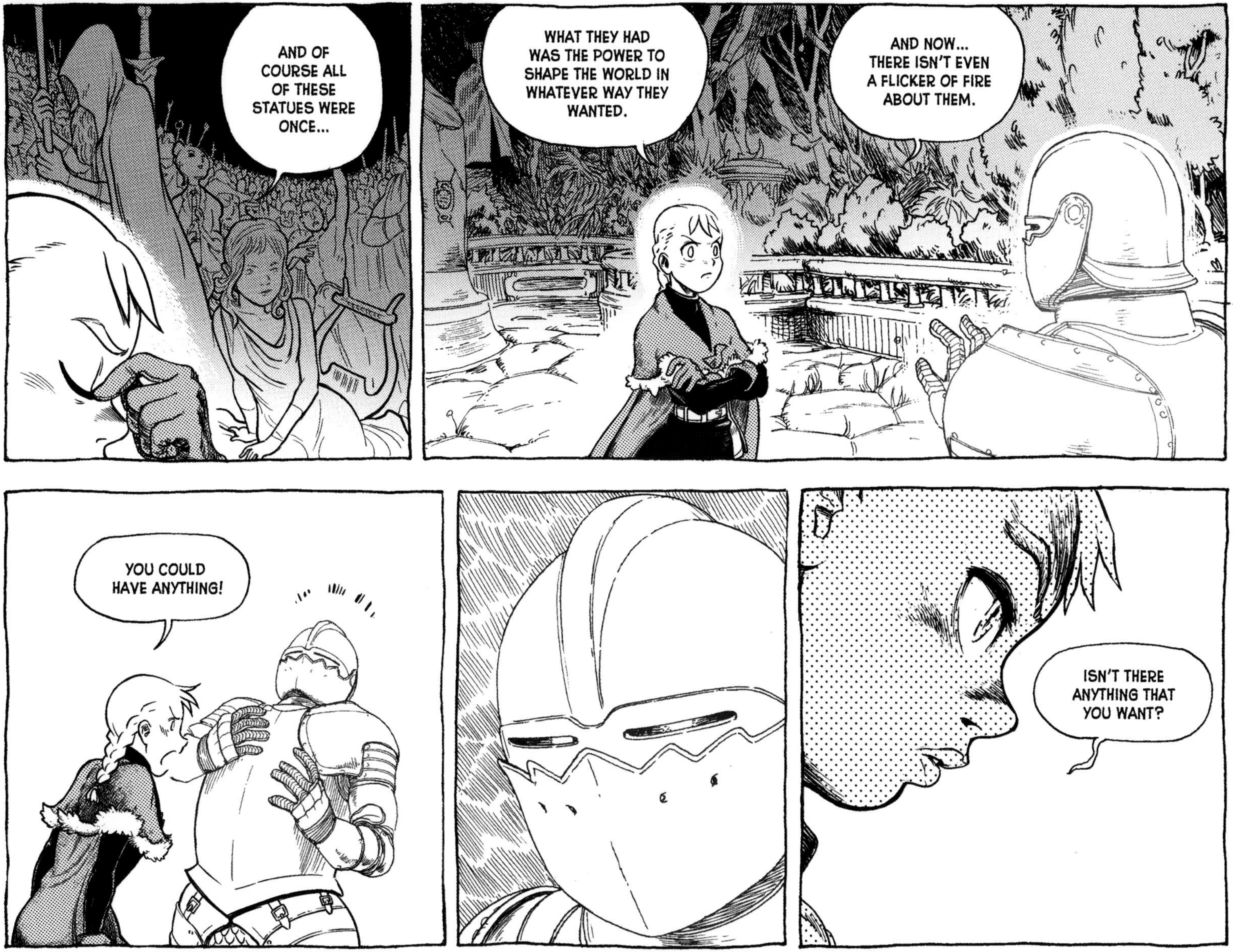
AND OF COURSE ALL OF THESE STATUES WERE ONCE...
WHAT THEY HAD WAS THE POWER TO SHAPE THE WORLD IN WHATEVER WAY THEY WANTED.
AND NOW... THERE ISN'T EVEN A FLICKER OF FIRE ABOUT THEM.
YOU COULD HAVE ANYTHING!
ISN'T THERE ANYTHING THAT YOU WANT?

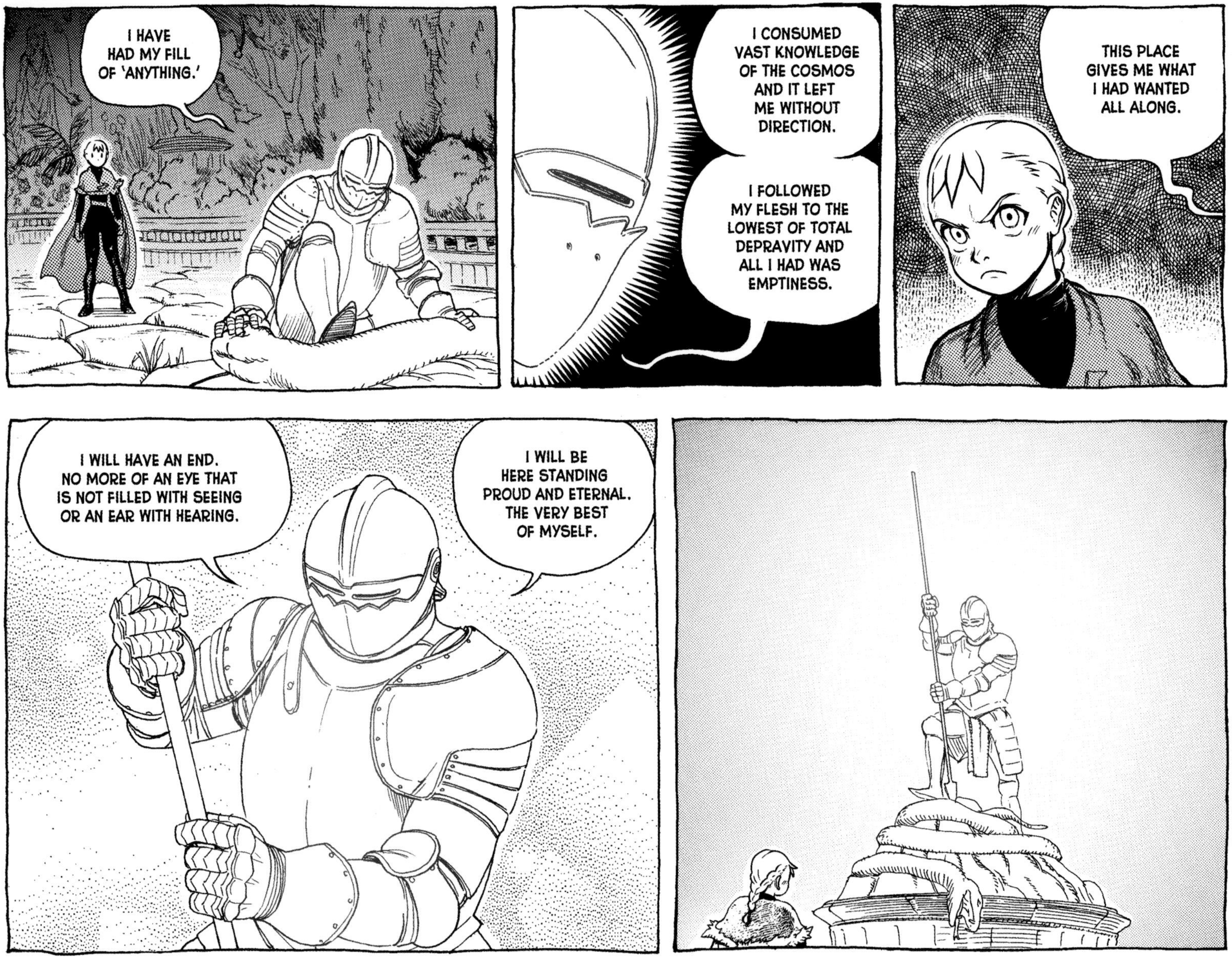
I HAVE HAD MY FILL OF 'ANYTHING.'
I CONSUMED VAST KNOWLEDGE OF THE COSMOS AND IT LEFT ME WITHOUT DIRECTION.
I FOLLOWED MY FLESH TO THE LOWEST OF TOTAL DEPRAVITY AND ALL I HAD WAS EMPTINESS.
THIS PLACE GIVES ME WHAT I HAD WANTED ALL ALONG.
I WILL HAVE AN END. NO MORE OF AN EYE THAT IS NOT FILLED WITH SEEING OR AN EAR WITH HEARING.
I WILL BE HERE STANDING PROUD AND ETERNAL. THE VERY BEST OF MYSELF.

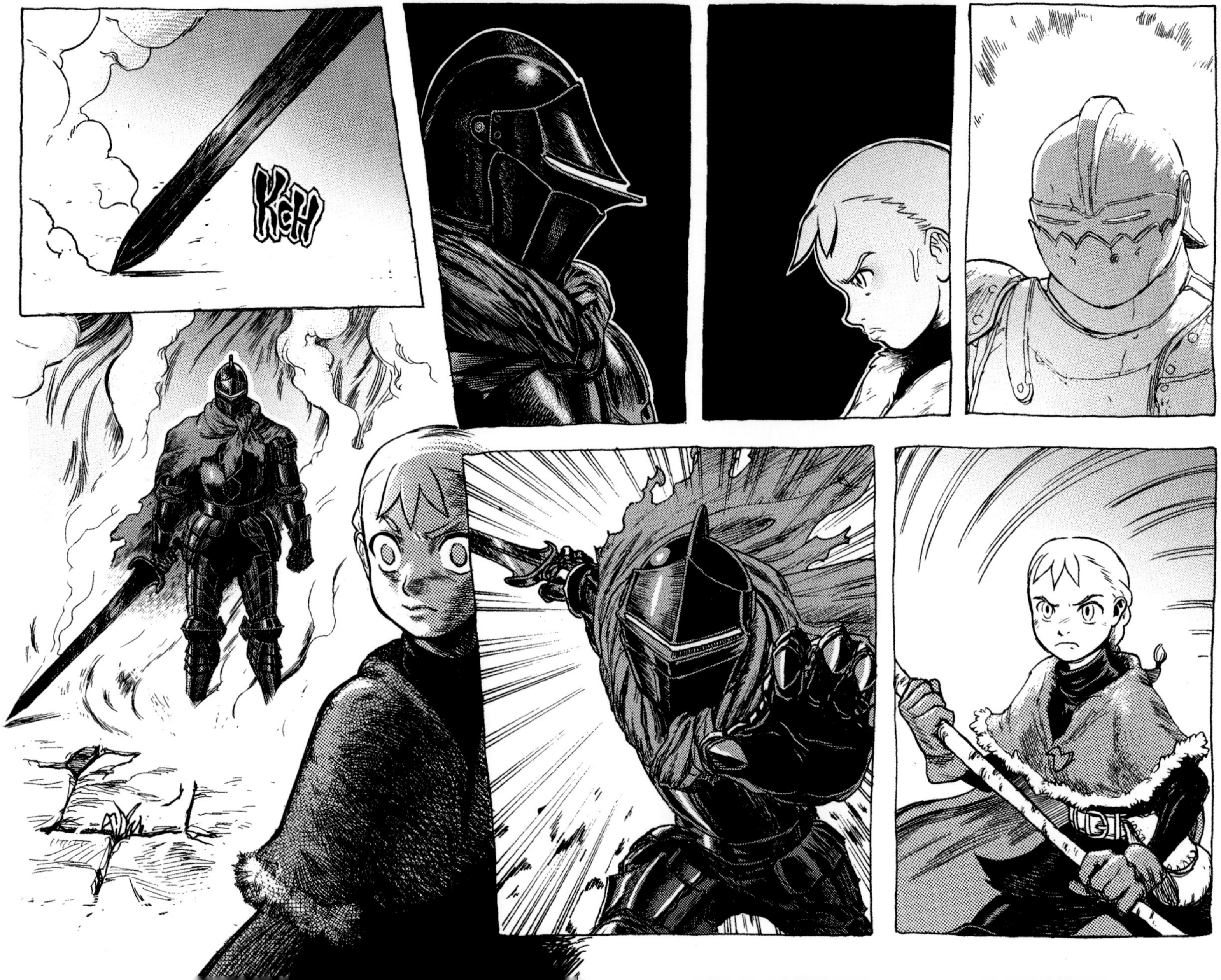
KCH

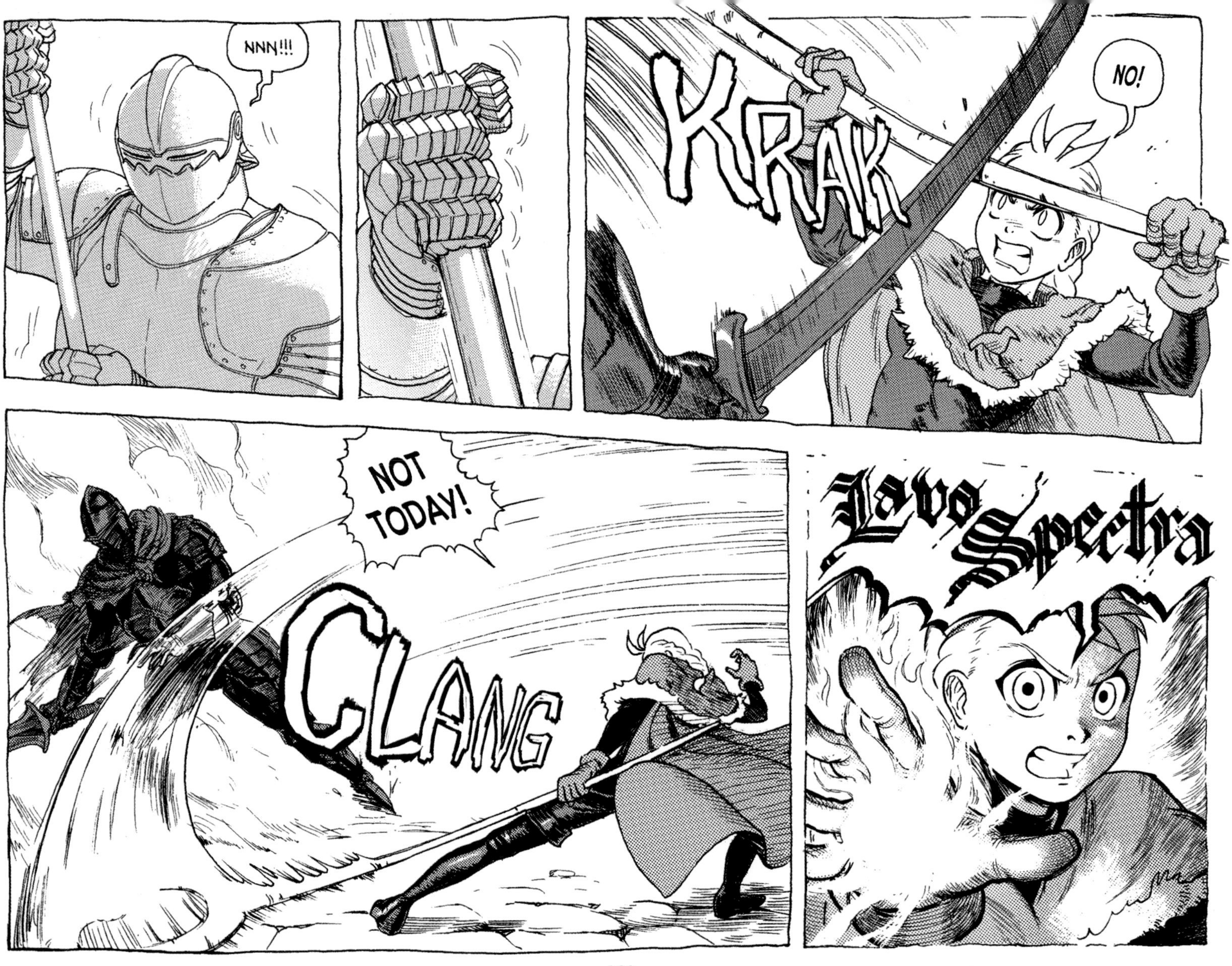
NNN!!!
NO!
KRAK
NOT TODAY!
CLANG
Lavo Spectra

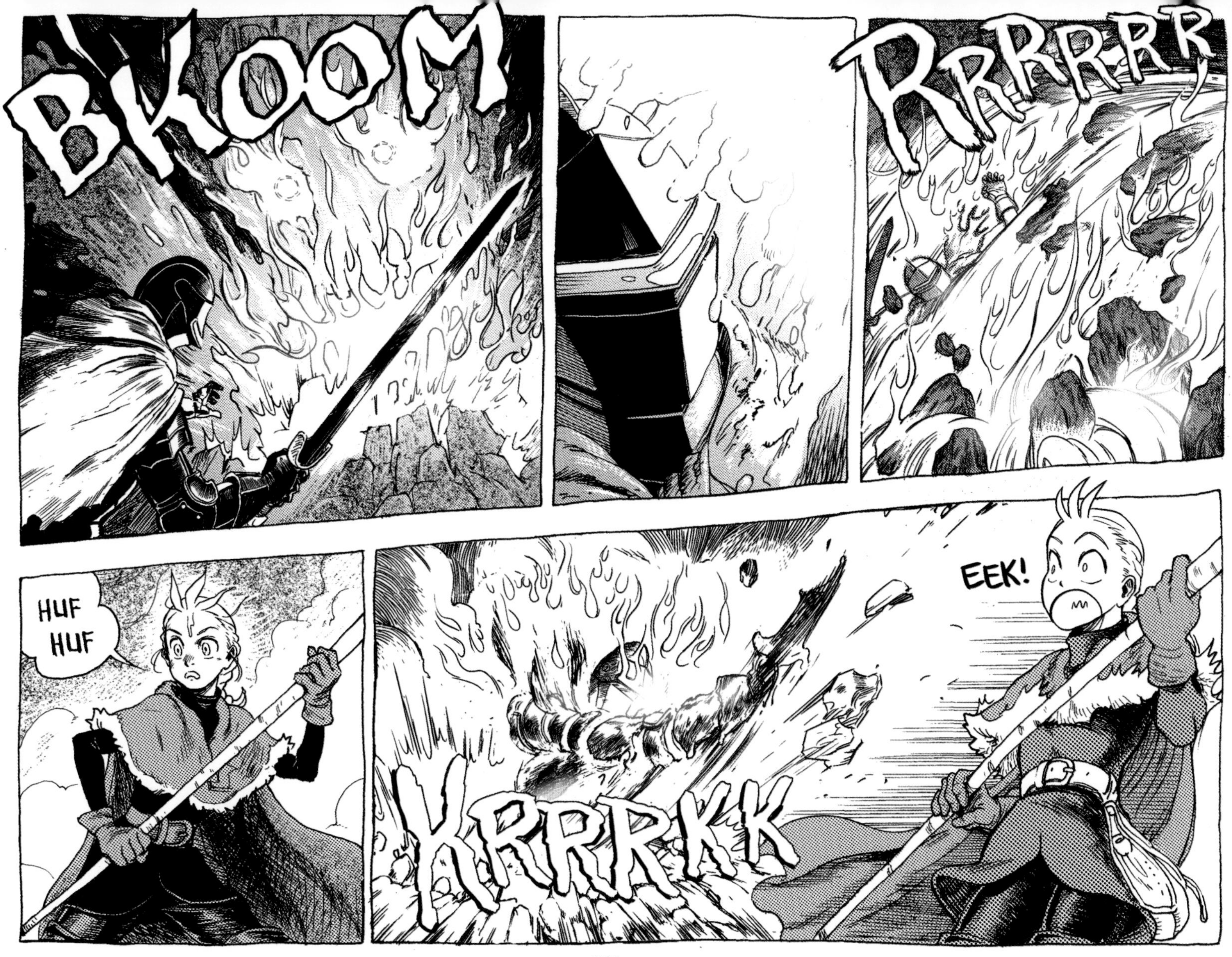
BKOOM
RRRRRR
HUF HUF
KRRRKK
EEK!

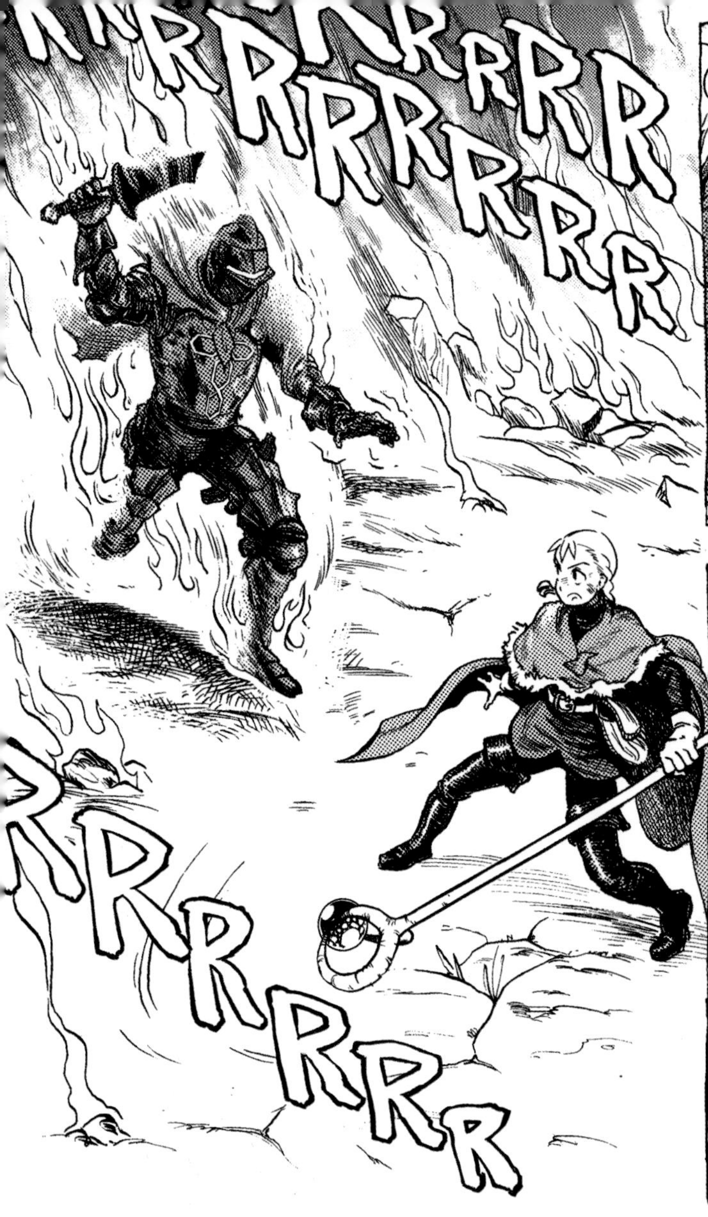
RRRRRRRRRRRRRRRRR
RRRRRRRR

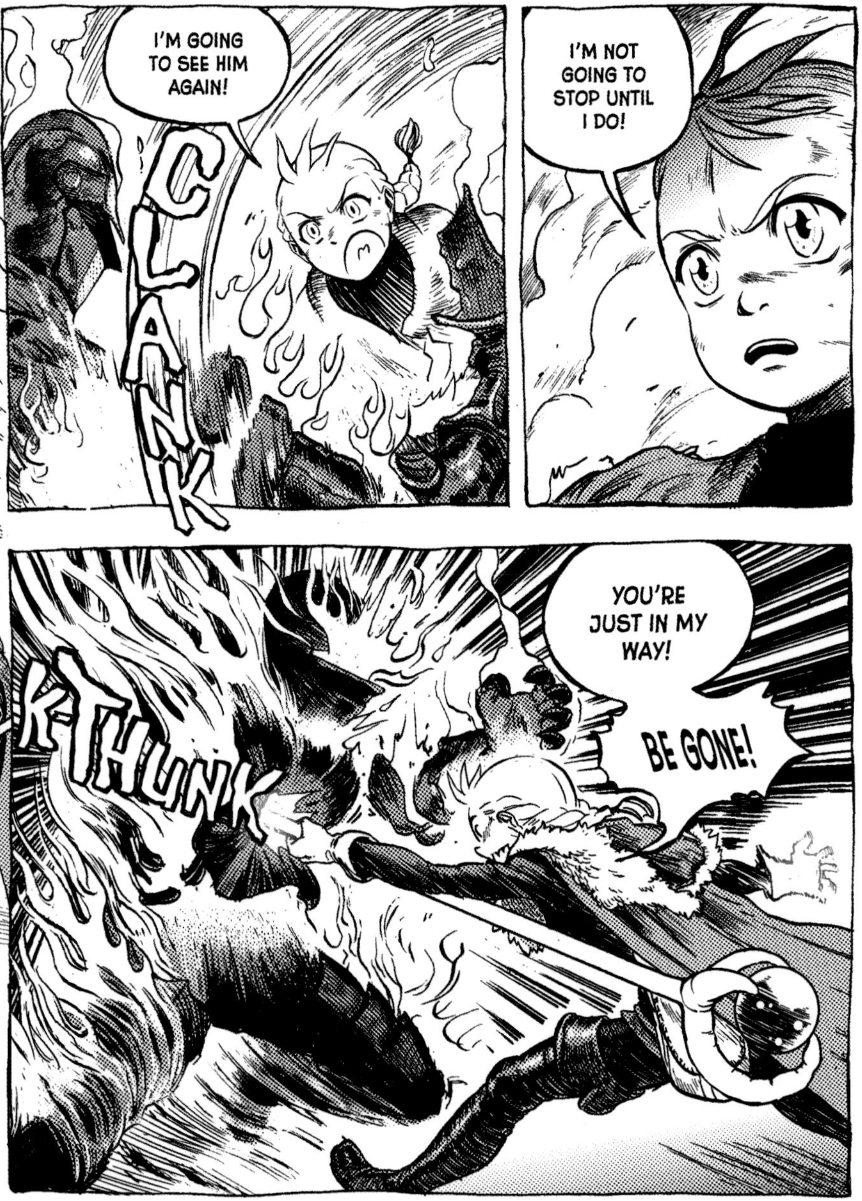
I'M GOING TO SEE HIM AGAIN!
CLANK
I'M NOT GOING TO STOP UNTIL I DO!
K-THUNK
YOU'RE JUST IN MY WAY!
BE GONE!

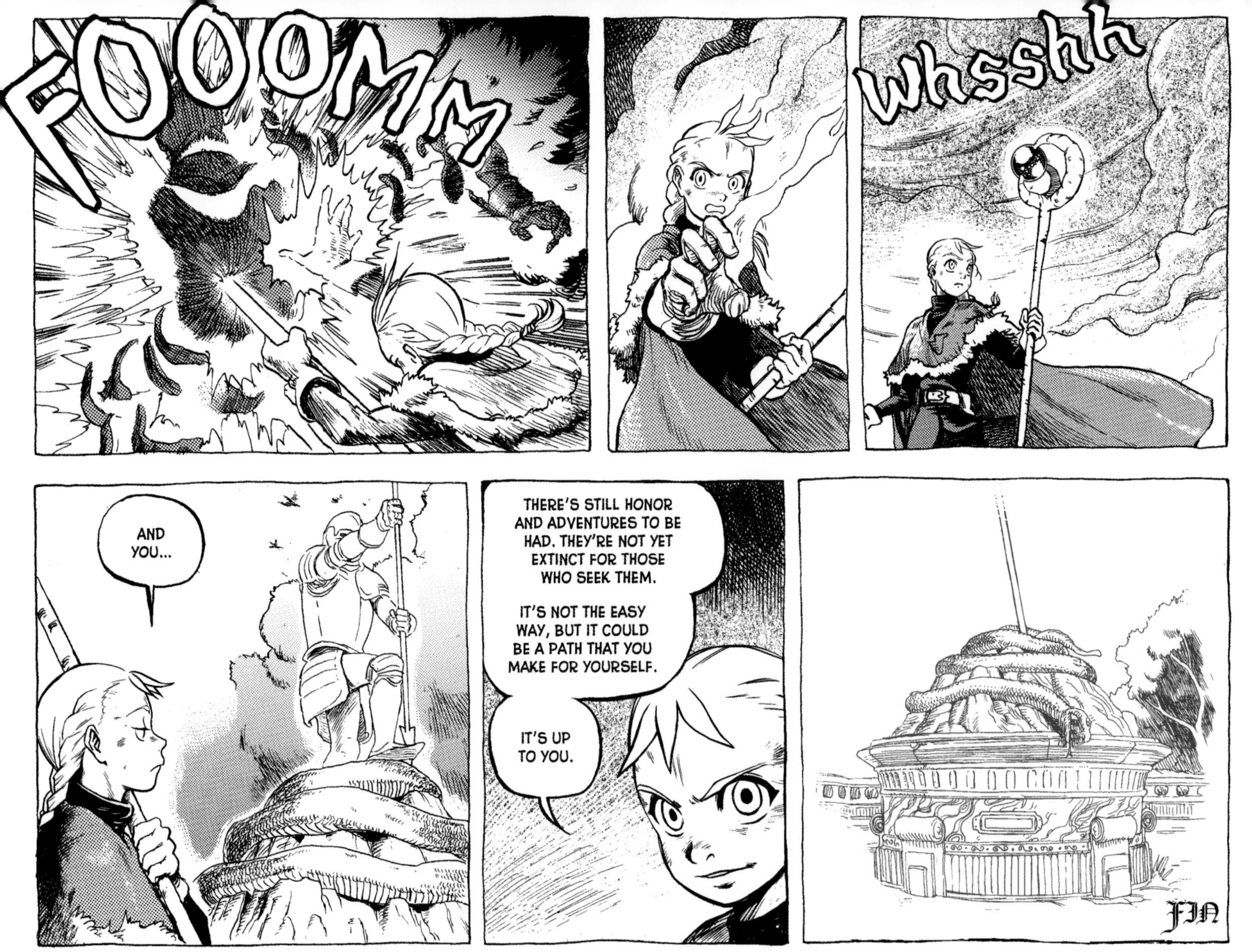
FOOOMM
whsshh
AND YOU...
THERE'S STILL HONOR AND ADVENTURES TO BE HAD. THEY'RE NOT YET EXTINCT FOR THOSE WHO SEEK THEM.
IT'S NOT THE EASY WAY, BUT IT COULD BE A PATH THAT YOU MAKE FOR YOURSELF.
IT'S UP TO YOU.
FIN

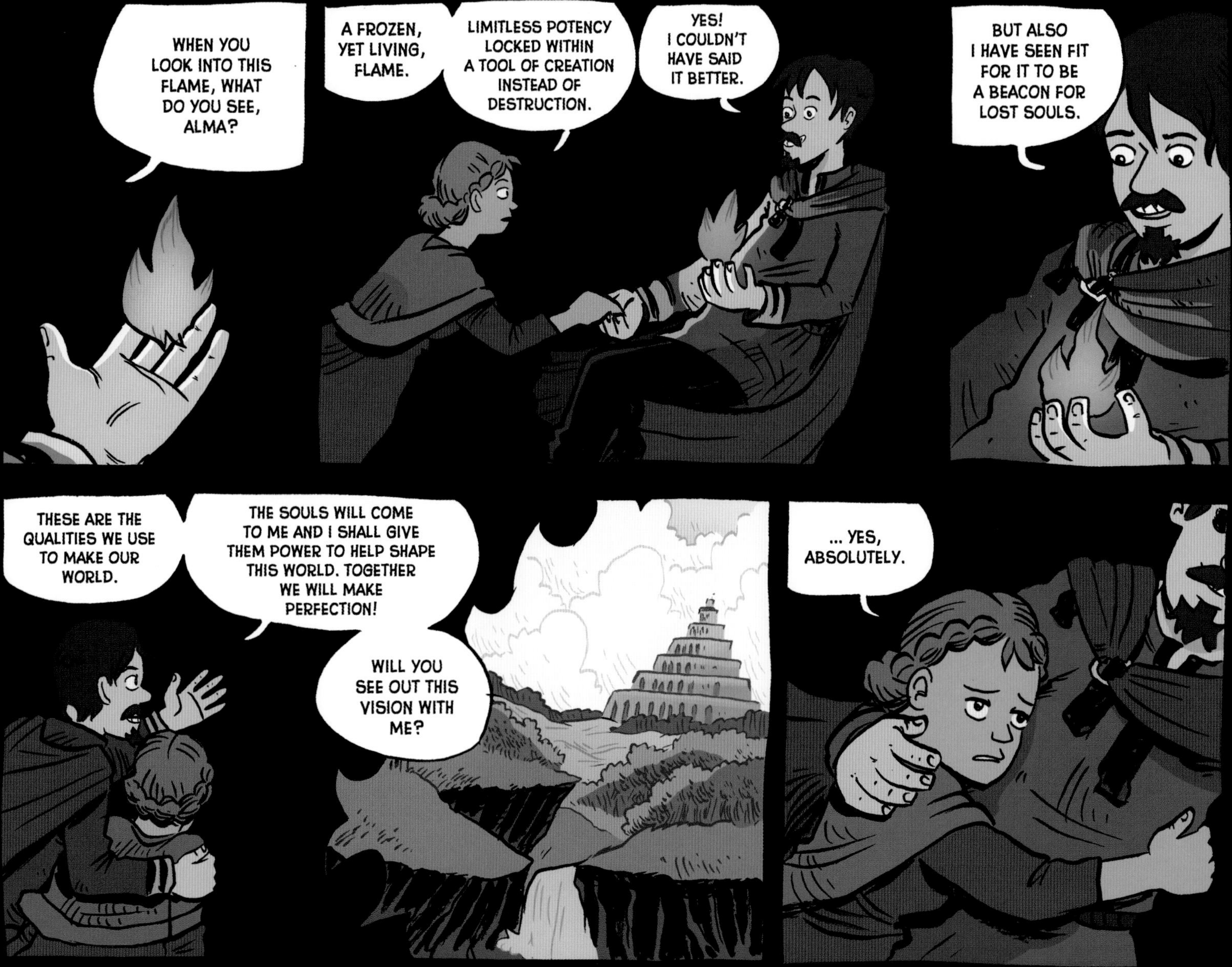
WHEN YOU LOOK INTO THIS FLAME, WHAT DO YOU SEE, ALMA?
A FROZEN, YET LIVING, FLAME.
LIMITLESS POTENCY LOCKED WITHIN A TOOL OF CREATION INSTEAD OF DESTRUCTION.
YES! I COULDN'T HAVE SAID IT BETTER.
BUT ALSO I HAVE SEEN FIT FOR IT TO BE A BEACON FOR LOST SOULS.
THESE ARE THE QUALITIES WE USE TO MAKE OUR WORLD.
THE SOULS WILL COME TO ME AND I SHALL GIVE THEM POWER TO HELP SHAPE THIS WORLD. TOGETHER WE WILL MAKE PERFECTION!
WILL YOU SEE OUT THIS VISION WITH ME?
... YES, ABSOLUTELY.

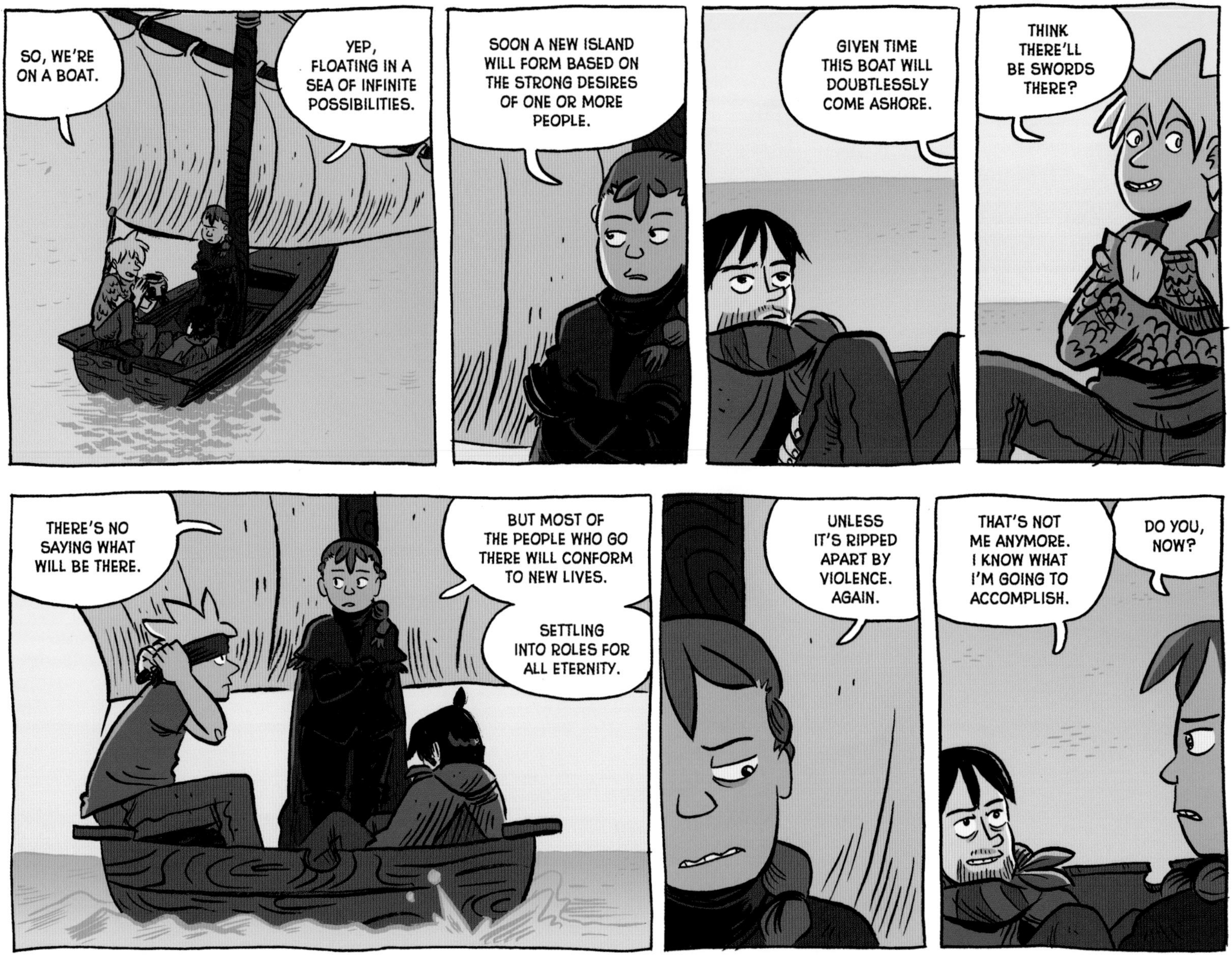
SO, WE'RE ON A BOAT.
YEP, FLOATING IN A SEA OF INFINITE POSSIBILITIES.
SOON A NEW ISLAND WILL FORM BASED ON THE STRONG DESIRES OF ONE OR MORE PEOPLE.
GIVEN TIME THIS BOAT WILL DOUBTLESSLY COME ASHORE.
THINK THERE'LL BE SWORDS THERE?
THERE'S NO SAYING WHAT WILL BE THERE.
BUT MOST OF THE PEOPLE WHO GO THERE WILL CONFORM TO NEW LIVES.
SETTLING INTO ROLES FOR ALL ETERNITY.
UNLESS IT'S RIPPED APART BY VIOLENCE. AGAIN.
THAT'S NOT ME ANYMORE. I KNOW WHAT I'M GOING TO ACCOMPLISH.
DO YOU, NOW?

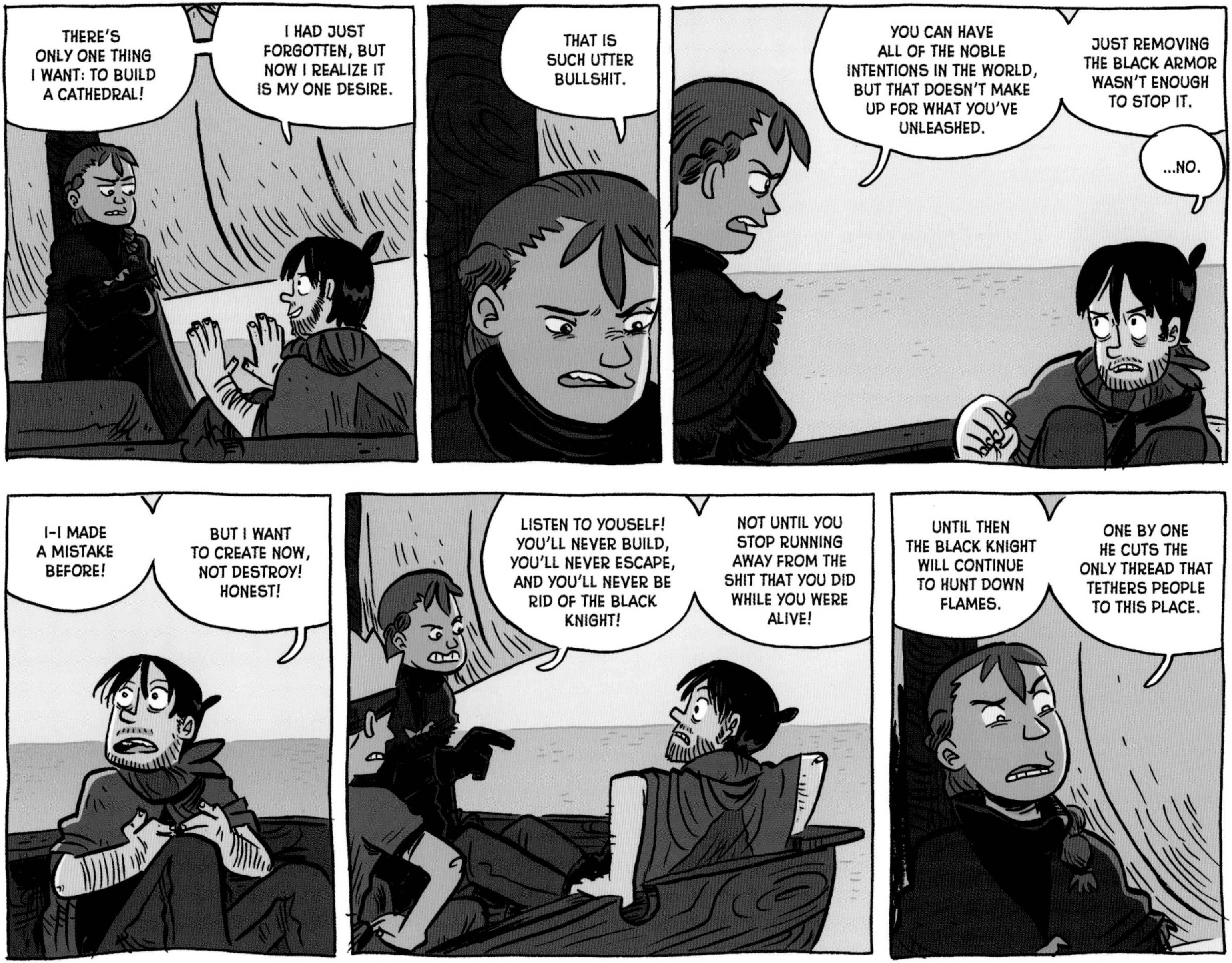
THERE'S ONLY ONE THING I WANT: TO BUILD A CATHEDRAL!
I HAD JUST FORGOTTEN, BUT NOW I REALIZE IT IS MY ONE DESIRE.
THAT IS SUCH UTTER BULLSHIT.
YOU CAN HAVE ALL OF THE NOBLE INTENTIONS IN THE WORLD, BUT THAT DOESN'T MAKE UP FOR WHAT YOU'VE UNLEASHED.
JUST REMOVING THE BLACK ARMOR WASN'T ENOUGH TO STOP IT.
...NO.
I-I MADE A MISTAKE BEFORE!
BUT I WANT TO CREATE NOW, NOT DESTROY! HONEST!
LISTEN TO YOUSELF! YOU'LL NEVER BUILD, YOU'LL NEVER ESCAPE, AND YOU'LL NEVER BE RID OF THE BLACK KNIGHT!
NOT UNTIL YOU STOP RUNNING AWAY FROM THE SHIT THAT YOU DID WHILE YOU WERE ALIVE!
UNTIL THEN THE BLACK KNIGHT WILL CONTINUE TO HUNT DOWN FLAMES.
ONE BY ONE HE CUTS THE ONLY THREAD THAT TETHERS PEOPLE TO THIS PLACE.

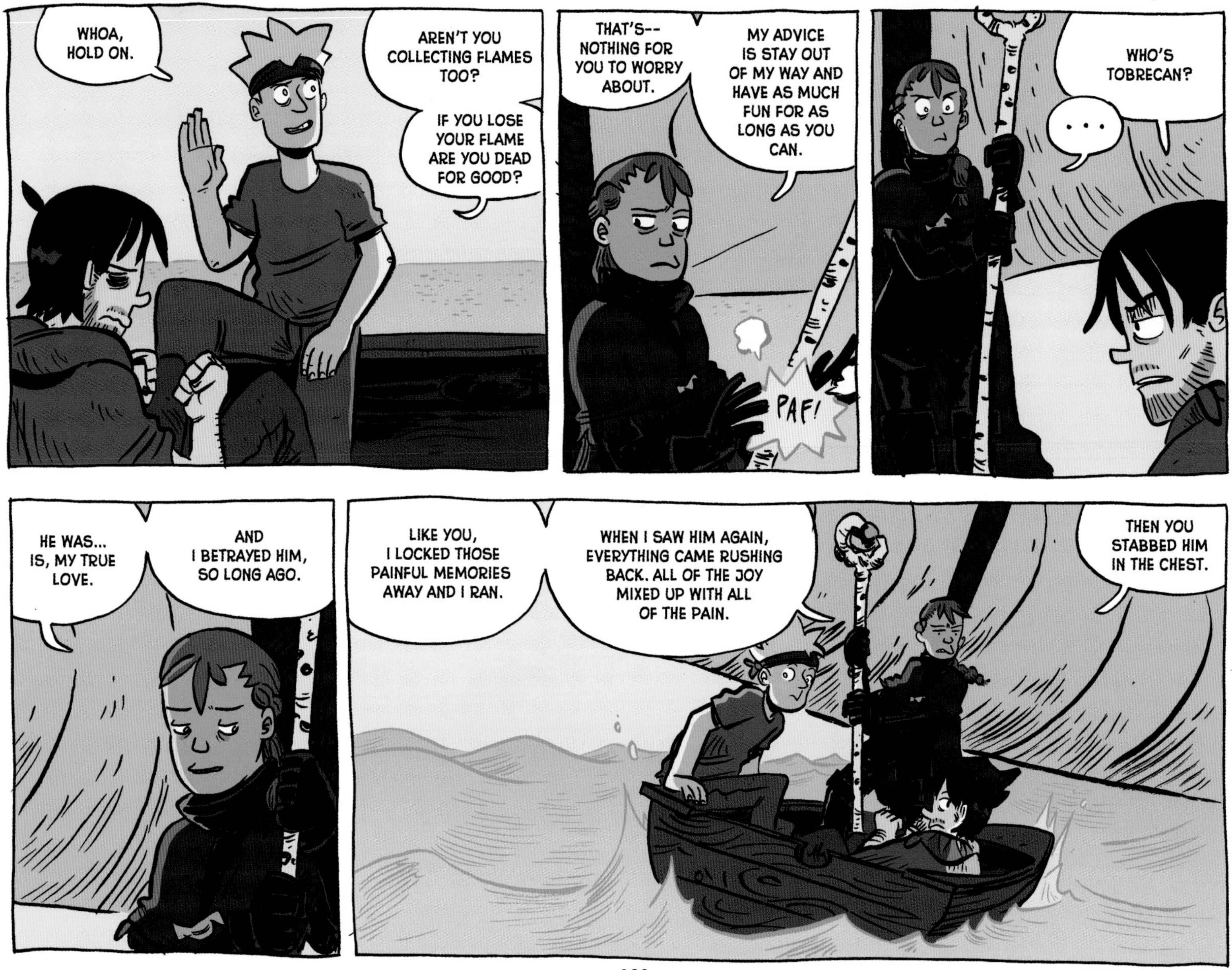
WHOA, HOLD ON.
AREN'T YOU COLLECTING FLAMES TOO?
IF YOU LOSE YOUR FLAME ARE YOU DEAD FOR GOOD?
THAT'S-- NOTHING FOR YOU TO WORRY ABOUT.
MY ADVICE IS STAY OUT OF MY WAY AND HAVE AS MUCH FUN FOR AS LONG AS YOU CAN.
PAF!
WHO'S TOBRECAN?
...
HE WAS... IS, MY TRUE LOVE.
AND I BETRAYED HIM, SO LONG AGO.
LIKE YOU, I LOCKED THOSE PAINFUL MEMORIES AWAY AND I RAN.
WHEN I SAW HIM AGAIN, EVERYTHING CAME RUSHING BACK. ALL OF THE JOY MIXED UP WITH ALL OF THE PAIN.
THEN YOU STABBED HIM IN THE CHEST.

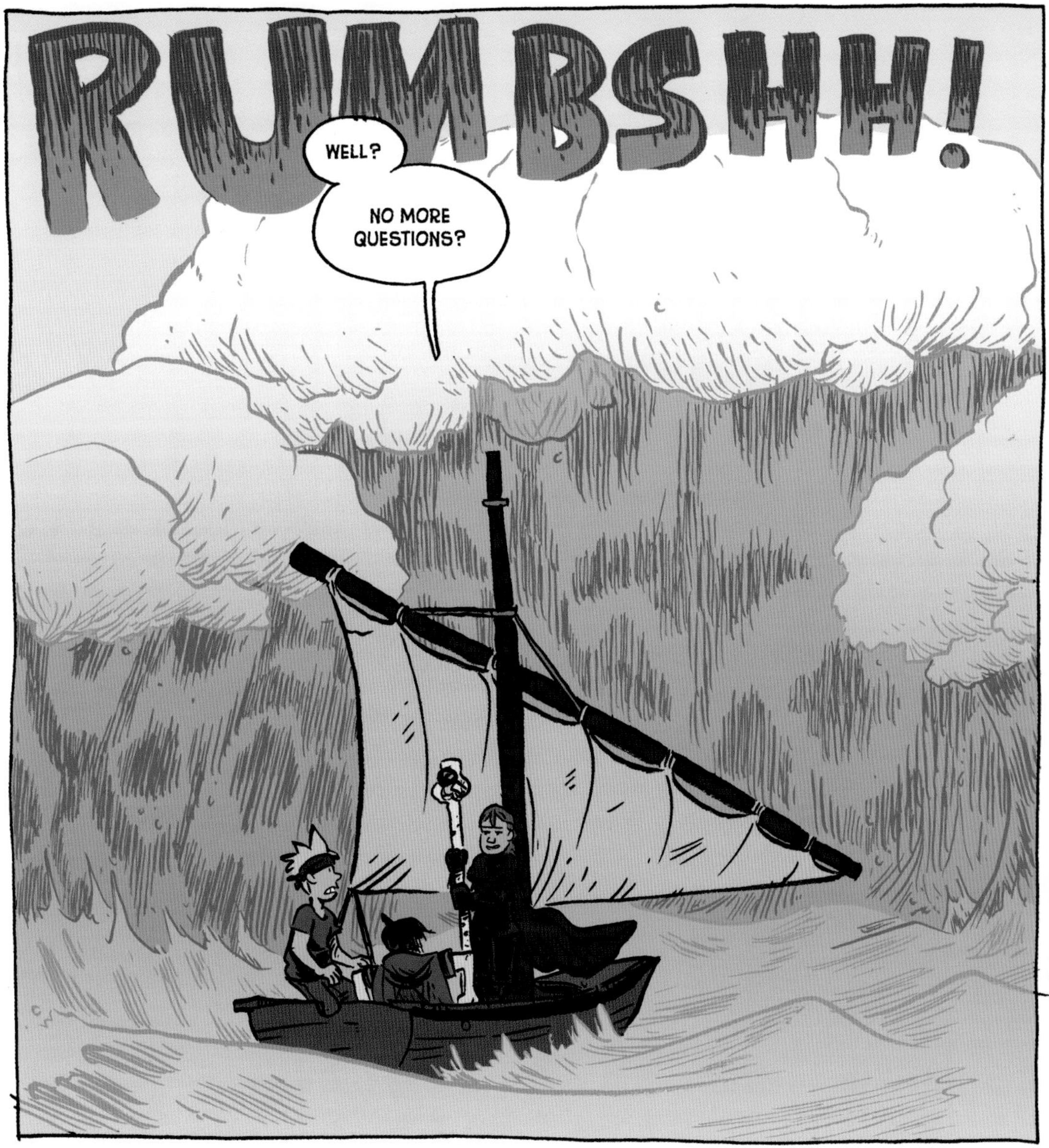
RUMBSHH!
WELL?
NO MORE QUESTIONS?

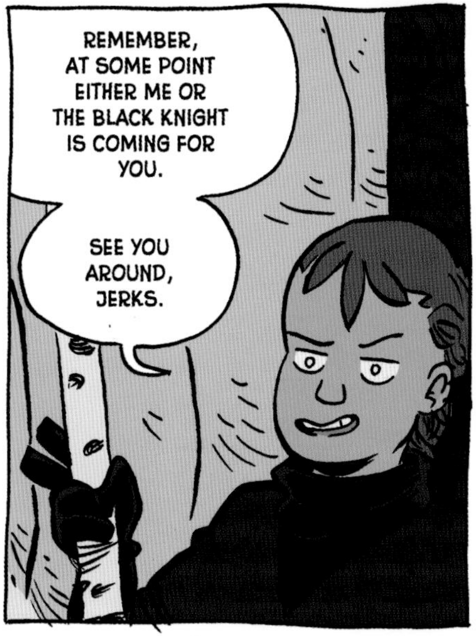
REMEMBER, AT SOME POINT EITHER ME OR THE BLACK KNIGHT IS COMING FOR YOU.
SEE YOU AROUND, JERKS.

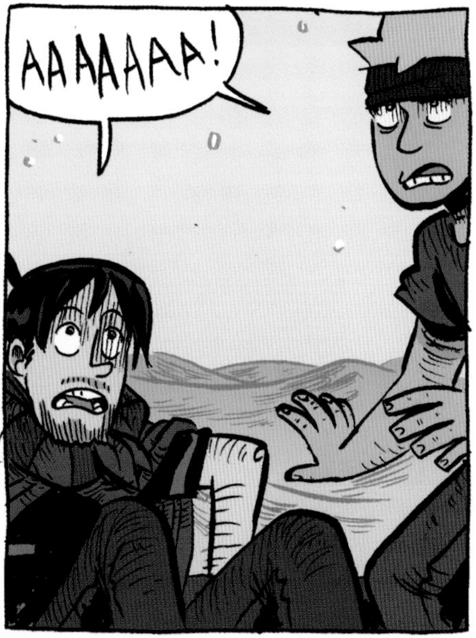
AAAAAAA!

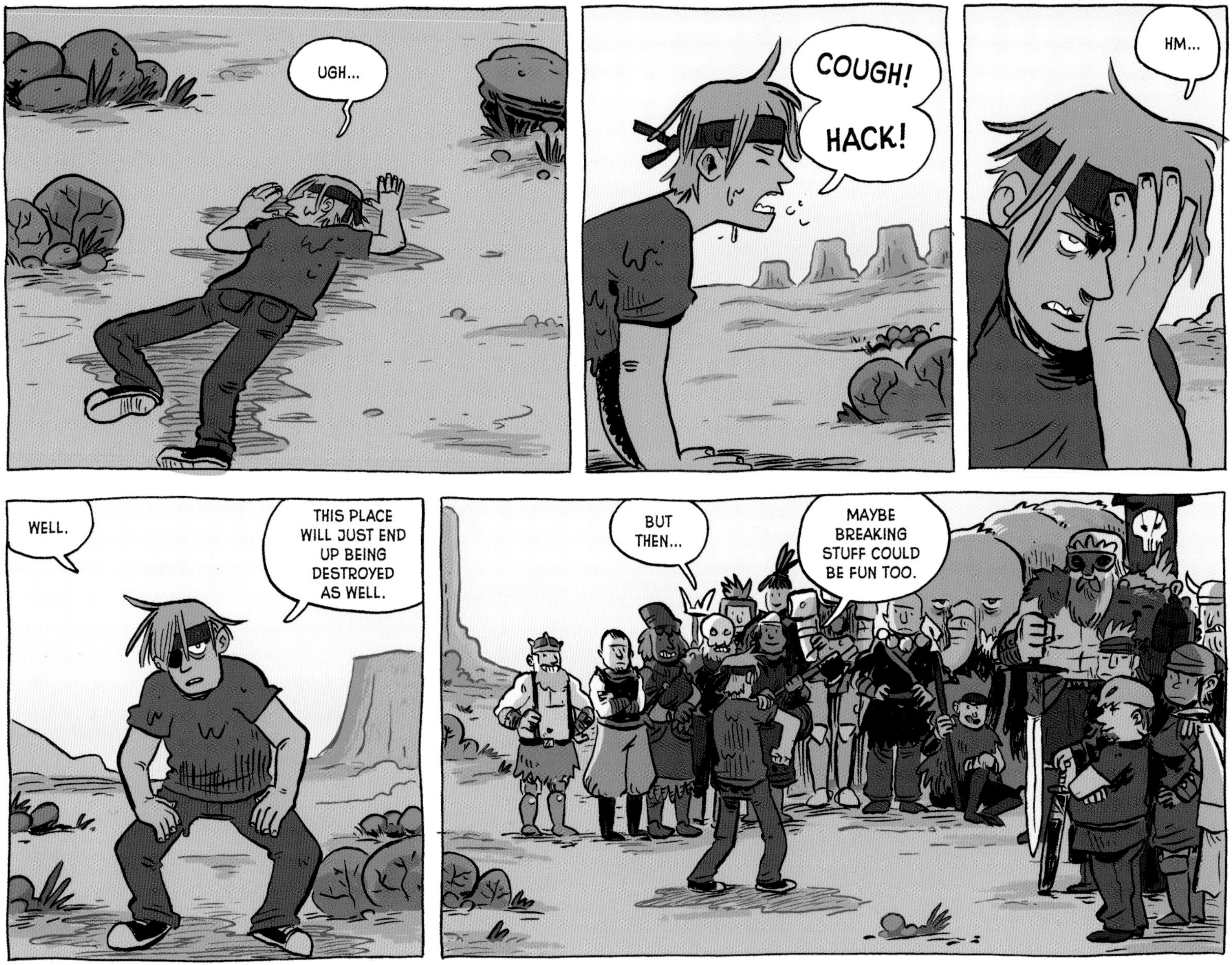
UGH...
COUGH!
HACK!
HM...
WELL.
THIS PLACE WILL JUST END UP BEING DESTROYED AS WELL.
BUT THEN...
MAYBE BREAKING STUFF COULD BE FUN TOO.

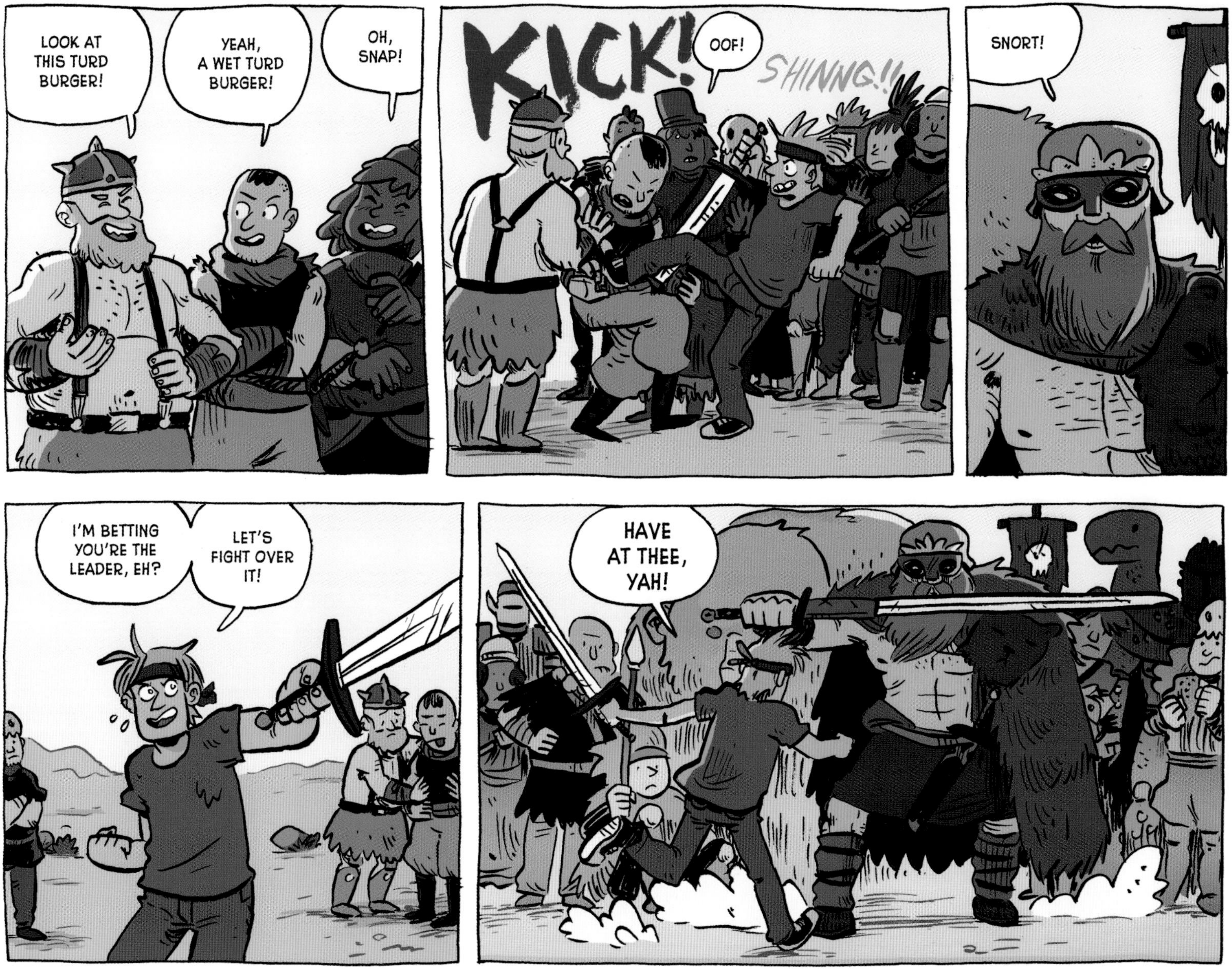
LOOK AT THIS TURD BURGER!
YEAH, A WET TURD BURGER!
OH, SNAP!
KICK!
OOF!
SHINNG!!
SNORT!
I'M BETTING YOU'RE THE LEADER, EH?
LET'S FIGHT OVER IT!
HAVE AT THEE, YAH!

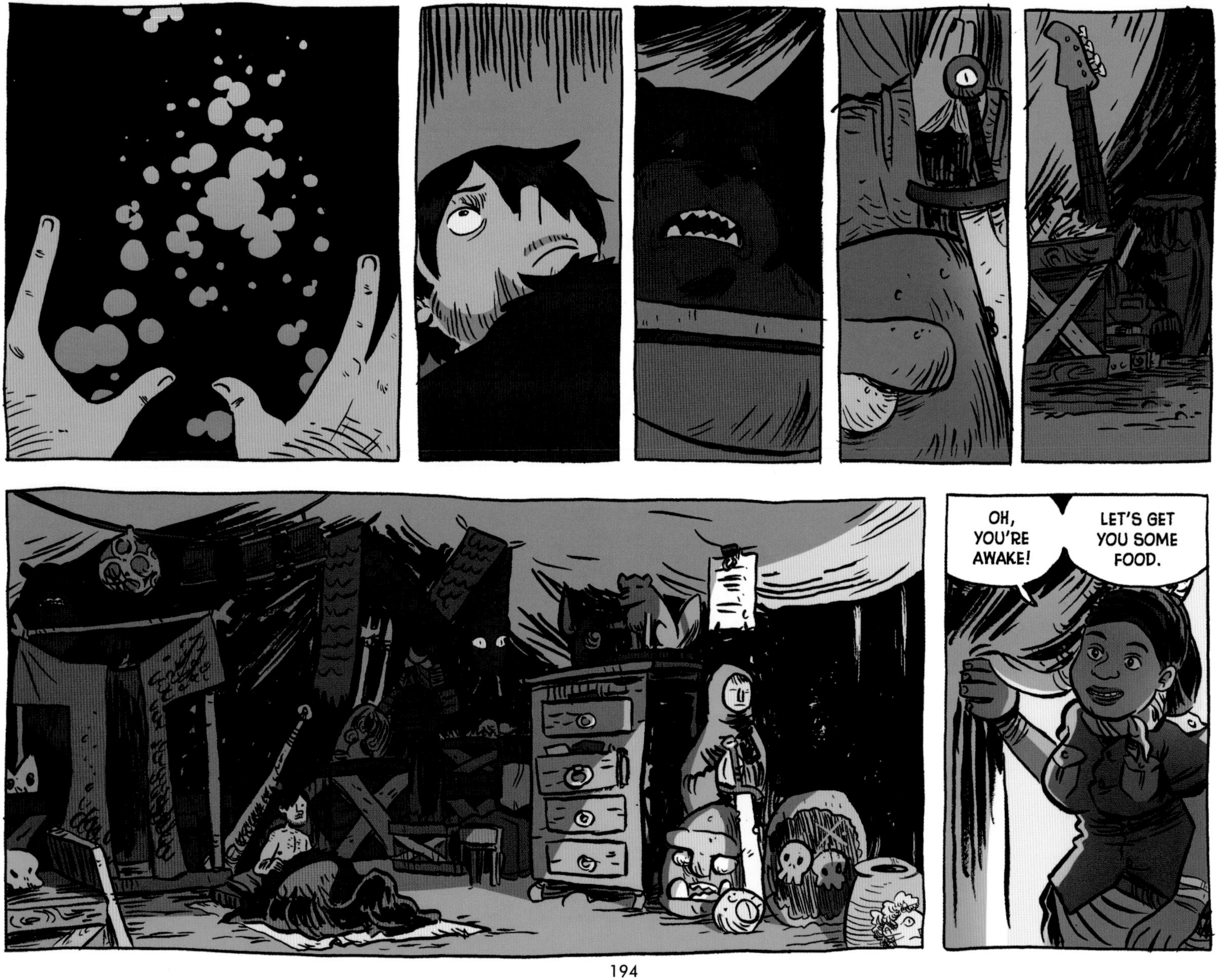
OH, YOU'RE AWAKE!
LET'S GET YOU SOME FOOD.

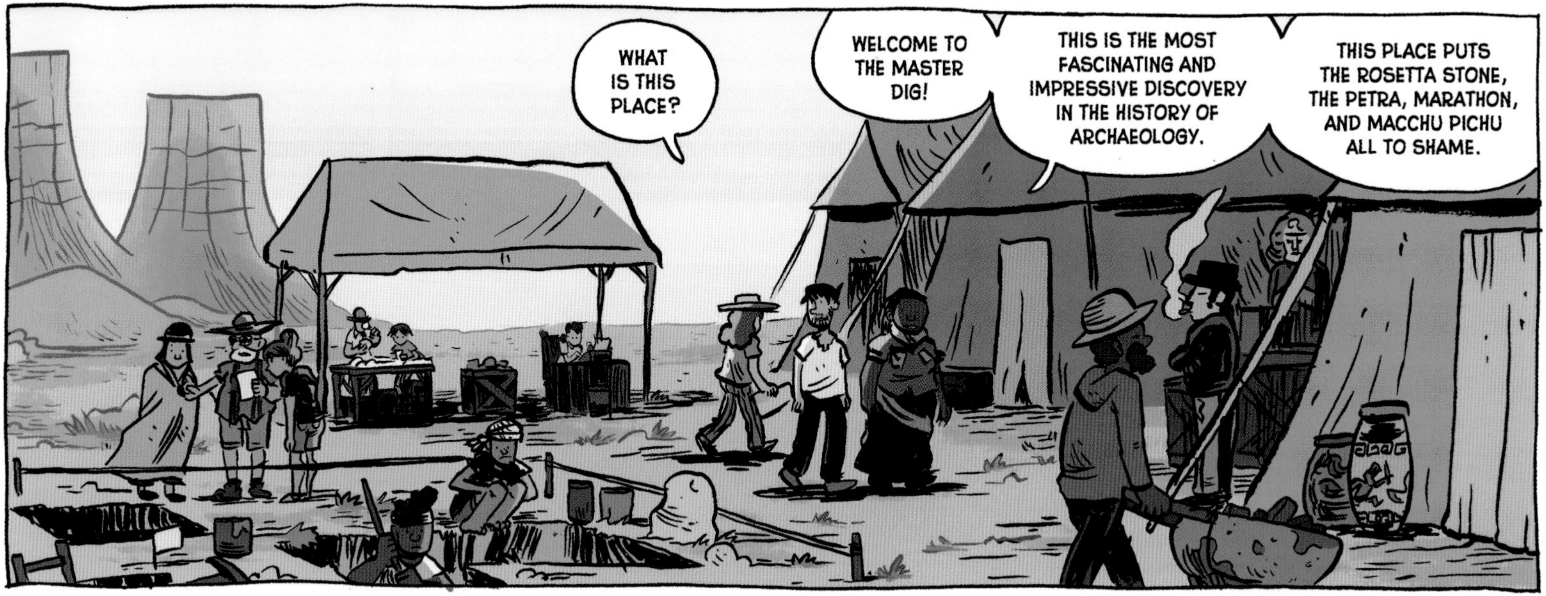
WHAT IS THIS PLACE?
WELCOME TO THE MASTER DIG!
THIS IS THE MOST FASCINATING AND IMPRESSIVE DISCOVERY IN THE HISTORY OF ARCHAEOLOGY.
THIS PLACE PUTS THE ROSETTA STONE, THE PETRA, MARATHON, AND MACCHU PICHU ALL TO SHAME.
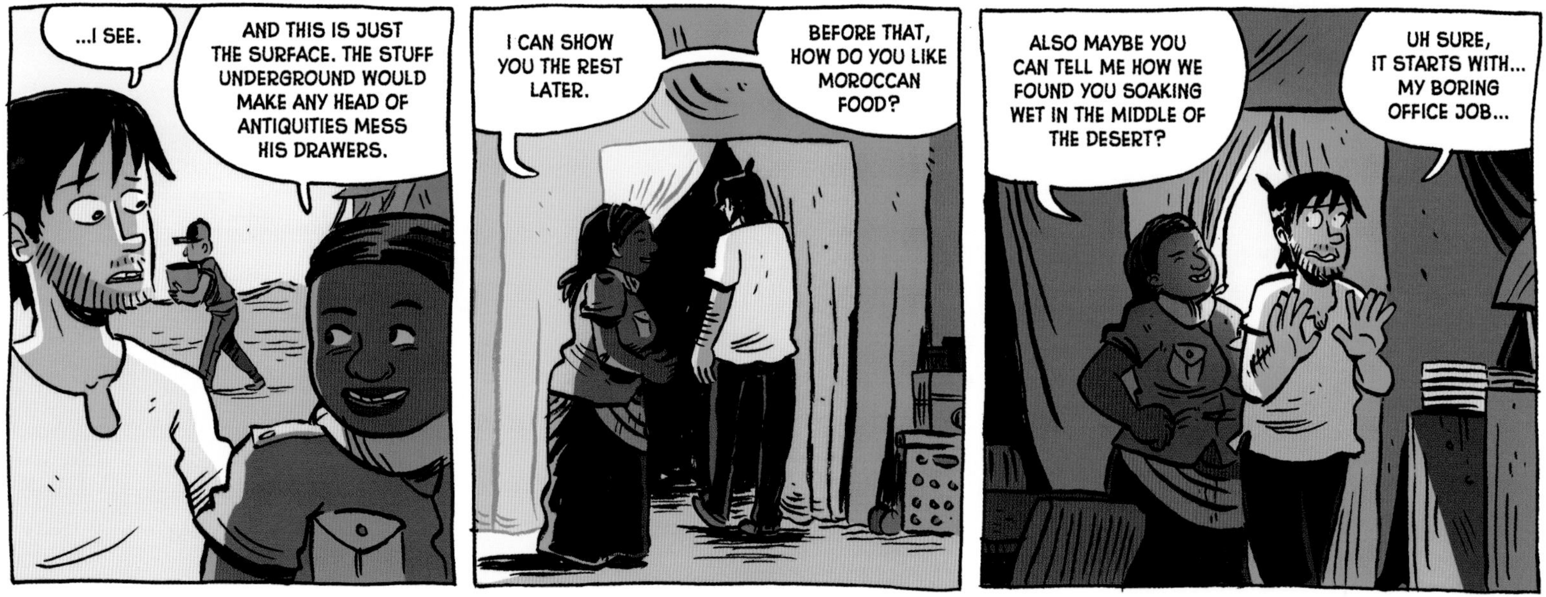
...I SEE.
AND THIS IS JUST THE SURFACE. THE STUFF UNDERGROUND WOULD MAKE ANY HEAD OF ANTIQUITIES MESS HIS DRAWERS.
I CAN SHOW YOU THE REST LATER.
BEFORE THAT, HOW DO YOU LIKE MOROCCAN FOOD?
ALSO MAYBE YOU CAN TELL ME HOW WE FOUND YOU SOAKING WET IN THE MIDDLE OF THE DESERT?
UH SURE, IT STARTS WITH... MY BORING OFFICE JOB...

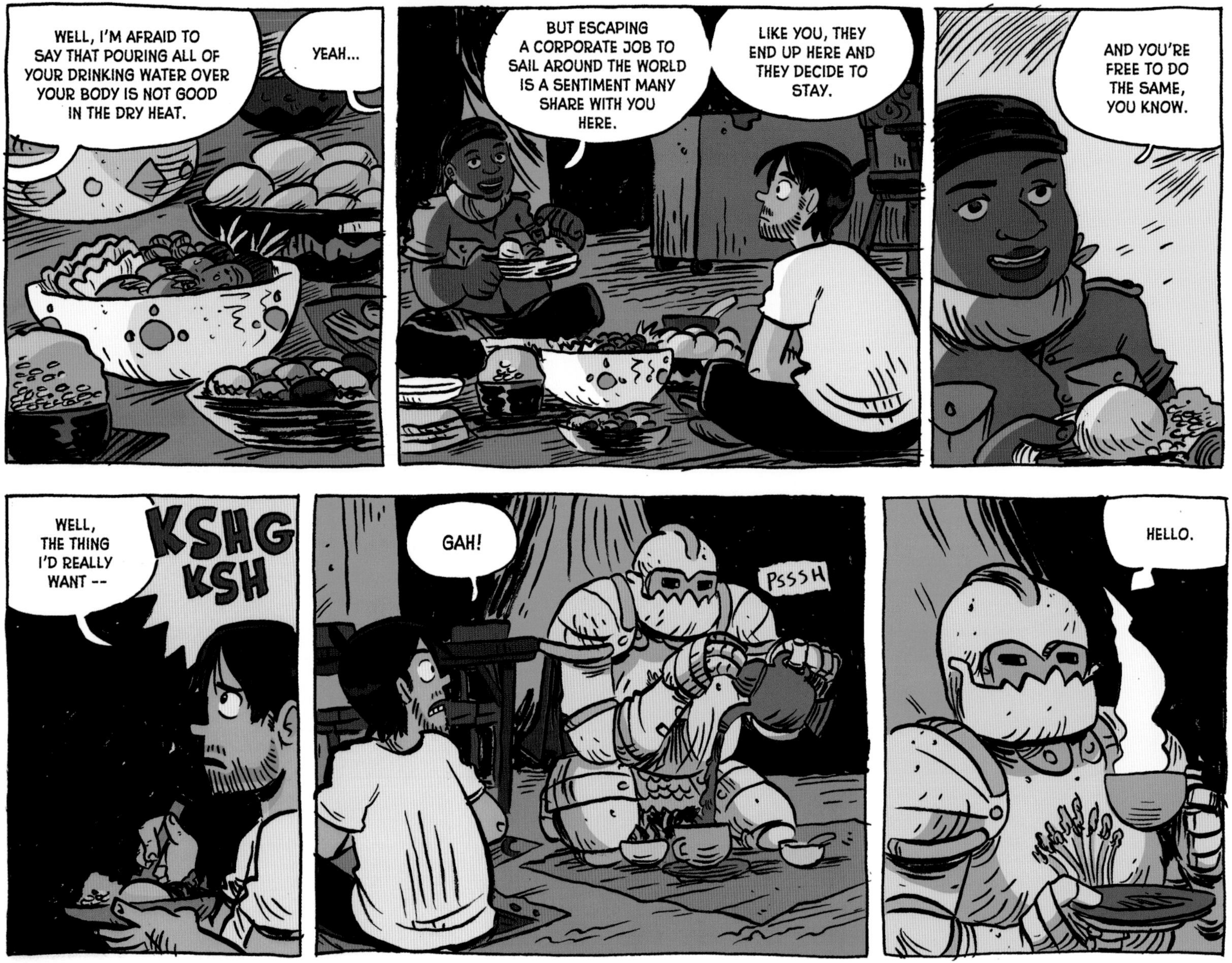
WELL, I'M AFRAID TO SAY THAT POURING ALL OF YOUR DRINKING WATER OVER YOUR BODY IS NOT GOOD IN THE DRY HEAT.
YEAH...
BUT ESCAPING A CORPORATE JOB TO SAIL AROUND THE WORLD IS A SENTIMENT MANY SHARE WITH YOU HERE.
LIKE YOU, THEY END UP HERE AND THEY DECIDE TO STAY.
AND YOU'RE FREE TO DO THE SAME, YOU KNOW.
WELL, THE THING I'D REALLY WANT --
KSHG KSH
GAH!
PSSSH
HELLO.

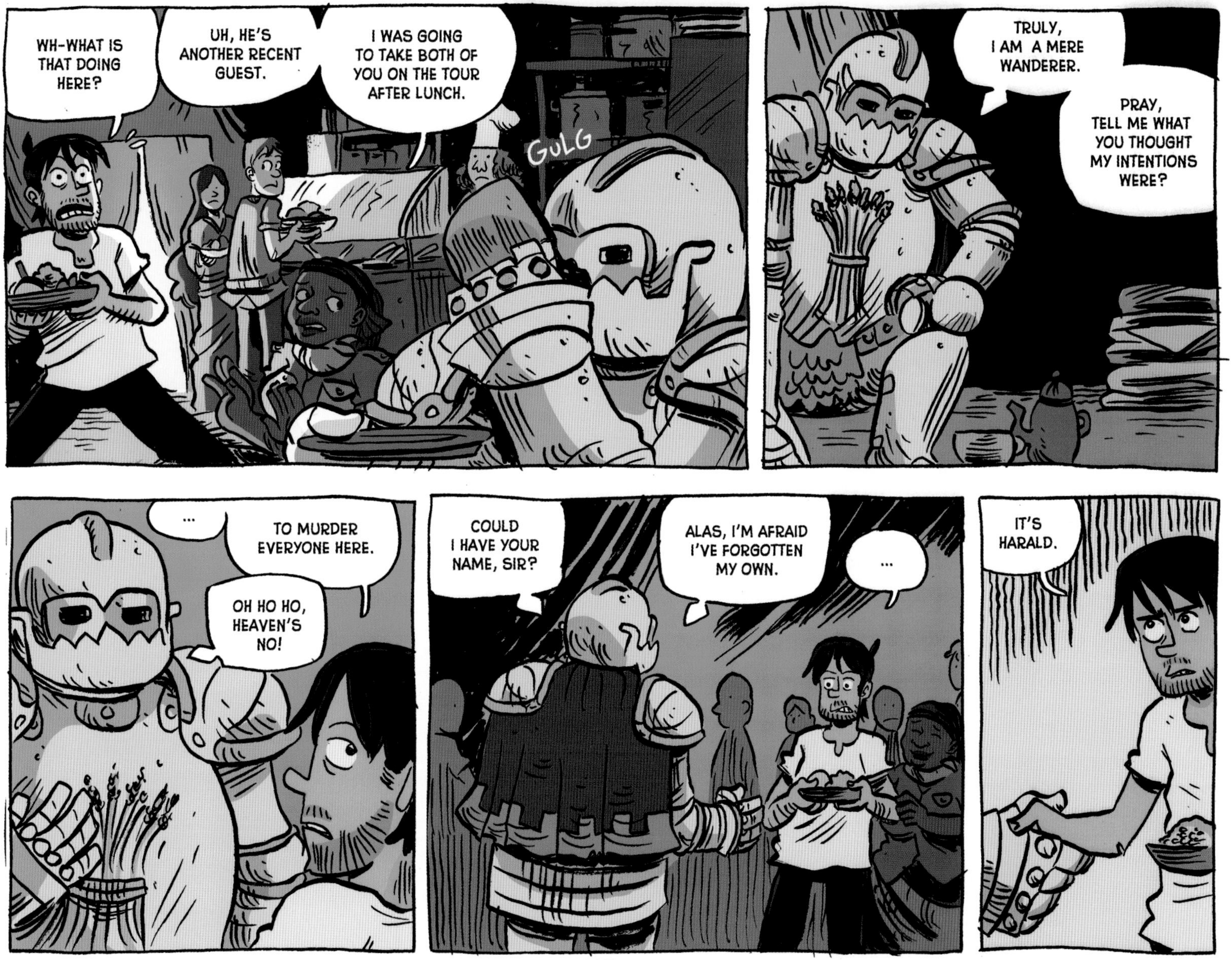
WH-WHAT IS THAT DOING HERE?
UH, HE'S ANOTHER RECENT GUEST.
I WAS GOING TO TAKE BOTH OF YOU ON THE TOUR AFTER LUNCH.
GULG
TRULY, I AM A MERE WANDERER.
PRAY, TELL ME WHAT YOU THOUGHT MY INTENTIONS WERE?
...
TO MURDER EVERYONE HERE.
OH HO HO, HEAVEN'S NO!
COULD I HAVE YOUR NAME, SIR?
ALAS, I'M AFRAID I'VE FORGOTTEN MY OWN.
...
IT'S HARALD.

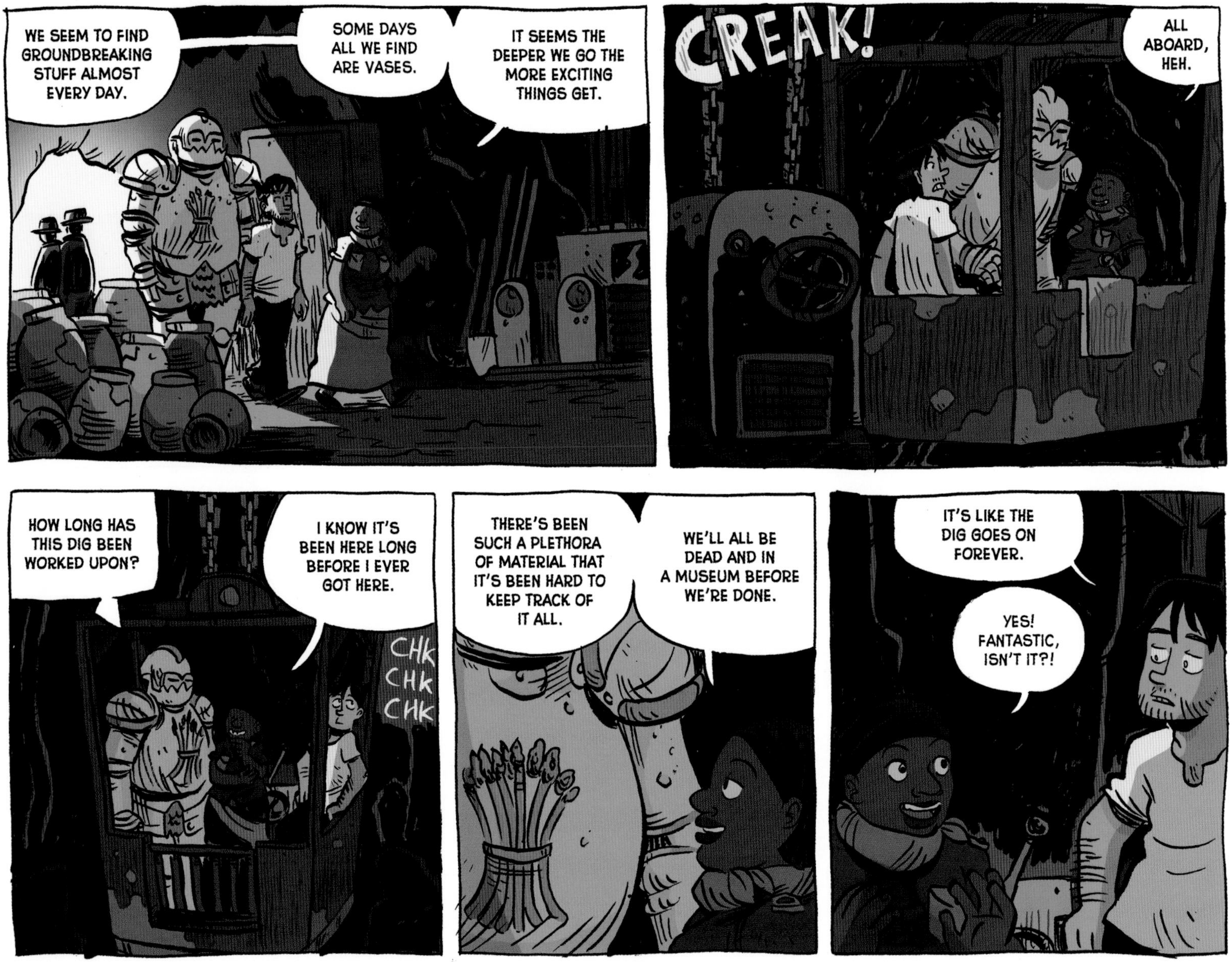

WE SEEM TO FIND GROUNDBREAKING STUFF ALMOST EVERY DAY.
SOME DAYS ALL WE FIND ARE VASES.
IT SEEMS THE DEEPER WE GO THE MORE EXCITING THINGS GET.
CREAK!
ALL ABOARD, HEH.
HOW LONG HAS THIS DIG BEEN WORKED UPON?
I KNOW IT'S BEEN HERE LONG BEFORE I EVER GOT HERE.
CHK CHK CHK
THERE'S BEEN SUCH A PLETHORA OF MATERIAL THAT IT'S BEEN HARD TO KEEP TRACK OF IT ALL.
WE'LL ALL BE DEAD AND IN A MUSEUM BEFORE WE'RE DONE.
IT'S LIKE THE DIG GOES ON FOREVER.
YES! FANTASTIC, ISN'T IT?!

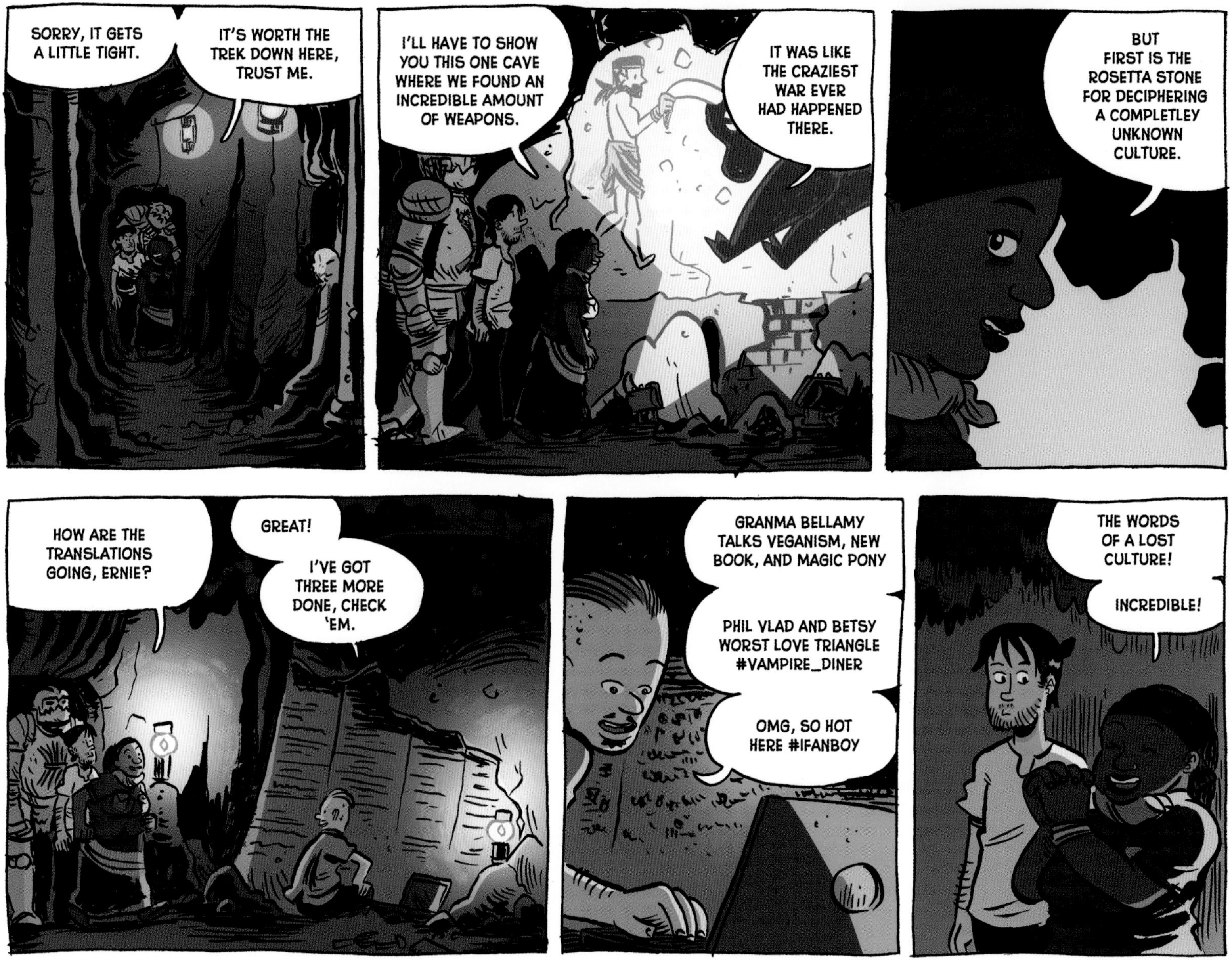
SORRY, IT GETS A LITTLE TIGHT.
IT'S WORTH THE TREK DOWN HERE, TRUST ME.
I'LL HAVE TO SHOW YOU THIS ONE CAVE WHERE WE FOUND AN INCREDIBLE AMOUNT OF WEAPONS.
IT WAS LIKE THE CRAZIEST WAR EVER HAD HAPPENED THERE.
BUT FIRST IS THE ROSETTA STONE FOR DECIPHERING A COMPLETLEY UNKNOWN CULTURE.
HOW ARE THE TRANSLATIONS GOING, ERNIE?
GREAT!
I'VE GOT THREE MORE DONE, CHECK 'EM.
GRANMA BELLAMY TALKS VEGANISM, NEW BOOK, AND MAGIC PONY
PHIL VLAD AND BETSY WORST LOVE TRIANGLE #VAMPIRE_DINER
OMG, SO HOT HERE #IFANBOY
THE WORDS OF A LOST CULTURE!
INCREDIBLE!

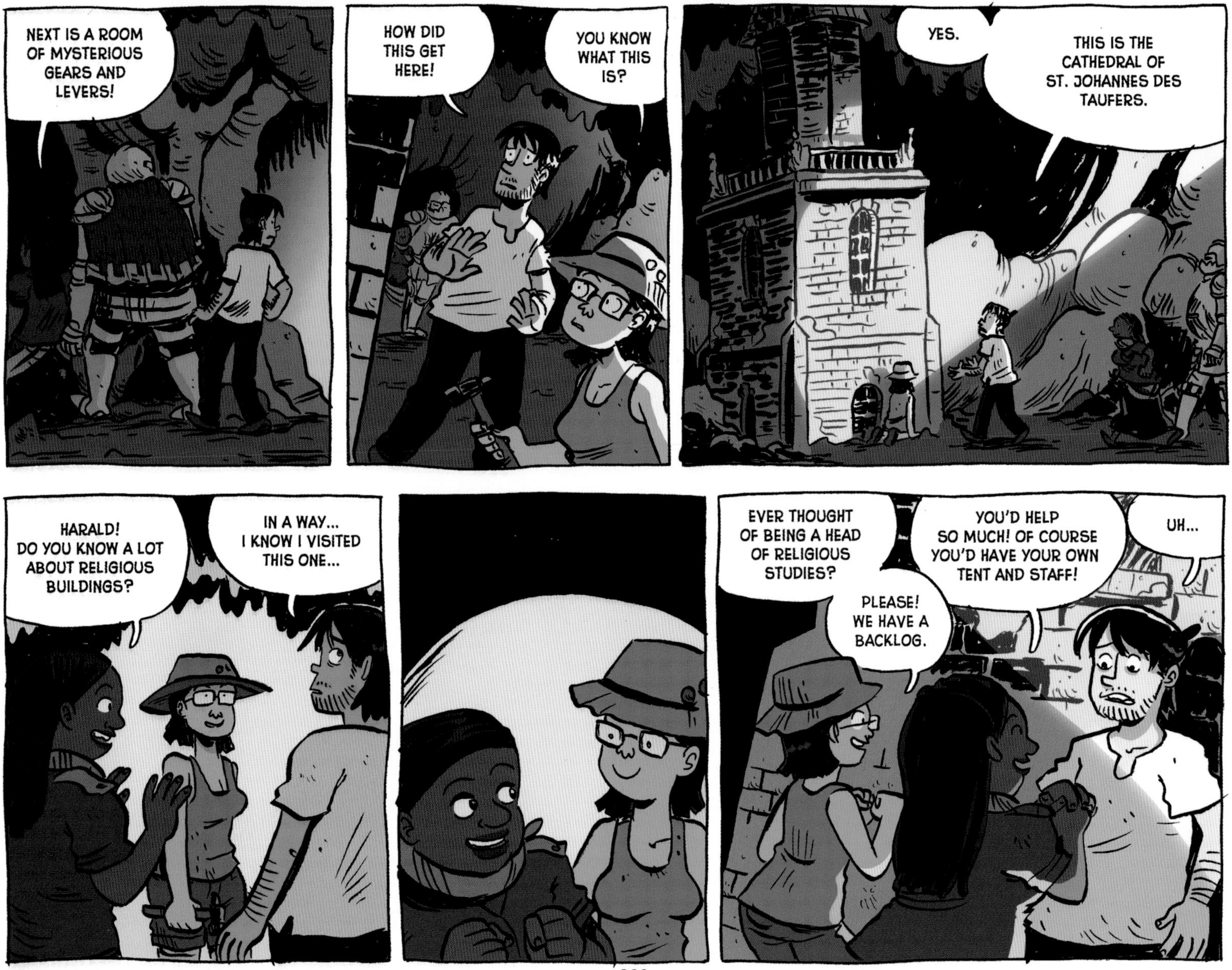
NEXT IS A ROOM OF MYSTERIOUS GEARS AND LEVERS!
HOW DID THIS GET HERE!
YOU KNOW WHAT THIS IS?
YES.
THIS IS THE CATHEDRAL OF ST. JOHANNES DES TAUFERS.
HARALD! DO YOU KNOW A LOT ABOUT RELIGIOUS BUILDINGS?
IN A WAY... I KNOW I VISITED THIS ONE...
EVER THOUGHT OF BEING A HEAD OF RELIGIOUS STUDIES?
PLEASE! WE HAVE A BACKLOG.
YOU'D HELP SO MUCH! OF COURSE YOU'D HAVE YOUR OWN TENT AND STAFF!
UH...

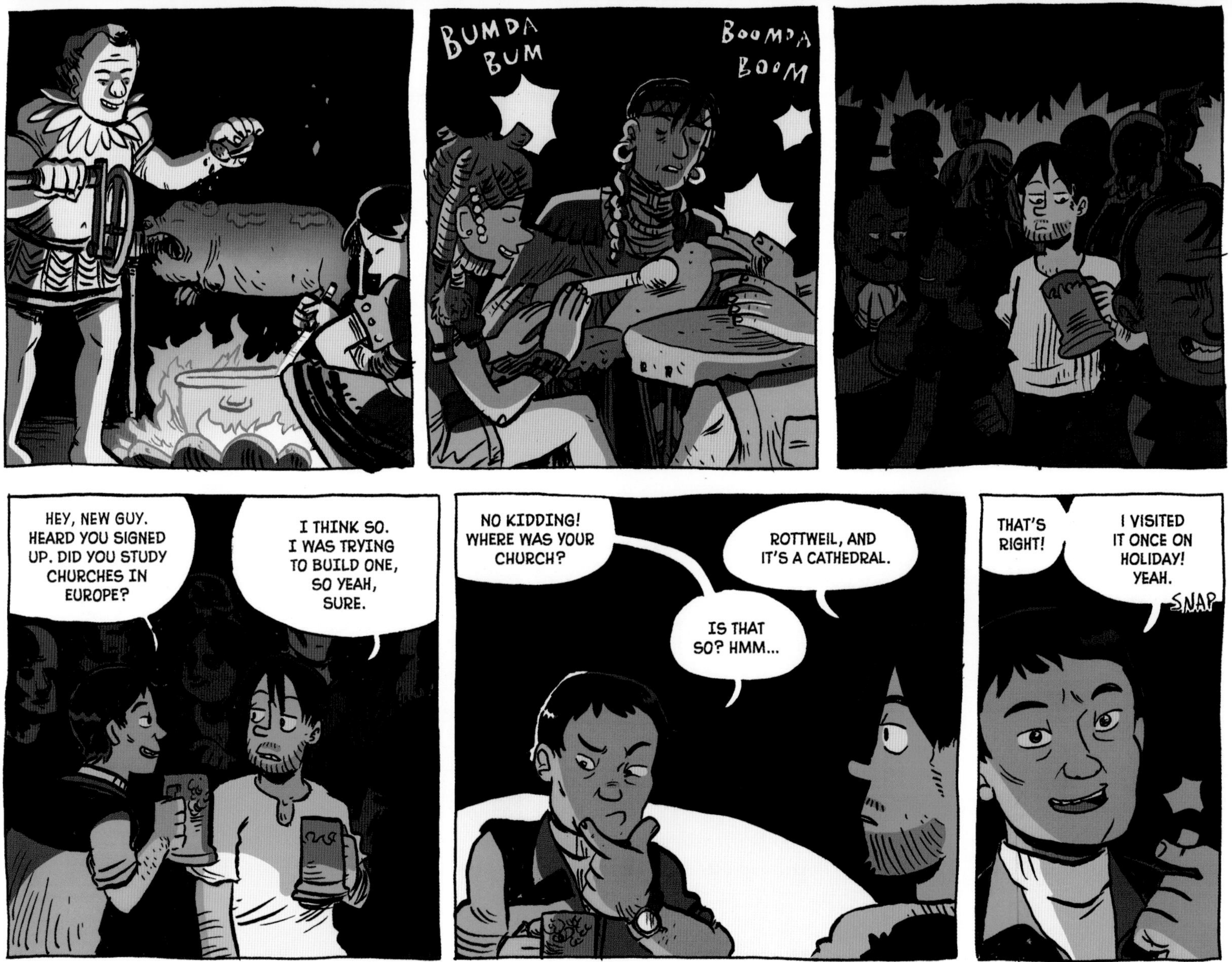

BUMDA BUM
BOOMDA BOOM
HEY, NEW GUY. HEARD YOU SIGNED UP. DID YOU STUDY CHURCHES IN EUROPE?
I THINK SO. I WAS TRYING TO BUILD ONE, SO YEAH, SURE.
NO KIDDING! WHERE WAS YOUR CHURCH?
ROTTWEIL, AND IT'S A CATHEDRAL.
IS THAT SO? HMM...
THAT'S RIGHT!
I VISITED IT ONCE ON HOLIDAY! YEAH.
SNAP

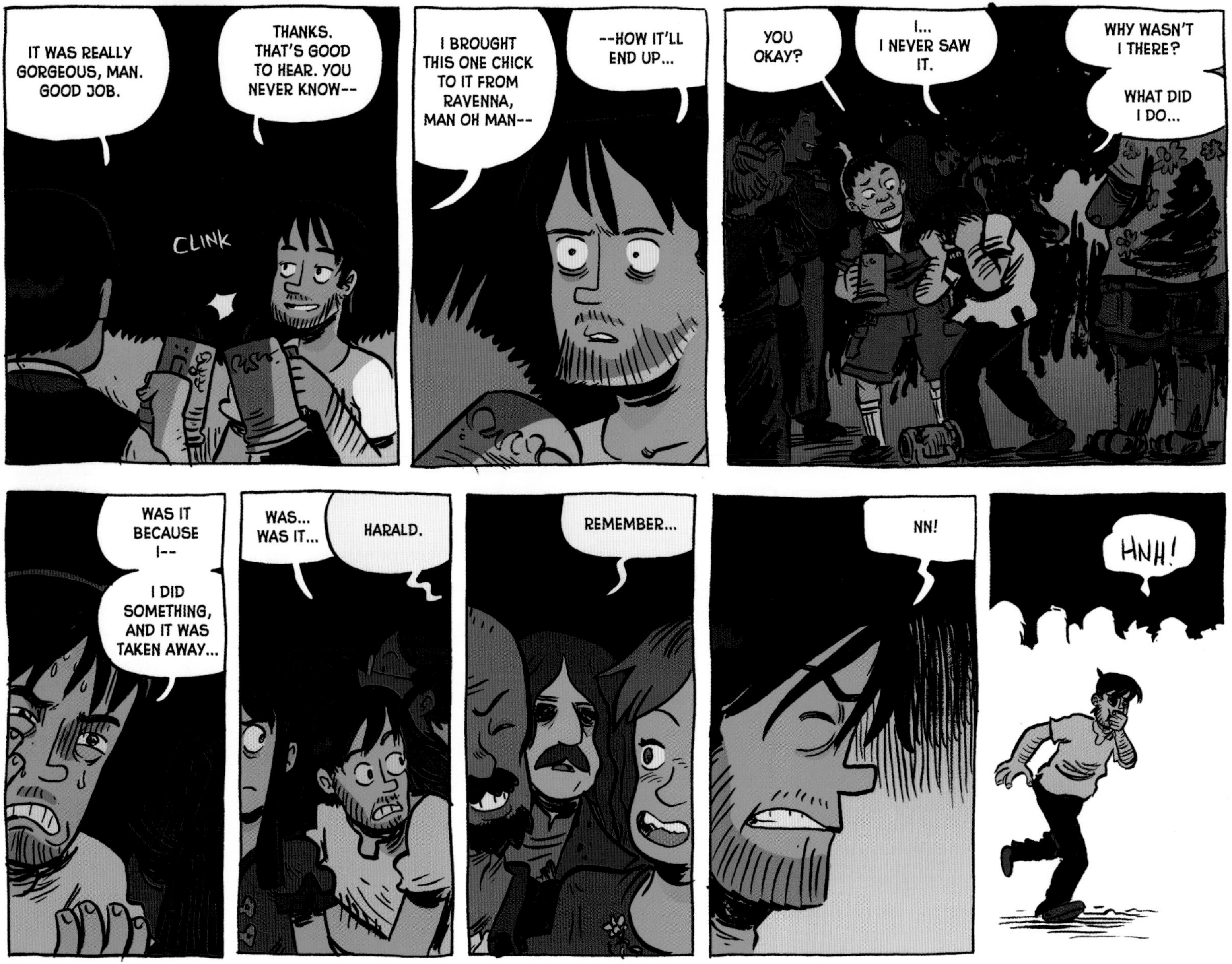
IT WAS REALLY GORGEOUS, MAN. GOOD JOB.
THANKS. THAT'S GOOD TO HEAR. YOU NEVER KNOW--
CLINK
I BROUGHT THIS ONE CHICK TO IT FROM RAVENNA, MAN OH MAN--
--HOW IT'LL END UP...
YOU OKAY?
I... I NEVER SAW IT.
WHY WASN'T I THERE?
WHAT DID I DO...
WAS IT BECAUSE I--
I DID SOMETHING, AND IT WAS TAKEN AWAY...
WAS... WAS IT...
HARALD.
REMEMBER...
NN!
HNH!

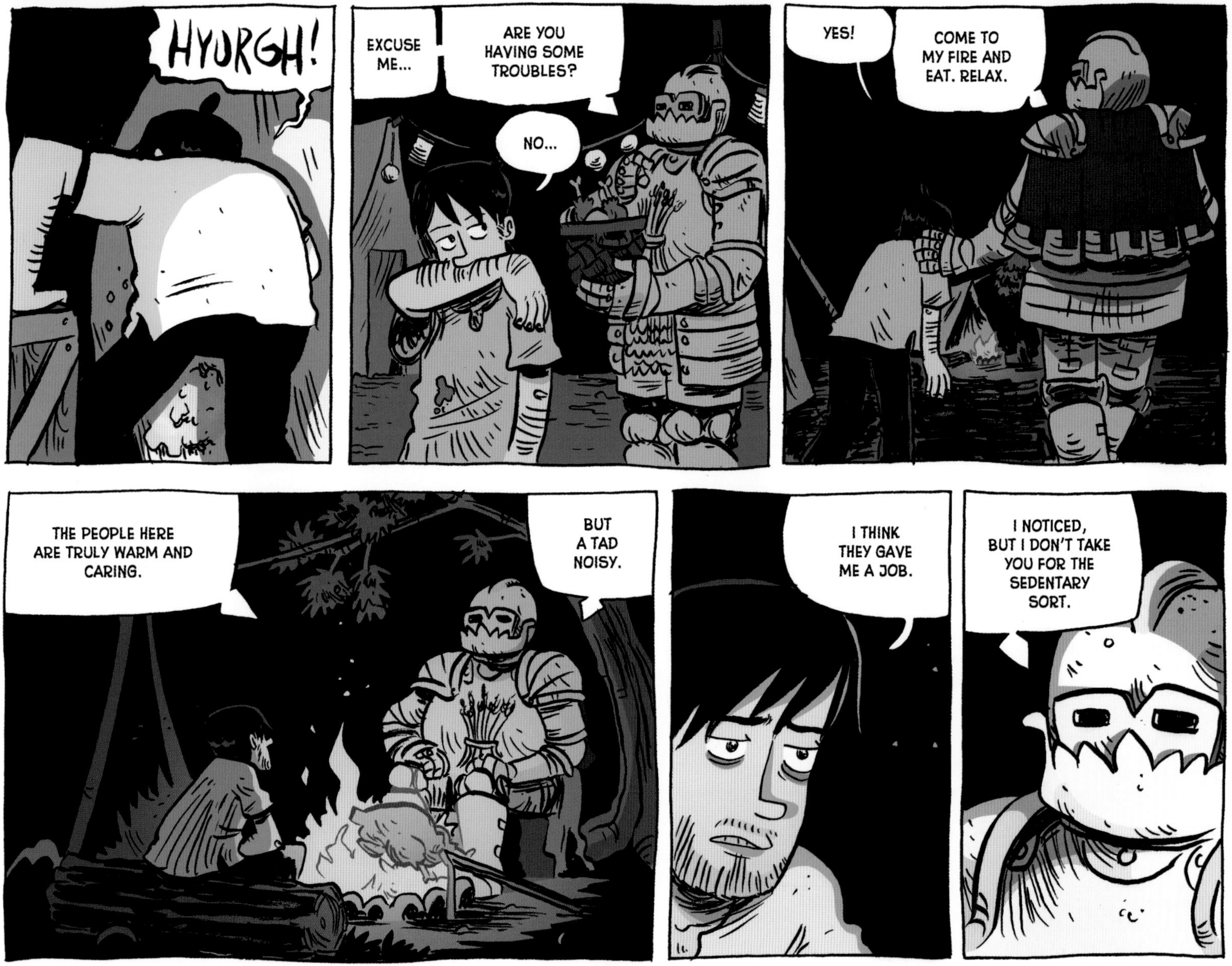
HYURGH!
EXCUSE ME...
ARE YOU HAVING SOME TROUBLES?
NO...
YES!
COME TO MY FIRE AND EAT. RELAX.
THE PEOPLE HERE ARE TRULY WARM AND CARING.
BUT A TAD NOISY.
I THINK THEY GAVE ME A JOB.
I NOTICED, BUT I DON'T TAKE YOU FOR THE SEDENTARY SORT.

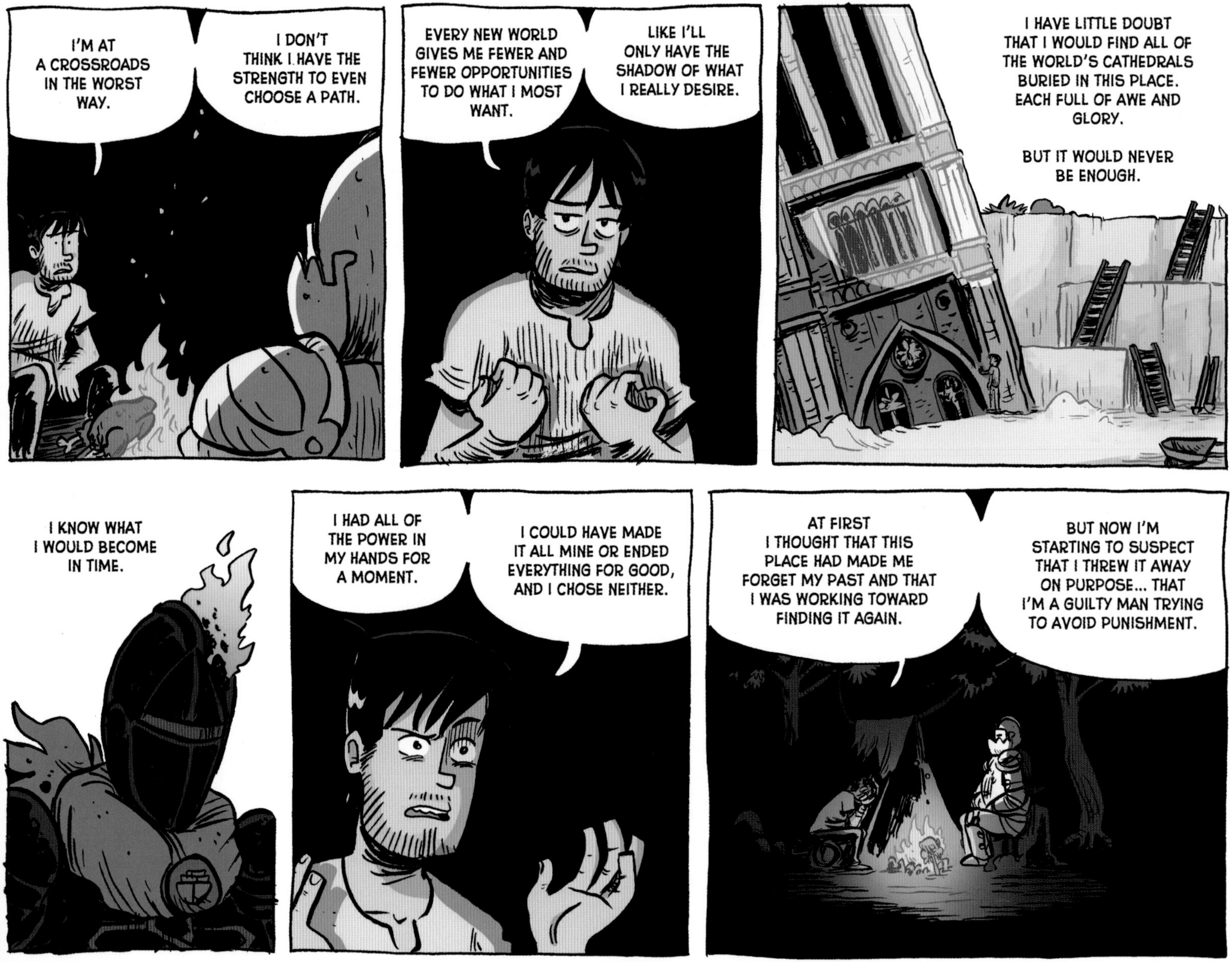
I'M AT A CROSSROADS IN THE WORST WAY.
I DON'T THINK I HAVE THE STRENGTH TO EVEN CHOOSE A PATH.
EVERY NEW WORLD GIVES ME FEWER AND FEWER OPPORTUNITIES TO DO WHAT I MOST WANT.
LIKE I'LL ONLY HAVE THE SHADOW OF WHAT I REALLY DESIRE.
I HAVE LITTLE DOUBT THAT I WOULD FIND ALL OF THE WORLD'S CATHEDRALS BURIED IN THIS PLACE. EACH FULL OF AWE AND GLORY.
BUT IT WOULD NEVER BE ENOUGH.
I KNOW WHAT I WOULD BECOME IN TIME.
I HAD ALL OF THE POWER IN MY HANDS FOR A MOMENT.
I COULD HAVE MADE IT ALL MINE OR ENDED EVERYTHING FOR GOOD, AND I CHOSE NEITHER.
AT FIRST I THOUGHT THAT THIS PLACE HAD MADE ME FORGET MY PAST AND THAT I WAS WORKING TOWARD FINDING IT AGAIN.
BUT NOW I'M STARTING TO SUSPECT THAT I THREW IT AWAY ON PURPOSE... THAT I'M A GUILTY MAN TRYING TO AVOID PUNISHMENT.

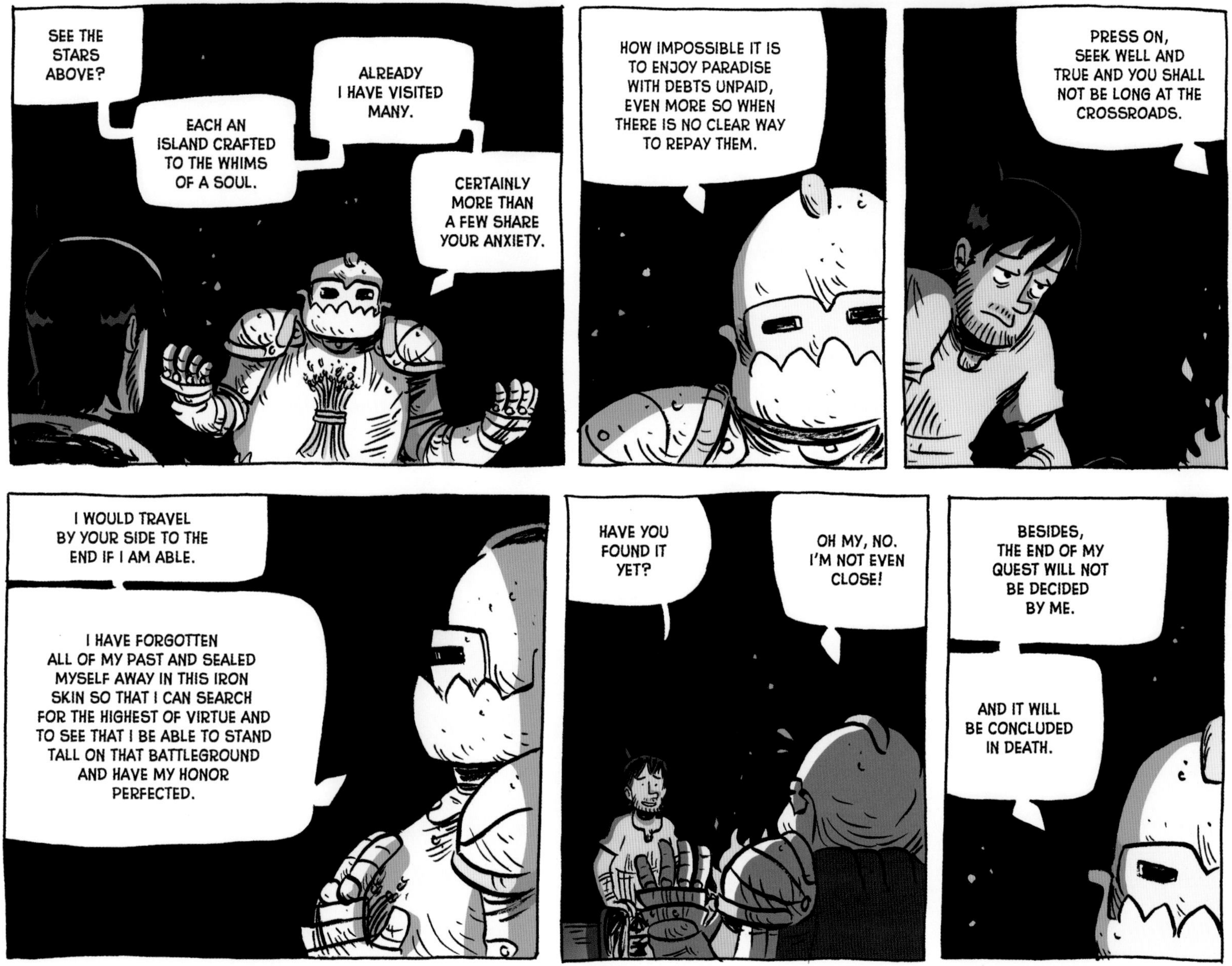
SEE THE STARS ABOVE?
EACH AN ISLAND CRAFTED TO THE WHIMS OF A SOUL.
ALREADY I HAVE VISITED MANY.
CERTAINLY MORE THAN A FEW SHARE YOUR ANXIETY.
HOW IMPOSSIBLE IT IS TO ENJOY PARADISE WITH DEBTS UNPAID, EVEN MORE SO WHEN THERE IS NO CLEAR WAY TO REPAY THEM.
PRESS ON, SEEK WELL AND TRUE AND YOU SHALL NOT BE LONG AT THE CROSSROADS.
I WOULD TRAVEL BY YOUR SIDE TO THE END IF I AM ABLE.
I HAVE FORGOTTEN ALL OF MY PAST AND SEALED MYSELF AWAY IN THIS IRON SKIN SO THAT I CAN SEARCH FOR THE HIGHEST OF VIRTUE AND TO SEE THAT I BE ABLE TO STAND TALL ON THAT BATTLEGROUND AND HAVE MY HONOR PERFECTED.
HAVE YOU FOUND IT YET?
OH MY, NO. I'M NOT EVEN CLOSE!
BESIDES, THE END OF MY QUEST WILL NOT BE DECIDED BY ME.
AND IT WILL BE CONCLUDED IN DEATH.

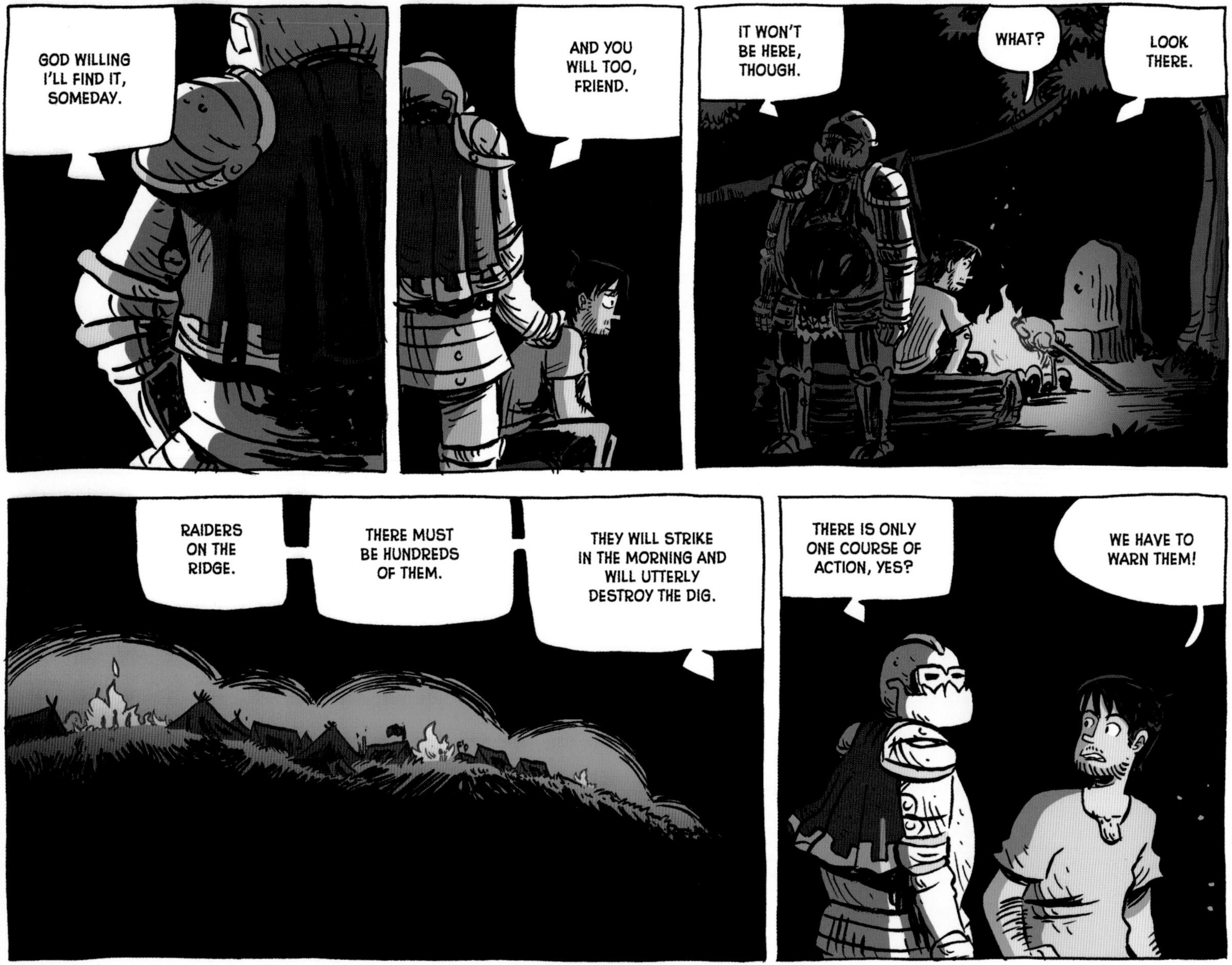
GOD WILLING I'LL FIND IT, SOMEDAY.
AND YOU WILL TOO, FRIEND.
IT WON'T BE HERE, THOUGH.
WHAT?
LOOK THERE.
RAIDERS ON THE RIDGE.
THERE MUST BE HUNDREDS OF THEM.
THEY WILL STRIKE IN THE MORNING AND WILL UTTERLY DESTROY THE DIG.
THERE IS ONLY ONE COURSE OF ACTION, YES?
WE HAVE TO WARN THEM!

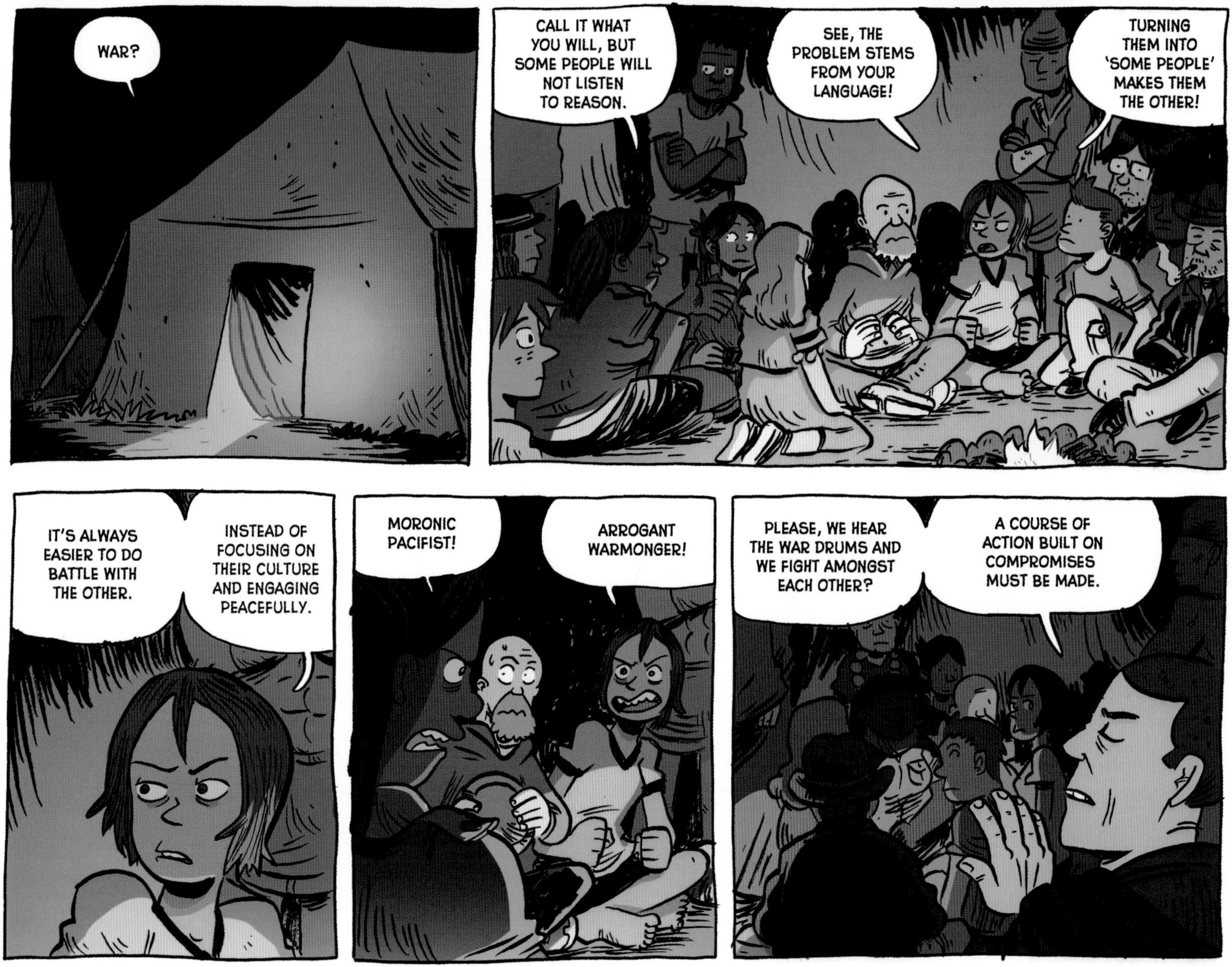
WAR?
CALL IT WHAT YOU WILL, BUT SOME PEOPLE WILL NOT LISTEN TO REASON.
SEE, THE PROBLEM STEMS FROM YOUR LANGUAGE!
TURNING THEM INTO 'SOME PEOPLE' MAKES THEM THE OTHER!
IT'S ALWAYS EASIER TO DO BATTLE WITH THE OTHER.
INSTEAD OF FOCUSING ON THEIR CULTURE AND ENGAGING PEACEFULLY.
MORONIC PACIFIST!
ARROGANT WARMONGER!
PLEASE, WE HEAR THE WAR DRUMS AND WE FIGHT AMONGST EACH OTHER?
A COURSE OF ACTION BUILT ON COMPROMISES MUST BE MADE.

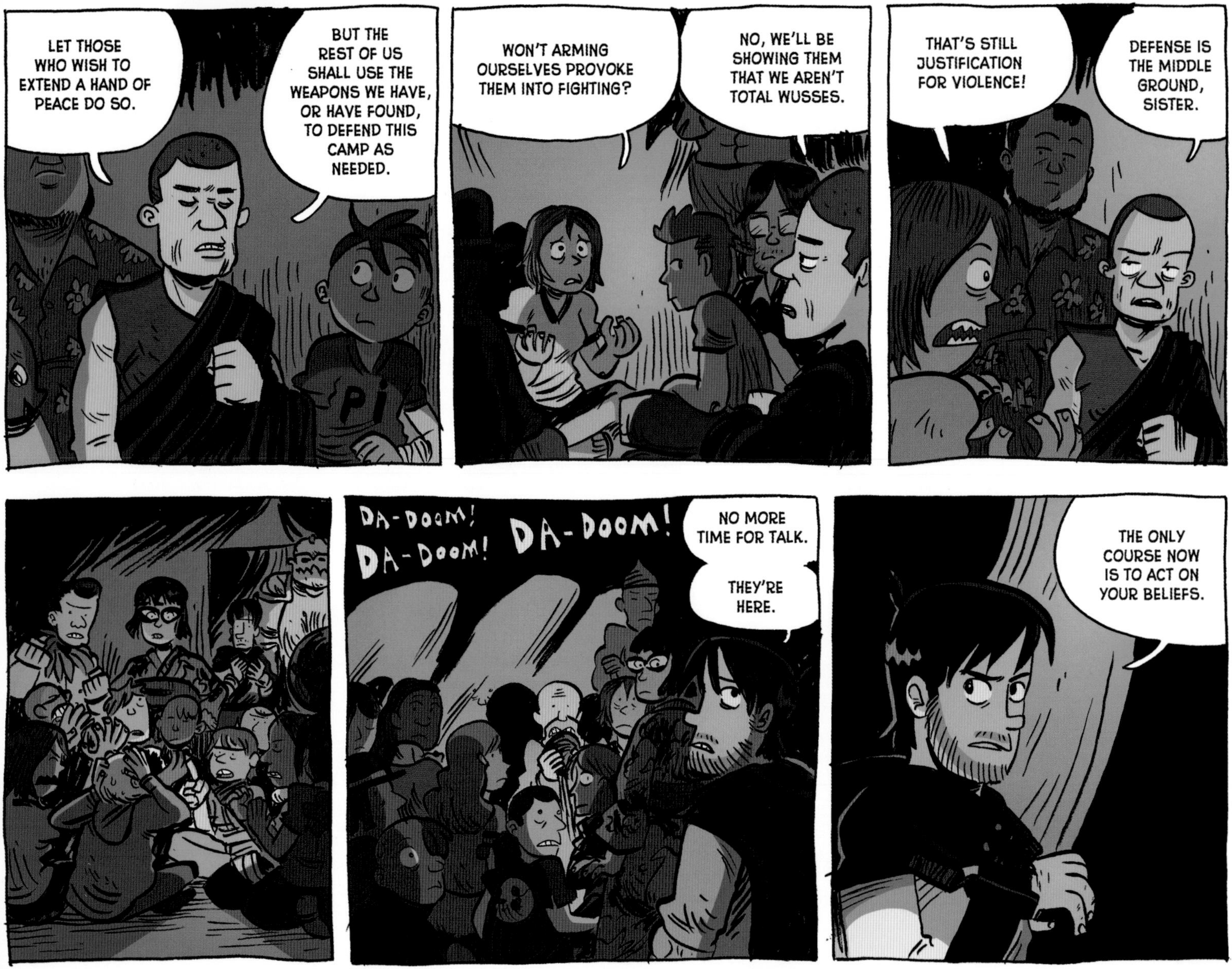
LET THOSE WHO WISH TO EXTEND A HAND OF PEACE DO SO.
BUT THE REST OF US SHALL USE THE WEAPONS WE HAVE, OR HAVE FOUND, TO DEFEND THIS CAMP AS NEEDED.
Pi
WON'T ARMING OURSELVES PROVOKE THEM INTO FIGHTING?
NO, WE'LL BE SHOWING THEM THAT WE AREN'T TOTAL WUSSES.
THAT'S STILL JUSTIFICATION FOR VIOLENCE!
DEFENSE IS THE MIDDLE GROUND, SISTER.
DA-DOOM!
DA-DOOM!
DA-DOOM!
NO MORE TIME FOR TALK.
THEY'RE HERE.
THE ONLY COURSE NOW IS TO ACT ON YOUR BELIEFS.

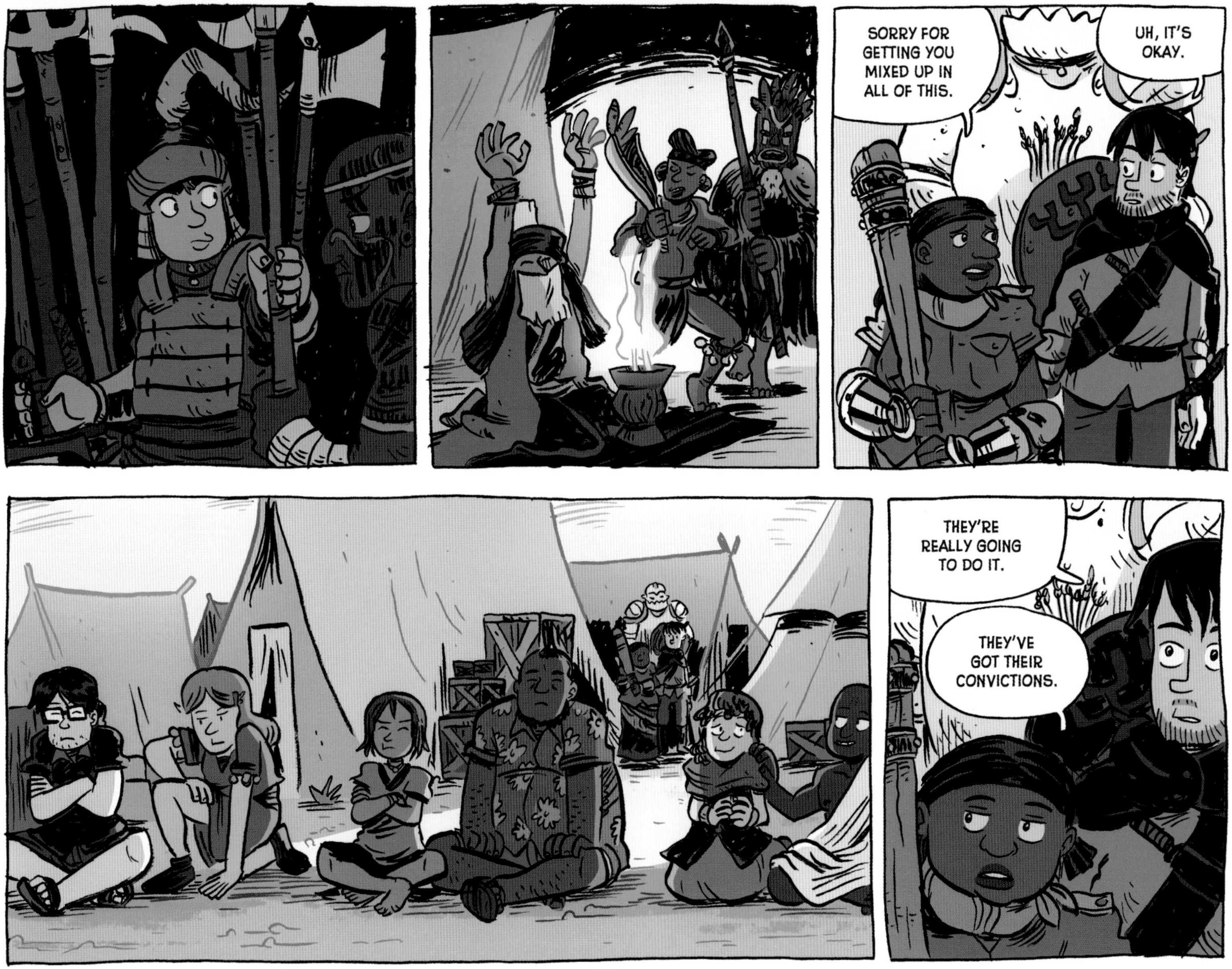
SORRY FOR GETTING YOU MIXED UP IN ALL OF THIS.
UH, IT'S OKAY.
THEY'RE REALLY GOING TO DO IT.
THEY'VE GOT THEIR CONVICTIONS.

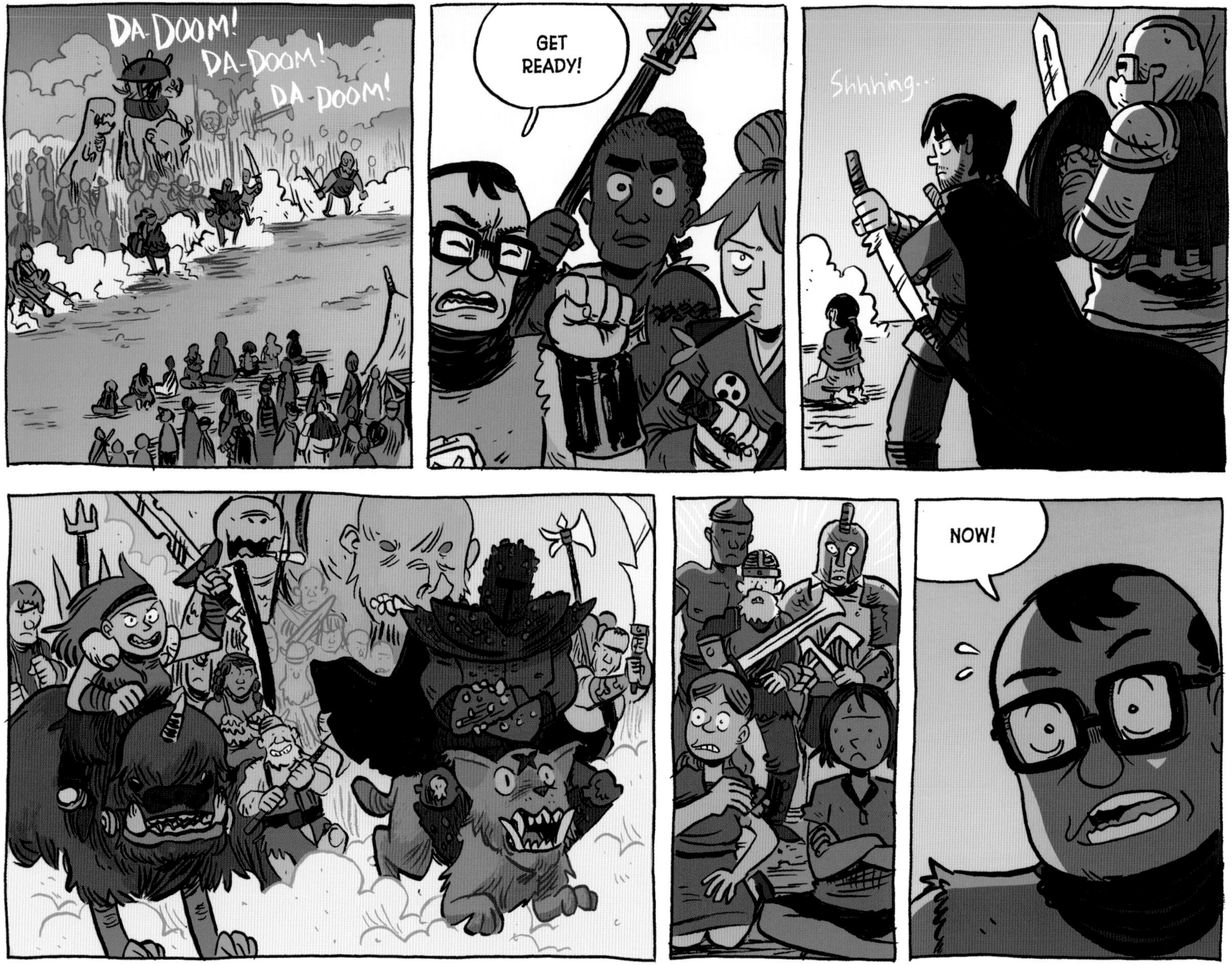
DA-DOOM!
DA-DOOM!
DA-DOOM!
GET READY!
Shhhing...
NOW!

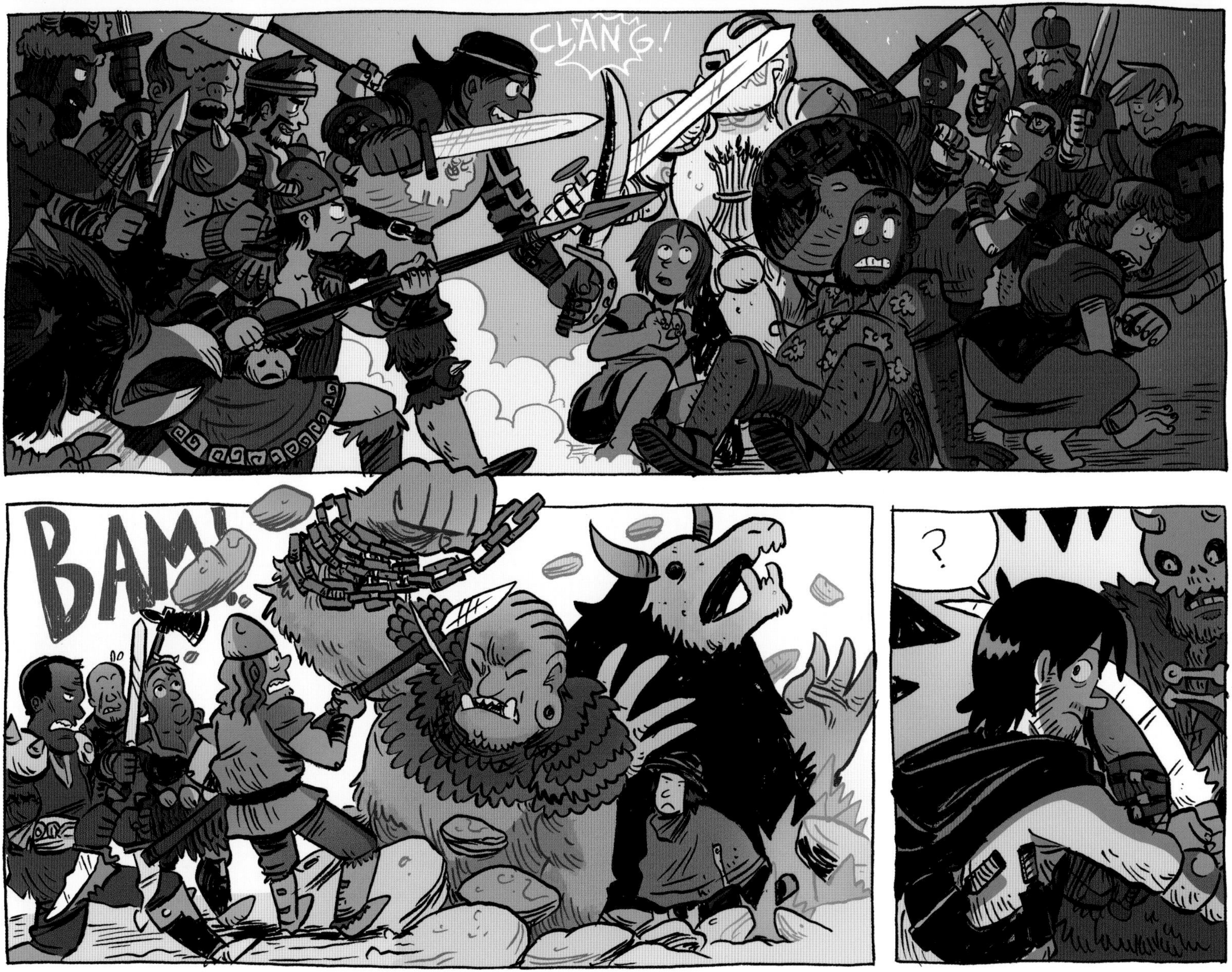
CLANG!
BAM!
?

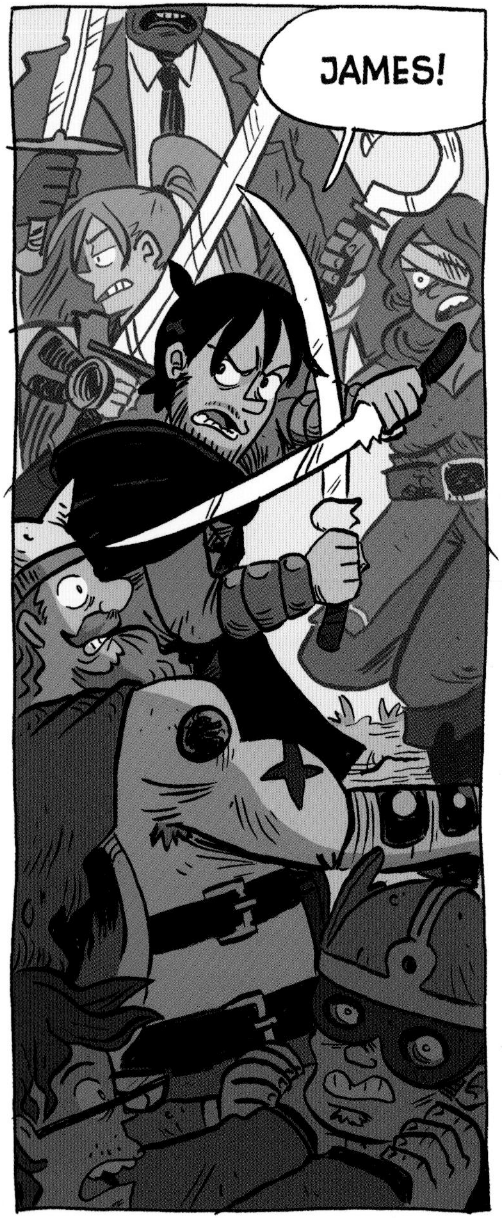
JAMES!

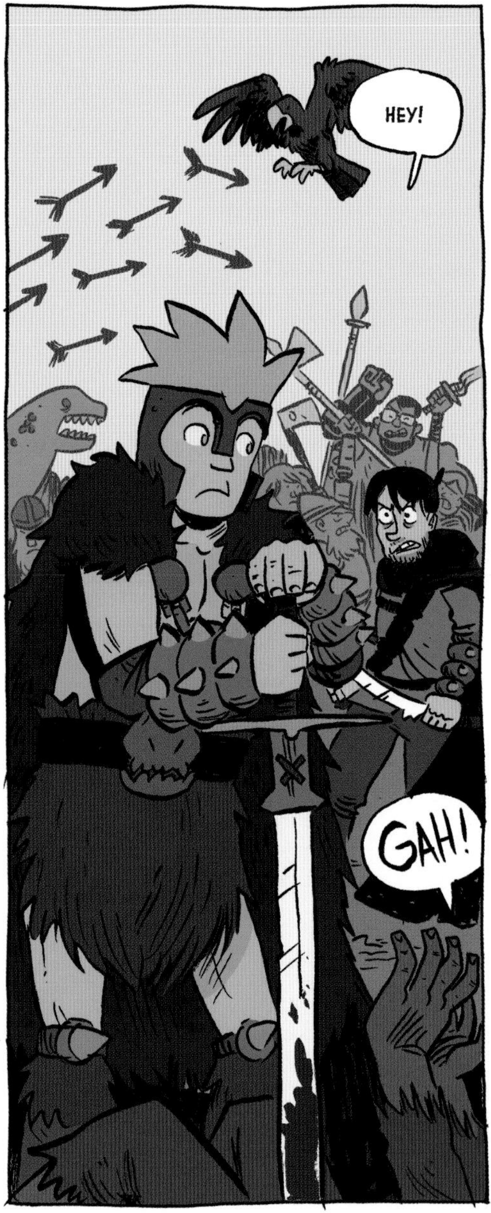
HEY!
GAH!

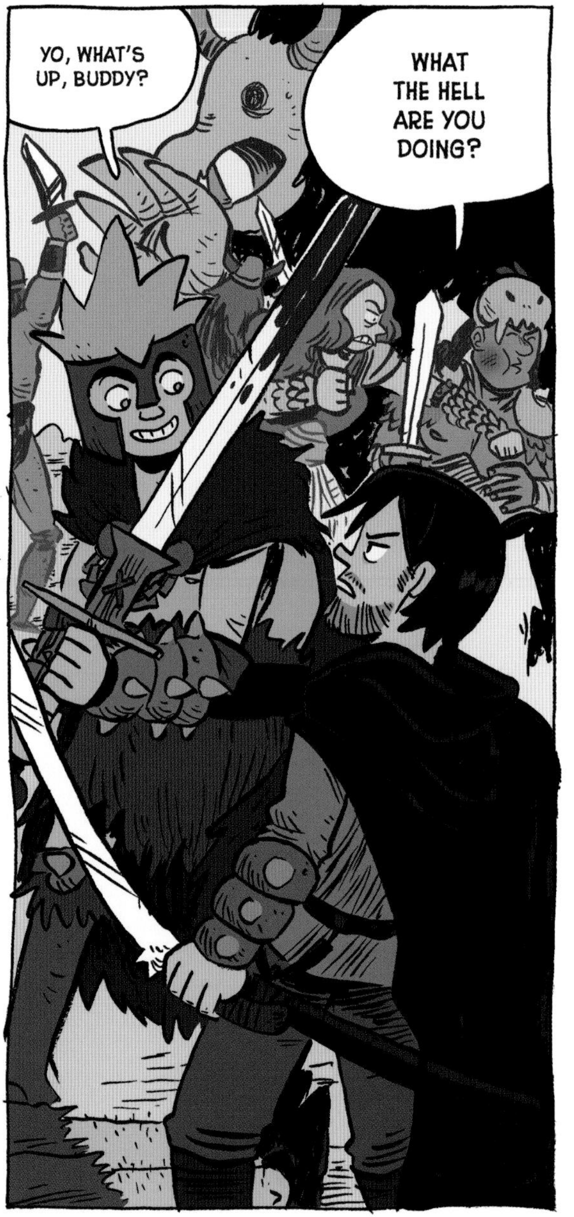
YO, WHAT'S UP, BUDDY?
WHAT THE HELL ARE YOU DOING?

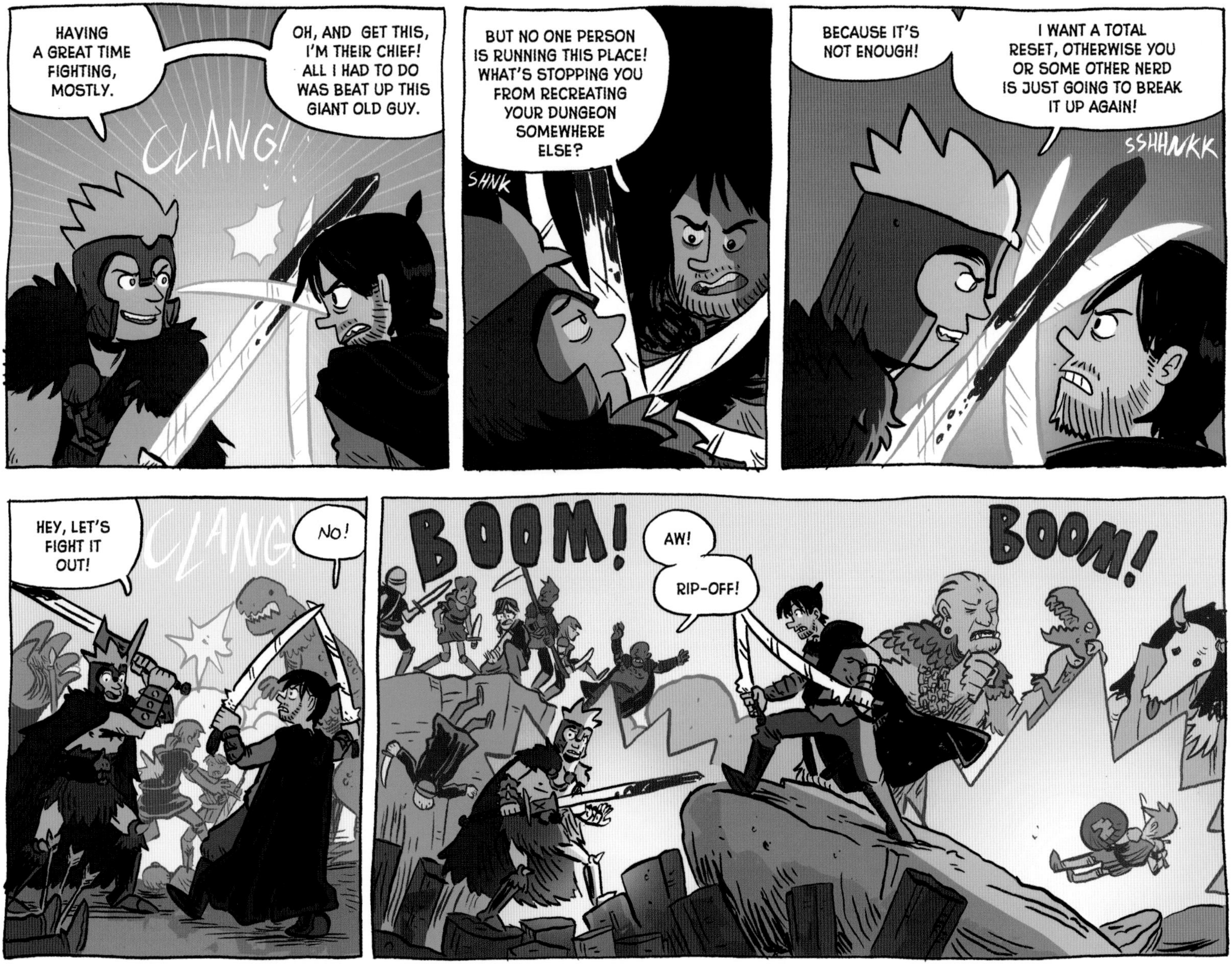
HAVING A GREAT TIME FIGHTING, MOSTLY.
OH, AND GET THIS, I'M THEIR CHIEF! ALL I HAD TO DO WAS BEAT UP THIS GIANT OLD GUY.
CLANG!
BUT NO ONE PERSON IS RUNNING THIS PLACE! WHAT'S STOPPING YOU FROM RECREATING YOUR DUNGEON SOMEWHERE ELSE?
SHNK
BECAUSE IT'S NOT ENOUGH!
I WANT A TOTAL RESET, OTHERWISE YOU OR SOME OTHER NERD IS JUST GOING TO BREAK IT UP AGAIN!
SSHHNKK
HEY, LET'S FIGHT IT OUT!
CLANG!
NO!
BOOM!
AW!
RIP-OFF!
BOOM!

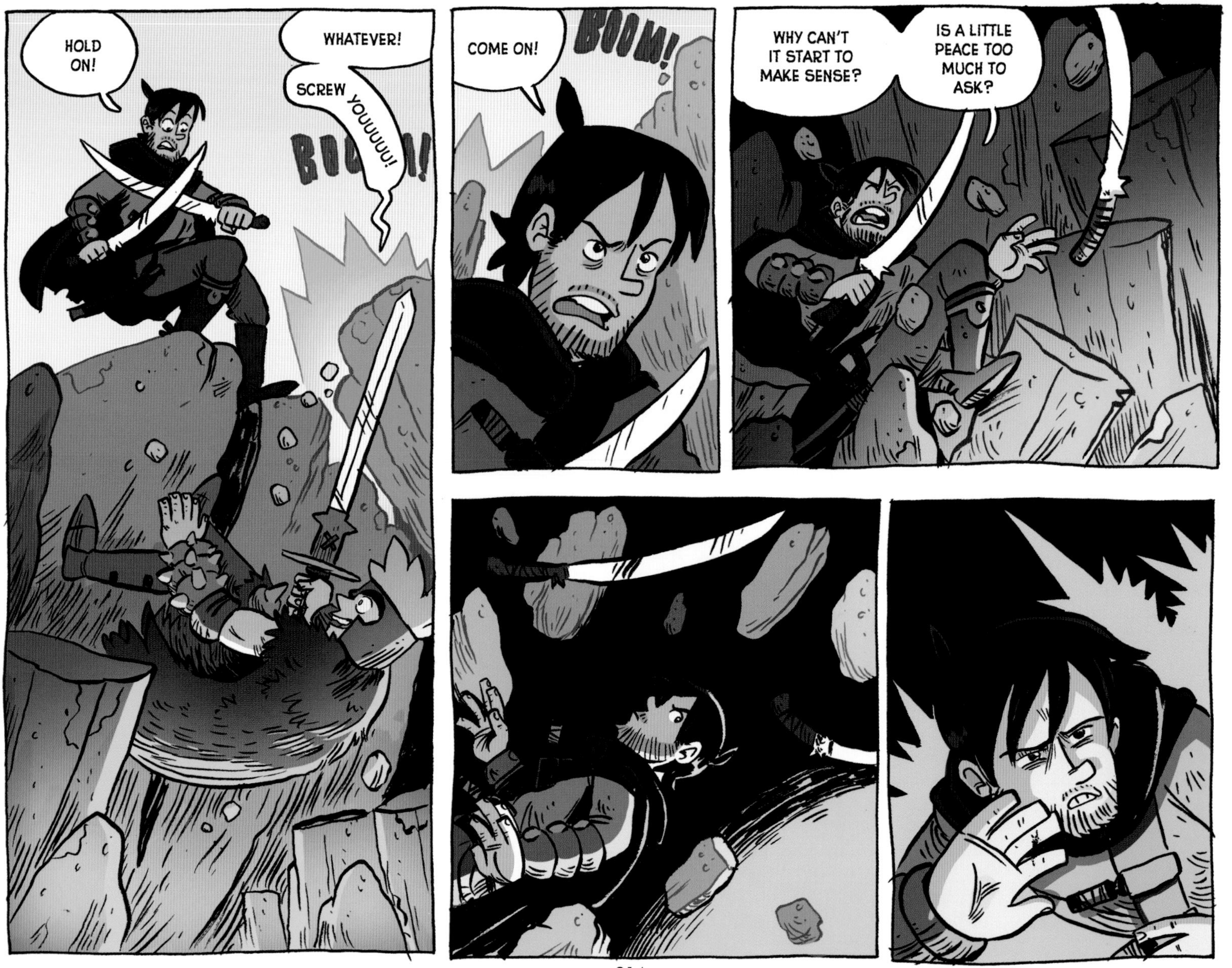
HOLD ON!
WHATEVER!
SCREW YOUUUUU!
COME ON!
BOOM!
WHY CAN'T IT START TO MAKE SENSE?
IS A LITTLE PEACE TOO MUCH TO ASK?

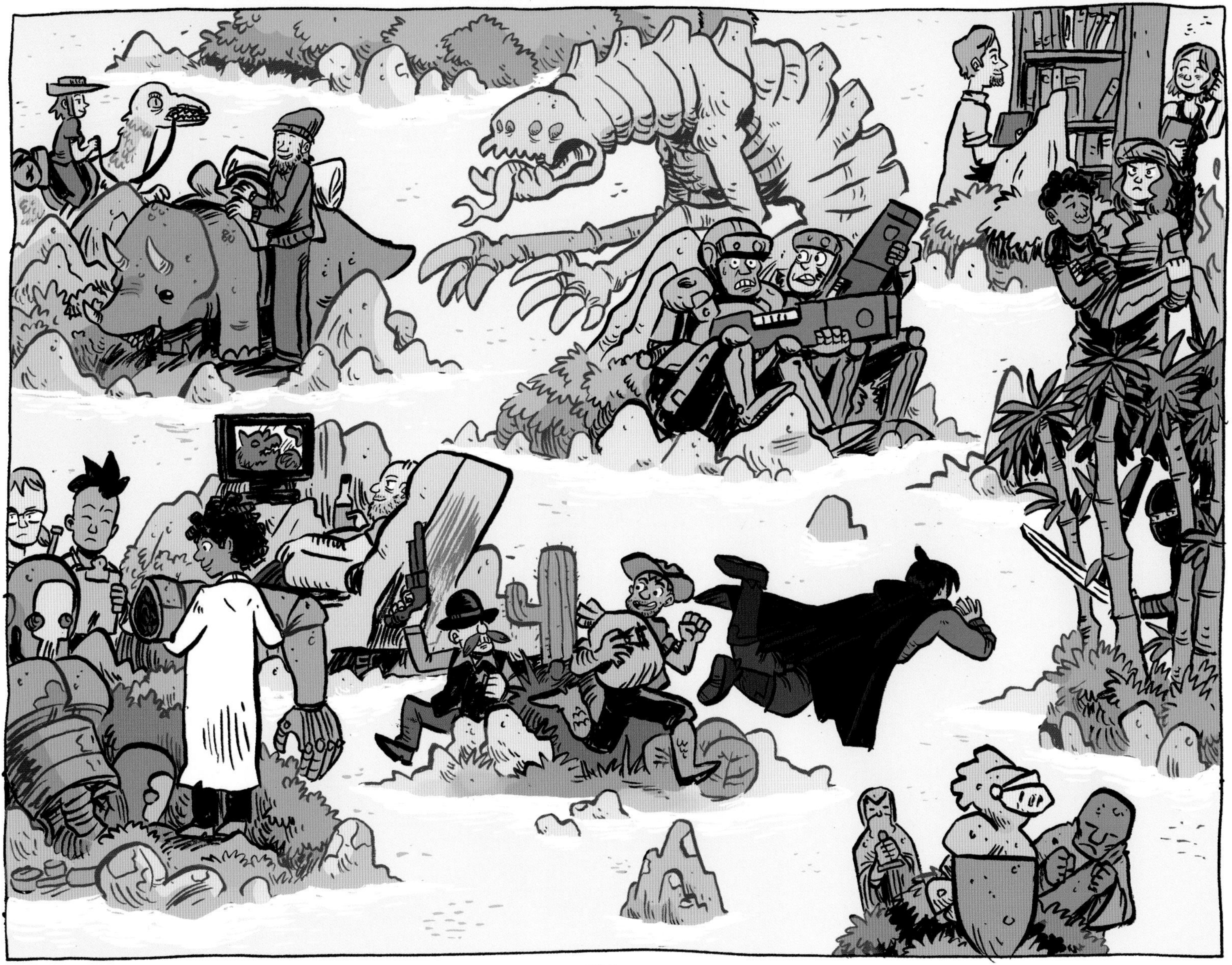

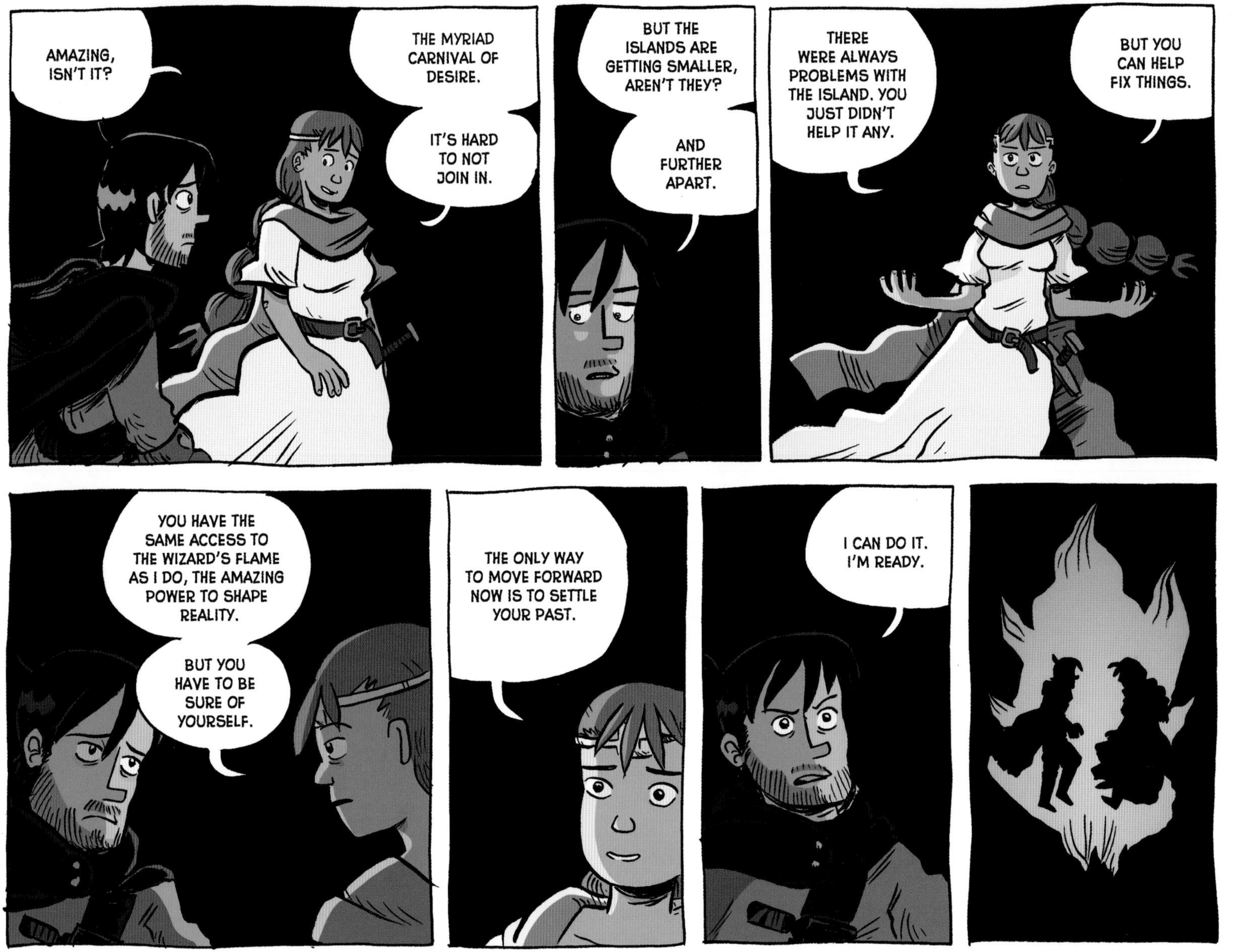
AMAZING, ISN'T IT?
THE MYRIAD CARNIVAL OF DESIRE.
IT'S HARD TO NOT JOIN IN.
BUT THE ISLANDS ARE GETTING SMALLER, AREN'T THEY?
AND FURTHER APART.
THERE WERE ALWAYS PROBLEMS WITH THE ISLAND. YOU JUST DIDN'T HELP IT ANY.
BUT YOU CAN HELP FIX THINGS.
YOU HAVE THE SAME ACCESS TO THE WIZARD'S FLAME AS I DO, THE AMAZING POWER TO SHAPE REALITY.
BUT YOU HAVE TO BE SURE OF YOURSELF.
THE ONLY WAY TO MOVE FORWARD NOW IS TO SETTLE YOUR PAST.
I CAN DO IT. I'M READY.

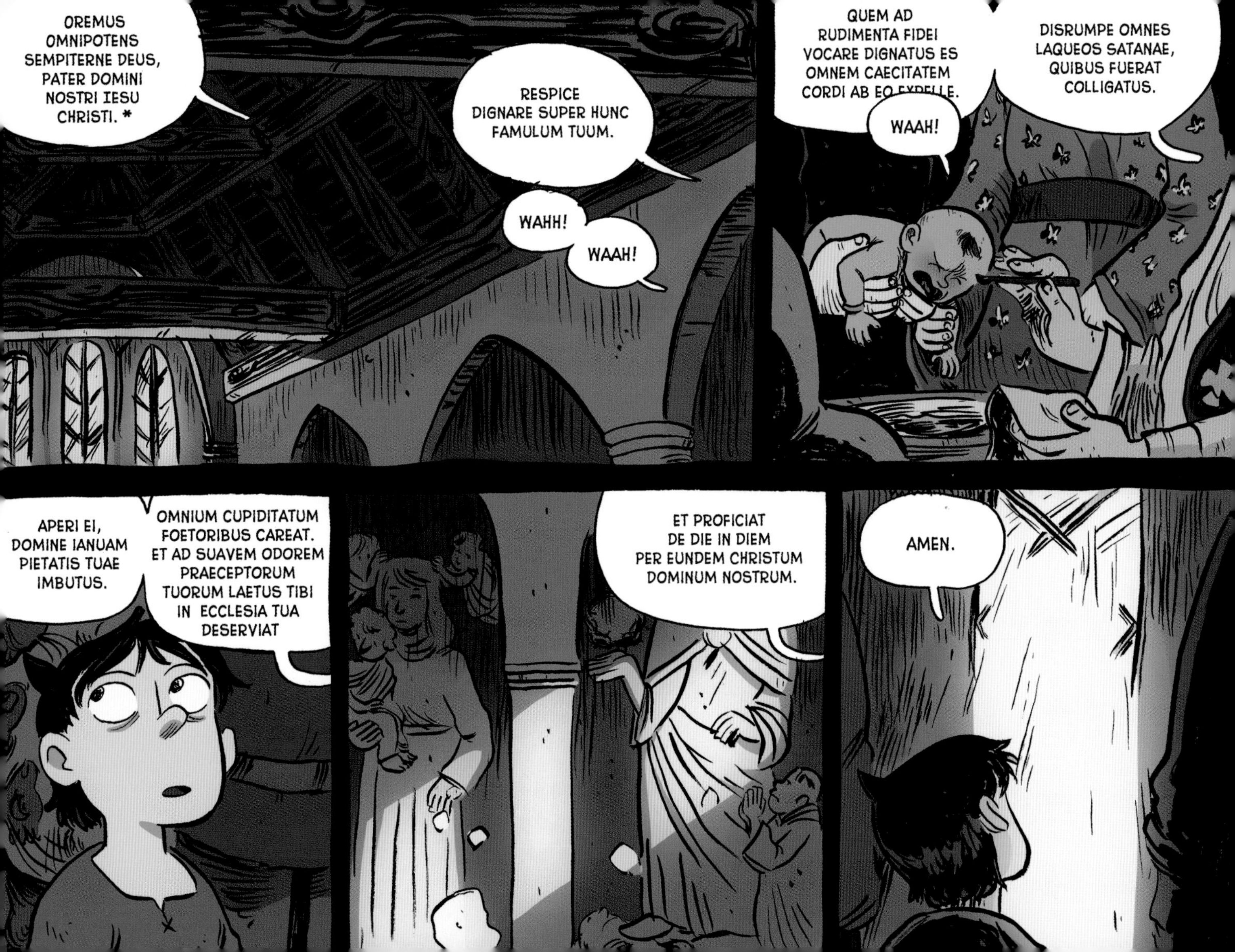
OREMUS OMNIPOTENS SEMPITERNE DEUS, PATER DOMINI NOSTRI IESU CHRISTI. *
RESPICE DIGNARE SUPER HUNC FAMULUM TUUM.
WAHH!
WAAH!
QUEM AD RUDIMENTA FIDEI VOCARE DIGNATUS ES OMNEM CAECITATEM CORDI AB EO EXPELLE.
WAAH!
DISRUMPE OMNES LAQUEOS SATANAE, QUIBUS FUERAT COLLIGATUS.
APERI EI, DOMINE IANUAM PIETATIS TUAE IMBUTUS.
OMNIUM CUPIDITATUM FOETORIBUS CAREAT. ET AD SUAVEM ODOREM PRAECEPTORUM TUORUM LAETUS TIBI IN ECCLESIA TUA DESERVIAT
ET PROFICIAT DE DIE IN DIEM PER EUNDEM CHRISTUM DOMINUM NOSTRUM.
AMEN.

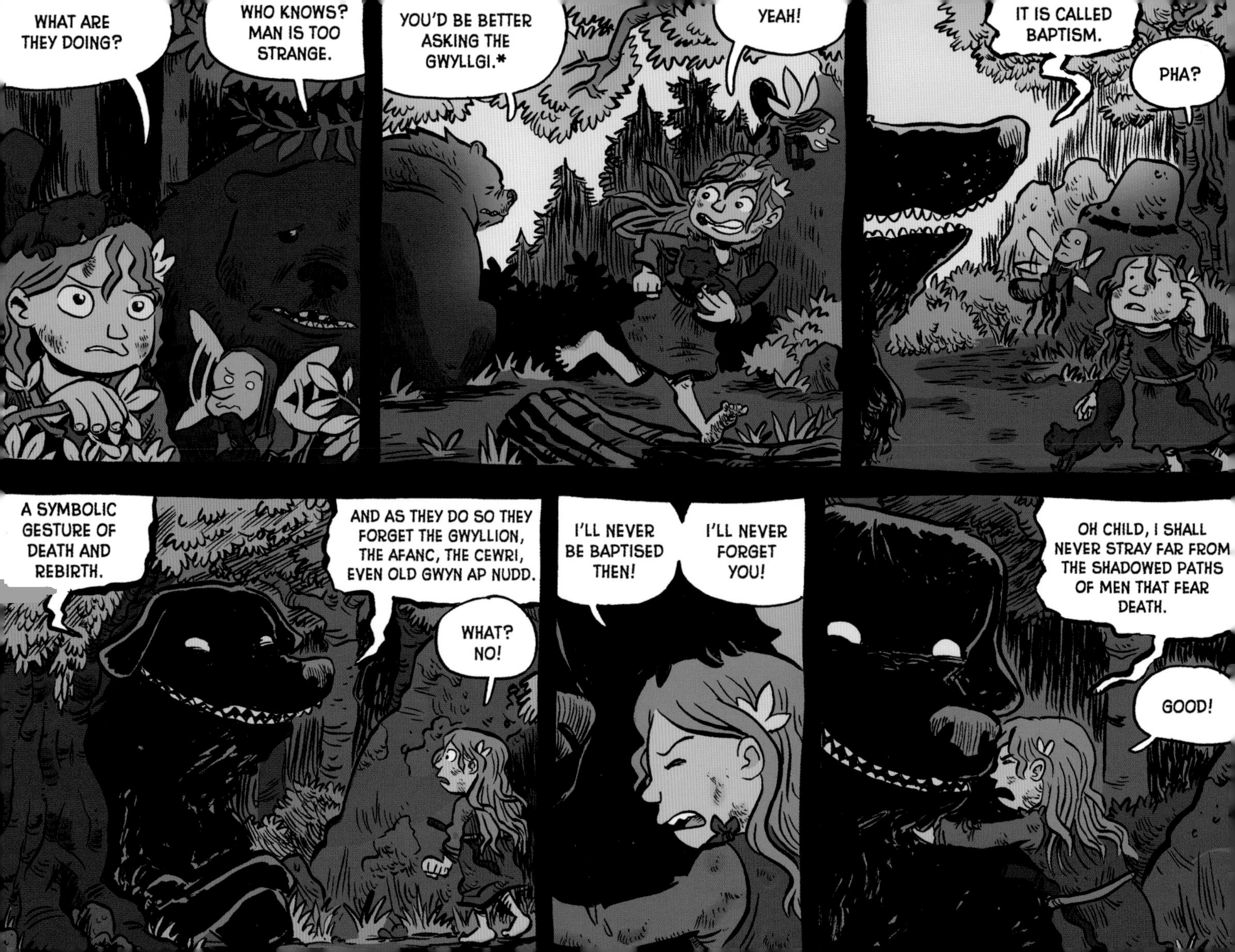
WHAT ARE THEY DOING?
WHO KNOWS? MAN IS TOO STRANGE.
YOU'D BE BETTER ASKING THE GWYLLGI.*
YEAH!
IT IS CALLED BAPTISM.
PHA?
A SYMBOLIC GESTURE OF DEATH AND REBIRTH.
AND AS THEY DO SO THEY FORGET THE GWYLLION, THE AFANC, THE CEWRI, EVEN OLD GWYN AP NUDD.
WHAT? NO!
I'LL NEVER BE BAPTISED THEN!
I'LL NEVER FORGET YOU!
OH CHILD, I SHALL NEVER STRAY FAR FROM THE SHADOWED PATHS OF MEN THAT FEAR DEATH.
GOOD!

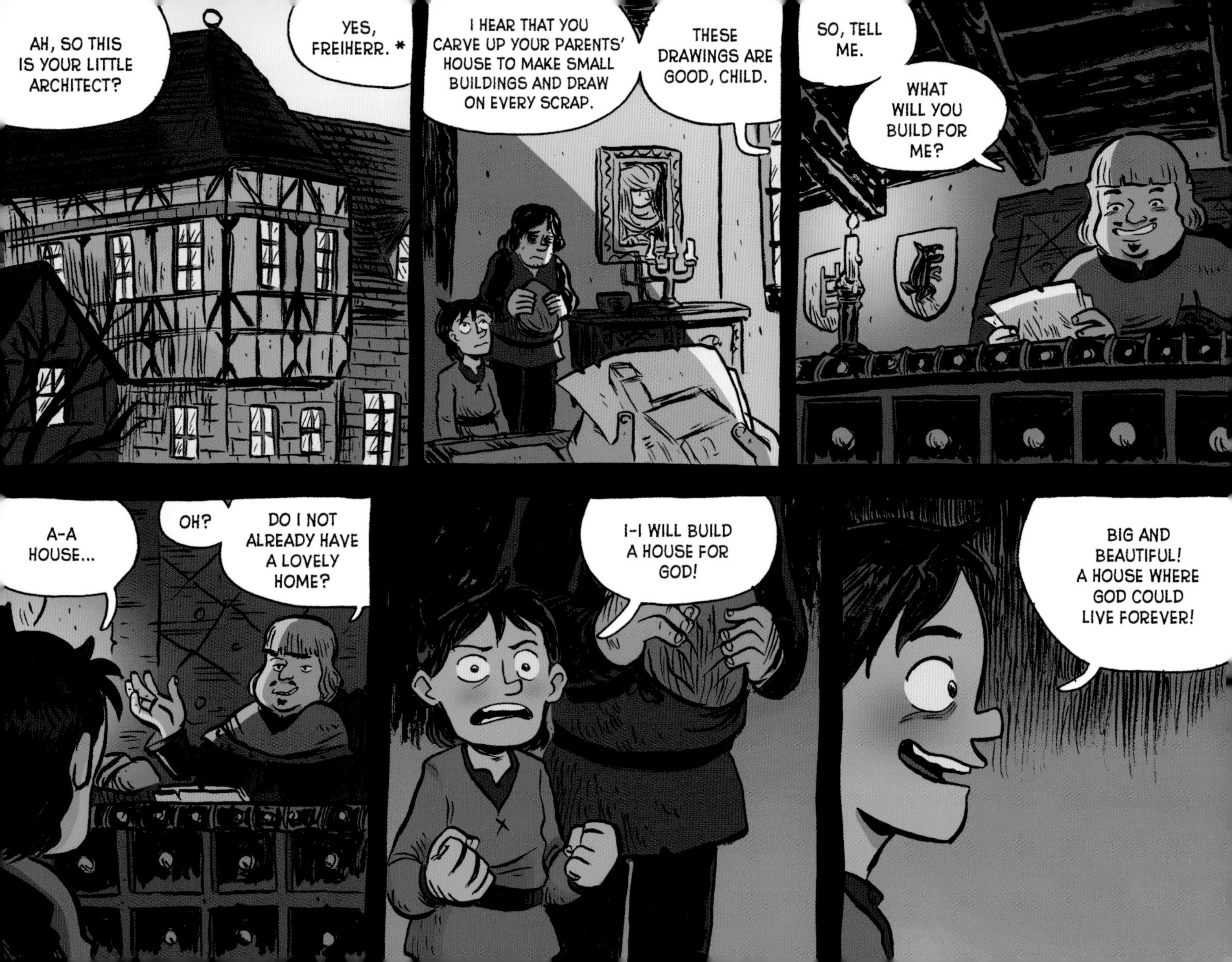
AH, SO THIS IS YOUR LITTLE ARCHITECT?
YES, FREIHERR. *
I HEAR THAT YOU CARVE UP YOUR PARENTS' HOUSE TO MAKE SMALL BUILDINGS AND DRAW ON EVERY SCRAP.
THESE DRAWINGS ARE GOOD, CHILD.
SO, TELL ME.
WHAT WILL YOU BUILD FOR ME?
A-A HOUSE...
OH?
DO I NOT ALREADY HAVE A LOVELY HOME?
I-I WILL BUILD A HOUSE FOR GOD!
BIG AND BEAUTIFUL! A HOUSE WHERE GOD COULD LIVE FOREVER!

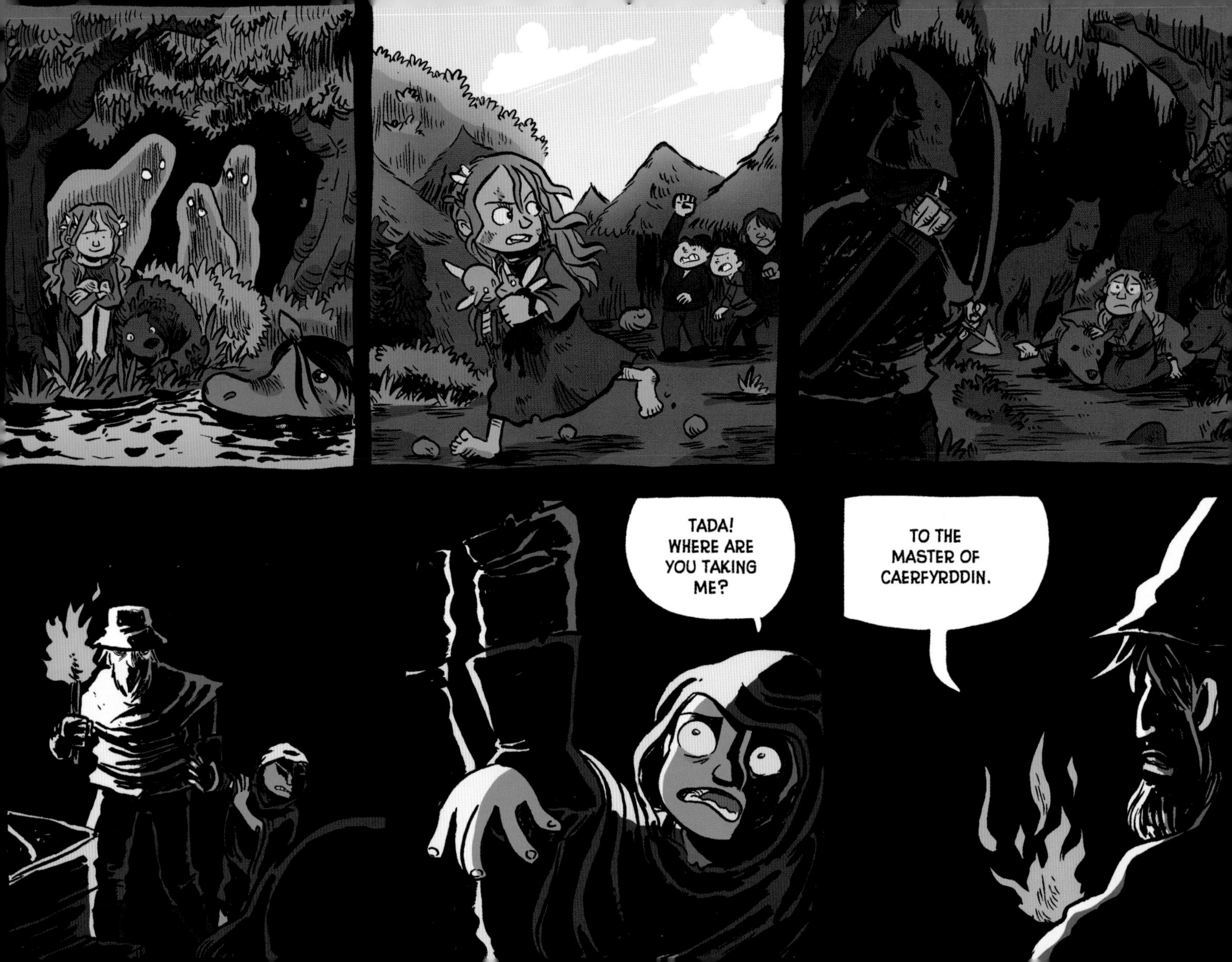
TADA! WHERE ARE YOU TAKING ME?
TO THE MASTER OF CAERFYRDDIN.

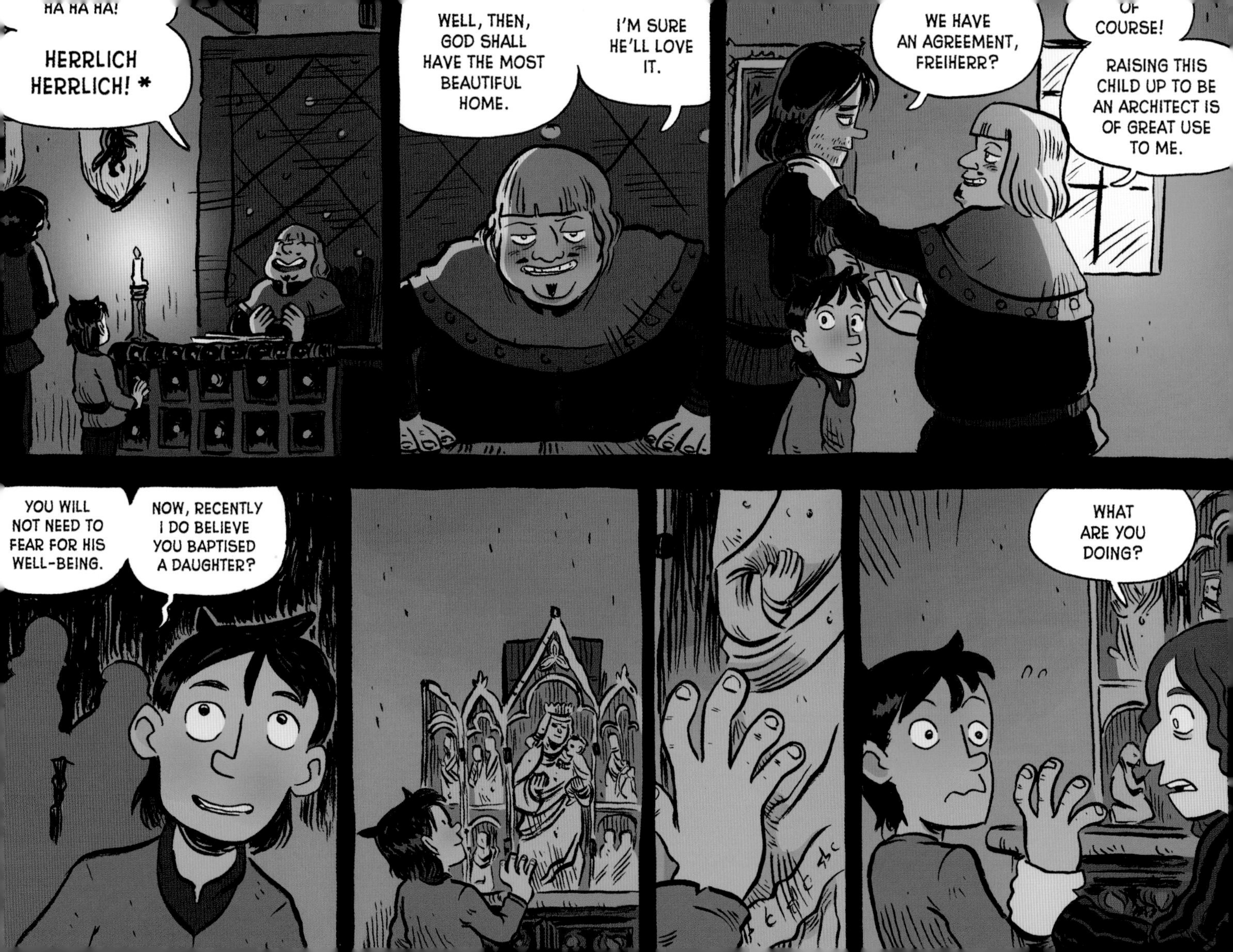
HA HA HA!
HERRLICH HERRLICH! *
WELL, THEN, GOD SHALL HAVE THE MOST BEAUTIFUL HOME.
I'M SURE HE'LL LOVE IT.
WE HAVE AN AGREEMENT, FREIHERR?
OF COURSE!
RAISING THIS CHILD UP TO BE AN ARCHITECT IS OF GREAT USE TO ME.
YOU WILL NOT NEED TO FEAR FOR HIS WELL-BEING.
NOW, RECENTLY I DO BELIEVE YOU BAPTISED A DAUGHTER?
WHAT ARE YOU DOING?

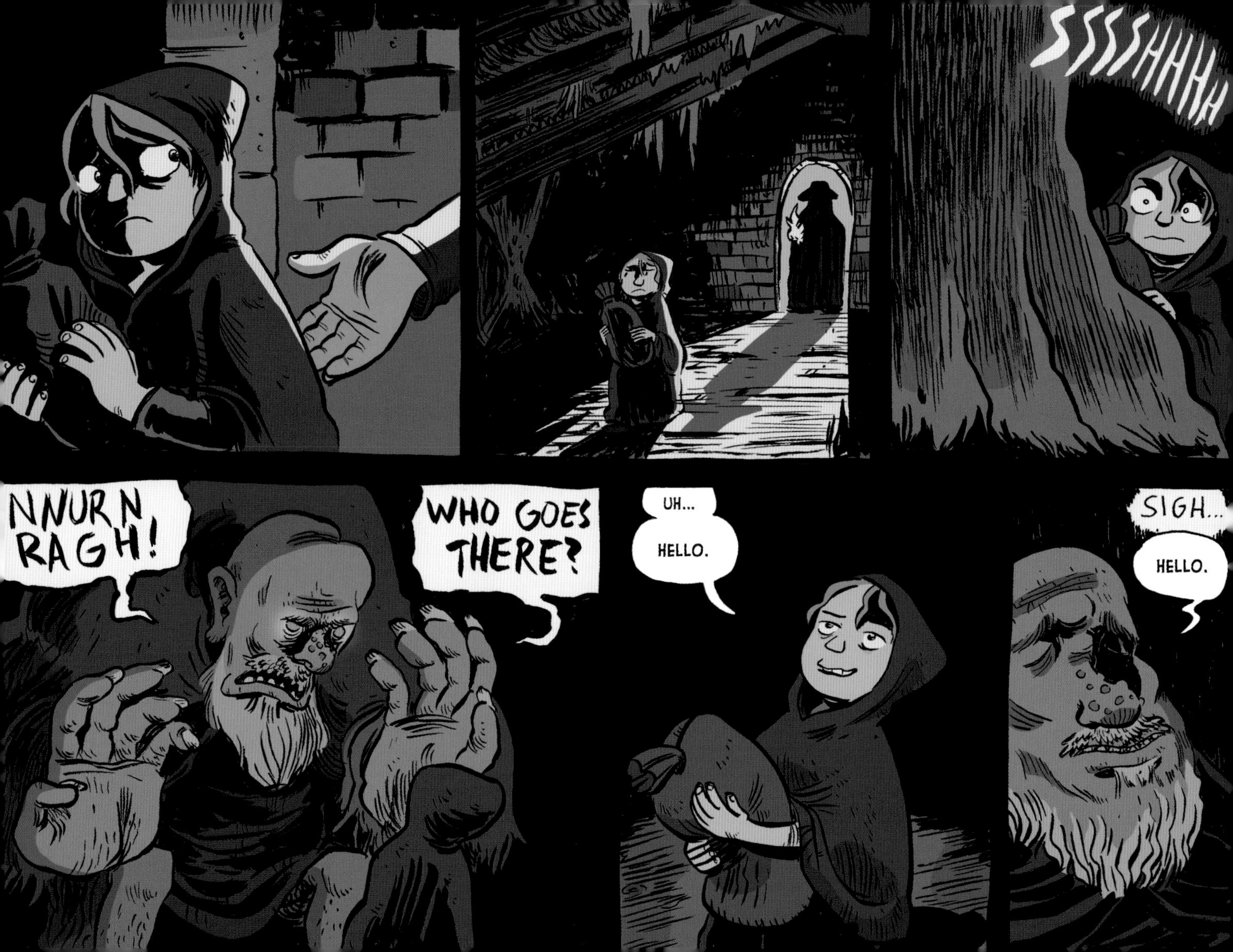
SSSSHHHH
NNURN RAGH!
WHO GOES THERE?
UH...
HELLO.
SIGH...
HELLO.

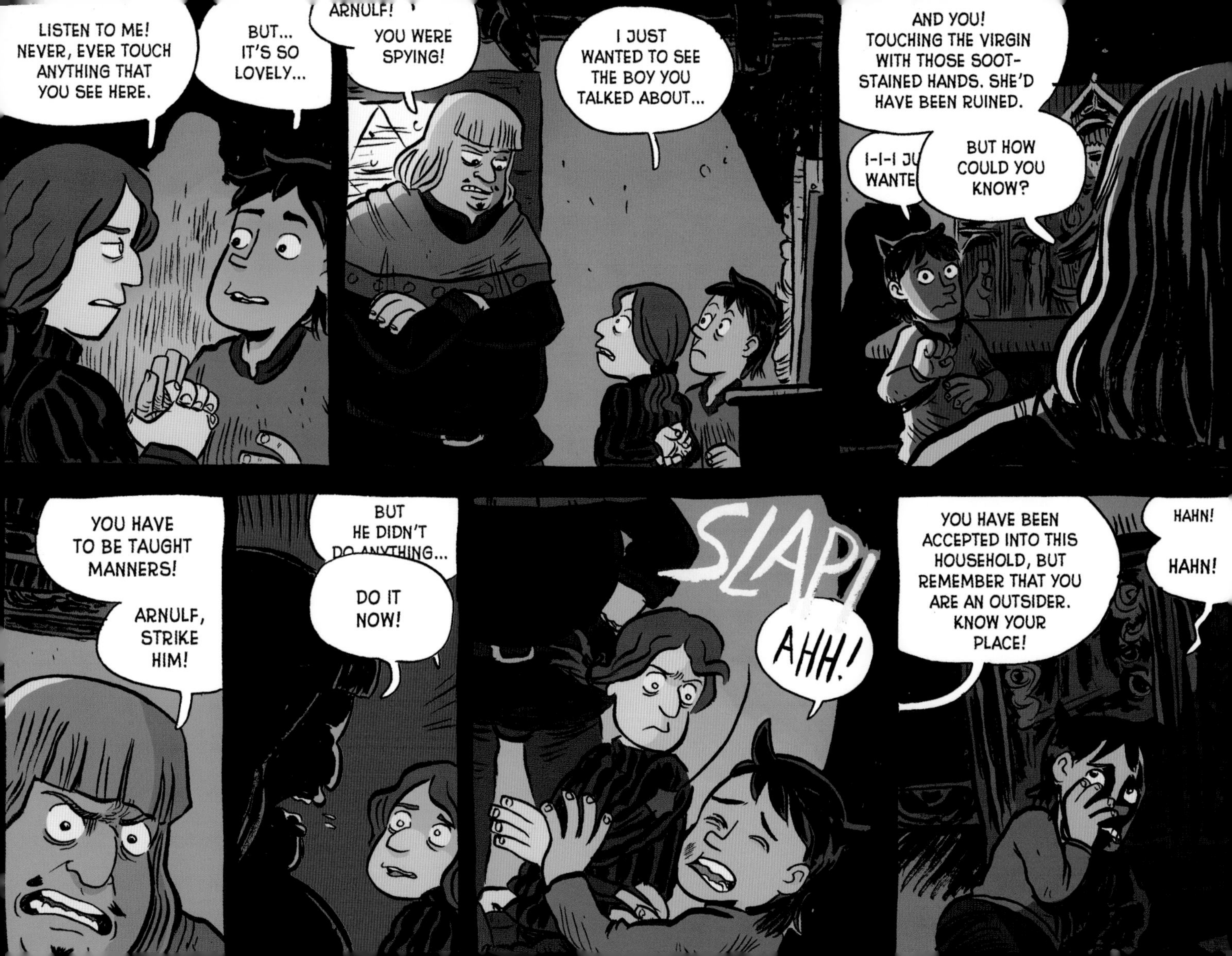

LISTEN TO ME! NEVER, EVER TOUCH ANYTHING THAT YOU SEE HERE.
BUT... IT'S SO LOVELY...
ARNULF!
YOU WERE SPYING!
I JUST WANTED TO SEE THE BOY YOU TALKED ABOUT...
AND YOU! TOUCHING THE VIRGIN WITH THOSE SOOT-STAINED HANDS. SHE'D HAVE BEEN RUINED.
BUT HOW COULD YOU KNOW?
YOU HAVE TO BE TAUGHT MANNERS!
ARNULF, STRIKE HIM!
BUT HE DIDN'T DO ANYTHING...
DO IT NOW!
SLAP!
AHH!
YOU HAVE BEEN ACCEPTED INTO THIS HOUSEHOLD, BUT REMEMBER THAT YOU ARE AN OUTSIDER. KNOW YOUR PLACE!
HAHN!
HAHN!

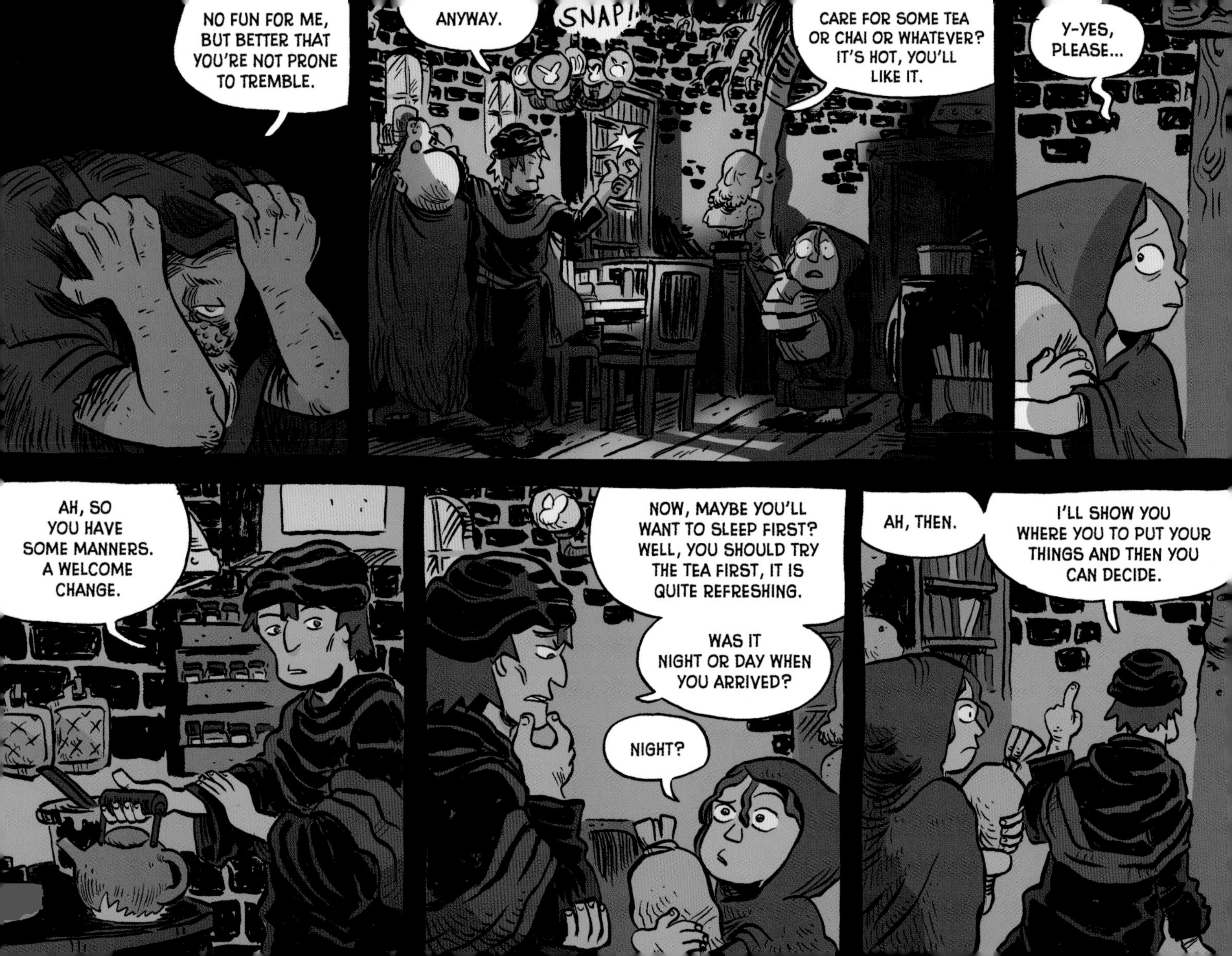
NO FUN FOR ME, BUT BETTER THAT YOU'RE NOT PRONE TO TREMBLE.
ANYWAY.
SNAP!
CARE FOR SOME TEA OR CHAI OR WHATEVER? IT'S HOT, YOU'LL LIKE IT.
Y-YES, PLEASE...
AH, SO YOU HAVE SOME MANNERS. A WELCOME CHANGE.
NOW, MAYBE YOU'LL WANT TO SLEEP FIRST? WELL, YOU SHOULD TRY THE TEA FIRST, IT IS QUITE REFRESHING.
WAS IT NIGHT OR DAY WHEN YOU ARRIVED?
NIGHT?
AH, THEN.
I'LL SHOW YOU WHERE YOU TO PUT YOUR THINGS AND THEN YOU CAN DECIDE.

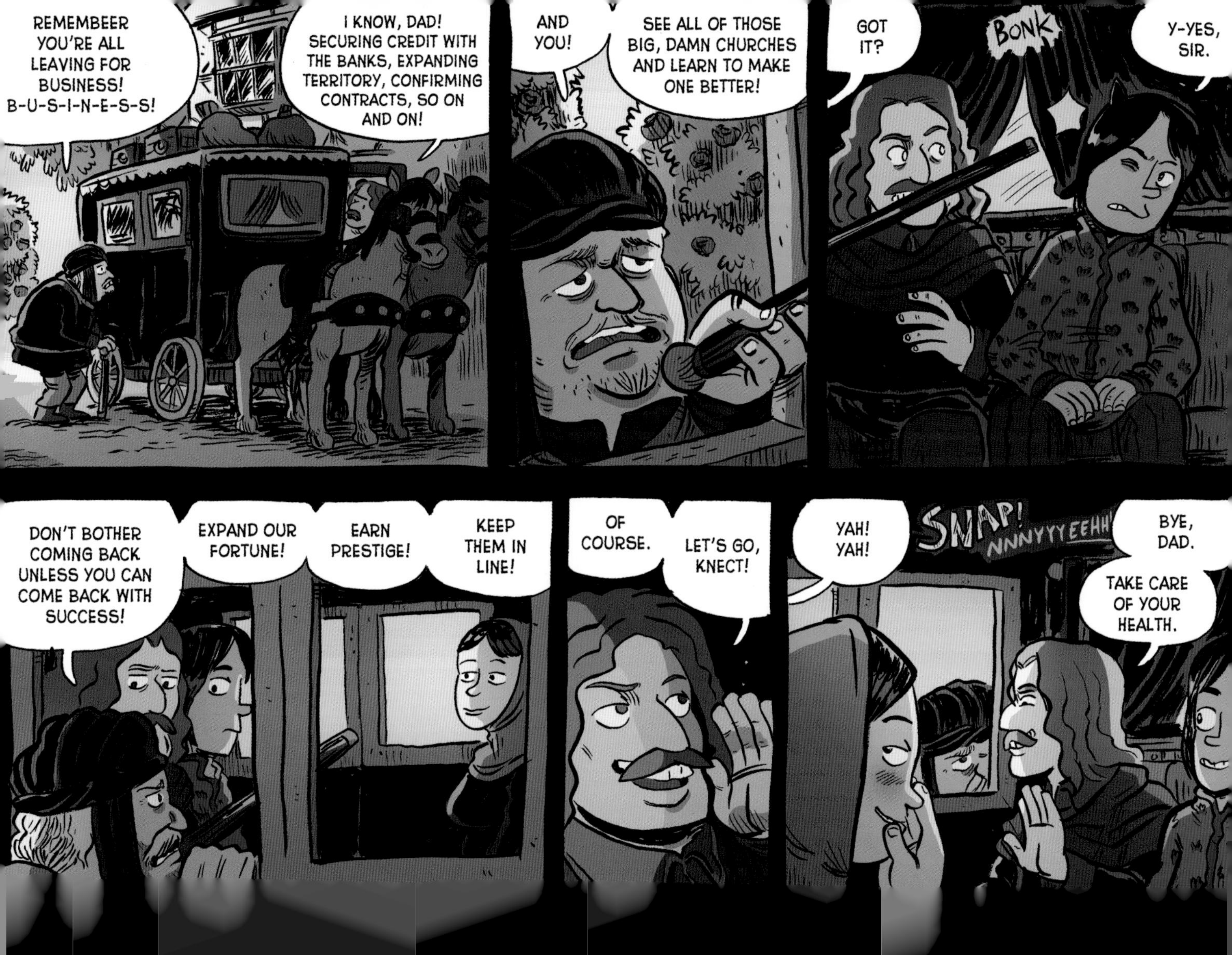
REMEMBEER YOU'RE ALL LEAVING FOR BUSINESS! B-U-S-I-N-E-S-S!
I KNOW, DAD! SECURING CREDIT WITH THE BANKS, EXPANDING TERRITORY, CONFIRMING CONTRACTS, SO ON AND ON!
AND YOU!
SEE ALL OF THOSE BIG, DAMN CHURCHES AND LEARN TO MAKE ONE BETTER!
GOT IT?
BONK
Y-YES, SIR.
DON'T BOTHER COMING BACK UNLESS YOU CAN COME BACK WITH SUCCESS!
EXPAND OUR FORTUNE!
EARN PRESTIGE!
KEEP THEM IN LINE!
OF COURSE.
LET'S GO, KNECT!
YAH! YAH!
SNAP!
NNNYYYEEHH
BYE, DAD.
TAKE CARE OF YOUR HEALTH.

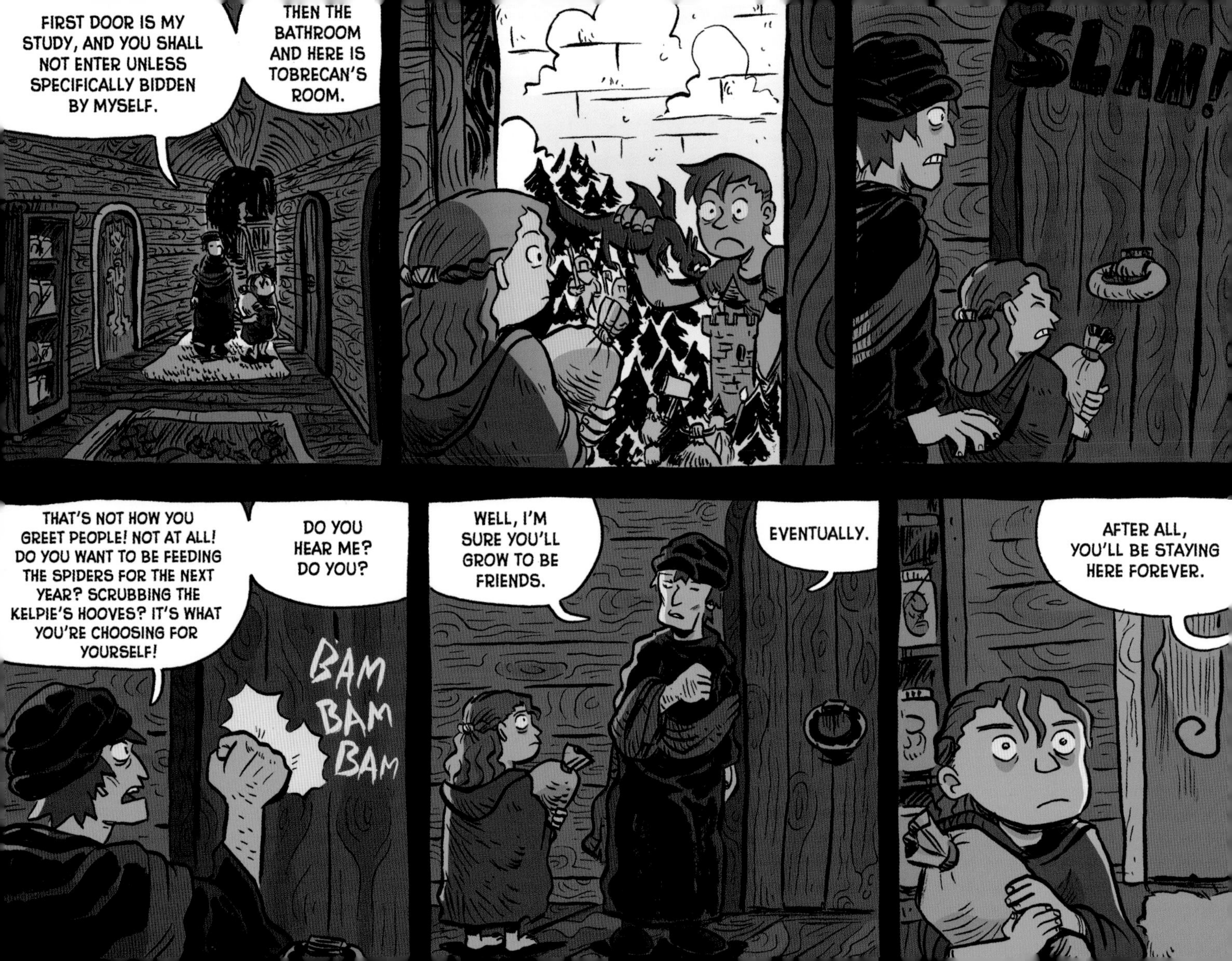
FIRST DOOR IS MY STUDY, AND YOU SHALL NOT ENTER UNLESS SPECIFICALLY BIDDEN BY MYSELF.
THEN THE BATHROOM AND HERE IS TOBRECAN'S ROOM.
SLAM!
THAT'S NOT HOW YOU GREET PEOPLE! NOT AT ALL! DO YOU WANT TO BE FEEDING THE SPIDERS FOR THE NEXT YEAR? SCRUBBING THE KELPIE'S HOOVES? IT'S WHAT YOU'RE CHOOSING FOR YOURSELF!
DO YOU HEAR ME? DO YOU?
BAM BAM BAM
WELL, I'M SURE YOU'LL GROW TO BE FRIENDS.
EVENTUALLY.
AFTER ALL, YOU'LL BE STAYING HERE FOREVER.

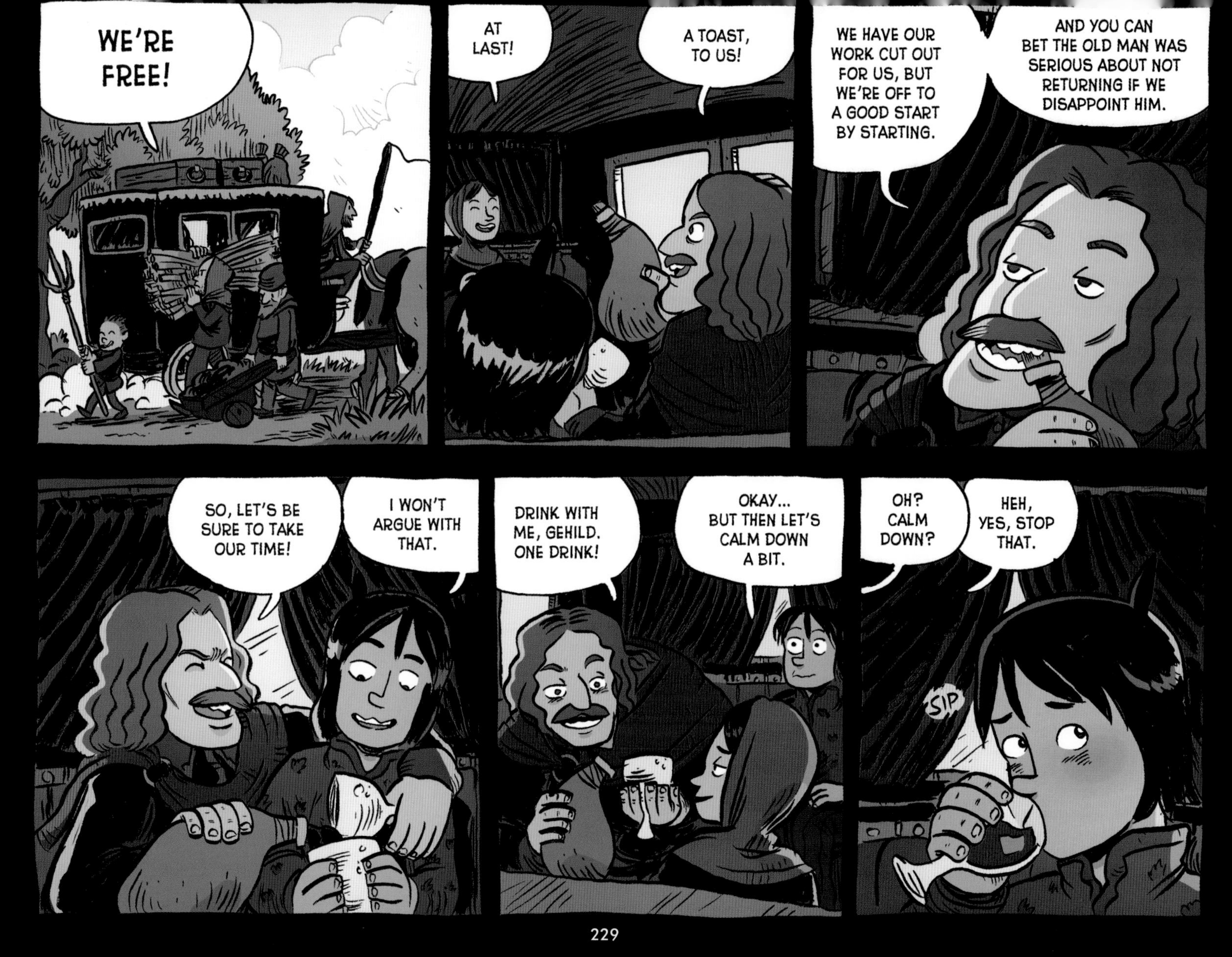
WE'RE FREE!
AT LAST!
A TOAST, TO US!
WE HAVE OUR WORK CUT OUT FOR US, BUT WE'RE OFF TO A GOOD START BY STARTING.
AND YOU CAN BET THE OLD MAN WAS SERIOUS ABOUT NOT RETURNING IF WE DISAPPOINT HIM.
SO, LET'S BE SURE TO TAKE OUR TIME!
I WON'T ARGUE WITH THAT.
DRINK WITH ME, GEHILD. ONE DRINK!
OKAY... BUT THEN LET'S CALM DOWN A BIT.
OH? CALM DOWN?
HEH, YES, STOP THAT.
SIP

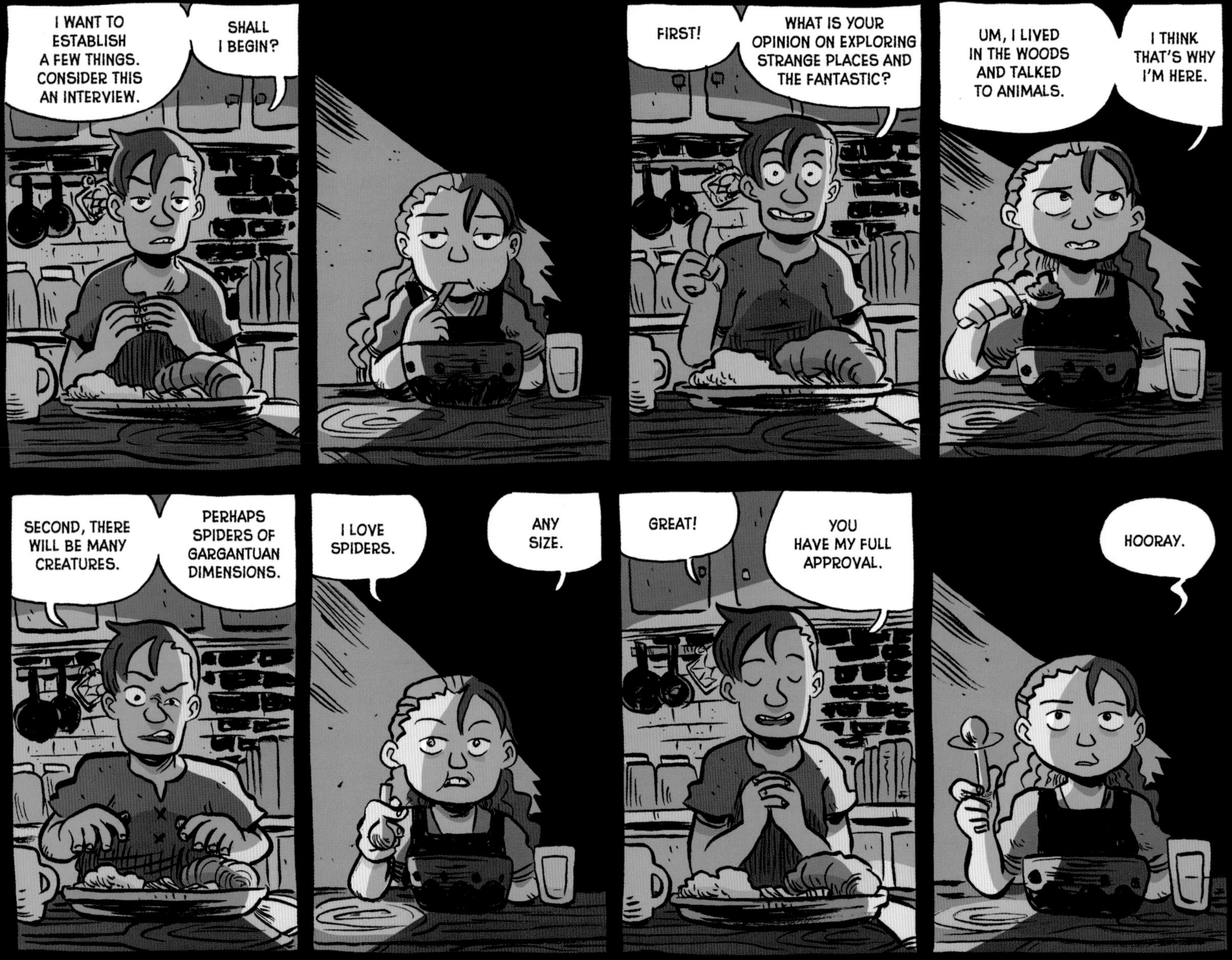
I WANT TO ESTABLISH A FEW THINGS. CONSIDER THIS AN INTERVIEW.
SHALL I BEGIN?
FIRST!
WHAT IS YOUR OPINION ON EXPLORING STRANGE PLACES AND THE FANTASTIC?
UM, I LIVED IN THE WOODS AND TALKED TO ANIMALS.
I THINK THAT'S WHY I'M HERE.
SECOND, THERE WILL BE MANY CREATURES.
PERHAPS SPIDERS OF GARGANTUAN DIMENSIONS.
I LOVE SPIDERS.
ANY SIZE.
GREAT!
YOU HAVE MY FULL APPROVAL.
HOORAY.

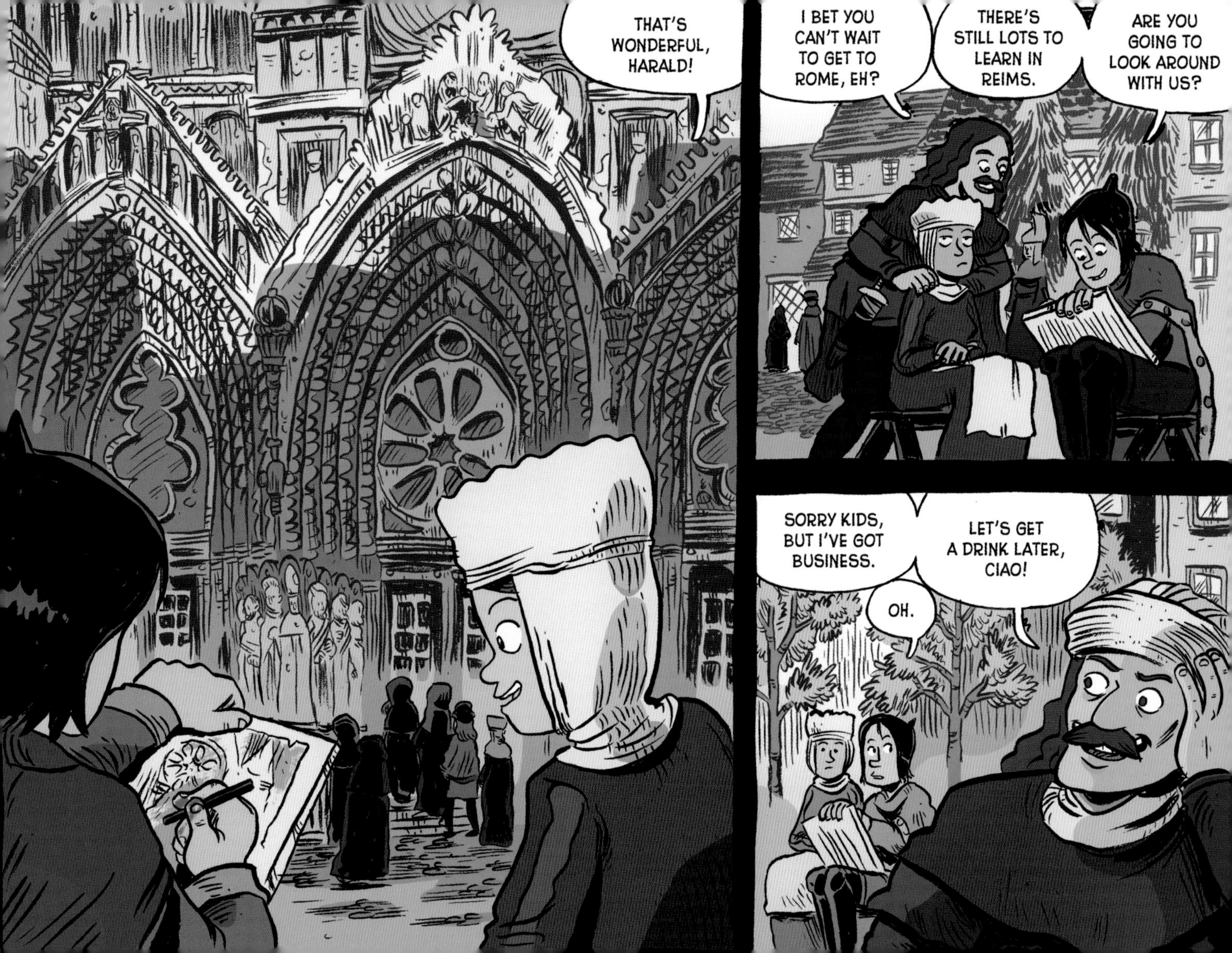
THAT'S WONDERFUL, HARALD!
I BET YOU CAN'T WAIT TO GET TO ROME, EH?
THERE'S STILL LOTS TO LEARN IN REIMS.
ARE YOU GOING TO LOOK AROUND WITH US?
SORRY KIDS, BUT I'VE GOT BUSINESS.
LET'S GET A DRINK LATER, CIAO!
OH.

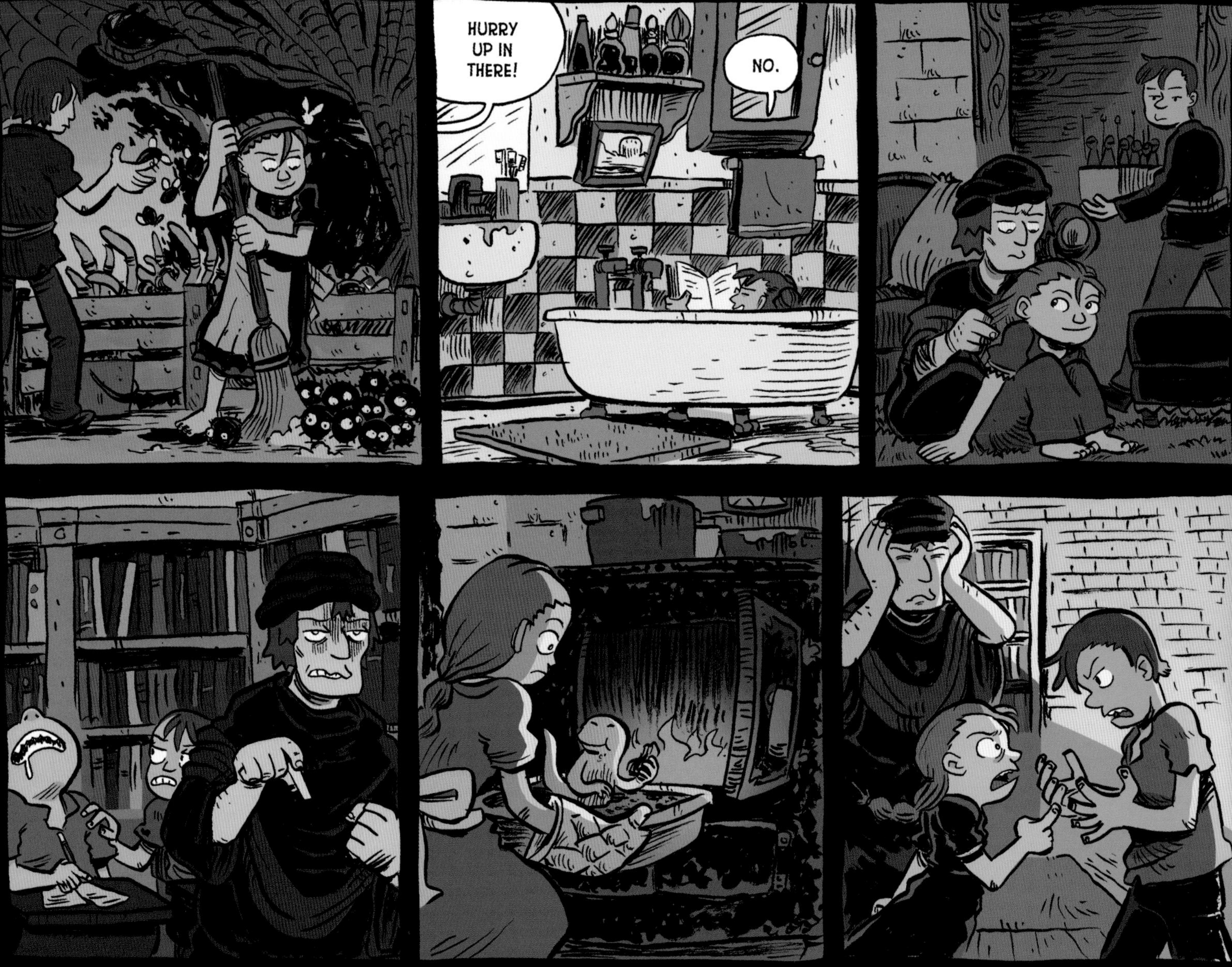
HURRY UP IN THERE!
NO.

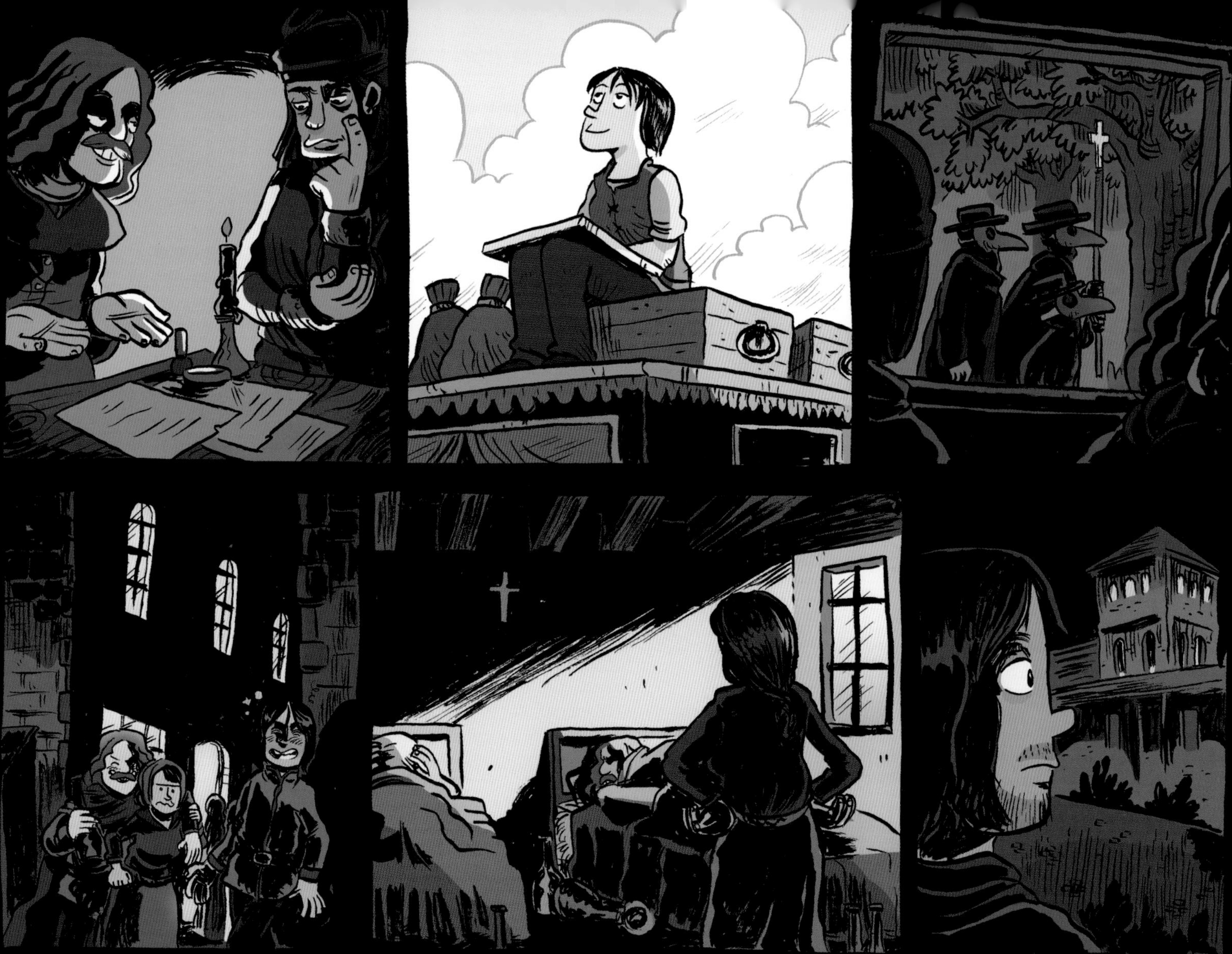

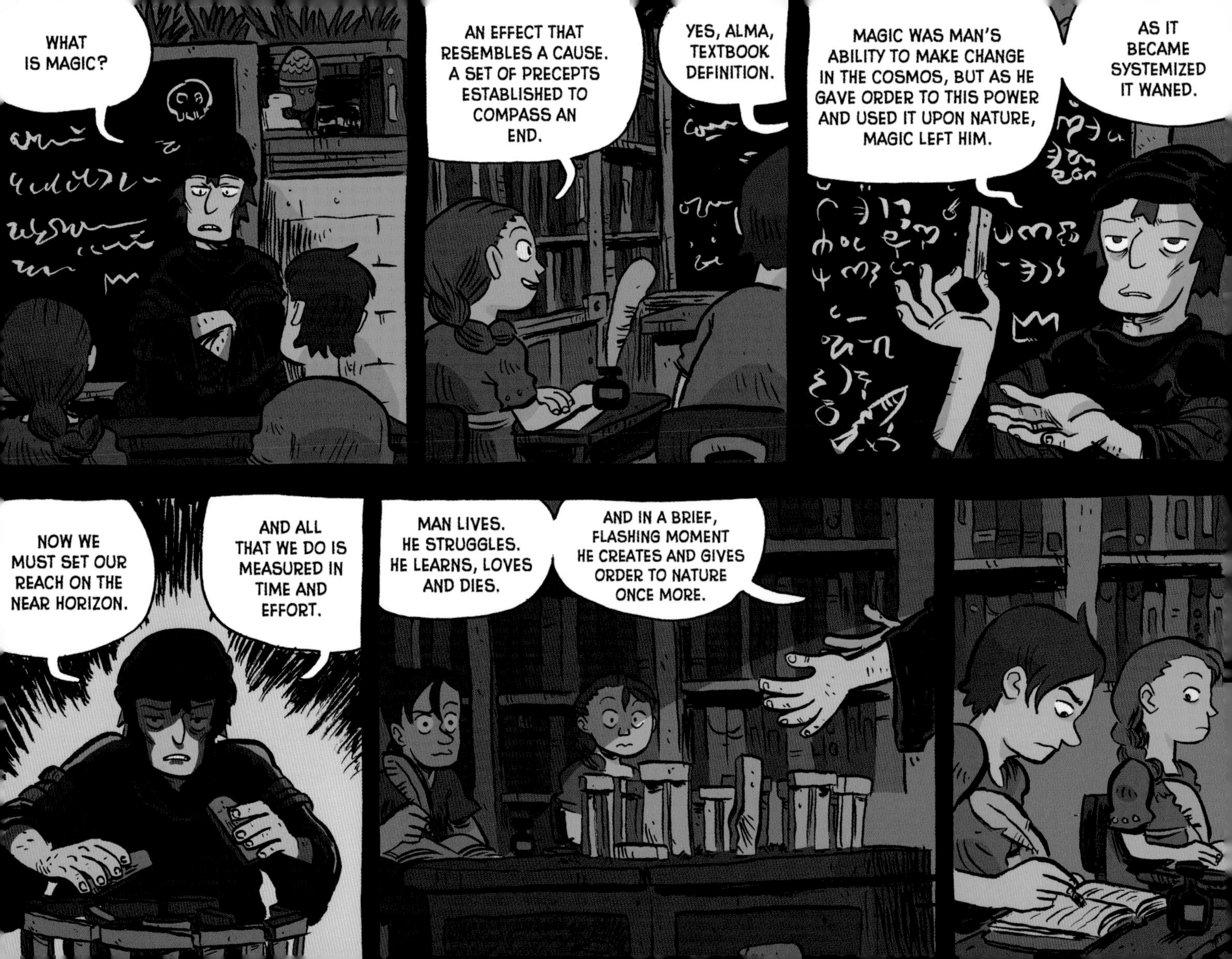

WHAT IS MAGIC?
AN EFFECT THAT RESEMBLES A CAUSE. A SET OF PRECEPTS ESTABLISHED TO COMPASS AN END.
YES, ALMA, TEXTBOOK DEFINITION.
MAGIC WAS MAN'S ABILITY TO MAKE CHANGE IN THE COSMOS, BUT AS HE GAVE ORDER TO THIS POWER AND USED IT UPON NATURE, MAGIC LEFT HIM.
AS IT BECAME SYSTEMIZED IT WANED.
NOW WE MUST SET OUR REACH ON THE NEAR HORIZON.
AND ALL THAT WE DO IS MEASURED IN TIME AND EFFORT.
MAN LIVES. HE STRUGGLES. HE LEARNS, LOVES AND DIES.
AND IN A BRIEF, FLASHING MOMENT HE CREATES AND GIVES ORDER TO NATURE ONCE MORE.

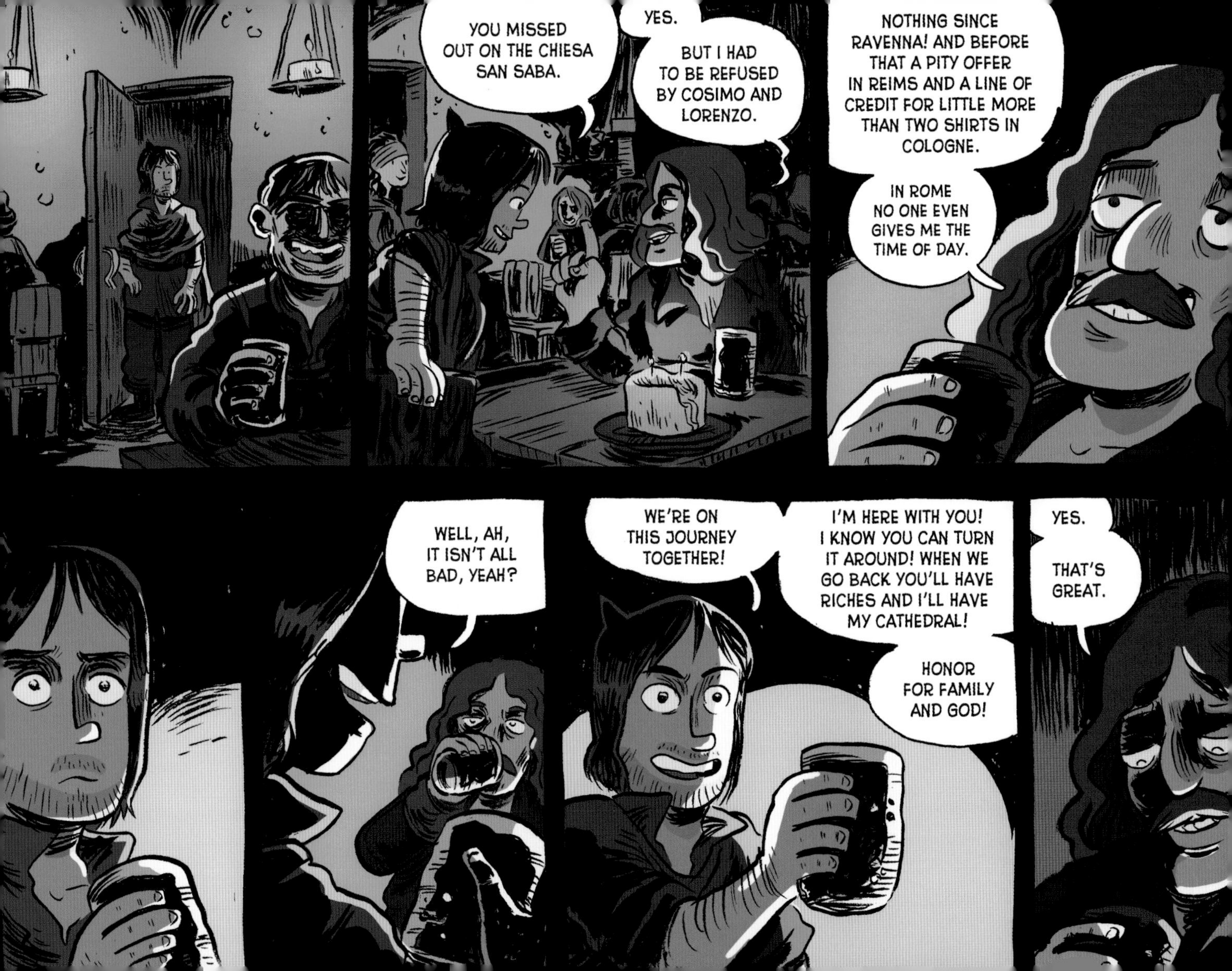
YOU MISSED OUT ON THE CHIESA SAN SABA.
YES.
BUT I HAD TO BE REFUSED BY COSIMO AND LORENZO.
NOTHING SINCE RAVENNA! AND BEFORE THAT A PITY OFFER IN REIMS AND A LINE OF CREDIT FOR LITTLE MORE THAN TWO SHIRTS IN COLOGNE.
IN ROME NO ONE EVEN GIVES ME THE TIME OF DAY.
WELL, AH, IT ISN'T ALL BAD, YEAH?
WE'RE ON THIS JOURNEY TOGETHER!
I'M HERE WITH YOU! I KNOW YOU CAN TURN IT AROUND! WHEN WE GO BACK YOU'LL HAVE RICHES AND I'LL HAVE MY CATHEDRAL!
HONOR FOR FAMILY AND GOD!
YES.
THAT'S GREAT.

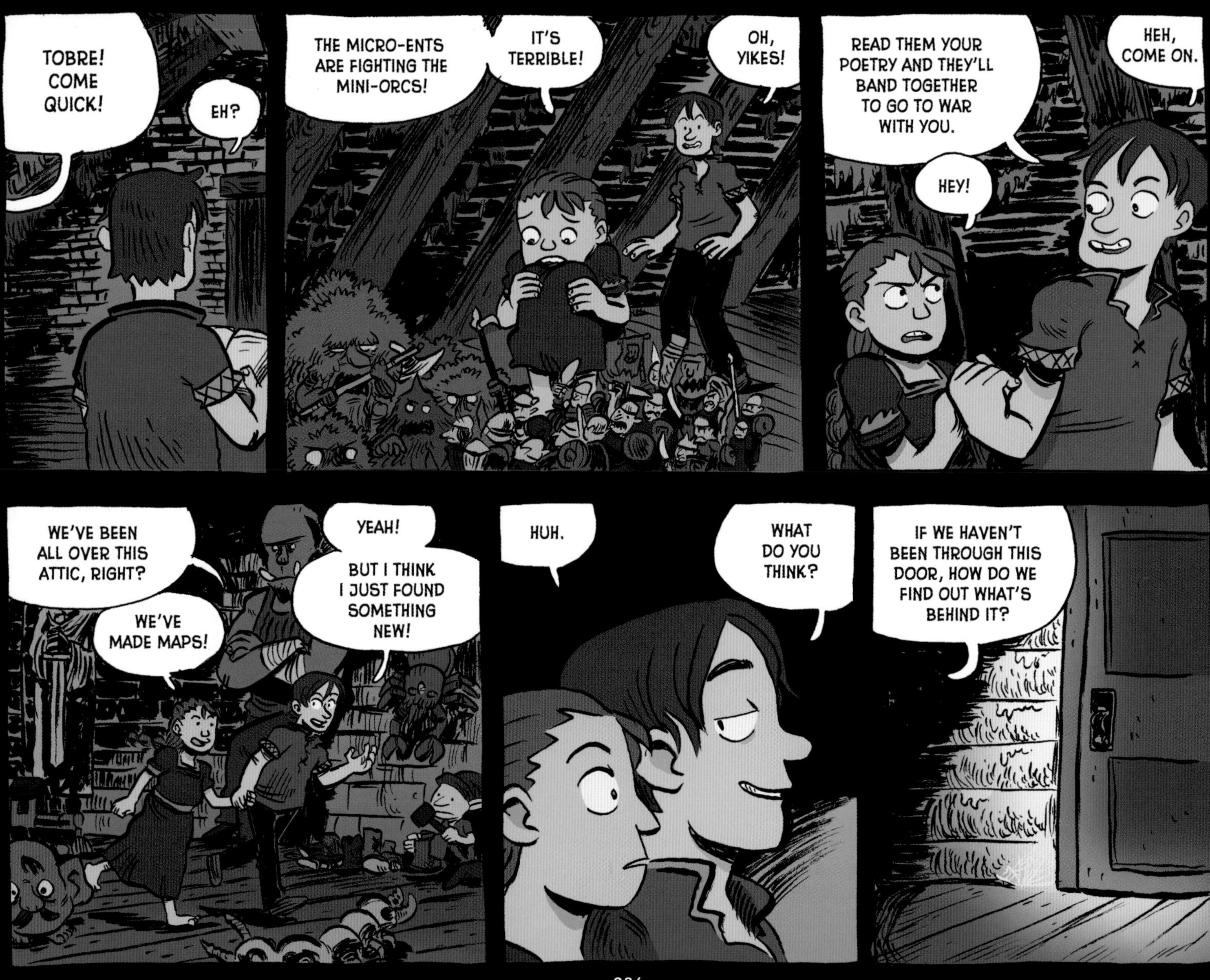
TOBRE! COME QUICK!
EH?
THE MICRO-ENTS ARE FIGHTING THE MINI-ORCS!
IT'S TERRIBLE!
OH, YIKES!
READ THEM YOUR POETRY AND THEY'LL BAND TOGETHER TO GO TO WAR WITH YOU.
HEY!
HEH, COME ON.
WE'VE BEEN ALL OVER THIS ATTIC, RIGHT?
WE'VE MADE MAPS!
YEAH!
BUT I THINK I JUST FOUND SOMETHING NEW!
HUH.
WHAT DO YOU THINK?
IF WE HAVEN'T BEEN THROUGH THIS DOOR, HOW DO WE FIND OUT WHAT'S BEHIND IT?

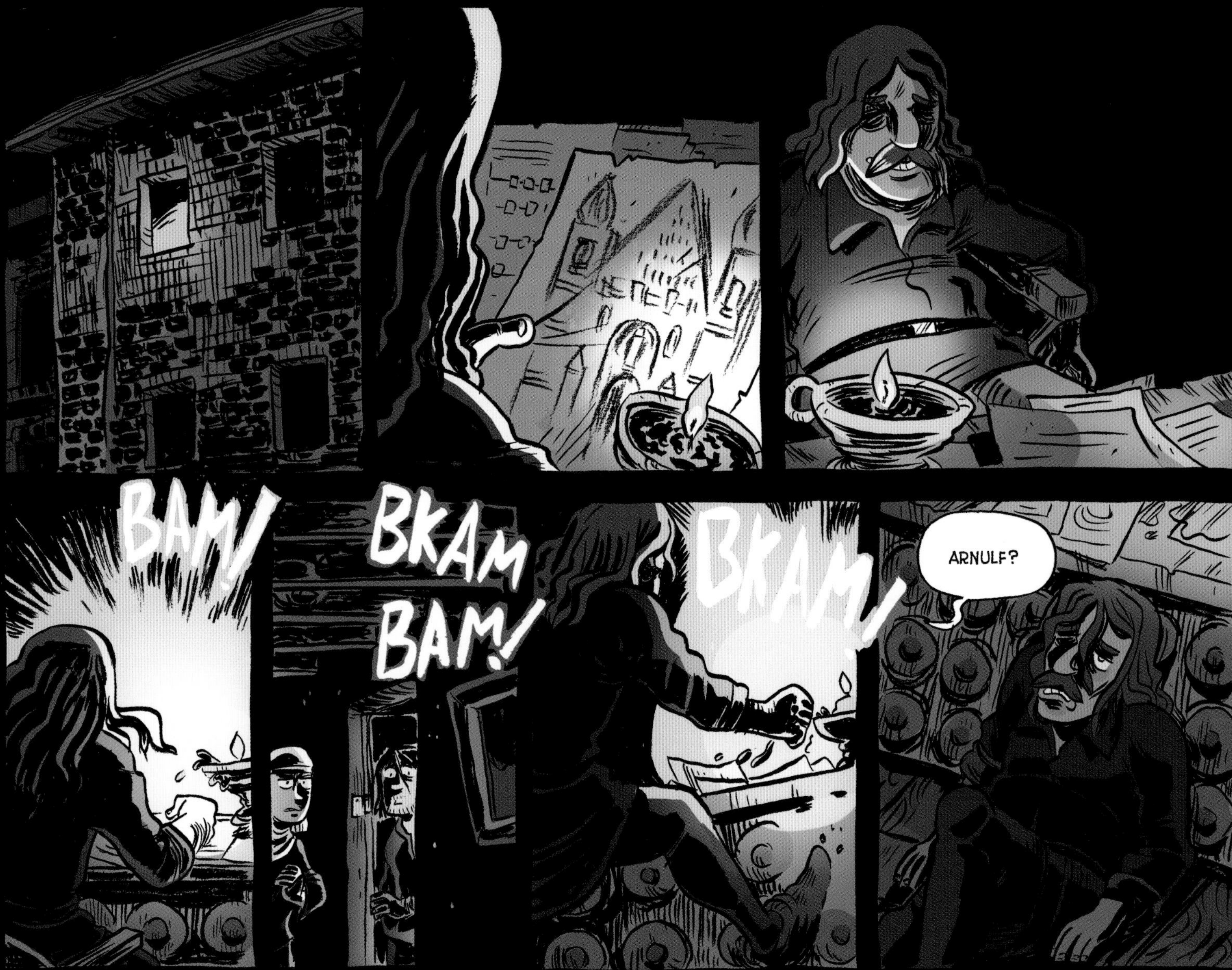
BAM!
BKAM
BAM!
BKAM!
ARNULF?

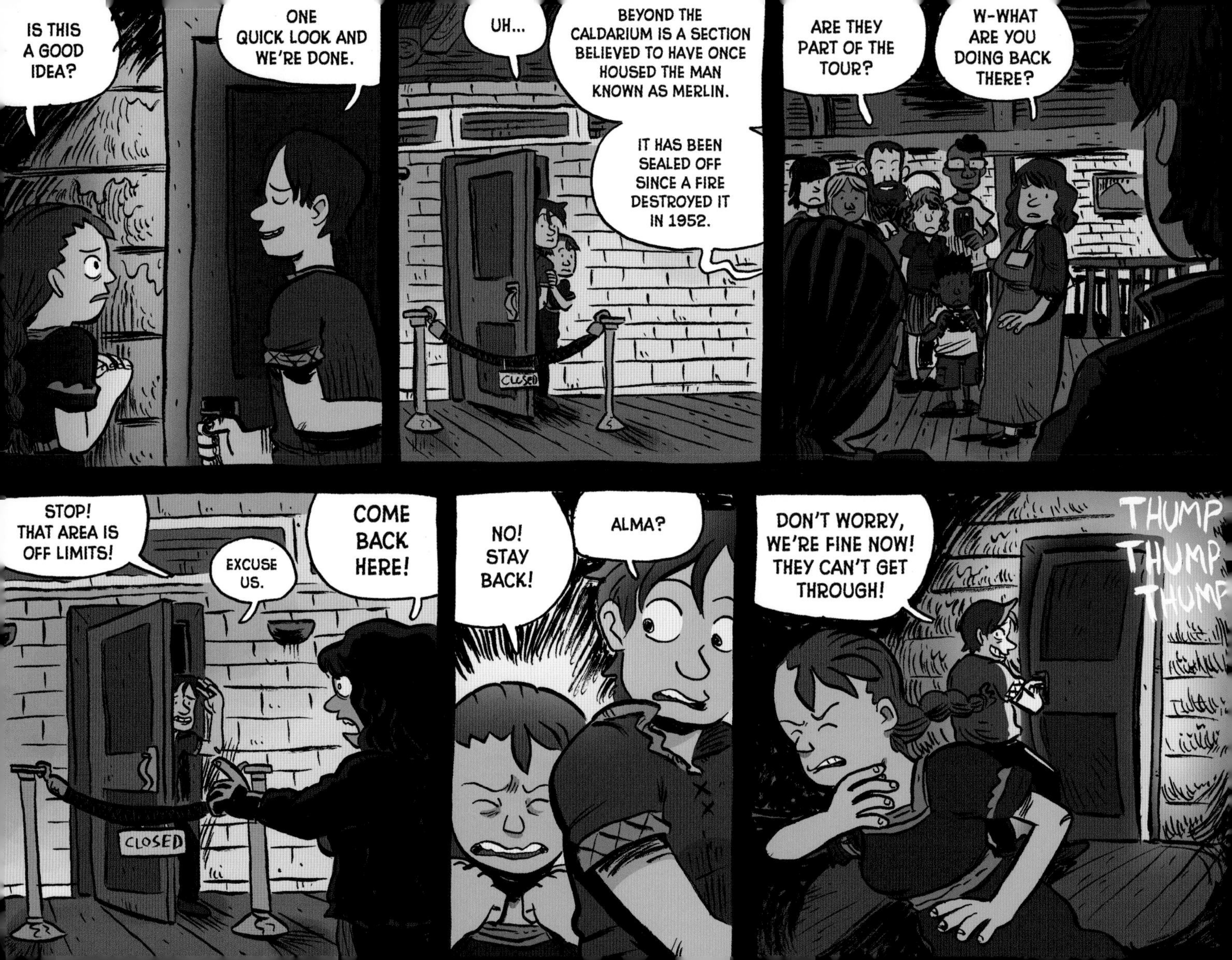
IS THIS A GOOD IDEA?
ONE QUICK LOOK AND WE'RE DONE.
UH...
BEYOND THE CALDARIUM IS A SECTION BELIEVED TO HAVE ONCE HOUSED THE MAN KNOWN AS MERLIN.
IT HAS BEEN SEALED OFF SINCE A FIRE DESTROYED IT IN 1952.
CLOSED
ARE THEY PART OF THE TOUR?
W-WHAT ARE YOU DOING BACK THERE?
STOP! THAT AREA IS OFF LIMITS!
EXCUSE US.
COME BACK HERE!
CLOSED
NO! STAY BACK!
ALMA?
DON'T WORRY, WE'RE FINE NOW! THEY CAN'T GET THROUGH!
THUMP THUMP THUMP

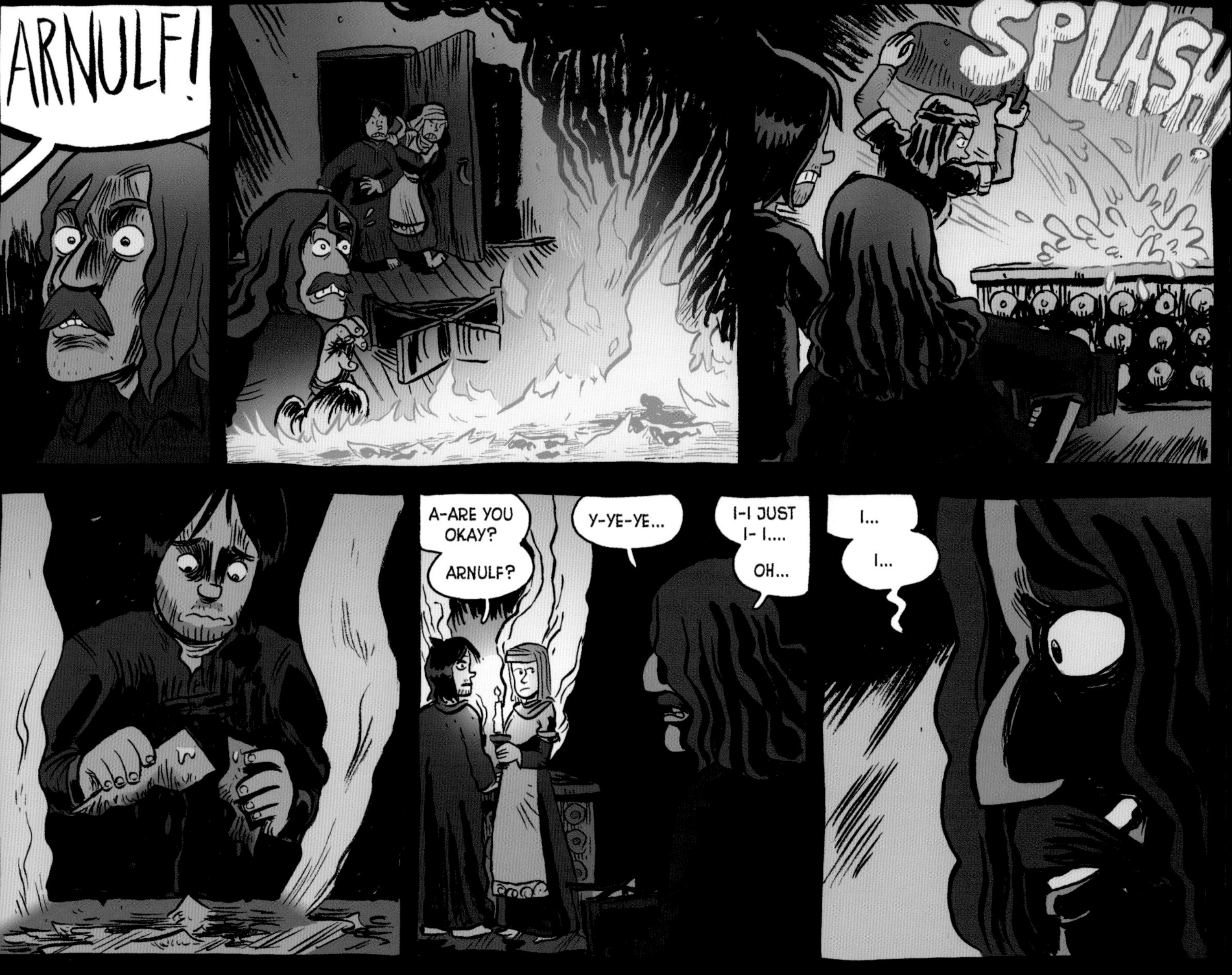
ARNULF!
SPLASH
A-ARE YOU OKAY?
ARNULF?
Y-YE-YE...
I-I JUST I- I....
OH...
I...
I...

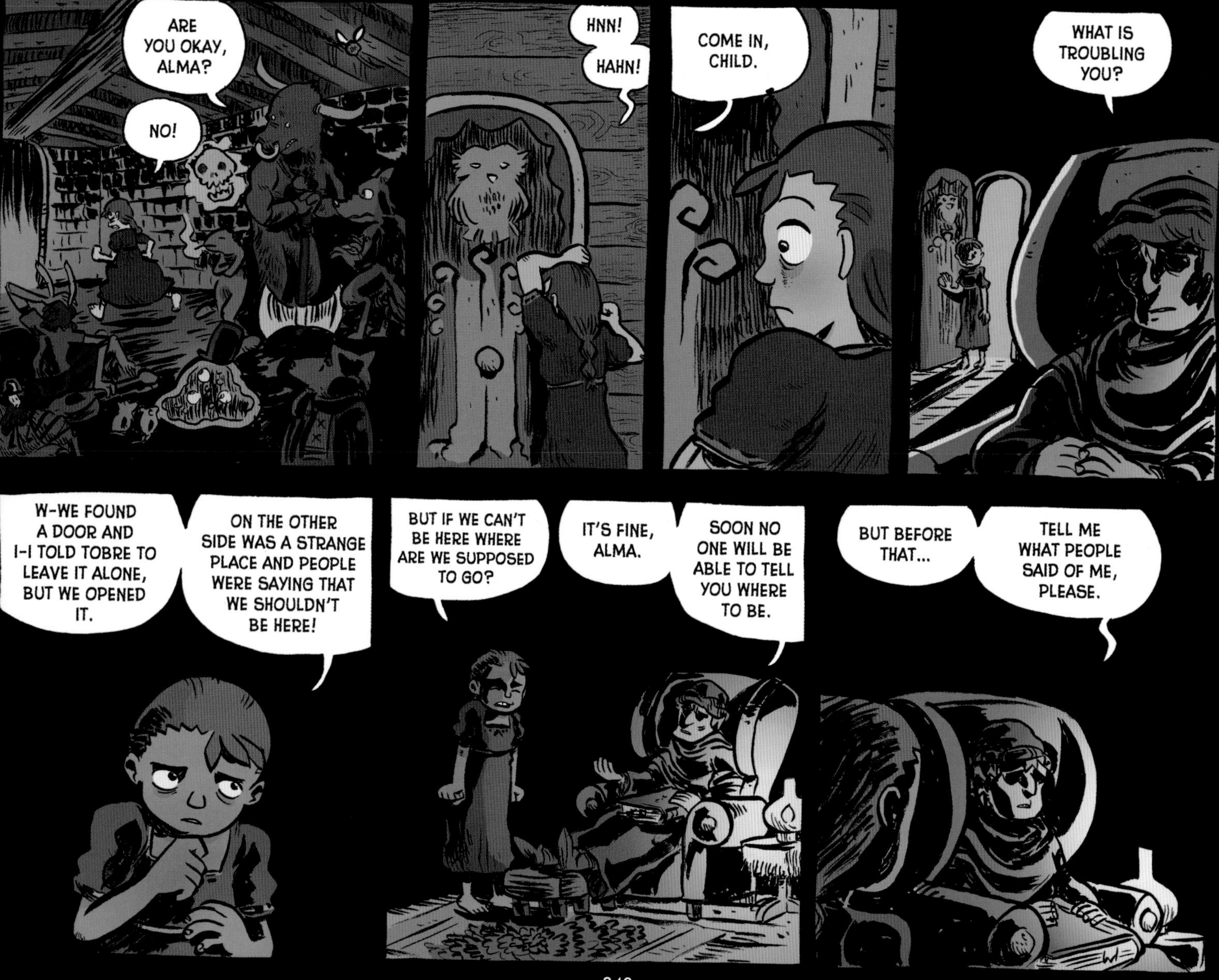

ARE YOU OKAY, ALMA?
NO!
HNN!
HAHN!
COME IN, CHILD.
WHAT IS TROUBLING YOU?
W-WE FOUND A DOOR AND I-I TOLD TOBRE TO LEAVE IT ALONE, BUT WE OPENED IT.
ON THE OTHER SIDE WAS A STRANGE PLACE AND PEOPLE WERE SAYING THAT WE SHOULDN'T BE HERE!
BUT IF WE CAN'T BE HERE WHERE ARE WE SUPPOSED TO GO?
IT'S FINE, ALMA.
SOON NO ONE WILL BE ABLE TO TELL YOU WHERE TO BE.
BUT BEFORE THAT...
TELL ME WHAT PEOPLE SAID OF ME, PLEASE.

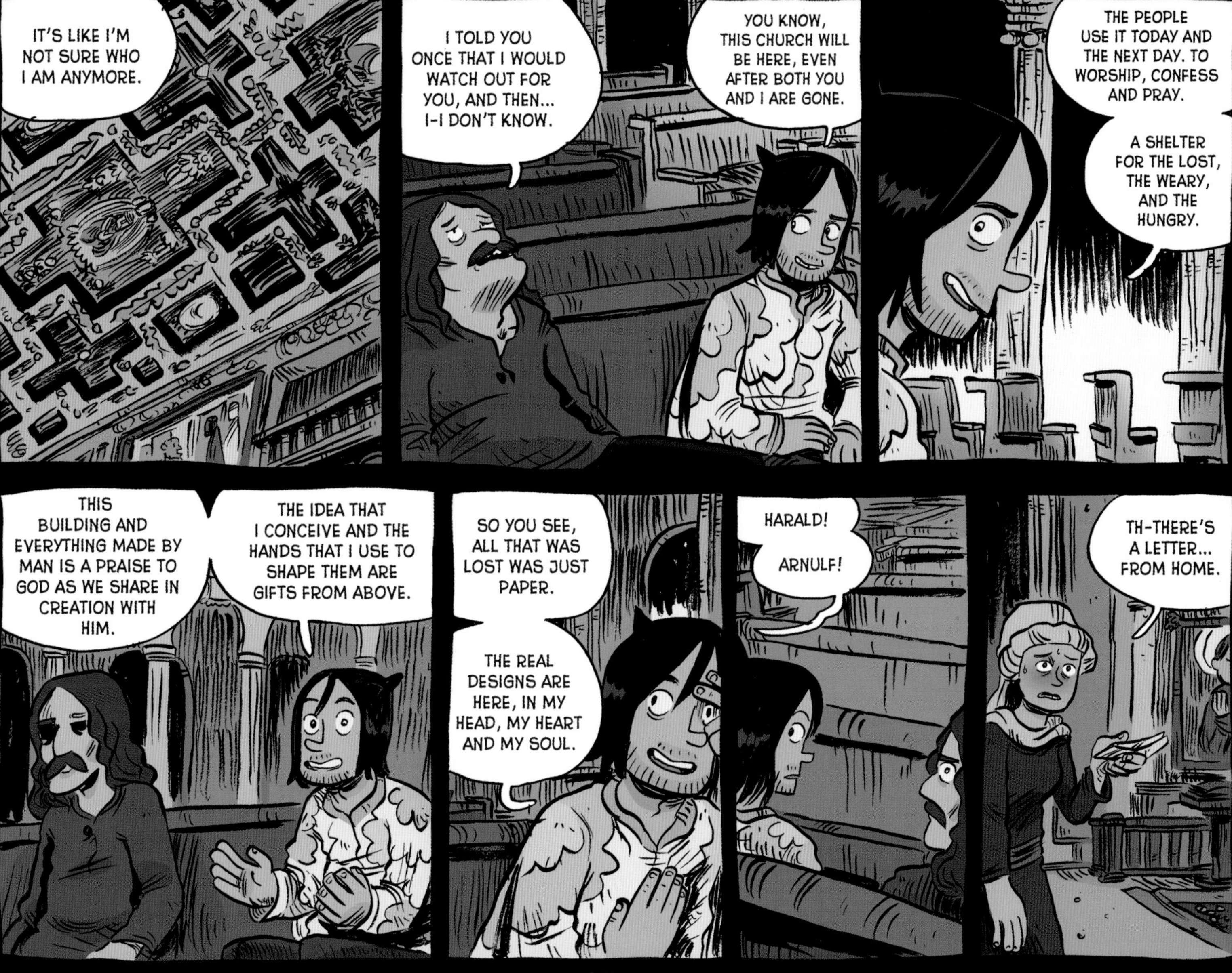
IT'S LIKE I'M NOT SURE WHO I AM ANYMORE.
I TOLD YOU ONCE THAT I WOULD WATCH OUT FOR YOU, AND THEN... I-I DON'T KNOW.
YOU KNOW, THIS CHURCH WILL BE HERE, EVEN AFTER BOTH YOU AND I ARE GONE.
THE PEOPLE USE IT TODAY AND THE NEXT DAY. TO WORSHIP, CONFESS AND PRAY.
A SHELTER FOR THE LOST, THE WEARY, AND THE HUNGRY.
THIS BUILDING AND EVERYTHING MADE BY MAN IS A PRAISE TO GOD AS WE SHARE IN CREATION WITH HIM.
THE IDEA THAT I CONCEIVE AND THE HANDS THAT I USE TO SHAPE THEM ARE GIFTS FROM ABOVE.
SO YOU SEE, ALL THAT WAS LOST WAS JUST PAPER.
THE REAL DESIGNS ARE HERE, IN MY HEAD, MY HEART AND MY SOUL.
HARALD!
ARNULF!
TH-THERE'S A LETTER... FROM HOME.

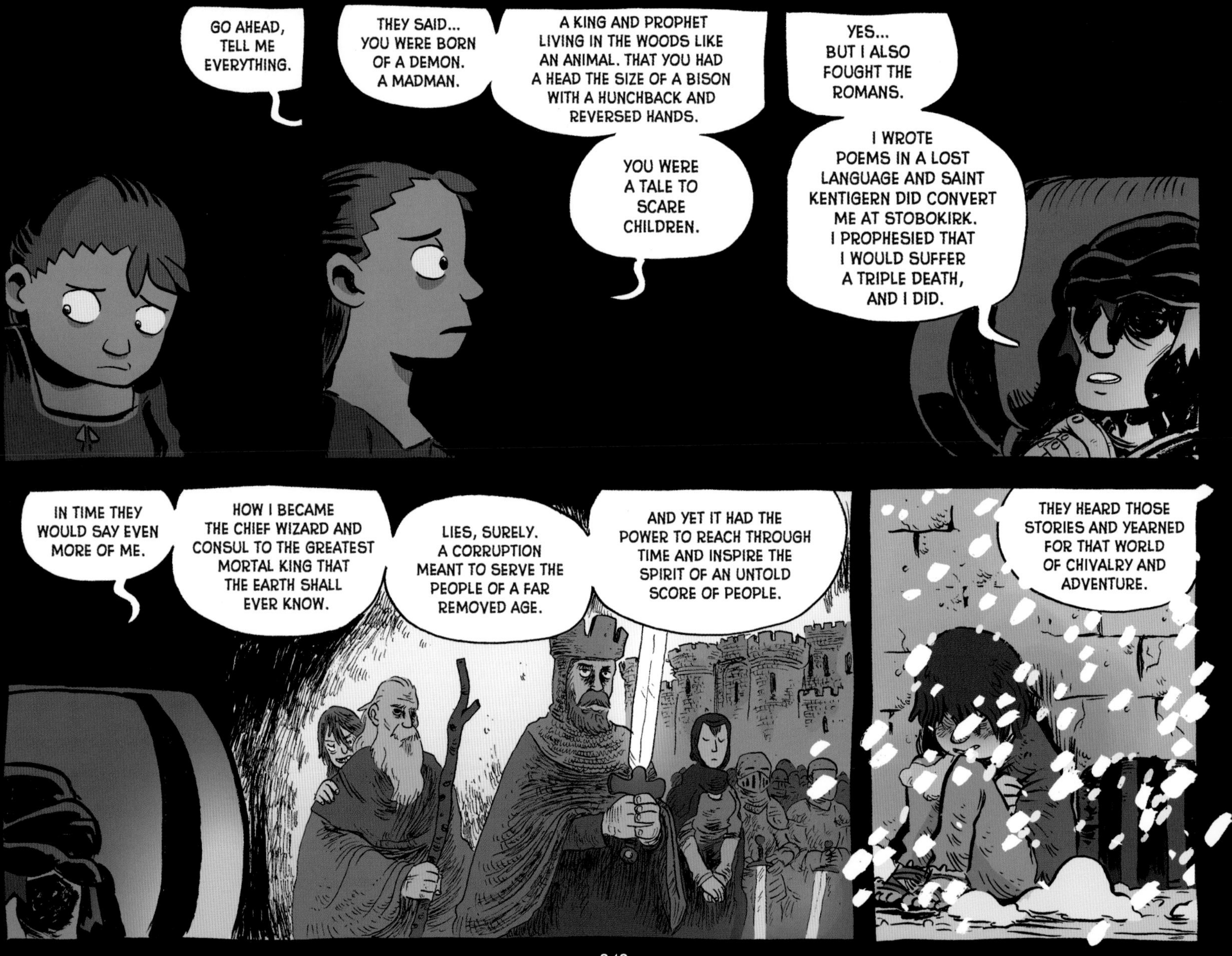
GO AHEAD, TELL ME EVERYTHING.
THEY SAID... YOU WERE BORN OF A DEMON. A MADMAN.
A KING AND PROPHET LIVING IN THE WOODS LIKE AN ANIMAL. THAT YOU HAD A HEAD THE SIZE OF A BISON WITH A HUNCHBACK AND REVERSED HANDS.
YOU WERE A TALE TO SCARE CHILDREN.
YES... BUT I ALSO FOUGHT THE ROMANS.
I WROTE POEMS IN A LOST LANGUAGE AND SAINT KENTIGERN DID CONVERT ME AT STOBOKIRK. I PROPHESIED THAT I WOULD SUFFER A TRIPLE DEATH, AND I DID.
IN TIME THEY WOULD SAY EVEN MORE OF ME.
HOW I BECAME THE CHIEF WIZARD AND CONSUL TO THE GREATEST MORTAL KING THAT THE EARTH SHALL EVER KNOW.
LIES, SURELY. A CORRUPTION MEANT TO SERVE THE PEOPLE OF A FAR REMOVED AGE.
AND YET IT HAD THE POWER TO REACH THROUGH TIME AND INSPIRE THE SPIRIT OF AN UNTOLD SCORE OF PEOPLE.
THEY HEARD THOSE STORIES AND YEARNED FOR THAT WORLD OF CHIVALRY AND ADVENTURE.

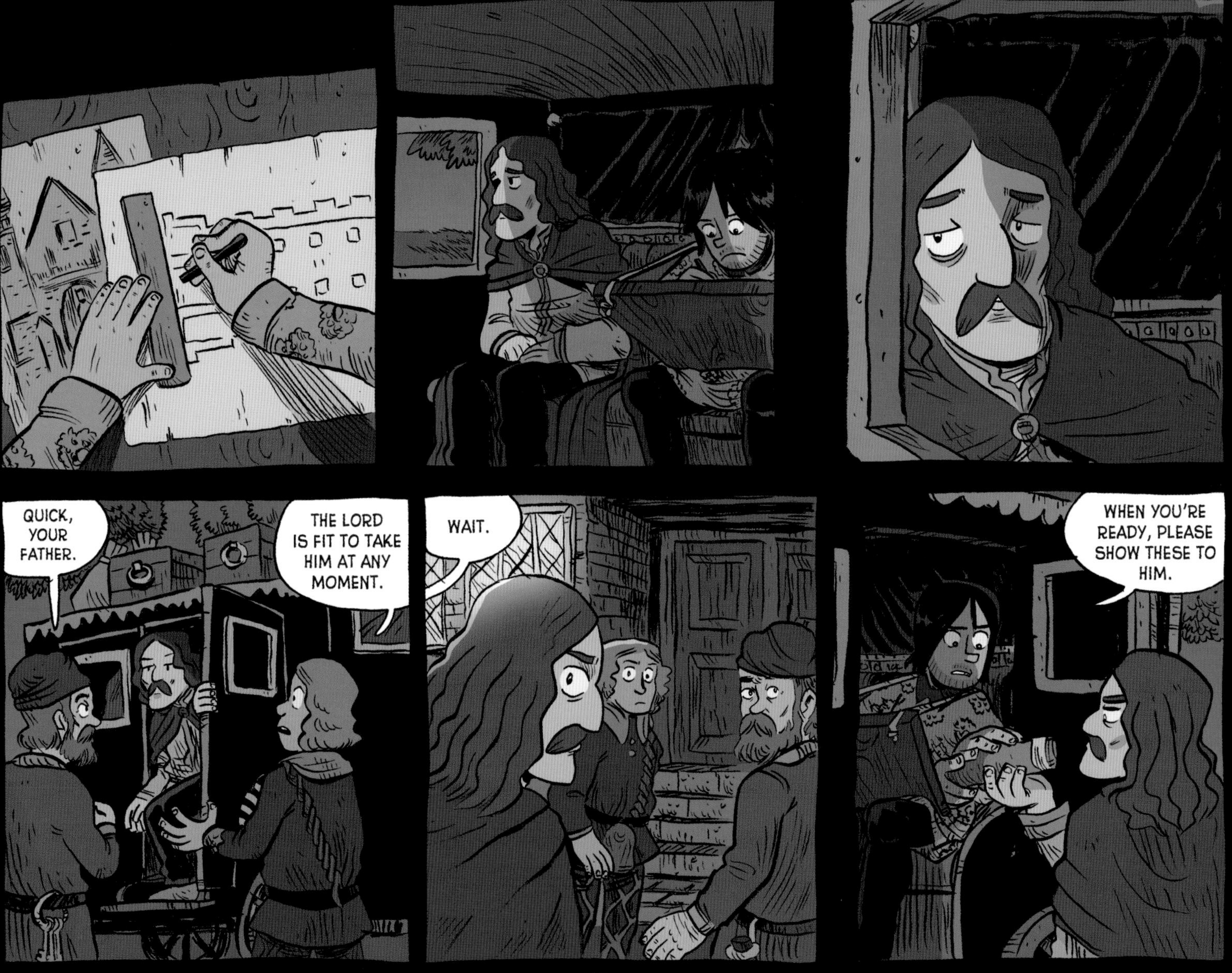
QUICK, YOUR FATHER.
THE LORD IS FIT TO TAKE HIM AT ANY MOMENT.
WAIT.
WHEN YOU'RE READY, PLEASE SHOW THESE TO HIM.

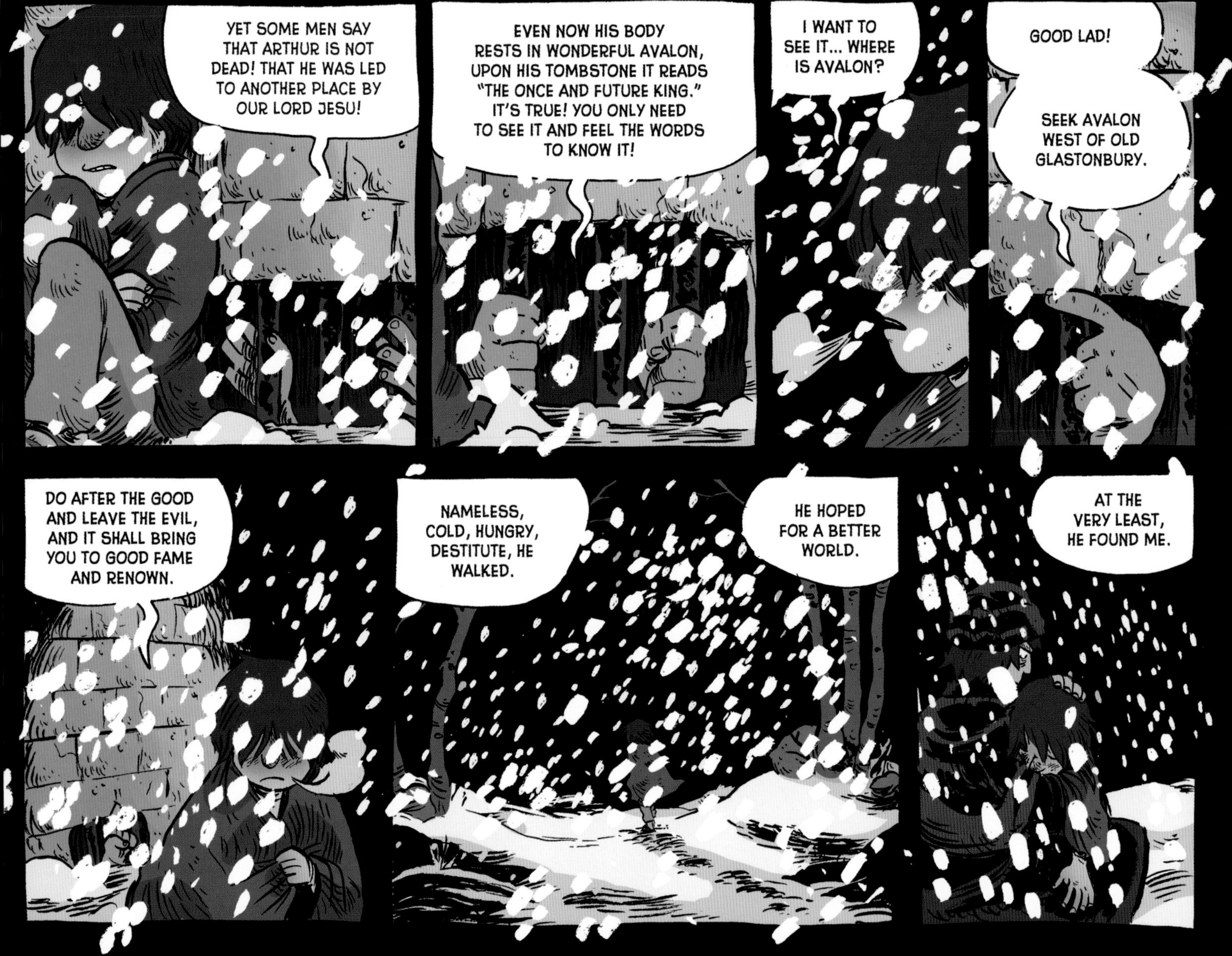

YET SOME MEN SAY THAT ARTHUR IS NOT DEAD! THAT HE WAS LED TO ANOTHER PLACE BY OUR LORD JESU!
EVEN NOW HIS BODY RESTS IN WONDERFUL AVALON, UPON HIS TOMBSTONE IT READS "THE ONCE AND FUTURE KING." IT'S TRUE! YOU ONLY NEED TO SEE IT AND FEEL THE WORDS TO KNOW IT!
I WANT TO SEE IT... WHERE IS AVALON?
GOOD LAD!
SEEK AVALON WEST OF OLD GLASTONBURY.
DO AFTER THE GOOD AND LEAVE THE EVIL, AND IT SHALL BRING YOU TO GOOD FAME AND RENOWN.
NAMELESS, COLD, HUNGRY, DESTITUTE, HE WALKED.
HE HOPED FOR A BETTER WORLD.
AT THE VERY LEAST, HE FOUND ME.

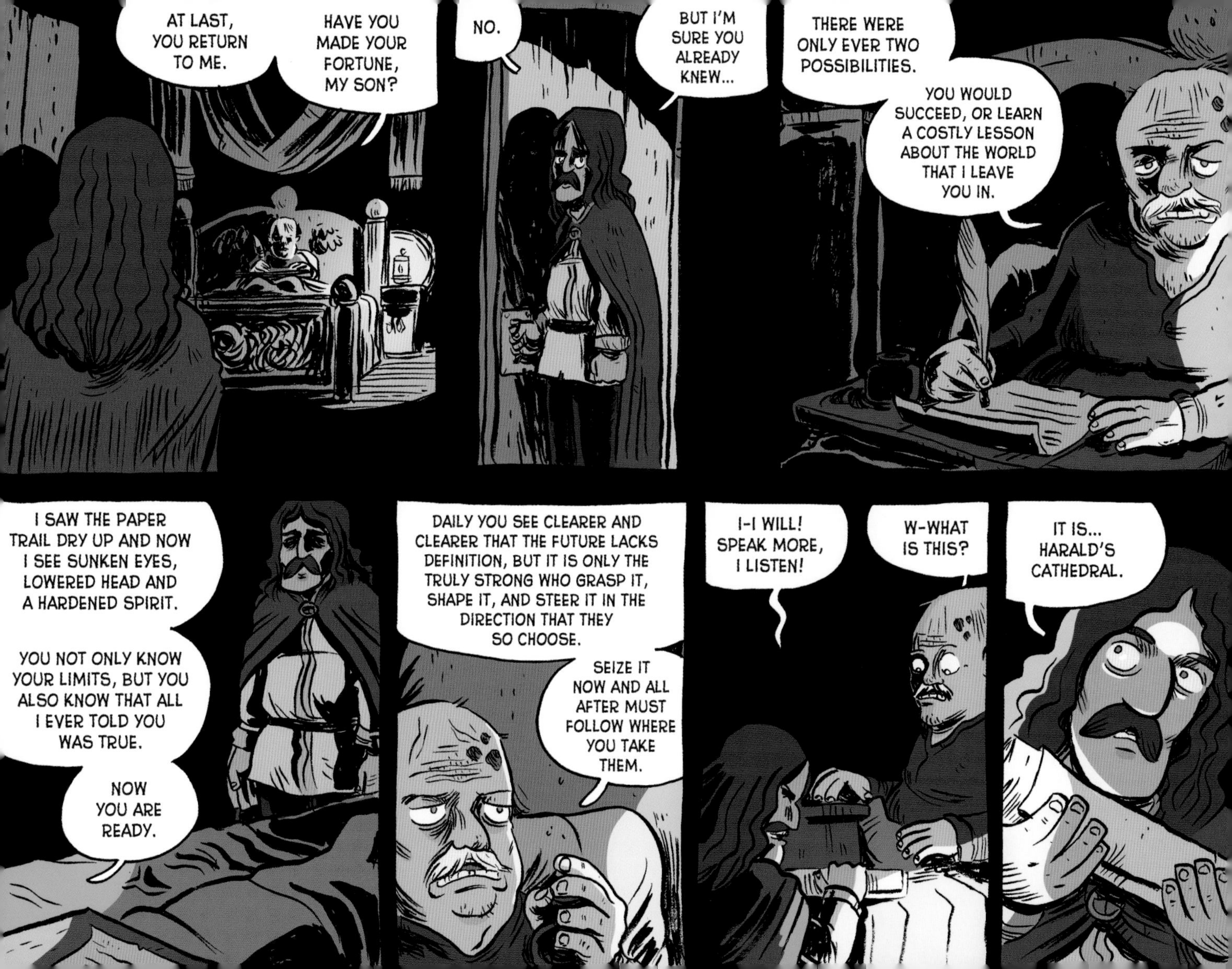
AT LAST, YOU RETURN TO ME.
HAVE YOU MADE YOUR FORTUNE, MY SON?
NO.
BUT I'M SURE YOU ALREADY KNEW...
THERE WERE ONLY EVER TWO POSSIBILITIES.
YOU WOULD SUCCEED, OR LEARN A COSTLY LESSON ABOUT THE WORLD THAT I LEAVE YOU IN.
I SAW THE PAPER TRAIL DRY UP AND NOW I SEE SUNKEN EYES, LOWERED HEAD AND A HARDENED SPIRIT.
YOU NOT ONLY KNOW YOUR LIMITS, BUT YOU ALSO KNOW THAT ALL I EVER TOLD YOU WAS TRUE.
NOW YOU ARE READY.
DAILY YOU SEE CLEARER AND CLEARER THAT THE FUTURE LACKS DEFINITION, BUT IT IS ONLY THE TRULY STRONG WHO GRASP IT, SHAPE IT, AND STEER IT IN THE DIRECTION THAT THEY SO CHOOSE.
SEIZE IT NOW AND ALL AFTER MUST FOLLOW WHERE YOU TAKE THEM.
I-I WILL! SPEAK MORE, I LISTEN!
W-WHAT IS THIS?
IT IS... HARALD'S CATHEDRAL.

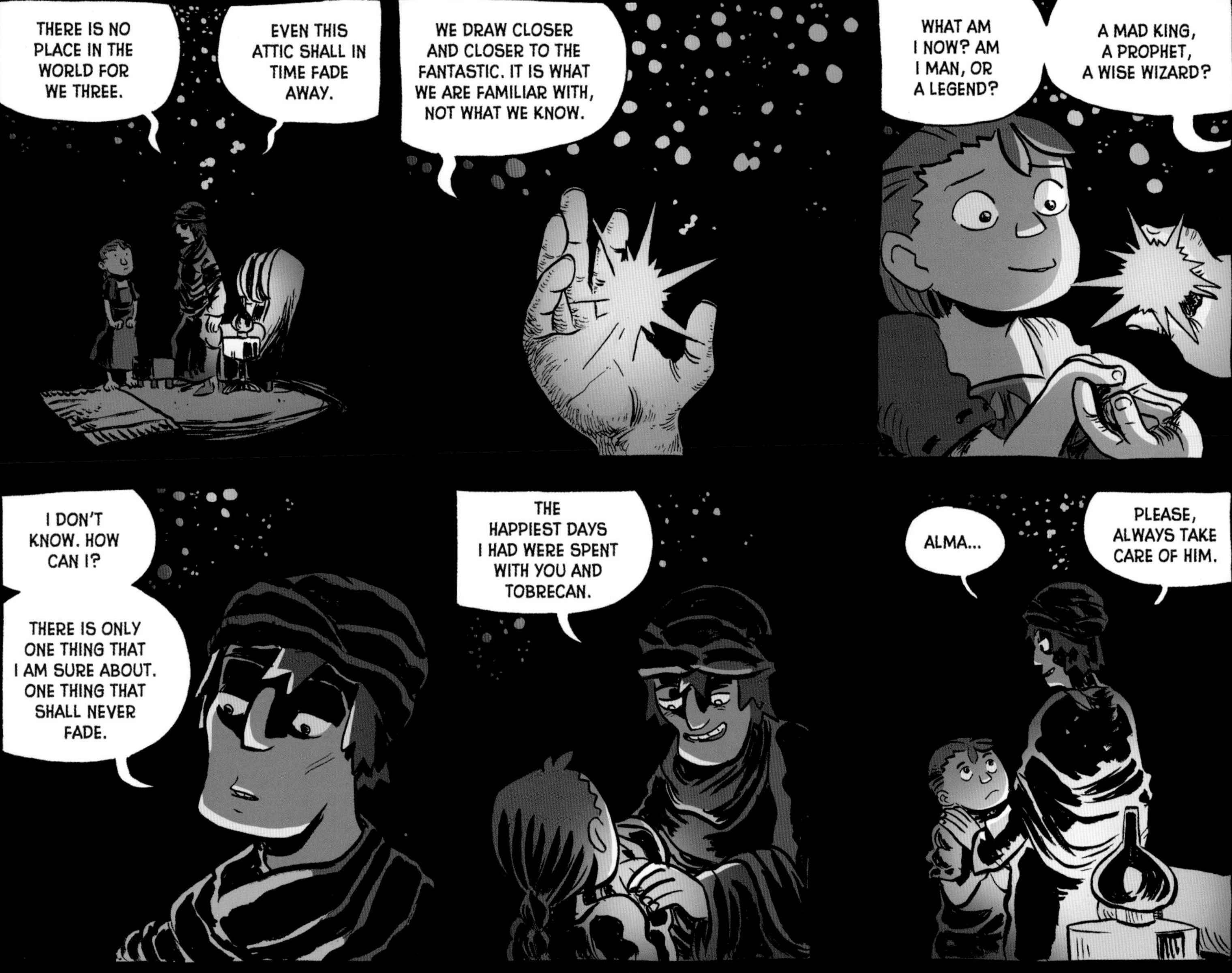
THERE IS NO PLACE IN THE WORLD FOR WE THREE.
EVEN THIS ATTIC SHALL IN TIME FADE AWAY.
WE DRAW CLOSER AND CLOSER TO THE FANTASTIC. IT IS WHAT WE ARE FAMILIAR WITH, NOT WHAT WE KNOW.
WHAT AM I NOW? AM I MAN, OR A LEGEND?
A MAD KING, A PROPHET, A WISE WIZARD?
I DON'T KNOW. HOW CAN I?
THERE IS ONLY ONE THING THAT I AM SURE ABOUT. ONE THING THAT SHALL NEVER FADE.
THE HAPPIEST DAYS I HAD WERE SPENT WITH YOU AND TOBRECAN.
ALMA...
PLEASE, ALWAYS TAKE CARE OF HIM.

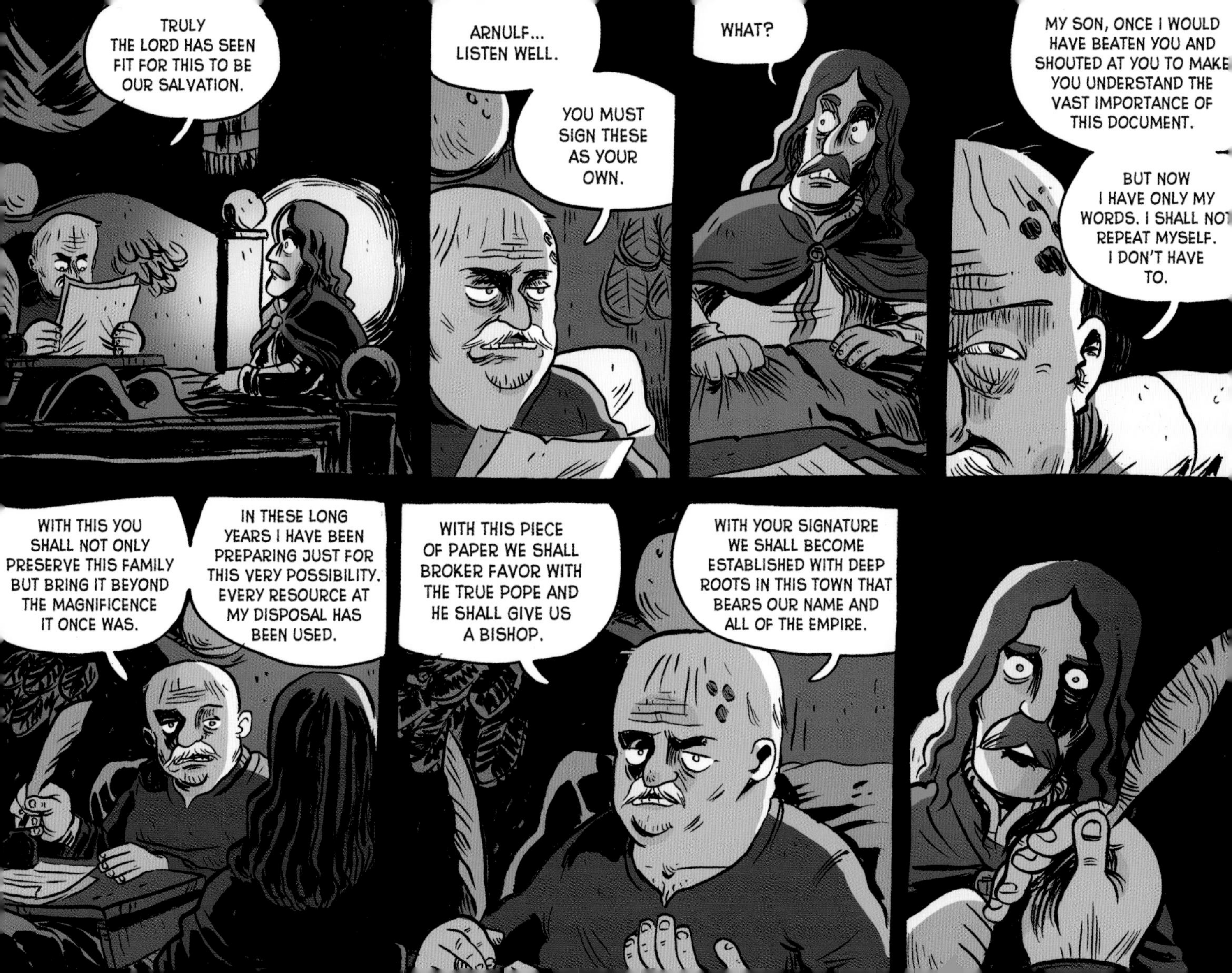
TRULY THE LORD HAS SEEN FIT FOR THIS TO BE OUR SALVATION.
ARNULF... LISTEN WELL.
YOU MUST SIGN THESE AS YOUR OWN.
WHAT?
MY SON, ONCE I WOULD HAVE BEATEN YOU AND SHOUTED AT YOU TO MAKE YOU UNDERSTAND THE VAST IMPORTANCE OF THIS DOCUMENT.
BUT NOW I HAVE ONLY MY WORDS. I SHALL NOT REPEAT MYSELF. I DON'T HAVE TO.
WITH THIS YOU SHALL NOT ONLY PRESERVE THIS FAMILY BUT BRING IT BEYOND THE MAGNIFICENCE IT ONCE WAS.
IN THESE LONG YEARS I HAVE BEEN PREPARING JUST FOR THIS VERY POSSIBILITY. EVERY RESOURCE AT MY DISPOSAL HAS BEEN USED.
WITH THIS PIECE OF PAPER WE SHALL BROKER FAVOR WITH THE TRUE POPE AND HE SHALL GIVE US A BISHOP.
WITH YOUR SIGNATURE WE SHALL BECOME ESTABLISHED WITH DEEP ROOTS IN THIS TOWN THAT BEARS OUR NAME AND ALL OF THE EMPIRE.

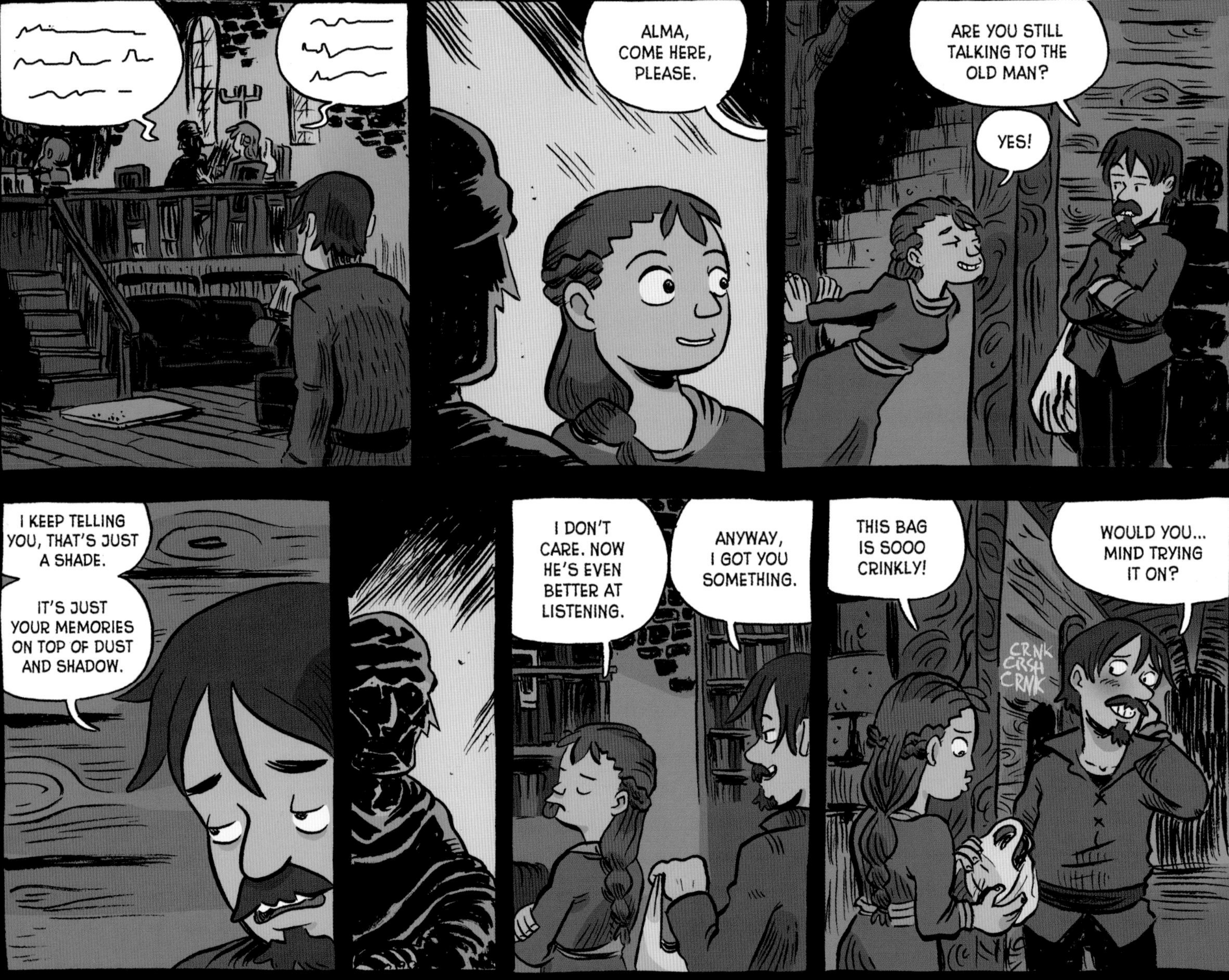
ALMA, COME HERE, PLEASE.
ARE YOU STILL TALKING TO THE OLD MAN?
YES!
I KEEP TELLING YOU, THAT'S JUST A SHADE.
IT'S JUST YOUR MEMORIES ON TOP OF DUST AND SHADOW.
I DON'T CARE. NOW HE'S EVEN BETTER AT LISTENING.
ANYWAY, I GOT YOU SOMETHING.
THIS BAG IS SOOO CRINKLY!
CRNK CRSH CRNK
WOULD YOU... MIND TRYING IT ON?

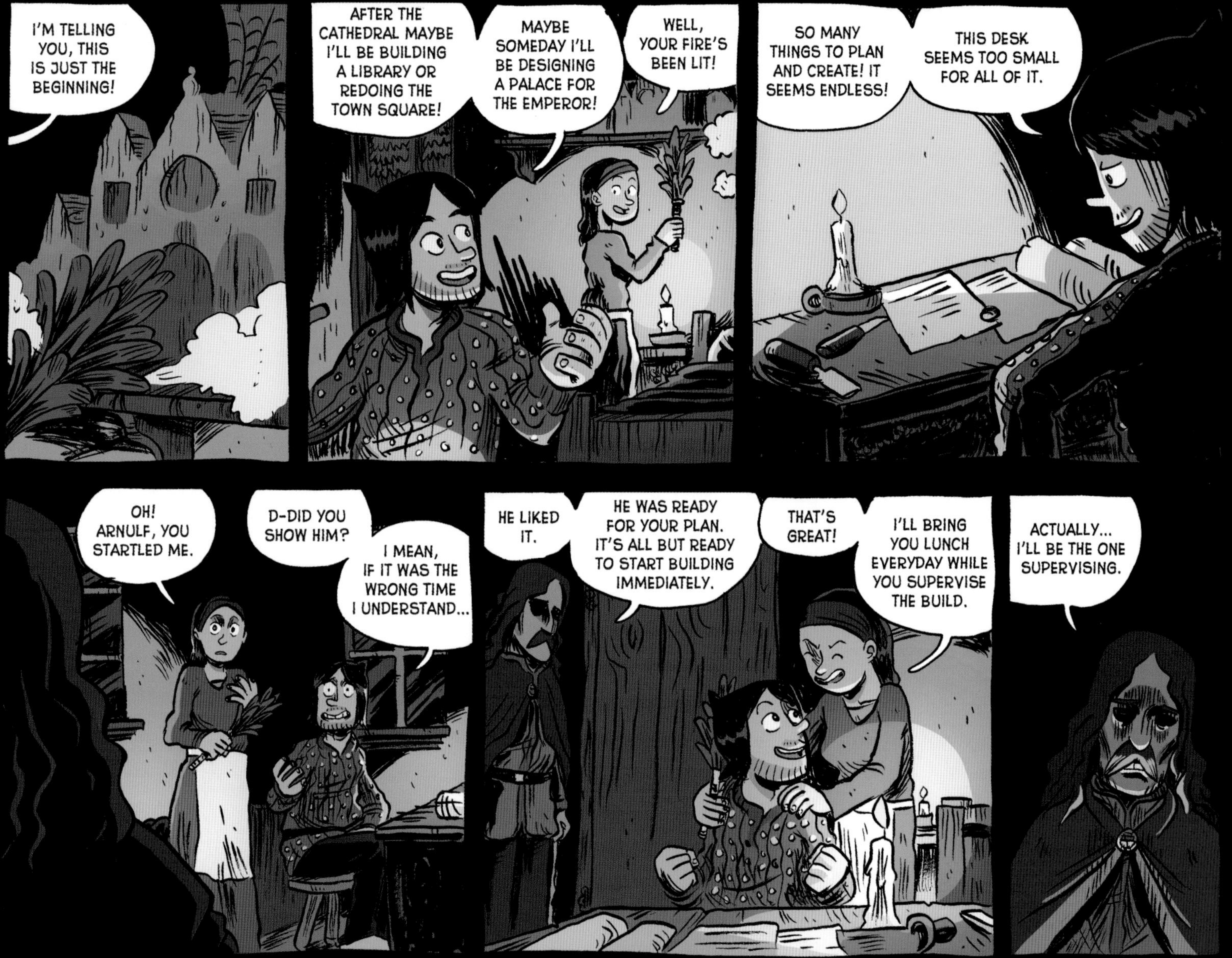
I'M TELLING YOU, THIS IS JUST THE BEGINNING!
AFTER THE CATHEDRAL MAYBE I'LL BE BUILDING A LIBRARY OR REDOING THE TOWN SQUARE!
MAYBE SOMEDAY I'LL BE DESIGNING A PALACE FOR THE EMPEROR!
WELL, YOUR FIRE'S BEEN LIT!
SO MANY THINGS TO PLAN AND CREATE! IT SEEMS ENDLESS!
THIS DESK SEEMS TOO SMALL FOR ALL OF IT.
OH! ARNULF, YOU STARTLED ME.
D-DID YOU SHOW HIM?
I MEAN, IF IT WAS THE WRONG TIME I UNDERSTAND...
HE LIKED IT.
HE WAS READY FOR YOUR PLAN. IT'S ALL BUT READY TO START BUILDING IMMEDIATELY.
THAT'S GREAT!
I'LL BRING YOU LUNCH EVERYDAY WHILE YOU SUPERVISE THE BUILD.
ACTUALLY... I'LL BE THE ONE SUPERVISING.

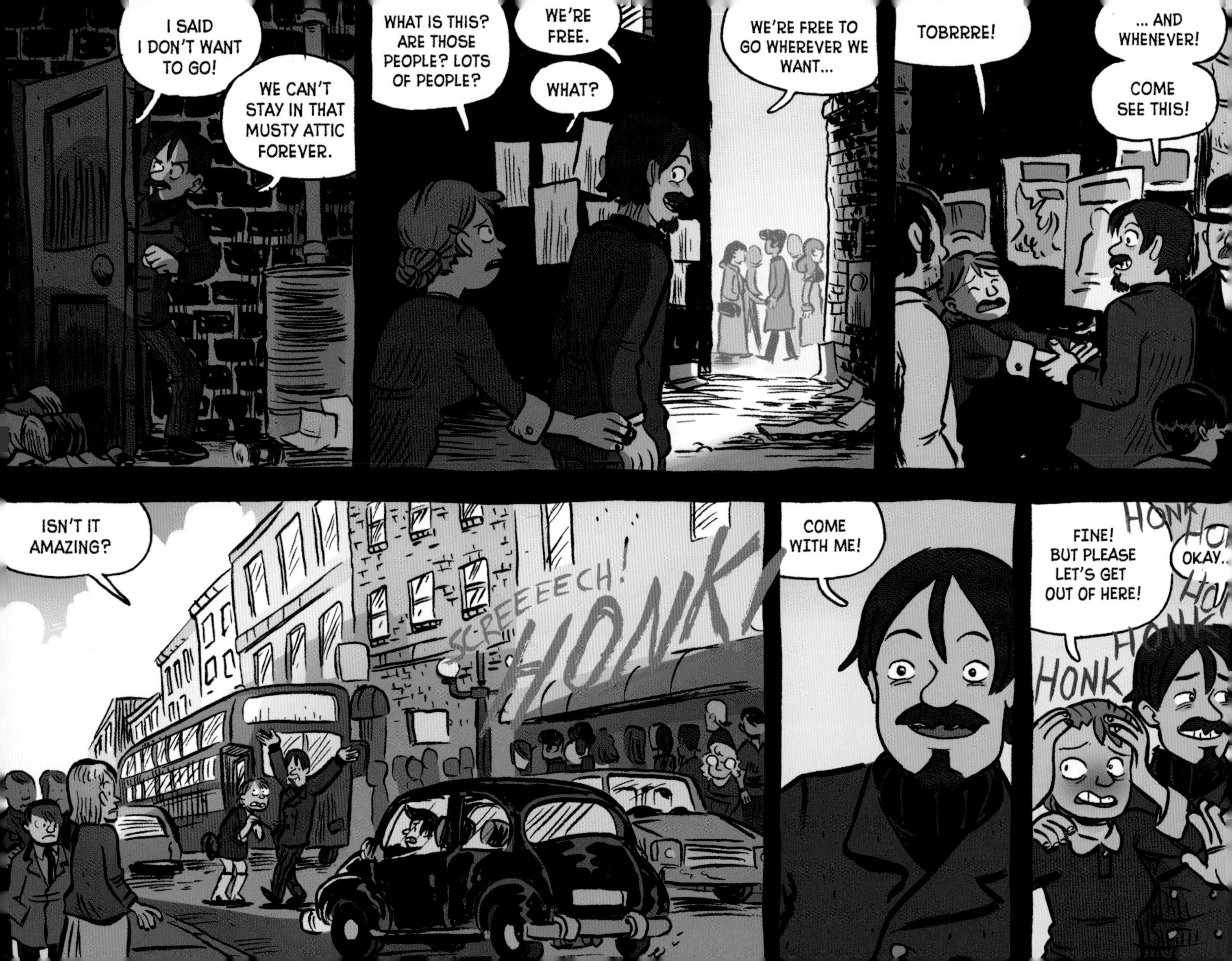
I SAID I DON'T WANT TO GO!
WE CAN'T STAY IN THAT MUSTY ATTIC FOREVER.
WHAT IS THIS? ARE THOSE PEOPLE? LOTS OF PEOPLE?
WE'RE FREE.
WHAT?
WE'RE FREE TO GO WHEREVER WE WANT...
TOBRRRE!
... AND WHENEVER!
COME SEE THIS!
ISN'T IT AMAZING?
SCREEEEECH!
HONK!
COME WITH ME!
HONK
FINE! BUT PLEASE LET'S GET OUT OF HERE!
OKAY...
HONK
HONK

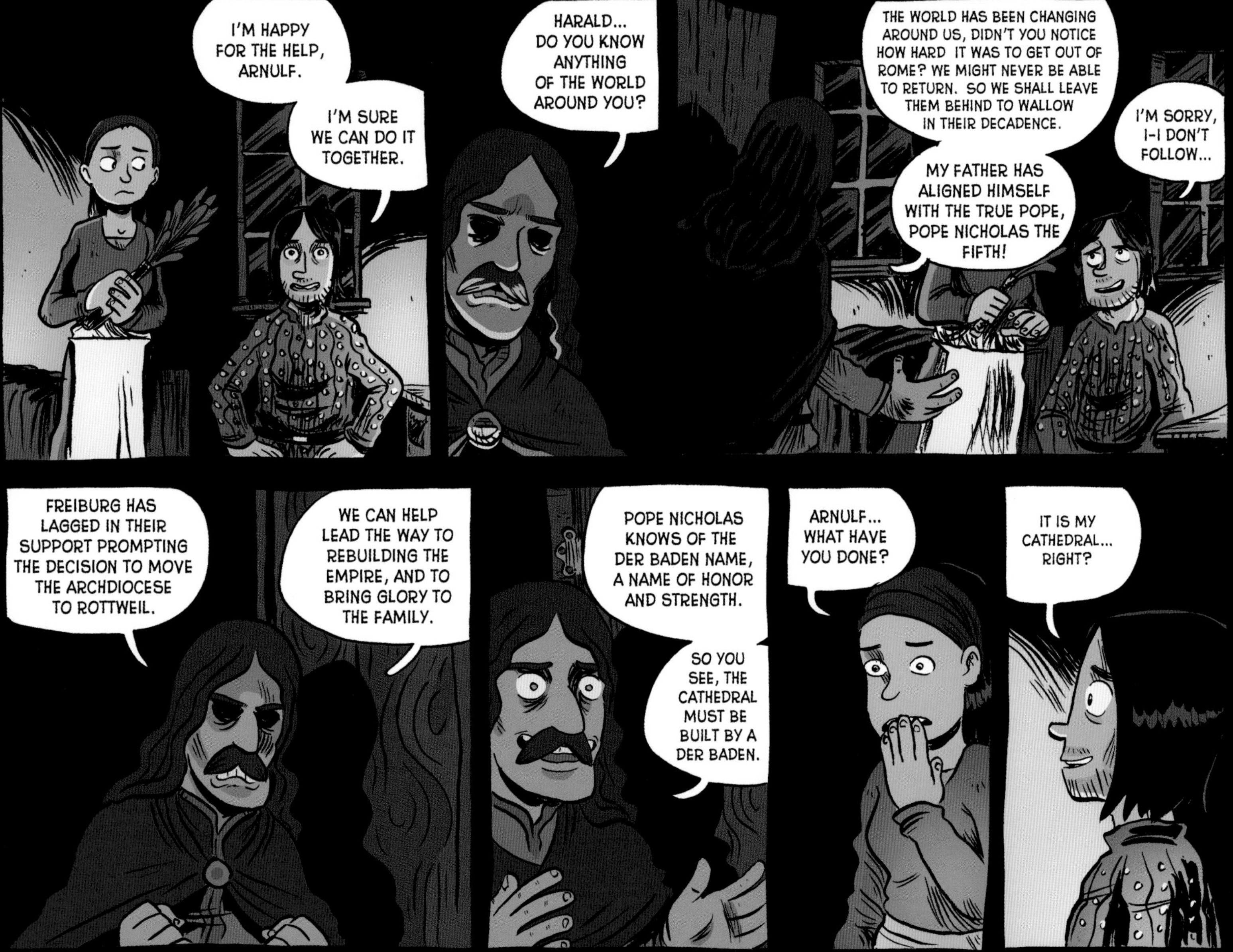
I'M HAPPY FOR THE HELP, ARNULF.
I'M SURE WE CAN DO IT TOGETHER.
HARALD... DO YOU KNOW ANYTHING OF THE WORLD AROUND YOU?
THE WORLD HAS BEEN CHANGING AROUND US, DIDN'T YOU NOTICE HOW HARD IT WAS TO GET OUT OF ROME? WE MIGHT NEVER BE ABLE TO RETURN. SO WE SHALL LEAVE THEM BEHIND TO WALLOW IN THEIR DECADENCE.
MY FATHER HAS ALIGNED HIMSELF WITH THE TRUE POPE, POPE NICHOLAS THE FIFTH!
I'M SORRY, I-I DON'T FOLLOW...
FREIBURG HAS LAGGED IN THEIR SUPPORT PROMPTING THE DECISION TO MOVE THE ARCHDIOCESE TO ROTTWEIL.
WE CAN HELP LEAD THE WAY TO REBUILDING THE EMPIRE, AND TO BRING GLORY TO THE FAMILY.
POPE NICHOLAS KNOWS OF THE DER BADEN NAME, A NAME OF HONOR AND STRENGTH.
SO YOU SEE, THE CATHEDRAL MUST BE BUILT BY A DER BADEN.
ARNULF... WHAT HAVE YOU DONE?
IT IS MY CATHEDRAL... RIGHT?

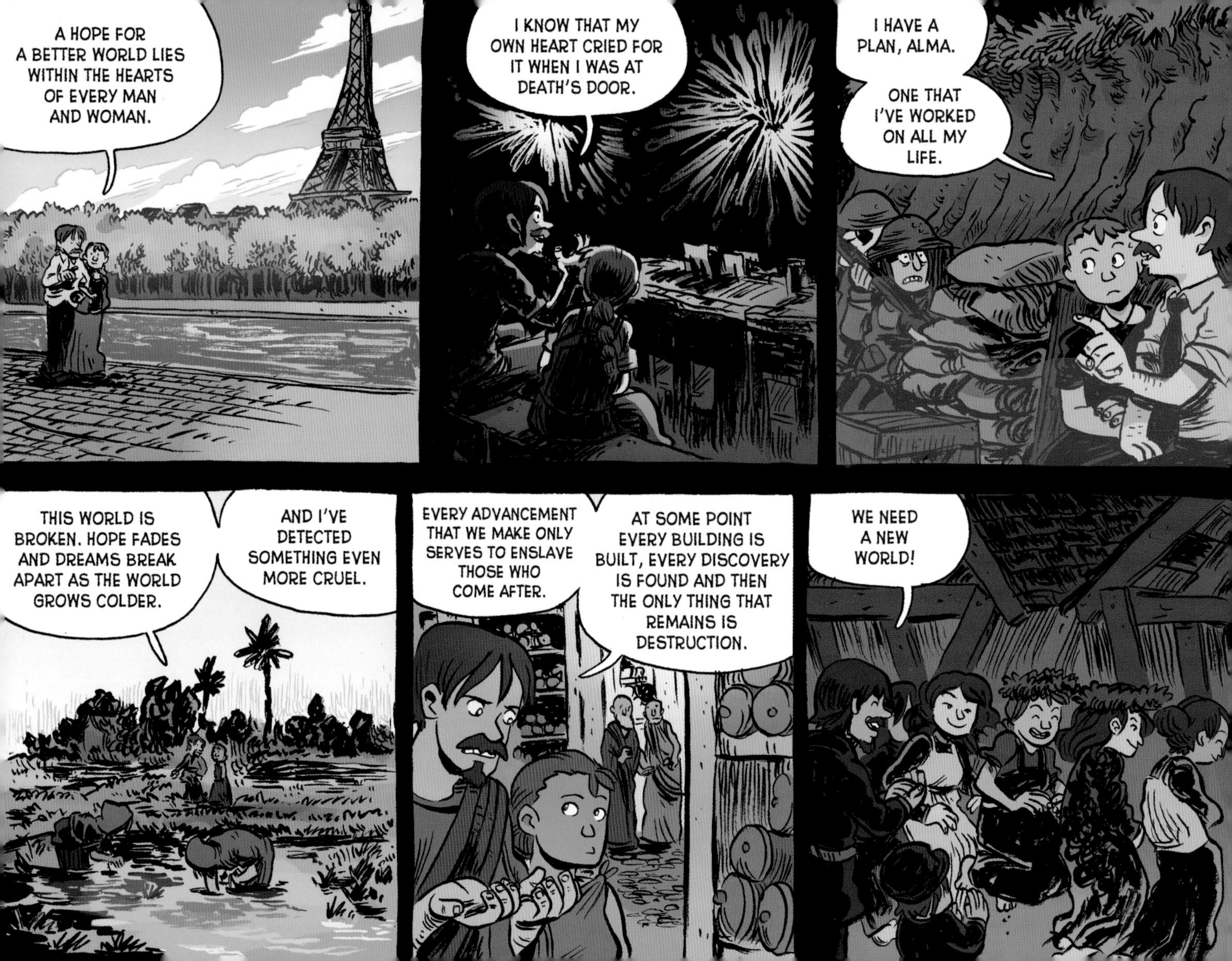
A HOPE FOR A BETTER WORLD LIES WITHIN THE HEARTS OF EVERY MAN AND WOMAN.
I KNOW THAT MY OWN HEART CRIED FOR IT WHEN I WAS AT DEATH'S DOOR.
I HAVE A PLAN, ALMA.
ONE THAT I'VE WORKED ON ALL MY LIFE.
THIS WORLD IS BROKEN. HOPE FADES AND DREAMS BREAK APART AS THE WORLD GROWS COLDER.
AND I'VE DETECTED SOMETHING EVEN MORE CRUEL.
EVERY ADVANCEMENT THAT WE MAKE ONLY SERVES TO ENSLAVE THOSE WHO COME AFTER.
AT SOME POINT EVERY BUILDING IS BUILT, EVERY DISCOVERY IS FOUND AND THEN THE ONLY THING THAT REMAINS IS DESTRUCTION.
WE NEED A NEW WORLD!

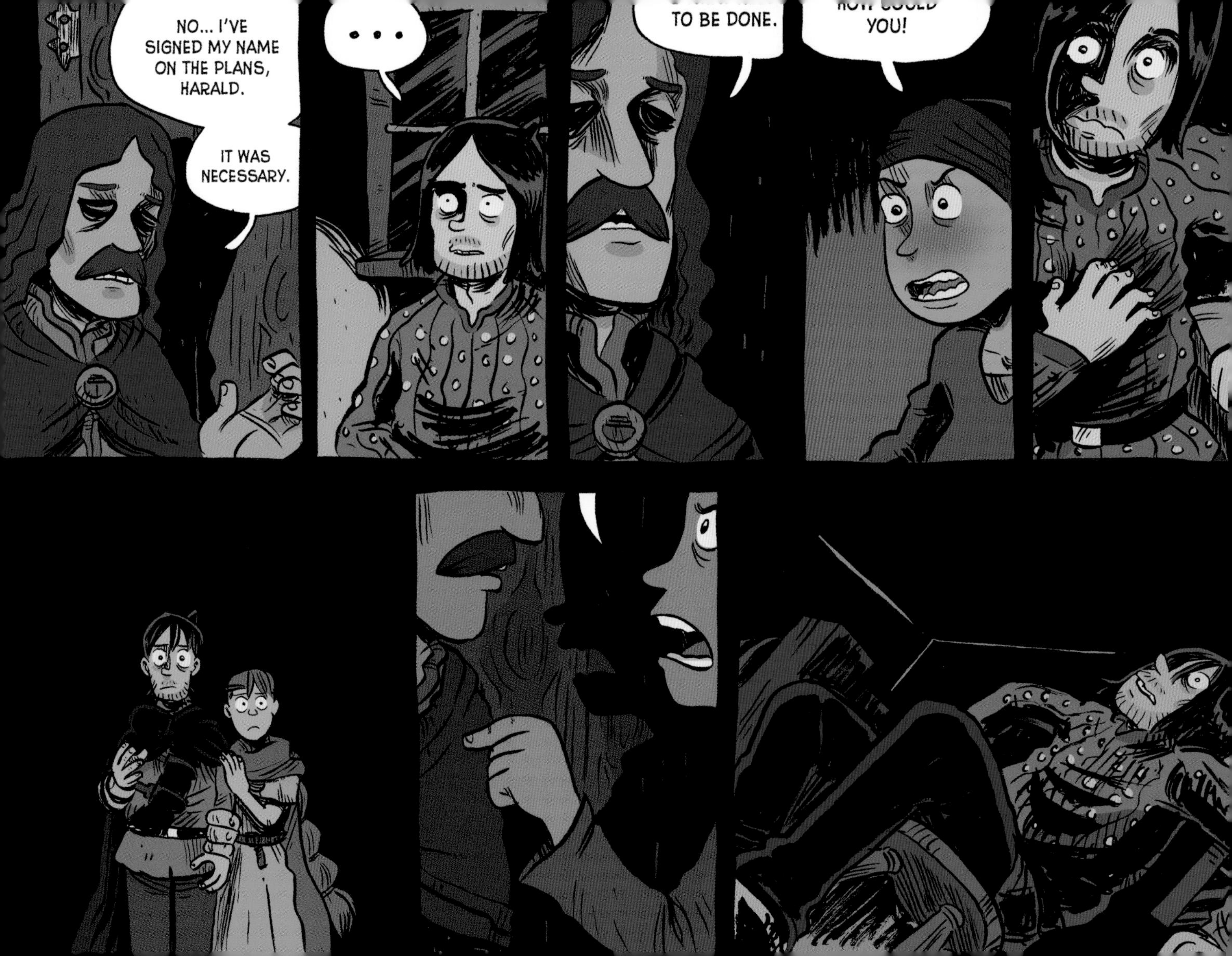
NO... I'VE SIGNED MY NAME ON THE PLANS, HARALD.
IT WAS NECESSARY.
...
TO BE DONE.
YOU!

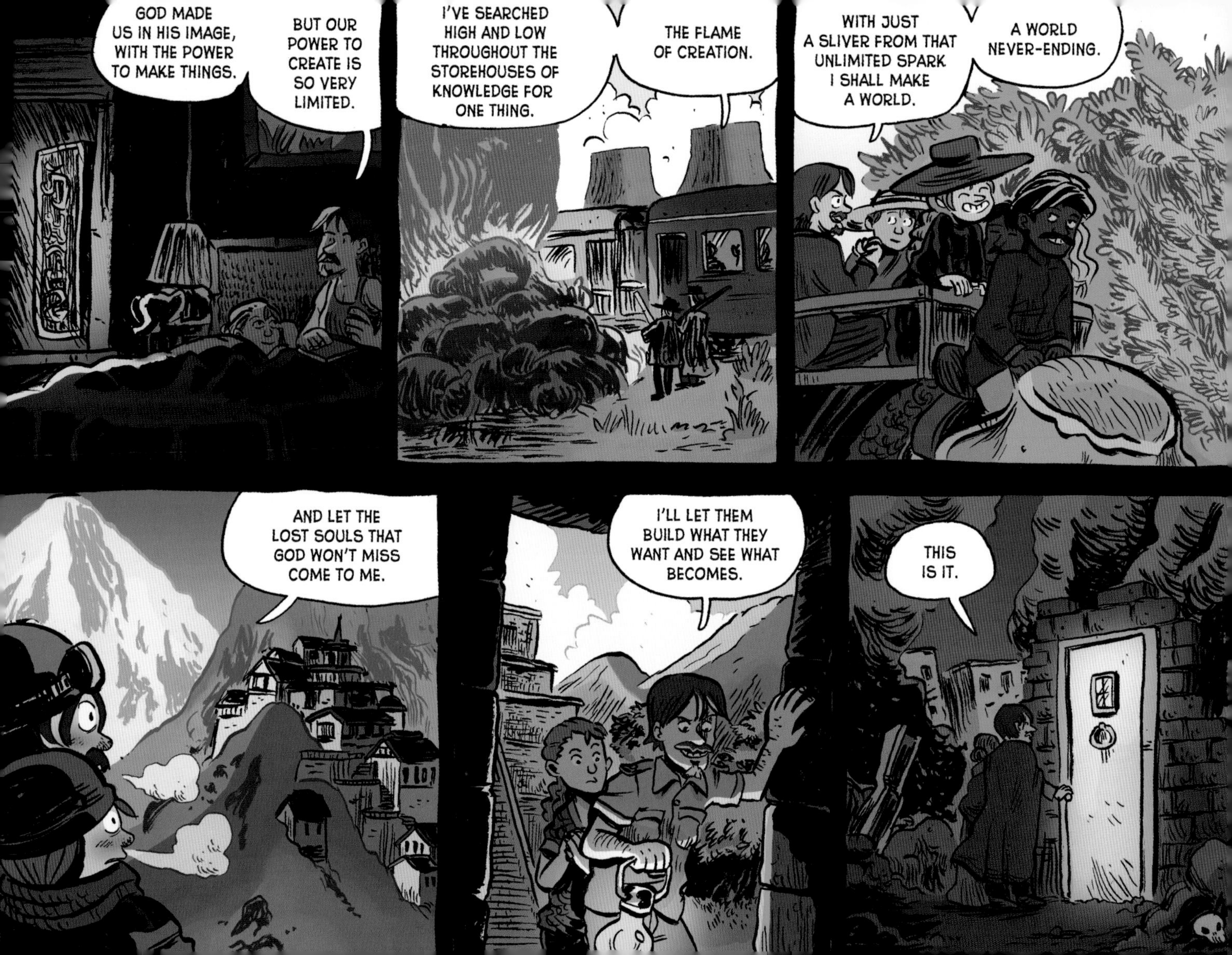
GOD MADE US IN HIS IMAGE, WITH THE POWER TO MAKE THINGS.
BUT OUR POWER TO CREATE IS SO VERY LIMITED.
I'VE SEARCHED HIGH AND LOW THROUGHOUT THE STOREHOUSES OF KNOWLEDGE FOR ONE THING.
THE FLAME OF CREATION.
WITH JUST A SLIVER FROM THAT UNLIMITED SPARK I SHALL MAKE A WORLD.
A WORLD NEVER-ENDING.
AND LET THE LOST SOULS THAT GOD WON'T MISS COME TO ME.
I'LL LET THEM BUILD WHAT THEY WANT AND SEE WHAT BECOMES.
THIS IS IT.

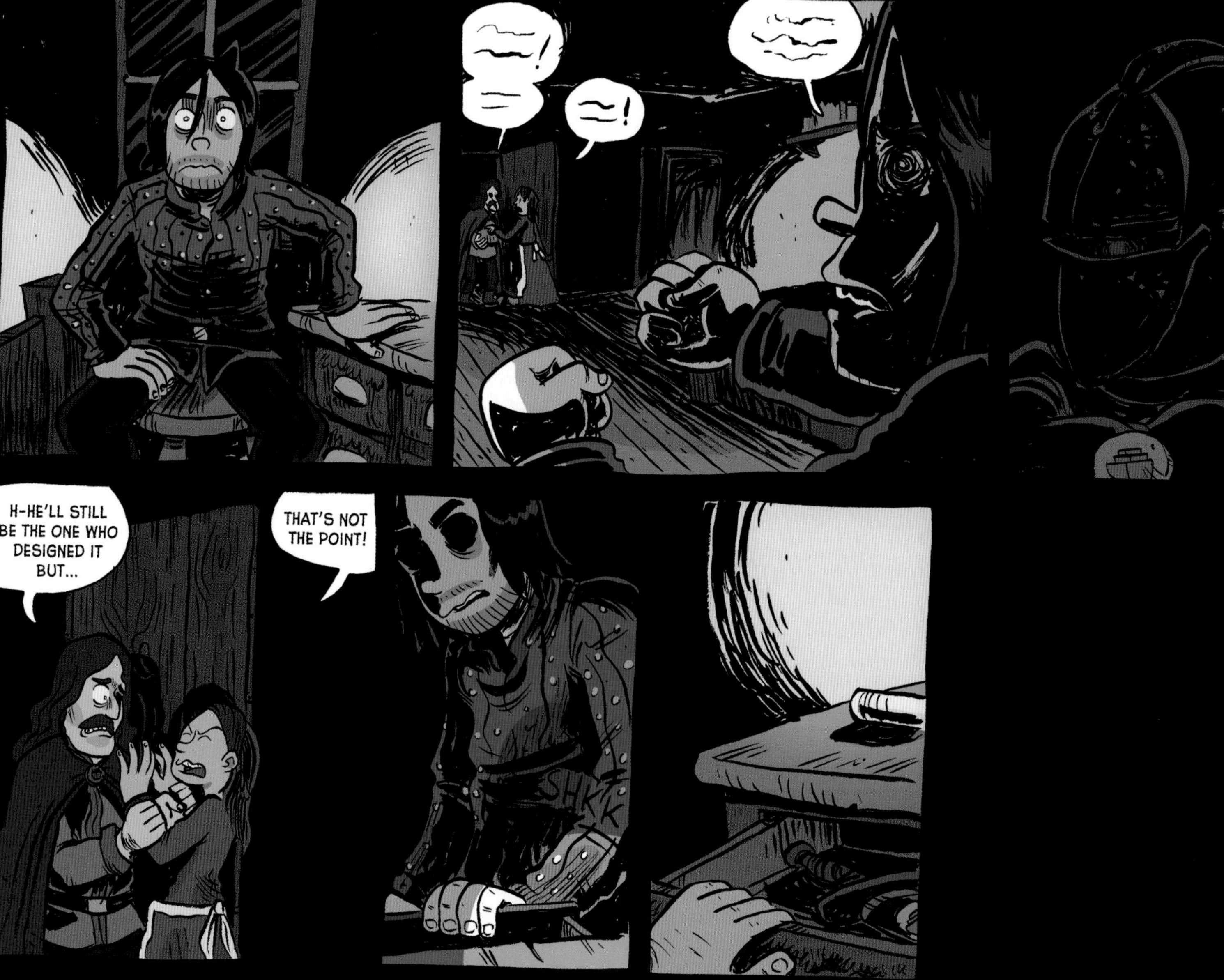
H-HE'LL STILL BE THE ONE WHO DESIGNED IT BUT...
THAT'S NOT THE POINT!
SHKK

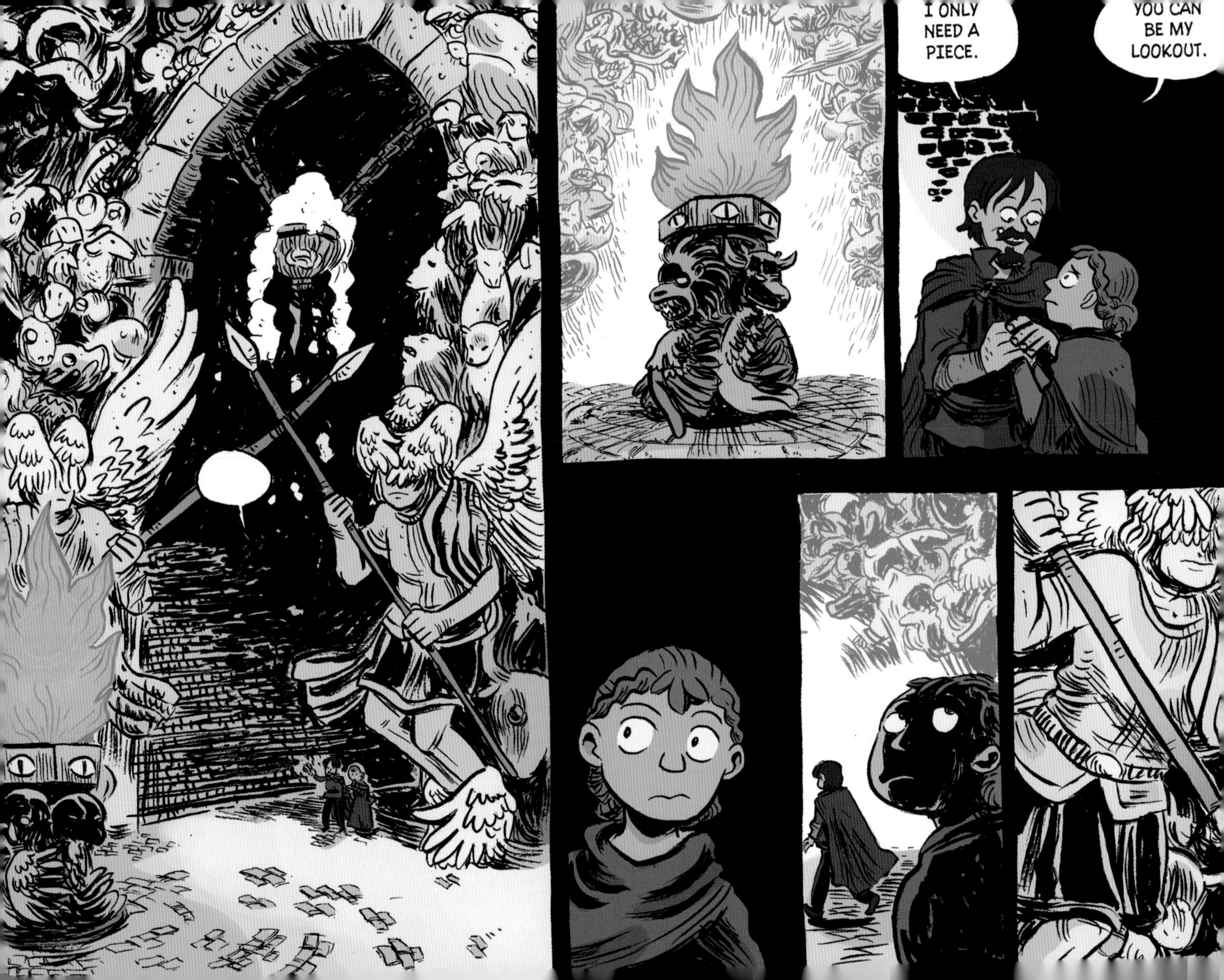
I ONLY NEED A PIECE.
YOU CAN BE MY LOOKOUT.

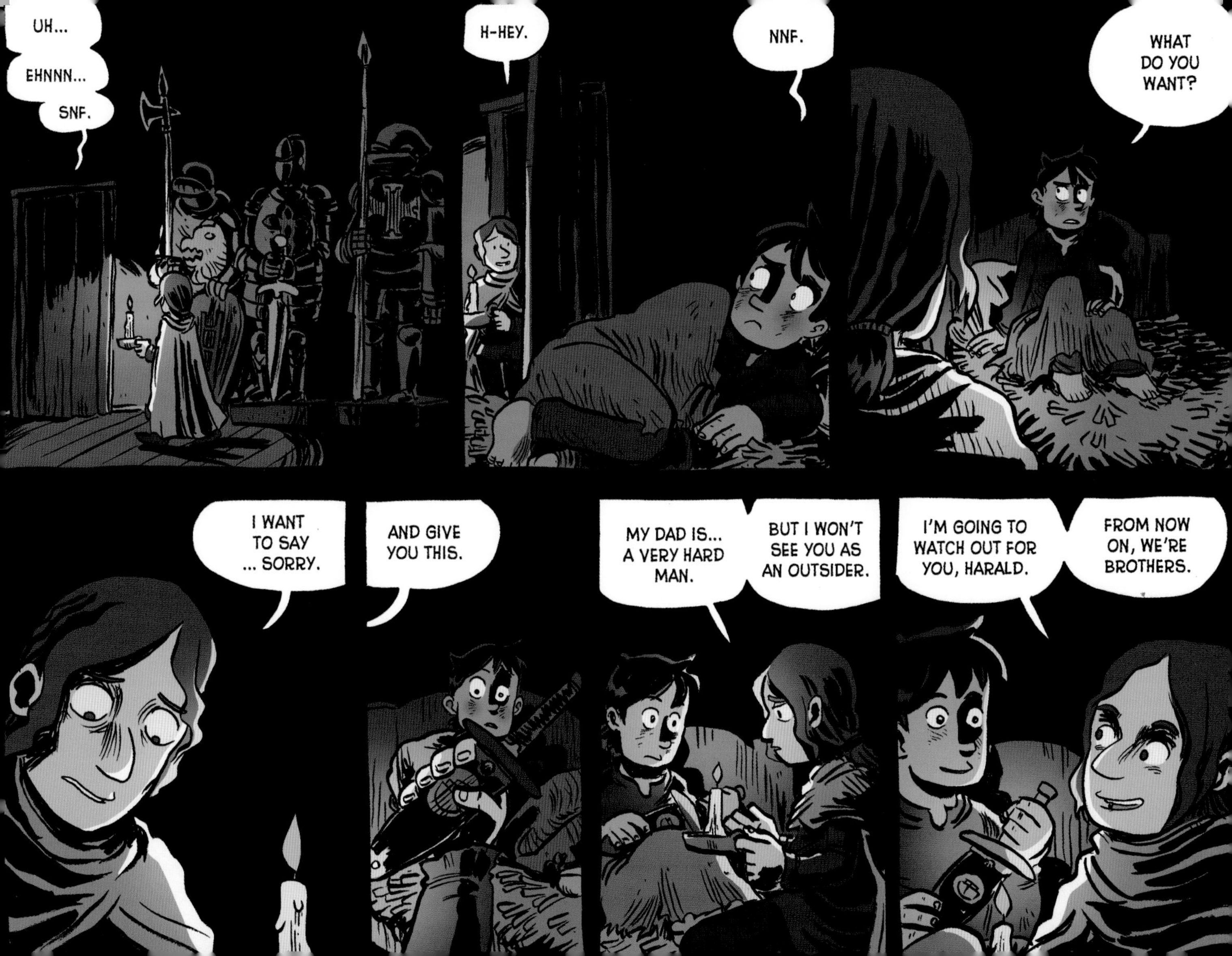
UH...
EHNNN...
SNF.
H-HEY.
NNF.
WHAT DO YOU WANT?
I WANT TO SAY ... SORRY.
AND GIVE YOU THIS.
MY DAD IS... A VERY HARD MAN.
BUT I WON'T SEE YOU AS AN OUTSIDER.
I'M GOING TO WATCH OUT FOR YOU, HARALD.
FROM NOW ON, WE'RE BROTHERS.

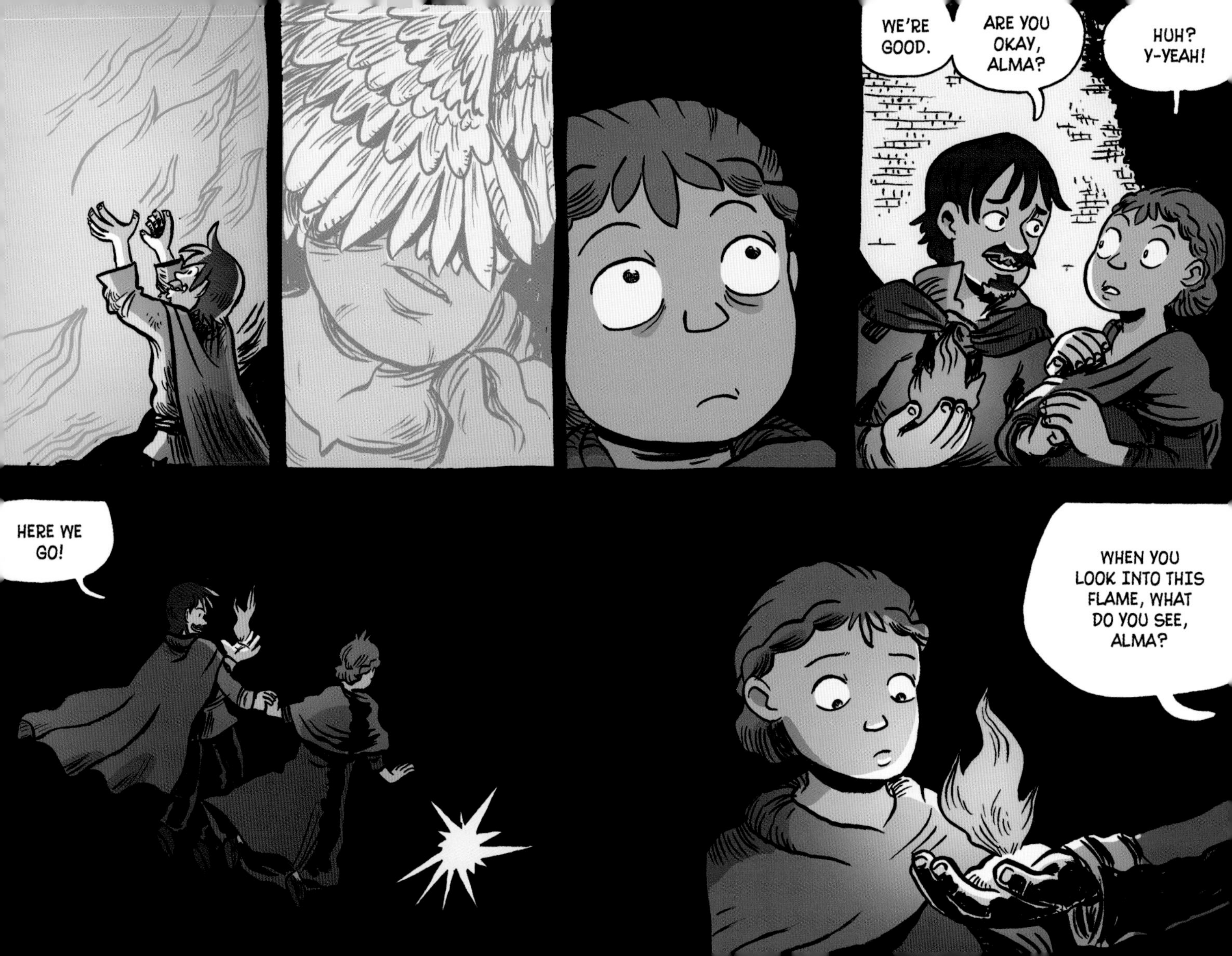
WE'RE GOOD.
ARE YOU OKAY, ALMA?
HUH? Y-YEAH!
HERE WE GO!
WHEN YOU LOOK INTO THIS FLAME, WHAT DO YOU SEE, ALMA?

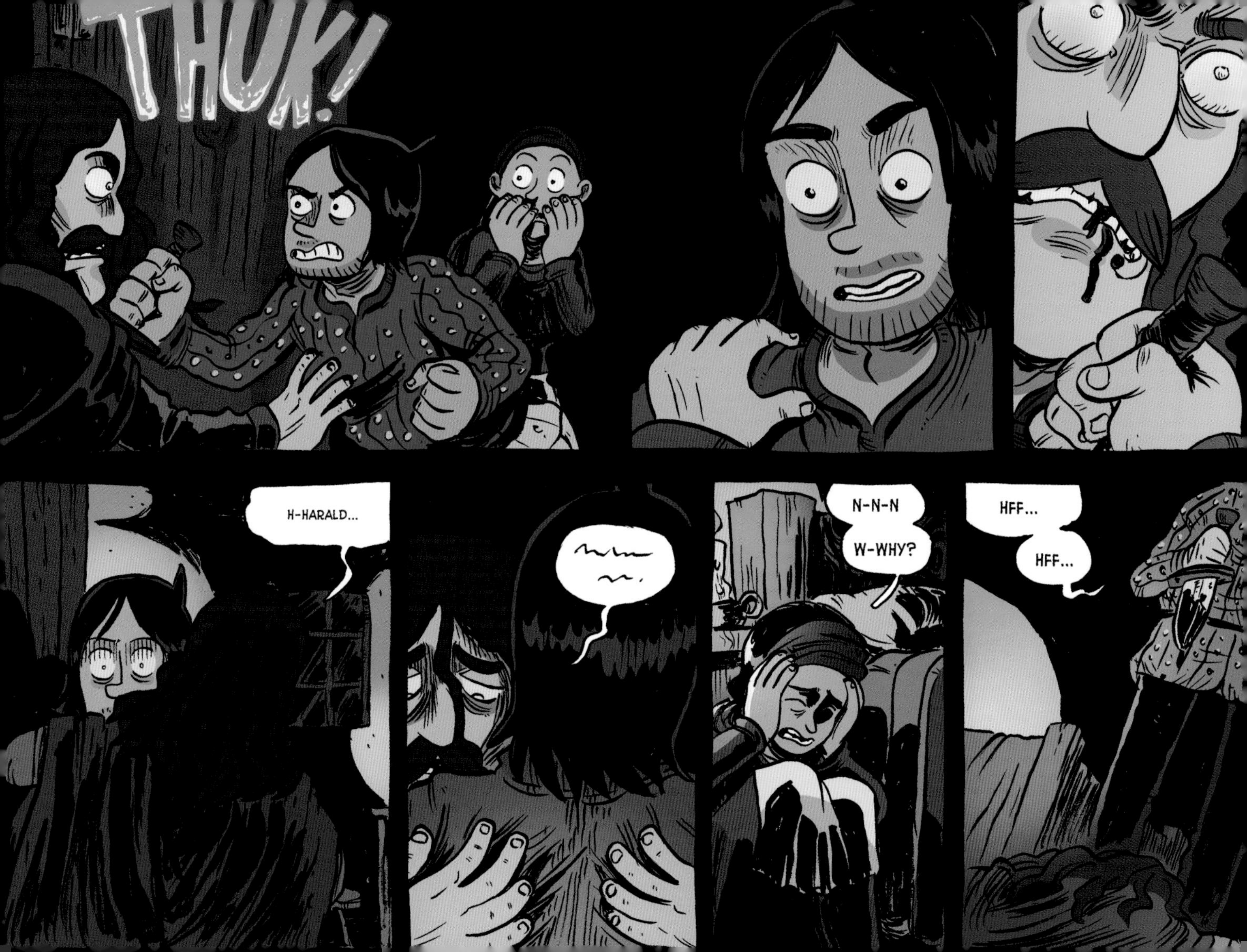
THUK!
H-HARALD...
N-N-N
W-WHY?
HFF...
HFF...

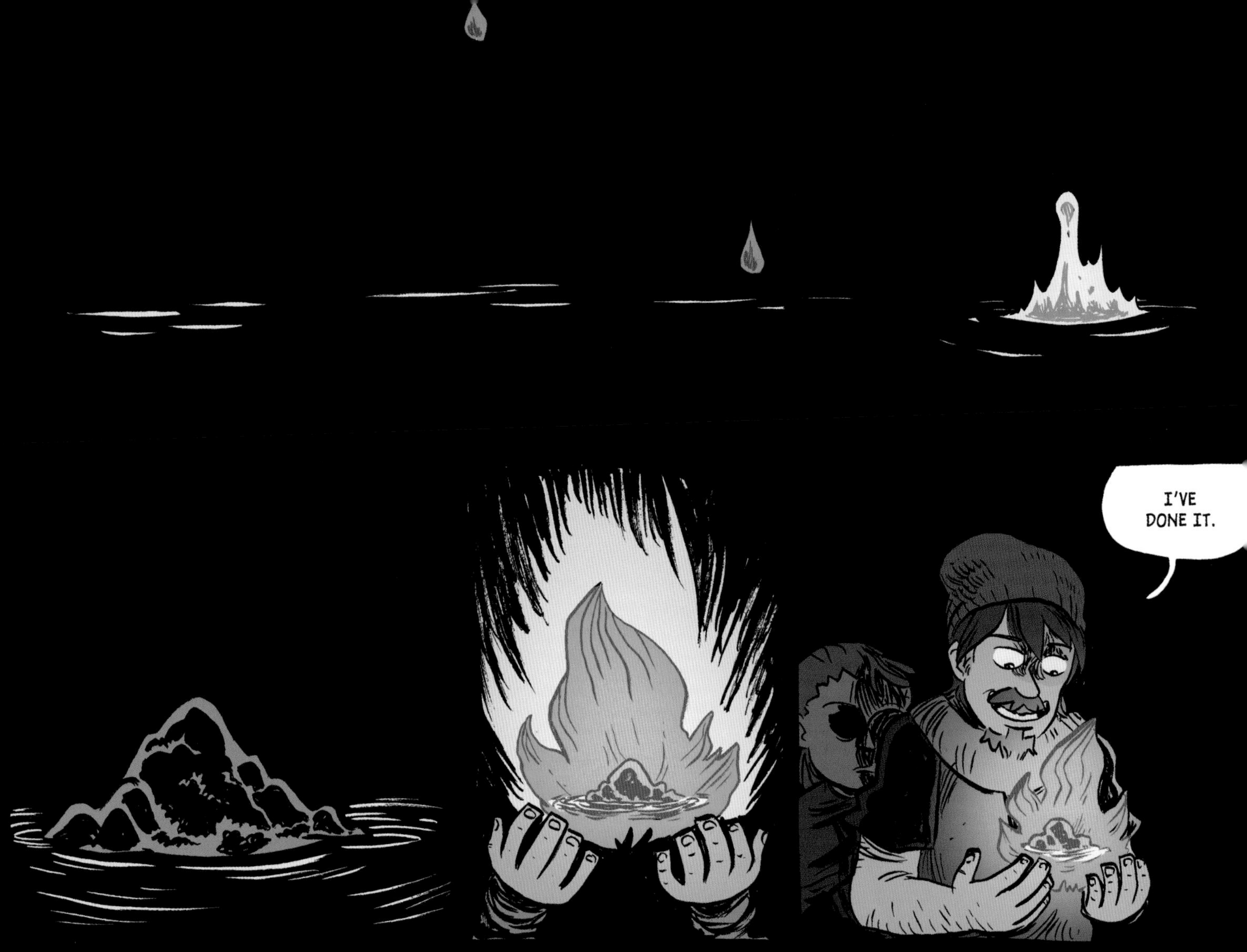
I'VE DONE IT.

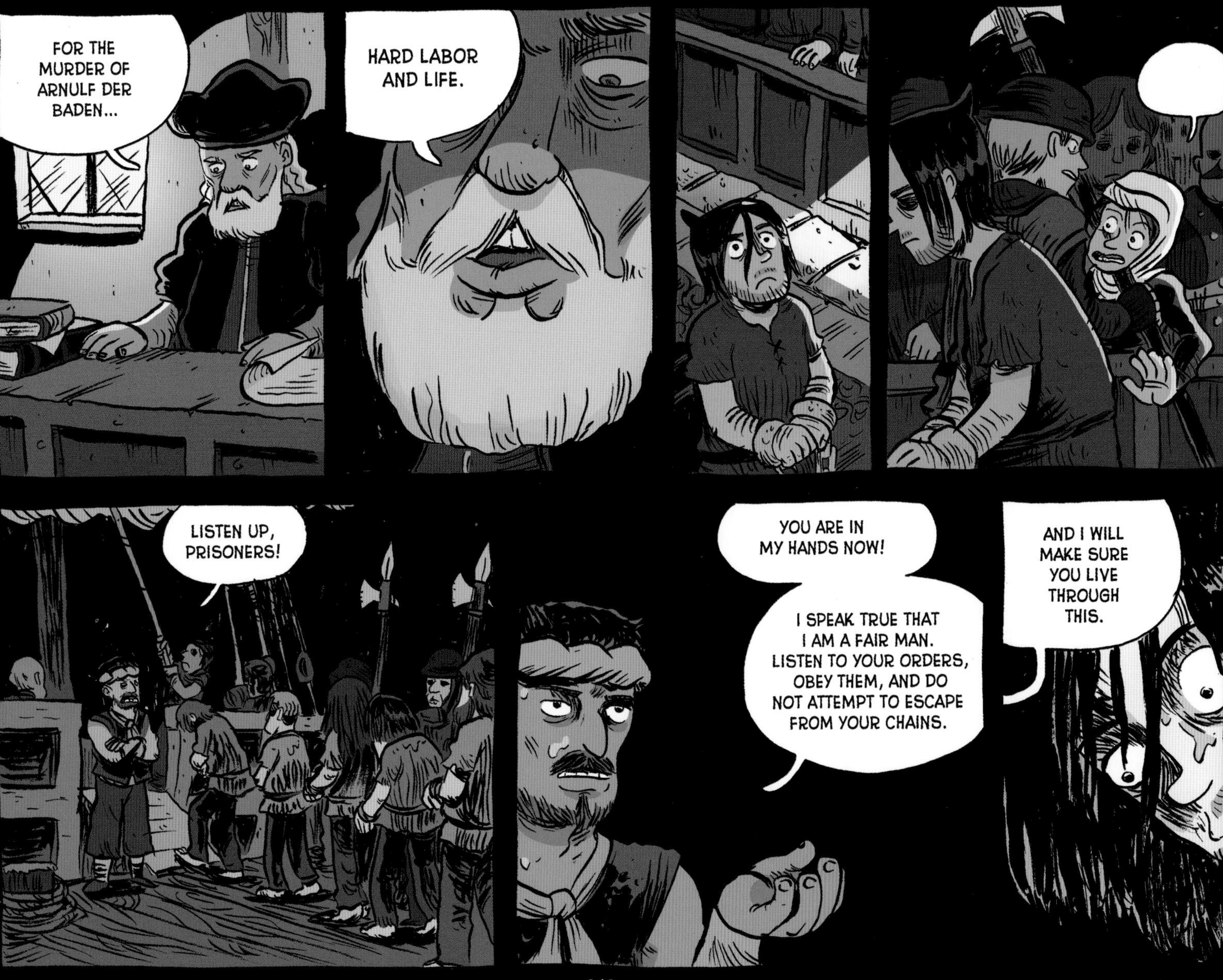
FOR THE MURDER OF ARNULF DER BADEN...
HARD LABOR AND LIFE.
LISTEN UP, PRISONERS!
YOU ARE IN MY HANDS NOW!
I SPEAK TRUE THAT I AM A FAIR MAN. LISTEN TO YOUR ORDERS, OBEY THEM, AND DO NOT ATTEMPT TO ESCAPE FROM YOUR CHAINS.
AND I WILL MAKE SURE YOU LIVE THROUGH THIS.

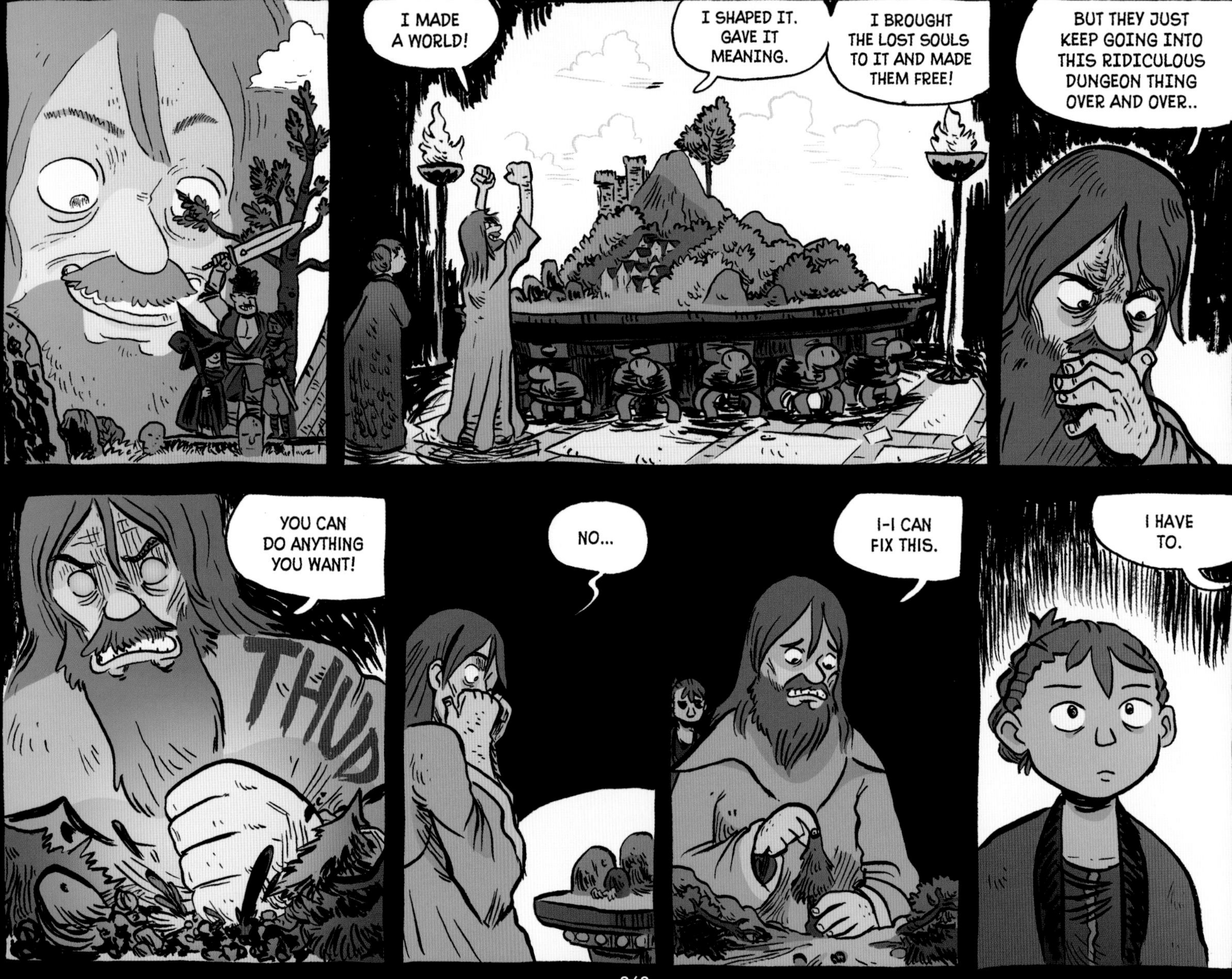
I MADE A WORLD!
I SHAPED IT. GAVE IT MEANING.
I BROUGHT THE LOST SOULS TO IT AND MADE THEM FREE!
BUT THEY JUST KEEP GOING INTO THIS RIDICULOUS DUNGEON THING OVER AND OVER..
YOU CAN DO ANYTHING YOU WANT!
THUD
NO...
I-I CAN FIX THIS.
I HAVE TO.

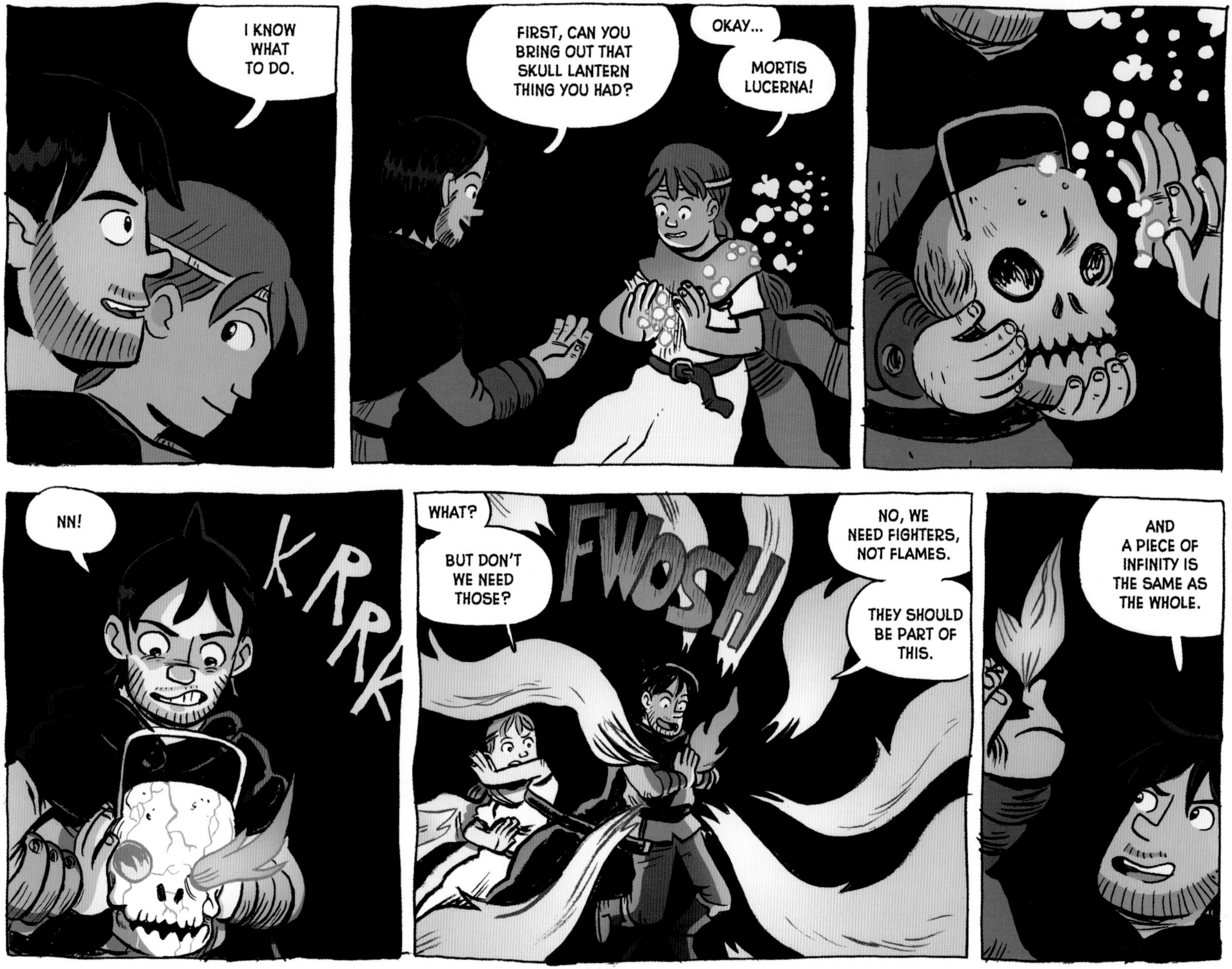
I KNOW WHAT TO DO.
FIRST, CAN YOU BRING OUT THAT SKULL LANTERN THING YOU HAD?
OKAY...
MORTIS LUCERNA!
NN!
KRRK
WHAT?
BUT DON'T WE NEED THOSE?
FWOSH
NO, WE NEED FIGHTERS, NOT FLAMES.
THEY SHOULD BE PART OF THIS.
AND A PIECE OF INFINITY IS THE SAME AS THE WHOLE.

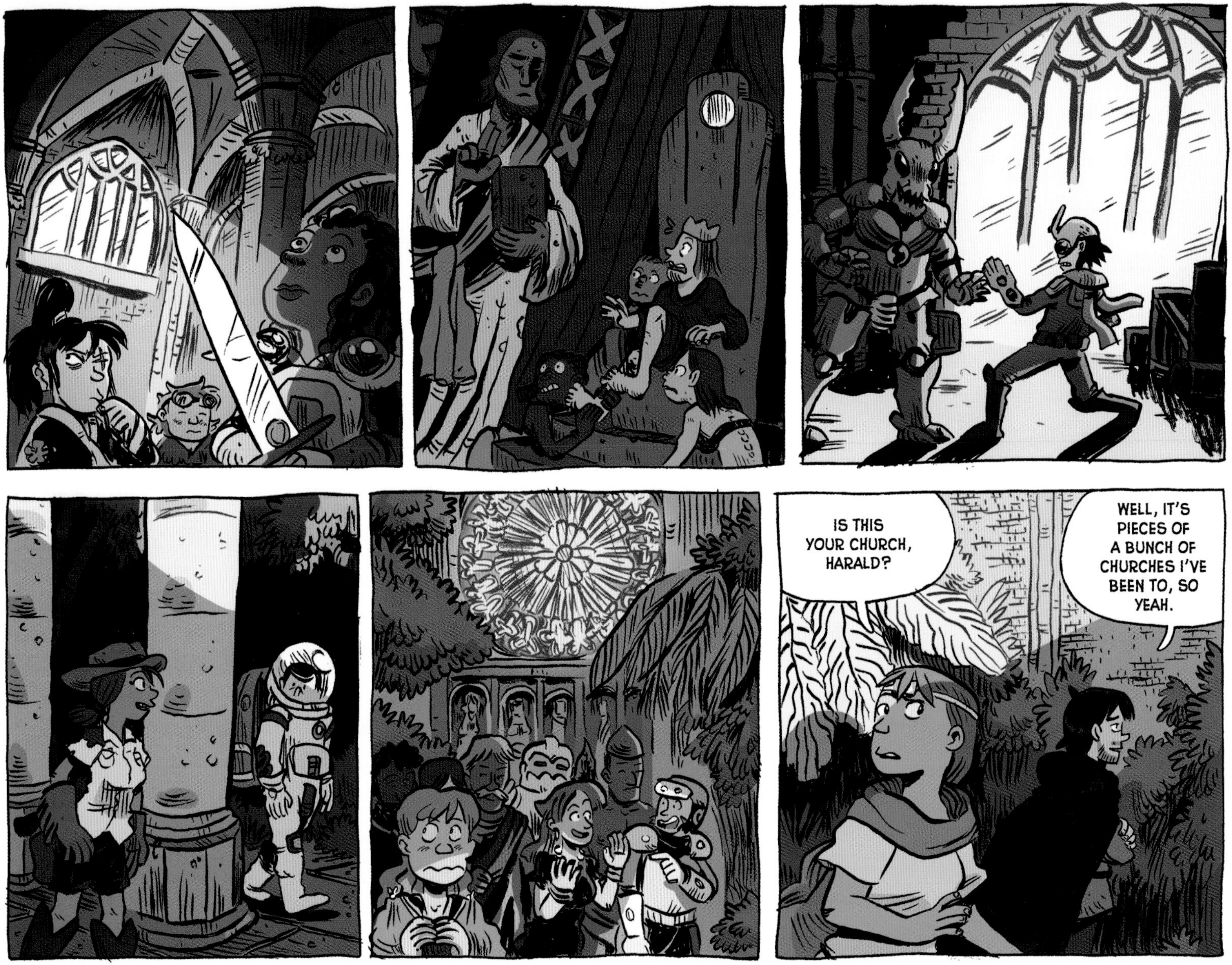
IS THIS YOUR CHURCH, HARALD?
WELL, IT'S PIECES OF A BUNCH OF CHURCHES I'VE BEEN TO, SO YEAH.

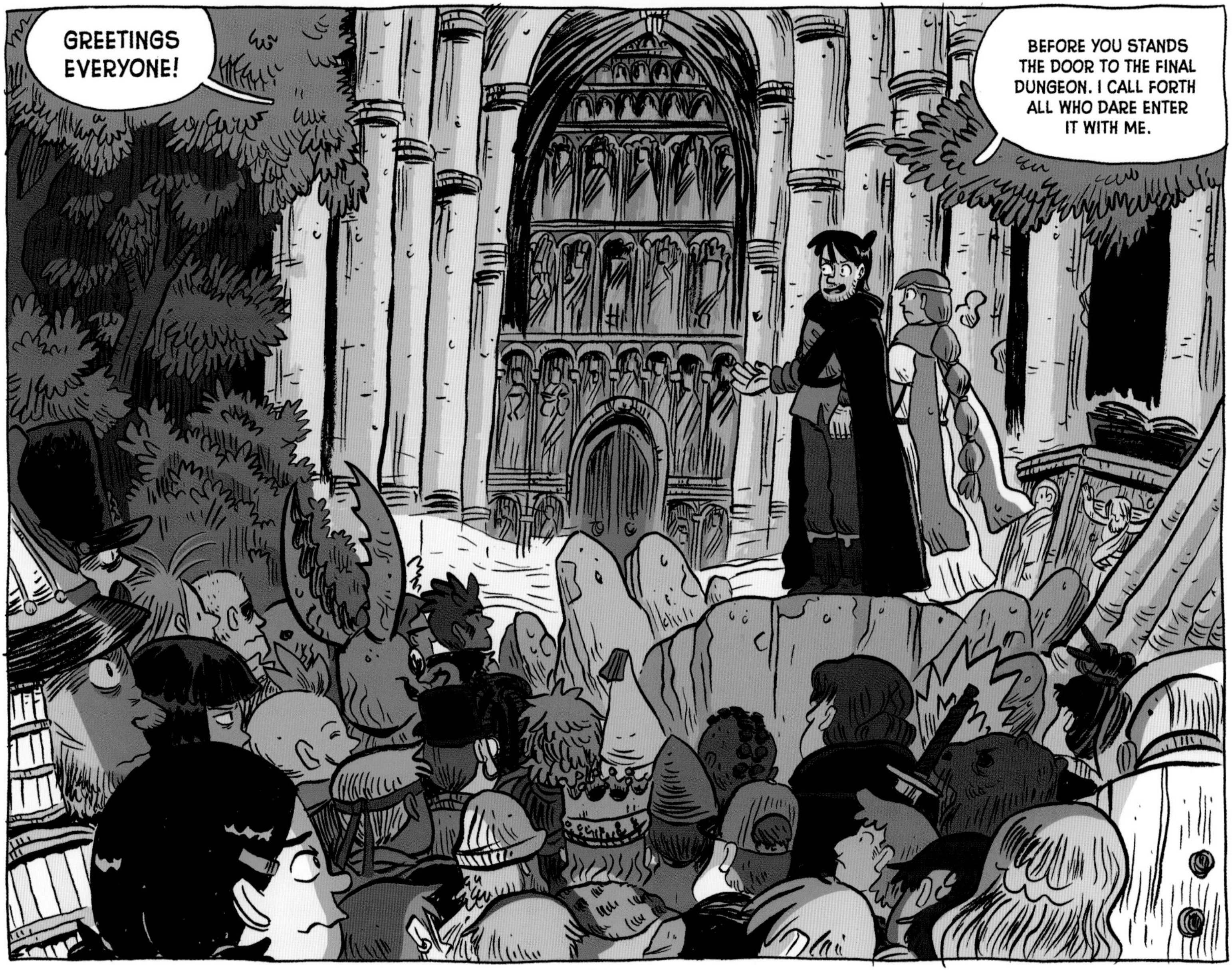
GREETINGS EVERYONE!
BEFORE YOU STANDS THE DOOR TO THE FINAL DUNGEON. I CALL FORTH ALL WHO DARE ENTER IT WITH ME.

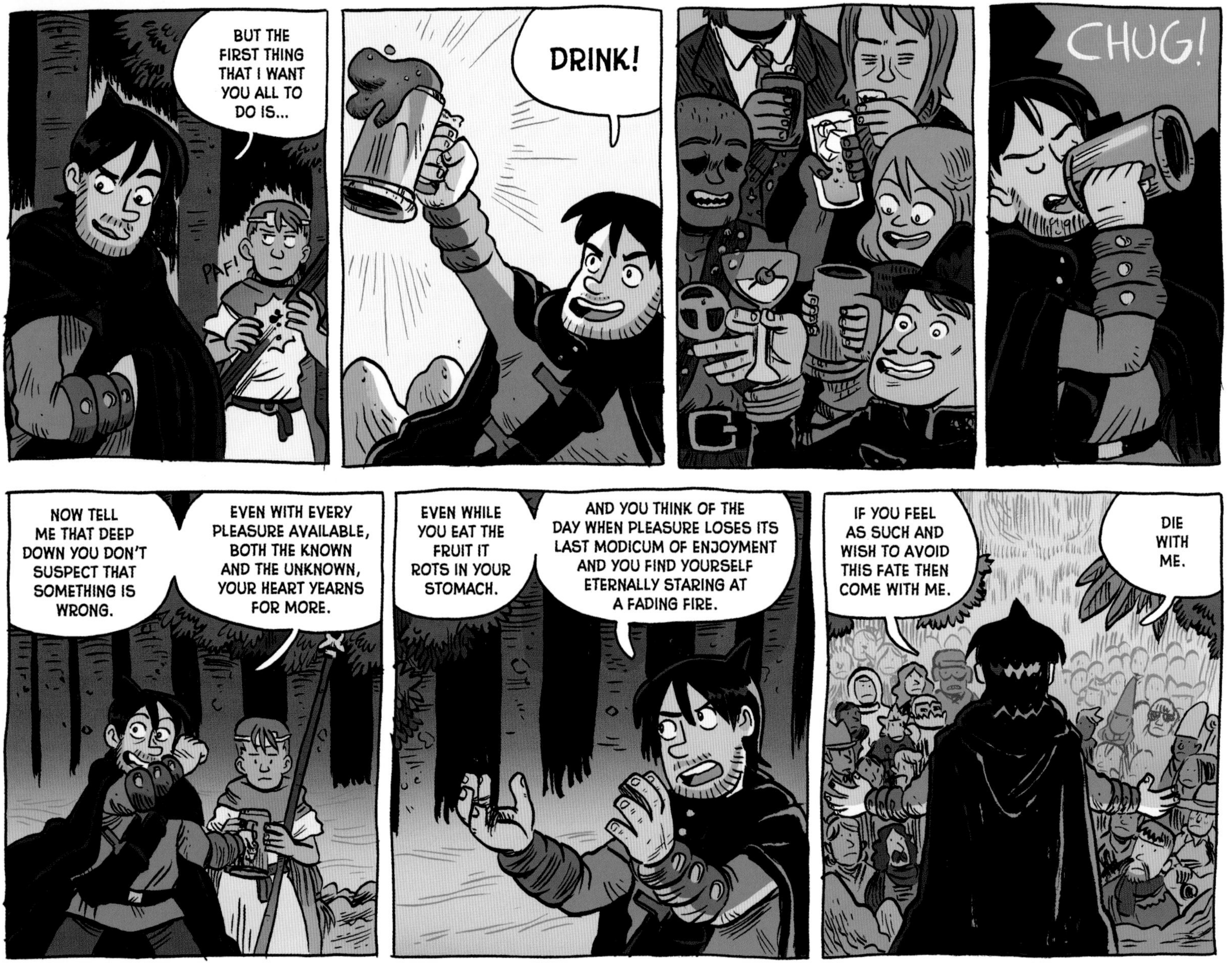
BUT THE FIRST THING THAT I WANT YOU ALL TO DO IS...
PAF!
DRINK!
CHUG!
NOW TELL ME THAT DEEP DOWN YOU DON'T SUSPECT THAT SOMETHING IS WRONG.
EVEN WITH EVERY PLEASURE AVAILABLE, BOTH THE KNOWN AND THE UNKNOWN, YOUR HEART YEARNS FOR MORE.
EVEN WHILE YOU EAT THE FRUIT IT ROTS IN YOUR STOMACH.
AND YOU THINK OF THE DAY WHEN PLEASURE LOSES ITS LAST MODICUM OF ENJOYMENT AND YOU FIND YOURSELF ETERNALLY STARING AT A FADING FIRE.
IF YOU FEEL AS SUCH AND WISH TO AVOID THIS FATE THEN COME WITH ME.
DIE WITH ME.

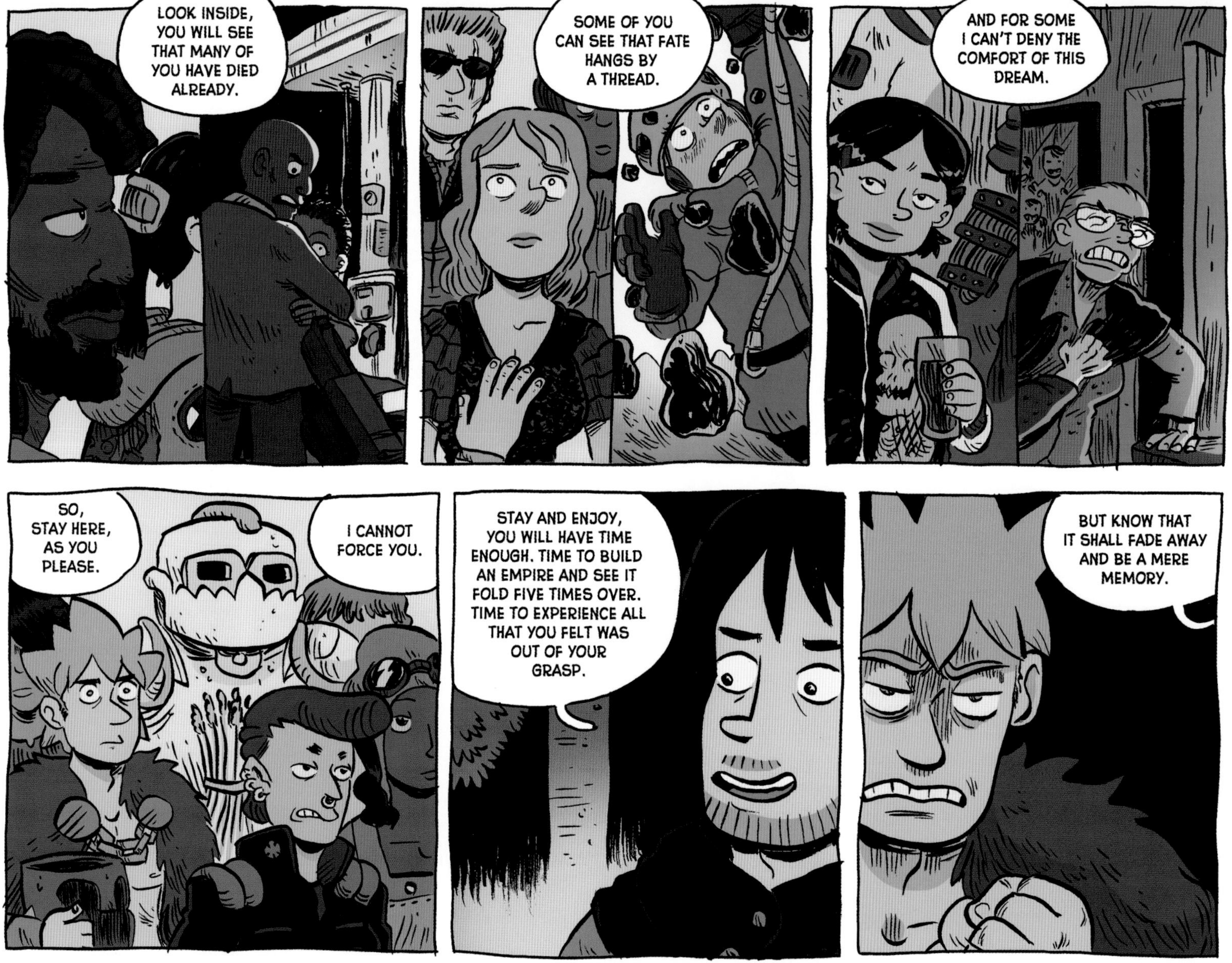
LOOK INSIDE, YOU WILL SEE THAT MANY OF YOU HAVE DIED ALREADY.
SOME OF YOU CAN SEE THAT FATE HANGS BY A THREAD.
AND FOR SOME I CAN'T DENY THE COMFORT OF THIS DREAM.
SO, STAY HERE, AS YOU PLEASE.
I CANNOT FORCE YOU.
STAY AND ENJOY, YOU WILL HAVE TIME ENOUGH. TIME TO BUILD AN EMPIRE AND SEE IT FOLD FIVE TIMES OVER. TIME TO EXPERIENCE ALL THAT YOU FELT WAS OUT OF YOUR GRASP.
BUT KNOW THAT IT SHALL FADE AWAY AND BE A MERE MEMORY.

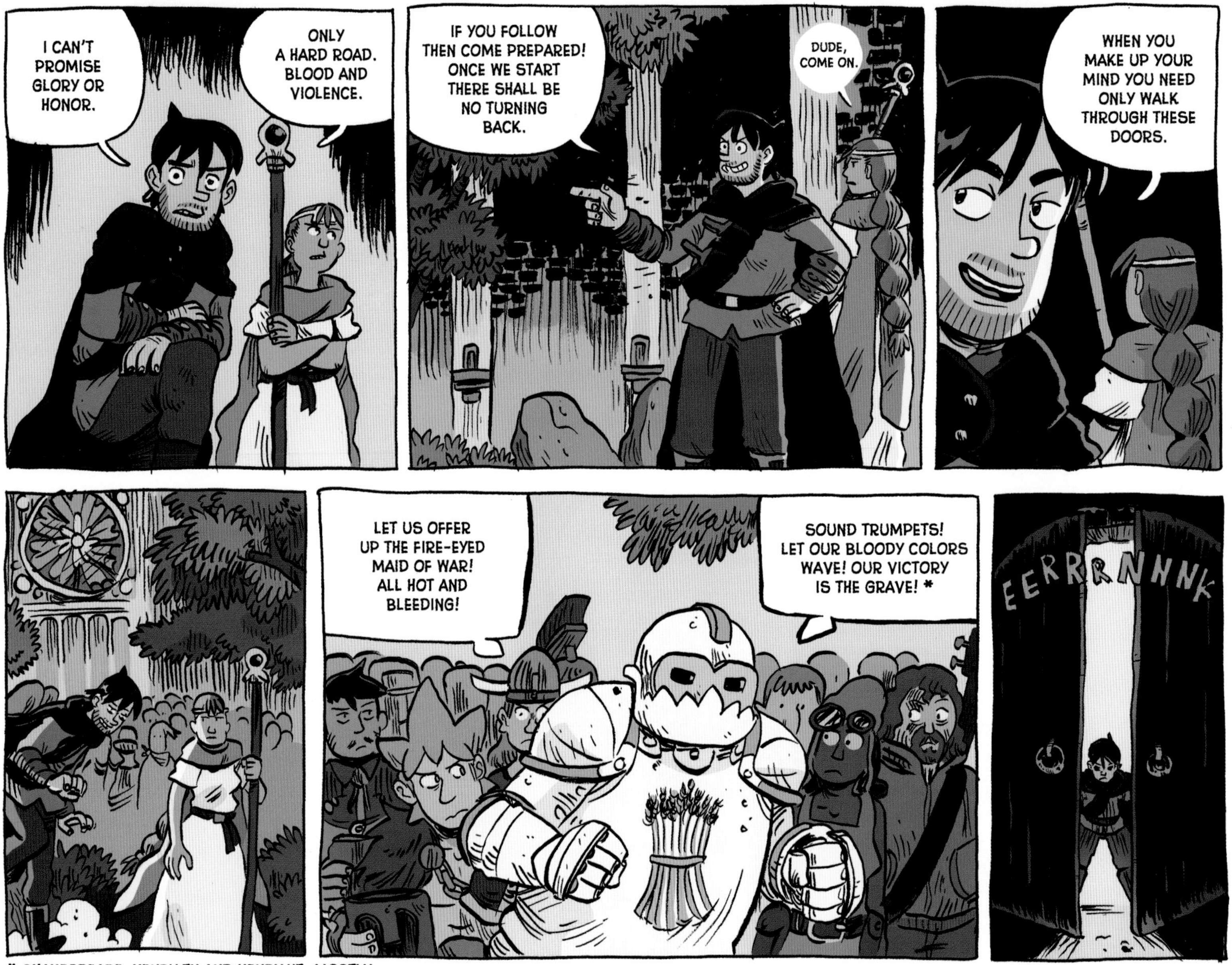
I CAN'T PROMISE GLORY OR HONOR.
ONLY A HARD ROAD. BLOOD AND VIOLENCE.
IF YOU FOLLOW THEN COME PREPARED! ONCE WE START THERE SHALL BE NO TURNING BACK.
DUDE, COME ON.
WHEN YOU MAKE UP YOUR MIND YOU NEED ONLY WALK THROUGH THESE DOORS.
LET US OFFER UP THE FIRE-EYED MAID OF WAR! ALL HOT AND BLEEDING!
SOUND TRUMPETS! LET OUR BLOODY COLORS WAVE! OUR VICTORY IS THE GRAVE! *
EERRRNNNK

* SHAKESPEARE, HENRY IV AND HENRY VI, MOSTLY

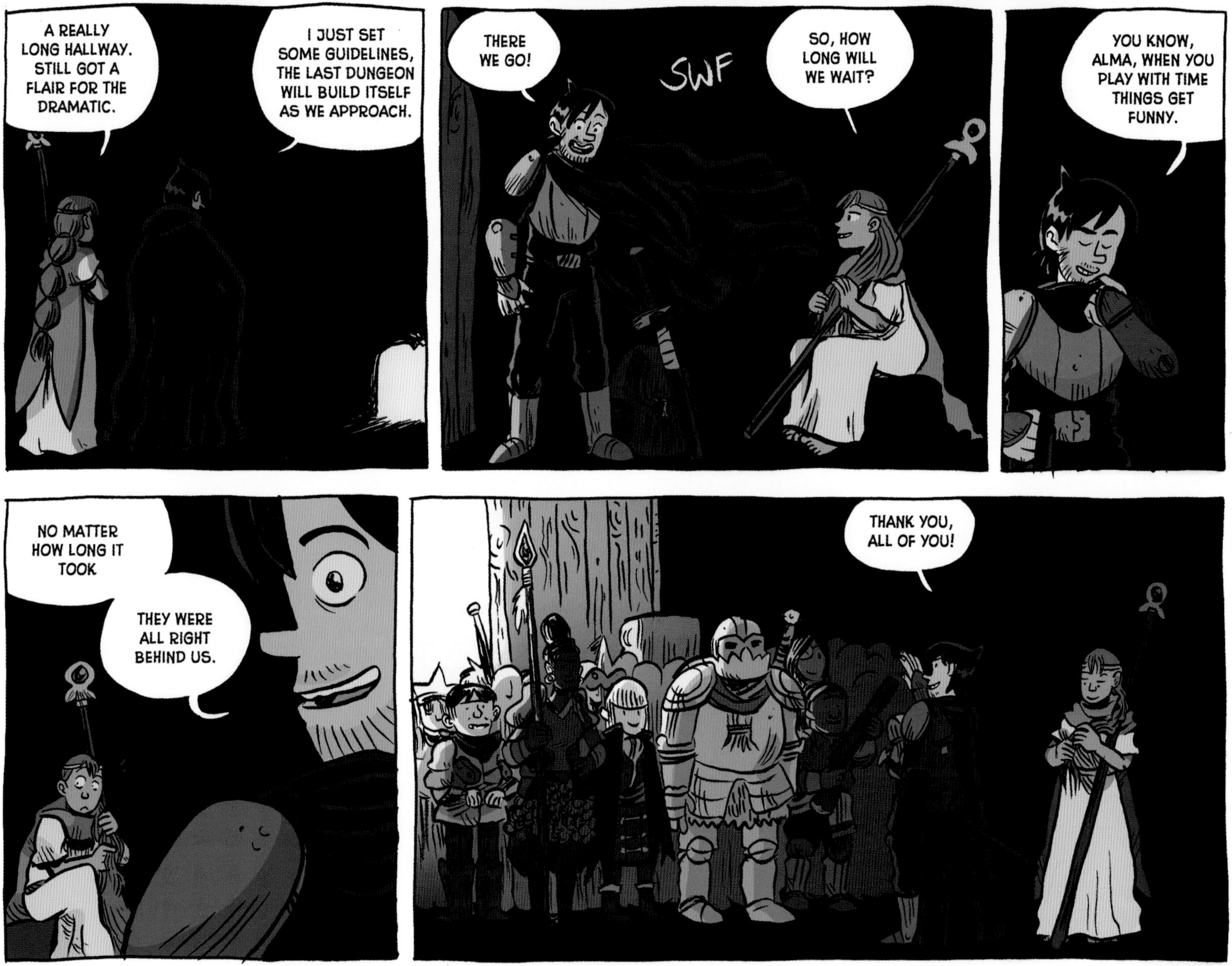
A REALLY LONG HALLWAY. STILL GOT A FLAIR FOR THE DRAMATIC.
I JUST SET SOME GUIDELINES, THE LAST DUNGEON WILL BUILD ITSELF AS WE APPROACH.
THERE WE GO!
SWF
SO, HOW LONG WILL WE WAIT?
YOU KNOW, ALMA, WHEN YOU PLAY WITH TIME THINGS GET FUNNY.
NO MATTER HOW LONG IT TOOK
THEY WERE ALL RIGHT BEHIND US.
THANK YOU, ALL OF YOU!

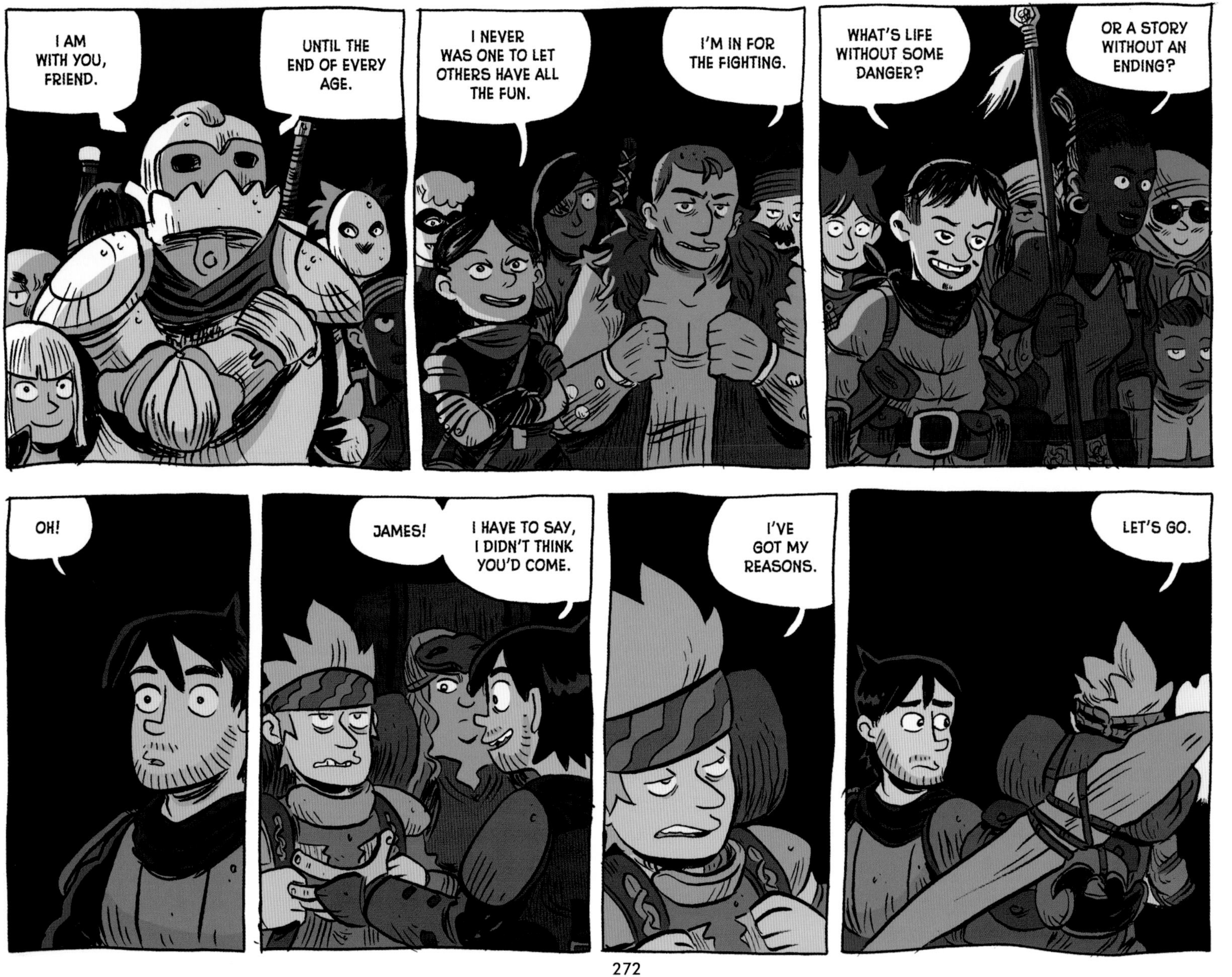
I AM WITH YOU, FRIEND.
UNTIL THE END OF EVERY AGE.
I NEVER WAS ONE TO LET OTHERS HAVE ALL THE FUN.
I'M IN FOR THE FIGHTING.
WHAT'S LIFE WITHOUT SOME DANGER?
OR A STORY WITHOUT AN ENDING?
OH!
JAMES!
I HAVE TO SAY, I DIDN'T THINK YOU'D COME.
I'VE GOT MY REASONS.
LET'S GO.

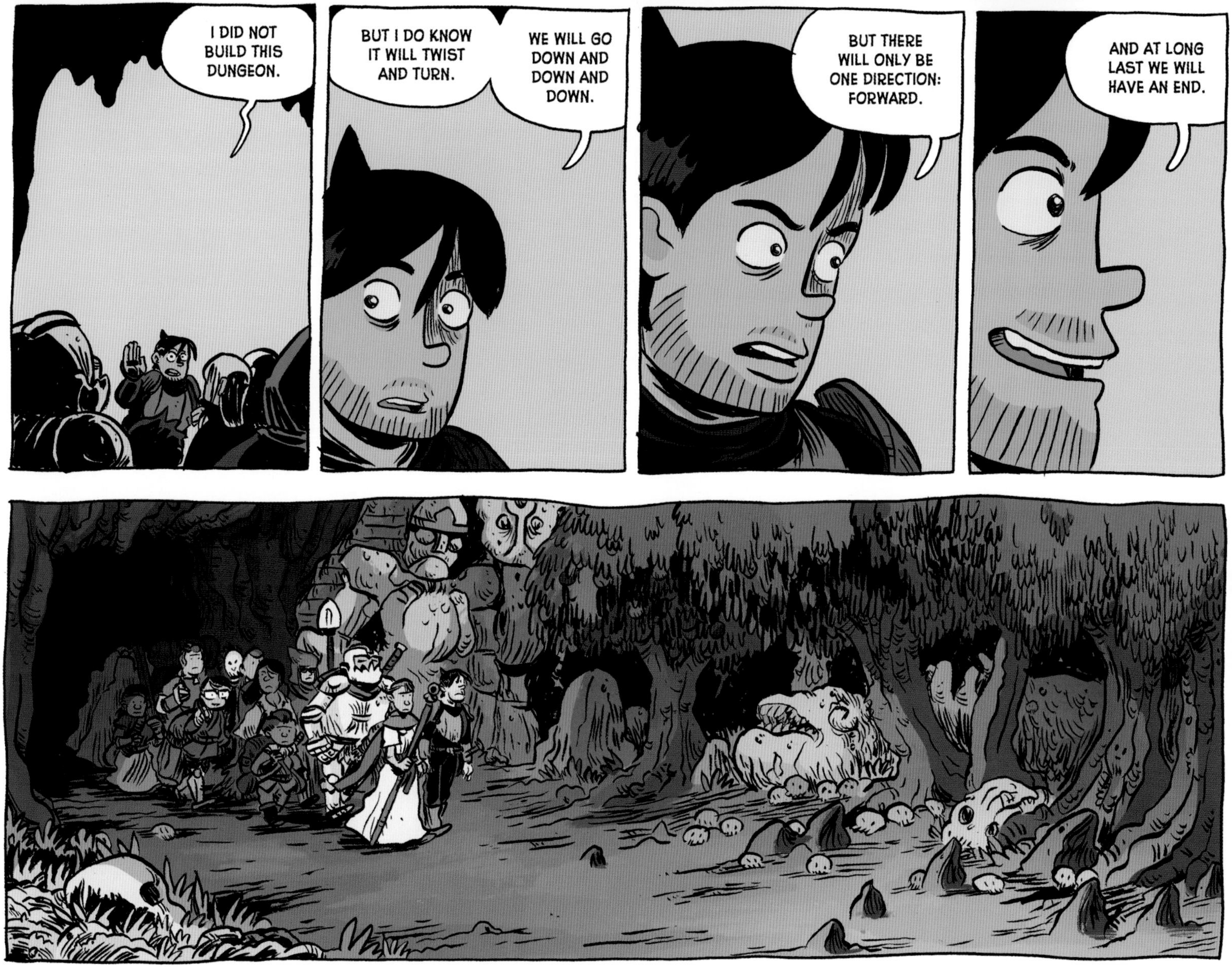
I DID NOT BUILD THIS DUNGEON.
BUT I DO KNOW IT WILL TWIST AND TURN.
WE WILL GO DOWN AND DOWN AND DOWN.
BUT THERE WILL ONLY BE ONE DIRECTION: FORWARD.
AND AT LONG LAST WE WILL HAVE AN END.

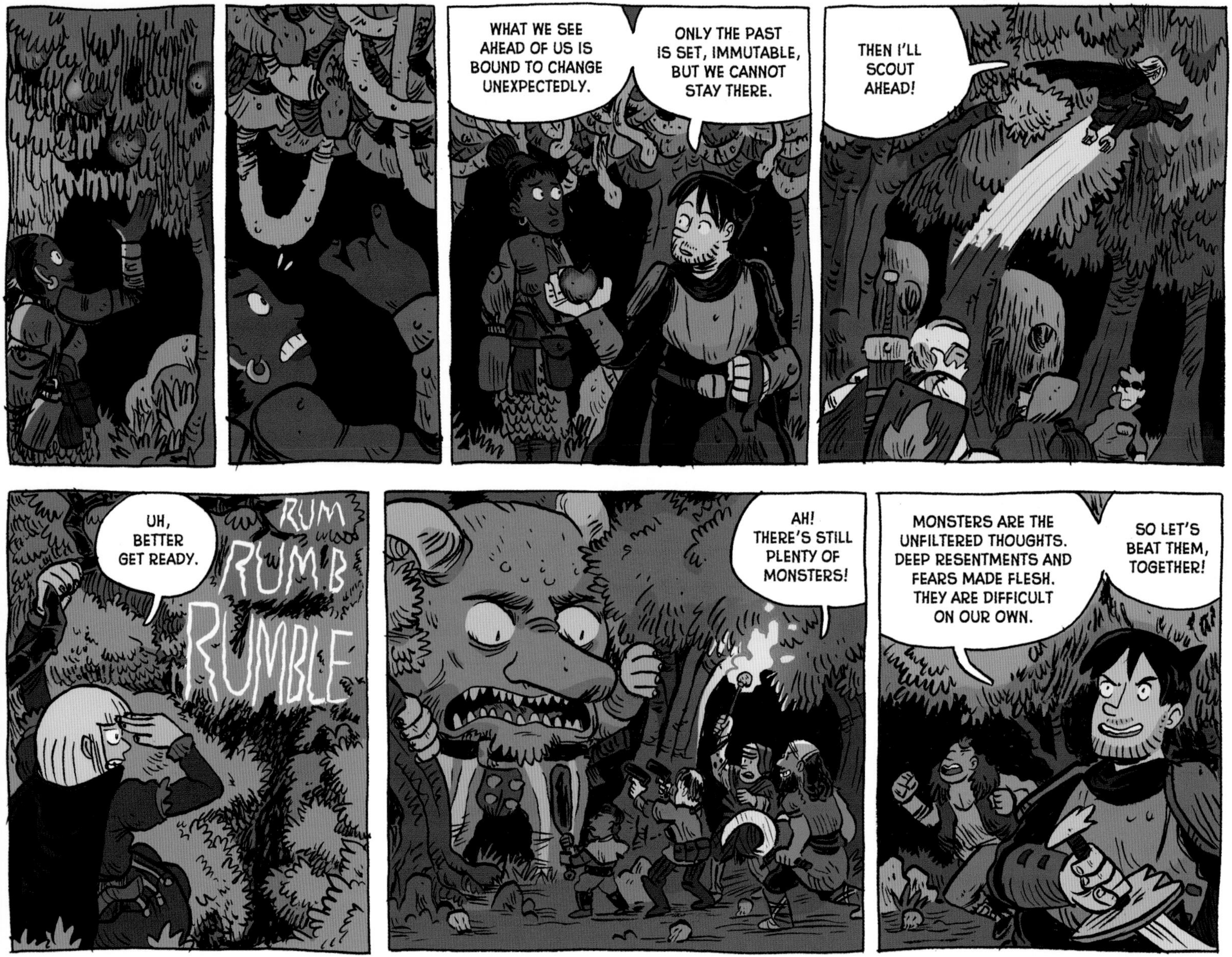

WHAT WE SEE AHEAD OF US IS BOUND TO CHANGE UNEXPECTEDLY.
ONLY THE PAST IS SET, IMMUTABLE, BUT WE CANNOT STAY THERE.
THEN I'LL SCOUT AHEAD!
UH, BETTER GET READY.
RUM
RUMB
RUMBLE
AH! THERE'S STILL PLENTY OF MONSTERS!
MONSTERS ARE THE UNFILTERED THOUGHTS. DEEP RESENTMENTS AND FEARS MADE FLESH. THEY ARE DIFFICULT ON OUR OWN.
SO LET'S BEAT THEM, TOGETHER!

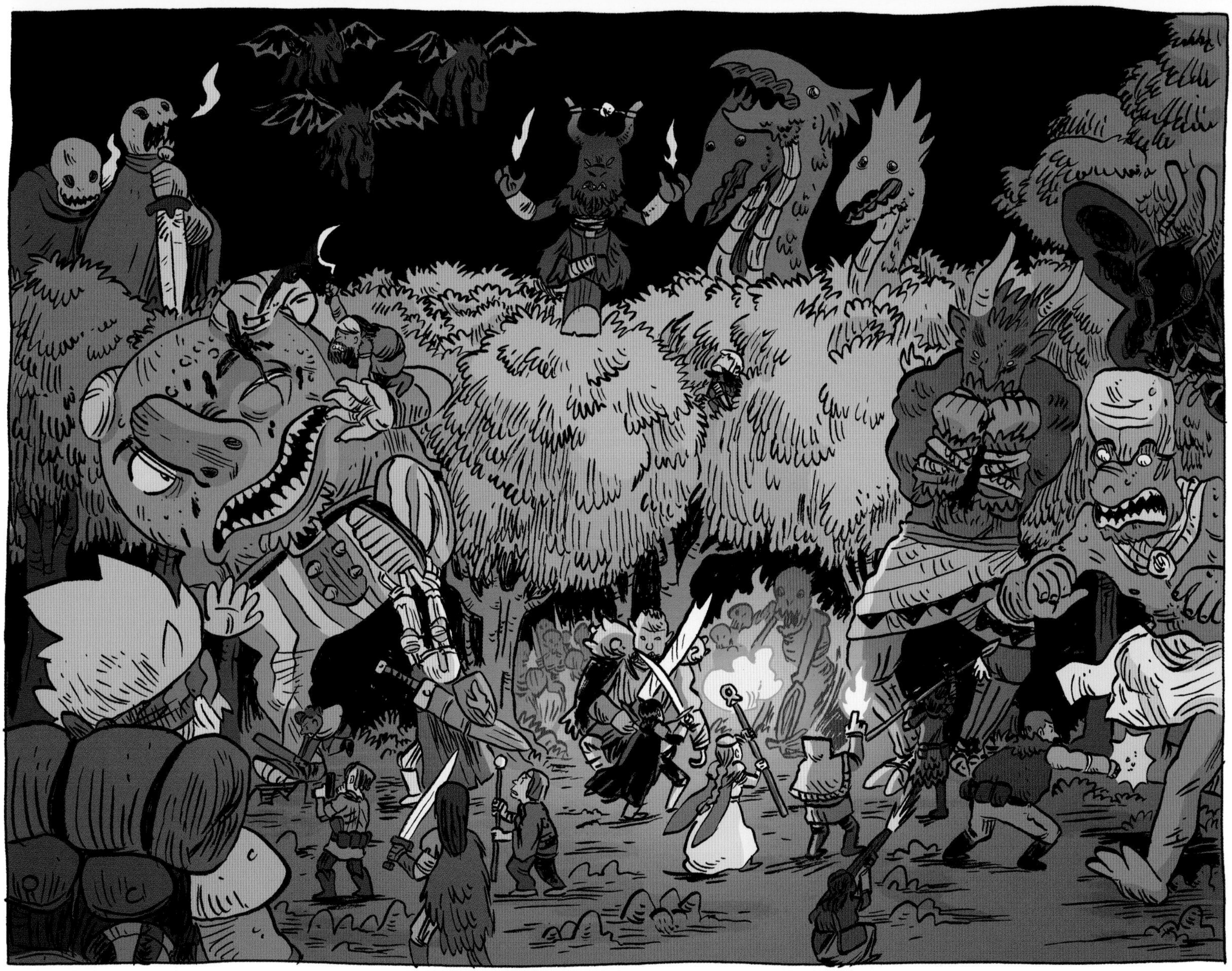

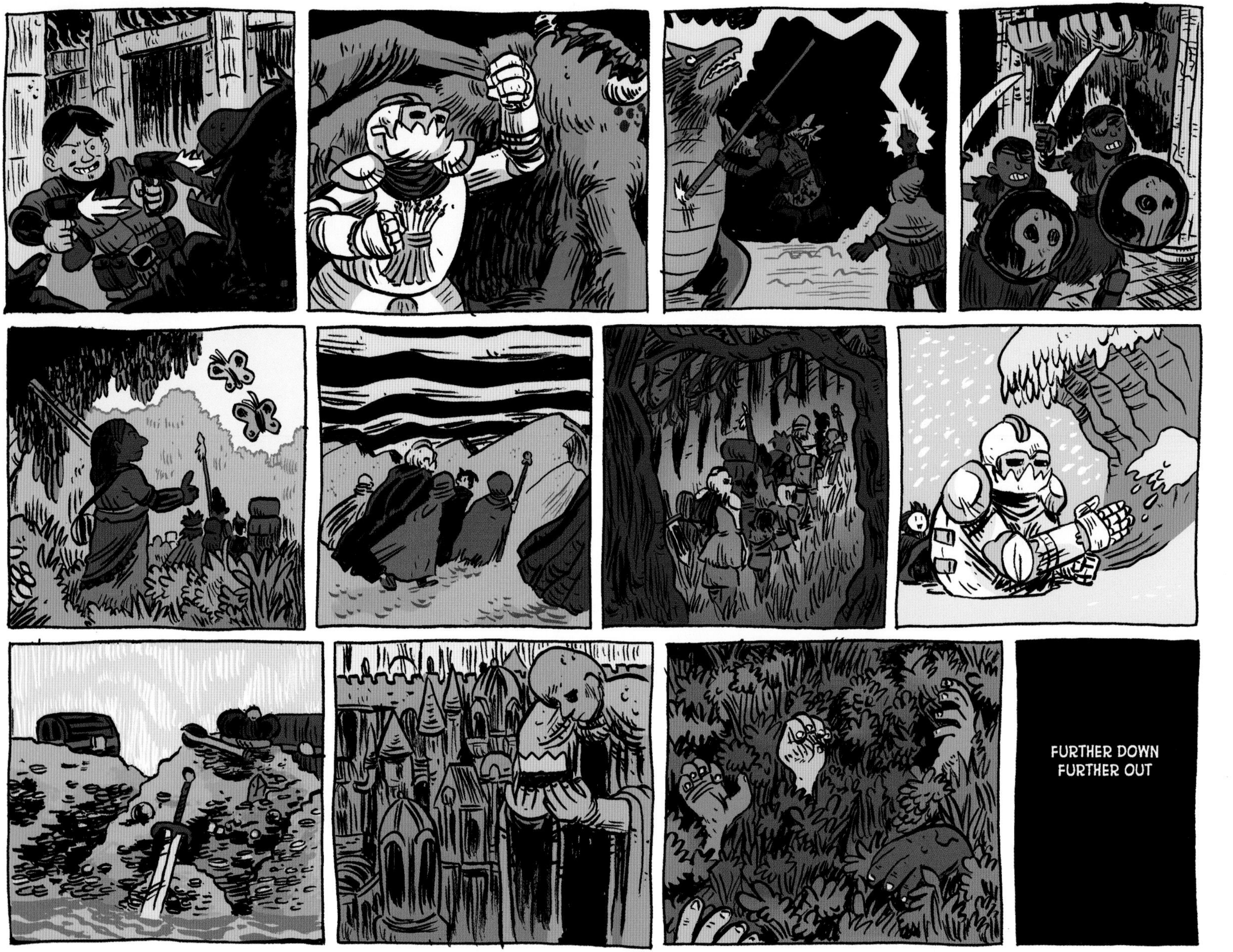
FURTHER DOWN
FURTHER OUT

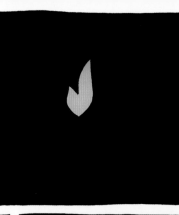

LESS LIKE
A JOURNEY AND
MORE LIKE UNDOING
A KNOT.

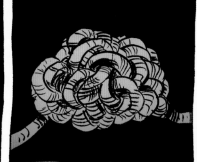

SLOWLY.
METICULOUSLY.
WARY NOT TO
MAKE IT STILL
TIGHTER.

WE SHOULD TAKE A BREAK.

WELL, TIME ISN'T AN ISSUE, BUT A SAFE HAVEN IS.

EXCEPT FOR THE RARE TIMES WHEN YOU HAVE IT WHEN YOU NEED IT.

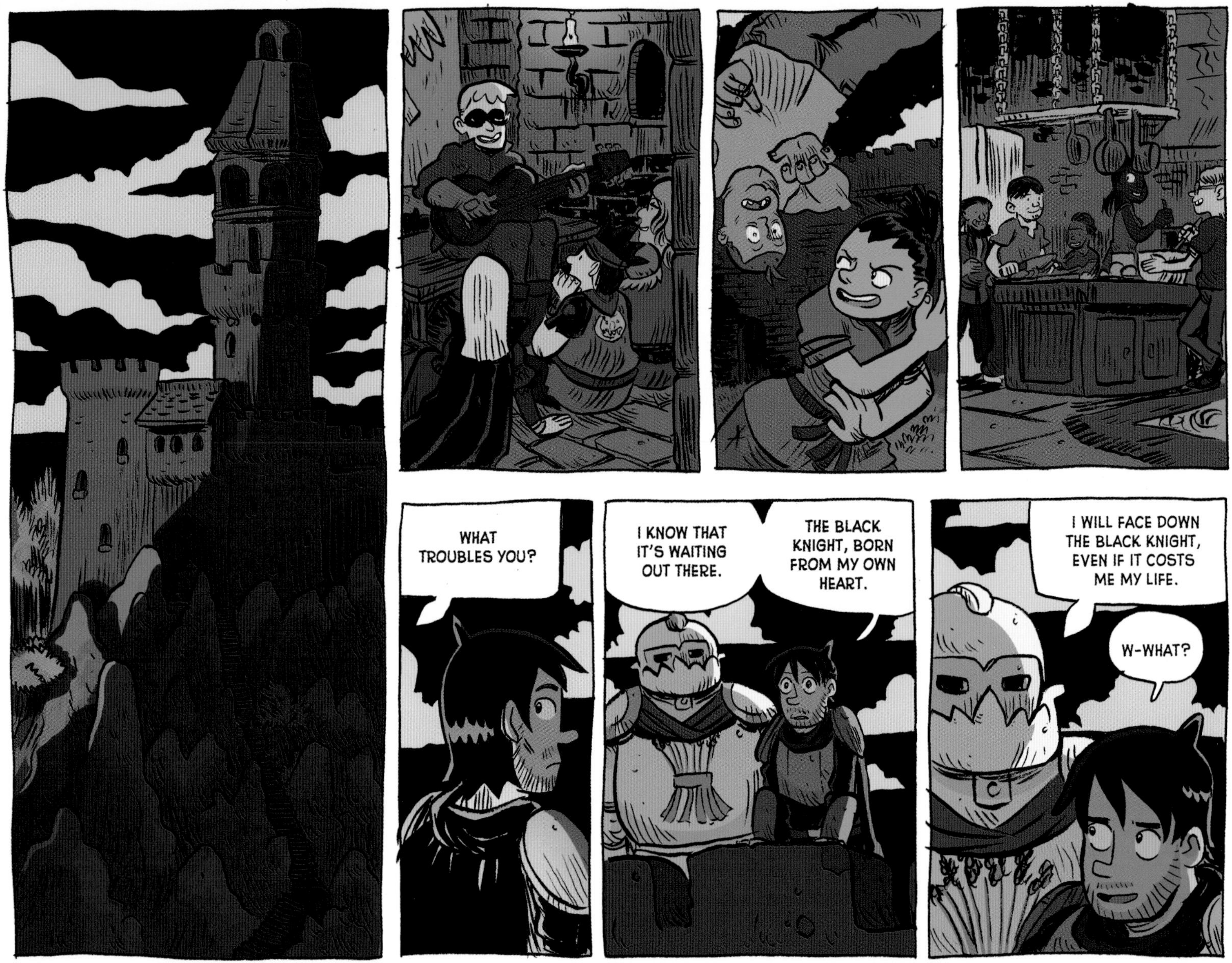
WHAT TROUBLES YOU?
I KNOW THAT IT'S WAITING OUT THERE.
THE BLACK KNIGHT, BORN FROM MY OWN HEART.
I WILL FACE DOWN THE BLACK KNIGHT, EVEN IF IT COSTS ME MY LIFE.
W-WHAT?

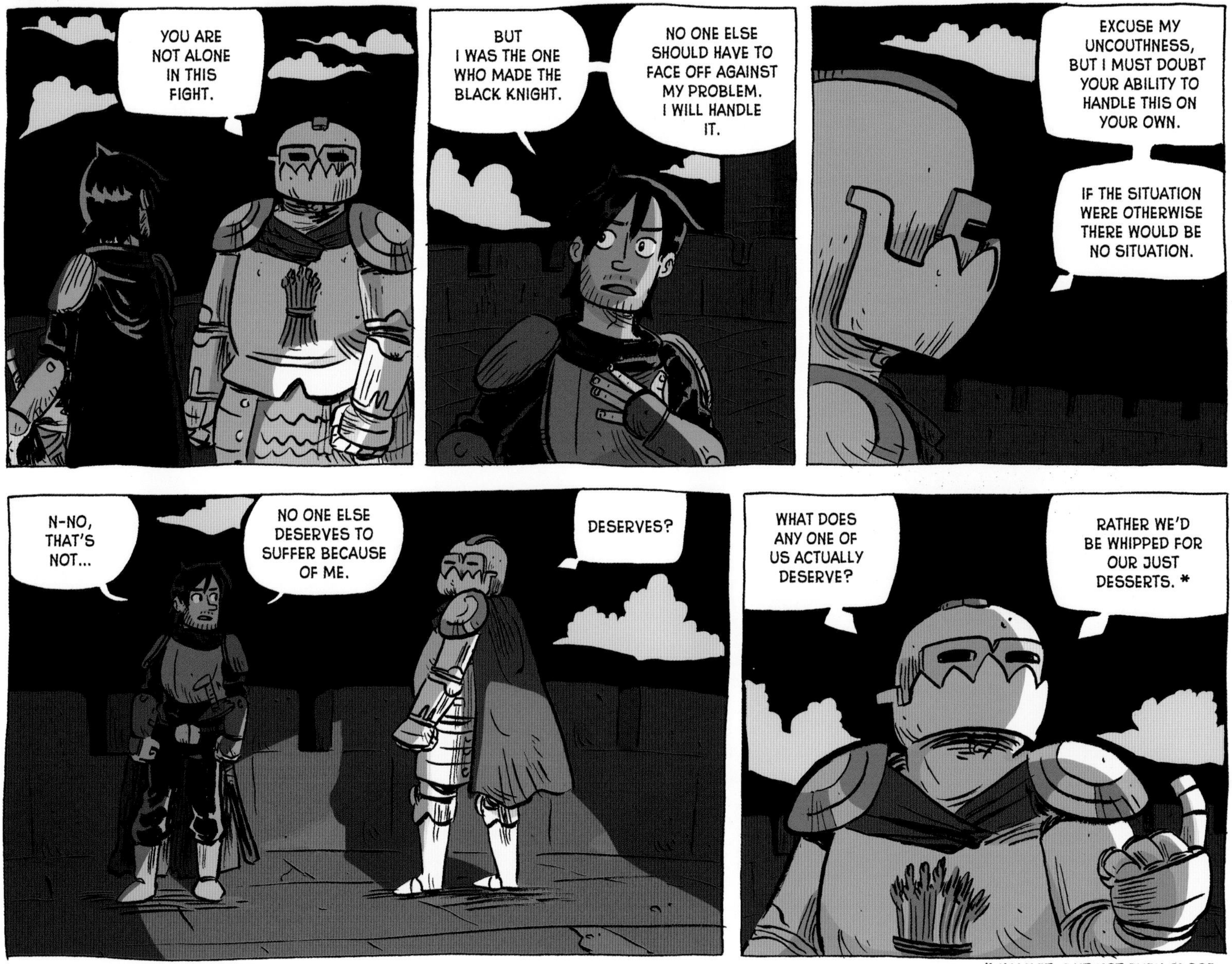
YOU ARE NOT ALONE IN THIS FIGHT.
BUT I WAS THE ONE WHO MADE THE BLACK KNIGHT.
NO ONE ELSE SHOULD HAVE TO FACE OFF AGAINST MY PROBLEM. I WILL HANDLE IT.
EXCUSE MY UNCOUTHNESS, BUT I MUST DOUBT YOUR ABILITY TO HANDLE THIS ON YOUR OWN.
IF THE SITUATION WERE OTHERWISE THERE WOULD BE NO SITUATION.
N-NO, THAT'S NOT...
NO ONE ELSE DESERVES TO SUFFER BECAUSE OF ME.
DESERVES?
WHAT DOES ANY ONE OF US ACTUALLY DESERVE?
RATHER WE'D BE WHIPPED FOR OUR JUST DESSERTS. *

* HAMLET, BUT NOT EVEN CLOSE.

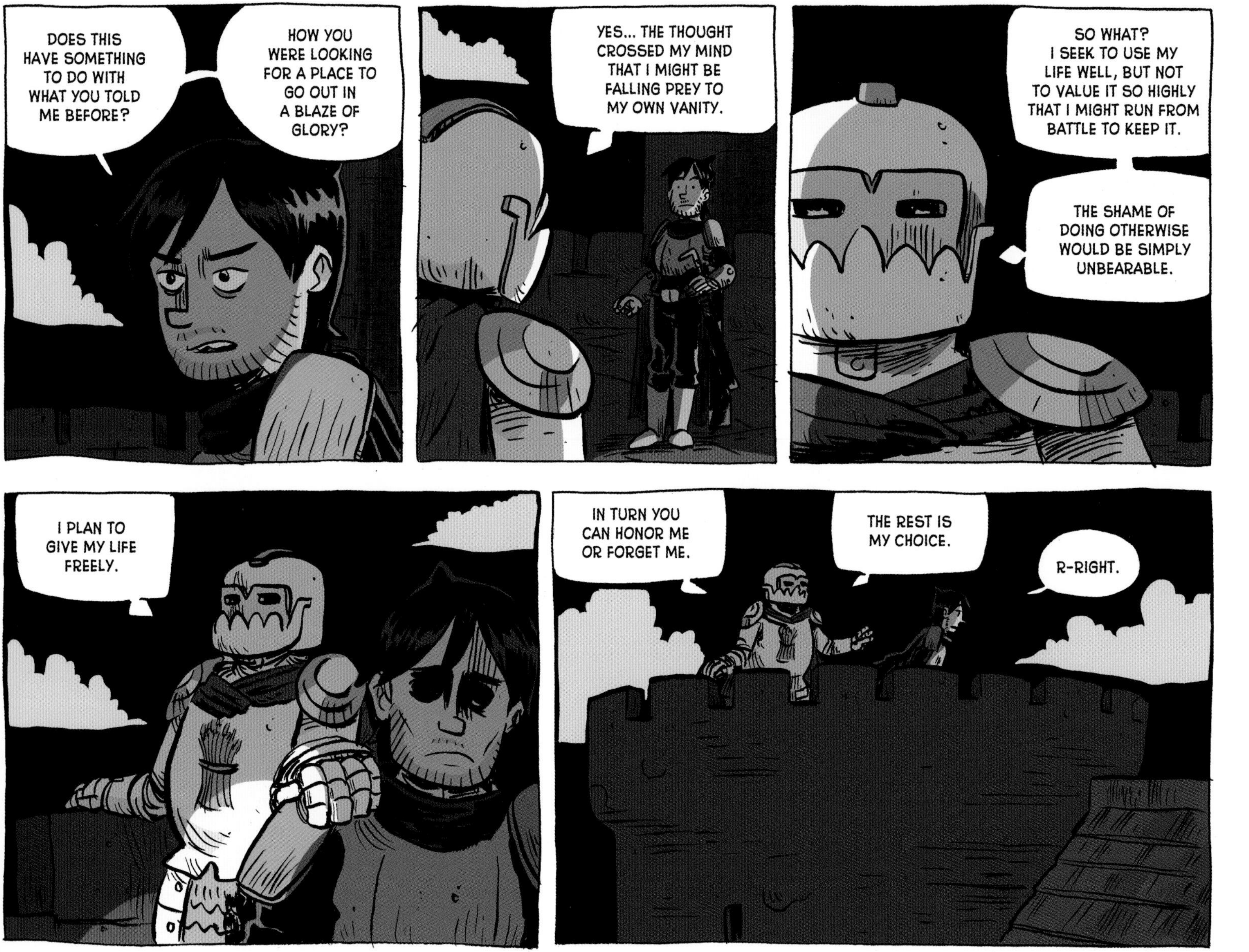
DOES THIS HAVE SOMETHING TO DO WITH WHAT YOU TOLD ME BEFORE?
HOW YOU WERE LOOKING FOR A PLACE TO GO OUT IN A BLAZE OF GLORY?
YES... THE THOUGHT CROSSED MY MIND THAT I MIGHT BE FALLING PREY TO MY OWN VANITY.
SO WHAT? I SEEK TO USE MY LIFE WELL, BUT NOT TO VALUE IT SO HIGHLY THAT I MIGHT RUN FROM BATTLE TO KEEP IT.
THE SHAME OF DOING OTHERWISE WOULD BE SIMPLY UNBEARABLE.
I PLAN TO GIVE MY LIFE FREELY.
IN TURN YOU CAN HONOR ME OR FORGET ME.
THE REST IS MY CHOICE.
R-RIGHT.

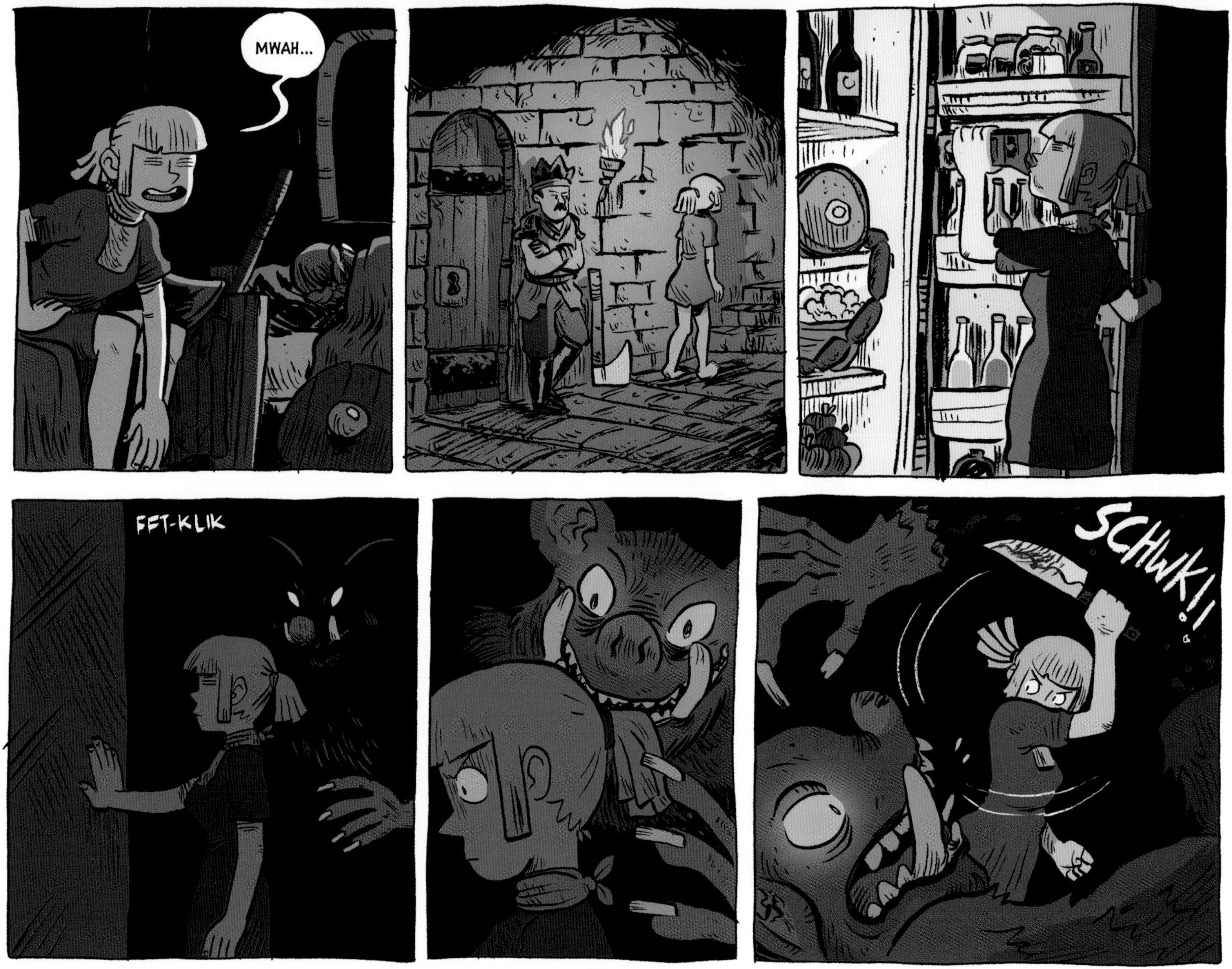
MWAH...
FFT-KLIK
SCHWK!!

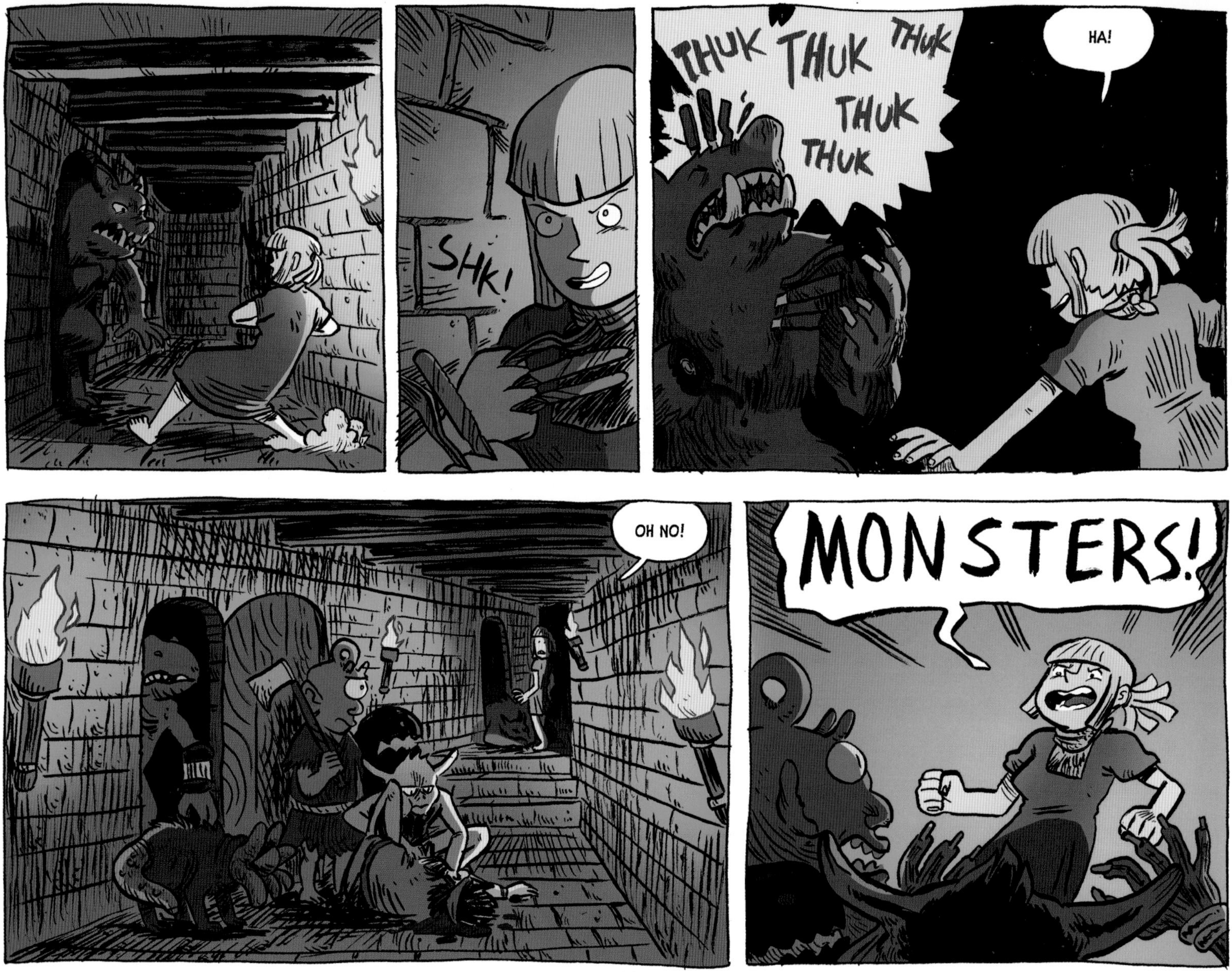
SHK!
THUK THUK THUK THUK THUK
HA!
OH NO!
MONSTERS!

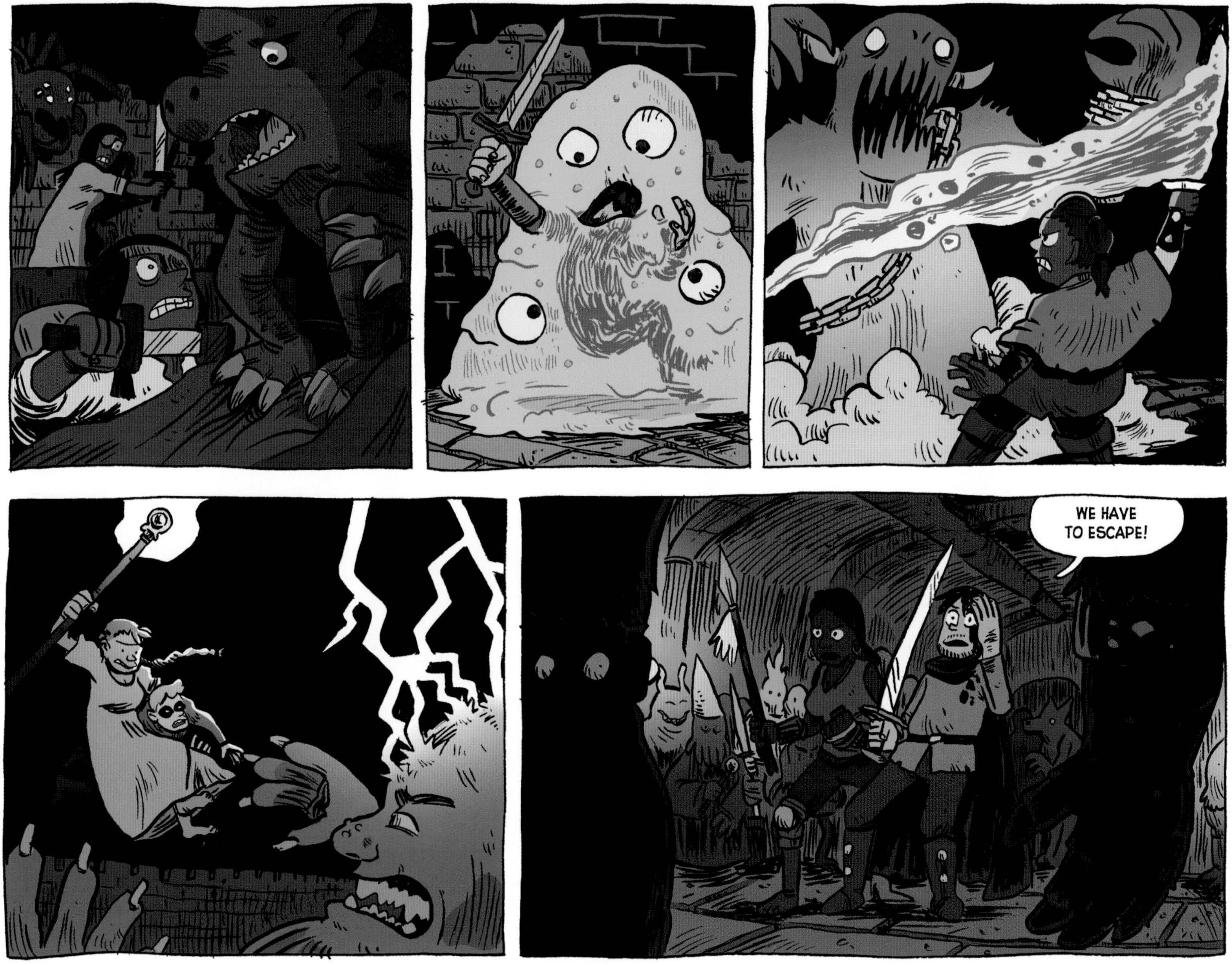
WE HAVE TO ESCAPE!

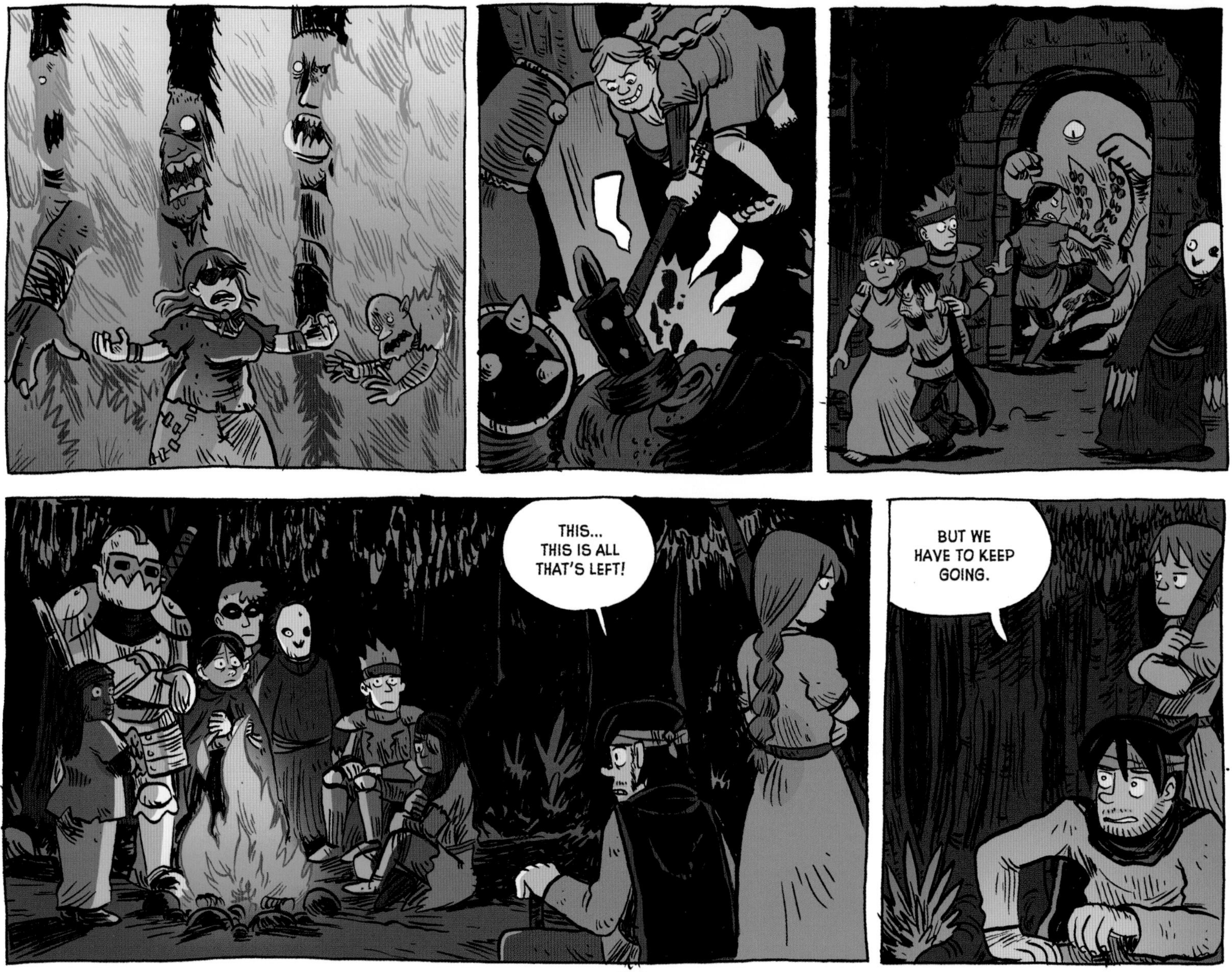
THIS... THIS IS ALL THAT'S LEFT!
BUT WE HAVE TO KEEP GOING.

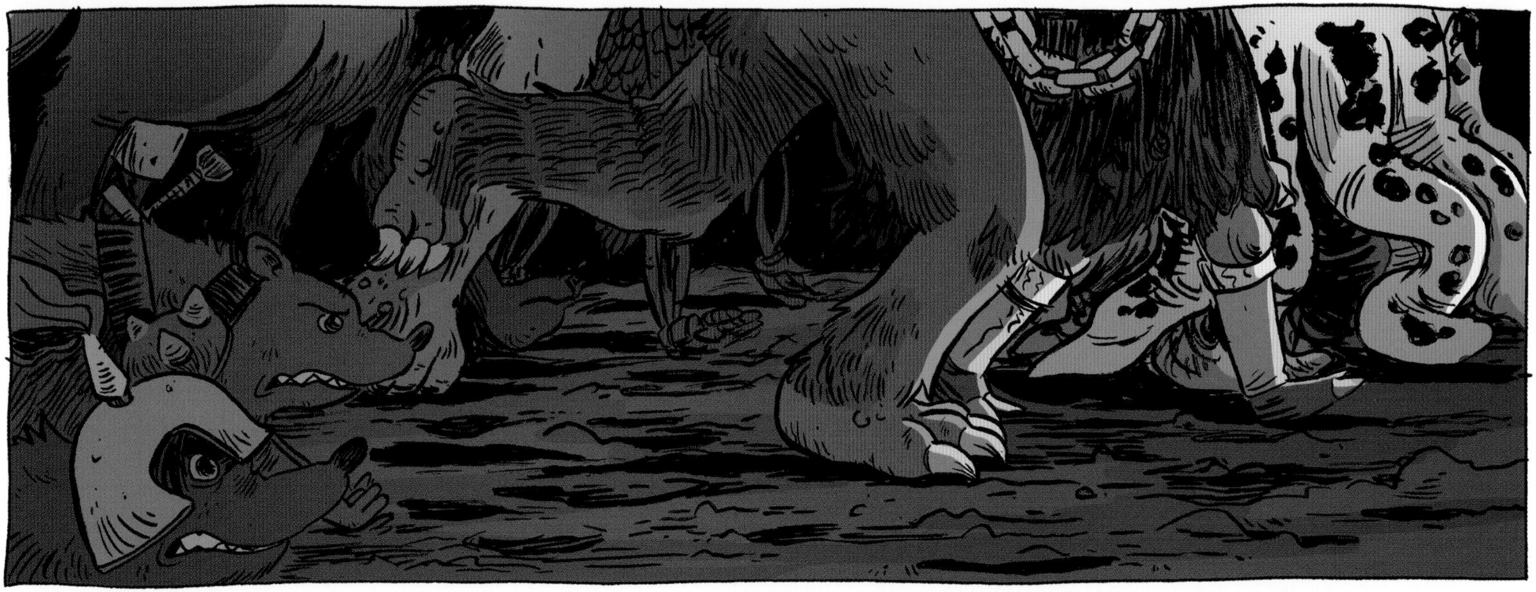

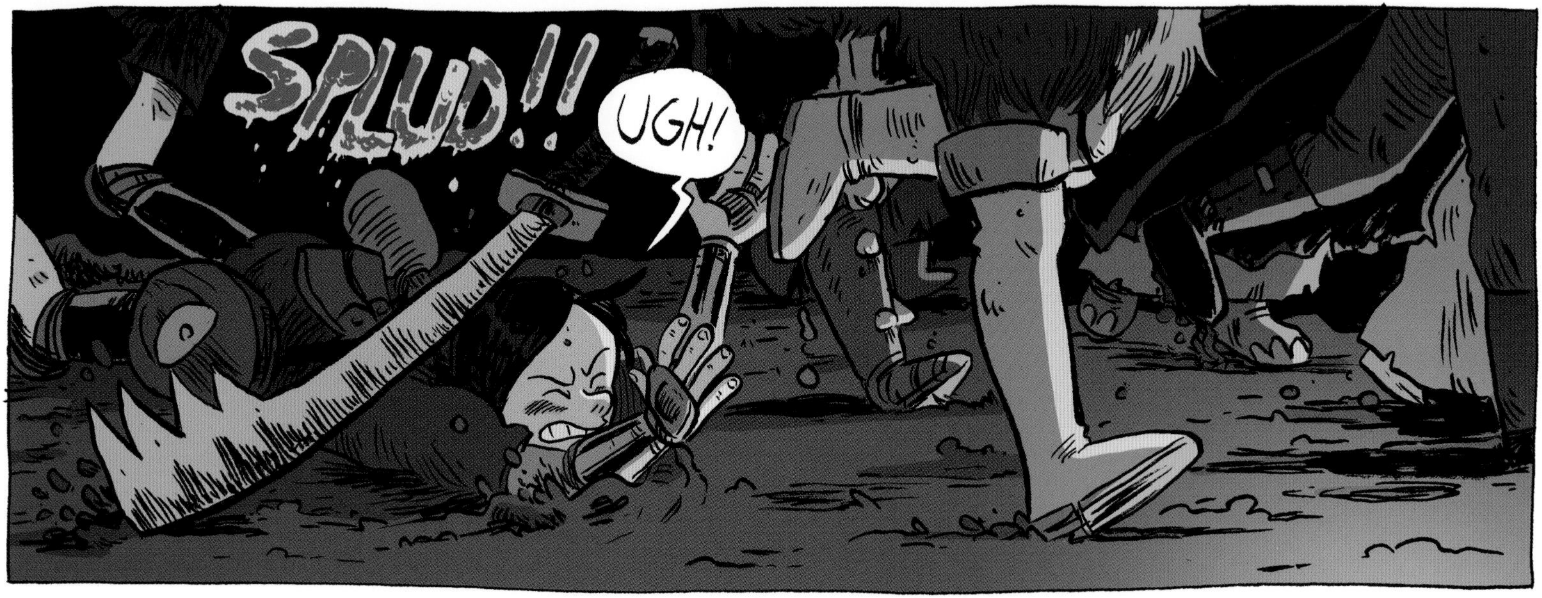
SPLUD!!
UGH!

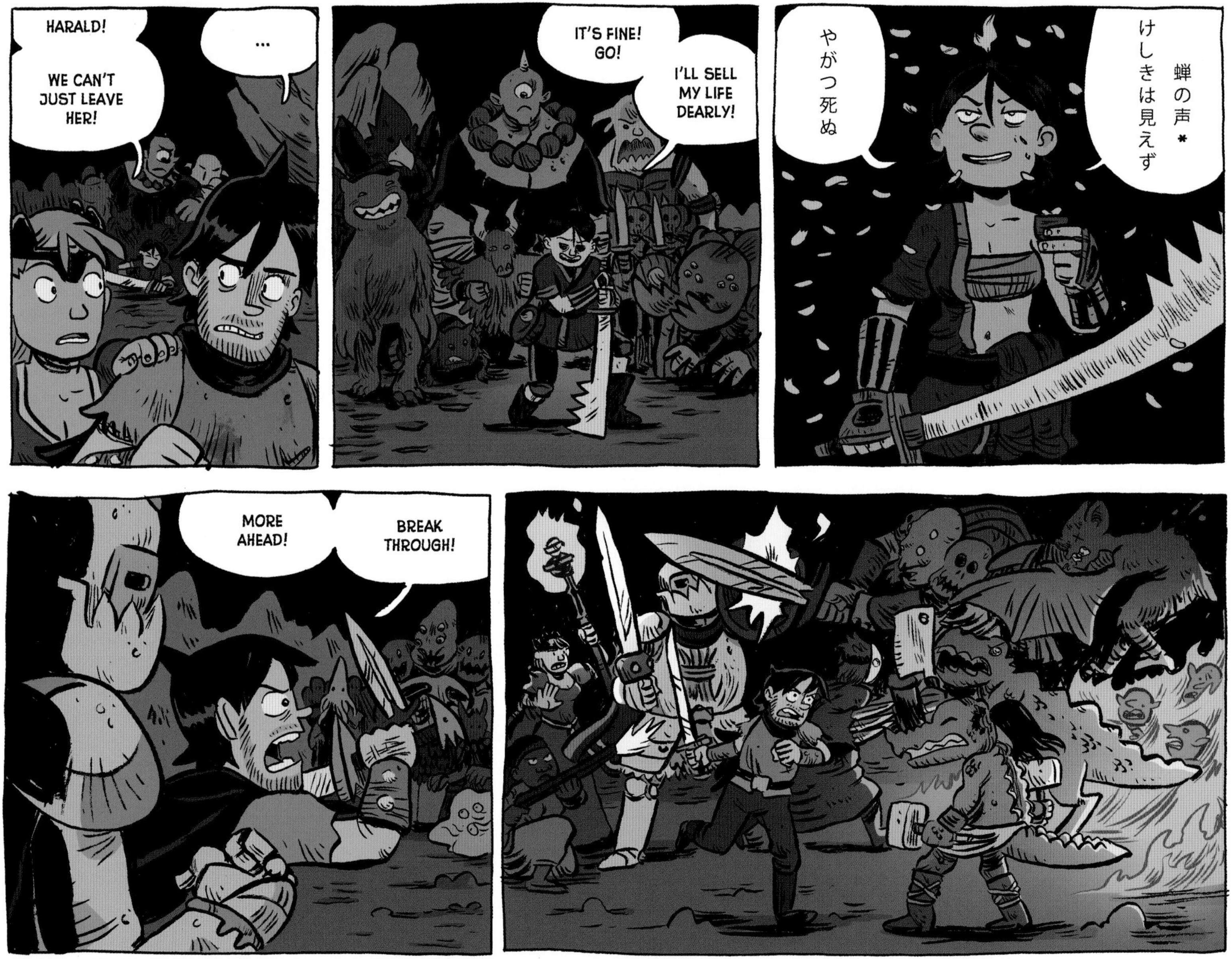
HARALD!
WE CAN'T JUST LEAVE HER!
...
IT'S FINE! GO!
I'LL SELL MY LIFE DEARLY!
やがつ死ぬ
蝉の声* けしきは見えず
MORE AHEAD!
BREAK THROUGH!

* BASHO, 17TH CENTURY "NOTHING IN THE VOICE OF THE CICADA INTIMATES HOW SOON IT WILL DIE."

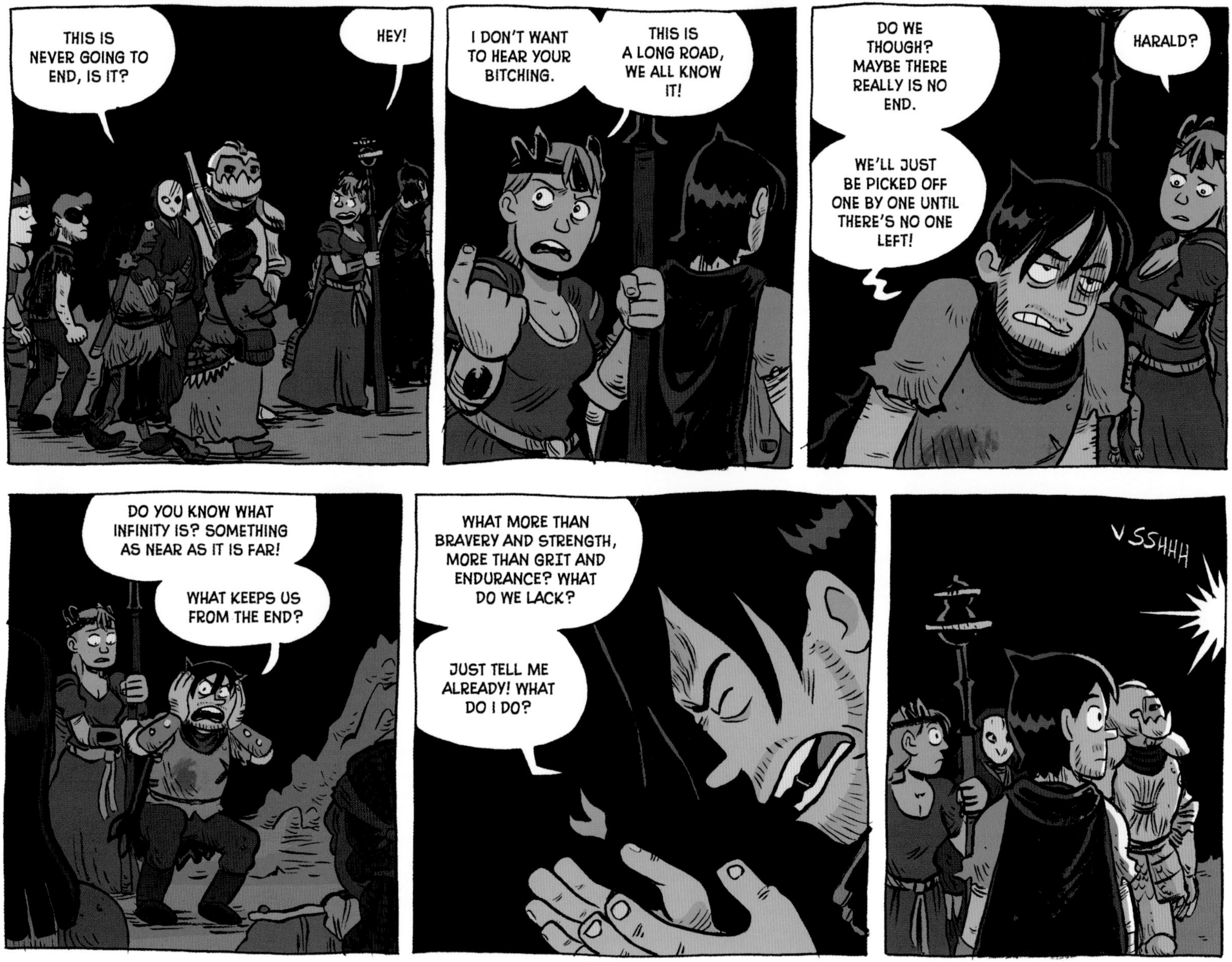
THIS IS NEVER GOING TO END, IS IT?
HEY!
I DON'T WANT TO HEAR YOUR BITCHING.
THIS IS A LONG ROAD, WE ALL KNOW IT!
DO WE THOUGH? MAYBE THERE REALLY IS NO END.
WE'LL JUST BE PICKED OFF ONE BY ONE UNTIL THERE'S NO ONE LEFT!
HARALD?
DO YOU KNOW WHAT INFINITY IS? SOMETHING AS NEAR AS IT IS FAR!
WHAT KEEPS US FROM THE END?
WHAT MORE THAN BRAVERY AND STRENGTH, MORE THAN GRIT AND ENDURANCE? WHAT DO WE LACK?
JUST TELL ME ALREADY! WHAT DO I DO?
VSSHHH

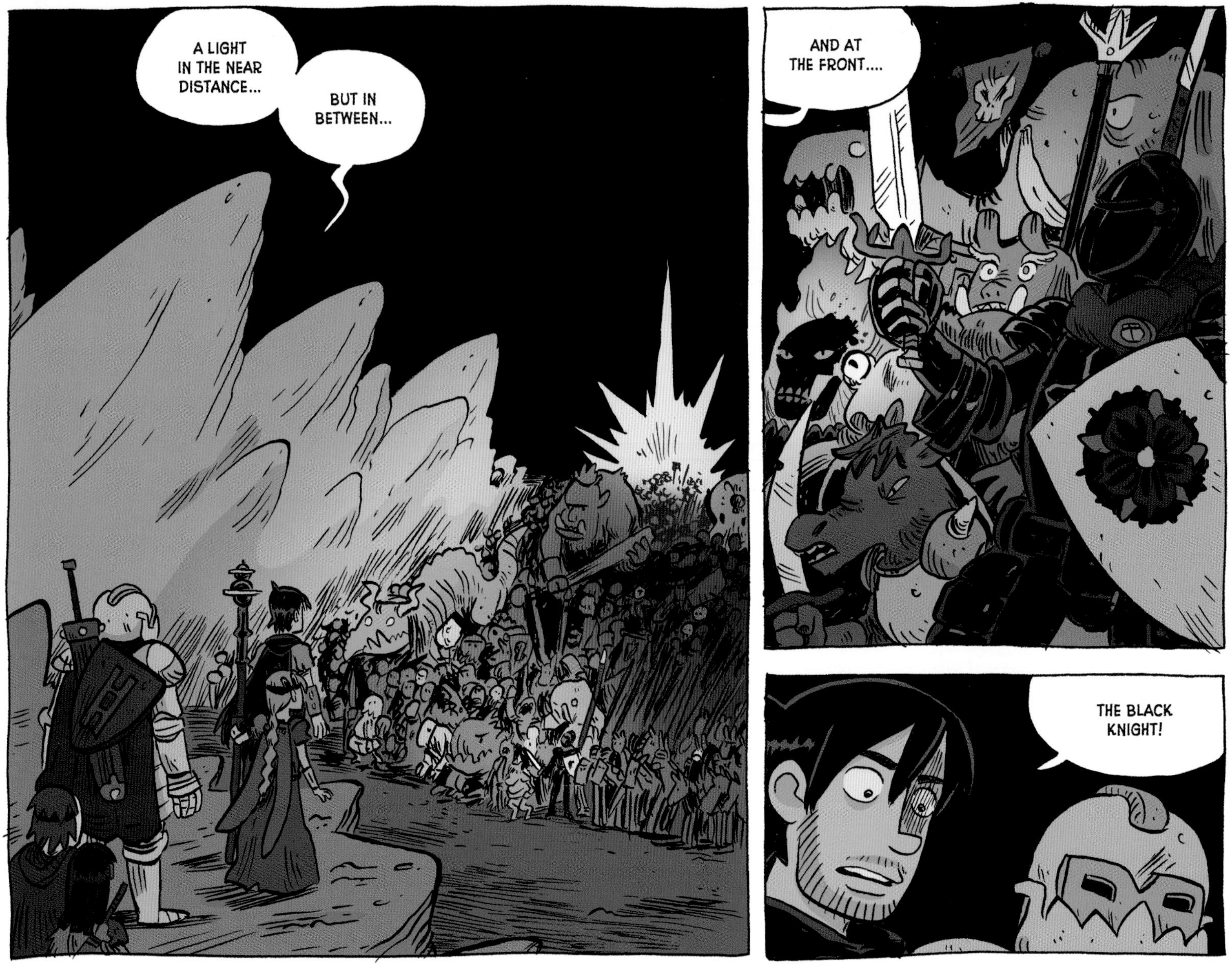
A LIGHT IN THE NEAR DISTANCE...
BUT IN BETWEEN...
AND AT THE FRONT....
THE BLACK KNIGHT!

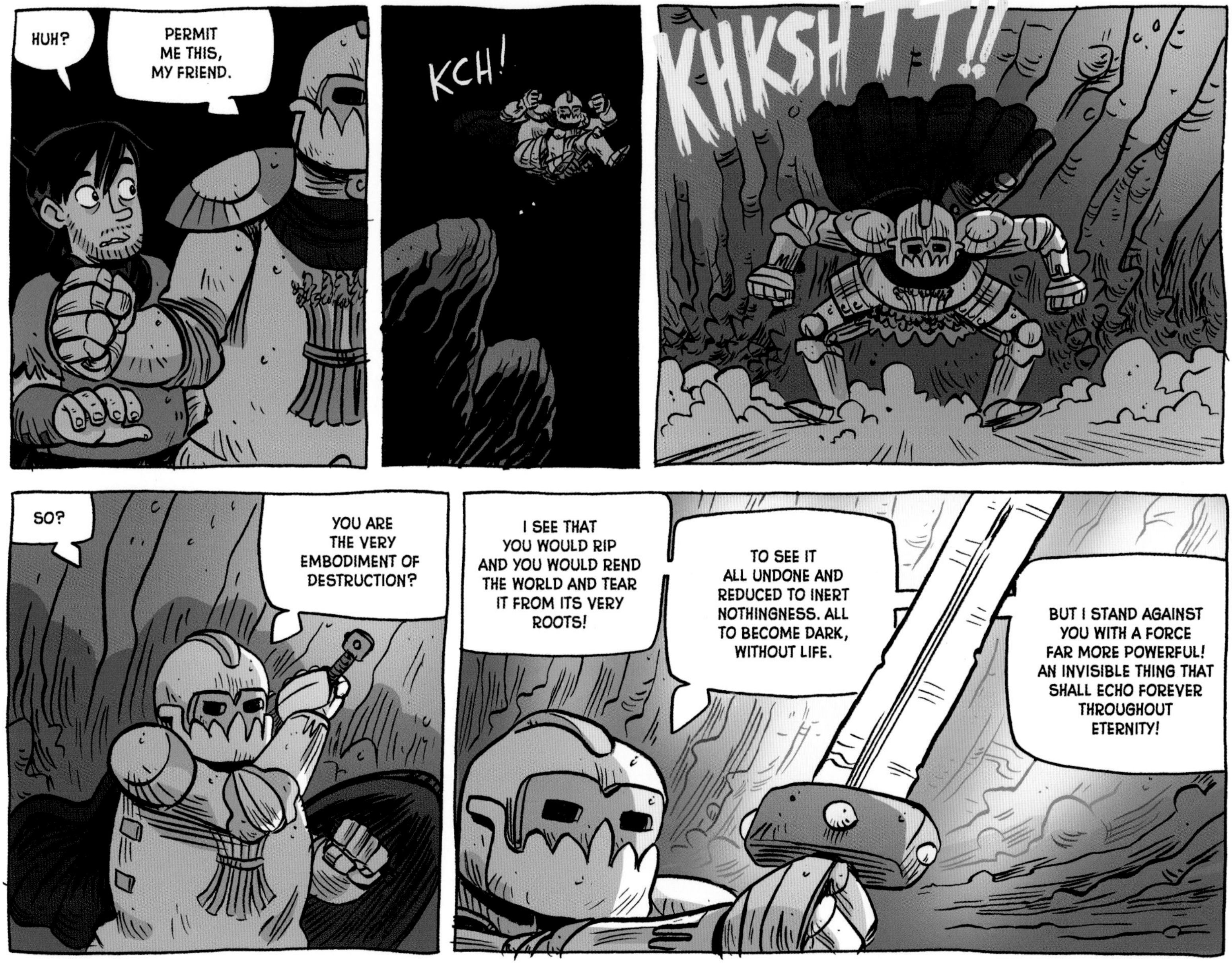
HUH?
PERMIT ME THIS, MY FRIEND.
KCH!
KHKSH T T!!
SO?
YOU ARE THE VERY EMBODIMENT OF DESTRUCTION?
I SEE THAT YOU WOULD RIP AND YOU WOULD REND THE WORLD AND TEAR IT FROM ITS VERY ROOTS!
TO SEE IT ALL UNDONE AND REDUCED TO INERT NOTHINGNESS. ALL TO BECOME DARK, WITHOUT LIFE.
BUT I STAND AGAINST YOU WITH A FORCE FAR MORE POWERFUL! AN INVISIBLE THING THAT SHALL ECHO FOREVER THROUGHOUT ETERNITY!

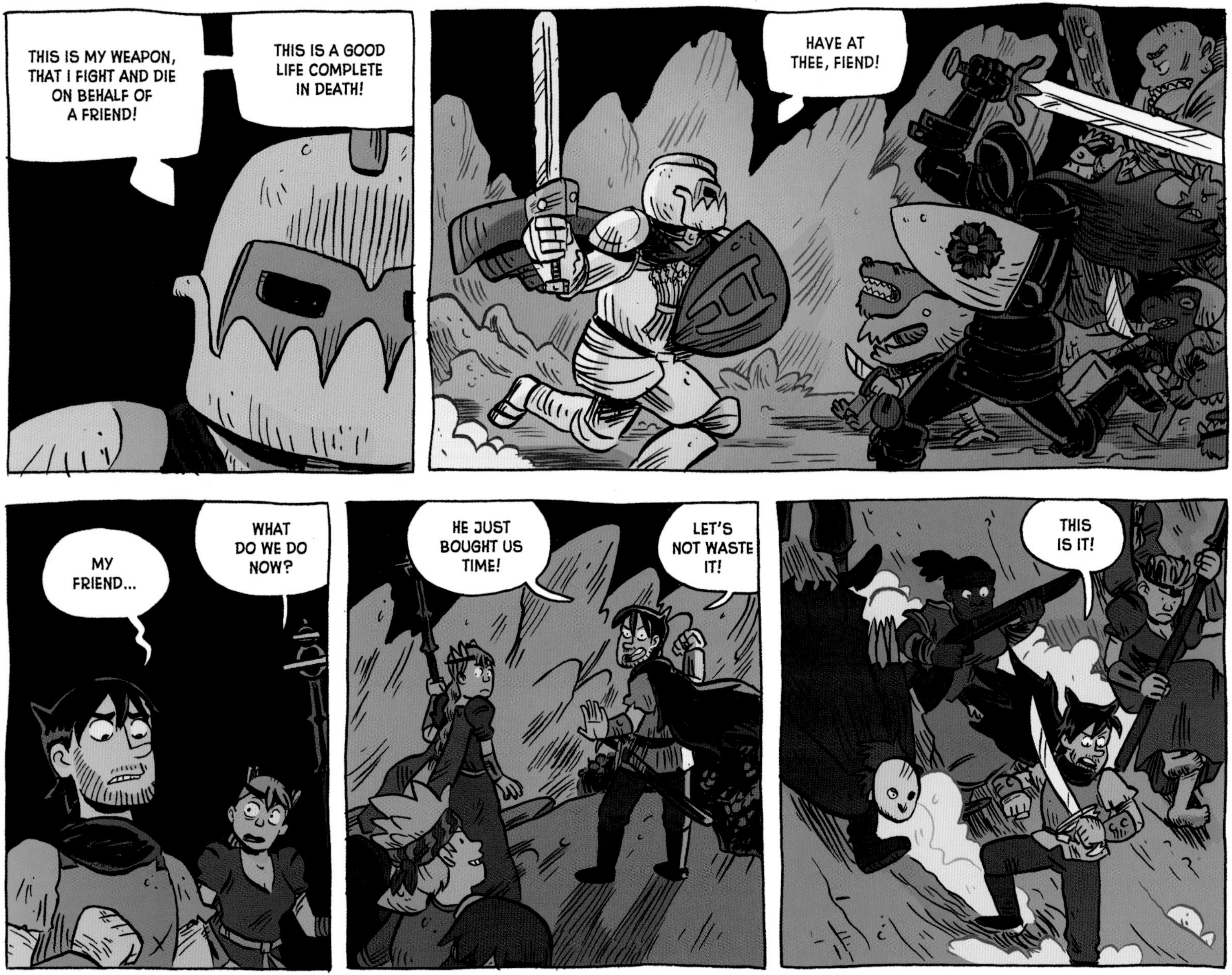
THIS IS MY WEAPON, THAT I FIGHT AND DIE ON BEHALF OF A FRIEND!
THIS IS A GOOD LIFE COMPLETE IN DEATH!
HAVE AT THEE, FIEND!
MY FRIEND...
WHAT DO WE DO NOW?
HE JUST BOUGHT US TIME!
LET'S NOT WASTE IT!
THIS IS IT!

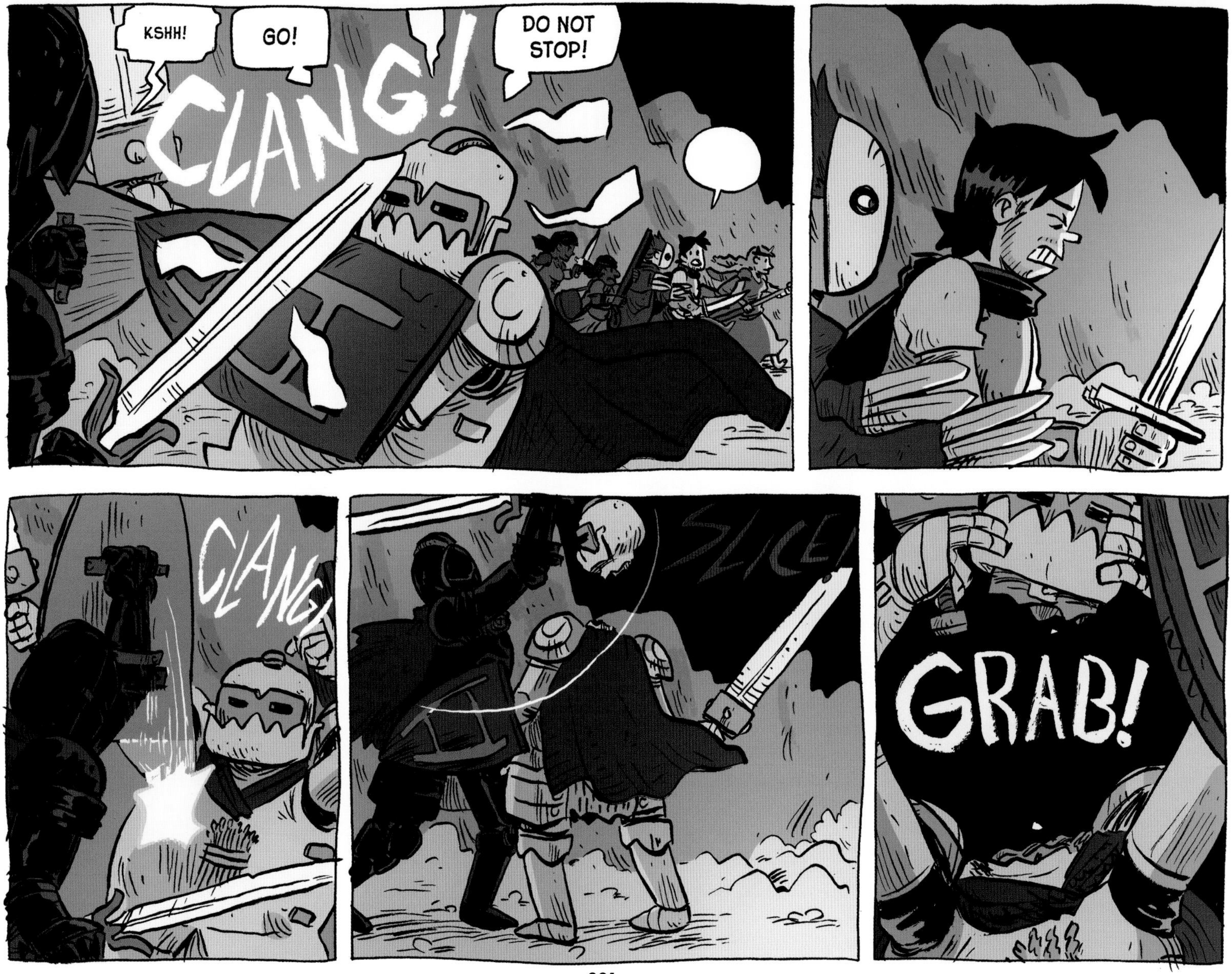
KSHH!
GO!
CLANG!
DO NOT STOP!
CLANG!
SLICE
GRAB!

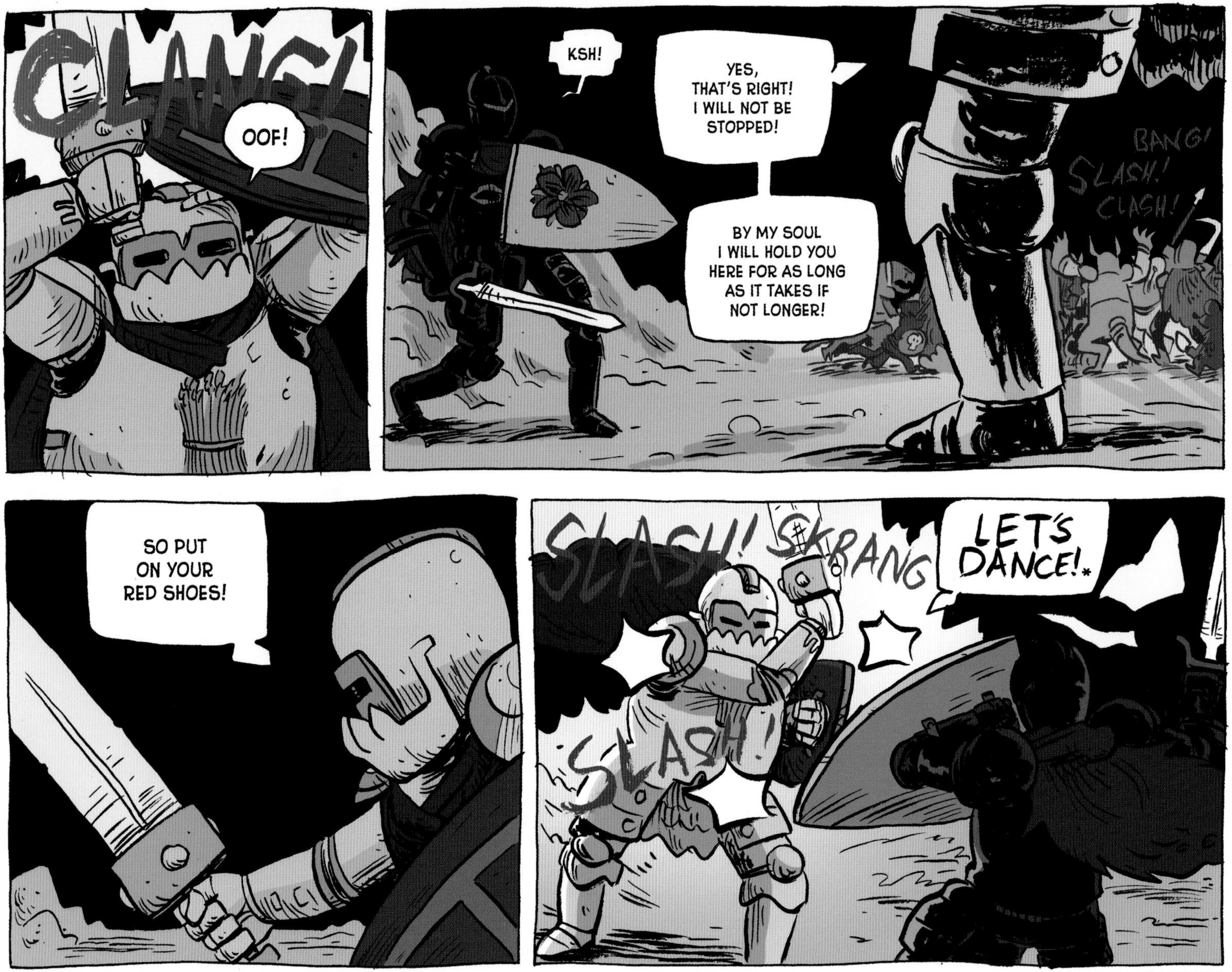
CLANG!
OOF!
KSH!
YES, THAT'S RIGHT! I WILL NOT BE STOPPED!
BY MY SOUL I WILL HOLD YOU HERE FOR AS LONG AS IT TAKES IF NOT LONGER!
BANG!
SLASH!
CLASH!
SO PUT ON YOUR RED SHOES!
SLASH!
SKRANG
LET'S DANCE!*
SLASH!

* DAVID BOWIE?!

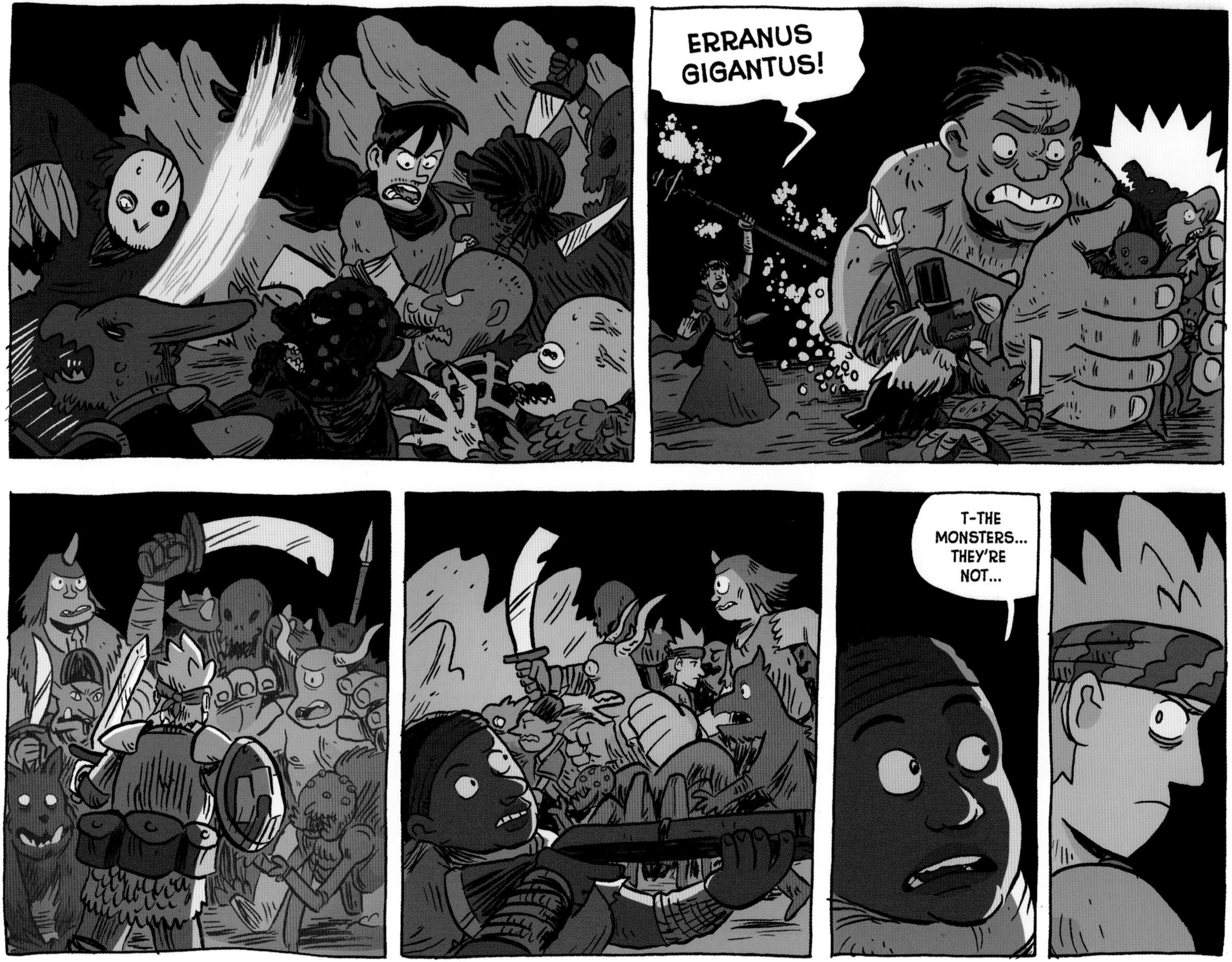
ERRANUS GIGANTUS!
T-THE MONSTERS... THEY'RE NOT...

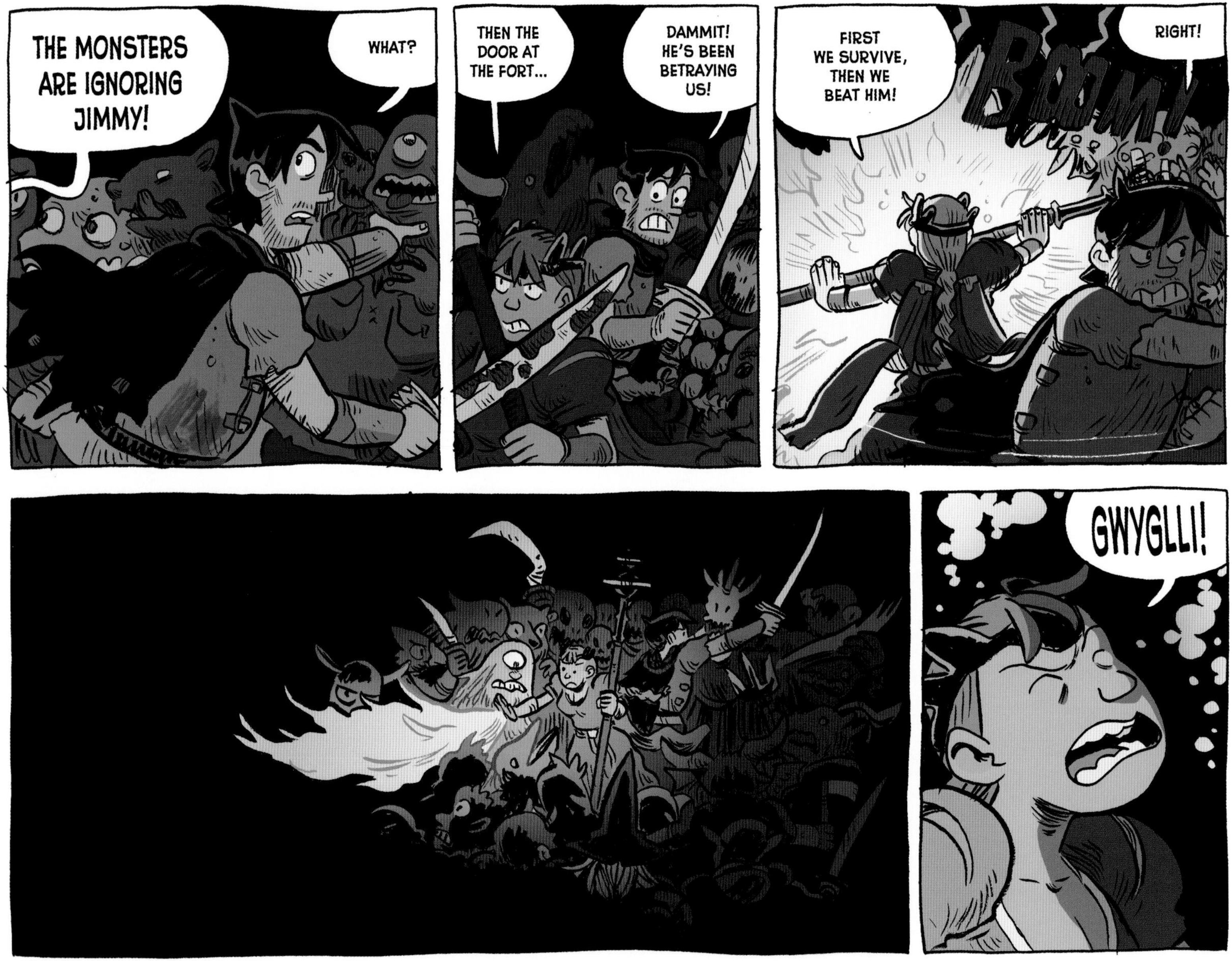
THE MONSTERS ARE IGNORING JIMMY!
WHAT?
THEN THE DOOR AT THE FORT...
DAMMIT! HE'S BEEN BETRAYING US!
FIRST WE SURVIVE, THEN WE BEAT HIM!
BOOM!
RIGHT!
GWYGLLI!

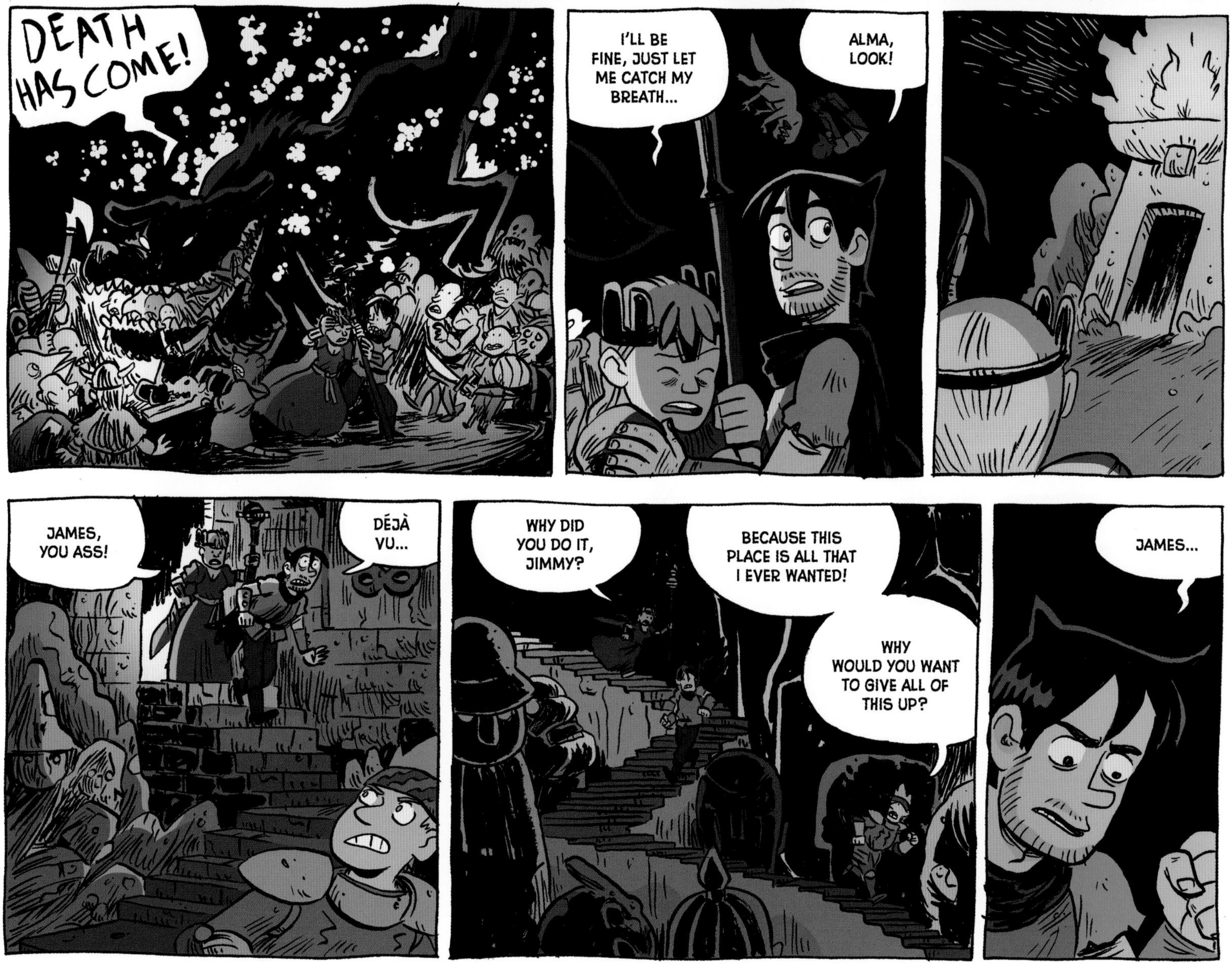
DEATH HAS COME!
I'LL BE FINE, JUST LET ME CATCH MY BREATH...
ALMA, LOOK!
JAMES, YOU ASS!
DÉJÀ VU...
WHY DID YOU DO IT, JIMMY?
BECAUSE THIS PLACE IS ALL THAT I EVER WANTED!
WHY WOULD YOU WANT TO GIVE ALL OF THIS UP?
JAMES...

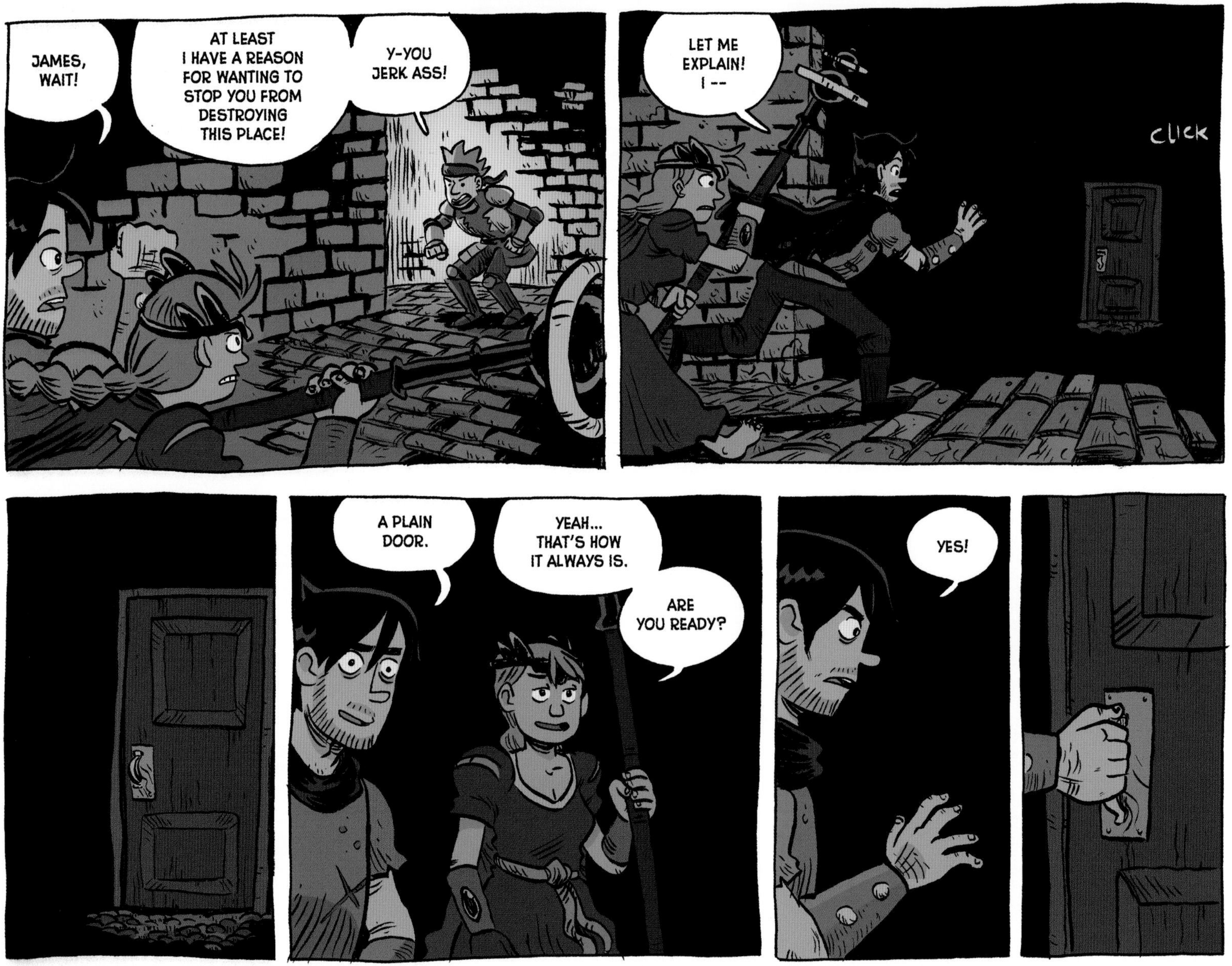
JAMES, WAIT!
AT LEAST I HAVE A REASON FOR WANTING TO STOP YOU FROM DESTROYING THIS PLACE!
Y-YOU JERK ASS!
LET ME EXPLAIN! I --
CLICK
A PLAIN DOOR.
YEAH... THAT'S HOW IT ALWAYS IS.
ARE YOU READY?
YES!

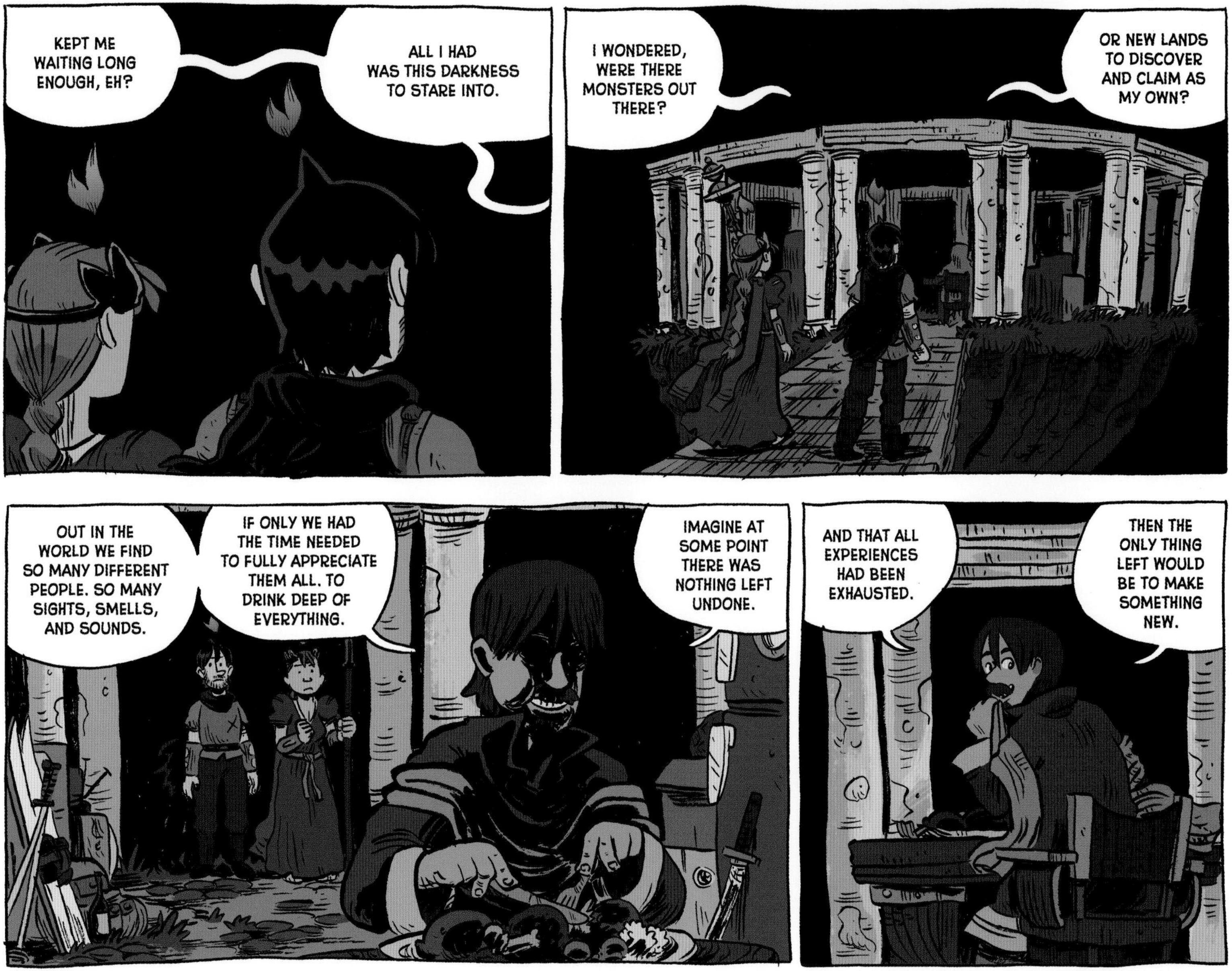
KEPT ME WAITING LONG ENOUGH, EH?
ALL I HAD WAS THIS DARKNESS TO STARE INTO.
I WONDERED, WERE THERE MONSTERS OUT THERE?
OR NEW LANDS TO DISCOVER AND CLAIM AS MY OWN?
OUT IN THE WORLD WE FIND SO MANY DIFFERENT PEOPLE. SO MANY SIGHTS, SMELLS, AND SOUNDS.
IF ONLY WE HAD THE TIME NEEDED TO FULLY APPRECIATE THEM ALL. TO DRINK DEEP OF EVERYTHING.
IMAGINE AT SOME POINT THERE WAS NOTHING LEFT UNDONE.
AND THAT ALL EXPERIENCES HAD BEEN EXHAUSTED.
THEN THE ONLY THING LEFT WOULD BE TO MAKE SOMETHING NEW.

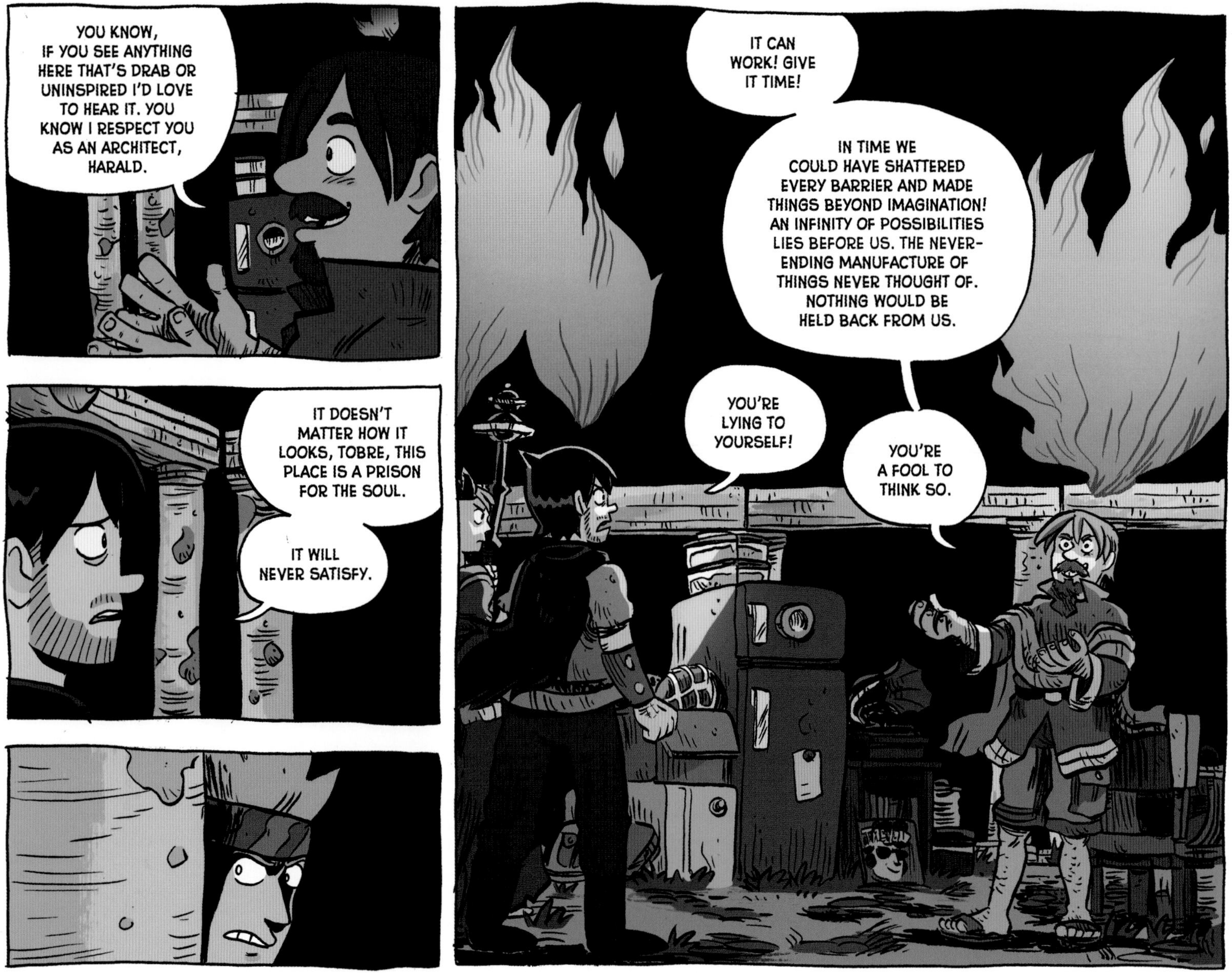
YOU KNOW, IF YOU SEE ANYTHING HERE THAT'S DRAB OR UNINSPIRED I'D LOVE TO HEAR IT. YOU KNOW I RESPECT YOU AS AN ARCHITECT, HARALD.
IT DOESN'T MATTER HOW IT LOOKS, TOBRE, THIS PLACE IS A PRISON FOR THE SOUL.
IT WILL NEVER SATISFY.
IT CAN WORK! GIVE IT TIME!
IN TIME WE COULD HAVE SHATTERED EVERY BARRIER AND MADE THINGS BEYOND IMAGINATION! AN INFINITY OF POSSIBILITIES LIES BEFORE US. THE NEVER-ENDING MANUFACTURE OF THINGS NEVER THOUGHT OF. NOTHING WOULD BE HELD BACK FROM US.
YOU'RE LYING TO YOURSELF!
YOU'RE A FOOL TO THINK SO.

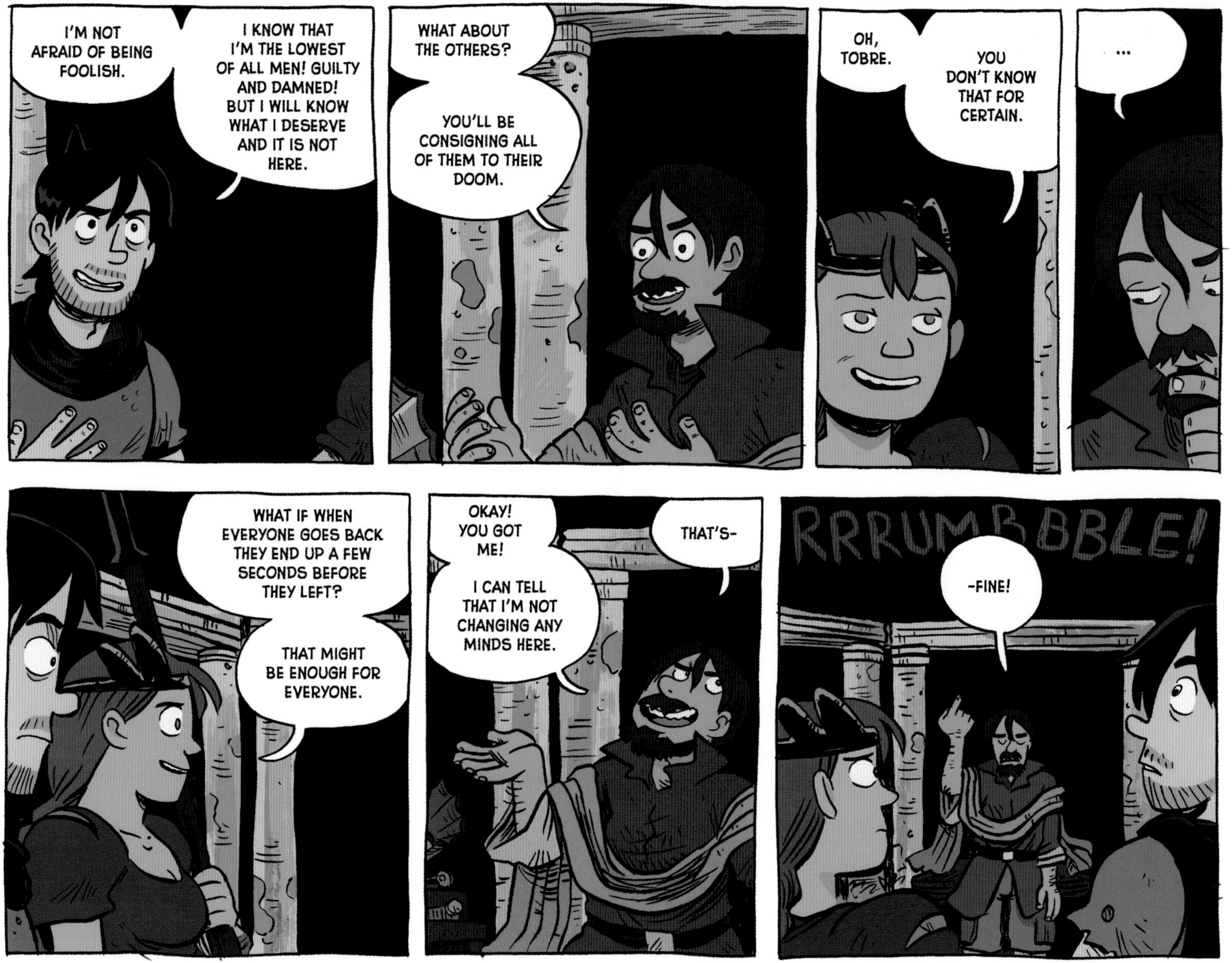
I'M NOT AFRAID OF BEING FOOLISH.
I KNOW THAT I'M THE LOWEST OF ALL MEN! GUILTY AND DAMNED! BUT I WILL KNOW WHAT I DESERVE AND IT IS NOT HERE.
WHAT ABOUT THE OTHERS?
YOU'LL BE CONSIGNING ALL OF THEM TO THEIR DOOM.
OH, TOBRE.
YOU DON'T KNOW THAT FOR CERTAIN.
...
WHAT IF WHEN EVERYONE GOES BACK THEY END UP A FEW SECONDS BEFORE THEY LEFT?
THAT MIGHT BE ENOUGH FOR EVERYONE.
OKAY! YOU GOT ME!
I CAN TELL THAT I'M NOT CHANGING ANY MINDS HERE.
THAT'S-
RRRUMBBBLE!
-FINE!

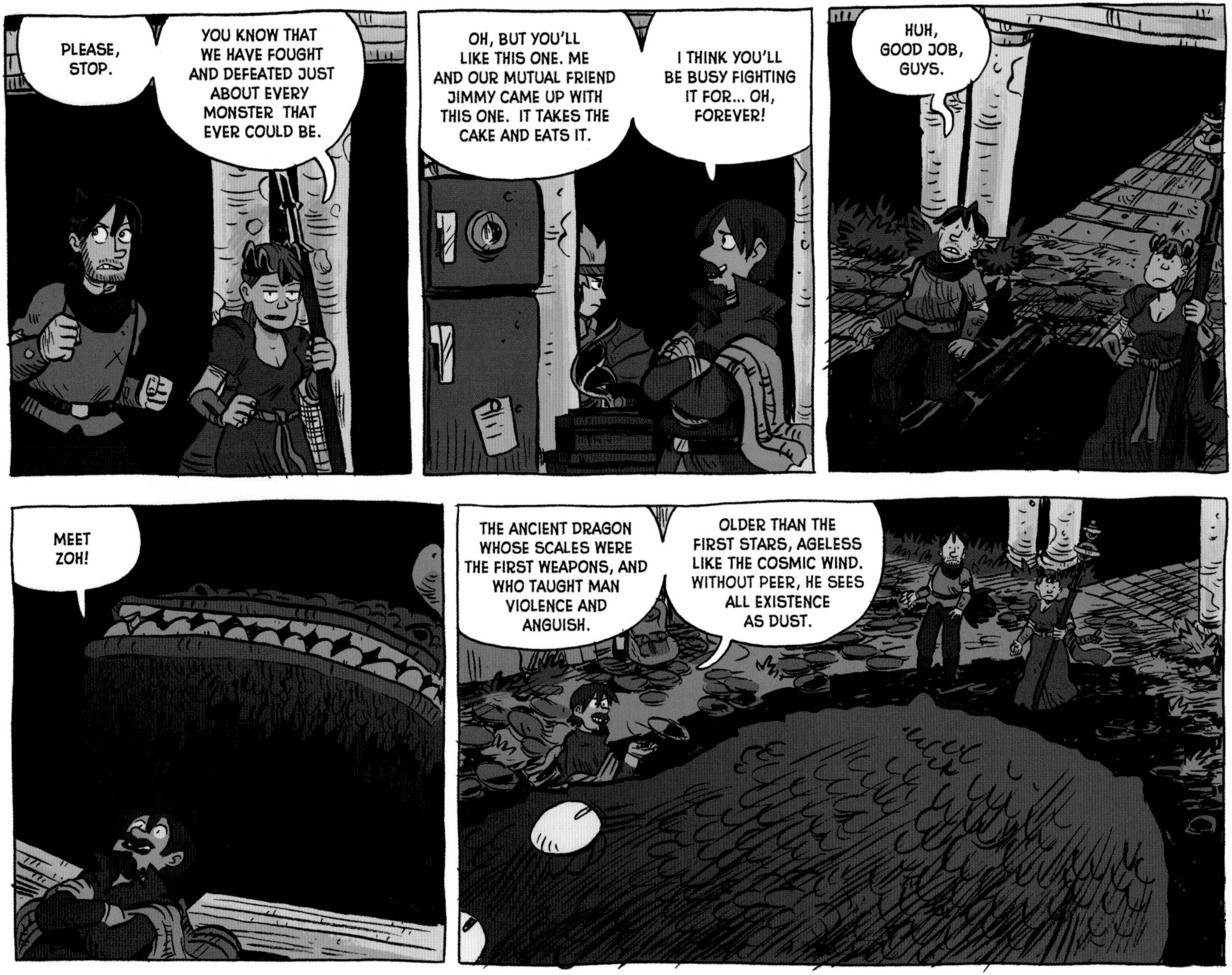
PLEASE, STOP.
YOU KNOW THAT WE HAVE FOUGHT AND DEFEATED JUST ABOUT EVERY MONSTER THAT EVER COULD BE.
OH, BUT YOU'LL LIKE THIS ONE. ME AND OUR MUTUAL FRIEND JIMMY CAME UP WITH THIS ONE. IT TAKES THE CAKE AND EATS IT.
I THINK YOU'LL BE BUSY FIGHTING IT FOR... OH, FOREVER!
HUH, GOOD JOB, GUYS.
MEET ZOH!
THE ANCIENT DRAGON WHOSE SCALES WERE THE FIRST WEAPONS, AND WHO TAUGHT MAN VIOLENCE AND ANGUISH.
OLDER THAN THE FIRST STARS, AGELESS LIKE THE COSMIC WIND. WITHOUT PEER, HE SEES ALL EXISTENCE AS DUST.

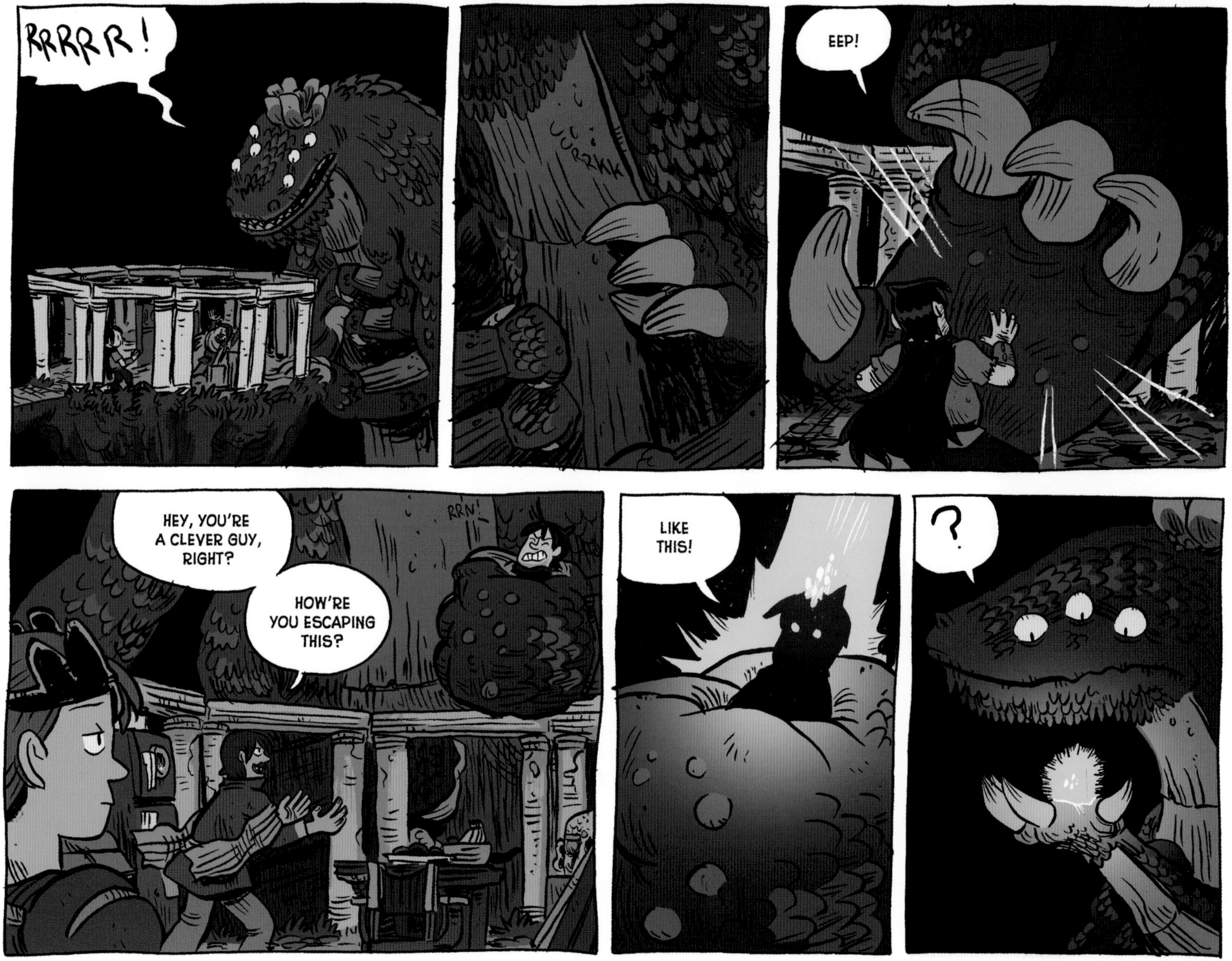
RRRRR!
URRKK
EEP!
HEY, YOU'RE A CLEVER GUY, RIGHT?
RRN!
HOW'RE YOU ESCAPING THIS?
LIKE THIS!
?

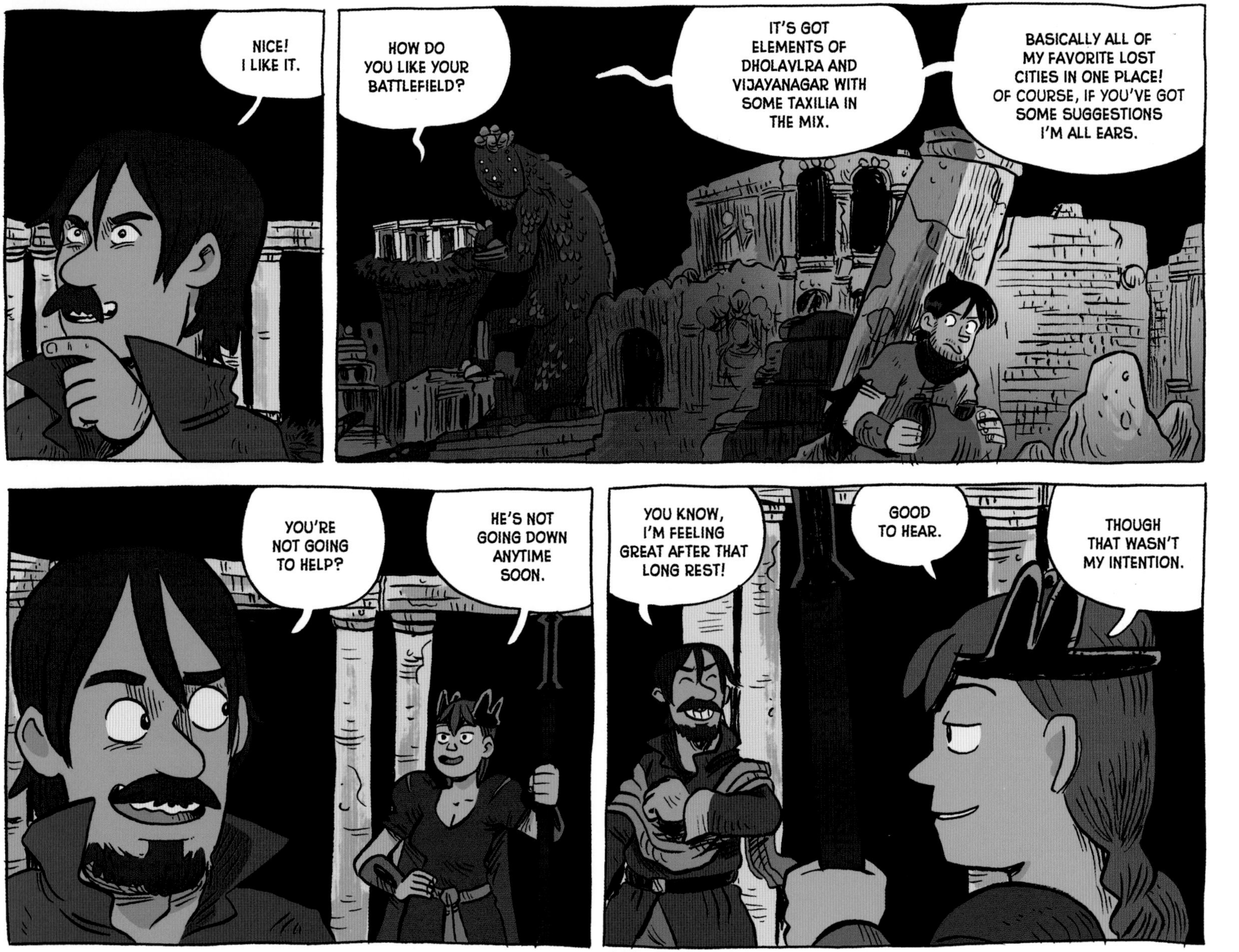
NICE! I LIKE IT.
HOW DO YOU LIKE YOUR BATTLEFIELD?
IT'S GOT ELEMENTS OF DHOLAVLRA AND VIJAYANAGAR WITH SOME TAXILIA IN THE MIX.
BASICALLY ALL OF MY FAVORITE LOST CITIES IN ONE PLACE! OF COURSE, IF YOU'VE GOT SOME SUGGESTIONS I'M ALL EARS.
YOU'RE NOT GOING TO HELP?
HE'S NOT GOING DOWN ANYTIME SOON.
YOU KNOW, I'M FEELING GREAT AFTER THAT LONG REST!
GOOD TO HEAR.
THOUGH THAT WASN'T MY INTENTION.

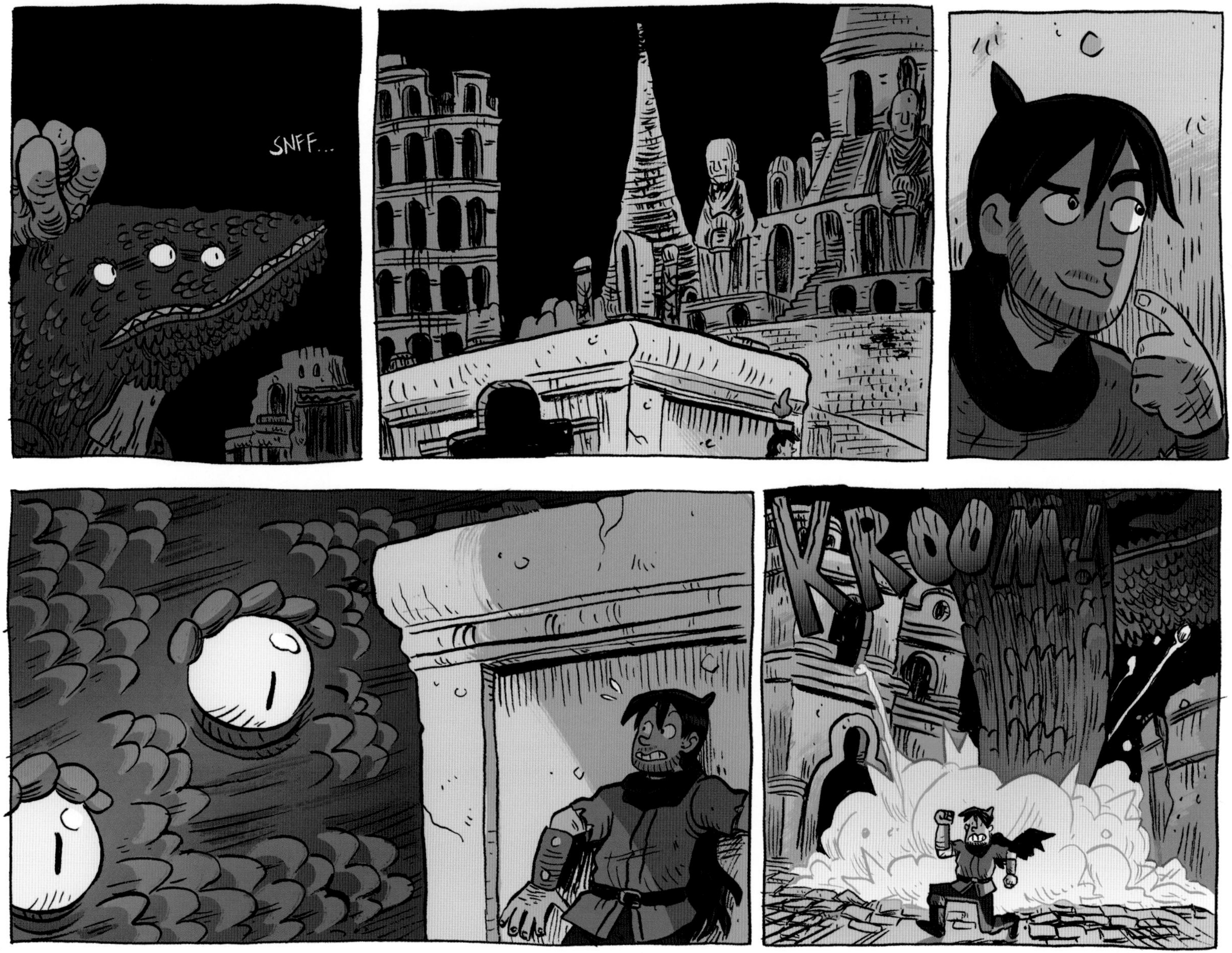
SNFF...
KROOM!

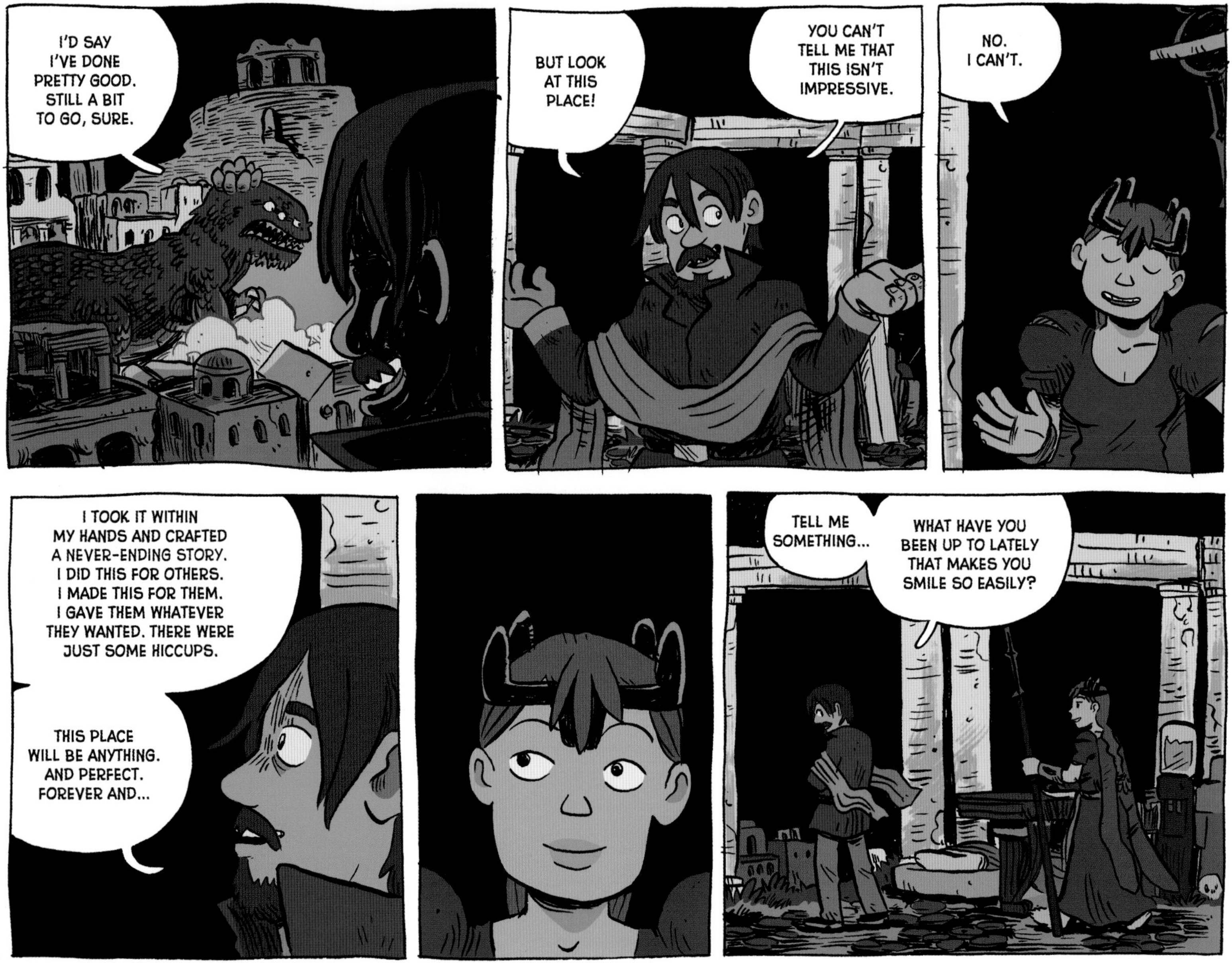
I'D SAY I'VE DONE PRETTY GOOD. STILL A BIT TO GO, SURE.
BUT LOOK AT THIS PLACE!
YOU CAN'T TELL ME THAT THIS ISN'T IMPRESSIVE.
NO. I CAN'T.
I TOOK IT WITHIN MY HANDS AND CRAFTED A NEVER-ENDING STORY. I DID THIS FOR OTHERS. I MADE THIS FOR THEM. I GAVE THEM WHATEVER THEY WANTED. THERE WERE JUST SOME HICCUPS.
THIS PLACE WILL BE ANYTHING. AND PERFECT. FOREVER AND...
TELL ME SOMETHING...
WHAT HAVE YOU BEEN UP TO LATELY THAT MAKES YOU SMILE SO EASILY?

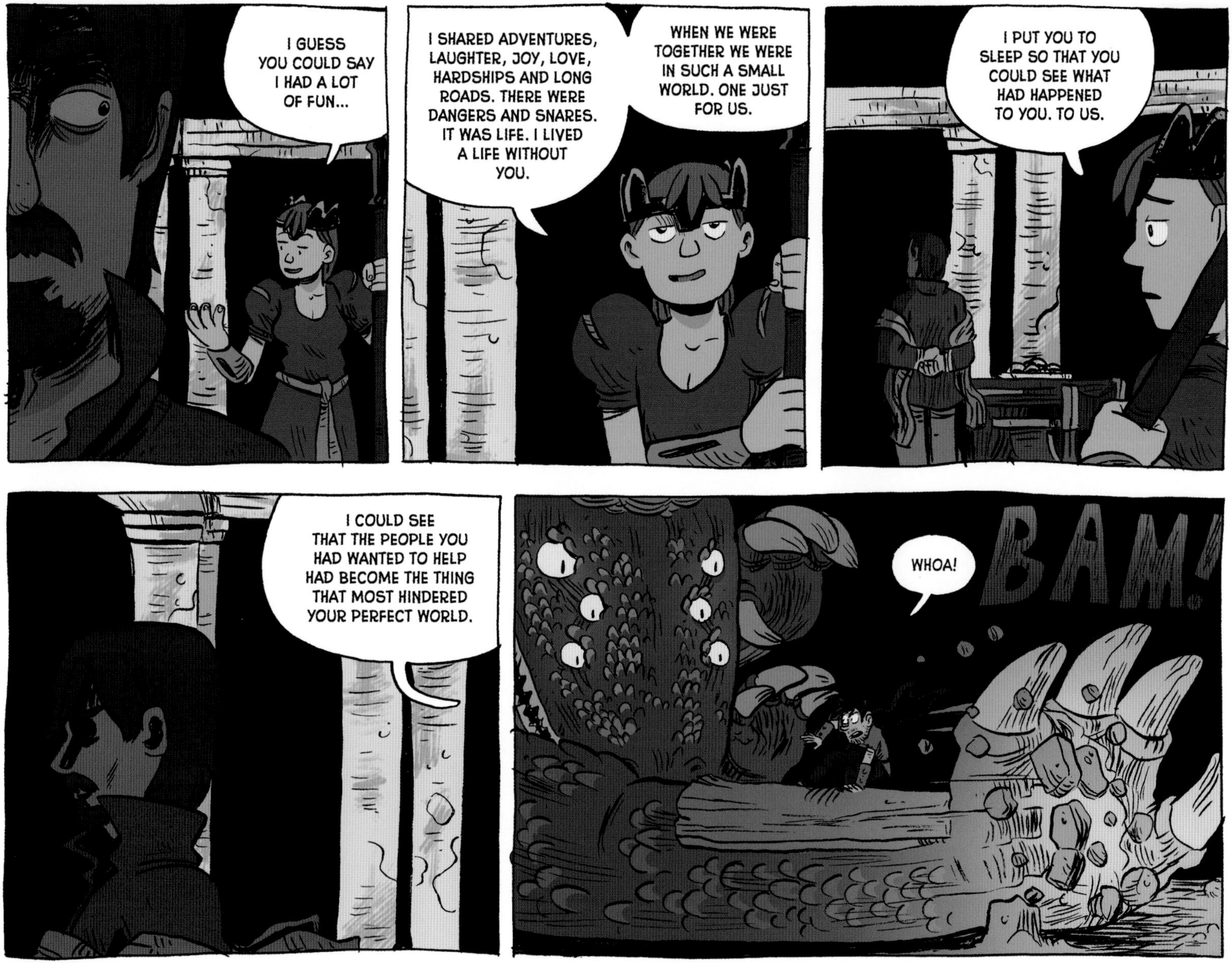
I GUESS YOU COULD SAY I HAD A LOT OF FUN...
I SHARED ADVENTURES, LAUGHTER, JOY, LOVE, HARDSHIPS AND LONG ROADS. THERE WERE DANGERS AND SNARES. IT WAS LIFE. I LIVED A LIFE WITHOUT YOU.
WHEN WE WERE TOGETHER WE WERE IN SUCH A SMALL WORLD. ONE JUST FOR US.
I PUT YOU TO SLEEP SO THAT YOU COULD SEE WHAT HAD HAPPENED TO YOU. TO US.
I COULD SEE THAT THE PEOPLE YOU HAD WANTED TO HELP HAD BECOME THE THING THAT MOST HINDERED YOUR PERFECT WORLD.
WHOA!
BAM!

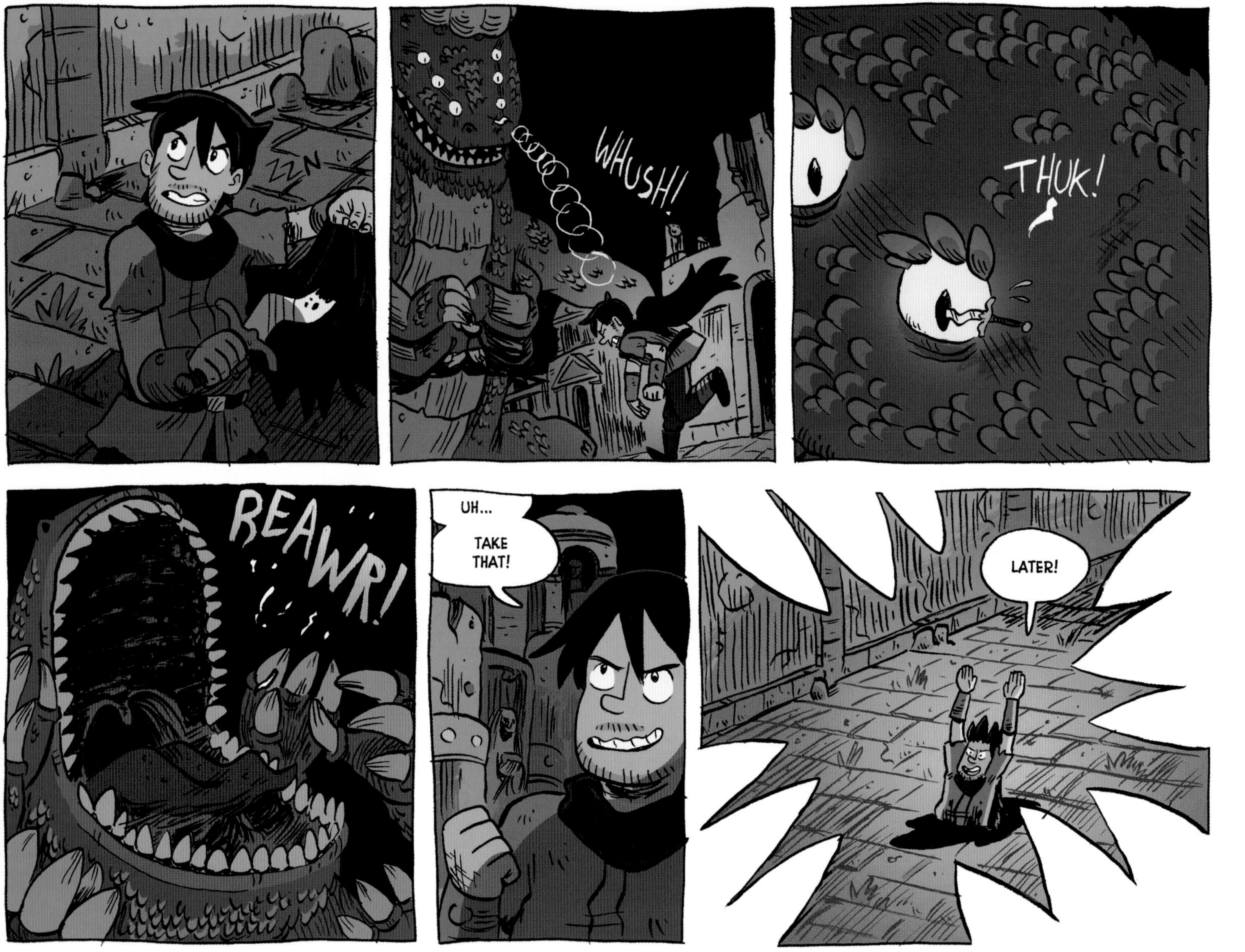

ZZN
WHUSH!
THUK!
REAWR!
UH... TAKE THAT!
LATER!

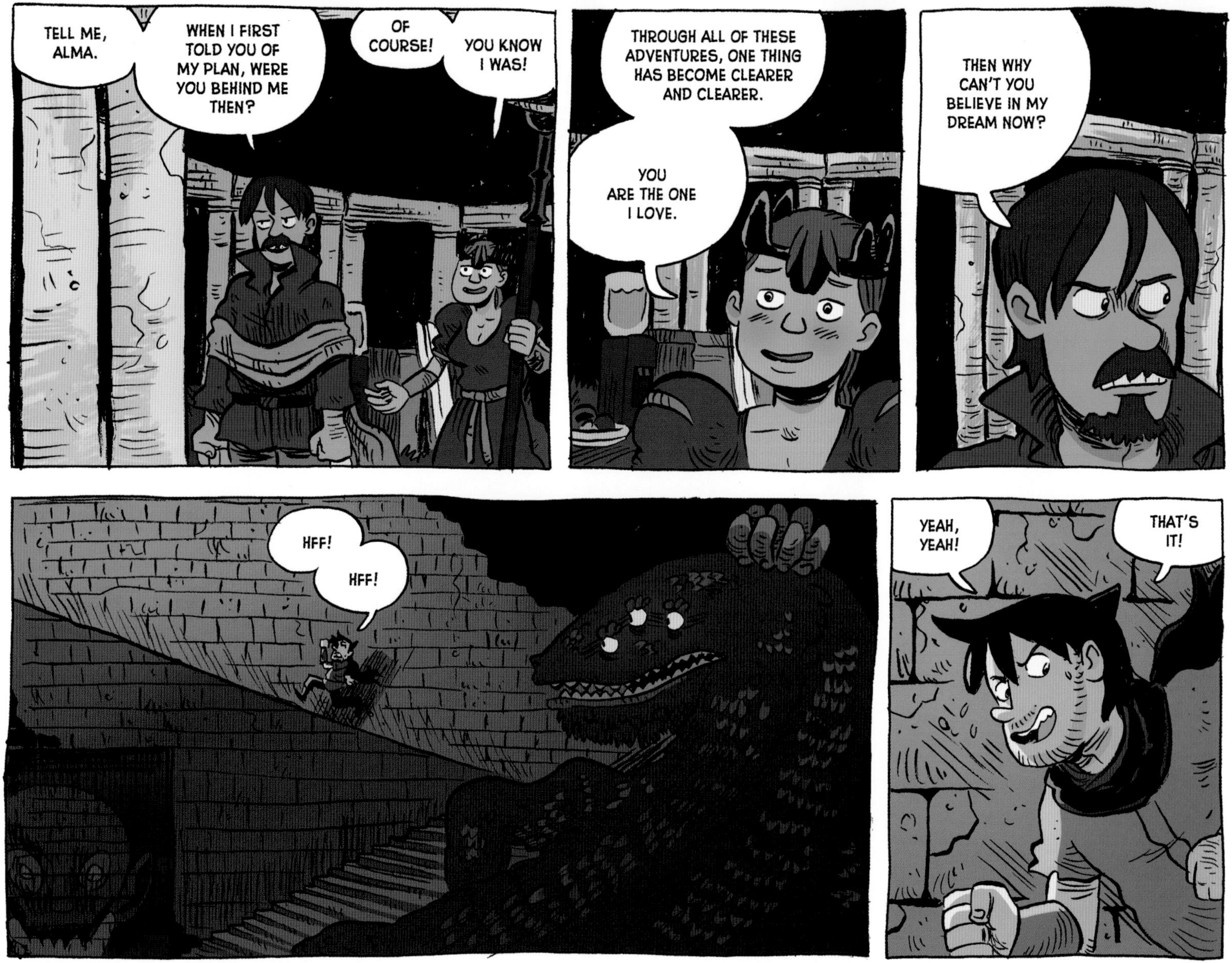
TELL ME, ALMA.
WHEN I FIRST TOLD YOU OF MY PLAN, WERE YOU BEHIND ME THEN?
OF COURSE!
YOU KNOW I WAS!
THROUGH ALL OF THESE ADVENTURES, ONE THING HAS BECOME CLEARER AND CLEARER.
YOU ARE THE ONE I LOVE.
THEN WHY CAN'T YOU BELIEVE IN MY DREAM NOW?
HFF!
HFF!
YEAH, YEAH!
THAT'S IT!

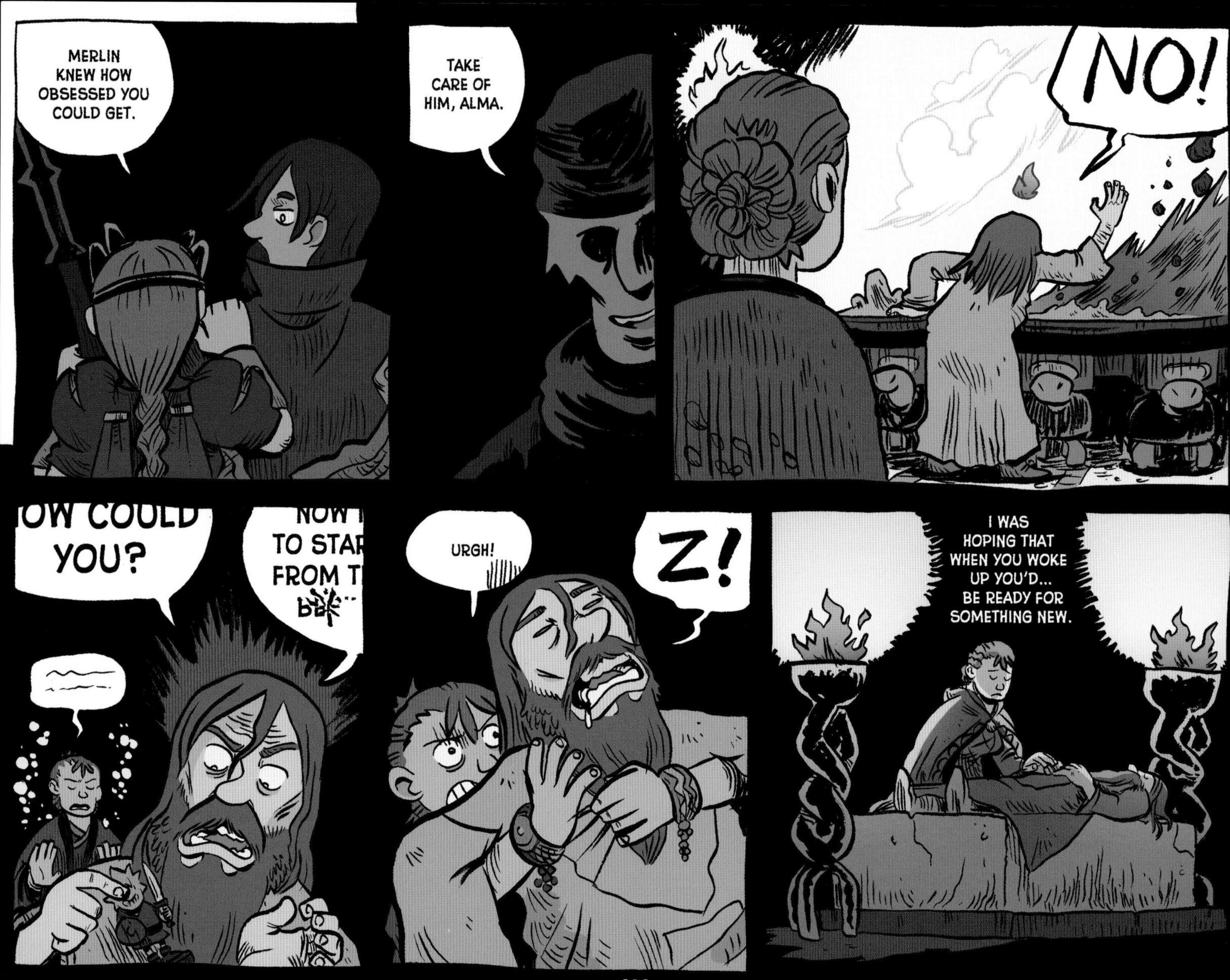

MERLIN KNEW HOW OBSESSED YOU COULD GET.
TAKE CARE OF HIM, ALMA.
NO!
OW COULD YOU?
NOW I
TO STAR
FROM T
URGH!
Z!
I WAS HOPING THAT WHEN YOU WOKE UP YOU'D... BE READY FOR SOMETHING NEW.

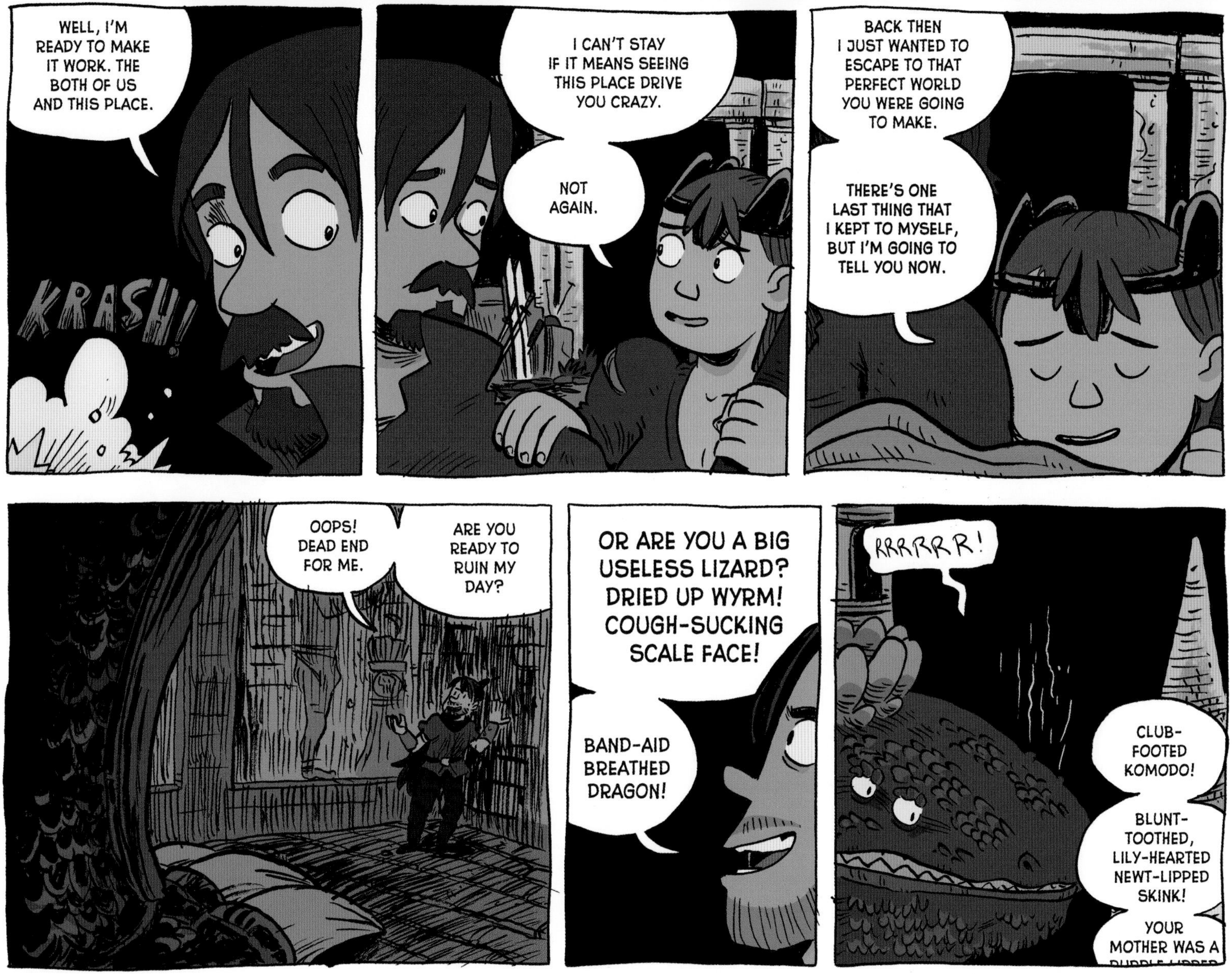
WELL, I'M READY TO MAKE IT WORK. THE BOTH OF US AND THIS PLACE.
KRASH!
I CAN'T STAY IF IT MEANS SEEING THIS PLACE DRIVE YOU CRAZY.
NOT AGAIN.
BACK THEN I JUST WANTED TO ESCAPE TO THAT PERFECT WORLD YOU WERE GOING TO MAKE.
THERE'S ONE LAST THING THAT I KEPT TO MYSELF, BUT I'M GOING TO TELL YOU NOW.
OOPS! DEAD END FOR ME.
ARE YOU READY TO RUIN MY DAY?
OR ARE YOU A BIG USELESS LIZARD? DRIED UP WYRM! COUGH-SUCKING SCALE FACE!
BAND-AID BREATHED DRAGON!
RRRRRR!
CLUB-FOOTED KOMODO!
BLUNT-TOOTHED, LILY-HEARTED NEWT-LIPPED SKINK!
YOUR MOTHER WAS A

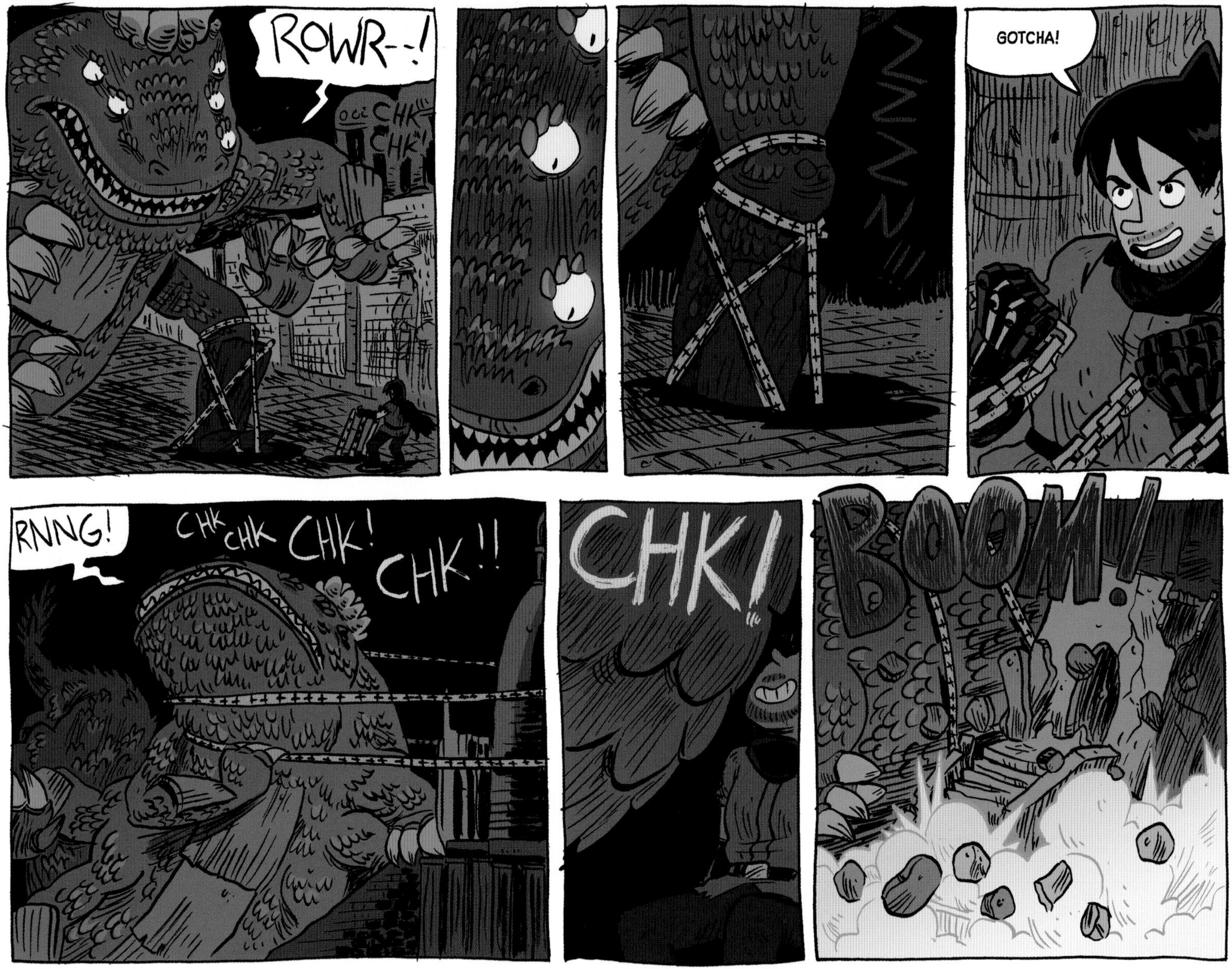
ROWR--!
CHK CHK!
GOTCHA!
RNNG!
CHK CHK CHK! CHK!!
CHK!
BOOM!

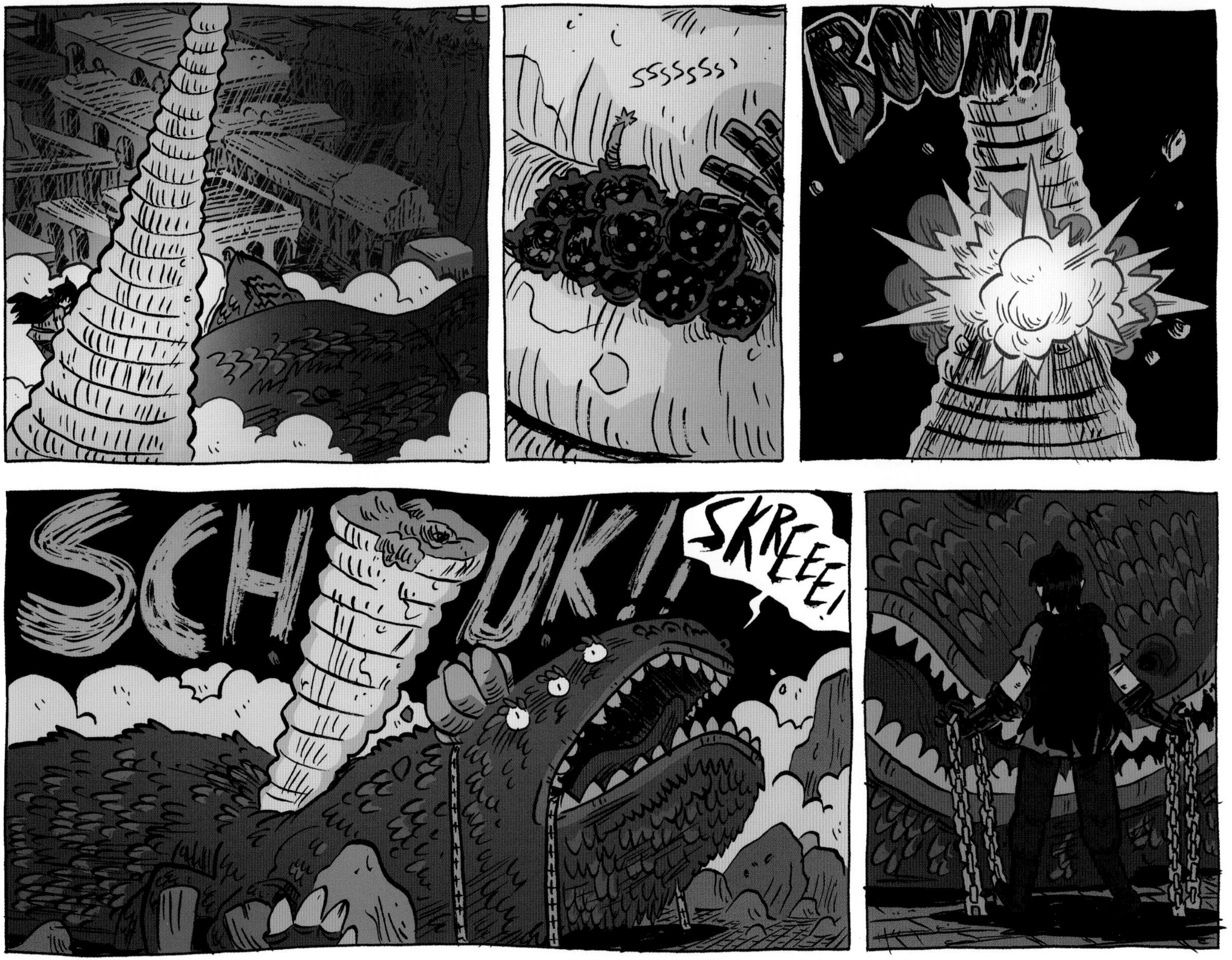
SSSSSSS
BOOM!!
SCH UK!!
SKREEE!

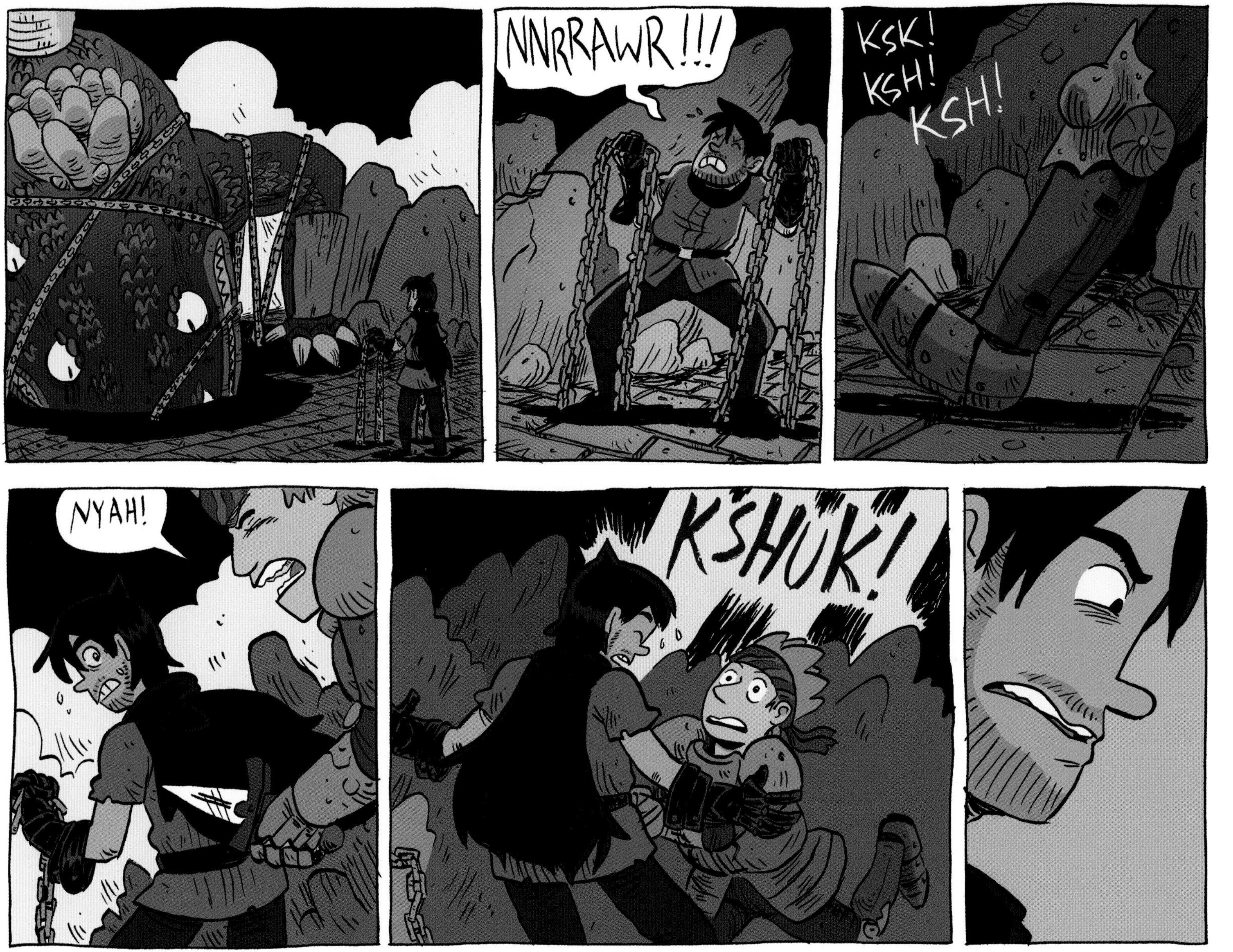

NNRRAWR!!!
KSK!
KSH!
KSH!
NYAH!
KSHUK!

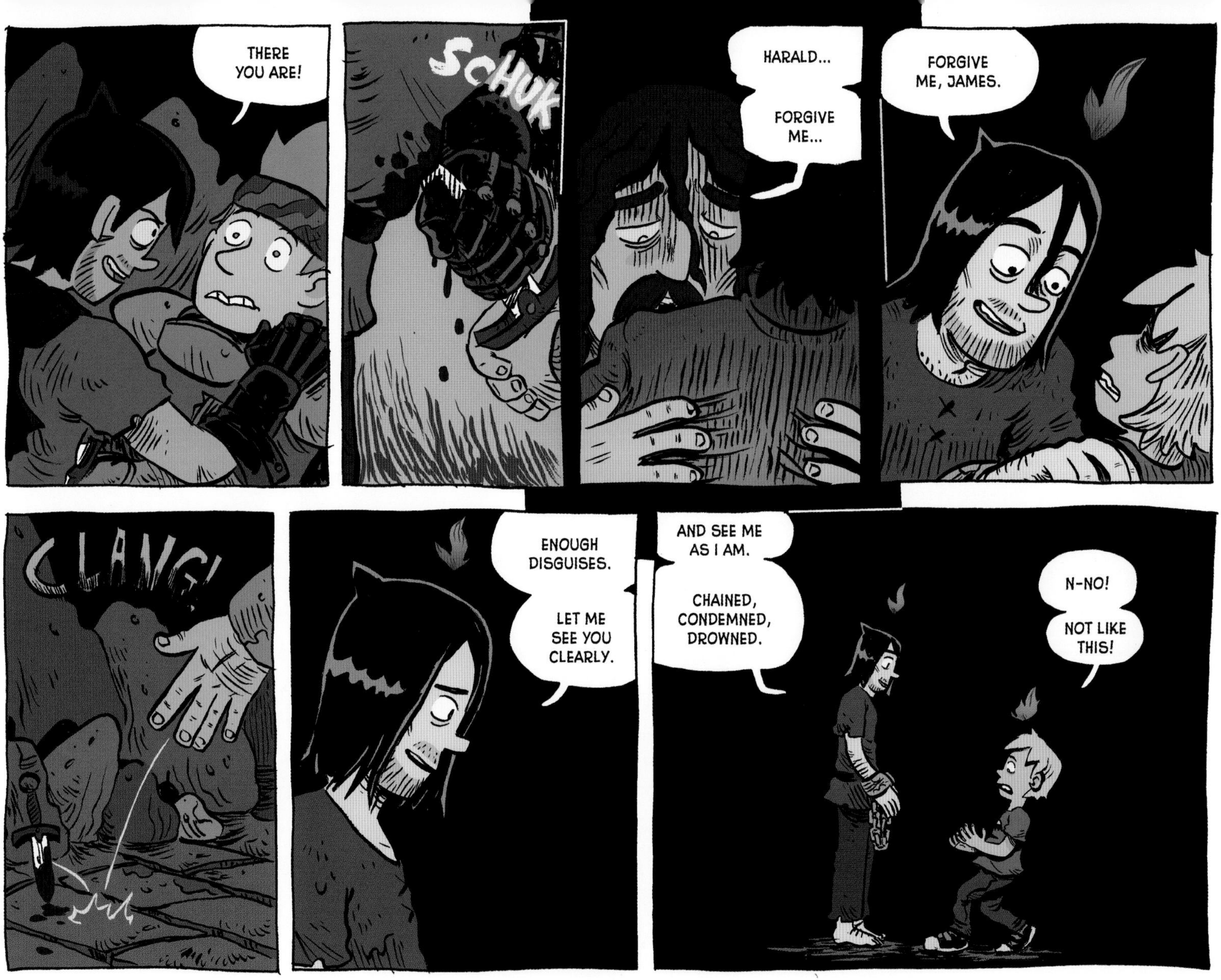
THERE YOU ARE!
SCHUK
HARALD...
FORGIVE ME...
FORGIVE ME, JAMES.
CLANG!
ENOUGH DISGUISES.
LET ME SEE YOU CLEARLY.
AND SEE ME AS I AM.
CHAINED, CONDEMNED, DROWNED.
N-NO!
NOT LIKE THIS!

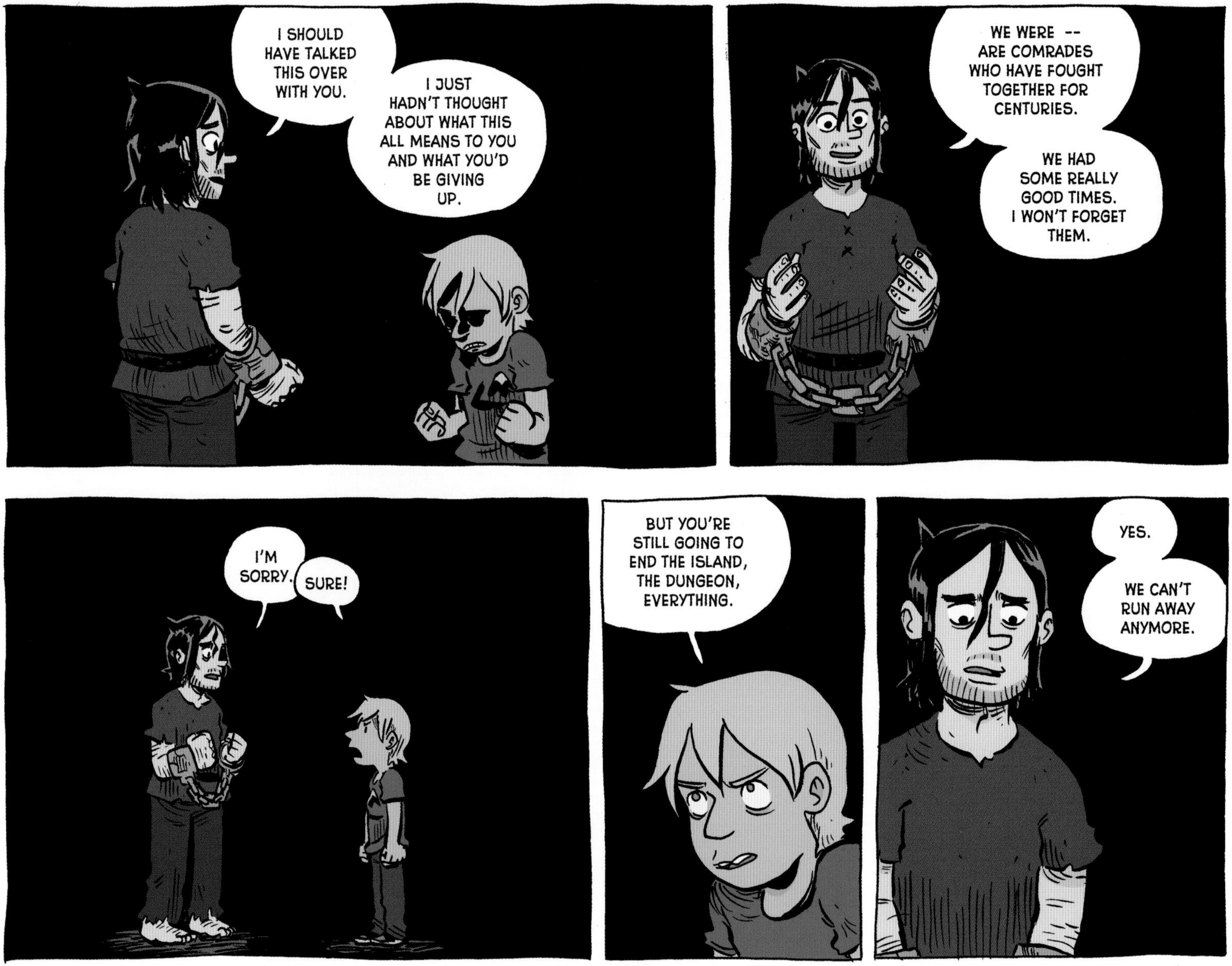
I SHOULD HAVE TALKED THIS OVER WITH YOU.
I JUST HADN'T THOUGHT ABOUT WHAT THIS ALL MEANS TO YOU AND WHAT YOU'D BE GIVING UP.
WE WERE -- ARE COMRADES WHO HAVE FOUGHT TOGETHER FOR CENTURIES.
WE HAD SOME REALLY GOOD TIMES. I WON'T FORGET THEM.
I'M SORRY.
SURE!
BUT YOU'RE STILL GOING TO END THE ISLAND, THE DUNGEON, EVERYTHING.
YES.
WE CAN'T RUN AWAY ANYMORE.

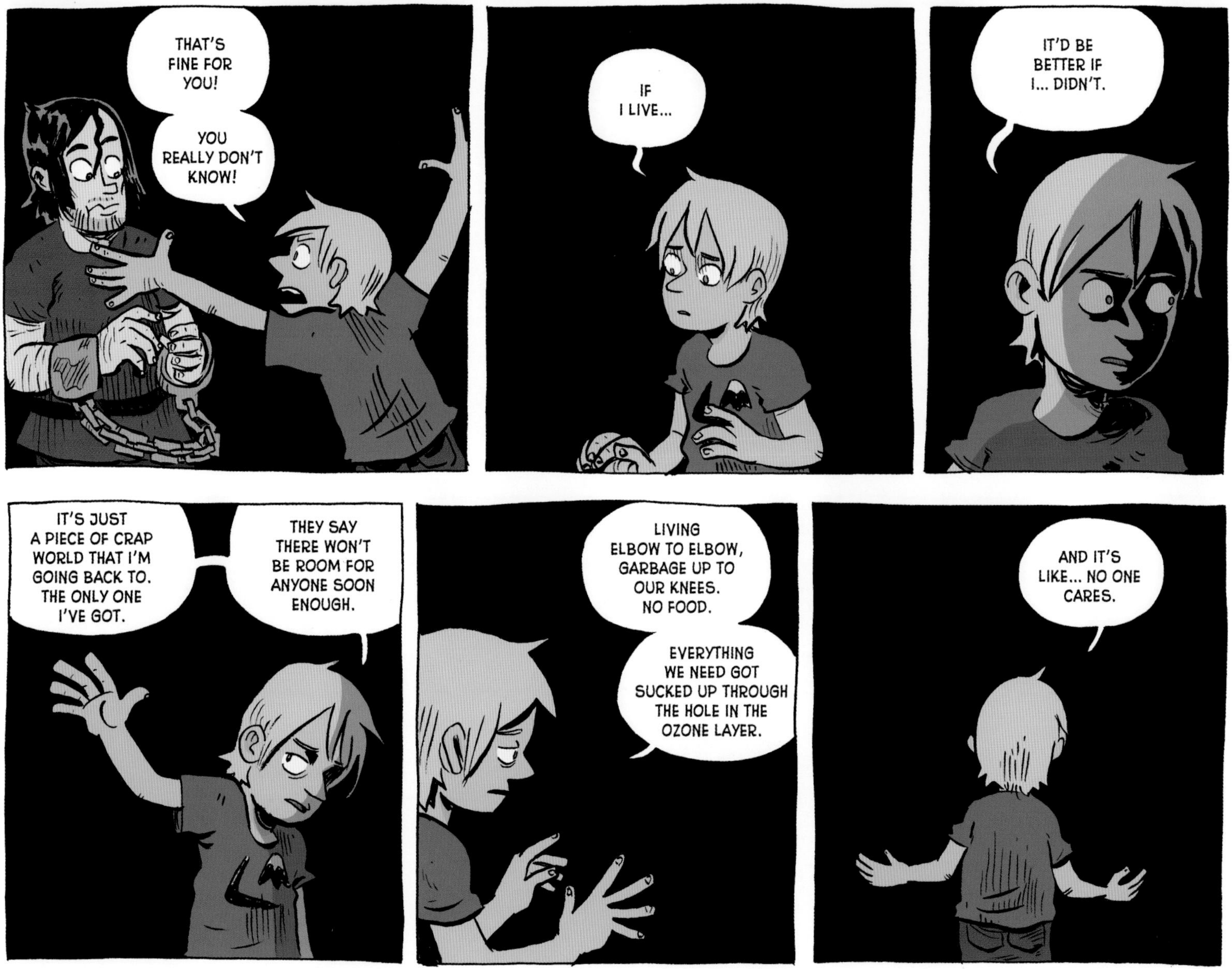
THAT'S FINE FOR YOU!
YOU REALLY DON'T KNOW!
IF I LIVE...
IT'D BE BETTER IF I... DIDN'T.
IT'S JUST A PIECE OF CRAP WORLD THAT I'M GOING BACK TO. THE ONLY ONE I'VE GOT.
THEY SAY THERE WON'T BE ROOM FOR ANYONE SOON ENOUGH.
LIVING ELBOW TO ELBOW, GARBAGE UP TO OUR KNEES. NO FOOD.
EVERYTHING WE NEED GOT SUCKED UP THROUGH THE HOLE IN THE OZONE LAYER.
AND IT'S LIKE... NO ONE CARES.

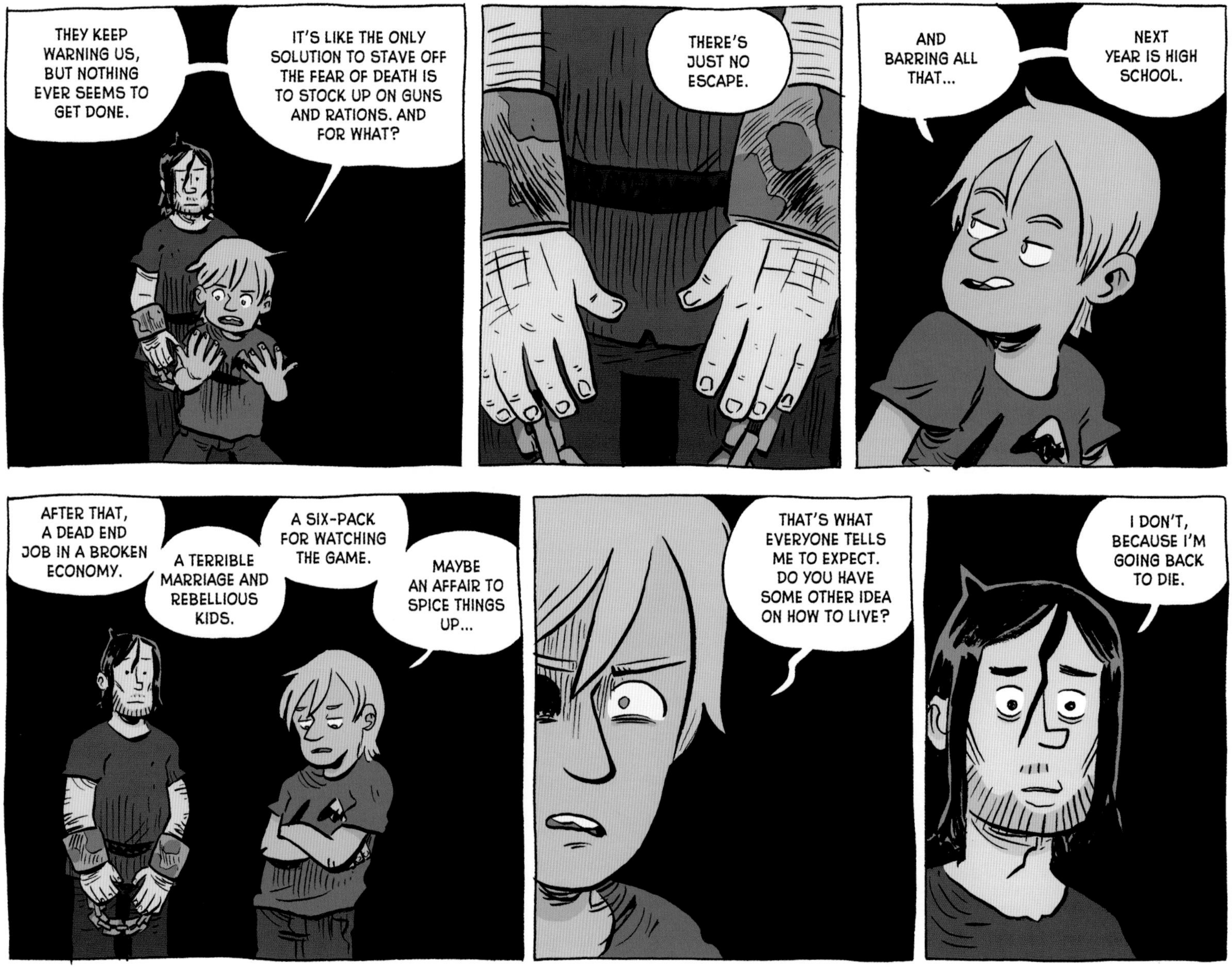
THEY KEEP WARNING US, BUT NOTHING EVER SEEMS TO GET DONE.
IT'S LIKE THE ONLY SOLUTION TO STAVE OFF THE FEAR OF DEATH IS TO STOCK UP ON GUNS AND RATIONS. AND FOR WHAT?
THERE'S JUST NO ESCAPE.
AND BARRING ALL THAT...
NEXT YEAR IS HIGH SCHOOL.
AFTER THAT, A DEAD END JOB IN A BROKEN ECONOMY.
A TERRIBLE MARRIAGE AND REBELLIOUS KIDS.
A SIX-PACK FOR WATCHING THE GAME.
MAYBE AN AFFAIR TO SPICE THINGS UP...
THAT'S WHAT EVERYONE TELLS ME TO EXPECT. DO YOU HAVE SOME OTHER IDEA ON HOW TO LIVE?
I DON'T, BECAUSE I'M GOING BACK TO DIE.

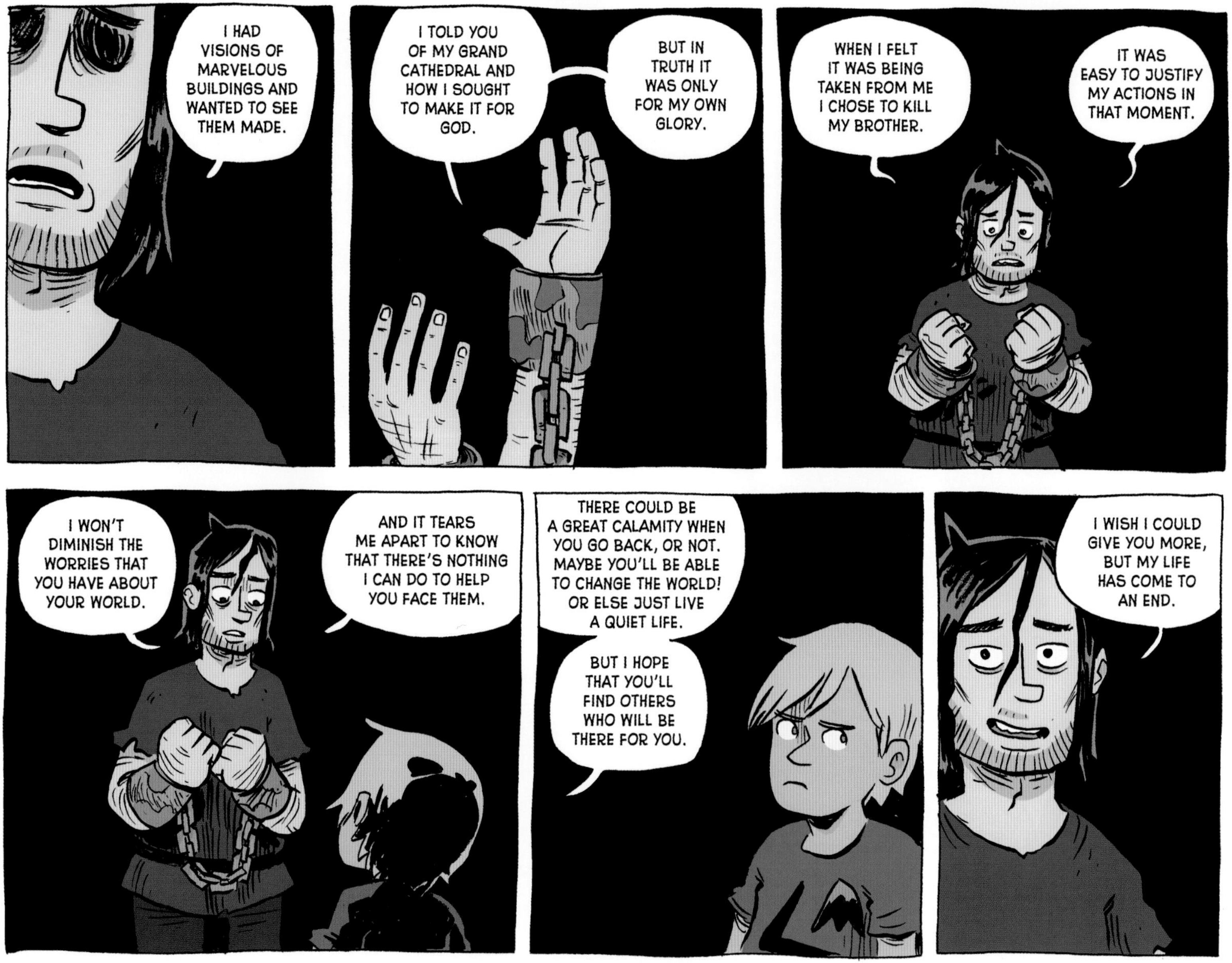
I HAD VISIONS OF MARVELOUS BUILDINGS AND WANTED TO SEE THEM MADE.
I TOLD YOU OF MY GRAND CATHEDRAL AND HOW I SOUGHT TO MAKE IT FOR GOD.
BUT IN TRUTH IT WAS ONLY FOR MY OWN GLORY.
WHEN I FELT IT WAS BEING TAKEN FROM ME I CHOSE TO KILL MY BROTHER.
IT WAS EASY TO JUSTIFY MY ACTIONS IN THAT MOMENT.
I WON'T DIMINISH THE WORRIES THAT YOU HAVE ABOUT YOUR WORLD.
AND IT TEARS ME APART TO KNOW THAT THERE'S NOTHING I CAN DO TO HELP YOU FACE THEM.
THERE COULD BE A GREAT CALAMITY WHEN YOU GO BACK, OR NOT. MAYBE YOU'LL BE ABLE TO CHANGE THE WORLD! OR ELSE JUST LIVE A QUIET LIFE.
BUT I HOPE THAT YOU'LL FIND OTHERS WHO WILL BE THERE FOR YOU.
I WISH I COULD GIVE YOU MORE, BUT MY LIFE HAS COME TO AN END.

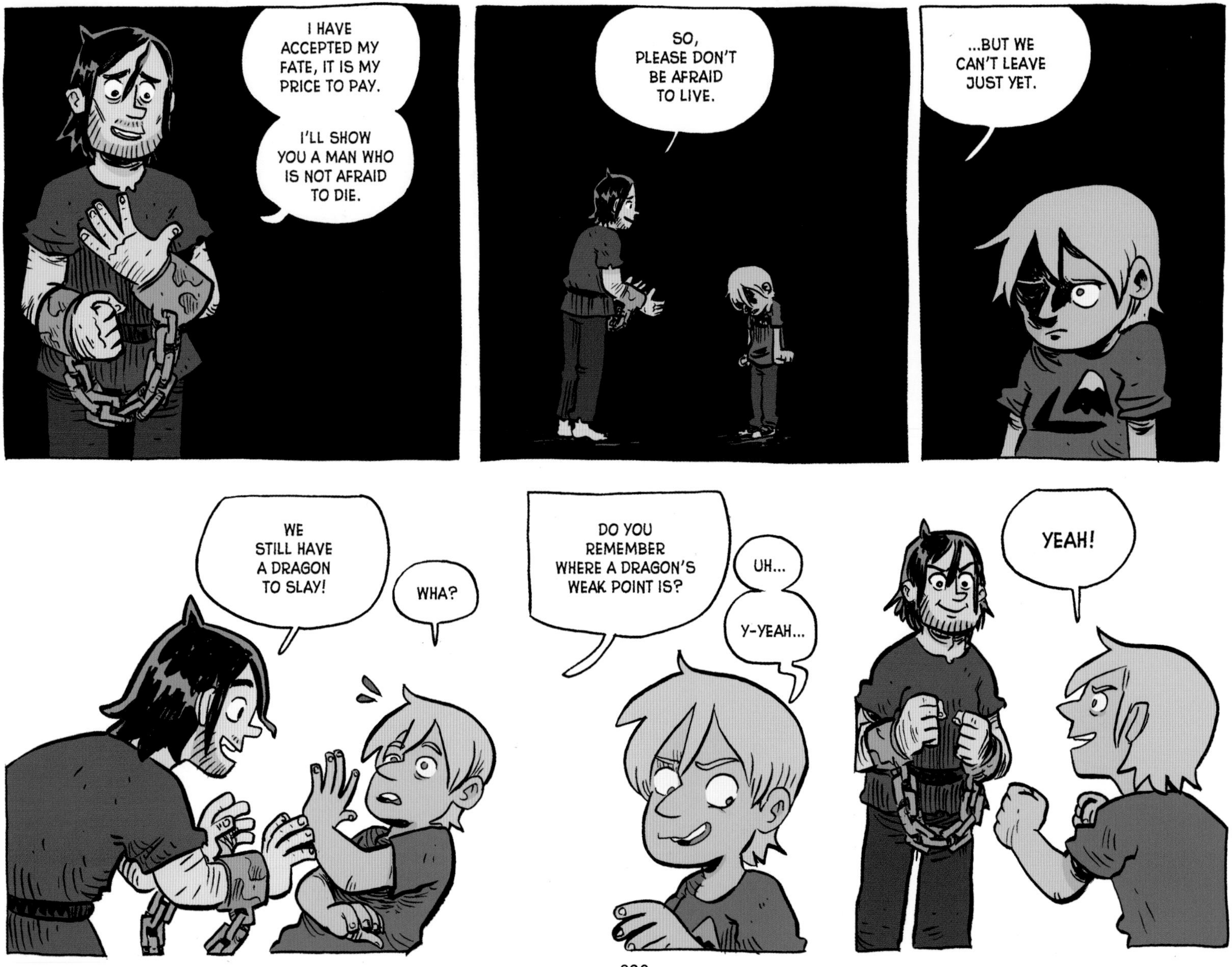
I HAVE ACCEPTED MY FATE, IT IS MY PRICE TO PAY.
I'LL SHOW YOU A MAN WHO IS NOT AFRAID TO DIE.
SO, PLEASE DON'T BE AFRAID TO LIVE.
...BUT WE CAN'T LEAVE JUST YET.
WE STILL HAVE A DRAGON TO SLAY!
WHA?
DO YOU REMEMBER WHERE A DRAGON'S WEAK POINT IS?
UH...
Y-YEAH...
YEAH!

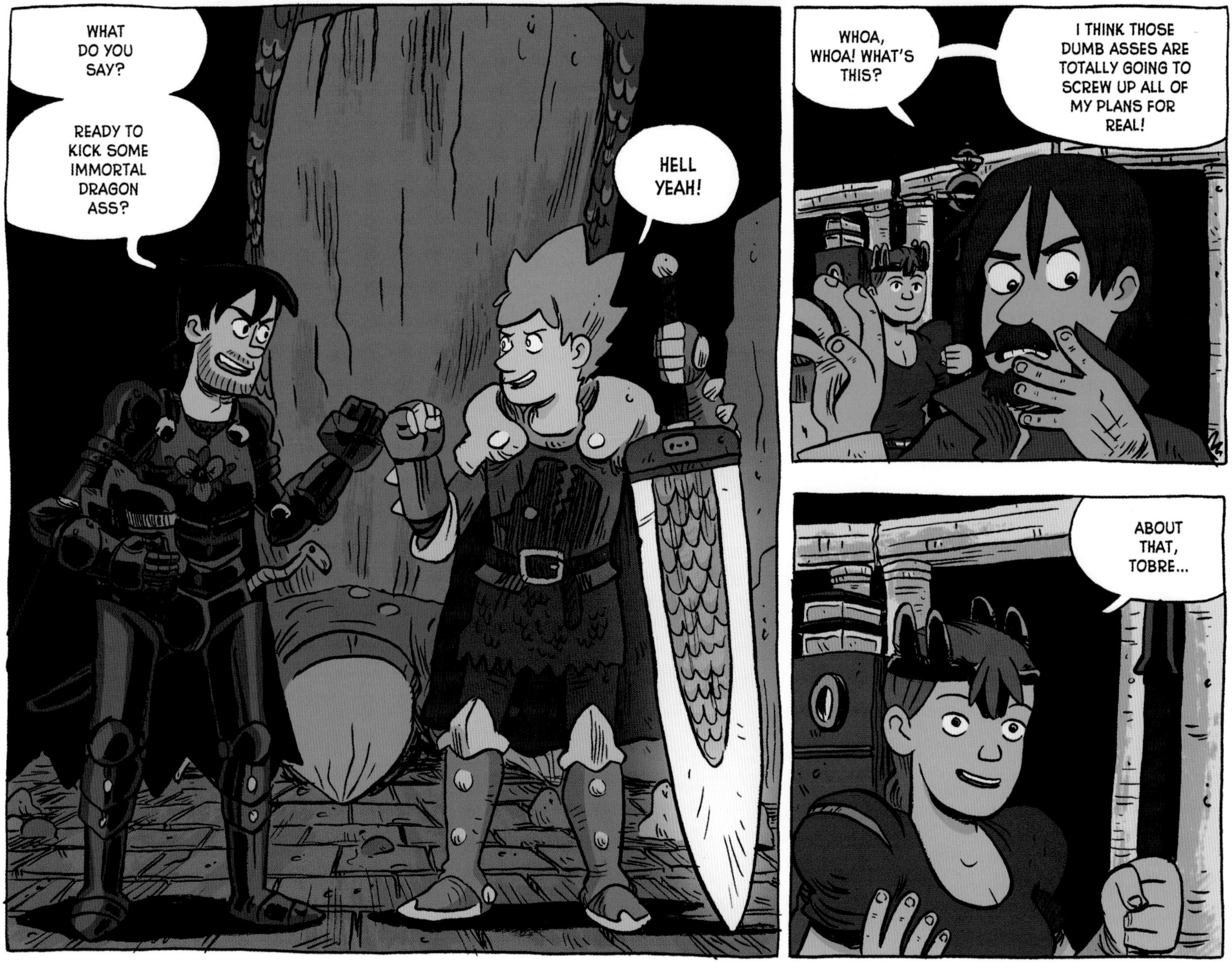
WHAT DO YOU SAY?
READY TO KICK SOME IMMORTAL DRAGON ASS?
HELL YEAH!
WHOA, WHOA! WHAT'S THIS?
I THINK THOSE DUMB ASSES ARE TOTALLY GOING TO SCREW UP ALL OF MY PLANS FOR REAL!
ABOUT THAT, TOBRE...

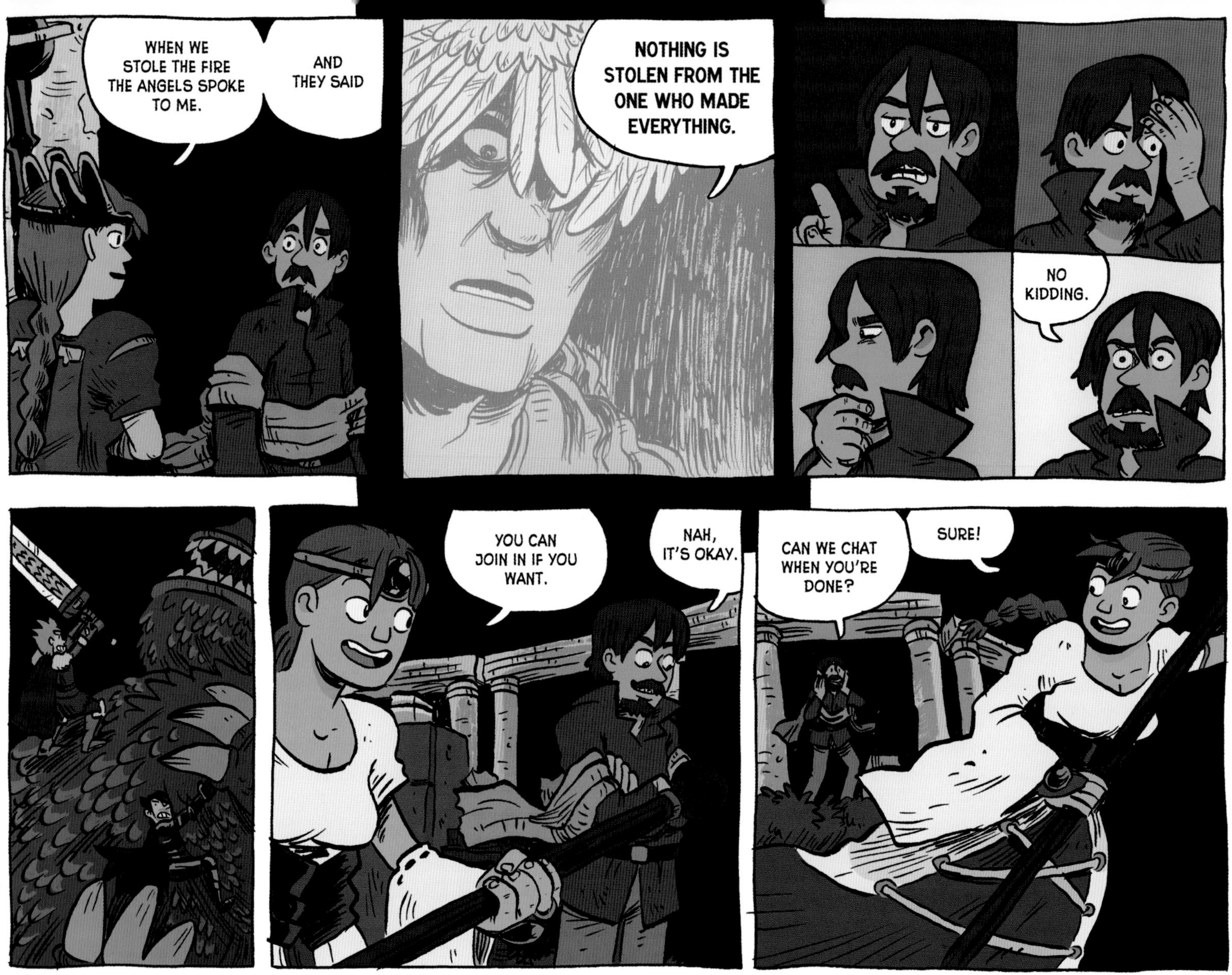
WHEN WE STOLE THE FIRE THE ANGELS SPOKE TO ME.
AND THEY SAID
NOTHING IS STOLEN FROM THE ONE WHO MADE EVERYTHING.
NO KIDDING.
YOU CAN JOIN IN IF YOU WANT.
NAH, IT'S OKAY.
CAN WE CHAT WHEN YOU'RE DONE?
SURE!

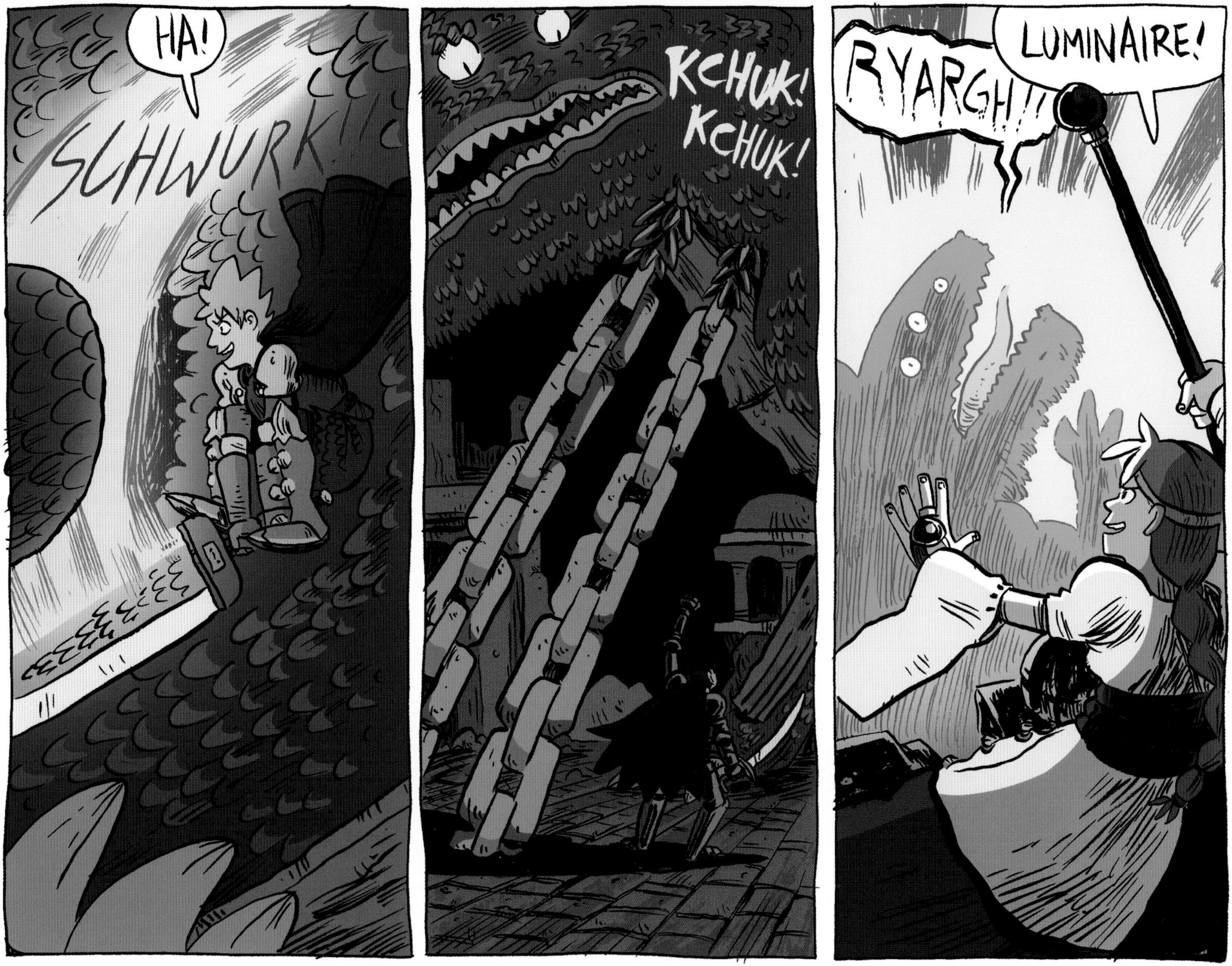
HA!
SCHWURK!!!
KCHUK! KCHUK!
RYARGH!!!
LUMINAIRE!

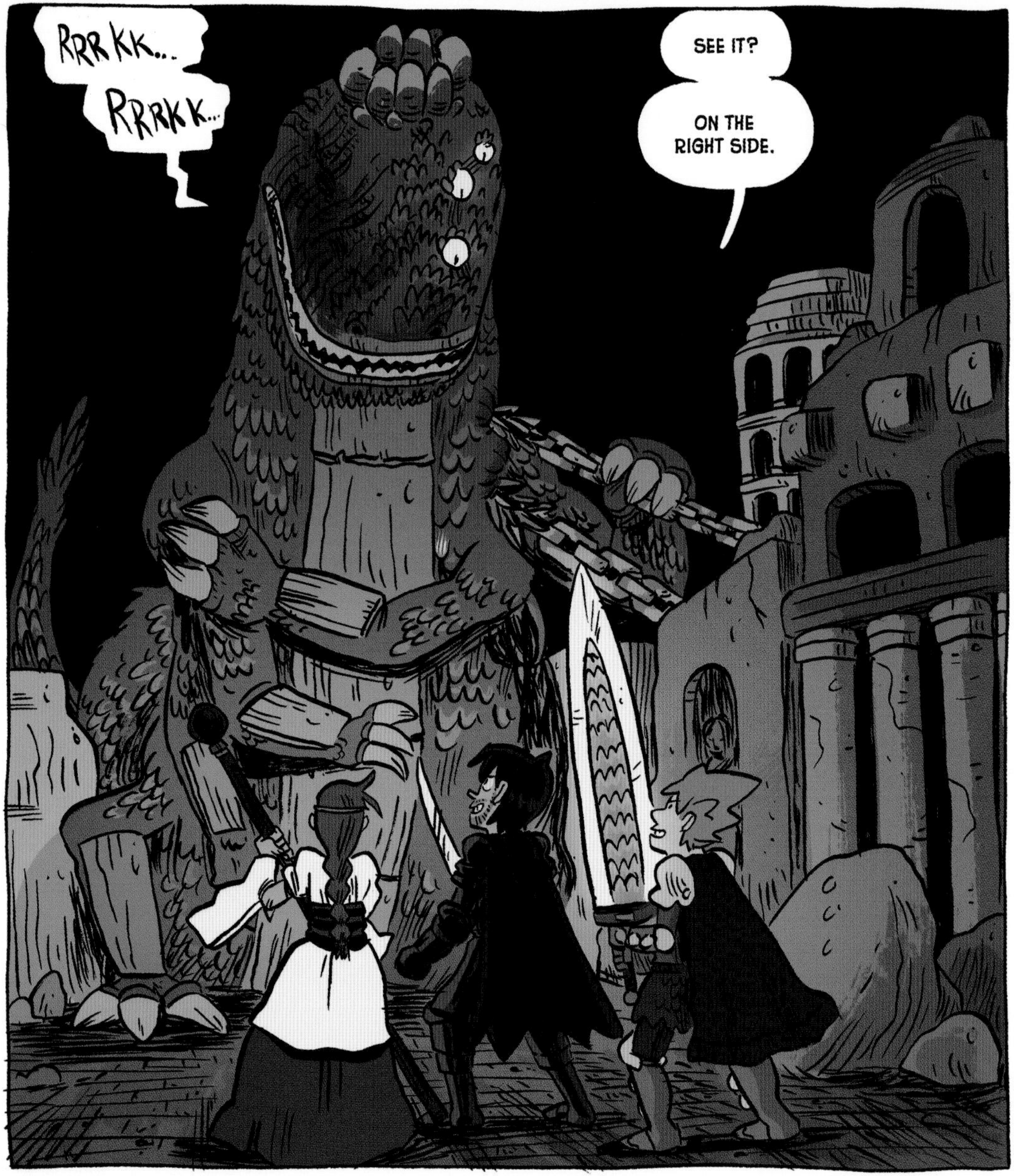
RRRKK...
RRRKK...
SEE IT?
ON THE RIGHT SIDE.
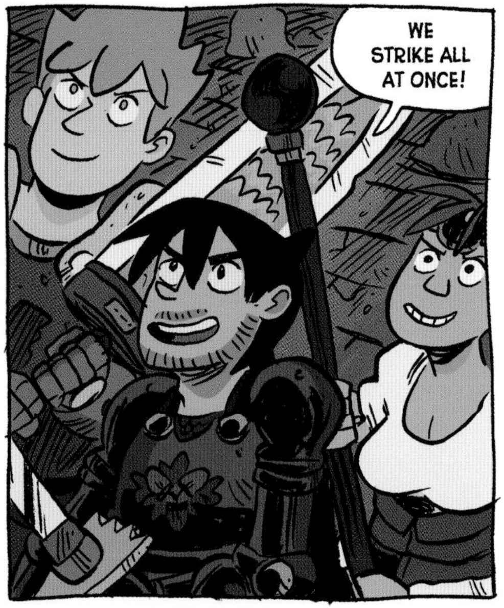
WE STRIKE ALL AT ONCE!
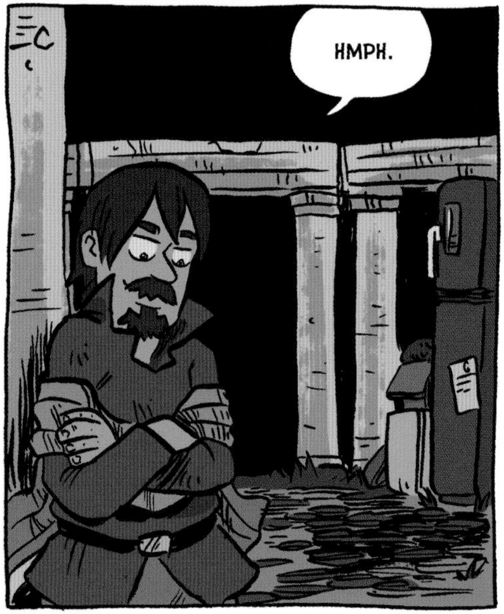
HMPH.

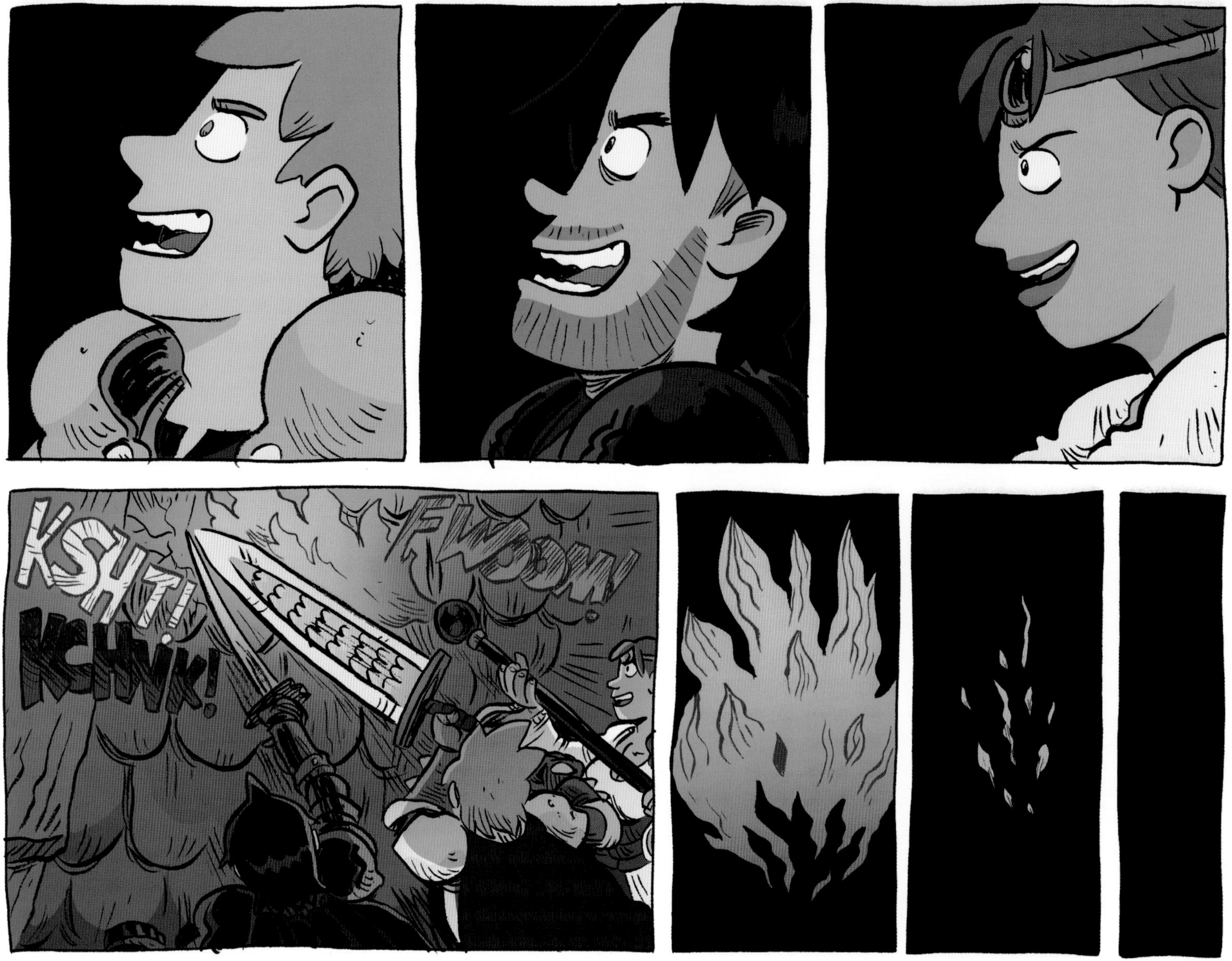
KSHT!
KCHNK!
FWOOM!

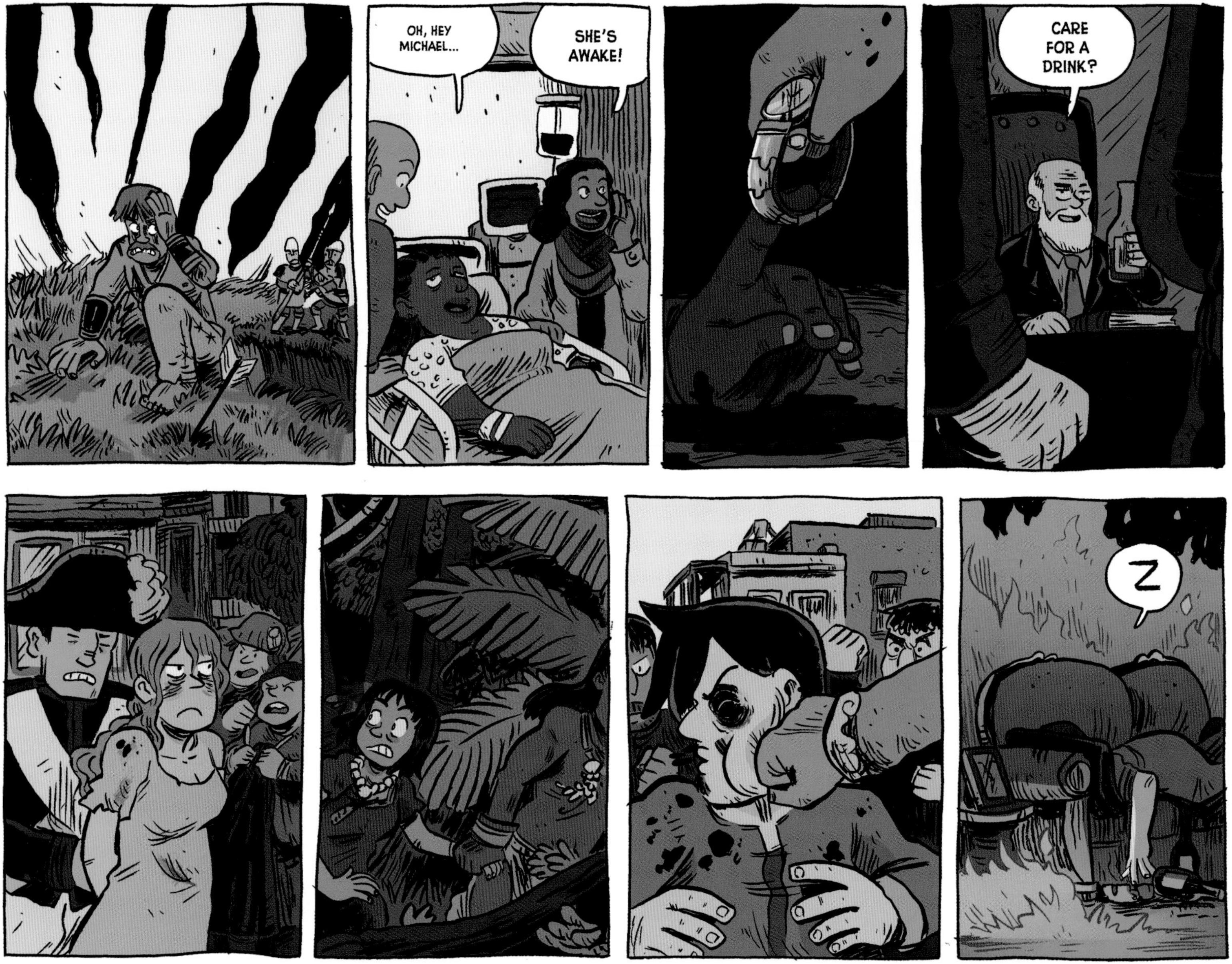
OH, HEY MICHAEL...
SHE'S AWAKE!
CARE FOR A DRINK?
Z

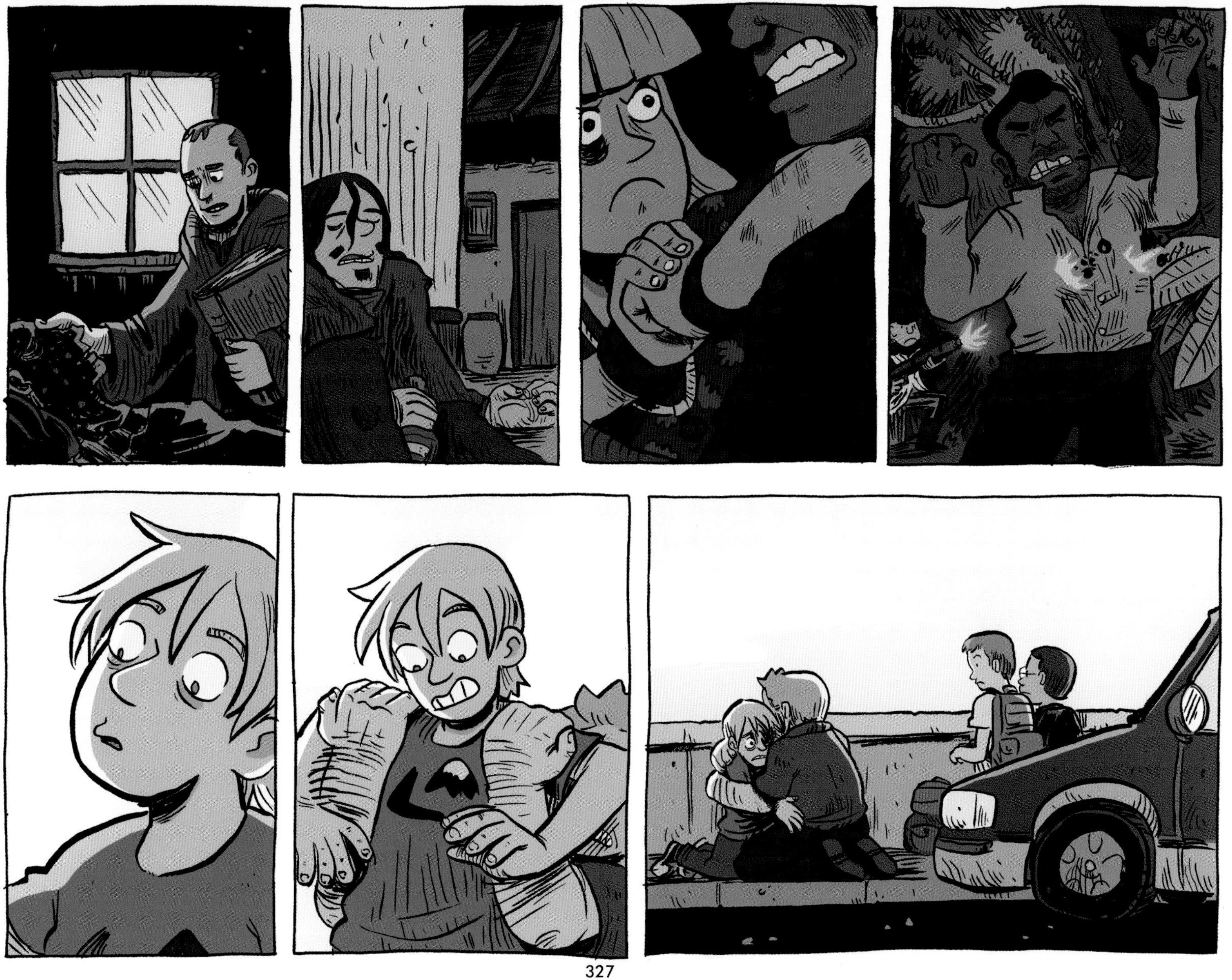

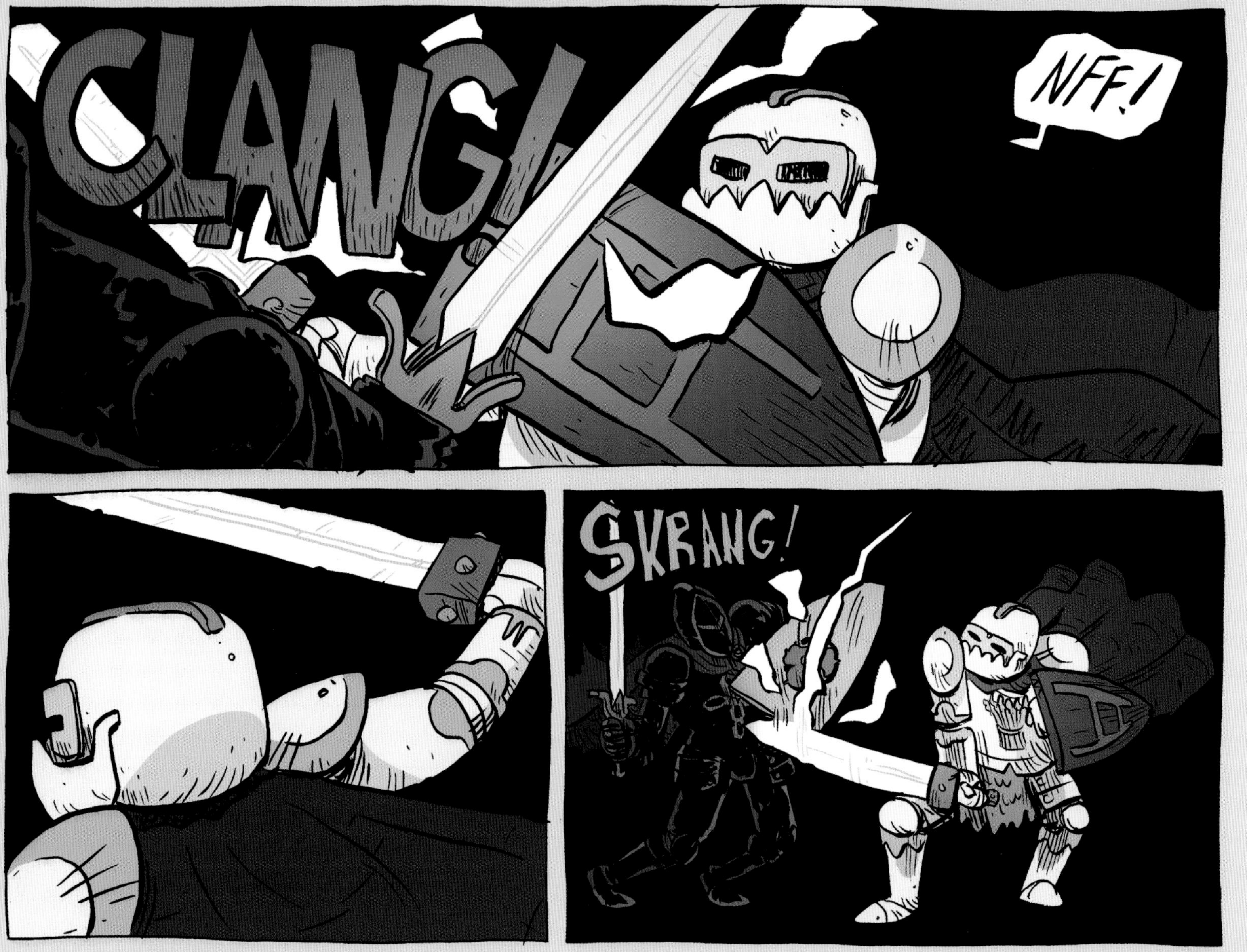
CLANG!
NFF!
SKRANG!

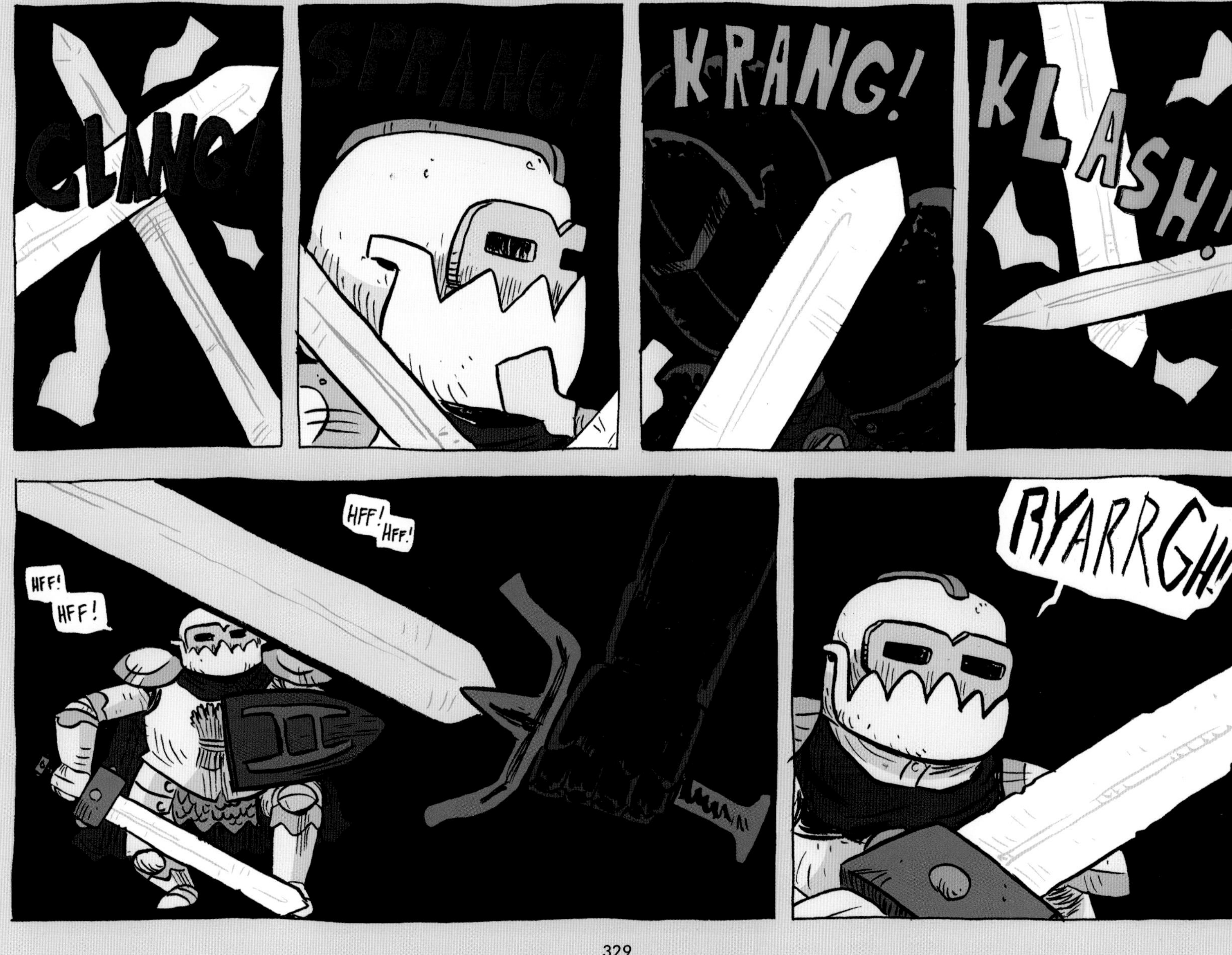
CLANG!
SPRANG!
KRANG!
KLASH!
HFF! HFF!
HFF! HFF!
RYARRGH!

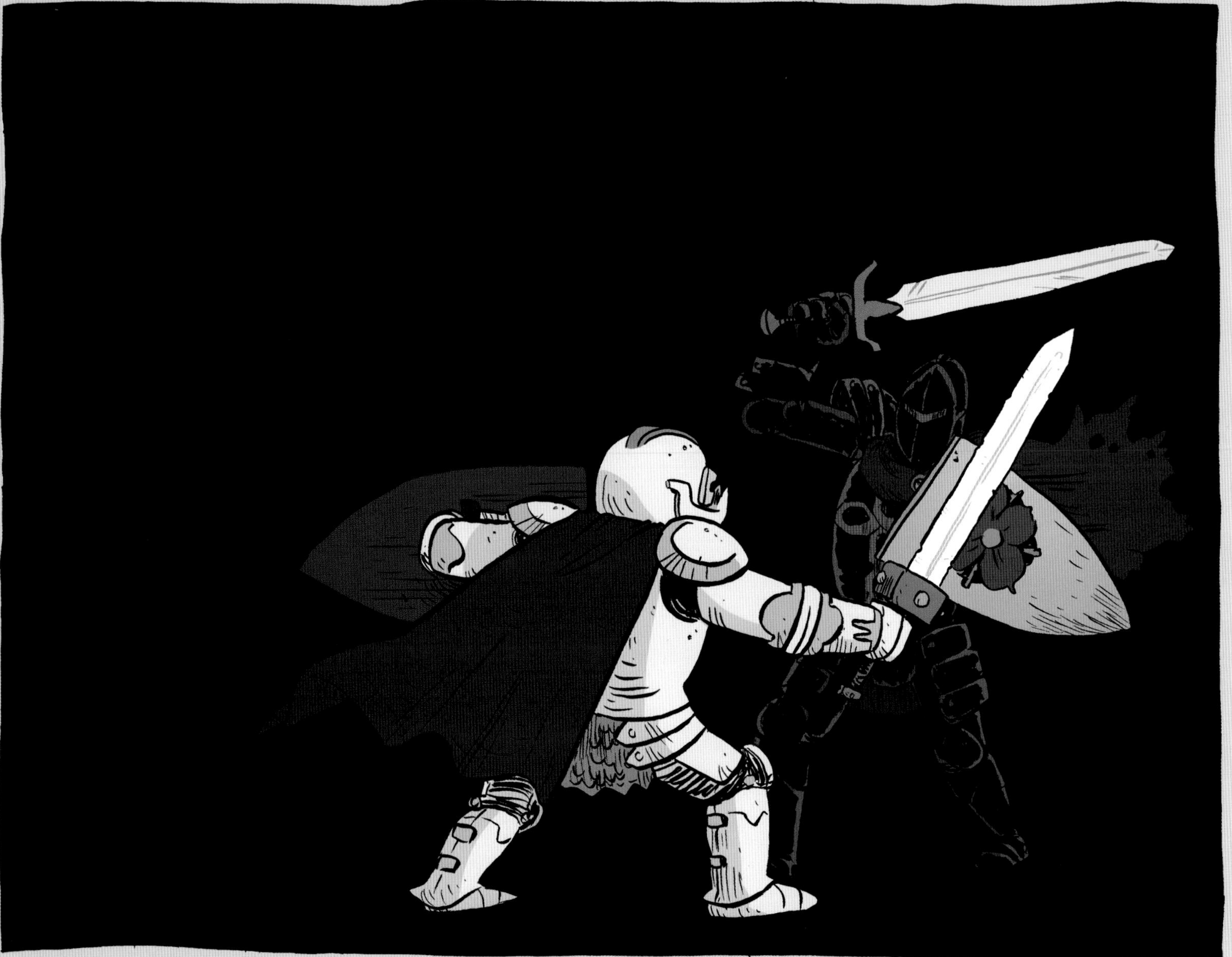

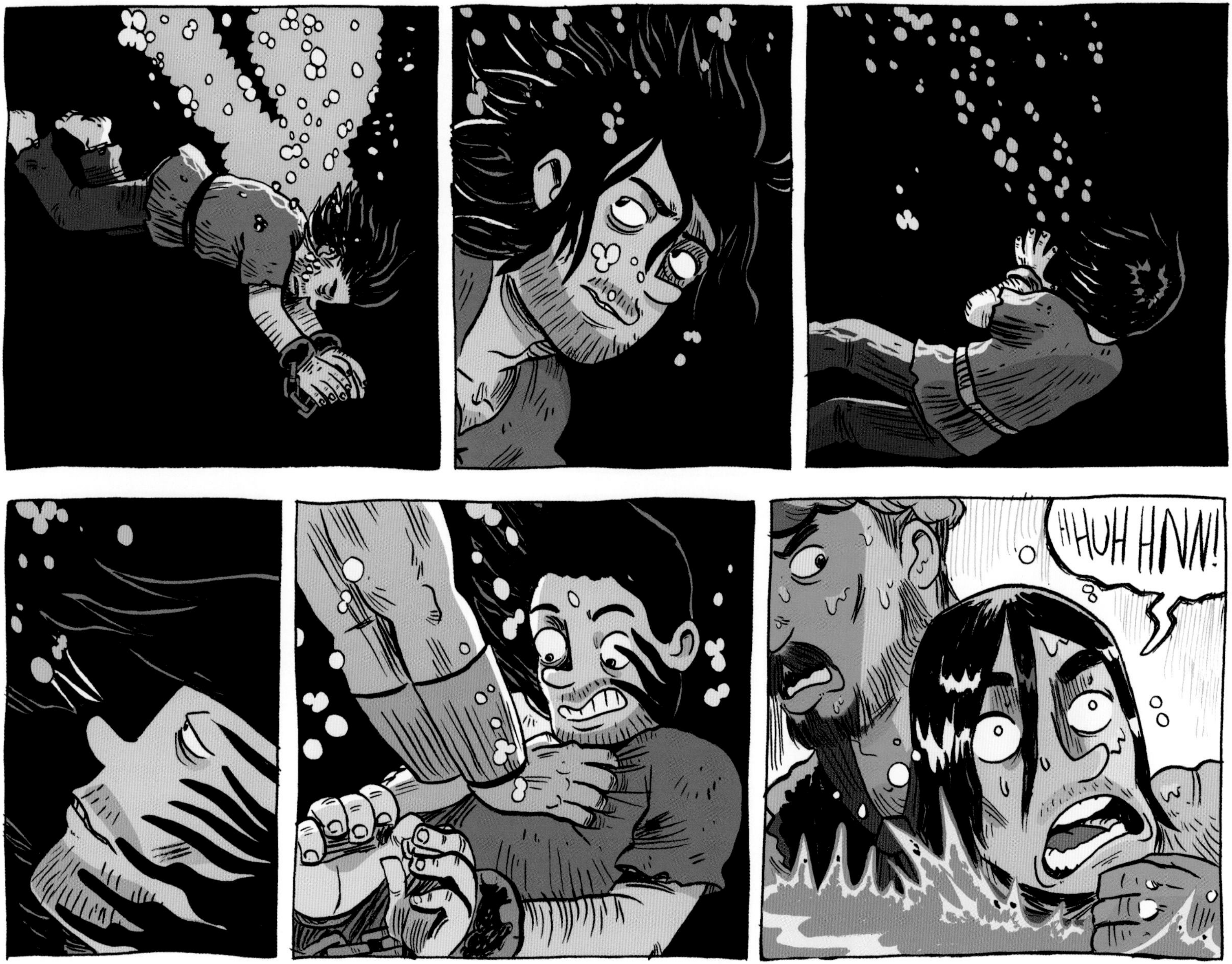
HHUH HNN!

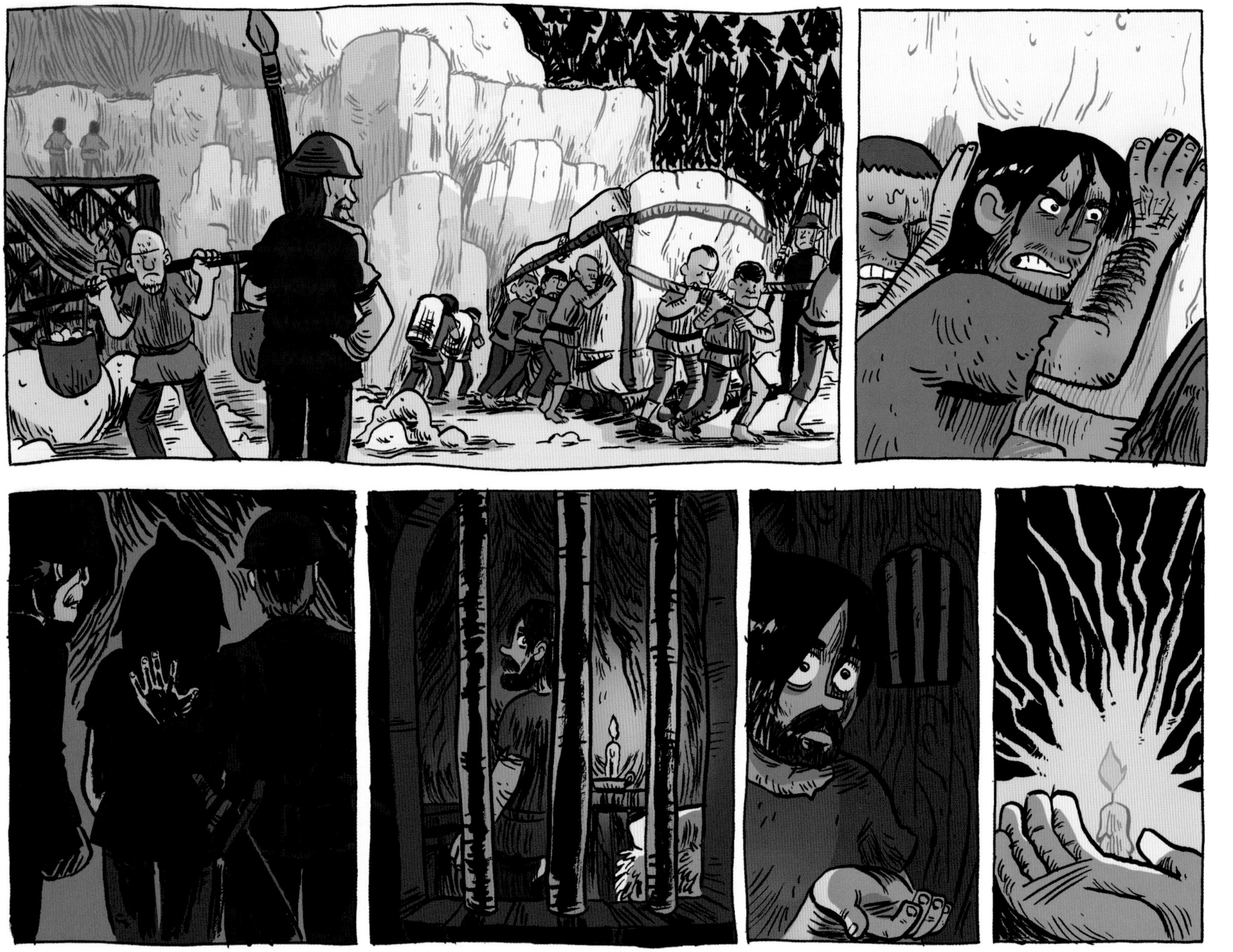

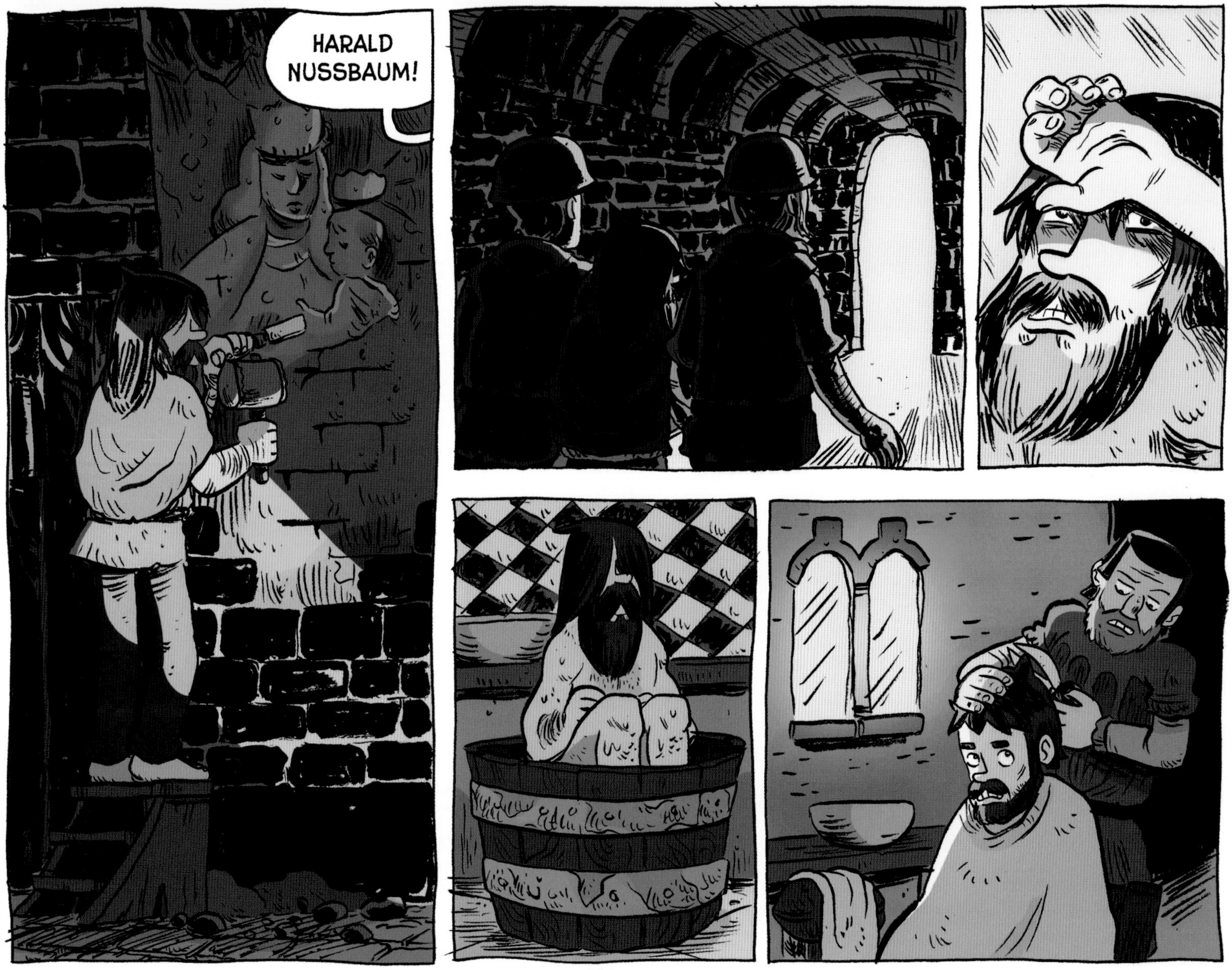
HARALD NUSSBAUM!

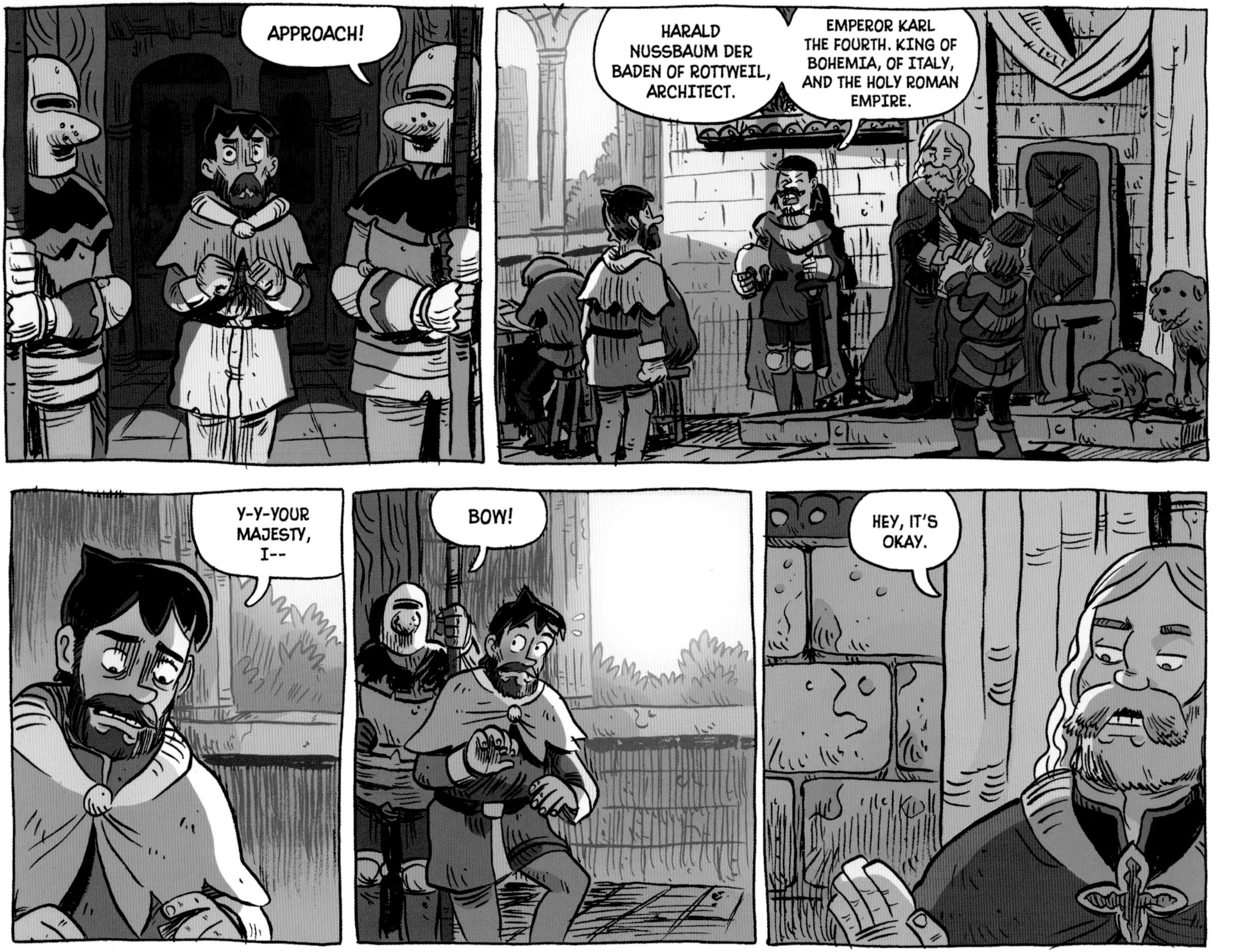
APPROACH!
HARALD NUSSBAUM DER BADEN OF ROTTWEIL, ARCHITECT.
EMPEROR KARL THE FOURTH. KING OF BOHEMIA, OF ITALY, AND THE HOLY ROMAN EMPIRE.
Y-Y-YOUR MAJESTY, I--
BOW!
HEY, IT'S OKAY.

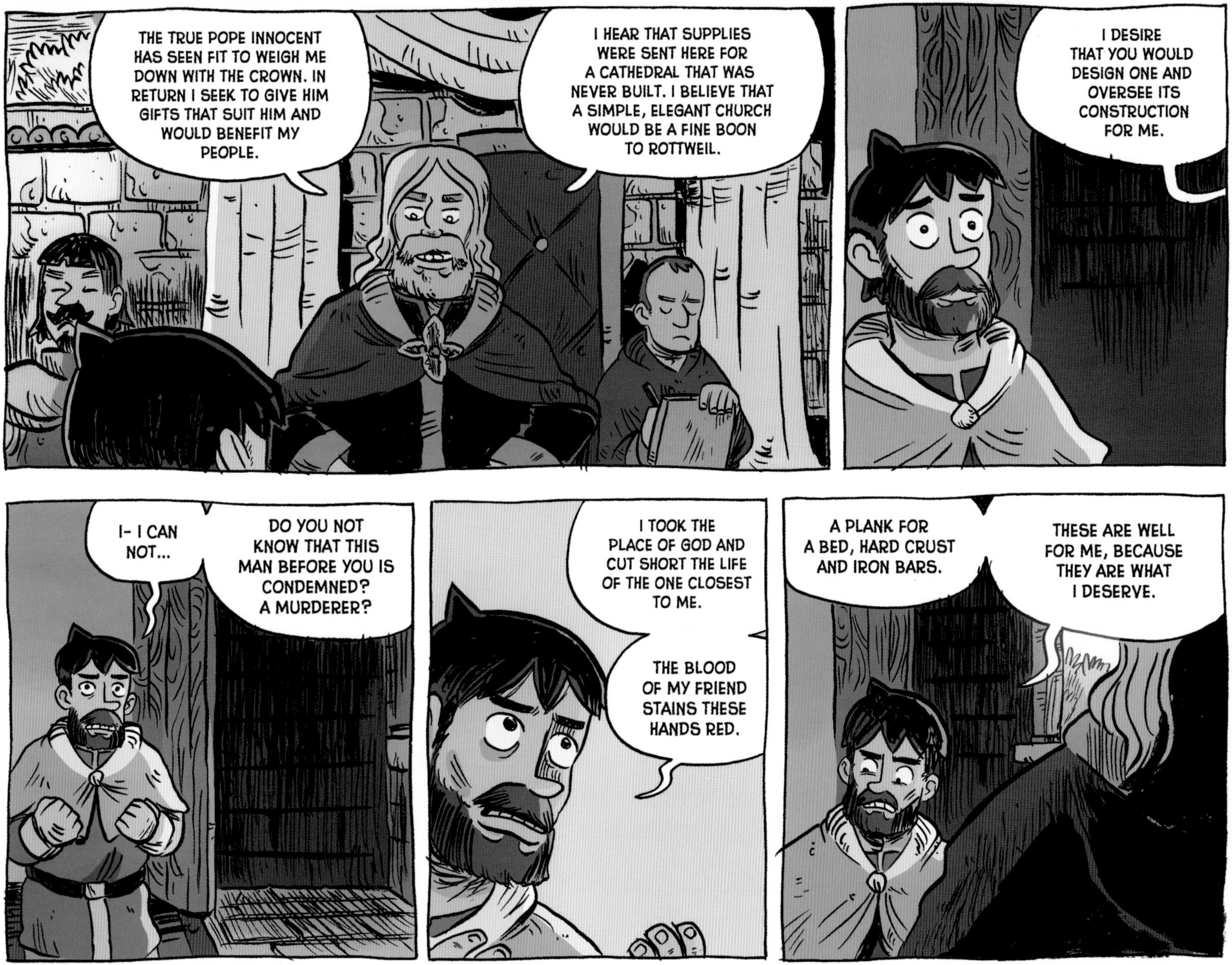
THE TRUE POPE INNOCENT HAS SEEN FIT TO WEIGH ME DOWN WITH THE CROWN. IN RETURN I SEEK TO GIVE HIM GIFTS THAT SUIT HIM AND WOULD BENEFIT MY PEOPLE.
I HEAR THAT SUPPLIES WERE SENT HERE FOR A CATHEDRAL THAT WAS NEVER BUILT. I BELIEVE THAT A SIMPLE, ELEGANT CHURCH WOULD BE A FINE BOON TO ROTTWEIL.
I DESIRE THAT YOU WOULD DESIGN ONE AND OVERSEE ITS CONSTRUCTION FOR ME.
I- I CAN NOT...
DO YOU NOT KNOW THAT THIS MAN BEFORE YOU IS CONDEMNED? A MURDERER?
I TOOK THE PLACE OF GOD AND CUT SHORT THE LIFE OF THE ONE CLOSEST TO ME.
THE BLOOD OF MY FRIEND STAINS THESE HANDS RED.
A PLANK FOR A BED, HARD CRUST AND IRON BARS.
THESE ARE WELL FOR ME, BECAUSE THEY ARE WHAT I DESERVE.

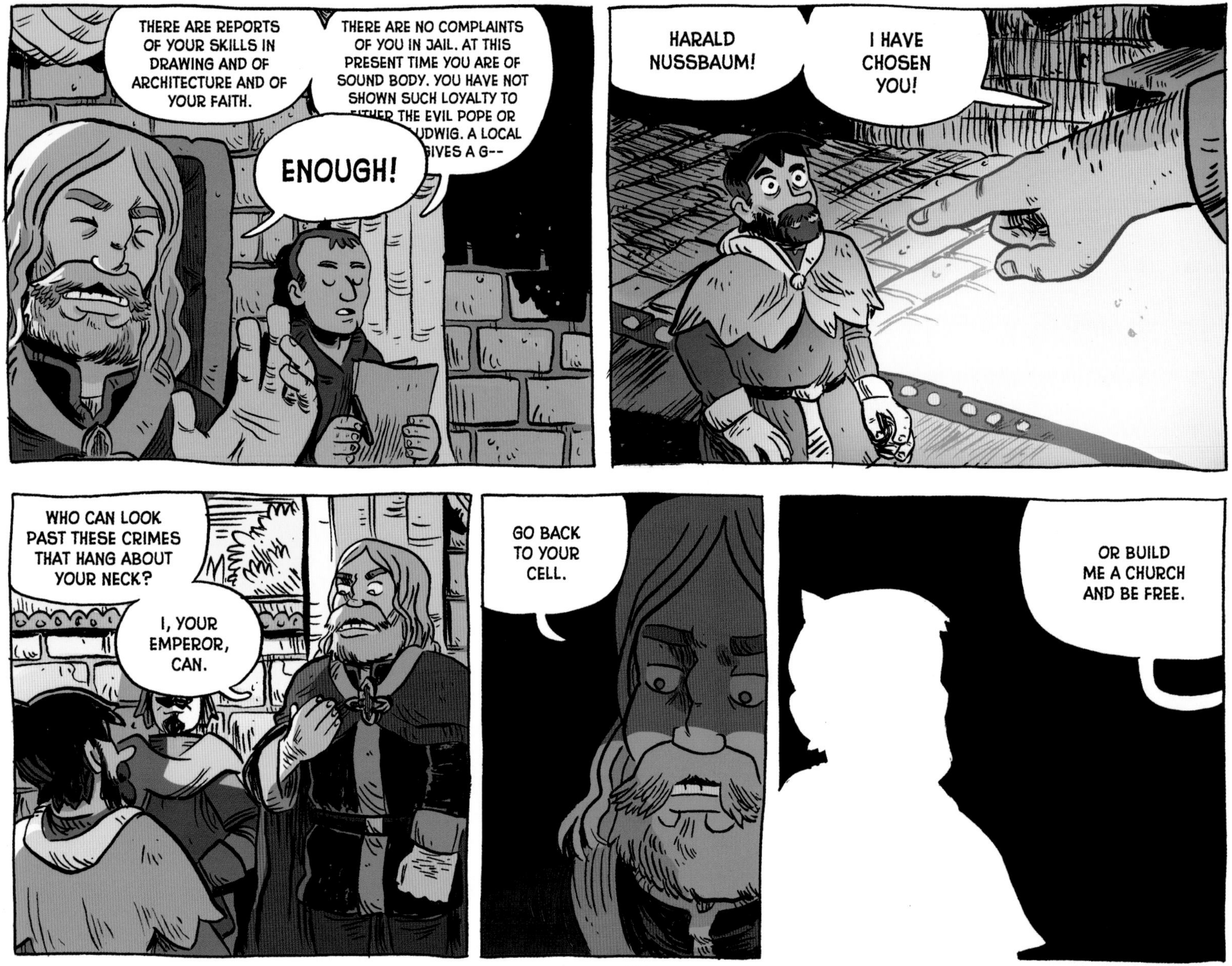
THERE ARE REPORTS OF YOUR SKILLS IN DRAWING AND OF ARCHITECTURE AND OF YOUR FAITH.
THERE ARE NO COMPLAINTS OF YOU IN JAIL. AT THIS PRESENT TIME YOU ARE OF SOUND BODY. YOU HAVE NOT SHOWN SUCH LOYALTY TO
THE EVIL POPE OR
UDWIG. A LOCAL
GIVES A G--
ENOUGH!
HARALD NUSSBAUM!
I HAVE CHOSEN YOU!
WHO CAN LOOK PAST THESE CRIMES THAT HANG ABOUT YOUR NECK?
I, YOUR EMPEROR, CAN.
GO BACK TO YOUR CELL.
OR BUILD ME A CHURCH AND BE FREE.

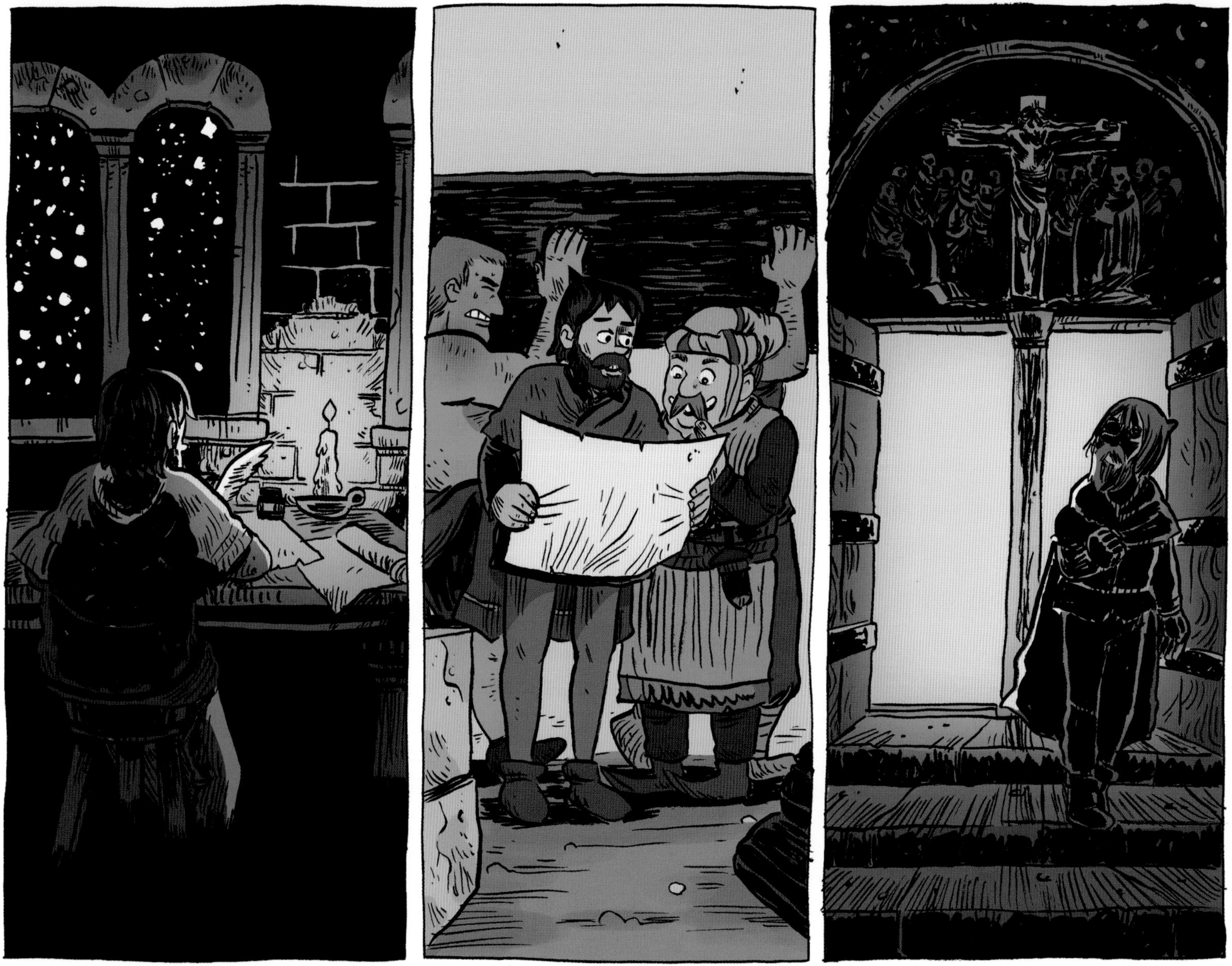

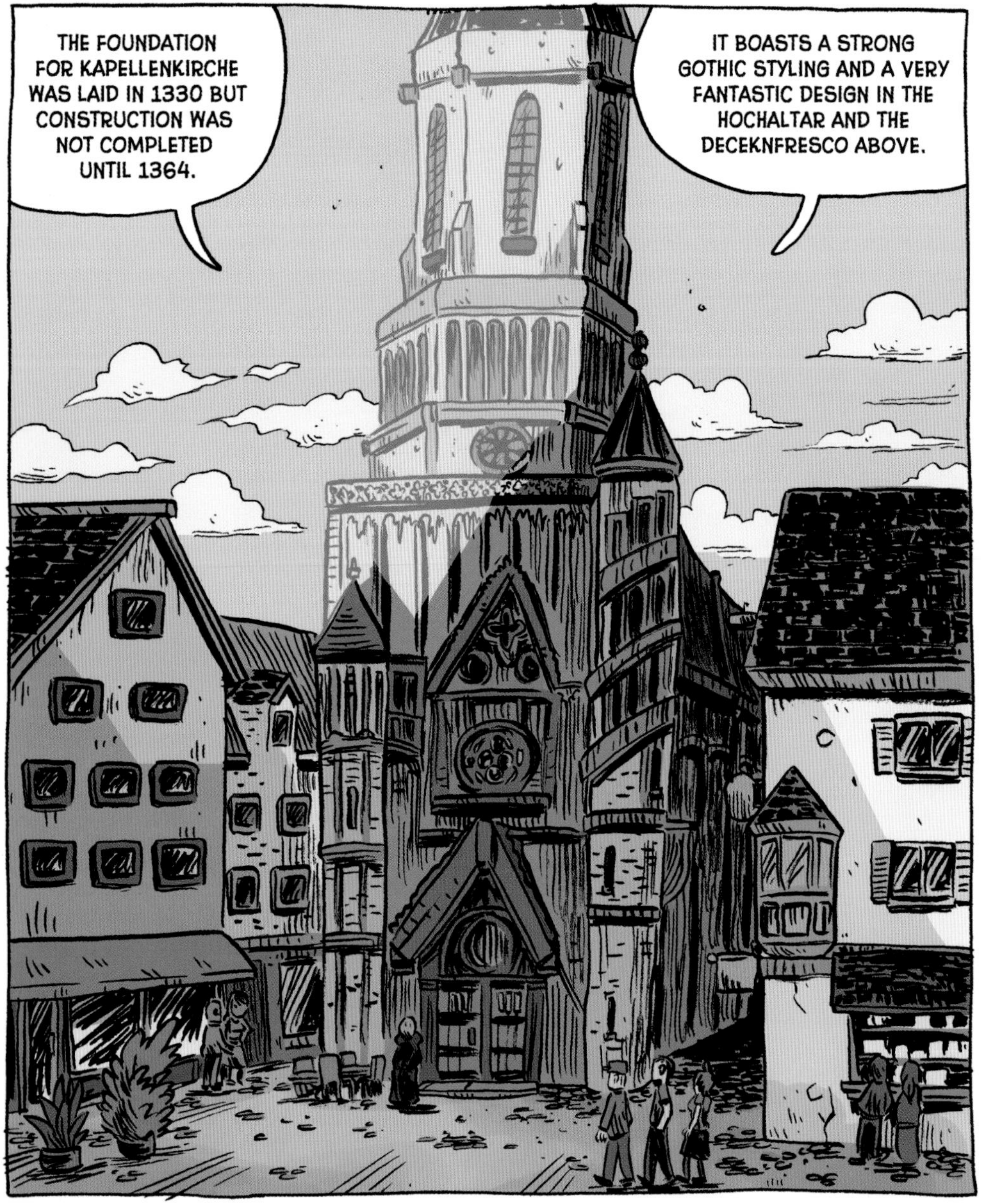
THE FOUNDATION FOR KAPELLENKIRCHE WAS LAID IN 1330 BUT CONSTRUCTION WAS NOT COMPLETED UNTIL 1364.
IT BOASTS A STRONG GOTHIC STYLING AND A VERY FANTASTIC DESIGN IN THE HOCHALTAR AND THE DECEKNFRESCO ABOVE.
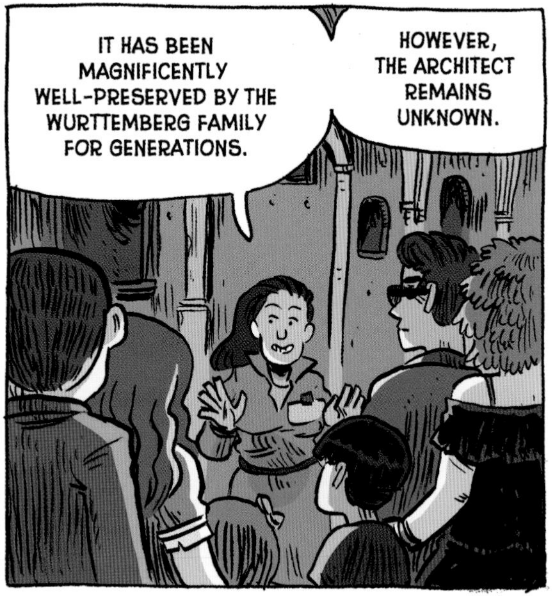
IT HAS BEEN MAGNIFICENTLY WELL-PRESERVED BY THE WURTTEMBERG FAMILY FOR GENERATIONS.
HOWEVER, THE ARCHITECT REMAINS UNKNOWN.
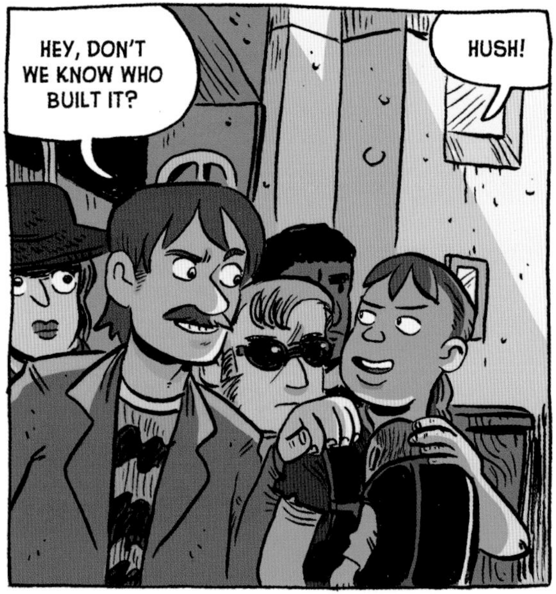
HEY, DON'T WE KNOW WHO BUILT IT?
HUSH!

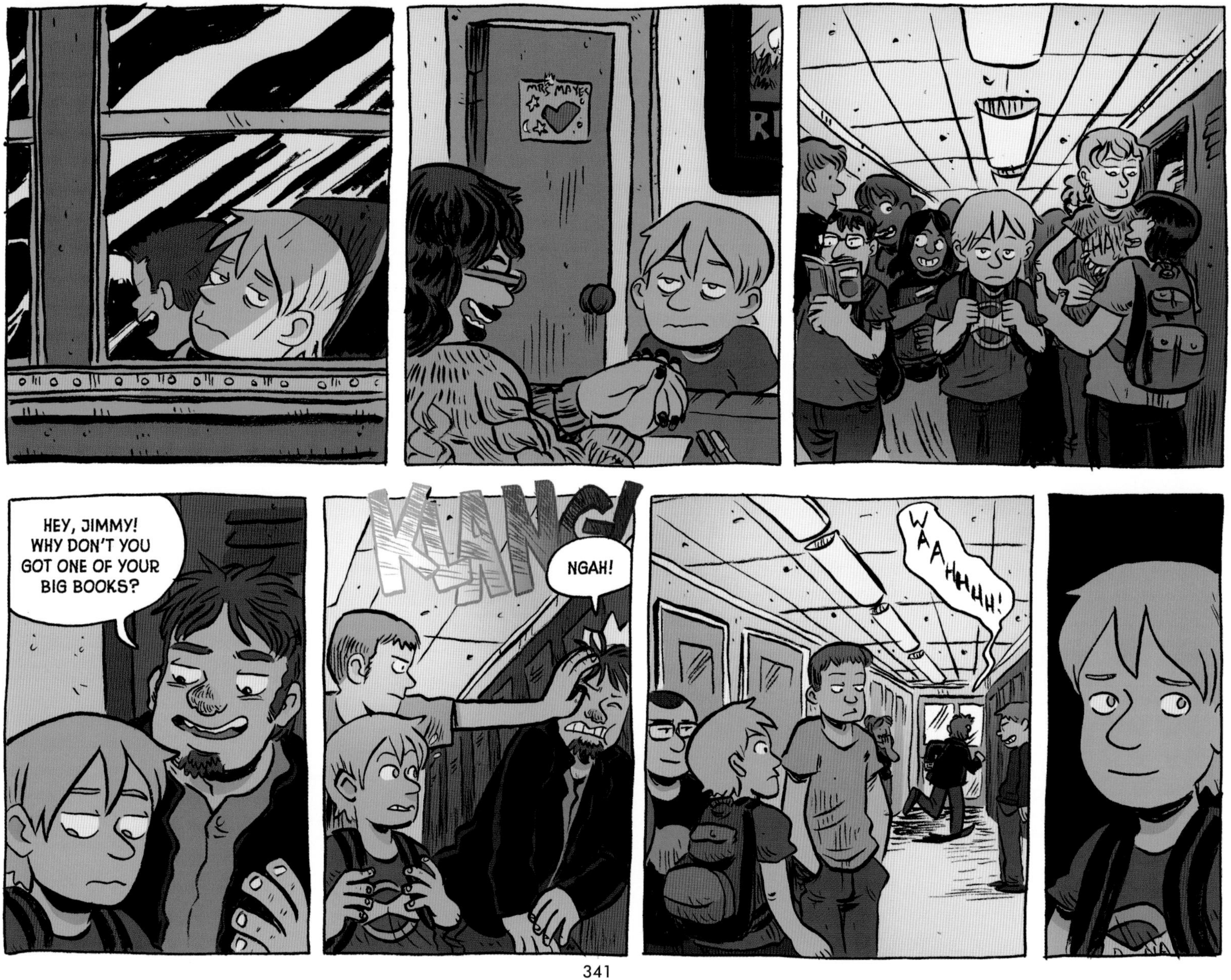
MRS MAYES
HEY, JIMMY! WHY DON'T YOU GOT ONE OF YOUR BIG BOOKS?
KLANG!
NGAH!
WAAHHHHH!

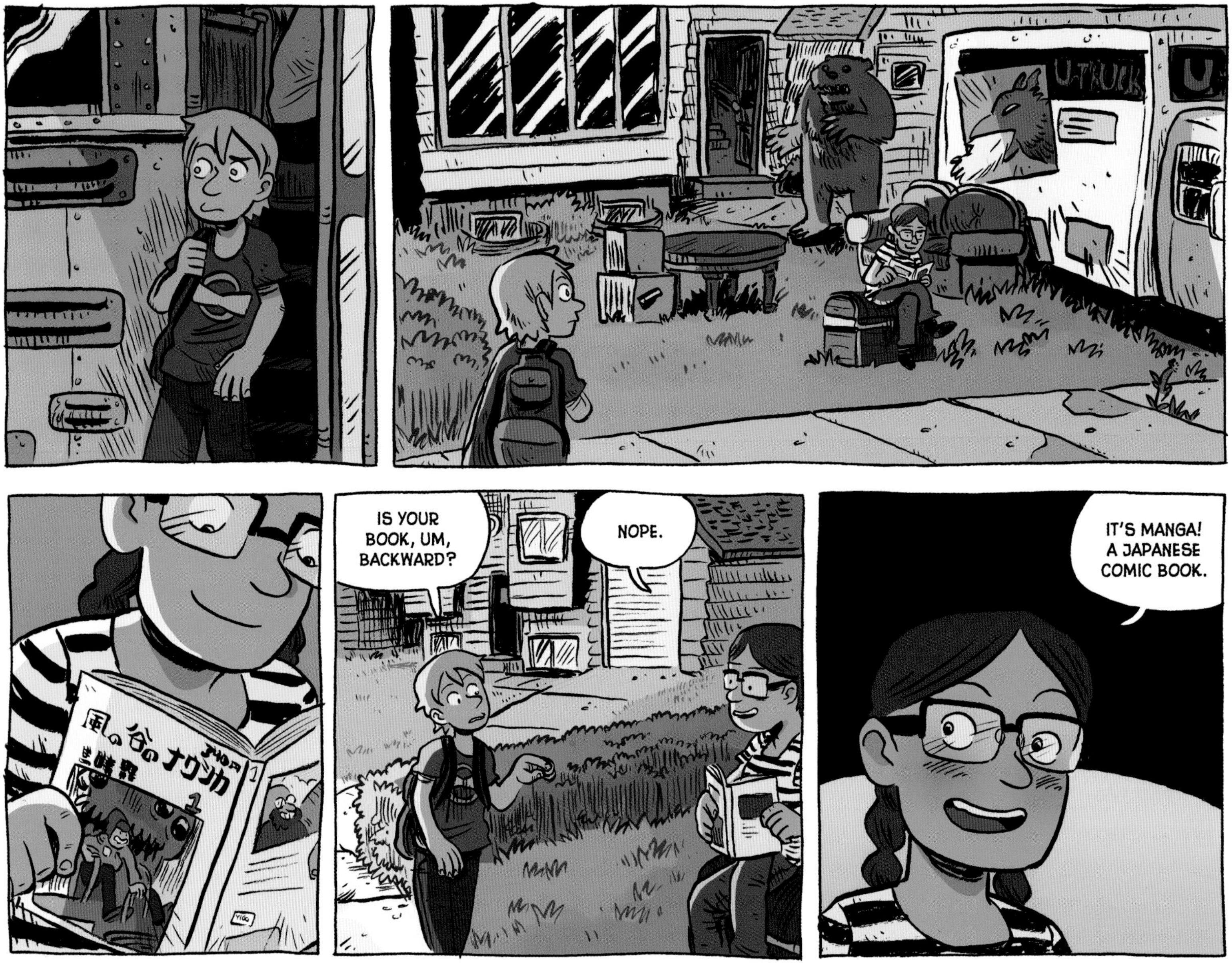
U-TRUCK
風の谷のナウシカ
IS YOUR BOOK, UM, BACKWARD?
NOPE.
IT'S MANGA! A JAPANESE COMIC BOOK.

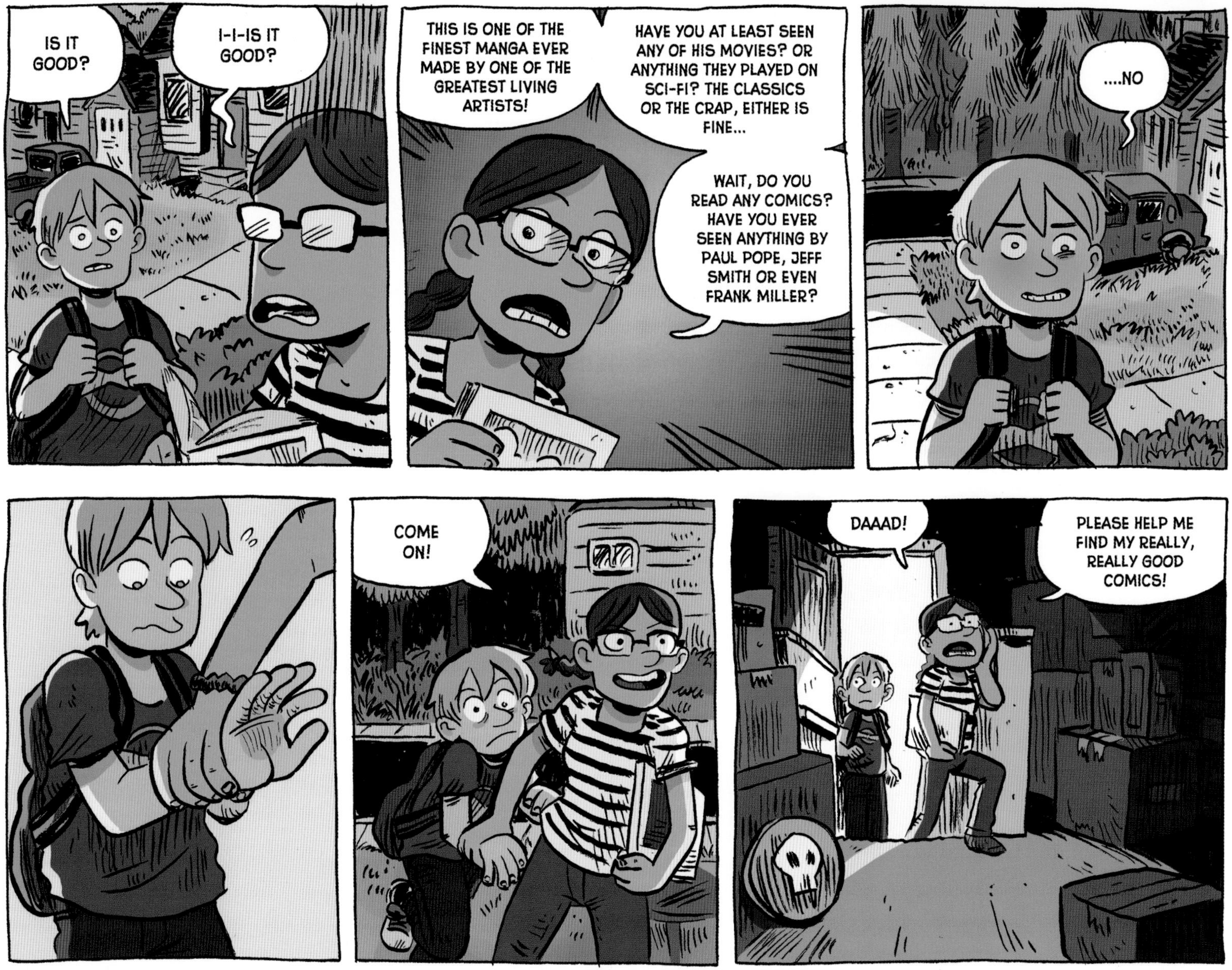
IS IT GOOD?
I-I-IS IT GOOD?
THIS IS ONE OF THE FINEST MANGA EVER MADE BY ONE OF THE GREATEST LIVING ARTISTS!
HAVE YOU AT LEAST SEEN ANY OF HIS MOVIES? OR ANYTHING THEY PLAYED ON SCI-FI? THE CLASSICS OR THE CRAP, EITHER IS FINE...
WAIT, DO YOU READ ANY COMICS? HAVE YOU EVER SEEN ANYTHING BY PAUL POPE, JEFF SMITH OR EVEN FRANK MILLER?
....NO
COME ON!
DAAAD!
PLEASE HELP ME FIND MY REALLY, REALLY GOOD COMICS!

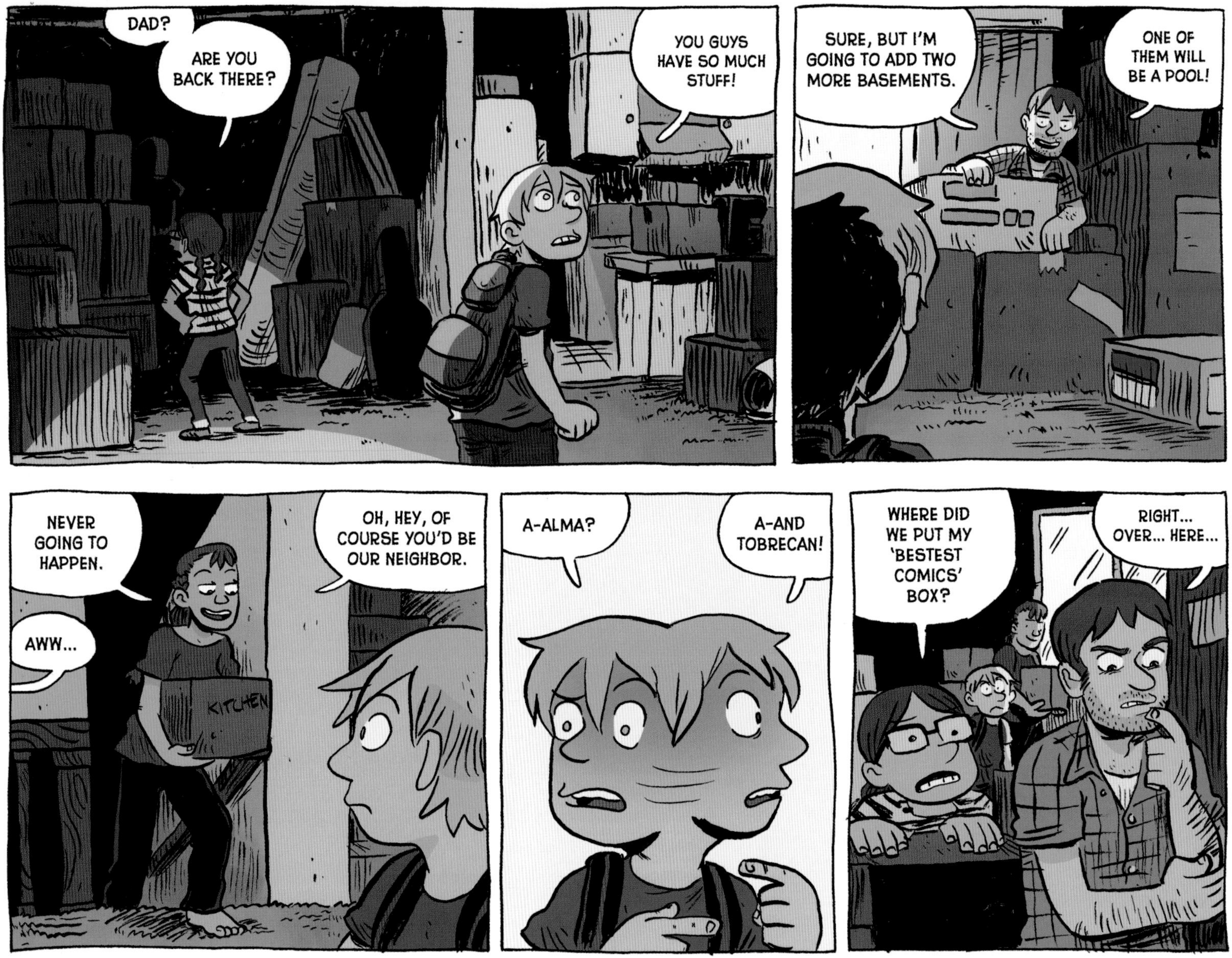
DAD?
ARE YOU BACK THERE?
YOU GUYS HAVE SO MUCH STUFF!
SURE, BUT I'M GOING TO ADD TWO MORE BASEMENTS.
ONE OF THEM WILL BE A POOL!
NEVER GOING TO HAPPEN.
AWW...
KITCHEN
OH, HEY, OF COURSE YOU'D BE OUR NEIGHBOR.
A-ALMA?
A-AND TOBRECAN!
WHERE DID WE PUT MY 'BESTEST COMICS' BOX?
RIGHT... OVER... HERE...

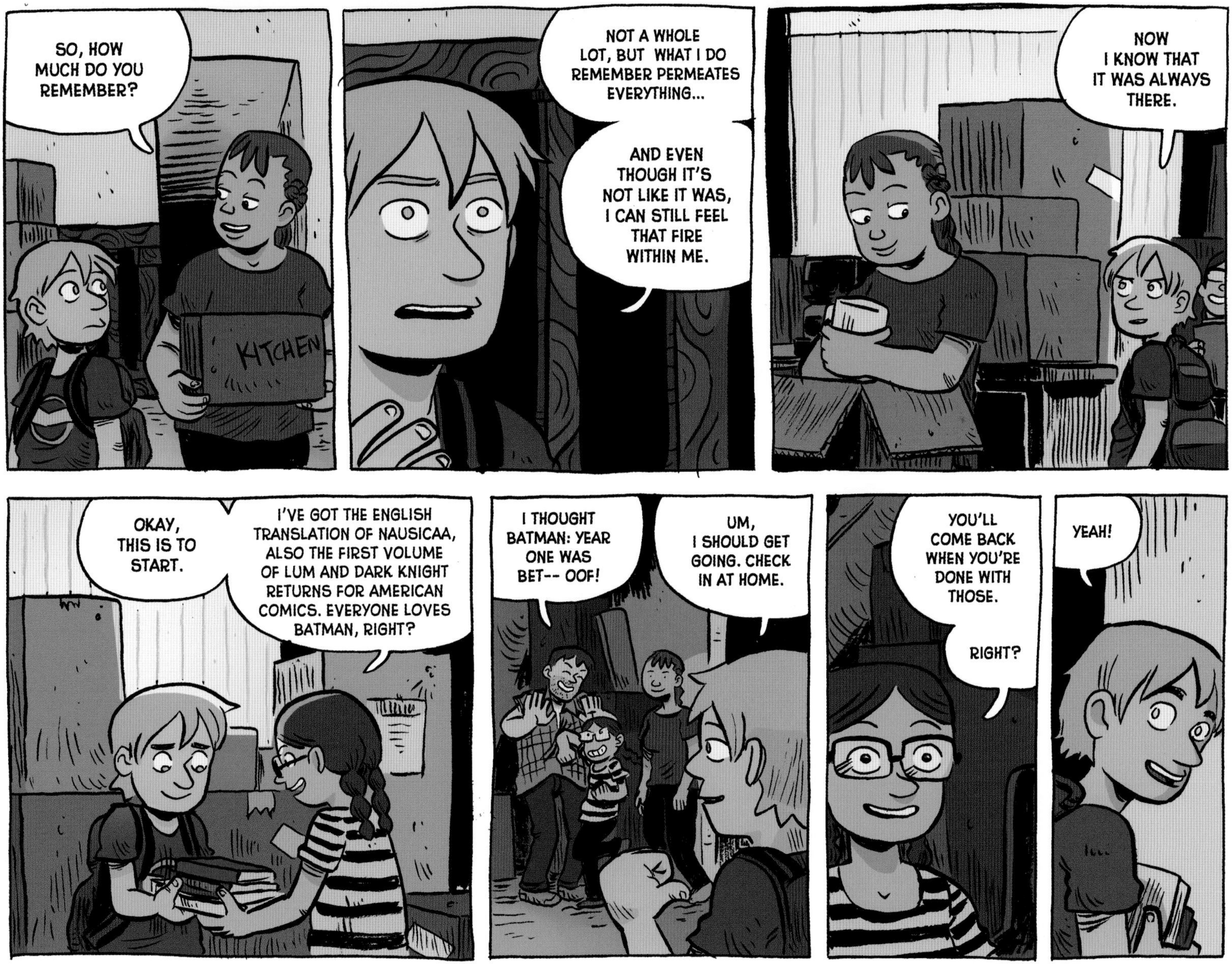
SO, HOW MUCH DO YOU REMEMBER?
KITCHEN
NOT A WHOLE LOT, BUT WHAT I DO REMEMBER PERMEATES EVERYTHING...
AND EVEN THOUGH IT'S NOT LIKE IT WAS, I CAN STILL FEEL THAT FIRE WITHIN ME.
NOW I KNOW THAT IT WAS ALWAYS THERE.
OKAY, THIS IS TO START.
I'VE GOT THE ENGLISH TRANSLATION OF NAUSICAA, ALSO THE FIRST VOLUME OF LUM AND DARK KNIGHT RETURNS FOR AMERICAN COMICS. EVERYONE LOVES BATMAN, RIGHT?
I THOUGHT BATMAN: YEAR ONE WAS BET-- OOF!
UM, I SHOULD GET GOING. CHECK IN AT HOME.
YOU'LL COME BACK WHEN YOU'RE DONE WITH THOSE.
RIGHT?
YEAH!

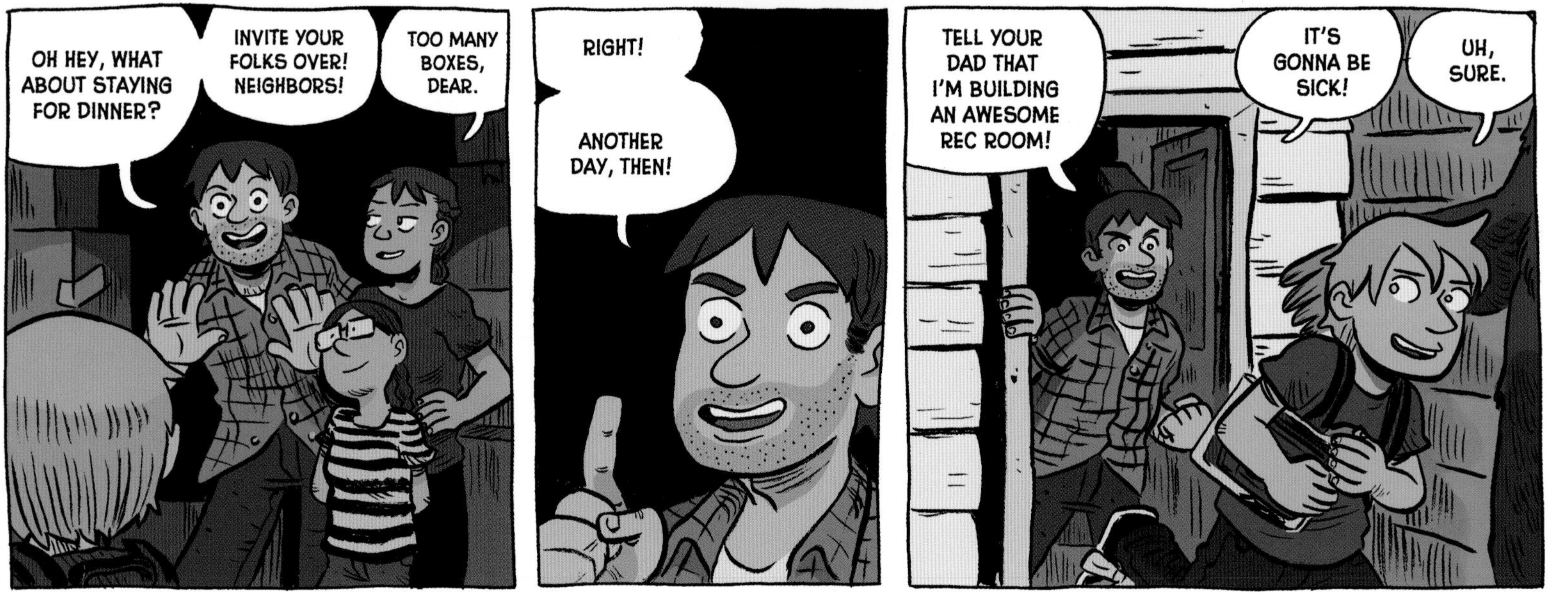
OH HEY, WHAT ABOUT STAYING FOR DINNER?
INVITE YOUR FOLKS OVER! NEIGHBORS!
TOO MANY BOXES, DEAR.
RIGHT!
ANOTHER DAY, THEN!
TELL YOUR DAD THAT I'M BUILDING AN AWESOME REC ROOM!
IT'S GONNA BE SICK!
UH, SURE.

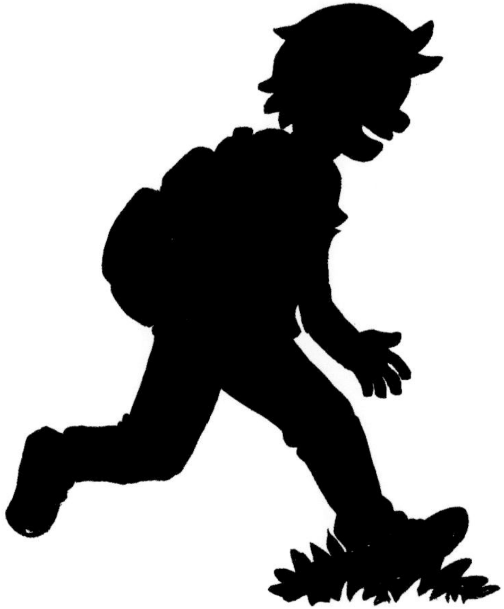

END

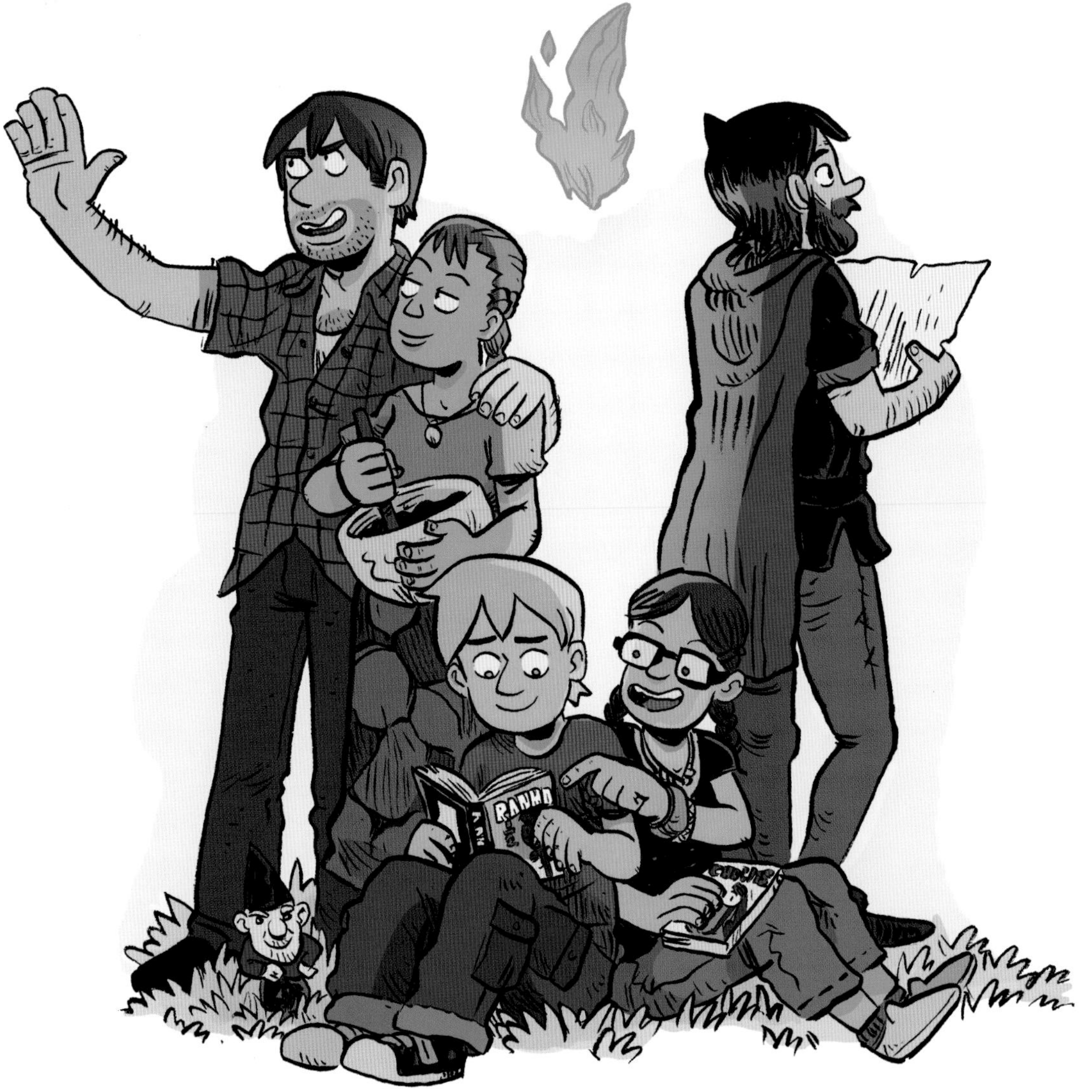

Lars Brown is a comic book author who lives in a small house with several other humans and animals in north Idaho. He is also the author of *North World* with Oni Press and several short stories in anthologies from Image Comics, New Reliable Press and the LavaPunch collective. He went to the University of Idaho for a degree in History. He is a self-taught artist. He has had twenty jobs which includes movie theater projectionist, substitute teacher and quality control at a stamp factory.

Bex Glendining (she/they) is a UK based, illustrator and comic colourist. Bex has worked with clients such as Lion Forge, Penguin Random House and Canterbury Christ Church University. They have also contributed to several zines and anthologies including, *Name and None*, *Faerie Fire: A 5e Supplemental*, *Ghibli Zine* and *Fortitudo: Dorian Pavus Art Book*. When not working, they can usually be found fussing their cat, playing games, or buying new plants.

John Kantz is a Seattle-based artist who previously co-created the book *Legends of Darkwood* and drew the backgrounds for *Scott Pilgrim*, volume 6.

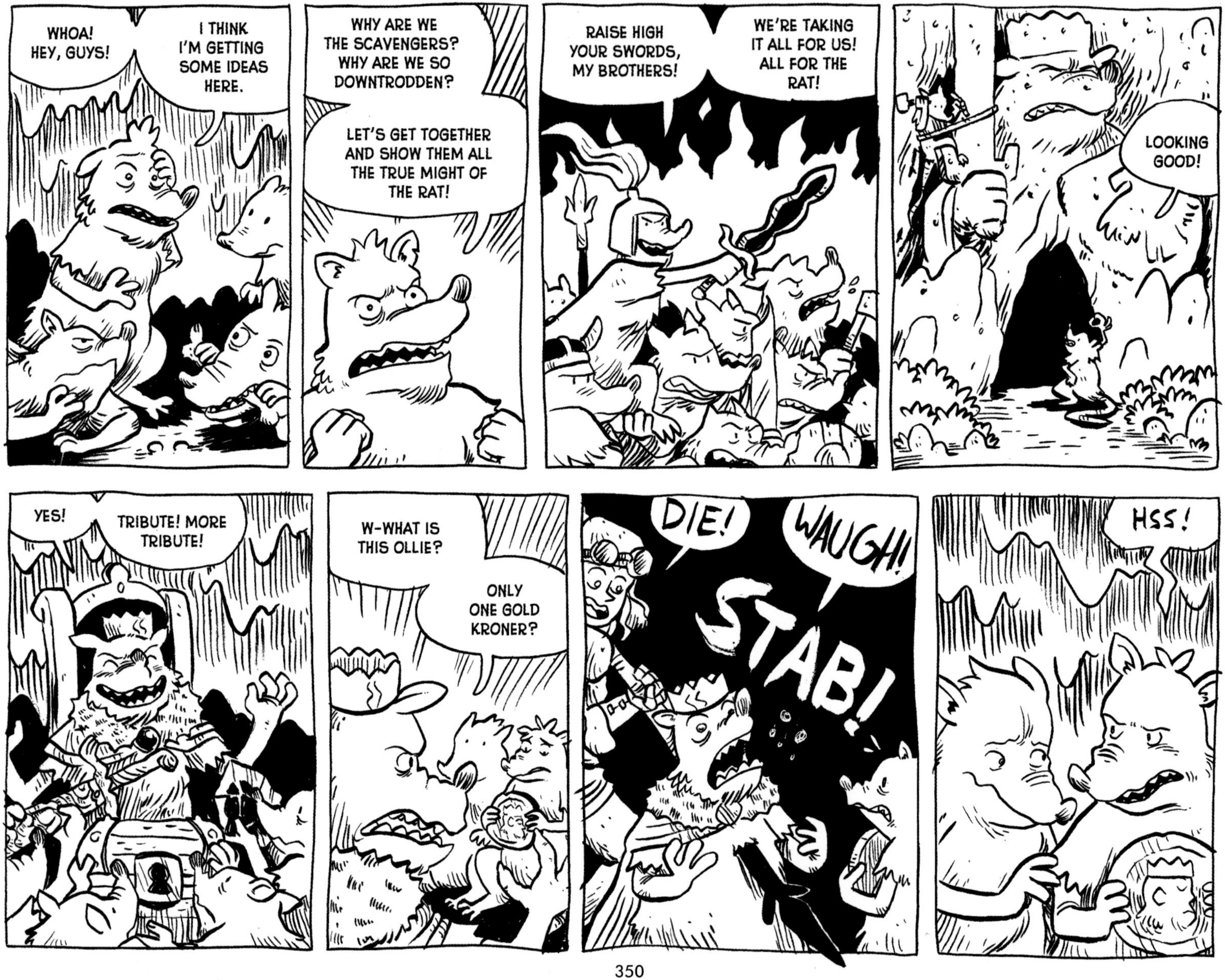
WHOA! HEY, GUYS!
I THINK I'M GETTING SOME IDEAS HERE.
WHY ARE WE THE SCAVENGERS? WHY ARE WE SO DOWNTRODDEN?
LET'S GET TOGETHER AND SHOW THEM ALL THE TRUE MIGHT OF THE RAT!
RAISE HIGH YOUR SWORDS, MY BROTHERS!
WE'RE TAKING IT ALL FOR US! ALL FOR THE RAT!
LOOKING GOOD!
YES!
TRIBUTE! MORE TRIBUTE!
W-WHAT IS THIS OLLIE?
ONLY ONE GOLD KRONER?
DIE!
WAUGH!
STAB!
HSS!

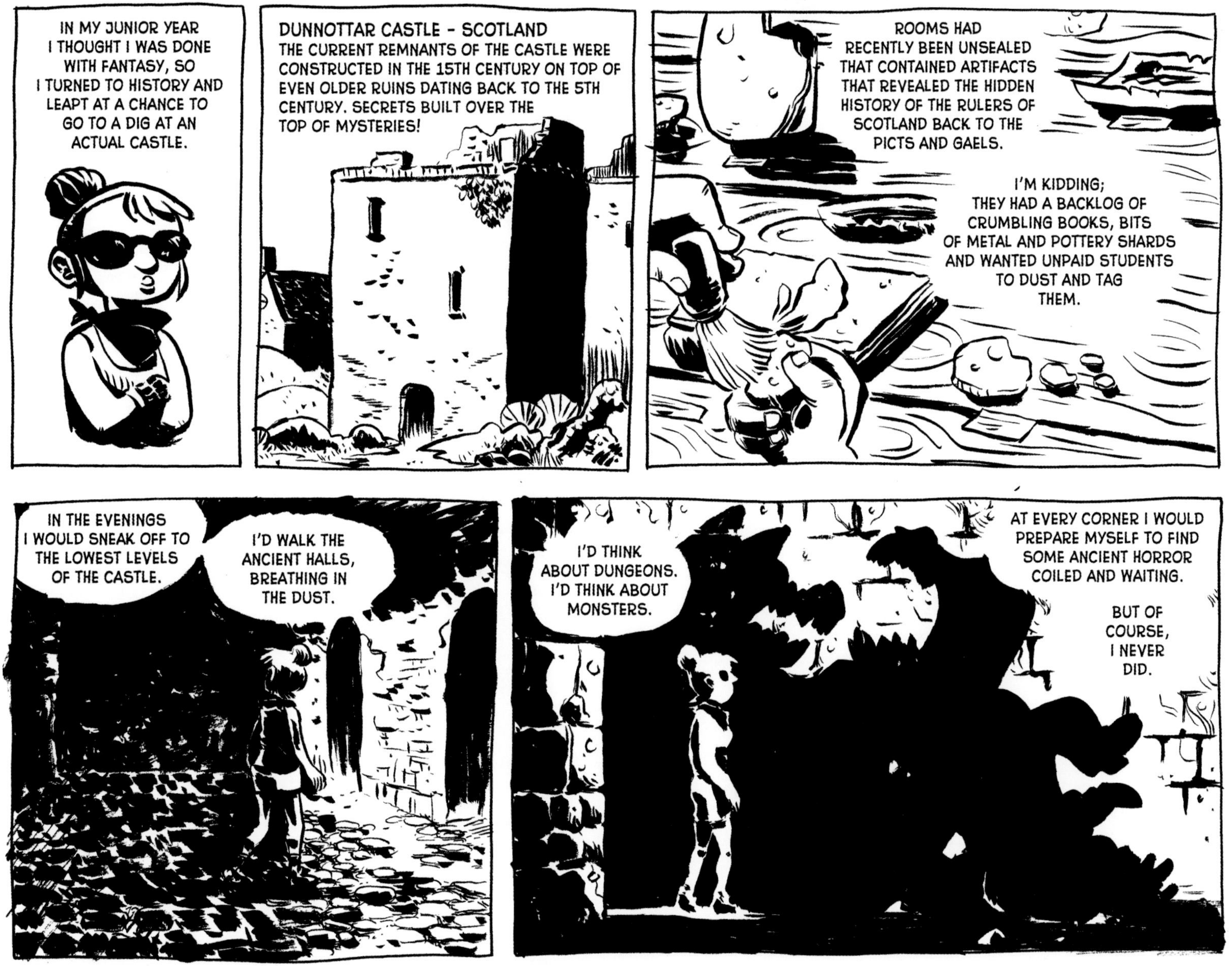
IN MY JUNIOR YEAR I THOUGHT I WAS DONE WITH FANTASY, SO I TURNED TO HISTORY AND LEAPT AT A CHANCE TO GO TO A DIG AT AN ACTUAL CASTLE.
DUNNOTTAR CASTLE - SCOTLAND
THE CURRENT REMNANTS OF THE CASTLE WERE CONSTRUCTED IN THE 15TH CENTURY ON TOP OF EVEN OLDER RUINS DATING BACK TO THE 5TH CENTURY. SECRETS BUILT OVER THE TOP OF MYSTERIES!
ROOMS HAD RECENTLY BEEN UNSEALED THAT CONTAINED ARTIFACTS THAT REVEALED THE HIDDEN HISTORY OF THE RULERS OF SCOTLAND BACK TO THE PICTS AND GAELS.
I'M KIDDING; THEY HAD A BACKLOG OF CRUMBLING BOOKS, BITS OF METAL AND POTTERY SHARDS AND WANTED UNPAID STUDENTS TO DUST AND TAG THEM.
IN THE EVENINGS I WOULD SNEAK OFF TO THE LOWEST LEVELS OF THE CASTLE.
I'D WALK THE ANCIENT HALLS, BREATHING IN THE DUST.
I'D THINK ABOUT DUNGEONS. I'D THINK ABOUT MONSTERS.
AT EVERY CORNER I WOULD PREPARE MYSELF TO FIND SOME ANCIENT HORROR COILED AND WAITING.
BUT OF COURSE, I NEVER DID.

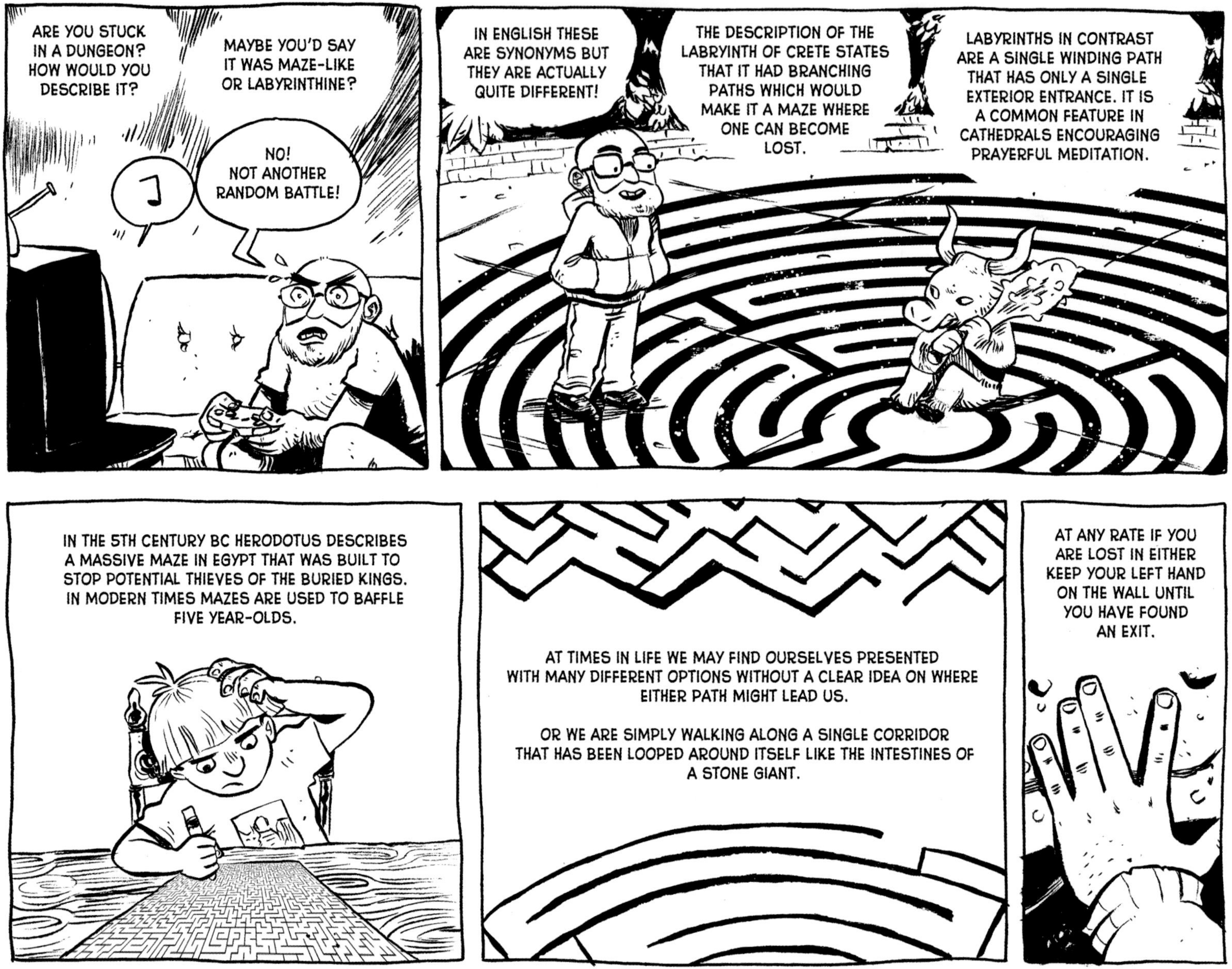

ARE YOU STUCK IN A DUNGEON? HOW WOULD YOU DESCRIBE IT?
MAYBE YOU'D SAY IT WAS MAZE-LIKE OR LABYRINTHINE?
NO! NOT ANOTHER RANDOM BATTLE!
IN ENGLISH THESE ARE SYNONYMS BUT THEY ARE ACTUALLY QUITE DIFFERENT!
THE DESCRIPTION OF THE LABRYINTH OF CRETE STATES THAT IT HAD BRANCHING PATHS WHICH WOULD MAKE IT A MAZE WHERE ONE CAN BECOME LOST.
LABYRINTHS IN CONTRAST ARE A SINGLE WINDING PATH THAT HAS ONLY A SINGLE EXTERIOR ENTRANCE. IT IS A COMMON FEATURE IN CATHEDRALS ENCOURAGING PRAYERFUL MEDITATION.
IN THE 5TH CENTURY BC HERODOTUS DESCRIBES A MASSIVE MAZE IN EGYPT THAT WAS BUILT TO STOP POTENTIAL THIEVES OF THE BURIED KINGS. IN MODERN TIMES MAZES ARE USED TO BAFFLE FIVE YEAR-OLDS.
AT TIMES IN LIFE WE MAY FIND OURSELVES PRESENTED WITH MANY DIFFERENT OPTIONS WITHOUT A CLEAR IDEA ON WHERE EITHER PATH MIGHT LEAD US.
OR WE ARE SIMPLY WALKING ALONG A SINGLE CORRIDOR THAT HAS BEEN LOOPED AROUND ITSELF LIKE THE INTESTINES OF A STONE GIANT.
AT ANY RATE IF YOU ARE LOST IN EITHER KEEP YOUR LEFT HAND ON THE WALL UNTIL YOU HAVE FOUND AN EXIT.